ROBERT LUDLUM

THE MATLOCK PAPER

THE CRY OF THE HALIDON

THE ROAD TO GANDOLFO

ROBERT LUDLUM

THE MATLOCK PAPER

THE CRY OF THE HALIDON

THE ROAD TO GANDOLFO

Harper CollinsPublishers

This omnibus edition published in 1999 by
HarperCollins*Publishers*
77-85 Fulham Palace Road,
Hammersmith, London W6 8JB

The Matlock Paper © Robert Ludlum 1973
The Cry of the Halidon © Jonathan Ryder 1974; Robert Ludlum 1996
Road to Gandolfo © Michael Shepherd 1975

ISBN 0 261 67285 1

Printed and bound in Great Britain by
Creative Print and Design (Wales), Ebbw Vale

ROBERT LUDLUM

THE MATLOCK PAPER

For Pat and Bill –
As the ancient Bagdhivi proverb says:
When giants cast shadows, hope for the shade.
The 'Due Macellis' are giants!

Chapter 1

Loring walked out the side entrance of the Justice Department and looked for a taxi. It was nearly five-thirty, a spring Friday, and the congestion in the Washington streets was awful. Loring stood by the curb and held up his left hand, hoping for the best. He was about to abandon the effort when a cab that had picked up a fare thirty feet down the block stopped in front of him.

'Going east, mister? It's OK. This gentleman said he wouldn't mind.'

Loring was always embarrassed when these incidents occurred. He unconsciously drew back his right forearm, allowing his sleeve to cover as much of his hand as possible – to conceal the thin black chain looped around his wrist, locked to the briefcase handle.

'Thanks, anyway. I'm heading south at the next corner.'

He waited until the taxi re-entered the flow of traffic and then resumed his futile signaling.

Usually, under such conditions, his mind was alert, his feelings competitive. He would normally dart his eyes in both directions, ferreting out cabs about to disgorge passengers, watching the corners for those dimly lit roof signs that meant this particular vehicle was for hire if you ran fast enough.

Today, however, Ralph Loring did not feel like running. On this particular Friday, his mind was obsessed with a terrible reality. He had just borne witness to a man's being sentenced to death. A man he'd never met but knew a great deal about. An unknowing man of thirty-three who lived and worked in a small New England town four

7

hundred miles away and who had no idea of Loring's existence, much less of the Justice Department's interest in him.

Loring's memory kept returning to the large conference room with the huge rectangular table around which sat the men who'd pronounced the sentence.

He had objected strenuously. It was the least he could do for the man he'd never met, the man who was being maneuvered with such precision into such an untenable position.

'May I remind you, Mr Loring,' said an assistant attorney general who'd once been a judge advocate in the navy, 'that in any combat situation basic risks are assumed. A percentage of casualties is anticipated.'

'The circumstances are different. This man isn't trained. He won't know who or where the enemy is. How could he? We don't know ourselves.'

'Just the point.' The speaker then had been another assistant AG, this one a recruit from some corporation law office, fond of committee meetings, and, Loring suspected, incapable of decisions without them. 'Our subject is highly mobile. Look at the psychological profile, "flawed but mobile in the extreme." That's exactly what it says. He's a logical choice.'

'"Flawed but mobile"! What in heaven's name does that mean? May *I* remind this committee that I've worked in the field for fifteen years. Psychological profiles are only screening guidelines, hit-and-miss judgments. I would no more send a man into an infiltration problem without knowing him thoroughly than I would assume the responsibility for NASA mathematics.'

The chairman of the committee, a career professional, had answered Loring.

'I understand your reservations; normally, I'd agree. However, these aren't normal conditions. We have barely three weeks. The time factor overrides the usual pre-cautions.'

'It's the risk we have to assume,' said the former judge advocate pontifically.

'*You're* not assuming it,' Loring replied.

'Do you wish to be relieved of the contact?' The chairman made the offer in complete sincerity.

'No, sir. I'll make it. Reluctantly. I want that on the record.'

'One thing before we adjourn.' The corporation lawyer leaned forward on the table. 'And this comes right from the top. We've all agreed that our subject is motivated. The profile makes that clear. What must also be made clear is that any assistance given this committee by the subject is given freely and on a voluntary basis. We're vulnerable here. We cannot, repeat *cannot*, be responsible. If it's possible, we'd like the record to indicate that the subject came to *us*.'

Ralph Loring had turned away from the man in disgust.

If anything, the traffic was heavier now. Loring had about made up his mind to start walking the twenty-odd blocks to his apartment when a white Volvo pulled up in front of him.

'Get in! You look silly with your hand up like that.'

'Oh, it's you. Thanks very much.' Loring opened the door and slid into the small front seat, holding his briefcase on his lap. There was no need to hide the thin black chain around his wrist. Cranston was a field man, too; an overseas route specialist. Cranston had done most of the background work on the assignment which was now Loring's responsibility.

'That was a long meeting. Accomplish anything?'

'The green light.'

'It's about time.'

'Two assistant AGs and a concerned message from the White House were responsible.'

'Good. Geo division got the latest reports from Force-Mediterranean this morning. It's a regular mass conversion of source routes. It's confirmed. The fields in Ankara and Konya in the north, the projects in Sidi Barrani and Rashid, even the Algerian contingents are systematically cutting production. It's going to make things very difficult.'

'What the hell do you want? I thought the objective was to rip them out. You people are never satisfied.'

'Neither would you be. We can exert controls over routes we know about; what in God's name do we know about places like . . . Porto Belocruz, Pilcomayo, a half dozen unpronounceable names in Paraguay, Brazil, Guiana? It's a whole goddamn new ballgame, Ralph.'

'Bring in the SA specialists. CIA's crawling with them.'

'No way. We're not even allowed to ask for maps.'

'That's asinine.'

'That's espionage. We stay clean. We're strictly according to Interpol-Hoyle; no funny business. I thought you knew that.'

'I do,' replied Loring wearily. 'It's still asinine.'

'You worry about New England, USA. We'll handle the pampas, or whatever they are – it is.'

'New England, USA, is a goddamn microcosm. That's what's frightening. What happened to all those poetic descriptions of rustic fences and Yankee spirit and ivied brick walls?'

'New poetry. Get with it.'

'Your sympathy is overwhelming. Thanks.'

'You sound discouraged.'

'There isn't enough time . . .'

'There never is.' Cranston steered the small car into a faster lane only to find it bottlenecked at Nebraska and

Eighteenth. With a sigh, he shoved the gearshift into neutral and shrugged his shoulders. He looked at Loring, who was staring blankly at the windshield. 'At least you got the green light. That's something.'

'Sure. With the wrong personnel.'

'Oh . . . I see. Is that him?' Cranston gestured his head toward Loring's briefcase.

'That's him. From the day he was born.'

'What's his name?'

'Matlock. James B. Matlock II. The *B* is for Barbour, very old family – two very old families. James Matlock, BA, MA, PhD. A leading authority in the field of social and political influences on Elizabethan literature. How about that?'

'Jesus! Are those his qualifications? Where does he start asking questions? At faculty teas for retired professors?'

'No. That part of it's all right; he's young enough. His qualifications are included in what Security calls "flawed but mobile in the extreme." Isn't that a lovely phrase?'

'Inspiring. What does it mean?'

'It's supposed to describe a man who isn't very nice. Probably because of a loused-up army record, or a divorce – I'm sure it's the army thing – but in spite of that insurmountable handicap, is very well liked.'

'I like him already.'

'That's my problem. I do, too.'

The two men fell into silence. It was clear that Cranston had been in the field long enough to realize when a fellow professional had to think by himself. Reach certain conclusions – or rationalizations – by himself. Most of the time, it was easy.

Ralph Loring thought about the man whose life was detailed so completely in his briefcase, culled from a score of data-bank sources. James Barbour Matlock was the name, but the person behind the name refused to come

11

into focus. And that bothered Loring; Matlock's life had been shaped by disturbing, even violent, inconsistencies.

He was the surviving son of two elderly, immensely wealthy parents who lived in handsome retirement in Scarsdale, New York. His education had been properly Eastern Establishment: Andover and Amherst, with the proper expectations of a Manhattan-based profession – banking, brokerage, advertising. There was nothing in his precollege or undergraduate record to indicate a deviation from this pattern. Indeed, marriage to a socially prominent girl from Greenwich seemed to confirm it.

And then things happened to James Barbour Matlock, and Loring wished he understood. First came the army.

It was the early sixties, and by the simple expedient of agreeing to a six-month extension of service, Matlock could have sat comfortably behind a desk as a supply officer somewhere – most likely, with his family's connections, in Washington or New York. Instead, his service file read like a hoodlum's: a series of infractions and insubordinations that guaranteed him the least desirable of assignments – Vietnam and its escalating hostilities. While in the Mekong Delta, his military behavior also guaranteed him two summary courts-martial.

Yet there appeared to be no ideological motivation behind his actions, merely poor, if any, adjustment.

His return to civilian life was marked by continuing difficulties, first with his parents and then with his wife. Inexplicably, James Barbour Matlock, whose academic record had been gentlemanly but hardly superior, took a small apartment in Morningside Heights and attended Columbia University's graduate school.

The wife lasted three and a half months, opting for a quiet divorce and a rapid exit from Matlock's life.

The following several years were monotonous intelligence material. Matlock, the incorrigible, was in the process of becoming Matlock, the scholar. He worked around the calendar, receiving his master's degree in fourteen months, his doctorate two years later. There was a reconciliation of sorts with his parents, and a position with the English department at Carlyle University in Connecticut. Since then Matlock had published a number of books and articles and acquired an enviable reputation in the academic community. He was obviously popular – 'mobile in the extreme.' (silly goddamn expression); he was moderately well-off and apparently possessed none of the antagonistic traits he'd displayed during the hostile years. Of course, there was damn little reason for him to be discontented, thought Loring. James Barbour Matlock II had his life nicely routined; he was covered on all flanks, thank you, including a girl. He was currently, with discretion, involved with a graduate student named Patricia Ballantyne. They kept separate residences, but according to the data, were lovers. As near as could be determined, however, there was no marriage in sight. The girl was completing her doctoral studies in archeology, and a dozen foundation grants awaited her. Grants that led to distant lands and unfamiliar facts. Patricia Ballantyne was not for marriage; not according to the data banks.

But what of Matlock? wondered Ralph Loring. What did the facts tell him? How could they possibly justify the choice?

They didn't. They couldn't. Only a trained professional could carry out the demands of the current situation. The problems were far too complex, too filled with traps for an amateur.

The terrible irony was that if this Matlock made errors, fell into traps, he might accomplish far more far quicker than any professional.

And lose his life doing so.

'What makes you all think he'll accept?' Cranston

13

was nearing Loring's apartment and his curiosity was piqued.

'What? I'm sorry, what did you say?'

'What's the motive for the subject's acceptance? Why would he agree?'

'A younger brother. Ten years younger, as a matter of fact. The parents are quite old. Very rich, very detached. This Matlock holds himself responsible.'

'For what?'

'The brother. He killed himself three years ago with an overdose of heroin.'

Ralph Loring drove his rented car slowly down the wide, tree-lined street past the large old houses set back beyond manicured lawns. Some were fraternity houses, but there were far fewer than had existed a decade ago. The social exclusivity of the fifties and early sixties was being replaced. A few of the huge structures had other identifications now. *The House, Aquarius* (naturally), *Afro-Commons, Warwick, Lumumba Hall*.

Connecticut's Carlyle University was one of those medium-sized 'prestige' campuses that dot the New England landscape. An administration, under the guidance of its brilliant president, Dr Adrian Sealfont, was restructuring the college, trying to bring it into the second half of the twentieth century. There were inevitable protests, proliferation of beards, and African studies balanced against the quiet wealth, club blazers, and alumni-sponsored regattas. Hard rock and faculty tea dances were groping for ways to coexist.

Loring reflected, as he looked at the peaceful campus in the bright spring sunlight, that it seemed inconceivable that such a community harbored any real problems.

Certainly not the problem that had brought him there.

Yet it did.

14

Carlyle was a time bomb which, when detonated, would claim extraordinary victims in its fallout. That it *would* explode, Loring knew, was inevitable. What happened before then was unpredictable. It was up to him to engineer the best possible probabilities. The key was James Barbour Matlock, BA, MA, PhD.

Loring drove past the attractive two-story faculty residence that held four apartments, each with a separate entrance. It was considered one of the better faculty houses and was usually occupied by bright young families before they'd reached the tenure necessary for outlying homes of their own. Matlock's quarters were on the first floor, west section.

Loring drove around the block and parked diagonally across the street from Matlock's door. He couldn't stay long; he kept turning in the seat, scanning the cars and Sunday morning pedestrians, satisfied that he himself wasn't being observed. That was vital. On Sunday, according to Matlock's surveillance file, the young professor usually read the papers till around noon and then drove to the north end of Carlyle where Patricia Ballantyne lived in one of the efficiency apartments reserved for graduate students. That is, he drove over if she hadn't spent the night with him. Then the two generally went out into the country for lunch and returned to Matlock's apartment or went south into Hartford or New Haven. There were variations, of course. Often the Ballantyne girl and Matlock took weekends together, registering as man and wife. Not this weekend, however. Surveillance had confirmed that.

Loring looked at his watch. It was twelve-forty, but Matlock was still in his apartment. Time was running short. In a few minutes, Loring was expected to be at Crescent Street. 217 Crescent. It was where he would make cover-contact for his second vehicle transfer.

15

He knew it wasn't necessary for him to physically watch Matlock. After all, he'd read the file thoroughly, looked at scores of photographs, and even talked briefly with Dr Sealfont, Carlyle's president. Nevertheless, each agent had his own working methods, and his included watching subjects for a period of hours before making contact. Several colleagues at Justice claimed it gave him a sense of power. Loring knew only that it gave him a sense of confidence.

Matlock's front door opened and a tall man walked out into the sunlight. He was dressed in khaki trousers, loafers, and a tan turtleneck sweater. Loring saw that he was modestly good looking with sharp features and fairly long blond hair. He checked the lock on his door, put on a pair of sunglasses, and walked around the sidewalk to what Loring presumed was a small parking area. Several minutes later, James Matlock drove out of the driveway in a Triumph sportscar.

The government man reflected that his subject seemed to have the best of a pleasant life. Sufficient income, no responsibilities, work he enjoyed, even a convenient relationship with an attractive girl.

Loring wondered if it would all be the same for James Barbour Matlock three weeks from then. For Matlock's world was about to be plunged into an abyss.

Chapter 2

Chapter 2

Matlock pressed the Triumph's accelerator to the floor and the low-slung automobile vibrated as the speedometer reached sixty-two miles per hour. It wasn't that he was in a hurry – Pat Ballantyne wasn't going anywhere – just that he was angry. Well, not angry, really; just irritated. He was usually irritated after a phone call from home. Time would never eliminate that. Nor money, if ever he made any to speak of – amounts his father considered respectable. What caused his irritation was the infuriating condescension. It grew worse as his mother and father advanced in years. Instead of making peace with the situation, they dwelled on it. They insisted that he spend the spring midterm vacation in Scarsdale so that he and his father could make daily trips into the city. To the banks, to the attorneys. To make ready for the inevitable, when and if it ever happened.

'. . . There's a lot you'll have to digest, son,' his father had said sepulchrally. 'You're not exactly prepared, you know . . .'

'. . . You're all that's left, darling,' his mother had said with obvious pain.

Matlock knew they enjoyed their anticipated, martyred leavetaking of this world. They'd made their mark – or at least his father had. The amusing part was that his parents were as strong as pack mules, as healthy as wild horses. They'd no doubt outlast him by decades.

The truth was that they wanted him with them far more than he wished to be there. It had been that way for the past three years, since David's death at the Cape.

17

Perhaps, thought Matlock, as he drew up in front of Pat's apartment, the roots of his irritation were in his own guilt. He'd never quite made peace with himself about David. He never would.

And he didn't want to be in Scarsdale during the midterm holidays. He didn't want the memories. He had someone now who was helping him forget the awful years – of death, no love, and indecision. He'd promised to take Pat to St Thomas.

The name of the country inn was the Cheshire Cat, and, as its title implied, it was Englishy and pubbish. The food was decent, the drinks generous, and those factors made it a favorite spot of Connecticut's exurbia. They'd finished their second Bloody Mary and had ordered roast beef and Yorkshire pudding. There were perhaps a dozen couples and several families in the spacious dining area. In the corner sat a single man reading *The New York Times* with the pages folded vertically, commuter fashion.

'He's probably an irate father waiting for a son who's about to splash out. I know the type. They take the Scarsdale train every morning.'

'He's too relaxed.'

'They learn to hide tension. Only their druggists know. All that Gelusil.'

'There are always signs, and he hasn't any. He looks positively self-satisfied. You're wrong.'

'You just don't know Scarsdale. Self-satisfaction is a registered trademark. You can't buy a house without it.'

'Speaking of such things, what are you going to do? I really think we should cancel St Thomas.'

'I don't. It's been a rough winter; we deserve a little sun. Anyway, they're being unreasonable. There's nothing I want to learn about the Matlock manipulations; it's a waste of time. In the unlikely event that they ever *do* go, others'll be in charge.'

'I thought we agreed that was only an excuse. They want you around for a while. I think it's touching they do it this way.'

'It's not touching, it's my father's transparent attempt at bribery . . . Look. Our commuter's given up.' The single man with the newspaper finished his drink and was explaining to the waitress that he wasn't ordering lunch. 'Five'll get you ten he pictured his son's hair and leather jacket – maybe bare feet – and just panicked.'

'I think you're wishing it on the poor man.'

'No, I'm not. I'm too sympathetic. I can't stand the aggravation that goes with rebellion. Makes me self-conscious.'

'You're a very funny man, Private Matlock,' said Pat, alluding to Matlock's inglorious army career. 'When we finish, let's go down to Hartford. There's a good movie.'

'Oh, I'm sorry, I forgot to tell you. We can't today . . . Sealfont called me this morning for an early evening conference. Said it was important.'

'About what?'

'I'm not sure. The African studies may be in trouble. That "Tom" I recruited from Howard turned out to be a beaut. I think he's a little to the right of Louis XIV.'

She smiled. 'Really, you're terrible.'

Matlock took her hand.

The residence of Dr Adrian Sealfont was imposingly appropriate. It was a large white colonial mansion with wide marble steps leading up to thick double doors carved in relief. Along the front were Ionic pillars spanning the width of the building. Floodlights from the lawn were turned on at sundown.

Matlock walked up the stairs to the door and rang the

bell. Thirty seconds later he was admitted by a maid, who ushered him through the hallway toward the rear of the house, into Dr Sealfont's huge library.

Adrian Sealfont stood in the center of the room with two other men. Matlock, as always, was struck by the presence of the man. A shade over six feet, thin, with aquiline features, he radiated a warmth that touched all who were near him. There was about him a genuine humility which concealed his brilliance from those who did not know him. Matlock liked him immensely.

'Hello, James.' Sealfont extended his hand to Matlock. 'Mr Loring, may I present Dr Matlock?'

'How do you do? Hi, Sam,' Matlock addressed this last to the third man, Samuel Kressel, dean of colleges at Carlyle.

'Hello, Jim.'

'We've met before, haven't we?' asked Matlock, looking at Loring. 'I'm trying to remember.'

'I'm going to be very embarrassed if you do.'

'I'll bet you will!' laughed Kressel with his sardonic, slightly offensive, humor. Matlock also liked Sam Kressel, more because he knew the pain of Kressel's job – what he had to contend with – than for the man himself.

'What do you mean, Sam?'

'I'll answer you,' interrupted Adrian Sealfont. 'Mr Loring is with the federal government, the Justice Department. I agreed to arrange a meeting between the three of you, but I did not agree to what Sam and Mr Loring have just referred to. Apparently Mr Loring has seen fit to have you – what is the term – under surveillance. I've registered my strong objections.' Sealfont looked directly at Loring.

'You've had me *what*?' asked Matlock quietly.

'I apologize,' said Loring persuasively. 'It's a personal idiosyncrasy and has nothing to do with our business.'

'You're the commuter in the Cheshire Cat.'

'The what?' asked Sam Kressel.

'The man with the newspaper.'

'That's right. I knew you'd noticed me this afternoon. I thought you'd recognized me the minute you saw me again. I didn't know I looked like a commuter.'

'It was the newspaper. We called you an irate father.'

'Sometimes I am. Not often, though. My daughter's only seven.'

'I think we should begin,' Sealfont said. 'Incidentally, James, I'm relieved your reaction is so understanding.'

'My only reaction is curiosity. And a healthy degree of fear. To tell you the truth, I'm scared to death.' Matlock smiled haltingly. 'What's it all about?'

'Let's have a drink while we talk.' Adrian Sealfont smiled back and walked to his copper-topped dry bar in the corner of the room. 'You're a bourbon and water man, aren't you, James? And Sam, a double Scotch over ice, correct? What's yours, Mr Loring?'

'Scotch'll be fine. Just water.'

'Here, James, give me a hand.' Matlock crossed to Sealfont and helped him.

'You amaze me, Adrian,' said Kressel, sitting down in a leather armchair. 'What in heaven's name prompts you to remember your subordinates' choice of liquor?'

Sealfont laughed. 'The most logical reason of all. And it certainly isn't confined to my . . . colleagues. I've raised more money for this institution with alcohol than with hundreds of reports prepared by the best analytic minds in fund-raising circles.' Here Adrian Sealfont paused and chuckled – as much to himself as to those in the room. 'I once gave a speech to the Organization of University Presidents. In the question and answer period, I was asked to what I attributed Carlyle's endowment . . . I'm afraid I replied, "To those ancient peoples who developed the art

21

of fermenting the vineyards." . . . My late wife roared but told me later I'd set the fund back a decade.'

The three men laughed; Matlock distributed the drinks.

'Your health,' said the president of Carlyle, raising his glass modestly. The toast, however, was brief. 'This is a bit awkward, James . . . Sam. Several weeks ago I was contacted by Mr Loring's superior. He asked me to come to Washington on a matter of utmost importance, relative to Carlyle. I did so and was briefed on a situation I still refuse to accept. Certain information which Mr Loring will impart to you seems incontrovertible on the surface. But that is the surface: rumor; out-of-context statements, written and verbal; constructed evidence which may be meaningless. On the other hand, there might well be a degree of substance. It is on that possibility that I've agreed to this meeting. I must make it clear, however, that I cannot be a party to it. Carlyle *will not* be a party to it. Whatever may take place in this room has my unacknowledged approval but not my official sanction. You act as individuals, not as members of the faculty or staff of Carlyle. If, indeed, you decide to act at all . . . Now, James, if that doesn't "scare you," I don't know what will.' Sealfont smiled again, but his message was clear.

'It scares me,' said Matlock without emphasis.

Kressel put down his glass and leaned forward on the chair. 'Are we to assume from what you've said that you don't endorse Loring's presence here? Or whatever it is he wants?'

'It's a gray area. If there's substance to his charges, I certainly cannot turn my back. On the other hand, no university president these days will openly collaborate with a government agency on speculation. You'll forgive me, Mr Loring, but too many people in Washington have taken advantage of the academic communities. I refer specifically to Michigan, Columbia, Berkeley . . . among

22

others. Simple police matters are one thing, infiltration
. . . well, that's something else again.'

'Infiltration? That's a pretty strong word,' said Matlock.

'Perhaps too strong. I'll leave the terms to Mr Loring.'

Kressel picked up his glass. 'May I ask why we – Matlock
and I – have been chosen?'

'That, again, will be covered in Mr Loring's discussion.
However, since I'm responsible for *your* being here, Sam,
I'll tell you *my* reasons. As dean, you're more closely
attuned to campus affairs than anyone else . . . You will
also be aware of it if Mr Loring or his associates overstep
their bounds . . . I think that's all I have to say. I'm going
over to the assembly. That filmmaker, Strauss, is speaking
tonight and I've got to put in an appearance.' Sealfont
walked back to the bar and put his glass on the tray. The
three other men rose.

'One thing before you go,' said Kressel, his brow
wrinkled. 'Suppose one or both of us decide we want
no part of Mr Loring's . . . business?'

'Then refuse.' Adrian Sealfont crossed to the library
door. 'You are under no obligation whatsoever; I want that
perfectly clear. Mr Loring understands. Good evening,
gentlemen.' Sealfont walked out into the hallway, closing
the door behind him.

Chapter 3

The three men remained silent, standing motionless. They could hear the front entrance open and close. Kressel turned and looked at Loring.

'It seems to me you've been put on the spot.'

'I usually am in these situations. Let me clarify my position; it will partly explain this meeting. The first thing you should know is that I'm with the Justice Department, *Narcotics* Bureau.'

Kressel sat down and sipped at his drink. 'You haven't traveled up here to tell us forty per cent of the student body is on pot and a few other items, have you? Because if so, it's nothing we don't know.'

'No, I haven't. I assume you *do* know about such things. Everyone does. I'm not sure about the percentage, though. It could be a low estimate.'

Matlock finished his bourbon and decided to have another. He spoke as he crossed to the copper bar table. 'It may be low or high, but comparatively speaking – in relation to other campuses – we're not in a panic.'

'There's no reason for you to be. Not about that.'

'There's something else?'

'Very much so.' Loring walked to Sealfont's desk and bent down to pick up his briefcase from the floor. It was apparent that the government man and Carlyle's president had talked before Matlock and Kressel arrived. Loring put the briefcase on the desk and opened it. Matlock walked back to his chair and sat down.

'I'd like to show you something.' Loring reached into the briefcase and withdrew a thick page of silver-colored

24

stationery, cut diagonally as if with pinking shears. The silver coating was now filthy with repeated handling and blotches of grease or dirt. He approached Matlock's chair and handed it to him. Kressel got up and came over.

'It's some kind of letter. Or announcement. With numbers,' said Matlock. 'It's in French; no, Italian, I think. I can't make it out.'

'Very good, professor,' said Loring. 'A lot of both and not a predominance of either. Actually, it's a Corsican dialect, written out. It's called the Oltremontan strain, used in the southern hill country. Like Etruscan, it's not entirely translatable. But what codes are used are simple to the point of not being codes at all. I don't think they were meant to be; there aren't too many of these. So there's enough here to tell us what we need to know.'

'Which is?' asked Kressel, taking the strange-looking paper from Matlock.

'First I'd like to explain how we got it. Without that explanation, the information is meaningless.'

'Go ahead.' Kressel handed the filthy silver paper back to the government agent, who carried it to the desk and carefully returned it to his briefcase.

'A narcotics courier – that is, a man who goes into a specific source territory carrying instructions, money, messages – left the country six weeks ago. He was more than a courier, actually; he was quite powerful in the distribution hierarchy; you might say he was on a busman's holiday, Mediterranean style. Or perhaps he was checking investments . . . At any rate, he was killed by some mountain people in the Toros Daglari – that's Turkey, a growing district. The story is, he canceled operations there and the violence followed. We accept that; the Mediterranean fields are closing down right and left, moving into South America . . . The paper was found on his body, in a skin belt. As you saw, it's been handed around a bit. It brought a succession of prices from Ankara to Marrakesh. An Interpol undercover man finally made the purchase and it was turned over to us.'

'From Toros Dag-whatever-it-is to Washington. That paper's had quite a journey,' said Matlock.

'And an expensive one,' added Loring. 'Only it's not in Washington now, it's here. From Toros Daglari to Carlyle, Connecticut.'

'I assume that means something.' Sam Kressel sat down, apprehensively watching the government man.

'It means the information in that paper concerns Carlyle.' Loring leaned back against the desk and spoke calmly, with no sense of urgency at all. He could have been an instructor in front of a class explaining a dry but necessary mathematics theorem. 'The paper says there'll be a conference on the tenth of May, three weeks from tomorrow. The numbers are the map coordinates of the Carlyle area – precision decimals of longitude and latitude in Greenwich units. The paper itself identifies the holder to be one of those summoned. Each paper has either a matching half or is cut from a pattern that can be matched – simple additional security. What's missing is the precise location.'

'Wait a minute.' Kressel's voice was controlled but sharp; he was upset. 'Aren't you ahead of yourself, Loring? You're giving us information – obviously restricted – before you state your request. This university administration isn't interested in being an investigative arm of the government. Before you go into facts, you'd better say what you want.'

'I'm sorry, Mr Kressel. You said I was on the spot and I am. I'm handling it badly.'

'Like hell. You're an expert.'

'Hold it, Sam.' Matlock raised his hand off the arm of the chair. Kressel's sudden antagonism seemed uncalled for. 'Sealfont said we had the option to refuse whatever he wants. If we exercise that option – and we probably will – I'd like to think we did so out of judgment, not blind reaction.'

'Don't be naïve, Jim. You receive restricted or classified information and instantly, *post facto*, you're involved. You can't deny receiving it; you can't say it didn't happen.'

Matlock looked up at Loring. 'Is that true?'

'To a degree, yes. I won't lie about it.'

'Then why should we listen to you?'

'Because Carlyle University *is* involved; has been for years. And the situation is critical. So critical that there are only three weeks left to act on the information we have.'

Kressel got out of his chair, took a deep breath, and exhaled slowly. 'Create the crisis – without proof – and force the involvement. The crisis fades but the records show the university was a silent participant in a federal investigation. That was the pattern at the University of Wisconsin.' Kressel turned to Matlock. 'Do you remember that one, Jim? Six days of riots on campus. Half a semester lost on teach-ins.'

'That was Pentagon oriented,' said Loring. 'The circumstances were entirely different.'

'You think the Justice Department makes it more palatable? Read a few campus newspapers.'

'For Christ's sake, Sam, let the man talk. If you don't want to listen, go home. I want to hear what he has to say.'

Kressel looked down at Matlock. 'All right. I think I understand. Go ahead, Loring. Just remember, no obligations. And we're not bound to respect any conditions of confidence.'

'I'll gamble on your common sense.'

'That may be a mistake.' Kressel walked to the bar and replenished his drink.

Loring sat on the edge of the desk. 'I'll start by asking both of you if you've ever heard of the word *nimrod*?'

'Nimrod is a Hebrew name,' Matlock answered. 'Old Testament. A descendant of Noah, ruler of Babylon and Nineveh. Legendary prowess as a hunter, which obscures the more important fact that he founded, or built, the great cities in Assyria and Mesopotamia.'

Loring smiled. 'Very good again, professor. A *hunter* and a *builder*. I'm speaking in more contemporary terms, however.'

'Then, no, I haven't. Have you, Sam?'

Kressel walked back to his chair, carrying his glass. 'I didn't even know what you just said. I thought a nimrod was a casting fly. Very good for trout.'

'Then I'll fill in some background . . . I don't mean to bore you with narcotics statistics. I'm sure you're bombarded with them constantly.'

'Constantly,' said Kressel.

'But there's an isolated geographical statistic you may not be aware of. The concentration of drug traffic in the New England states is growing at a rate exceeding that of any other section of the country. It's a startling pattern. Since 1968, there's been a systematic erosion of enforcement procedures . . . Let me put it into perspective, geographically. In California, Illinois, Louisiana, narcotics controls have improved to the point of at least curtailing the growth curves. It's really the best we can hope for until the international agreements have teeth. But not in the New England area. Throughout this section, the expansion has gone wild. It's hit the colleges hard.'

'How do you know that?' asked Matlock.

'Dozens of ways and always too late to prevent distribution. Informers, marked inventories from Mediterranean,

Asian, and Latin American sources, traceable Swiss deposits; that *is* restricted data.' Loring looked at Kressel and smiled.

'Now I know you people are crazy.' Kressel spoke disagreeably. 'It seems to me that if you can substantiate those charges, you should do so publicly. And loud.'

'We have our reasons.'

'Also restricted, I assume,' said Kressel with faint disgust.

'There's a side issue,' continued the government man, disregarding him. 'The eastern prestige campuses – large and small, Princeton, Amherst, Harvard, Vassar, Williams, Carlyle – a good percentage of their enrollments include VIP kids. Sons and daughters of very important people, especially in government and industry. There's a blackmail potential, and we think it's been used. Such people are painfully sensitive to drug scandals.'

Kressel interrupted. 'Granting what you say is true, and I don't, we've had less trouble here than most other colleges in the northeast area.'

'We're aware of that. We even think we know why.'

'That's esoteric, Mr Loring. Say what you want to say.' Matlock didn't like the games some people played.

'Any distribution network which is capable of systematically servicing, expanding, and controlling an entire section of the country has got to have a base of operations. A clearing house – you might say, a command post. Believe me when I tell you that this base of operations, the command post for the narcotics traffic throughout the New England states, is Carlyle University.'

Samuel Kressel, dean of the colleges, dropped his glass on Adrian Sealfont's parquet floor.

Ralph Loring continued his incredible story. Matlock and Kressel remained in their chairs. Several times during his

29

calm, methodical explanation, Kressel began to interrupt, to object, but Loring's persuasive narrative cut him short. There was nothing to argue.

The investigation of Carlyle University had begun eighteen months ago. It had been triggered by an accounts ledger uncovered by the French Sureté during one of its frequent narcotics investigations in the port of Marseilles. Once the ledger's American origins were established, it was sent to Washington under Interpol agreement. Throughout the ledger's entries were references to 'C – 22°–59°' consistently followed by the name *Nimrod*. The numbered degree marks were found to be map co-ordinates of northern Connecticut, but not decimally definitive. After tracing hundreds of possible trucking routes from Atlantic seaboard piers and airports relative to the Marseilles operation, the vicinity of Carlyle was placed under maximum surveillance.

As part of the surveillance, telephone taps were ordered on persons known to be involved with narcotics distribution from such points as New York, Hartford, Boston, and New Haven. Tapes were made of conversations of underworld figures. All calls regarding narcotics to and from the Carlyle area were placed to and from public telephone booths. It made the intercepts difficult, but not impossible. Again, restricted methods.

As the information files grew, a startling fact became apparent. The Carlyle group was independent. It had no formal ties with structured organized crime; it was beholden to no-one. It *used* known criminal elements, was not used *by* them. It was a tightly knit unit, reaching into the majority of New England universities. And it did not – apparently – stop at drugs.

There was evidence of the Carlyle unit's infiltration into gambling, prostitution, even postgraduate employment placement. Too, there seemed to be a purpose,

30

an objective beyond the inherent profits of the illegal activities. The Carlyle unit could have made far greater profit with less complications by dealing outright with known criminals, acknowledged suppliers in all areas. Instead, it spent its own money to set up its organization. It was its own master, controlling its own sources, its own distribution. But what its ultimate objectives were was unclear.

It had become so powerful that it threatened the leadership of organized crime in the Northeast. For this reason, leading figures of the underworld had demanded a conference with those in charge of the Carlyle operation. The key here was a group, or an individual, referred to as *Nimrod*.

The purpose of the conference, as far as could be determined, was for an accommodation to be reached between Nimrod and the overlords of crime who felt threatened by Nimrod's extraordinary growth. The conference would be attended by dozens of known and unknown criminals throughout the New England states.

'Mr Kressel.' Loring turned to Carlyle's dean and seemed to hesitate. 'I suppose you have lists – students, faculty, staff – people you know or have reason to suspect are into the drug scene. I can't assume it because I don't know, but most colleges do have.'

'I won't answer that question.'

'Which, of course, gives me my answer,' said Loring quietly, even sympathetically.

'Not for a minute! You people have a habit of assuming exactly what you want to assume.'

'All right, I stand rebuked. But even if you'd said yes, it wasn't my purpose to ask for them. It was merely by way of telling you that we *do* have such a list. I wanted you to know that.'

Sam Kressel realized he'd been trapped; Loring's ingenuousness only annoyed him further. 'I'm sure you do.'

'Needless to say, we'd have no objection to giving you a copy.'

'That won't be necessary.'

'You're pretty obstinate, Sam,' said Matlock. 'You burying your head?'

Before Kressel could reply, Loring spoke. 'The dean knows he can change his mind. And we've agreed, there's no crisis here. You'd be surprised how many people wait for the roof to cave in before asking for help. Or accepting it.'

'But there aren't many surprises in your organization's proclivity for turning difficult situations into disasters, are there?' countered Sam Kressel antagonistically.

'We've made mistakes.'

'Since you have names,' continued Sam, 'why don't you go after them? Leave us out of it; do your own dirty work. Make arrests, press charges. Don't try to deputize *us*.'

'We don't want to do that . . . Besides, most of our evidence is inadmissible.'

'That occurred to me,' interjected Kressel.

'And what do we gain? What do *you* gain?' Loring leaned forward, returning Sam's stare. 'We pick up a couple of hundred potheads, a few dozen speedfreaks; users and low-level pushers. Don't you understand, that doesn't *solve* anything.'

'Which brings us to what you really want, doesn't it?' Matlock sank back into the chair; he watched the persuasive agent closely.

'Yes,' answered Loring softly. 'We want Nimrod. We want to know the location of that conference on May 10. It could be anywhere within a radius of fifty to a hundred miles. We want to be prepared for it. We want to break the back of the Nimrod operation, for reasons that go way beyond Carlyle University. As well as narcotics.'

'How?' asked James Matlock.

'Dr Sealfont said it. Infiltration . . . Professor Matlock, you are what's known in intelligence circles as a highly mobile person within your environment. You're widely accepted by diverse, even conflicting factions – within both the faculty and the student body. We have the names, you have the mobility.' Loring reached into his briefcase and withdrew the scissored page of filthy stationery. 'Somewhere out there is the information we need. Somewhere there's someone who has a paper like this; someone who knows what we have to know.'

James Barbour Matlock remained motionless in his chair, staring at the government man. Neither Loring nor Kressel could be sure what he was thinking but both had an idea. If thoughts were audible, there would have been full agreement in that room at that moment. James Matlock's mind had wandered back three, almost four years ago. He was remembering a blond-haired boy of nineteen. Immature for his age, perhaps, but good, kind. A boy with problems.

They'd found him as they'd found thousands like him in thousands of cities and towns across the country. Other times, other Nimrods.

James Matlock's brother, David, had inserted a needle in his right arm and had shot up thirty mg. of white fluid. He had performed the act in a catboat in the calm waters of a Cape Cod inlet. The small sailboat had drifted into the reeds near shore. When they found it, James Matlock's brother was dead.

Matlock made his decision.

'Can you get me the names?'

'I have them with me.'

'Just hold it.' Kressel stood up, and when he spoke, it wasn't in the tone of an angry man – it was with fear. 'Do you realize what you're asking him to do? He has no

33

experience in this kind of work. He's not trained. Use one of your *own* men.'

'There isn't time. There's no time for one of our men. He'll be protected; you can help.'

'I can *stop* you!'

'No, you can't, Sam,' said Matlock from the chair.

'Jim, for Christ's sake, do you know what he's asking? If there's *any* truth to what he's said, he's placing you in the worst position a man can be in. An informer.'

'You don't have to stay. My decision doesn't have to be your decision. Why don't you go home?' Matlock rose and walked slowly to the bar, carrying his glass.

'That's impossible now,' said Kressel, turning toward the government agent. 'And *he knows it*.'

Loring felt a touch of sadness. This Matlock was a good man; he was doing what he was doing because he felt he owed a debt. And it was coldly, professionally projected that by accepting the assignment, James Matlock was very possibly going to his death. It was a terrible price, that possibility. But the objective was worth it. The conference was worth it.

Nimrod was worth it.

That was Loring's conclusion.

It made his assignment bearable.

34

Chapter 4

Nothing could be written down; the briefing was slow, repetition constant. But Loring was a professional and knew the value of taking breaks from the pressures of trying to absorb too much too rapidly. During these periods, he attempted to draw Matlock out, learn more about this man whose life was so easily expendable. It was nearly midnight; Sam Kressel had left before eight o'clock. It was neither necessary nor advisable that the dean be present during the detailing of the specifics. He was a liaison, not an activist. Kressel was not averse to the decision.

Ralph Loring learned quickly that Matlock was a private man. His answers to innocuously phrased questions were brief, thrown-away replies constituting no more than self-denigrating explanations. After a while, Loring gave up. Matlock had agreed to do a job, not make public his thoughts or his motives. It wasn't necessary; Loring understood the latter. That was all that mattered. He was just as happy not to know the man too well.

Matlock, in turn – while memorizing the complicated information – was, on another level, reflecting on his own life, wondering in his own way why he'd been selected. He was intrigued by an evaluation that could describe him as being *mobile*; what an awful word to have applied!

Yet he knew he was precisely what the term signified. He *was* mobile. The professional researchers, or psychologists, or whatever they were, were accurate. But he doubted they understood the reasons behind his . . . 'mobility.'

The academic world had been a refuge, a sanctuary. Not an objective of long-standing ambition. He had fled into it in order to buy time, to organize a life that was falling apart, to understand. To get his *head straight*, as the kids said these days.

He had tried to explain it to his wife, his lovely, quick, bright, ultimately hollow wife, who thought he'd lost his senses. What was there to understand but an *awfully* good job, an *awfully* nice house, an *awfully* pleasant club, and a *good* life with an *awfully* rewarding social and financial world? For her, there *was* nothing more to understand. And he understood that.

But for him that world had lost its meaning. He had begun to drift away from its core in his early twenties, during his last year at Amherst. The separation became complete with his army experience.

It was no one single thing that had triggered his rejection. And the rejection itself was not a violent act, although violence played its role in the early days of the Saigon mess. It had begun at home, where most life-styles are accepted or rejected, during a series of disagreeable confrontations with his father. The old gentleman – too old, too gentlemanly – felt justified in demanding a better performance from his first son. A direction, a sense of purpose not at all in evidence. The senior Matlock belonged to another era – if not another century – and believed the gap between father and son a desirable thing, the lower element being dismissible until it had proved itself in the marketplace. Dismissible but, of course, malleable. In ways, the father was like a benign ruler who, after generations of power, was loathe to have the throne abandoned by his rightful issue. It was inconceivable to the elder Matlock that his son would not assume the leadership of the family business. Businesses.

But for the younger Matlock, it was all *too* conceivable.

36

And preferable. He was not only uncomfortable thinking about a future in his father's *marketplace*, he was also afraid. For him there was no joy in the regimented pressures of the financial world; instead, there was an awesome fear of inadequacy, emphasized by his father's strong – overpowering – competence. The closer he came to entering that world, the more pronounced was his fear. And it occurred to him that along with the delights of extravagant shelter and unnecessary creature comforts had to come the justification for doing what was expected in order to possess these things. He could not find that justification. Better the shelter should be less extravagant, the creature comforts somewhat limited, than face the prospects of continuing fear and discomfort.

He had tried to explain *that* to his father. Whereas his wife had claimed he'd lost his senses, the old gentleman pronounced him a misfit.

Which didn't exactly refute the army's judgment of him.

The army.

A disaster. Made worse by the knowledge that it was of his own making. He found that blind physical discipline and unquestioned authority were abhorrent to him. And he was large enough and strong enough and had a sufficient vocabulary to make his unadjustable, immature objections known – to his disadvantage.

Discreet manipulations by an uncle resulted in a discharge before his tour of service was officially completed; for that he *was* grateful to an influential family.

And at this juncture of his life, James Barbour Matlock II was a mess. Separated from the service less than gloriously, divorced by his wife, dispossessed – symbolically if not actually – by his family, he felt the panic of belonging nowhere, of being without motive or purpose.

So he'd fled into the secure confines of graduate school,

hoping to find an answer. And as in a love affair begun on a sexual basis but growing into psychological dependence, he had married that world; he'd found what had eluded him for nearly five vital years. It was the first real commitment he'd ever experienced.

He was free.

Free to enjoy the excitement of a meaningful challenge; free to revel in the confidence that he was equal to it. He plunged into his new world with the enthusiasm of a convert but without the blindness. He chose a period of history and literature that teemed with energy and conflict and contradictory evaluations. The apprentice years passed swiftly; he was consumed and pleasantly surprised by his own talents. When he emerged on the professional plateau, he brought fresh air into the musty archives. He made startling innovations in long-unquestioned methods of research. His doctoral thesis on court interference with English Renaissance literature – news management – blew into the historical ashcan several holy theories about one benefactress named Elizabeth.

He was the new breed of scholar: restless, sceptical, unsatisfied, always searching while imparting what he'd learned to others. Two and a half years after receiving his doctorate, he was elevated to the tenured position of associate professor, the youngest instructor at Carlyle to be so contracted.

James Barbour Matlock II made up for the lost years, the awful years. Perhaps best of all was the knowledge that he could communicate his excitement to others. He was young enough to enjoy sharing his enthusiasm, old enough to direct the inquiries.

Yes, he was *mobile*; God, was he! He couldn't, *wouldn't* turn anyone off, shut anyone out because of disagreement – even dislike. The depth of his own gratitude, the profoundness of his relief was such that he unconsciously

38

promised himself never to discount the concerns of another human being.

'Any surprises?' Loring had completed a section of the material that dealt with narcotics purchases as they'd been traced.

'More a clarification, I'd say,' replied Matlock. 'The old-line fraternities or clubs – mostly white, mostly rich – get their stuff from Hartford. The black units like Lumumba Hall go to New Haven. Different sources.'

'Exactly; that's student orientation. The point being that none buy from the Carlyle suppliers. From Nimrod.'

'You explained that. The Nimrod people don't want to be advertised.'

'But they're here. They're used.'

'By whom?'

'Faculty and staff,' answered Loring calmly, flipping over a page. 'This *may* be a surprise. Mr and Mrs Archer Beeson . . .'

Matlock immediately pictured the young history instructor and his wife. They were Ivy League conformity itself – falsely arrogant, aesthetically precious. Archer Beeson was a young man in an academic hurry; his wife, the perfect faculty ingenue, carelessly sexy, always in awe.

'They're with LSD and the methedrines. Acid and speed.'

'Good Lord! They fooled the hell out of me. How do you know?'

'It's too complicated to go into, also restricted. To oversimplify: they, he, used to purchase heavily from a distributor in Bridgeport. The contact was terminated and he didn't show up on any other lists. But he's not off. We think he made the Carlyle connection. No proof, though . . . Here's another.'

It was the coach of varsity soccer, a jock who worked in physical education. His items were marijuana and

39

amphetamines; his previous source, Hartford. He was considered a pusher on campus, not a user. Although the Hartford source was no longer employed, the man's varied and dummied bank accounts continued to grow. Assumption: Nimrod.

And another. This one frightening to Matlock. The assistant dean of admissions. An alumnus of Carlyle who returned to the campus after a brief career as a salesman. He was a flamboyant, open-handed man; a proselytizer for the cause of Carlyle. A popular enthusiast in these days of cynicism. He, too, was considered a distributor, not a user. He covered himself well through second- and third-level pushers.

'We think he came back here through the Nimrod organization. Good positioning on Nimrod's part.'

'Goddamn scarey. That son of a bitch makes parents think he's a combination of astronaut and chaplain.'

'Good positioning, as I said. Remember? I told you and Kressel: the Nimrod people have interests that go beyond drugs.'

'But you don't know what they are.'

'We'd better find out . . . Here's the breakdown of the kids.'

The names of the students seemed endless to Matlock. There were 563 out of a total enrollment of 1200 plus. The government man admitted that many were included not because of confirmation of individual use, but due to their campus affiliations. Clubs and fraternities were known to pool resources for the purchase of narcotics.

'We haven't the time to ascertain the validity of every name. We're looking for relationships; any, no matter how remote. You've got to have all kinds of avenues; we can't restrict them . . . And there's one aspect to this list; I don't know whether you see it or not.'

'I certainly do. At least, I think I do. Twenty or thirty

40

names here ring loud bells in several high places. Some very influential parents. Industry, government. Here.' Matlock pointed. 'The president's cabinet, if I'm not mistaken. And I'm not.'

'You see.' Loring smiled.

'Has any of this had any effect?'

'We don't know. Could have, could be. The Nimrod tentacles are spreading out fast. That's why the alarms are sounding; louder than your bells. Speaking unofficially, there could be repercussions no-one's dreamed of . . . Defence overruns, union contracts, forced installations. You name it. It *could* be related.'

'Jesus Christ,' said Matlock softly.

'Exactly.'

The two men heard the front door of Sealfont's mansion open and shut. As if by reflex, Loring calmly took the papers from Matlock's hand and quickly replaced them in his briefcase. He closed the case and then did an unexpected thing. He silently, almost unobtrusively, whipped back his jacket and curled his fingers around the handle of a revolver in a small holster strapped to his chest. The action startled Matlock. He stared at the hidden hand.

The library door opened and Adrian Sealfont walked in. Loring casually removed his hand from inside his coat. Sealfont spoke kindly.

'I *do try*. I honestly do. I understand the words and the pictures and take no offence whatsoever at the braided hair. What confuses me is the hostility. Anyone past thirty is the natural enemy of these fellows.'

'That was Strauss, wasn't it?' asked Matlock.

'Yes. Someone inquired about the New Wave influence. He replied that the New Wave was ancient history. Prehistoric, was his word . . . I won't interrupt you gentlemen. I would, however, like to know Kressel's status, Mr Loring. Obviously, James has accepted.'

'So has Mr Kressel, sir. He'll act as liaison between us.'

'I see.' Sealfont looked at Matlock. There was a sense of relief in his eyes. 'James, I can tell you now. I'm extremely grateful you've decided to help.'

'I don't think there's an alternative.'

'There isn't. What's frightening is the possibility of such total involvement. Mr Loring, I'll want to be advised the minute you have anything concrete. At that point, I shall do whatever you wish, follow any instructions. All I ask is that you supply me with proof and you'll have my complete, my official cooperation.'

'I understand, sir. You've been very helpful. More than we had a right to expect. We appreciate it.'

'As James said, there is no alternative. But I must impose limits; my first obligation is to this institution. The campuses these days might appear dormant; I think that's a surface evaluation . . . You have work to do and I have some reading to finish. Good night, Mr Loring. James.'

Matlock and the government man nodded their good nights as Adrian Sealfont closed the library door.

By one o'clock, Matlock could absorb no more. The main elements – names, sources, conjectures – were locked in; he would never forget them. Not that he could recite everything by rote; that wasn't expected. But the sight of any particular individual on the lists would trigger a memory response. He knew Loring was right about that. It was why the agent insisted that he say the names out loud, repeating them several times each. It would be enough.

What he needed now was a night's sleep, if sleep would come. Let everything fall into some kind of perspective. Then in the morning he could begin to make initial decisions, determine which individuals should be approached, selecting those least likely to come in contact with one another. And this meant familiarizing himself with immediate friends, faculty or student body status – dozens of isolated fragments of information beyond the data supplied by Loring. Kressel's files – the ones he disclaimed having – would help.

Once in conversations he'd have to make his way carefully – thrusting, parrying, watching for signs, looks, betrayals.

Somewhere, with someone, it would happen.

'I'd like to go back to something,' said Loring. 'Background material.'

'We've covered an awful lot. Maybe I should digest what I've got.'

'This won't take a minute. It's important.' The agent reached into his briefcase and withdrew the filthy, scissored paper. 'Here, this is yours.'

'Thanks for I-don't-know-what.' Matlock took the once-shining silver paper and looked at the strange script.

'I told you it was written in Oltremontan-Corsican and, except for two words, that's correct. At the bottom, on a single line, you'll see the phrase *Venerare Omerta*. That's not Corsican, it's Sicilian. Or a Sicilian contraction, to be precise.'

'I've seen it before.'

'I'm sure you have. It's been given wide distribution in newspapers, movies, fiction. But that doesn't lessen its impact on those concerned by it. It's very real.'

'What does it mean?'

'Roughly translated: Respect the law of Omerta. Omerta is an oath of allegiance *and* silence. To betray either is asking to be killed.'

'Mafia?'

'It's involved. You might say it's the party of the second part. Bear in mind that this little announcement

43

was issued jointly by two factions trying to reach an accommodation. "Omerta" goes across the board; it's understood by both.'

'I'll bear it in mind, but I don't know what I'm supposed to do with it.'

'Just know about it.'

'OK.'

'One last item. Everything we've covered here tonight is related to narcotics. But if our information is correct, the Nimrod people are involved in other fields. Sharking, prostitution, gambling . . . perhaps, and it's only perhaps, municipal controls, state legislatures, even the federal government . . . Experience tells us that narcotics is the weakest action, the highest rate of collapse among these activities, and that's why we've centered on it. In other words, concentrate on the drug situation but be aware that other avenues exist.'

'It's no secret.'

'Maybe not to you. Let's call it a night.'

'Shouldn't you give me a number where I can reach you?'

'Negative. Use Kressel. We'll check with him several times a day. Once you start asking questions, you may be put under a microscope. Don't call Washington. And *don't* lose our Corsican invitation. It's your ultimate clout. Just find another one.'

'I'll try.'

Matlock watched as Loring closed his briefcase, looped the thin black chain around his wrist, and snapped the built-in lock.

'Looks very cloak-and-daggerish, doesn't it?' Loring laughed.

'I'm impressed.'

'Don't be. The custom began with diplomatic couriers who'd take their pouches to hell with them, but today it's simply a protection against purse-snatching. . . . So help me, that's what they think of us.'

'I don't believe a word you say. That's one of those cases that make smoke screens, send out radio signals, and trigger bombs.'

'You're right. It does all those things and more. It's got secret compartments for sandwiches, laundry, and God knows what else.' Loring swung the briefcase off the desk. 'I think it'd be a good idea if we left separately. Preferably one from the front, one from the rear. Ten minutes apart.'

'You think that's necessary?'

'Frankly, no, but that's the way my superiors want it.'

'OK. I know the house. I'll leave ten minutes after you do, from the kitchen.'

'Fine.' Loring extended his right hand by steadying the bottom of his case with his left. 'I don't have to tell you how much we appreciate what you're doing.'

'I think you know why I'm doing it.'

'Yes, we do. Frankly, we counted on it.'

Loring let himself out of the library and Matlock waited until he heard the outer door open and close. He looked at his watch. He'd have one more drink before he left.

By one-twenty Matlock was several blocks away from the house. He walked slowly west toward his apartment, debating whether to detour around the campus. It often helped him to walk out a problem; he knew sleep would come fitfully. He passed a number of students and several faculty members, exchanging low-keyed, end of the weekend greetings with those he recognized. He'd about made up his mind to turn north on High Street, away from the direction of his apartment, when he heard the footsteps behind him. First the footsteps, then the harshly whispered voice.

45

'Matlock! Don't turn around. It's Loring. Just keep walking and listen to me.'

'What is it?'

'Someone knows I'm here. My car was searched . . .'

'Christ! How do you know?'

'Field threads, preset markings. All over the car. Front, back, trunk. A very thorough, very professional job.'

'You're sure?'

'So goddamn sure I'm not going to start that engine!'

'Jesus!' Matlock nearly stopped.

'Keeping walking. If anyone was watching me – and you can be damned sure someone was – I made it clear I'd lost my ignition key. Asked several people who passed by where a pay phone was and waited till I saw you far enough away.'

'What do you want me to do? There's a phone booth on the next corner . . .'

'I know. I don't think you'll have to do anything, and for both our sakes, I hope I'm right. I'm going to jostle you as I pass – pretty hard. Lose your balance, I'll shout my apologies. Pretend you twisted an ankle, a wrist, anything you like; *but buy time!* Keep me in sight until a car comes for me and *I nod that it's OK.* Do you have all that? I'll get to the booth in a hurry.'

'Suppose you're still phoning when I get there?'

'Keep walking but *keep checking*. The car's cruising.'

'What's the point?'

'This briefcase. That's the point. There's only one thing Nimrod – if it *is* Nimrod – would like more than this briefcase. And that's the paper in your coat pocket. So be careful.'

Without warning, he rushed up beside Matlock and pushed him off the sidewalk.

'Sorry, fella! I'm in an awful hurry!'

Matlock looked up from the ground, reflecting that he'd

46

had no reason to *pretend* to fall. The force of Loring's push eliminated that necessity. He swore and rose awkwardly. Once on his feet, he limped slowly toward the phone booth several hundred yards away. He wasted nearly a minute lighting a cigarette. Loring was inside the booth now, sitting on the plastic seat, hunched over the phone.

Any second, Matlock expected Loring's car to drive up the street.

Yet none come.

Instead, there was the tiniest break in the spring noises. A rush of air through the new leaves. Or was it the crush of a stone beneath a foot, or a small twig unable to take the weight of the new growth in the trees? Or was it Matlock's imagination? He couldn't be sure.

He approached the booth and remembered Loring's orders. *Walk by and pay no attention*. Loring was still huddled over the phone, his briefcase resting on the floor, its chain visible. But Matlock could hear no conversation, could see no movement from the man within. Instead, again, there was a sound: now, the sound of a dial tone.

Despite his instructions, Matlock approached the booth and opened the door. There was nothing else he could do. The government man had not even *begun* his call.

And in an instant, he understood why.

Loring had fallen into the gleaming gray metal of the telephone. He was dead. His eyes wide, blood trickling out of his forehead. A small circular hole no larger than a shirt button, surrounded by a spray of cracked glass, was ample evidence of what had happened.

Matlock stared at the man who had briefed him for hours and left him minutes ago. The dead man who had thanked him, joked with him, then finally warned him. He was petrified, unsure of what he should do, *could* do.

He backed away from the booth toward the steps of the nearest house. Instinct told him to stay away but not to

47

run away. Someone was out there in the street. Someone with a rifle.

When the words came, he realized they were his, but he didn't know when he'd decided to shout them. They just emerged involuntarily.

'Help . . . *Help*! There's a man out here! He's been *shot*!'

Matlock raced up the steps of the corner house and began pounding on the door with all his strength. Several lights went on in several different homes. Matlock continued shouting.

'For God's *sake*, someone call the *police*! *There's a dead man out here!*'

Suddenly, from the shadows underneath the full trees in the middle of the block, Matlock heard the roar of an automobile engine, then the sound of swerving tires as the vehicle pulled out into the middle of the street and started forward. He rushed to the edge of the porch. The long black automobile plunged out of the darkness and sped to the corner. Matlock tried to see the license plates and, realizing that was impossible, took a step down to identify the make of the car. Suddenly he was blinded. The beam of a searchlight pierced the dimly lit spring night and focused itself on him. He pulled his hands up to shield his eyes and then heard the quiet slap, the instant rush of air he had heard minutes ago.

A rifle was being fired at him. A rifle with a silencer.

He dove off the porch into the shrubbery. The black car sped away.

Chapter 5

He waited alone. The room was small, the window glass meshed with wire. The Carlyle Police Station was filled with officers and plainclothesmen called back on duty; no-one could be sure what the killing signified. And none discounted the possibility that others might follow.

Alert. It was the particular syndrome of midcentury America, thought Matlock.

The gun.

He'd had the presence of mind after reaching the police to call Sam Kressel. Kressel, in shock, told him he would somehow contact the appropriate men in Washington and then drive down to the station house.

Until further instructions, they both agreed Matlock would restrict himself to a simple statement on finding the body and seeing the automobile. He had been out for a late night walk, that was all.

Nothing more.

His statement was typed out; questions as to time, his reasons for being in the vicinity, descriptions of the 'alleged perpetrator's vehicle,' direction, estimated speed – all were asked routinely and accepted without comment.

Matlock was bothered by his unequivocal negative to one question.

'Did you ever see the deceased before?'

'No.'

That hurt. Loring deserved more than a considered, deliberate lie. Matlock recalled that the agent said he had a seven-year-old daughter. A wife and a child; the husband and father killed and he could not admit he knew his name.

He wasn't sure why it bothered him, but it did. Perhaps, he thought, because he knew it was the beginning of a great many lies.

He signed the short deposition and was about to be released when he heard a telephone ring inside an office beyond the desk. Not *on* the desk, beyond it. Seconds later, a uniformed policeman emerged and said his name in a loud voice, as if to make sure he had not left the building.

'Yes, officer?'

'We'll have to ask you to wait. If you'll follow me, please.'

Matlock had been in the small room for nearly an hour; it was 2:45 A.M. and he had run out of cigarettes. It was no time to run out of cigarettes.

The door opened and a tall, thin man with large, serious eyes walked in. He was carrying Loring's briefcase. 'Sorry to detain you, Dr Matlock. It is "Doctor," isn't it?'

'"Mister" is fine.'

'My identification. Name's Greenberg, Jason Greenberg. Federal Bureau of Investigation. I had to confirm your situation . . . It's a hell of a note, isn't it?'

'"A hell of a note"? Is that all you can say?'

The agent looked at Matlock quizzically. 'It's all I care to share,' he said quietly. 'If Ralph Loring had completed his call, he would have reached me.'

'I'm sorry.'

'Forget it. I'm out-briefed – that is, I know something but not much about the Nimrod situation; I'll get filled in before morning. Incidentally, this fellow Kressel is on his way over. He knows I'm here.'

'Does this change anything? . . . That sounds stupid,

doesn't it? A man is killed and I ask you if it changes anything. I apologize again.'

'No need to; you've had a terrible experience . . . Any change is up to you. We accept the fact that Ralph's death could alter tonight's decision. We ask only that you keep your own counsel in what was revealed to you.'

'You're offering me a chance to renege?'

'Of course. You're under no obligation to us.'

Matlock walked to the small, rectangular window with the wire-enclosed glass. The police station was at the south end of the town of Carlyle, about a half a mile from the campus, the section of town considered industrialized. Still, there were trees along the streets. Carlyle was a very clean town, a neat town. The trees by the station house were pruned and shaped.

And Carlyle was also something else.

'Let me ask you a question,' he said. 'Does the fact that I found Loring's body associate me with him? I mean, would I be considered a part of whatever he was doing?'

'We don't think so. The way you behaved tends to remove you from any association.'

'What do you mean?' Matlock turned to face the agent.

'Frankly, you panicked. You didn't run, you didn't take yourself out of the area; you flipped out and started shouting your head off. Someone who's programmed for an assignment wouldn't react like that.'

'I wasn't programmed for *this*.'

'Same results. You just found him and lost your head. If this Nimrod even *suspects* we're involved . . .'

'Suspects!' interrupted Matlock. 'They *killed* him!'

'*Someone* killed him. It's unlikely that it's any part of Nimrod. Other factions, maybe. No cover's absolutely foolproof, even Loring's. But his was the closest.'

'I don't understand you.'

51

Greenberg leaned against the wall and folded his arms, his large, sad eyes reflective. 'Ralph's field cover was the best at Justice. For damn near fifteen years.' The agent looked down at the floor. His voice was deep, with faint bitterness. 'The kind of goddamn cover that works best when it doesn't matter to a man any more. When it's finally used, it throws everyone off balance. And insults his family.'

Greenberg looked up and tried to smile, but no smile would come.

'I still don't understand you.'

'It's not necessary. The main point is that you simply stumbled on the scene, went into panic, and had the scare of your life. You're dismissible, Mr Matlock . . . So?'

Before Matlock could respond, the door swung open and Sam Kressel entered, his expression nervous and frightened.

'Oh, Christ! This is terrible! Simply terrible. You're Greenberg?'

'And you're Mr Kressel.'

'Yes. What's going to happen?' Kressel turned to Matlock, speaking in the same breath. 'Are you all right, Jim?'

'Sure.'

'Well, Greenberg, what's *happening*!? They told me in Washington that you'd let us know!'

'I've been talking to Mr Matlock and . . .'

'Listen to me,' interrupted Kressel suddenly. 'I called Sealfont and we're of the same opinion. What happened was terrible . . . tragic. We express our sympathies to the man's family, but we're most anxious that any use of the Carlyle name be cleared with us. We assume this puts everything in a different light and, therefore, we insist we be kept out of it. I think that's understandable.'

Greenberg's face betrayed his distaste. 'You race in

52

here, ask me what's happening, and before you give me a chance to answer, you tell me what *must* happen. Now, how do you want it? Do I call Washington and let them have *your* version or do you want to listen first? Doesn't make a particle of difference to me.'

'There's no reason for antagonism. We never asked to be involved.'

'Nobody does.' Greenberg smiled. 'Just please let me finish. I've offered Matlock his out. He hasn't given me his answer, so I can't give you mine. However, if he says what I think he's going to say, Loring's cover will be activated immediately. It'll be activated anyway, but if the professor's in, we'll blow it up a bit.'

'What the hell are you talking about?' Kressel stared at the agent.

'For years Ralph was a partner in just about the most disreputable law firm in Washington. Its clients read like a cross section of a Mafia index . . . Early this morning, there was the first of two vehicle transfers. It took place in a Hartford suburb, Elmwood. Loring's car with the DC plates was left near the home of a well-advertised capo. A rented automobile was waiting for him a couple of blocks away. He used that to drive to Carlyle and parked it in front of 217 Crescent Street, five blocks from Sealfont's place. 217 Crescent is the residence of a Dr Ralston . . .'

'I've met him,' interjected Matlock. 'I've heard he's . . .'

'. . . an abortionist,' completed Greenberg.

'He's in no way associated with this university!' said Kressel emphatically.

'You've had worse,' countered Greenberg quietly. 'And the doctor is still a Mafia referral. At any rate, Ralph positioned the car and walked into town for the second transfer. I covered him; this briefcase is prime material. He was picked up by a Bell Telephone truck which made routine stops – including one at a restaurant called the

53

Cheshire Cat – and finally delivered him to Sealfont's. No-one could have known he was there. If they had, they would have intercepted him outside; they were watching the car on Crescent.'

'That's what he told me,' said Matlock.

'He knew it was possible; the trace to Crescent was intentionally left open. When he confirmed it, to his satisfaction, he acted fast. I don't know what he did, but he probably used whatever stragglers he could find until he spotted you.'

'That's what he did.'

'He wasn't fast enough.'

'What in God's name does this have to do with *us*? What *possible* bearing can it have?' Kressel was close to shouting.

'If Mr Matlock wants to go on, Loring's death will be publicized as an underworld killing. Disreputable lawyer, maybe a bag man; undesirable clients. The capo and the doctor will be hauled in; they're expendable. The smoke screen's so thick everyone's off balance. Even the killers. Matlock's forgotten. It'll work; it's worked before.'

Kressel seemed astonished at Greenberg's assured glibness, his confidence, his calm professionalism. 'You talk awfully fast, don't you?'

'I'm very bright.'

Matlock couldn't help but smile. He liked Greenberg; even in – perhaps because of – the sadly disagreeable circumstances. The agent used the language well; his mind was fast. He was, indeed, bright.

'And if Jim says he washes his hands of it?'

Greenberg shrugged. 'I don't like to waste words. Let's hear him say it.'

Both the men looked at Matlock.

'I'm afraid I'm not going to, Sam. I'm still in.'

'You can't be serious! That man was killed!'

54

'I know. I found him.'

Kressel put his hand on Matlock's arm. It was the gesture of a friend. 'I'm not an hysterical shepherd watching over a flock. I'm concerned. I'm *frightened*. I see a man being manipulated into a situation he's not qualified to handle.'

'That's subjective,' broke in Greenberg quietly. 'We're concerned, too. If we didn't think he was capable, we never would have approached him.'

'I think you would,' said Kressel. 'I don't for a minute believe such a consideration would stop you. You use the word *expendable* too easily, Mr Greenberg.'

'I'm sorry you think so. Because I don't. We don't . . . I haven't gotten the detailed briefing, Kressel, but aren't you supposed to act as liaison? Because if that's true, I suggest you remove yourself. We'll have someone else assigned to the job.'

'And give you a clear field? Let you run roughshod over this campus? Not on your life.'

'Then we work together. As disagreeable as that may be for both of us . . . You're hostile; perhaps that's good. You'll keep me on my toes. You protest too much.'

Matlock was startled by Greenberg's statement. It was one thing to form an antagonistic coalition, quite another to make veiled accusations; insulting to use a literary cliché.

'That remark requires an explanation,' said Kressel, his face flushed with anger.

When Greenberg replied, his voice was soft and reasonable, belying the words he spoke. 'Pound sand, mister. I lost a very good friend tonight. Twenty minutes ago I spoke with his wife. I don't give explanations under those conditions. That's where my employers and me part company. Now, shut up and I'll write out the hours of contact and give you the emergency

55

telephone numbers. If you don't want them, get the hell out of here.'

Greenberg lifted the briefcase on to a small table and opened it. Sam Kressel, stunned, approached the agent silently.

Matlock stared at the worn leather briefcase, only hours ago chained to the wrist of a dead man. He knew the deadly pavanne had begun. The first steps of the dance had been taken violently.

There were decisions to make, people to confront.

Chapter 6

The implausible name below the door bell on the two-family faculty house read: Mr and Mrs Archer Beeson. Matlock had elicited the dinner invitation easily. History instructor Beeson had been flattered by his interest in coordinating a seminar between two of their courses. Beeson would have been flattered if a faculty member of Matlock's attainments had asked him how his wife was in bed (and most wondered). And since Matlock was very clearly male, Archer Beeson felt that 'drinks and din' with his wife wriggling around in a short skirt might help cement a relationship with the highly regarded professor of English literature.

Matlock heard the breathless shout from the second-floor landing. 'Just a sec!'

It was Beeson's wife, and her broad accent, over-cultivated at Miss Porter's and Finch, sounded caricatured. Matlock pictured the girl racing around checking the plates of cheese and dip – very unusual cheese and dip, conversation pieces, really – while her husband put the final touches on the visual aspects of his bookcases – perhaps several obscure tomes carelessly, carefully, placed on tables, impossible for a visitor to miss.

Matlock wondered if these two were also secreting small tablets of lysergic acid or capsules of methedrine.

The door opened and Beeson's petite wife, dressed in the expected short skirt and translucent silk blouse that loosely covered her large breasts, smiled ingenuously.

'Hi! I'm Ginny Beeson. We met at several *mad* cocktail

57

parties. I'm *so* glad you could come. Archie's just finishing a paper. Come on up.' She preceded Matlock up the stairs, hardly giving him a chance to acknowledge. 'These stairs are *horrendous*! Oh, well, the price of starting at the bottom.'

'I'm sure it won't be for long,' said Matlock.

'That's what Archie keeps saying. He'd better be right or I'll have muscles all over my legs!'

'I'm sure he is,' said Matlock looking at the soft, unmuscular, large expanse of legs in front of him.

Inside the Beeson apartment, the cheese and dip were prominently displayed on an odd-shaped coffee table, and the anticipated showcase volume was one of Matlock's own. It was titled *Interpolations in Richard II* and it resided on a table underneath a fringed lamp. Impossible for a visitor to miss.

The minute Ginny closed the door, Archie burst into the small living room from what Matlock presumed was Beeson's study – also small. He carried a sheaf of papers in his left hand; his right was extended.

'Good-oh! Glad you could make it, old man! . . . Sit, sit. Drinks are due and overdue! Good! I'm flaked out for one! . . . Just spent three hours reading twenty versions of the Thirty Years' War!'

'It happens. Yesterday I got a theme on *Volpone* with the strangest ending I ever heard of. Turned out the kid never read it but saw the film in Hartford.'

'With a new ending?'

'Totally.'

'God! That's marvy!' injected Ginny semihysterically. 'What's your drink preference, Jim? I may call you Jim, mayn't I, Doctor?'

'Bourbon and a touch of water, and you certainly better, Ginny. I've never gotten used to the "doctor." My father calls it fraud. Doctors carry stethoscopes, not books.'

Matlock sat in an easy chair covered with an Indian serape.

'Speaking of doctors, I'm working on my dissertation now. That and two more hectic summers'll do the trick.' Beeson took the ice bucket from his wife and walked to a long table underneath a window where bottles and glasses were carelessly arranged.

'It's worth it,' said Ginny Beeson emphatically. 'Isn't it worth it, Jim?'

'Almost essential. It'll pay off.'

'That and *publishing*.' Ginny Beeson picked up the cheese and crackers and carried them to Matlock. 'This is an interesting little Irish *fromage*. Would you believe, it's called "Blarney"? Found it in a little shop in New York two weeks ago.'

'Looks great. Never heard of it.'

'Speaking of publishing. I picked up your *Interpolations* book the other day. *Damned fascinating!* Really!'

'Lord, I've almost forgotten it. Wrote it four years ago.'

'It should be a *required text*! That's what Archie said, isn't it, Archie?'

'Damned right! Here's the poison, old man,' said Beeson, bringing Matlock his drink. 'Do you work through an agent, Jim? Not that I'm nosy. I'm years from writing anything.'

'That's not true, and you know it,' Ginny pouted vocally.

'Yes, I do. Irving Block in Boston. If you're working on something, perhaps I could show it to him.'

'Oh, no, I wouldn't . . . that'd be awfully presumptuous of me . . .' Beeson retreated with feigned humility to the couch with his drink. He sat next to his wife and they – involuntarily, thought Matlock – exchanged satisfied looks.

'Come on, Archie. You're a bright fellow. A real comer on this campus. Why do you think I asked you about the seminar! *You* could be doing *me* the favor. I might be bringing Block a winner. That rubs off, you know.'

Beeson's expression had the honesty of gratitude. It embarrassed Matlock to return the instructor's gaze until he saw something else in Beeson's eyes. He couldn't define it, but it was there. A slight wildness, a trace of panic.

The look of a man whose mind and body knew drugs.

'That's *damned* good-oh of you, Jim. I'm touched, *really*.'

The cheese, drinks, and dinner somehow passed. There were moments when Matlock had the feeling he was outside himself, watching three characters in a scene from some old movie. Perhaps on board ship or in a sloppily elegant New York apartment with the three of them wearing tightly fitted formal clothes. He wondered why he visualized the scene in such fashion – and then he knew. The Beesons had a thirties quality about them. The thirties that he had observed on the late night television films. They were somehow an anachronism, of this time but not of the time. It was either more than camp or less than put-on; he couldn't be sure. They were not artificial in themselves, but there was a falseness in their emphatic small talk, their dated expressions. Yet the truth was that they were the *now* of the present generation.

Lysergic acid and methedrine.

Acid heads. Pill poppers.

The Beesons were somehow forcing themselves to show themselves as part of a past and carefree era. Perhaps to deny the times and conditions in which they found themselves.

Archie Beeson and his wife were frightening.

By eleven, after considerable wine with the 'interesting-

60

'little-veal-dish-from-a-recipe-in-an-old-Italian-cookbook,' the three of them sat down in the living room. The last of the proposed seminar problems was ironed out. Matlock knew it was time to begin; the awful, awkward moment. He wasn't sure how; the best he could do was to trust his amateur instincts.

'Look, you two . . . I hope to hell this won't come as too great a shock, but I've been a long time without a stick.' He withdrew a thin cigarette case from his pocket and opened it. He felt foolish, uncomfortably clumsy. But he knew he could not show those feelings. 'Before you make any judgments, I should tell you I don't go along with the pot laws and I never have.'

Matlock selected a cigarette from the dozen in the case and left the case open on the table. Was that the proper thing to do? He wasn't sure; he didn't know. Archie and his wife looked at each other. Through the flame in front of his face, Matlock watched their reaction. It was cautious yet positive. Perhaps it was the alcohol in Ginny, but she smiled hesitantly, as if she was relieved to find a friend. Her husband wasn't quite so responsive.

'Go right ahead, old man,' said the young instructor with a trace of condescension. 'We're hardly on the attorney general's payroll.'

'Hardly!' giggled the wife.

'The laws are archaic,' continued Matlock, inhaling deeply. 'In all areas. Control and an abiding sense of discretion – self-discretion – are all that matter. To deny experience is the real crime. To prohibit any intelligent individual's right to fulfillment is . . . goddamn it, it's repressive.'

'Well, I think the key word is *intelligent*, Jim. *In*discriminate use among the *un*intelligent leads to chaos.'

'Socratically, you're only half right. The other half is "control." Effective control among the "iron" and "bronze" then frees the "gold" – to borrow from *The Republic*. If the intellectually superior were continually kept from thinking, experimenting, because their thought processes were beyond the comprehension of their fellow citizens, there'd be no great works – artistically, technically, politically. We'd still be in the Dark Ages.'

Matlock inhaled his cigarette and closed his eyes. Had he been too strong, too positive? Had he sounded too much the false proselytizer? He waited, and the wait was not long. Archie spoke quietly, but urgently nevertheless.

'Progress is being made every day, old man. Believe that. It's the truth.'

Matlock half opened his eyes in relief and looked at Beeson through the cigarette smoke. He held his gaze steady without blinking and then shifted his stare to Beeson's wife. He spoke only two words.

'You're children.'

'That's a relative supposition under the circumstances,' answered Beeson still keeping his voice low, his speech precise.

'And that's talk.'

'Oh, don't be so sure about that!' Ginny Beeson had had enough alcohol in her to be careless. Her husband reached for her arm and held it. It was a warning. He spoke again, taking his eyes off Matlock, looking at nothing.

'I'm not at all sure we're on the same wavelength . . .'

'No, probably not. Forget it . . . I'll finish this and shove off. Be in touch with you about the seminar.' Matlock made sure his reference to the seminar was offhanded, almost disinterested.

Archie Beeson, the young man in an academic hurry, could not stand that disinterest.

'Would you mind if I had one of those?'

'If it's your first, yes, I would . . . Don't try to impress me. It doesn't really matter.'

'My first? . . . Of what?' Beeson rose from the couch and walked to the table where the cigarette case lay open. He reached down, picked it up, and held it to his nostrils. 'That's passable grass. I might add, just passable. I'll try one . . . for openers.'

'For openers?'

'You seem to be very sincere but, if you'll forgive me, you're a bit out of touch.'

'From what?'

'From where it's at.' Beeson withdrew two cigarettes and lit them in *Now, Voyager* fashion. He inhaled deeply, nodding and shrugging a reserved approval, and handed one to his wife.

'Let's call this an hors d'oeuvre. An appetizer.'

He went into his study and returned with a Chinese lacquered box, then showed Matlock the tiny peg which, when pushed, enabled the holder to flip up a thin layer of wood on the floor of the box, revealing a false bottom. Beneath were two dozen or so white tablets wrapped in transparent plastic.

'This is the main course . . . the entrée, if you're up to it.'

Matlock was grateful for what knowledge he possessed and the intensive homework he'd undertaken during the past forty-eight hours. He smiled but his tone of voice was firm.

'I only take white trips under two conditions. The first is at *my* home with very good, very old friends. The second is with very good, very old friends at *their* homes. I don't know you well enough, Archie. Self-destruction . . . I'm not averse to a small red journey, however. Only I didn't come prepared.'

'Say no more. I just may be.' Beeson took the Chinese box back into his study and returned with a small leather pouch, the sort pipe smokers use for tobacco, and

63

approached Matlock's chair. Ginny Beeson's eyes grew wide; she undid a button on her half-unbuttoned blouse and stretched her legs.

'Dunhill's best.' Beeson opened the top flap and held the pouch down for Matlock to see inside. Again there was the clear plastic wrapped around tablets. However, these were deep red and slightly larger than the white pills in the Chinese box. There were at least fifty to sixty doses of Seconal.

Ginny jumped out of the chair and squealed. 'I *love* it! It's the pinky-groovy!'

'Beats the hell out of brandy,' added Matlock.

'We'll trip. Not too much, old man. Limit's five. That's the house rules for new old friends.'

The next two hours were blurred for James Matlock, but not as blurred as they were for the Beesons. The history instructor and his wife quickly reached their 'highs' with the five pills – as would have Matlock had he not been able to pocket the final three while pretending to have swallowed them. Once on the first plateau, it wasn't hard for Matlock to imitate his companions and then convince Beeson to go for another dosage.

'Where's the almighty discretion, Doctor?' chuckled Beeson, sitting on the floor in front of the couch, reaching occasionally for one of his wife's legs.

'You're better friends than I thought you were.'

'Just the *beginning* of a beautiful, *beautiful* friendship.' The young wife slowly reclined on the couch and giggled. She seemed to writhe and put her right hand on her husband's head, pushing his hair forward.

Beeson laughed with less control than he had shown earlier and rose from the floor. 'I'll get the magic then.'

When Beeson walked into his study, Matlock watched his wife. There was no mistaking her action. She looked at

64

Matlock, opened her mouth slowly, and pushed her tongue out at him. Matlock realized that one of Seconal's side effects was showing. As was most of Virginia Beeson.

The second dosage was agreed to be three, and Matlock was now easily able to fake it. Beeson turned on his stereo and played a recording of 'Carmina Burana.' In fifteen minutes Ginny Beeson was sitting on Matlock's lap, intermittently rubbing herself against his groin. Her husband was spread out in front of the stereo speakers, which were on either side of the turntable. Matlock spoke as though exhaling, just loud enough to be heard over the music.

'These are some of the best I've had, Archie . . . Where? Where's the supply from?'

'Probably the same as yours, old man.' Beeson turned over and looked at Matlock and his wife. He laughed. 'Now, I don't know what you mean. The magic or the girl on your lap. Watch her, Doctor. She's a minx.'

'No kidding. Your pills are a better grade than mine and my grass barely passed inspection. Where? Be a good friend.'

'You're funny, man. You keep asking. Do I ask you? No . . . It's not polite . . . Play with Ginny. Let me listen.' Beeson rolled back over face down on the floor.

The girl on Matlock's lap suddenly put her arms around his neck and pressed her breasts against his chest. She put her head to the side of his face and began kissing his ears. Matlock wondered what would happen if he lifted her out of the chair and carried her into the bedroom. He wondered, but he didn't want to find out. Not then. Ralph Loring had not been murdered to increase his, Matlock's, sex life.

'Let me try one of your joints. Let me see just how advanced your taste is. You may be a phony, Archie.'

Suddenly Beeson sat up and stared at Matlock. He

65

wasn't concerned with his wife. Something in Matlock's voice seemed to trigger an instinctive doubt. Or was it the words? Or was it the too normal pattern of speech Matlock used? The English professor thought of all these things as he returned Beeson's look over the girl's shoulder. Archie Beeson was suddenly a man warned, and Matlock wasn't sure why. Beeson spoke haltingly.

'Certainly, old man . . . Ginny, don't annoy Jim.' He began to rise.

'Pinky groovy . . .'

'I've got several in the kitchen . . . I'm not sure where but I'll look. Ginny, I told you not to tease Jim . . . Be nice to him, be good to him.' Beeson kept staring at Matlock, his eyes wide from the Seconal, his lips parted, the muscles of his face beyond relaxation. He backed away toward the kitchen door, which was open. Once inside, Archie Beeson did a strange thing. Or so it appeared to James Matlock.

He slowly closed the swing-hinged door and held it shut.

Matlock quickly eased the drugged girl off his lap and she quietly stretched out on the floor. She smiled angelically and reached her arms up for him. He smiled down, stepping over her.

'Be right back,' he whispered. 'I want to ask Archie something.' The girl rolled over on her stomach as Matlock walked cautiously toward the kitchen door. He ruffled his hair and purposely, silently, lurched, holding on to the dining room table as he neared the entrance. If Beeson suddenly came out, he wanted to appear irrational, drugged. The stereo was a little louder now, but through it Matlock could hear the sound of Archie's voice talking quietly, excitedly on the kitchen telephone.

He leaned against the wall next to the kitchen door and tried to analyze the disjointed moments that caused Archie Beeson to panic, to find it so imperative to reach someone on the telephone.

66

Why? What?

Had the grand impersonation been so obvious? Had he blown his first encounter?

If he had, the least he could do was try to find out who was on the other end of the line, who it was that Beeson ran to in his disjointed state of anxiety.

One fact seemed clear: whoever it was had to be more important than Archer Beeson. A man – even a drug addict – did not panic and contact a lesser figure on his own particular totem.

Perhaps the evening wasn't a failure; or his failure – conversely – a necessity. In Beeson's desperation, he might let slip information he never would have revealed if he *hadn't* been desperate. It wasn't preposterous to force it out of the frightened, drugged instructor. On the other hand, that was the least desirable method. If he failed in that, too, he was finished before he'd begun. Loring's meticulous briefing would have been for nothing; his death a rather macabre joke, his terrible cover – so painful to his family, so inhuman somehow – made fruitless by a bumbling amateur.

There was no other way, thought Matlock, but to try. Try to find out who Beeson had reached *and* try to put the pieces of the evening back where Beeson might accept him again. For some insane reason, he pictured Loring's briefcase and the thin black chain dangling from the handle. For an even crazier reason, it gave him confidence; not much, but some.

He assumed a stance as close to the appearance of collapse as he could imagine, then moved his head to the door frame and slowly, quarter inch by quarter inch, pushed it inward. He fully expected to be met by Beeson's staring eyes. Instead, the instructor's back was to him; he was hunched over like a small boy trying to control his bladder, the phone clutched to his thin scrunched neck, his head bent to the side. It was obvious that Beeson thought his voice was muffled, indistinguishable beneath the sporadic crescendos of the 'Carmina Burana.' But the Seconal had played one of its tricks. Beeson's ear and his speech were no longer synchronized. His words were not only clear. They were emphasized by being spaced out and repeated.

'. . . You *do not* understand me. I want you to understand me. *Please*, understand. He keeps asking questions. He's not *with* it. He *is not with it*. I swear to Christ he's a plant. Get hold of Herron. Tell Herron to reach him for *God's* sake. Reach him, *please*! I could lose everything! . . . No. No, I can tell! I *see* what I *see, man*! When that bitch turns horny I have *problems*. I mean there are appearances, old man . . . Get Lucas . . . For Christ's sake *get* to him! I'm in *trouble* and I can't . . .'

Matlock let the door swing slowly back into the frame. His shock was such that thought and feeling were suspended; he saw his hand still on the kitchen door, yet he felt no wood against his fingers. What he had just heard was no less horrible than the sight of Ralph Loring's lifeless body in the telephone booth.

Herron. *Lucas Herron!*

A seventy-year-old legend. A quiet scholar who was as much revered for his perceptions of the human condition as he was for his brilliance. A lovely man, an honored man. There had to be a mistake, an explanation.

There was no time to ponder the inexplicable.

Archer Beeson thought he was a 'plant.' And now, someone else thought so, too. He couldn't allow that. He had to think, force himself to *act*.

Suddenly he understood. Beeson himself had told him what to do.

No informer – no-one not narcotized – would attempt it.

Matlock looked over at the girl lying face down on the living room floor. He crossed rapidly around the dining table and ran to her side, unbuckling his belt as he did so. In swift movements, he took off his trousers and reached down, rolling her over on her back. He lay down beside her and undid the remaining two buttons on her blouse, pulling her brassiere until the hasp broke. She moaned and giggled, and when he touched her exposed breasts, she moaned again and lifted one leg over Matlock's hip.

'Pinky groovy, pinky groovy . . .' She began breathing through her mouth, pushing her pelvis into Matlock's groin; her eyes half open, her hands reaching down, stroking his leg, her fingers clutching at his skin.

Matlock kept his eyes toward the kitchen door, praying it would open.

And then it did, and he shut his eyes.

Archie Beeson stood in the dining area looking down at his wife and guest. Matlock, at the sound of Beeson's footsteps, snapped his head back and feigned terrified confusion. He rose from the floor and immediately fell back down again. He grabbed his trousers and held them in front of his shorts, rising once more unsteadily and finally falling on to the couch.

'Oh, Jesus! Oh, sweet Jesus, Archie! Christ, young fella! I didn't think I was this freaked out! . . . I'm far out, Archie! What the hell, what do I *do*? I'm *gone*, man, I'm sorry! Christ, I'm sorry!'

Beeson approached the couch, his half-naked wife at his feet. From his expression it was impossible to tell what he was thinking. Or the extent of his anger.

Or was it anger?

His audible reaction was totally unexpected. He started to laugh. At first softly, and then with gathering momentum, until he became nearly hysterical.

'Oh, *God*, old man! I said it! I *said* she was a minx! . . .

Don't worry. No tattle tales. No rapes, no dirty-old-man-on-the-faculty. But we'll have our *seminar*. Oh, Christ, yes! That'll be some *seminar*! And you'll tell them all you picked *me*! Won't you? Oh, yes! That's what you'll tell them, isn't it?'

Matlock looked into the wild eyes of the addict above him.

'Sure. Sure, Archie. Whatever you say.'

'You better believe it, old man! And don't apologize. No apologies are necessary! The apologies are mine!' Archer Beeson collapsed on the floor in laughter. He reached over and cupped his wife's left breast; she moaned and giggled her maddening, high-pitched giggle.

And Matlock knew he had won.

Chapter 7

He was exhausted, both by the hour and by the tensions of the night. It was ten minutes past three and the choral strains of the 'Carmina Burana' were still hammering in his ears. The image of the bare-breasted wife and the jackal-sounding husband – both writhing on the floor in front of him – added revulsion to the sickening taste in his mouth.

But what bothered him most was the knowledge that Lucas Herron's name was used within the context of such an evening.

It was inconceivable.

Lucas Herron. The 'grand old bird,' as he was called. A reticent but obvious fixture of the Carlyle campus. The chairman of the Romance languages department and the embodiment of the quiet scholar with a deep and abiding compassion. There was always a glint in his eyes, a look of bemusement mixed with tolerance.

To associate him – regardless of how remotely – with the narcotics world was unbelievable. To have heard him sought after by an hysterical addict – for essentially, Archer Beeson was an addict, psychologically if not chemically – as though Lucas were some sort of power under the circumstances was beyond rational comprehension.

The explanation had to lie somewhere in Lucas Herron's immense capacity for sympathy. He was a friend to many, a dependable refuge for the troubled, often the deeply troubled. And beneath his placid, aged, unruffled surface, Herron was a strong man, a leader. A quarter of a century ago, he had spent countless months of hell in the Solomon

71

Islands as a middle-aged infantry officer. A lifetime ago, Lucas Herron had been an authentic hero in a vicious moment of time during a savage war in the Pacific. Now over seventy, Herron was an institution.

Matlock rounded the corner and saw his apartment half a block away. The campus was dark; aside from the street lamps, the only light came from one of his rooms. Had he left one on? He couldn't remember.

He walked up the path to his door and inserted his key. Simultaneously with the click of the lock, there was a loud crash from within. Although it startled him, his first reaction was amusement. His clumsy, long-haired house cat had knocked over a stray glass or one of those pottery creations Patricia Ballantyne had inflicted on him. Then he realized such a thought was ridiculous, the product of an exhausted mind. The crash was too loud for pottery, the shattering of glass too violent.

He rushed into the small foyer, and what he saw pushed fatigue out of his brain. He stood immobile in disbelief.

The entire room was in shambles. Tables were overturned; books pulled from the shelves, their pages torn from the bindings, scattered over the floor, his stereo turntable and speakers smashed. Cushions from his couch and armchairs were slashed, the stuffing and foam rubber strewn everywhere; the rugs upended, lumped in folds; the curtains ripped from their rods, thrown over the upturned furniture.

He saw the reason for the crash. His large casement window, on the far right wall bordering the street, was a mass of twisted lead and broken glass. The window consisted of two panels; he remembered clearly that he had opened both before leaving for the Beesons. He liked the spring breezes, and it was too early in the season for screens. So there was no reason for the window to be smashed; the ground was perhaps four or five feet

72

below the casement, sufficient to dissuade an intruder, low enough for a panicked burglar to negotiate easily.

The smashing of the window, therefore, was not for escape. It was intended.

He had been watched, and a signal had been given.

It was a warning.

And Matlock knew he could not acknowledge that warning. To do so was to acknowledge more than a robbery; he was not prepared to do that.

He crossed rapidly to his bedroom door and looked inside. If possible, his bedroom was in more of a mess than the living room. The mattress was thrown against the wall, ripped to shreds. Every drawer of his bureau was dislodged, lying on the floor, the contents scattered all around the room. His closet was like the rest – suits and jackets pulled from the clothes rod, shoes yanked from their recesses.

Even before he looked he knew his kitchen would be no better off than the rest of his apartment. The foodstuffs in cans and boxes had not been thrown on the floor, simply moved around, but the soft items had been torn to pieces. Matlock understood again. One or two crashes from the other rooms were tolerable noise levels; a continuation of the racket from his kitchen might arouse one of the other families in the building. As it was, he could hear the faint sounds of footsteps above him. The final crash of the window had gotten someone up.

The warning was explicit, but the act itself was a search.

He thought he knew the object of that search, and again he realized he could not acknowledge it. Conclusions were being made as they had been made at Beeson's; he had to ride them out with the most convincing denials he could manufacture. That much he knew instinctively.

But before he began that pretense, he had to find out if the search was successful.

He shook the stammering lethargy out of his mind and body. He looked once again at his living room; he studied it. All the windows were bare, and the light was sufficient for someone with a pair of powerful binoculars stationed in a nearby building or standing on the inclining lawn of the campus beyond the street to observe every move he made. If he turned off the lights, would such an unnatural action lend credence to the conclusions he wanted denied?

Without question. A man didn't walk into a house in shambles and proceed to turn off lights.

Yet he had to reach his bathroom, at that moment the most important room in the apartment. He had to spend less than thirty seconds inside to determine the success or failure of the ransacking, and do so in such a way as to seem innocent of any abnormal concerns. If anyone *was* watching.

It was a question of appearance, of gesture, he thought. He saw that the stereo turntable was the nearest object to the bathroom door, no more than five feet away. He walked over and bent down, picking up several pieces, including the metal arm. He looked at it, then suddenly dropped the arm and brought his finger to his mouth, feigning an imagined puncture on his skin. He walked into the bathroom rapidly.

Once inside, he quickly opened the medicine cabinet and grabbed a tin of Band-Aids from the glass shelf. He then swiftly reached down to the left of the toilet bowl where the cat's yellow plastic box was placed and picked up a corner of the newspaper underneath the granules of litter. Beneath the newspaper he felt the coarse grain of the two layers of canvas he had inserted and lifted up an edge.

The scissored page was still intact. The silver Corsican

paper that ended in the deadly phrase *Venerare Omerta* had not been found.

He replaced the newspaper, scattered the litter, and stood up. He saw that the frosted glass of the small window above the toilet was partially opened, and he swore.

There was no time to think of that.

He walked back into the living room, ripping the plastic off a Band-Aid.

The search had failed. Now the warning had to be ignored, the conclusions denied. He crossed to the telephone and called the police.

'Can you give me a list of what's missing?' A uniformed patrolman stood in the middle of the debris. A second policeman wandered about the apartment making notes.

'I'm not sure yet. I haven't really checked.'

'That's understandable. It's a mess. You'd better look, though. The quicker we get a list, the better.'

'I don't think anything *is* missing, officer. What I mean is, I don't have anything particularly valuable to anyone else. Except perhaps the stereo . . . and that's smashed. There's a television set in the bedroom, that's okay. Some of the books could bring a price, but look at them.'

'No cash, jewelry, watches?'

'I keep money in the bank and cash in my wallet. I wear my watch and haven't any jewelry.'

'How about exam papers? We've been getting a lot of that.'

'In my office. In the English department.'

The patrolman wrote in a small black notebook and called to his partner, who had gone into the bedroom. 'Hey, Lou, did the station confirm the print man?'

'They're getting him up. He'll be over in a few minutes.'

'Have you touched anything, Mr Matlock?'

75

'I don't know. I may have. It was a shock.'

'Particularly any of the broken items, like that record player? It'd be good if we could show the fingerprint man specific things you haven't touched.'

'I picked up the arm, not the casing.'

'Good. It's a place to start.'

The police stayed for an hour and a half. The fingerprint specialist arrived, did his work, and departed. Matlock thought of phoning Sam Kressel, but reasoned that there wasn't anything Kressel could do at that hour. And in the event someone outside *was* watching the building, Kressel shouldn't be seen. Various people from the other apartments had wakened and had come down offering sympathy, help, and coffee.

As the police were leaving, a large patrolman turned in the doorway. 'Sorry to take so much time, Mr Matlock. We don't usually lift prints in a break and entry unless there's injury or loss of property, but there's been a lot of this sort of thing recently. Personally, I think it's those weirdos with the hair and the beads. Or the niggers. We never had trouble like this before the weirdos and the niggers got here.'

Matlock looked at the uniformed officer, who was so confident of his analysis. There was no point in objecting; it would be useless, and Matlock was too tired. 'Thanks for helping me straighten up.'

'Sure thing.' The patrolman started down the cement path, then turned again. 'Oh, Mr Matlock.'

'Yes?' Matlock pulled the door back.

'It struck us that maybe someone was looking for something. What with all the slashing and books and everything . . . you know what I mean?'

'Yes.'

'You'd tell us if that was the case, wouldn't you?'

76

'Of course.'

'Yeah. It'd be stupid to withhold information like that.'

'I'm not stupid.'

'No offense. Just that sometimes you guys get all involved and forget things.'

'I'm not absentminded. Very few of us are.'

'Yeah.' The patrolman laughed somewhat derisively. 'I just wanted to bring it up. I mean, we can't do our jobs unless we got all the facts, you know?'

'I understand.'

'Yeah. Good.'

'Good night.'

'Good night, Doctor.'

He closed the door and walked into his living room. He wondered if his insurance would cover the disputable value of his rarer books and prints. He sat down on the ruined couch and surveyed the room. It was still a mess; the carnage had been thorough. It would take more than picking up debris and righting furniture. The warning had been clear, violent.

The startling fact was that the warning existed at all.

Why? From whom?

Archer Beeson's hysterical telephone call? That was possible, even preferable, perhaps. It might encompass a motive unrelated to Nimrod. It could mean that Beeson's circle of users and pushers wanted to frighten him enough to leave Archie alone. Leave them all alone; and Loring had specifically said there was no proof that the Beesons were involved with the Nimrod unit.

There was no proof that they weren't, either.

Nevertheless, if it *was* Beeson, the alarm would be called off in the morning. There was no mistaking the conclusion of the night's engagement. The 'near-rape' by a dirty, drugged 'old man.' He was Beeson's academic ladder.

On the other hand, and far less preferable, there was the

77

possibility that the warning *and* the search were centered on the Corsican paper. What had Loring whispered behind him on the sidewalk?

'. . . There's only one thing they want more than this briefcase; that's the paper in your pocket.'

It was then reasonable to assume that he'd been linked to Ralph Loring.

Washington's assessment that his panic at finding Loring dissociated him from the agent was in error, Jason Greenberg's confidence misplaced.

Still again, as Greenberg had suggested, they might test him. Press him before issuing a clean bill of health.

Might, could, possible, still again.

Conjectures.

He had to keep his head; he couldn't allow himself to overreact. If he was to be of *any* value, he had to play the innocent.

Might have, could have, it was possible.

His body ached. His eyes were swollen and his mouth still had the terrible aftertaste of the combined dosages of Seconal, wine, and marijuana. He was exhausted; the pressures of trying to reach unreachable conclusions were overtaking him. His memory wandered back to the early days in 'Nam and he recalled the best advice he'd ever been given in those weeks of unexpected combat. That was to rest whenever he could, to sleep if it was at all possible. The advice had come from a line sergeant who, it had been rumored, had survived more assaults than any man in the Mekong Delta. Who, it was also rumored, had slept through an ambush which had taken most of his company.

Matlock stretched out on the barely recognizable couch. There was no point in going into the bedroom – his mattress was destroyed. He unbuckled his belt and kicked off his shoes. He could sleep for a few hours; then he'd talk to Kressel. Ask Kressel and Greenberg to work out a story for him to use about the invasion of his apartment. A story approved by Washington and, perhaps, the Carlyle police.

The police.

Suddenly he sat up. It hadn't struck him at the time, but now he considered it. The crass but imperiously polite patrolman whose primitive detection powers had centered on the 'weirdos and niggers' had addressed him as 'Mister' throughout the nearly two hours of police investigation. Yet when he was leaving, when he insultingly referred to the possibility of Matlock's withholding information, he had called him 'Doctor.' The 'mister' was normal. The 'doctor' was most unusual. No one outside the campus community – and rarely there – ever called him 'Doctor,' ever called *any* PhD 'Doctor.' It struck most holders of such degrees as fatuous, and only the fatuous expected it.

Why had the patrolman used it? He didn't know him, he had never seen him to his knowledge. How would the patrolman know he was even entitled to the name 'doctor'?

As he sat there, Matlock wondered if the combined efforts and pressures of the last hours were taking their toll. Was he now finding unreasonable meanings where no meanings existed? Was it not entirely plausible that the Carlyle police had a list of the Carlyle faculty and that a desk sergeant, or whoever took emergency calls, had checked his name against the list and casually stated his title? Was he not, perhaps, consigning the patrolman to a plateau of ignorance because he disliked the officer's prejudices?

A lot of things were possible.

And disturbing.

Matlock fell back on to the couch and closed his eyes.

At first the noise reached him as a faint echo might from the far end of a long, narrow tunnel. Then the noise became identifiable as rapid, incessant tapping. Tapping which would not stop, tapping which became louder and louder.

Matlock opened his eyes and saw the blurred light coming from two table lamps across from the couch. His feet were drawn up under him, his neck perspiring against the rough surface of the sofa's corduroy cover. Yet there was a cool breeze coming through the smashed, lead-framed window.

The tapping continued, the sound of flesh against wood. It came from the foyer, from his front door. He flung his legs over the side onto the floor and found that they both were filled with pins and needles. He struggled to stand.

The tapping and the knocking became louder. Then the voice. 'Jamie! Jamie!'

He walked awkwardly toward the door.

'Coming!' He reached the door and opened it swiftly. Patricia Ballantyne, dressed in a raincoat, silk pajamas evident underneath, walked rapidly inside.

'Jamie, for God's sake, I've been trying to call you.'

'I've been here. The phone didn't ring.'

'I know it didn't. I finally got an operator and she said it was out of order. I borrowed a car and drove over as fast as I could and . . .'

'It's not out of order, Pat. The police – the police were here and a quick look around will explain why – they used it a dozen times.'

'Oh, good Lord!' The girl walked past him into the still-disheveled room. Matlock crossed to the telephone and picked it up from the table. He quickly held it away from his ear as the piercing tone of a disengaged instrument whistled out of the receiver.

80

'The bedroom,' he said, replacing the telephone and going to his bedroom door.

On his bed, on top of the slashed remains of his mattress, was his bedside phone. The receiver was off the hook, *underneath* the pillow, muffling the harsh sound of the broken connection so it would not be heard. Someone had not wanted it to ring.

Matlock tried to remember everyone who'd been there. All told, more than a dozen people. Five or six policemen – in and out of uniform; husbands and wives from other apartments; several late-night passersby who had seen the police cars and wandered up to the front door. It had been cumulatively blurred. He couldn't remember all the faces.

He put the telephone back on the bedside table and was aware that Pat stood in the doorway. He gambled that she hadn't seen him remove the pillow.

'Someone must have knocked it over straightening out things,' he said, pretending irritation. 'That's rotten; I mean your having to borrow a car . . . Why did you? What's the matter?'

She didn't reply. Instead, she turned and looked back into the living room. 'What happened?'

Matlock remembered the patrolman's language. 'They call it "break and entry." A police phrase covering human tornadoes, as I understand it. . . . Robbery. I got myself robbed for the first time in my life. It's quite an experience. I think the poor bastards were angry because there wasn't anything of any value so they ripped the place apart . . . Why'd you come over?'

She spoke softly, but the intensity of her voice made Matlock realize that she was close to panic. As always, she imposed a control on herself when she became emotional. It was an essential part of the girl.

'A couple of hours ago – at quarter to four to be exact

81

– my phone rang. The man, it was a man, asked for you. I was asleep, and I suppose I didn't make much sense, but I pretended to be upset that anyone would think you were there . . . I didn't know what to do. I was confused . . .'

'Okay, I understand that. So?'

'He said he didn't believe me. I was a liar. I . . . I was so surprised that anyone would phone then – at quarter to four – and called me a liar . . . I was confused . . .'

'What did you say?'

'It's not what *I* said. It's what *he* said. He told me to tell you to . . . not to stay "behind the globe" or "light the lower world." He said it *twice*! He said it was an awful joke but you'd understand. It was frightening! . . . Do you? Do you understand?'

Matlock walked past her into the living room. He looked for his cigarettes and tried to remain calm. She followed him. 'What did he mean?'

'I'm not sure.'

'Has it anything to do with . . . this?' She gestured her hand over the apartment.

'I don't think so.' He lit his cigarette and wondered what he should tell her. The Nimrod people hadn't wasted any time finding associations. If it *was* Nimrod.

'What did he mean by . . . "standing behind the globe"? It sounds like a riddle.'

'It's a quote, I think.' But Matlock did not have to think. He knew. He recalled Shakespeare's words precisely: *Knowest thou not that when the searching eye of heaven is hid behind the globe and lights the lower world . . . then thieves and robbers range abroad unseen . . . in murders and in outrage bloody here.*

'What does it mean?'

'I don't *know*! I can't remember it . . . Somebody's confusing me with someone else. That's the only thing I can imagine . . . What did he sound like?'

'Normal. He was angry but he didn't shout or anything.'

'No one you recognized? Not specifically, but did you ever hear the voice before?'

'I'm not sure. I don't think so. No one I could pick out, but . . .'

'But what?'

'Well, it was a . . . cultivated voice. A little actorish, I think.'

'A man used to lecturing.' Matlock made a statement, he did not ask a question. His cigarette tasted sour so he crushed it out.

'Yes, I guess that would describe it.'

'And probably not in a science lab . . . That reduces the possibilities to roughly eighty people on campus.'

'You're making assumptions I don't understand! That phone call *did* have something to do with what happened here.'

He knew he was talking too much. He didn't want to involve Pat; he *couldn't* involve her. Yet someone else had – and that fact was a profound complication. 'It might have. According to the best sources – naturally I refer to television detectives – thieves make sure people aren't home before they rob a place. They were probably checking me out.'

The girl held his wavering eyes with her gaze. 'Weren't you home then? At quarter to four? . . . The question is not inquisitorial, my darling, simply a point of information.'

He swore at himself silently. It was the exhaustion, the Beeson episode, the shock of the apartment. Of course the question wasn't inquisitorial. He was a free agent. And, of course, he was at home at quarter to four.

'I'm not sure. I wasn't that concerned with the time. It was one hell of a long evening.' He laughed feebly. 'I was at Archie Beeson's. Proposed seminars with young instructors promote a lot of booze.'

She smiled. 'I don't think you understand me. I really don't mind what Poppa Bear was doing . . . Well, of course, I do, but right now I don't understand why you're lying to me . . . You were *here* two hours ago, and that phone call wasn't any thief checking your whereabouts and you *know* it.'

'Momma Bear's reaching. That doesn't go with the territory.' Matlock was rude. It, too, like the lying, was obviously false. Whatever his past rebellions, whatever his toughness, he was a kind person and she knew that.

'All right. I apologize. I'll ask one more question and then I'll leave . . . What does *Omerta* mean?'

Matlock froze. 'What did you say?'

'The man on the phone. He used the word *Omerta*.'

'How?'

'Very casually. Just a reminder, he said.'

84

Chapter 8

Field Agent Jason Greenberg walked through the border-less door of the squash court. 'You're working up quite a sweat there, Dr Matlock.'

'I'd hate to have it analyzed . . . Anyway, it was your idea. I would have been just as happy at Kressel's office or even downtown somewhere.'

'This is better . . . We've got to talk quickly, though. The gym registry has me listed as an insurance surveyor. I'm checking the extinguishers in the corridors.'

'They probably need checking.' Matlock walked to a corner where a gray sweatshirt was wrapped in a towel. He unwound it and slipped it over his head. 'What have you come up with? Last night was a little hairy.'

'If you discount confusion, we haven't come up with a thing. At least nothing specific. A couple of theories, that's all . . . We think you handled yourself very well.'

'Thanks. I was confused. What are the theories? You sound academic, and I'm not sure I like that.'

Greenberg's head suddenly shifted. From the right wall there could be heard a dull thumping. 'Is that another court?'

'Yes. There are six of them on this side. They're practice courts, no balconies. But you know that.'

Greenberg picked up the ball and threw it hard against the front wall. Matlock understood and caught it on the bounce. He threw it back; Greenberg returned it. They maintained a slow rhythm, neither man moving more than a foot or two, each taking his turn to throw. Greenberg spoke softly, in a monotone.

'We think you're being tested. That's the most logical explanation. You *did* find Ralph. You made a statement about seeing the car. Your reasons for being in the area were weak; so weak we thought they were plausible. They want to make sure, that's why they brought in the girl. They're being thorough.'

'Okay. Theory number one. What's number two?'

'I said that was the most logical . . . It's the only one, really.'

'What about Beeson?'

'What about him? You were there.'

Matlock held the squash ball in his hand for a few seconds before lobbing it against the side wall. The wall away from Greenberg's stare.

'Could Beeson have been smarter than I thought and sent out an alarm?'

'He could have. We think it's doubtful . . . The way you described the evening.'

But Matlock had *not* described the *entire* evening. He had not told Greenberg or anyone of Beeson's telephone call. His reasons weren't rational, they were emotional. Lucas Herron was an old man, a gentle man. His sympathy for troubled students was legendary; his concern for young, untried, often arrogant new instructors was a welcomed sedative in faculty crises. Matlock had convinced himself that the 'grand old bird' had befriended a desperate young man, helping him in a desperate situation. He had no right to surface Herron's name on the basis of a phone call made by a panicked drug user. There were too many possible explanations. Somehow he'd speak with Herron, perhaps over coffee at the Commons, or in the bleachers at a baseball game – Herron loved baseball – talk to him, tell him he should back away from Archer Beeson.

'– about Beeson?'

86

'What?' Matlock had not heard Greenberg.

'I asked you if you had second thoughts about Beeson.'

'No. No, I haven't. He's not important. As a matter of fact, he'll probably throw away the grass and the pills – except for *my* benefit – if he thinks he can use me.'

'I won't try to follow that.'

'Don't. I just had momentary doubts . . . I can't believe you arrived at only one theory. Come on. What else?'

'All right. Two others and they're not even plausible – both from the same egg. The first is that there might be a leak in Washington. The second – a leak here at Carlyle.'

'Why not plausible?'

'Washington first. There are fewer than a dozen men who know about this operation, and that includes Justice, Treasury, and the White House. They're the calibre of men who exchange secret messages with the Kremlin. Impossible.'

'And Carlyle?'

'You, Adrian Sealfont, and the obnoxious Samuel Kressel . . . I'd like nothing better than pointing at Kressel – he's a prick – but, again, impossible. I'd also take a certain ethnic delight in knocking a venerated WASP like Sealfont off his pedestal, but there, too – no sense. That leaves you. Are you the one?'

'Your wit is staggering.' Matlock had to run to catch the ball which Greenberg threw into a corner. He held it in his hand and looked at the agent. 'Don't misunderstand me – I like Sam, or at least I think I do – but why is he "impossible"?'

'Same as Sealfont . . . In an operation like this we start at the beginning. And I *mean* the *beginning*. We don't give a goddamn about positions, status, or reputation – good or bad. We use every trick in the books to prove someone guilty, not innocent. We try to find even the flimsiest reason *not* to clear him. Kressel's as clean as John the Baptist. Still a prick, but clean. Sealfont's worse. He's everything they say. A goddamn saint – Church of England, of course. So, again, that leaves you.'

Matlock whipped the ball up in a spinning reverse shot into the rear left ceiling. Greenberg stepped back and slashed the ball in midair into the right wall. It bulleted back between Matlock's legs.

'I gather you've played the game,' said Matlock with an embarrassed grin.

'The bandit of Brandeis. What about the girl? Where is she?'

'In my apartment. I made her promise not to leave till I got back. Outside of safety, it's one way to get the place cleaned up.'

'I'm assigning a man to her. I don't think it's necessary, but it'll make *you* feel better.' Greenberg looked at his watch.

'It will and thanks.'

'We'd better hurry . . . Now, listen. We're letting everything take its normal course. Police blotter, newspapers, everything. No covers, no counter stories, nothing to obstruct normal curiosity or your perfectly normal reactions. Someone broke into your apartment and smashed up the place. That's all you know . . . And there's something else. You may not like it, but we think it's best – and safest.'

'What?'

'We think Miss Ballantyne should report the phone call she received to the police.'

'Hey, come on! The caller expected to find me there at four o'clock in the morning. You don't spell that kind of thing out. Not if you're on a fellowship and expect to work for museum foundations. They still revere McKinley.'

'The eye of the beholder, Dr Matlock . . . She just

received a phone call; some man asked for you, quoted Shakespeare, and made an unintelligible reference to some foreign word or city. She was goddamn mad. It wouldn't rate five lines in a newspaper, but since your apartment was broken into, it's logical she'd report it.'

Matlock was silent. He walked over to the corner of the squash court where the ball had settled and picked it up. 'We're a couple of ciphers who got pushed around. We don't know what happened; just that we don't like it.'

'That's the idea. Nothing is so convincing as someone who's a bewildered injured party and lets everybody know it. Make an insurance issue about those old books of yours . . . I've got to go. There aren't that many extinguishers in the building. Anything else? What are you doing next?'

Matlock bounced the ball on the floor. 'A fortuitous invitation. Fortuitously received over a number of beers at the Afro-Commons. I'm invited to a staged version of the original puberty rites of the Mau Mau tribes. Tonight at ten o'clock in the cellars of Lumumba Hall . . . It used to be the Alpha Delta fraternity house. I can tell you there are a lot of white Episcopalians spinning in hell over that one.'

'Again, I'm not following, Doctor.'

'You don't do your homework, either . . . Lumumba Hall is very large on your list.'

'Sorry. You'll phone me in the morning?'

'In the morning.'

'I'll call you Jim if you'll call me Jason.'

'No kiss, but agreed.'

'OK. Practice some more in here. I'll take you when this is over.'

'You're on.'

Greenberg let himself out. He looked up and down the narrow corridor, satisfied that no one was there; no one had seen him enter or leave the court. Continuous thumping could be heard within the walls. All the courts were in use. Greenberg wondered, as he was about to turn the corner into the main hallway, why the Carlyle gymnasium was so heavily attended at eleven o'clock in the morning. It was never the case at Brandeis; not fifteen years ago. Eleven o'clock in the morning was a time for class.

He heard a strange noise that was not the sound of a hard ball against thick wood and turned quickly.

No one.

He entered the main hall and turned once again. No one. He left quickly.

The sound he heard was that of a stubborn latch. It came from the door next to Matlock's court. Out of that door a man emerged. He, too, as Greenberg had done less than a minute before, looked up and down the narrow corridor. But instead of being satisfied that no one was there, he was annoyed. The obstinate latch had caused him to miss seeing the man who'd met with James Matlock.

Now the door of court four opened and Matlock himself stepped into the corridor. The man ten feet away was startled, pulled his towel up to his face, and walked away, coughing.

But the man wasn't quick enough. Matlock knew that face.

It was the patrolman from his apartment at four o'clock in the morning.

The patrolman who had called him 'Doctor.' The man in uniform who knew beyond a doubt that the campus troubles were caused by the 'weirdos and the niggers.'

Matlock stared at the retreating figure.

Chapter 9

Over the large cathedral doors one could see – if one looked closely, or the sun was shining at a certain angle – the faded imprint of the Greek letters A△∅. They had been there in bas-relief for decades, and no amount of sand blasting or student damage could eradicate them completely. The fraternity house of Alpha Delta Phi had gone the way of other such buildings at Carlyle. Its holy order of directors could not find it within themselves to accept the inevitable. The house had been sold – lock, stock, leaking roof, and bad mortgage – to the blacks.

The blacks had done well, even extremely well, with what they had to work with. The decrepit old house had been totally refurbished inside and out. All past associations with its former owners were obliterated wherever possible. The scores of faded photographs of venerated alumni were replaced with wildly theatrical portraits of the new revolutionaries – African, Latin American, Black Panther. Throughout the ancient halls were the new commands, screeched in posters and psychedelic art: *Death to the Pigs! Up Whitey! Malcolm Lives! Lumumba the Black Christ!*

Between these screams for recognition were replicas of primitive African artifacts – fertility masks, spears, shields, animal skins dipped in red paint, shrunken heads suspended by hair with complexions unmistakably white.

Lumumba Hall wasn't trying to fool anyone. It reflected anger. It reflected fury.

Matlock didn't have to use the brass knocker set beside the grotesque iron mask at the edge of the door frame.

The large door opened as he approached it, and a student greeted him with a bright smile.

'I was hoping you'd make it! It's gonna be a groove!'

'Thanks, Johnny. Wouldn't miss it.' Matlock walked in, struck by the proliferation of lighted candles throughout the hallway and adjoining rooms. 'Looks like a wake. Where's the casket?'

'That's later. Wait'll you see!'

A black Matlock recognized as one of the campus extremists walked up to them. Adam Williams' hair was long – African style and clipped in a perfect semicircle above his head. His features were sharp; Matlock had the feeling that if they met in the veldt, Williams would be assumed to be a tribal chief.

'Good evening,' Williams said with an infectious grin. 'Welcome to the seat of revolution.'

'Thanks very much.' They shook hands. 'You don't look so revolutionary as you do funereal. I was asking Johnny where the casket was.'

Williams laughed. His eyes were intelligent, his smile genuine, without guile or arrogance. In close quarters, the black radical had little of the firebrand quality he displayed on the podium in front of cheering supporters. Matlock wasn't surprised. Those of the faculty who had Williams in their courses often remarked on his subdued, good-humored approach. So different from the image he projected in campus – rapidly becoming national – politics.

'Oh, Lord! We're lousing up the picture then! This is a happy occasion. A little gruesome, I suppose, but essentially joyful.'

'I'm not sure I understand,' Matlock smiled.

'A youngster from the tribe reaches the age of manhood, the brink of an active, responsible life. A jungle Bar Mitzvah. It's a time for rejoicing. No caskets, no weeping shrouds.'

92

'That's right! That's right, Adam!' said the boy named Johnny enthusiastically.

'Why don't you get Mr Matlock a drink, brother.' And then he turned to Matlock. 'It's all the same drink until after the ceremony – it's called Swahili punch. Is that OK?'

'Of course.'

'Right.' Johnny disappeared into the crowd toward the dining room and the punch bowl. Adam smiled as he spoke.

'It's a light rum drink with lemonade and cranberry juice. Not bad, really . . . Thank you for coming. I mean that.'

'I was surprised to be invited. I thought this was a very "in" thing. Restricted to the tribe . . . That didn't come out the way I meant it.'

Williams laughed. 'No offense. I used the word. It's good to think in terms of tribes. Good for the brothers.'

'Yes, I imagine it is . . .'

'The collective, protective social group. Possessing an identity of its own.'

'If that's the purpose – the constructive purpose – I endorse it.'

'Oh, it is. Tribes in the bush don't always make war on each other, you know. It's not all stealing, looting, carrying away women. That's a Robert Ruark hang-up. They trade, share hunting and farming lands together, coexist in the main probably better than nations or even political subdivisions.'

It was Matlock's turn to laugh. 'All right, professor. I'll make notes *after* the lecture.'

'Sorry. Avocational hazard.'

'Avocational or occupational?'

'Time will tell, won't it? . . . One thing I should make clear, however. We don't need your endorsement.'

93

Johnny returned with Matlock's cup of Swahili punch. 'Hey, you know what? Brother Davis, that's Bill Davis, says you told him you were going to flunk him, then at midterm you gave him a High Pass!'

'Brother Davis got off his fat ass and did a little work.' Matlock looked at Adam Williams. 'You don't object to that kind of endorsement, do you?'

Williams smiled broadly and placed his hand on Matlock's arm. 'No, sir, bwana . . . In that area you run King Solomon's Mines. Brother Davis is here to work as hard as he can and go as far as his potential will let him. No argument there. Bear down on the brother.'

'You're positively frightening.' Matlock spoke with a lightness he did not feel.

'Not at all. Just pragmatic . . . . I've got some last-minute preparations to look after. See you later.' Williams hailed a passing student and walked through the crowd toward the staircase.

'Come on, Mr Matlock. I'll show you the new alterations.' Johnny led Matlock into what used to be Alpha Delta's common room.

In the sea of dark faces, Matlock saw a minimum of guarded, hostile looks. There were, perhaps, less overt greetings than he might expect outside on the campus, but by and large, his presence was accepted. He thought for a moment that if the brothers knew why he had come, the inhabitants of Lumumba Hall might turn on him angrily. He was the only white person there.

The alterations in the common room were drastic. Gone were the wide moldings of dark wood, the thick oak window seats beneath the huge cathedral windows, the solid, heavy furniture with the dark red leather. Instead, the room was transformed into something else entirely. The arched windows were no longer. They were now squared at the top, bordered by jet-black dowels an inch or two in diameter, which looked like long, rectangular slits. Spreading out from the windows into the walls was a textured pattern of tiny wooden bamboo strips shellacked to a high polish. This same wall covering was duplicated on the ceiling, thousands of highly glossed reeds converging towards the center. In the middle of the ceiling was a large circle, perhaps three feet in width, in which there was placed a thick pane of rippled glass. Beyond the glass shone a bright yellowish white light, its flood diffused in ripples over the room. What furniture he could see through the mass of bodies was not really furniture at all. There were various low-cut slabs of thick wood in differing shapes on short legs – these Matlock assumed were tables. Instead of chairs, there were dozens of pillows in vibrant colors scattered about the edge of the walls.

It didn't take Matlock long to realize the effect.

Alpha Delta Phi's common room had been transformed brilliantly into the replica of a large thatched African hut. Even to the point of the blazing equatorial sun streaming through the enclosure's vent to the skies.

'This is remarkable! Really remarkable. It must have taken months.'

'Almost a year and a half,' Johnny said. 'It's very comfortable, very relaxing. Did you know that lots of top designers are going in for this sort of thing now? I mean the back-to-nature look. It's very functional and easy to maintain.'

'That sounds dangerously like an apology. You don't have to apologize. It's terrific.'

'Oh, I'm *not* apologizing.' Johnny retreated from his explanation. 'Adam says there's a certain majesty in the primitive. A very proud heritage.'

'Adam's right. Only he's not the first person to make that observation.'

'Please don't put us down, Mr Matlock . . . .'

Matlock looked at Johnny over the rim of his cup of Swahili punch. Oh, Christ, he thought, the more things change, the more they remain the same.

The high-ceilinged chapter room of Alpha Delta Phi had been carved out of the cellars at the farthest end of the fraternity house. It had been built shortly after the turn of the century when impressive alumni had poured impressive sums into such hobbies as secret societies and debutante cotillions. Such activities promulgated and propagandized a way of life, yet assuredly kept it selective.

Thousands of starched young men had been initiated in this chapel-like enclosure, whispering the secret pledges, exchanging the unfamiliar handshakes explained to them by stern-faced older children, vowing till death to keep the selected faith. And afterward, getting drunk and vomiting in corners.

Matlock thought these thoughts as he watched the Mau Mau ritual unfold before him. It was no less childish, no less absurd than the preceding scenes in this room, he considered. Perhaps the physical aspects – the simulated physical aspects – were more brutal in what they conveyed, but then the roots of the ceremony were not based in the delicate steps of a cotillion's pavanne but, instead, in harsh, animal-like pleas to primitive gods. Pleas for strength and survival. Not supplications for continued exclusivity.

The tribal rite itself was a series of unintelligible chants, each one growing in intensity, over the body of a black student – obviously the youngest brother in Lumumba Hall – stretched out on the concrete floor, naked except for a red loincloth strapped around his waist and legs, covering his genitals. At the finish of each chant, signifying the end of one canto and the commencement of the succeeding song, the boy's body was raised above the crowd by

96

four extremely tall students, themselves naked to the waist, wearing jet-black dance belts, their legs encased in spirals of rawhide strips. The room was lighted by dozens of thick candles mounted on stands, causing shadows to dance across the upper wall and the ceiling. Adding to this theatrical effect was the fact that the five active participants in the ritual had their skins covered with oil, their faces streaked in diabolical patterns. As the singing grew wilder, the young boy's rigid body was thrown higher and higher until it left the hands of its four supporters, returning split seconds later into the outstretched arms. Each time the black body with the red loincloth was flung into the air, the crowd responded with growing volumes of guttural shouts.

And then Matlock, who had been watching with a degree of detachment, suddenly found himself frightened. Frightened for the small Negro whose stiff, oiled body was being flung into air with such abandon. For two additional blacks, dressed like the others, had joined the four in the center of the floor. However, instead of helping toss the now soaring figure, the two blacks crouched between the rectangular foursome – beneath the body – and withdrew long-bladed knives, one in each hand. Once in their squatting positions, they stretched out their arms so that the blades were held upright, as rigid, as stiff as the body above them. Each time the small Negro descended, the four blades inched closer to the falling flesh. One slip, one oily miscalculation on the part of just one of the four blacks, and the ritual would end in death for the small student. In murder.

Matlock, feeling that the ritual had gone as far as he could allow, began scanning the crowd for Adam Williams. He saw him in front, on the edge of the circle, and started pushing his way toward him. He was stopped – quietly but firmly – by the blacks around him. He looked angrily at a

97

Negro who held his arm. The black didn't acknowledge his stare; he was hypnotized by the action now taking place in the center of the room.

Matlock saw why instantly. For the body of the small boy was now being *spun*, alternately face up and face down with each elevation. The danger of error was increased tenfold. Matlock grabbed the hand on his arm, twisted it inward, and flung it off him. He looked once more in the direction of Adam Williams.

He wasn't there. He was nowhere in sight! Matlock stood still, undecided. If he raised his voice between the crowd's roaring crescendos, it was entirely possible that he might cause a break in the concentration of those handling the body. He couldn't risk that, and yet he couldn't allow the dangerous absurdity to continue.

Suddenly Matlock felt another hand, this one on his shoulder. He turned and saw the face of Adam Williams behind him. It startled him. Had some primitive tribal signal been transmitted to Williams? The black radical gestured with his head for Matlock to follow him through the shouting crowd to the outer edge of the circle. Williams spoke between the roars.

'You look worried. Don't be.'

'Look! This crap's gone far enough! That kid could be killed!'

'No chance. The brothers have rehearsed for months . . . It's really the most simplistic of the Mau Mau rites. The symbolism is fundamental . . . See? The child's eyes remain open. First to the sky, then facing the blades. He is constantly aware – every second – that his life is in the hands of his brother warriors. He cannot, he *must* not show fear. To do so would betray his peers. Betray the confidence he must place in their hands – as they will someday place their lives in *his* hands.'

'It's childish, *dangerous stupidity*, and you *know* it!' cut

98

in Matlock. 'Now, I'm telling you, Williams, you put a stop to it or I will!'

'Of course,' continued the black radical, as if Matlock had not spoken, 'there are anthropologists who insist that the ceremony is essentially one of fertility. The unsheathed knives representing erections, the four protectors guarding the child through its formative years. Frankly, I think that's reaching. Also, it strikes me as contradictory even for the primitive mind . . .'

'Goddamn you!' Matlock grabbed Williams by the front of his shirt. Immediately other blacks closed in on him.

Suddenly there was total silence in the eerily lit room. The silence lasted only a moment. It was followed by a series of mind-shattering screams from the mouths of the four Negroes in the center of the crowd in whose hands the life of the young student depended. Matlock whipped around and saw the shining black body descending downward from an incredible height above the outstretched hands.

It couldn't be true! It wasn't happening! Yet it was!

The four blacks suddenly, in unison, crouched into kneeling positions *away* from the center, their arms slashed to their sides. The young student came crashing down, *face toward the blades*. Two further screams followed. In a fraction of a second, the students holding the huge knives swung their weapons across one another and in an unbelievable display of wrist strength, *caught* the body on the flat of the blades.

The crowd of blacks went wild.

The ceremony was over.

'Do you believe me now?' Williams asked, speaking in a corner with Matlock.

'Whether I do or not doesn't change what I said. You can't *do* this sort of thing! It's too goddamn dangerous!'

'You exaggerate . . . Here, let me introduce another guest.' Williams raised his hand and a tall thin black with close-cropped hair and glasses, dressed in an expensively cut tan suit, joined them. 'This is Julian Dunois, Mr Matlock. Brother Julian is our expert. Our choreographer, if you like.'

'A pleasure.' Dunois extended his hand, speaking with a slight accent.

'Brother Julian is from Haiti . . . Harvard Law out of Haiti. A most unusual progression, I think you'll agree.'

'It certainly is . . .'

'Many Haitians, even the Ton Ton Macoute, still get upset when they hear his name.'

'You exaggerate, Adam,' said Julian Dunois with a smile.

'That's what I just said to Mr Matlock. *He* exaggerates. About the danger of the ceremony.'

'Oh, there's danger – as there's danger if one crosses the Boston Commons wearing a blindfold. The petcock of safety, Mr Matlock, is that those holding the knives watch closely. In the training there is as much emphasis on being able to drop the knives instantly as there is in holding them up.'

'That may be so,' Matlock acknowledged. 'But the margin for error terrifies me.'

'It's not as narrow as you think.' The lilt in the Haitian's voice was as reassuring as it was attractive. 'Incidentally, I'm a fan of yours. I've enjoyed your works on the Elizabethans. May I add, you're not exactly what I expected. I mean, you're far, far younger.'

'You flatter me. I didn't think I was known in law schools.'

'My undergraduate major was English literature.'

Adam interrupted politely. 'You two enjoy yourselves. There'll be drinks upstairs in a few minutes; just follow the crowd. I've got things to do . . . I'm glad you've met. You're both strangers, in a way. Strangers should meet in unfamiliar areas. It's comforting.'

He gave Dunois an enigmatic look and walked rapidly away through the crowd.

'Why does Adam feel he has to talk in what I'm sure he considers are profound riddles?' Matlock asked.

'He's very young. He strives constantly to make emphasis. Very bright, but very young.'

'You'll pardon me, but you're not exactly ancient. I doubt more than a year or two older than Adam.'

The black in the expensively cut tan suit looked into Matlock's eyes and laughed gently.

'Now you flatter *me*,' he said. 'If the truth were known – and why shouldn't it be? – and if my tropic color did not disguise the years so well, you'd know that I was precisely one year, four months, and sixteen days *older* than *you*.'

Matlock stared at the Negro, speechless. It took him nearly a full minute to assimilate the lawyer's words and the meaning behind those words. The black's eyes did not waver. He returned Matlock's stare in equal measure. Finally, Matlock found his voice.

'I'm not sure I like this game.'

'Oh, come, we're both here for the same reason, are we not? You from your vantage point, I from mine . . . Let's go upstairs and have a drink . . . Bourbon and soda, isn't it? Sour mash, if it's available, I understand.'

Dunois preceded Matlock through the crowd, and Matlock had no other course but to follow.

Dunois leaned against the brick wall.

'All right,' Matlock said, 'the amenities are over. Everyone's acknowledged your show downstairs, and there's no-one left for me to impress my white skin on. I think it's time you started explaining.'

101

They were alone now, outside on the porch. Both held drinks.

'My, aren't we professional? Would you care for a cigar? I can assure you it's Havana.'

'No cigar. Just talk. I came here tonight because these are my friends. I felt privileged to be invited . . . Now, you've attached something else and I don't like it.'

'Bravo! Bravo!' said Dunois, raising his glass. 'You do that very well . . . Don't worry, they know nothing. Perhaps they suspect, but believe me, only in the vaguest terms.'

'What the hell are you talking about?'

'Finish your drink and let's walk out on the lawn.' Dunois drained his rum and, as if by reflex, Matlock drank the remainder of his bourbon. The two men walked down the steps of the Lumumba Hall, Matlock following the black to the base of a large elm tree. Dunois turned suddenly and grabbed Matlock by the shoulders.

'Take your goddamn hands off me!'

'Listen to me! I want that paper! I *must have* that paper! And you must tell me *where it is*!'

Matlock flung his hands up to break Dunois's grip. But his arms did not respond. They were suddenly heavy, terribly heavy. And there was a whistling. A growing, piercing whistling in his head.

'What? What? . . . What paper? I don't have any paper . . .'

'Don't be difficult! We'll get it, you know! . . . Now, just tell me where it is!'

Matlock realized that he was being lowered to the ground. The outline of the huge tree above him began to spin, and the whistling in his brain became louder and louder. It was unendurable. He fought to find his mind again.

'What are you doing? What are you doing to me!?'

'The paper, Matlock! Where is the Corsican *paper*?'

'Get *off* me!' Matlock tried to yell. But nothing came from his lips.

'*The silver paper, goddamn you to hell!*'

'No paper . . . no. Haven't paper! No!'

'Listen to me! You just had a drink, remember the drink? . . . You just finished that drink. Remember? . . . You can't be alone now! You don't *dare* be alone!'

'What? . . . What? Get off me! You're crushing me!'

'I'm not even *touching* you. The drink is! You just consumed three tabs of *lysergic acid*! You're in trouble, Doctor! . . . *Now! You tell me where that paper is!*'

From his inner recesses he found an instant of clarity. From the spinning, turning, whirling spirals of mind-blasting colors, he saw the form of the man above him and he lashed out. He grabbed at the white shirt between the dark borders of the jacket and pulled it down with all the strength he could summon. He brought his fist up and hit the descending face as hard as he could. Once the face was jarred, he began hammering at the throat beneath it mercilessly. He could feel the shattering of the glasses and he knew his fist had found the eyes and crushed the glass into the rolling head.

It was over in a period of time he could never ascertain. Dunois's body was beside him, unconscious.

And he knew he had to run. Run furiously away! What had Dunois said? . . . Don't dare be alone. Don't *dare*! He had to find Pat! Pat would know what to do. He had to find her! The chemical in his body was going to take full effect soon and he knew it. Run, for Christ's sake!

But where?! Which way?! He didn't know *the way*! *The goddamn, fucking way*! The street was there, he raced along the street, but was it the *right way*?! Was it the *right street*?!

Then he heard a car. It *was* a car, and it was coming close

103

to the curb and the driver was looking at him. Looking at him, so he ran faster, tripping once over the curb and falling into the pavement and rising again. Running, for Christ Almighty's sake, running till the breath in his lungs was gone and he could no longer control the movement of his feet. He felt himself swerve, unable to stop himself, toward the wide gulf of the street, which suddenly became a river, a black putrid river in which he would drown.

He vaguely heard the screech of the brakes. The lights blinded him, and the figure of a man reached down and poked at his eyes. He didn't care any longer. Instead, he laughed. Laughed through the blood which flowed into his mouth and over his face.

He laughed hysterically as Jason Greenberg carried him to the car.

And then the earth, the world, the planet, the galaxy, and the entire solar system went crazy.

Chapter 10

The night was agony.

The morning brought a degree of reality, less so for Matlock than for the two people sitting beside him, one on either side of the bed. Jason Greenberg, his large, sad eyes drooping, his hands calmly crossed on his lap, leaned forward. Patricia Ballantyne, her arm stretched out, held a cool washcloth on Matlock's forehead.

'The schvugs gave you one hell of a party, friend.'

'Shh!' whispered the girl. 'Leave him alone.'

Matlock's eyes wandered as best they could around the room. He was in Pat's apartment, in her bedroom, her bed.

'They gave me acid.'

'You're telling *us* . . . We had a doctor – a real doctor – brought in from Litchfield. He's the nice fella you kept trying to take the eyeballs from . . . Don't worry, he's federal. No names.'

'Pat? How come . . .'

'You're a very sweet acid head, Jamie. You kept yelling my name.'

'It also made the best sense,' interrupted Greenberg. 'No hospitals. No out-patient records. Nice and private; good thinking. Also, you're very persuasive when you're violent. You're a hell of a lot stronger than I thought. Especially for such a lousy handball player.'

'You shouldn't have brought me here. Goddamn it, Greenberg, you shouldn't have *brought* me here!'

'Forgetting for the moment that it was your idea . . .'

'I was drugged!'

'It was a *good* idea. What would you have preferred? The emergency clinic? . . . "Who's that on the stretcher, Doctor? The one screaming." . . . "Oh, just Associate Professor Matlock, Nurse. He's on an acid trip."'

'You know what I mean! You could have taken me home. Strapped me down.'

'I'm relieved to see you don't know much about acid,' said Greenberg.

'What he means, Jamie . . .' Pat took his hand, '. . . if it's bad, you should be with someone you know awfully well. The reassurance is necessary.'

Matlock looked at the girl. And then at Greenberg. 'What have you told her?'

'That you volunteered to help us; that we're grateful. With your help we may be able to prevent a serious situation from getting worse.' Greenberg spoke in a monotone; it was obvious that he didn't wish to expand.

'It was a very cryptic explanation,' Pat said. 'He wouldn't have given me that if I hadn't threatened him.'

'She was going to call the police.' Greenberg sighed, his sad eyes sadder. 'She was going to have me locked up for dosing you. I had no choice.'

Matlock smiled.

'Why are you doing this, Jamie?' Pat found nothing amusing.

'The man said it: the situation's serious.'

'But why *you*?'

'Because I can.'

'What? Turn in kids?'

'I told you,' said Jason. 'We're not interested in students . . .'

'What's Lumumba Hall, then? A branch of General Motors?'

'It's one contact point; there are others. Frankly, we'd

106

rather *not* have gotten involved with that crowd; it's ticklish. Unfortunately, we can't choo_e.'

'That's offensive.'

'I don't think there's much I could say that wouldn't be offensive to you, Miss Ballantyne.'

'Perhaps not. Because I thought the FBI had more important work to do than harassing young blacks. Obviously, you don't.'

'Hey, come on.' Matlock squeezed the girl's hand. She took it from him.

'No, I mean that, Jamie! No games, no radical chic. There are drugs all over this place. Some of it's a bad scene, most of it's pretty standard. We *both* know that. Why all of a sudden are the kids at Lumumba singled out?'

'We wouldn't *touch* those kids. Except to help them.' Greenberg was weary from the long night. His irritation showed.

'I don't like the way you people help people and I don't like what happened to Jamie! Why did you send him there?'

'He didn't *send* me. I maneuvered that myself.'

'Why?'

'It's too complicated and I'm too washed out to explain it.'

'Oh, Mr Greenberg did that. He explained all right. They've given you a badge, haven't they? They can't do it themselves so they pick a nice, easygoing fellow to do it for them. You take all the risks; and when it's over, you'll never be trusted on this campus again. Jamie, for God's sake, this is your *home*, your *work*!'

Matlock held the girl's eyes with his own, doing his best to calm her. 'I know that better than you do. My home needs to be helped – and that's no game either, Pat. I think the risks are worth it.'

'I won't pretend to understand that.'

'You can't understand it, Miss Ballantyne, because we can't tell you enough to make it reasonable. You'll have to accept that.'

'Do I?'

'I'm asking you to,' said Matlock. 'He saved my life.'

'I wouldn't go that far, Professor.' Greenberg shrugged as he spoke.

Pat stood up. 'I think he threw you overboard and tossed you a rope as an afterthought . . . Are you all right?'

'Yes,' answered Matlock.

'I have to go; I won't if you don't want me to.'

'No, you go ahead. I'll call you later. Thanks for the ministrations.'

The girl looked briefly at Greenberg – it was not a pleasant look – and crossed to her dresser. She picked up a brush and rapidly stroked her hair, slipping an orange headband into place. She watched Greenberg through the mirror. He returned the stare.

'The man who's been following me, Mr Greenberg. Is he one of your men?'

'Yes.'

'I don't like it.'

'I'm sorry.'

Pat turned. 'Will you remove him, please?'

'I can't do that. I'll tell him to be less obvious.'

'I see.' She took her purse from the dresser top and reached down to the floor, picking up her accordion briefcase. Without speaking further, the girl walked out of the bedroom. Several seconds later, the two men could hear the apartment door open and shut firmly.

'That is one very strong-willed young lady,' said Jason.

'There's a good reason.'

'What do you mean?'

108

'I thought you fellows were so familiar with the people you had to deal with . . .'

'I'm still getting briefed. I'm the back-up, remember?'

'Then I'll save you time. In the late fifties her father got McCarthyized out of the State Department. Of course, he was very dangerous. He was a language consultant. He was cleared for translating newspapers.'

'Shit.'

'That's the word, brother. He never made it back. She's had scholarships all her life; the cupboard's bare. She's a little sensitive to your type.'

'Boy, do you pick 'em!'

'You picked *me*, remember?'

Matlock opened the door to his apartment and walked into the foyer. Pat had done a good job putting the rooms in order – as he knew she would. Even the curtains were rehung. It was a little after three – most of the day wasted. Greenberg had insisted that the two of them drive over to Litchfield for a re-examination by the doctor. Shaken but operable, was the verdict.

They stopped for lunch at the Cheshire Cat. During the meal, Matlock kept looking over at the small table where four days ago Ralph Loring had sat with his folded newspaper. The lunch was quiet. Not strained – the two men were comfortable in each other's company – but quiet, as if each had too much to think about.

On the road back to Carlyle, Greenberg told him to stay in his apartment until he contacted him. Washington hadn't issued any new instructions. They were evaluating the new information, and until they confirmed any further involvement, Matlock was to remain 'OOS' – a term the English professor found hard to equate with grownups: *out of strategy*.

It was just as well, he thought. He had his own strategy

109

to think about – Lucas Herron. The 'grand old bird,' the campus elder statesman. It was time to reach him, to warn him. The old man was out of his element, and the quicker he retreated, the better for everyone – Carlyle included. Yet he didn't want to telephone him, he didn't want to arrange a formal meeting – he had to be subtler than that. He didn't want to alarm old Lucas, have him talking to the wrong people.

It occurred to Matlock that he was acting as some sort of protector for Herron. That presumed Lucas was innocent of any serious involvement. He wondered if he had the right to make that assumption. On the other hand, by civilized standards, he had no right to make any other.

The telephone rang. It couldn't be Greenberg, he thought. He'd just left him at the curb. He hoped it wasn't Pat; he wasn't ready to talk to her yet. Reluctantly he lifted the instrument to his ear. 'Hello!'

'Jim! Where have you *been*!? I've been calling since eight this morning! I was so goddamn worried I went over there twice. Got your key from maintenance.' It was Sam Kressel. He sounded as though Carlyle had lost its accreditation.

'It's too involved to go into now, Sam. Let's get together later. I'll come over to your place after dinner.'

'I don't know if it can wait that long. Jesus! What the hell got *into* you?'

'I don't understand.'

'At Lumumba last night!'

'What are you talking about? What have you heard?'

'That black bastard, Adam Williams, handed in a report to my office accusing you of just about everything short of advocating slavery! He claims the only reason he's not filing police charges is that you were blind drunk! Of course, the alcohol stripped you of your pretenses and showed clearly what a racist you are!'

110

'What?!'

'You broke up furniture, slapped around some kids, smashed windows . . .'

'You know damned well that's bullshit!'

'I figured as much.' Kressel lowered his voice. He was calming down. 'But my knowing it doesn't help, can't you see that? This is the kind of thing we've got to *avoid*. Polarization! The government walks on to a campus, polarization follows.'

'Listen to me. Williams' statement is a decoy – if that's the word. It's camouflage. They drugged me last night. If it hadn't been for Greenberg, I don't know where I'd be right now.'

'Oh, God! . . . Lumumba's on your list, isn't it? That's all we *need*! The blacks'll scream persecution. Christ knows what'll happen.'

Matlock tried to speak calmly. 'I'll come over around seven. Don't do anything, don't say anything. I've got to get off the phone. Greenberg's supposed to call.'

'Wait a minute, Jim! One thing. This Greenberg . . . I don't trust him. I don't trust any of them. Just remember. Your loyalty's to Carlyle . . .' Kressel stopped, but he had not finished. Matlock realized he was at a loss for words.

'That's a strange thing to say.'

'I think you know what I mean.'

'I'm not sure I do. I thought the idea was to work together . . .'

'*Not at the expense of ripping this campus apart!*' The dean of colleges sounded nearly hysterical.

'Don't worry,' Matlock said. 'It won't tear. I'll see you later.' Matlock hung up the phone before Kressel could speak again. His mind needed a short rest, and Kressel never let anyone rest where his domain was concerned. Sam Kressel, in his own way, was as militant as any extremist, and, perhaps, quicker to cry 'foul.'

111

These thoughts led Matlock to another consideration – two considerations. Four days ago, he had told Pat that he didn't want to change their plans for St Thomas. Carlyle's midterm holiday, a short ten days at the end of April, would start after classes on Saturday, in three days. Under the circumstances, St Thomas was out – unless Washington decided to retire him, and he doubted that. He'd use his parents as the excuse. Pat would understand, even be sympathetic. The other thought was his own classes. He had fallen behind. His desk was piled with papers – mostly themes and essay exams. He had also missed his two classes earlier in the day. He was not so much concerned for his students – his method was to accelerate in the fall and winter and relax in the spring – but he didn't want to add any fuel to such fires as Williams' false complaint. An absentee associate professor was a target for gossip. His class load for the next three days was medium – three, two, and two. He'd organize the work later. Between now and seven o'clock, however, he had to find Lucas Herron. If Greenberg called while he was out, he'd blame it on a forgotten graduate conference.

He decided to shower, shave, and change clothes. Once in the bathroom, he checked the litter box. The Corsican paper was there – he knew it would be.

The shave and shower completed, Matlock walked into his bedroom, selecting clothes and a course of action. He didn't know Herron's daily schedule, although it would be a simple matter to find out if Lucas had any late afternoon classes or seminars. If he didn't, Matlock knew Herron's house; it would take about fifteen minutes to get there by car. Herron lived eight miles from the campus, on a rarely traveled back road in a section once a part of the old Carlyle family estate. Herron's home had been a carriage house. It was out of the way, but as Lucas kept saying, 'Once there, it's worth it.'

The rapid tapping of the door knocker broke his concentration. It also frightened him – he felt himself gasping for breath; that was disturbing.

'Be right there,' he yelled, slipping a white sport shirt over his head. He walked barefoot to the front door and opened it. It was impossible for him to conceal his shock. In the doorframe stood Adam Williams – alone.

'Afternoon.'

'Jesus! . . . I don't know whether to hit you in the mouth right now or first call the police! What the hell do you want? Kressel's already called me, if that's what you're checking on.'

'Please let me talk to you. I'll be quick.' The black spoke with urgency, trying, thought Matlock, to conceal his fear.

'Come on in. And *make* it quick.' Matlock slammed the door as Williams passed by him into the foyer. The black turned and tried to smile, but there was no humor in his eyes.

'I'm sorry about that report. Truly sorry. It was an unpleasant necessity.'

'I don't buy that and you can't sell it! What did you want Kressel to do? Bring me up before the board and burn me out of here? Did you think I'd just sit down and play doormat? You're a goddamn maniac!'

'We didn't think *anything* would happen. That's precisely why we did it . . . We couldn't be sure where you went. You disappeared, you know. You might say we had to take the offensive and then later agree that it was all a disagreeable misunderstanding . . . It's not a new tactic. I'll send Kressel another report, backing off – but not entirely. In a couple of weeks, it'll be forgotten.'

Matlock raged, as much against Williams' attitude as his conscienceless pragmatism. But when he spoke he did not raise his voice. 'Get out. You disgust me.'

113

'Oh, come off it, man! Haven't we *always disgusted* you?!' Matlock had hit a nerve and Williams responded in kind. But just as suddenly, he took hold of himself. 'Let's not argue theoretical practicalities. Let me get to the point and leave.'

'By all means.'

'All right. Listen to me. Whatever Dunois wanted from you, *give* it to him! . . . That is, give it to me and I'll send it on. No forked tongue; it's last-extremity language!'

'Too pat a phrase. No sale. Why would I have anything Brother Julian wanted? Did he say so? Why doesn't he come over himself?'

'Brother Julian doesn't stay long in any one place. His talents are in great demand.'

'Staging Mau Mau puberty rituals?'

'He really does that, you know. It's a hobby.'

'Send him to me.' Matlock crossed in front of Williams and went to the coffee table. He reached down and picked up a half-empty pack of cigarettes. 'We'll compare notes on associative body movements. I've a hell of a collection of sixteenth-century folk dances.'

'Talk seriously. There's no *time!*'

Matlock lit a cigarette. 'I've got all the time in the world. I just want to see Brother Julian again; I want to put him in jail.'

'No chance! No chance. I'm here for *your* benefit! If I leave without it, I can't *control* it!'

'Two pronouns signifying the same or different objects?'

'Oh, you're too much! You're really too much! Do you know who Julian Dunois *is*?'

'Part of the Borgia family? Ethiopian branch?'

'*Stop it, Matlock!* Do what he says! People could be hurt. Nobody wants that.'

'I *don't* know who Dunois is and I don't much give a damn. I just know he drugged me and assaulted me and

114

is exercising a dangerous influence on a bunch of children. Beyond this, I suspect he had my apartment broken into and many of my personal belongings destroyed. I want him put away. From you *and* from me.'

'Be reasonable, *please!*'

Matlock walked swiftly to the curtains in front of his casement window and with a flourish, yanked them down, displaying the shattered glass and twisted lead.

'Is this one of Brother Julian's calling cards?'

Adam Williams stared, obviously shocked, at the mass of destruction. 'No, man. Absolutely, no. That's not Julian's style . . . That's not even my style. That's some-one else.'

Chapter 11

The road to Lucas Herron's house was dotted with the potholes of winter. Matlock doubted that the town of Carlyle would fill them in; there were too many other commercially traveled streets still showing the effects of the New England freeze. As he approached the old carriage house, he slowed his Triumph to barely ten miles an hour. The bumps were jarring, and he wanted to reach Herron's house with little noise.

Thinking that Jason Greenberg might have had him followed, Matlock took the long route to Herron's, driving four miles north on a parallel road and then doubling back on Herron's street. There was no-one behind him. The nearest houses to Herron's were a hundred yards away on either side, none in front. There'd been talk of turning the area into a housing development just as there'd been talk of enlarging Carlyle University, but nothing came of either project. Actually, the first depended upon the second, and there was strong alumni opposition to any substantial physical change at Carlyle. The alumni were Adrian Sealfont's personal cross.

Matlock was struck by the serenity of Herron's home. He'd never really looked at the house before. A dozen times, more or less, he'd driven Lucas home after faculty meetings, but he'd always been in a hurry. He'd never accepted Lucas's invitations for a drink and, as a result, he had never been inside the house.

He got out of the car and approached the old brick structure. It was tall and narrow; the faded stone covered with thousands of strands of ivy heightened the feeling

116

of isolation. In front, on the large expanse of lawn, were two Japanese willow trees in full spring bloom, their purple flowers cascading toward the earth in large arcs. The grass was cut, the shrubbery pruned, and the white gravel on the various paths was gleaming. It was a house and grounds which were loved and cared for, yet one had the feeling that they were not shared. It was the work of and for one person, not two or a family. And then Matlock remembered that Lucas Herron had never married. There were the inevitable stories of a lost love, a tragic death, even a runaway bride-to-be, but whenever Lucas Herron heard about such youthful romanticizing he countered with a chuckle and a statement about being 'too damned selfish.'

Matlock walked up the short steps to the door and rang the bell. He tried practicing an opening smile, but it was false; he wouldn't be able to carry it off. He was afraid.

The door swung back and the tall, white-haired Lucas Herron, dressed in wrinkled trousers and a half-unbuttoned, oxford-blue shirt, stared at him.

It was less than a second before Herron spoke, but in that brief instant, Matlock knew that he'd been wrong. Lucas Herron knew why he had come.

'Well, Jim! Come in, come in, my boy. A pleasant surprise.'

'Thank you, Lucas. I hope I'm not interrupting anything.'

'Not a thing. You're just in time, as a matter of fact. I'm dabbling in alchemy. A fresh fruit gin Collins. Now I won't have to dabble alone.'

'Sounds good to me.'

The inside of Herron's house was precisely as Matlock thought it would be – as his own might be in thirty-odd years, if he lived that long alone. It was a mixed bag, an accumulated total of nearly half a century of unrelated

117

gatherings from a hundred unrelated sources. The only common theme was comfort; there was no concern for style or period or coordination. Several walls were lined with books, and those which were not were filled with enlarged photographs of places visited abroad – one suspected during sabbaticals. The armchairs were thick and soft, the tables within arm's reach – the sign of practiced bachelorhood, thought Matlock.

'I don't think you've ever been here – inside, I mean.'

'No, I haven't. It's very attractive. Very comfortable.'

'Yes, it's that. It's comfortable. Here, sit down, I'll finish the formula and bring us a drink.' Herron started across the living room toward what Matlock presumed was the door to the kitchen and then stopped and turned. 'I know perfectly well that you haven't come all the way out here to liven up an old man's cocktail hour. However, I have a house rule: at least one drink – religion and strong principles permitting – before any serious discussion.' He smiled and the myriad lines around his eyes and temples became more pronounced. He was an *old*, old man. 'Besides, you look terribly serious. The Collins'll lessen the degree, I promise you.'

Before Matlock could answer, Herron walked rapidly through the door. Instead of sitting, Matlock walked to the wall nearest him, against which was a small writing desk, above it a half-dozen photographs that hung in no discernible pattern. Several were of Stonehenge taken from the same position, the setting sun at dramatically different angles. Another was of a rock-bound coast, mountains in the distance, fishing boats moored offshore. It looked Mediterranean, possibly Greece or the Thracian Islands. Then there was a surprise. On the lower right side of the wall, only inches above the desk, was a small photograph of a tall, slender army officer standing by the trunk of a tree. Behind him the foliage was profuse, junglelike; to the sides were the shadows of other figures. The officer was helmetless, his shirt drenched with sweat, his large right hand holding the stock of a submachine gun. In his left hand the officer held a folded piece of paper – it looked like a map – and the man had obviously just made a decision. He was looking upward, as though toward some high terrain. The face was taut but not excited. It was a good face, a strong face. It was a dark-haired, middle-aged Lucas Herron.

'I keep that old photograph to remind me that time was not always so devastating.'

Matlock snapped up, startled. Lucas had re-entered and had taken him off guard. 'It's a good picture. Now I know who really won that war.'

'No doubt about it. Unfortunately, I never heard of that particular island either before or since. Someone said it was one of the Solomons. I think they blew it up in the fifties. Wouldn't take much. Couple of fire crackers'd do it. Here.' Herron crossed to Matlock, handing him his drink.

'Thanks. You're too modest. I've heard the stories.'

'So have I. Impressed the hell out of me. They grow better as I grow older . . . What do you say we sit in the back yard. Too nice to stay indoors.' Without waiting for a reply, Herron started out and Matlock followed.

Like the front of the house, the back was precisely manicured. On a flagstone patio, there were comfortable-looking, rubber-stranded beach chairs, each with a small table by its side. A large wrought-iron table with a sun umbrella was centered in the middle of the flagstones. Beyond, the lawn was close cropped and full. Dogwood trees were dotted about, each spaded around its trunk, and two lines of flowers – mostly roses – stretched lengthwise to the end of the lawn, about a hundred feet away. At the end of the lawn, however, the pastoral effect abruptly stopped. Suddenly there were huge trees, the underbrush

119

thick, mangled, growing within itself. The side borders were the same. Around the perimeters of the sculptured back lawn was an undisciplined, overgrown forest.

Lucas Herron was surrounded by a forbidding green wall.

'It *is* a good drink, you'll admit.' The two men were seated.

'It certainly is. You'll convert me to gin.'

'Only in spring and summer. Gin's not for the rest of the year . . . All right, young fellow, the house rule's been observed. What brings you to Herron's Nest?'

'I think you have an idea.'

'Do I?'

'Archie Beeson.' Matlock watched the old man, but Herron's concentration was on his glass. He showed no reaction.

'The young history man?'

'Yes.'

'He'll make a fine teacher one day. Nice little filly of a wife, too.'

'Nice . . . and promiscuous, I think.'

'*Appearances*, Jim.' Herron chuckled. 'Never thought of you as Victorian . . . One grows infinitely more tolerant of the appetites as one gets older. And the innocent whetting of them. You'll see.'

'Is that the key? The tolerance of appetites?'

'Key to what?'

'Come on. He wanted to reach you the other night.'

'Yes, he did. And you were there . . . I understand your behavior left something to be desired.'

'My behavior was calculated to leave that impression.' For the first time Herron betrayed a trace of concern. It was a small reaction, the blinking of his eyes in rapid succession.

'That was reprehensible.' Herron spoke softly and

120

looked up at his imposing green wall. The sun was going below the line of tall trees; long shadows were cast across the lawn and patio.

'It was necessary.' Matlock saw the old man's face wince in pain. And then he recalled his own reaction to Adam Williams' description of the 'unpleasant necessity' of sending Sam Kressel the false report of his actions at Lumumba Hall. The parallel hurt.

'The boy's in trouble. He's sick. It's a disease and he's trying to cure himself. That takes courage . . . This is no time for campus Gestapo tactics.' Herron took a long drink from his glass while his free hand gripped the arm of the chair.

'How did you know about it?'

'That might be privileged information. Let's say I heard from a respected co-worker of ours – in the medical line – who ran across the symptoms and became concerned. What difference does it make? I tried to help the boy and I'd do it again.'

'I'd like to believe that. It's what I wanted to believe.'

'Why is that difficult for you?'

'I don't know . . . Something at the front door a few minutes ago. Perhaps this house. I can't put my finger on it . . . I'm being completely honest with you.'

Herron laughed but still avoided Matlock's eyes. 'You're too wound up in the Elizabethans. The plots and counter-plots of *The Spanish Tragedy* . . . You young faculty crusaders should stop trying to be an amateur Scotland Yard. Not too long ago it was fashionable around here to have Red Dogs for breakfast. You're just magnifying the situation out of proportion.'

'That's not true. I'm not a faculty crusader. I'm no part of that crowd, and I think you know it.'

'What was it then? Personal interest? In the boy. Or his wife? . . . I'm sorry, I shouldn't have said that.'

'I'm glad you did. I have no interest in Virginia Beeson – sexual or otherwise. Although I can't imagine what else there would be.'

'Then you put on quite an act.'

'I certainly did. I took extreme measures to keep Beeson from knowing why I was there. It was that important.'

'To whom?' Herron slowly put his glass down with his right hand, his left still gripped the arm of the chair.

'To people beyond this campus. Washington people. The federal authorities . . .'

Lucas Herron took a sudden, sustained intake of breath through his nostrils. In front of Matlock's eyes, Herron's face began to drain itself of color. When he spoke, he did so barely above a whisper.

'What are you saying?'

'That I was approached by a man from the Justice Department. The information he showed me was frightening. Nothing was trumped up, nothing overdramatized. It was straight data. I was given a free choice whether to cooperate or not.'

'And you accepted?' Herron's words were uttered softly in disbelief.

'I didn't feel there was an alternative. My younger brother . . .'

'You didn't feel there was an *alternative*?' Herron rose from his chair, his hands began to shake, his voice grew in intensity. 'You didn't *feel* there was an *alternative*?!'

'No, I didn't,' Matlock remained calm. 'That's why I came out here. To warn you, old friend. It's much deeper – far more dangerous . . .'

'*You* came out here to warn *me*?! What have you *done*? What in the name of everything sacred *have you done*? . . . Now, you listen to me! You listen to what I say!' Herron backed off, bumping into the small side table. In one whip of his left arm, he sent it crashing onto

122

the flagstones. 'You let it go, do you hear me! You go back and tell them *nothing! Nothing exists!* It's all . . . all in their imaginations! *Don't touch it! Let it go!'*

'I can't do that,' said Matlock gently, suddenly afraid for the old man. 'Even Sealfont will have to agree. He can't fight it any longer. It's there, Lucas . . .'

'Adrian! Adrian's been told? . . . Oh, my God, do you know what you're doing? *You'll destroy so much.* So many, many . . . Get out of here! *Get out!* I don't know you! Oh, *Jesus! Jesus!'*

'Lucas, what is it?' Matlock got up and took several steps toward the old man. Herron continued backing away, an old man in panic.

'Don't come near me! Don't you *touch me!'*

Herron turned and started running as well as his ancient legs could carry him across the lawn. He stumbled, falling to the ground, and picked himself up. He didn't look back. Instead he ran with all his might toward the rear of the yard, toward the overgrown woods. And then he disappeared through his huge green wall.

'Lucas! For Christ's sake!' Matlock raced after the old man, reaching the edge of the woods only seconds behind him. Yet he was nowhere in sight. Matlock whipped at the overgrowth in front of him and stepped into the tangled mass of foliage. Branches slashed back at him, and the intricate webbings of giant weeds ensnared his feet as he kicked his way into the dense woods.

Herron was gone.

'Lucas! Where are you?!'

There was no answer, only the rustling of the disturbed growth behind him. Matlock went farther into the forest, ducking, crouching, sidling by the green barriers in front of him. There was no sign of Lucas Herron, no sound.

'Lucas! For God's sake, Lucas, answer me!'

Still no reply, no hint of presence.

123

Matlock tried to look around him, tried to spot a break in the patterns of foliage, a route to follow. He could see none. It was as if Lucas were matter one moment, vapor the next.

And then he heard it. Indistinct, from all sides of him, echoing softly from some unknown place. It was a deep-throated moan, a wail. Near, yet far in the dense distance. And then the wail diminished and became a plaintive sob. A single sob, punctuated by a single word – clear, and spoken in hatred.

The word was –

'Nimrod . . .'

Chapter 12

'Goddamn it, Matlock! I told you to stay put until I contacted you!'

'Goddamn it, Greenberg! How did you get into my apartment?!'

'You didn't get your window fixed.'

'You haven't offered to pay for it.'

'We're even. Where have you been?'

Matlock threw his car keys on the coffee table and looked at his broken stereo set in the corner. 'It's an involved story and I suspect . . . pathetic. I'll tell you all about it after I've had a drink. My last one was interrupted.'

'Get me one, too. I've also got a story and mine's *definitely* pathetic.'

'What do you drink?'

'Very little, so whatever you're having is fine.'

Matlock looked out his front window. The curtains were strewn on the floor where he had torn them in front of Adam Williams. The sun was almost down now. The spring day was over. 'I'm going to squeeze some lemons and have a fresh fruit Tom Collins.'

'Your file says you drink bourbon. Sour mash.'

Matlock looked at the federal agent. 'Does it?'

Greenberg followed Matlock into the kitchen and watched in silence as he fixed their drinks. Matlock handed the federal man his glass.

'Looks fancy.'

'It's not . . . Whose pathetic story gets first telling?'

'I'll want to hear yours, of course, but under the circumstances, mine has priority.'

'You sound ominous.'

'No. Just pathetic . . . I'll start by asking you if you'd care to know where I've been since I dropped you off.' Greenberg leaned against the counter.

'Not particularly, but you'll tell me anyway.'

'Yes, I will. It's part of the pathos. I was out at your local airport – Bradley Field – waiting for a jet despatched by Justice a few hours ago from Dulles. There was a man on the plane who brought me two sealed envelopes which I had to sign for. Here they are.' Greenberg reached into his jacket pocket and took out two long business envelopes. He put one on the counter and began to open the second.

'They look very official,' said Matlock, edging himself up so that he sat next to the sink, his long legs dangling over the side in front of the cabinets.

'They couldn't be more official . . . This envelope contains the summary of our conclusions based on information you gave us – gave me. It ends with a specific recommendation. I'm allowed to convey this information in my own words as long as I cover all the facts . . .'

'Jason Greenberg gets two points.'

'However,' continued the federal man without acknowledging Matlock's interruption, 'the contents of the second envelope must be delivered verbatim. You are to read it thoroughly – *should it be necessary* – and if it's acceptable, you've got to acknowledge that by your signature.'

'This gets better and better. Am I running for the Senate?'

'No, you're just running . . . I'll start as instructed.' Greenberg glanced at the unfolded paper and then looked across at Matlock. 'The man at Lumumba Hall named Julian Dunois – alias Jacques Devereaux, Jésus Dambert, and probably several others we don't know about – is a legal strategist for the Black Left militants. The term

126

legal strategist covers everything from court manipulations to agent provocateur. When involved with the former, he uses the name of Dunois, the latter – any number of aliases. He operates out of unusual places geographically. Algiers, Marseilles, the Caribbean – including Cuba – and, we suspect, Hanoi and probably Moscow. Perhaps even Peking. In the States he has a regular, bona fide law office in upper Harlem and a West Coast affiliate in San Francisco . . . He's generally in the background, but wherever he's in evidence, bad news usually follows. Needless to say, he's on the attorney general's list of undesirables, and these days that's not respectable any longer . . .'

'These days,' broke in Matlock, 'that includes almost everyone to the left of AT&T.'

'No comment. To continue. The surfacing of Dunois in this operation adds a dimension not anticipated – a new aspect not considered before. It goes beyond domestic lawbreakers and enters the area of international crime and/*or* subversion. *Or* a combination of both. In light of the fact that drugs were used on you, your apartment broken into and ripped apart, your friend, Miss Ballantyne, indirectly threatened – and don't kid yourself, that's what it was – in light of all this, the recommendation is as follows. You withdraw from any further participation in this investigation. Your involvement is beyond the realm of reasonable risk.' Greenberg dropped the paper on the counter and took several swallows of his drink. Matlock swung his legs slowly back and forth in front of the cabinet beneath him. 'What say you, in the docket?' asked Greenberg.

'I'm not sure. It seems to me you're not finished.'

'I'd like to be. Right here. The summary's accurate, and I think you should agree with the recommendation. Pull out, Jim.'

127

'Finish first. What's the other letter? The one I'm supposed to read verbatim?'

'It's only necessary if you reject the recommendation. Don't reject it. I'm not instructed to lean that way, so that's off the record.'

'You know damned well I'm going to reject it, so why waste time?'

'I *don't* know that. I don't want to *believe* that.'

'There's no way out.'

'There are counter explanations I can activate in an hour. Get you off the hook, out of the picture.'

'Not any longer.'

'What? Why?'

'That's *my* pathetic story. So you'd better continue.'

Greenberg searched Matlock's eyes for an explanation, found none, and so picked up the second envelope and opened it.

'In the unlikely and ill-advised event that you reject our recommendation to cease and desist, you must understand that you do so against the express wishes of the Justice Department. Although we will offer whatever protection we can – as we would any citizen – you act under your own responsibility. We cannot be held liable for any injuries or inconveniences of any nature.'

'Is that what it says?'

'No, that's *not* what it says, but that's what it means,' said Greenberg, unfolding the paper. 'It's much simpler and even more inclusive. Here.' The federal agent handed Matlock the letter.

It was a statement signed by an assistant attorney general with a separate line on the left for Matlock's signature.

'An investigative office of the Department of Justice accepted the offer of James B. Matlock to make inquiries of a minor nature with regard to certain illegal acts alleged to have occurred within the vicinity of Carlyle

128

University. However, the Department of Justice now considers the situation to be a professional matter, and any further participation on the part of Professor Matlock is deemed unwarranted and against the policies of the Department. Therefore, the Department of Justice hereby informs James B. Matlock that it appreciates his previous cooperation but requests him to remove himself from any further involvement in the interest of safety and investigatory progress. It is the opinion of the Department that further actions on the part of Professor Matlock might tend to interfere with the aims of the Investigation in the Carlyle area. Mr Matlock has received the original of this letter and so signifies by his signature below.'

'What the hell are you talking about? This says that I agree to pull out.'

'You'd make a lousy lawyer. Don't buy a bicycle on time before talking to me.'

'What?'

'Nowhere! *Nowhere* does your signing this little stinkpot say you *agree* to retire from the scene. Only that Justice *requested* you to.'

'Then why in hell should I sign it?'

'Excellent question. You may buy a bicycle . . . You sign it if, as you say, you reject the recommendation to pull out.'

'Oh, for Christ's sake!' Matlock slipped down from the edge of the sink and threw the paper across the counter next to Greenberg. 'I may not know law but I know language. You're talking in contradictions!'

'Only on the surface . . . Let me ask you a question. Say you continue playing undercover agent. Is it conceivable that you may want to ask for help? An emergency, perhaps?'

'Of course. Inevitable.'

'You get no help whatsoever without that letter going

129

back signed . . . Don't look at *me*! I'll be replaced in a matter of days. I've been in the area too long already.'

'Kind of hypocritical, isn't it? The only way I can count on any assistance – any protection – is to sign a statement that says I won't need it.'

'It's enough to send me into private practice . . . There's a new term for this sort of thing these days. It's called "hazardless progress." Use whatever – *who*ever – you can. But don't take the blame if a *game plan* gets fucked up. Don't be responsible.'

'And I jump without a parachute if I don't sign.'

'I told you. Take some free advice – I'm a good lawyer. Quit. Forget it. But *forget* it.'

'And I told *you* – I can't.'

Greenberg reached for his drink and spoke softly. 'No matter what you do, it's not going to bring your brother out of his grave.'

'I know that.' Matlock was touched, but he answered firmly.

'You might prevent other younger brothers but you probably won't. In either case, someone else can be recruited from professional ranks. I hate like hell to admit it, but Kressel was right. And if we don't get this conference – this convocation of peddlers in a couple of weeks – there'll be others.'

'I agree with everything you say.'

'Then why hesitate? Pull out.'

'Why? . . . I haven't told you *my* pathetic little story, that's why. Remember? You had priority, but I've still got my turn.'

'So tell.'

And Matlock told him. Everything he knew about Lucas Herron – legend, giant, the 'grand old bird' of Carlyle. The terror-stricken skeleton who had run into his personal forest. The wail of the single word: 'Nimrod.' Greenberg listened, and the longer Matlock talked, the sadder Jason Greenberg's eyes became. When Matlock finished, the federal agent drank the last of his drink and morosely nodded his head in slow motion.

'You spelled out everything for him, didn't you? You couldn't come to *me*, you had to go to *him*. Your campus saint with a bucket of blood in his hands . . . Loring was right. We had to reach a conscience-stricken amateur . . . Amateurs in front of us and amateurs behind us. At least I'll say this for you. You got a conscience. That's more than I can say for the rear flank.'

'What should I do?'

'Sign the stinkpot.' Greenberg picked up the Justice Department letter from the counter and handed it to Matlock. 'You're going to need help.'

Patricia Ballantyne preceded Matlock to the small side table at the far end of the Cheshire Cat. The drive out had been strained. The girl had hammered away – quietly, acidly – at Matlock's cooperating with the government, in particular and specifically the Federal Bureau of Investigation. She claimed not to be reacting to a programmed liberal response; there was simply too much overwhelming evidence that such organizations had brought the country ten steps from its own particular police state.

She knew firsthand. She'd witnessed the anguished aftermath of one FBI exercise and knew it wasn't isolated.

Matlock held her chair as she sat down, touching her shoulders as she did so. Touching, reaffirming, lessening the imagined hurt. The table was small, next to a window, several feet from a terrace that soon – in late May – would be in use for outside dining. He sat across from her and took her hand.

'I'm not going to apologize for what I'm doing. I think

131

it has to be done. I'm not a hero and I'm not a fink. I'm not asked to be heroic, and the information they want ultimately will help a lot of people. People who need help – desperately.'

'Will those people *get* help? Or will they simply be prosecuted? Instead of hospitals and clinics . . . will they find themselves in jail?'

'They're not interested in sick kids. They want the ones who make them sick. So do I.'

'But in the process, the kids get hurt.' A statement.

'Some may be. As few as possible.'

'That's contemptible.' The girl took her hand away from Matlock's. 'It's so condescending. Who makes *those* decisions? You?'

'You're beginning to sound like a one-track tape.'

'I've *been* there. It's not pleasant.'

'This is entirely different. I've met just two men; one . . . left. The other's Greenberg. They're not your nightmares from the fifties. Take my word for that.'

'I'd like to.'

The manager of the Cheshire Cat approached the table. 'There's a telephone call for you, Mr Matlock.'

Matlock felt a twinge of pain in his stomach. It was the nerves of fear. Only one person knew where he was – Jason Greenberg.

'Thanks, Harry.'

'You can take it by the reservations desk. The phone's off the hook.'

Matlock got out of his chair and looked briefly at Pat. In the months and months of their going out together, from restaurants to parties to dinners, he had never received a telephone call, had never been interrupted that way. He saw that realization in her eyes. He walked rapidly away from the table to the reservations desk.

'Hello?'

132

'Jim?' It *was* Greenberg, of course.

'Jason?'

'Sorry to bother you. I wouldn't if I didn't have to.'

'What is it, for heaven's sake?'

'Lucas Herron's dead. He committed suicide about an hour ago.'

The pain in Matlock's stomach suddenly returned. It wasn't a twinge this time, but instead a sharp blow that left him unable to breathe. All he could see in front of his eyes was the picture of the staggering, panicked old man running across the manicured lawn and disappearing into the dense foliage bordering his property. And then the wailing sound of a sob and the name of Nimrod whispered in hatred.

'Are you all right?'

'Yes. Yes, I'm all right.' For reasons he could not fathom, Matlock's memory focused on a small, black-framed photograph. It was an enlarged snapshot of a dark-haired, middle-aged infantry officer with a weapon in one hand, a map in the other, the face lean and strong, looking up toward the high ground.

A quarter of a century ago.

'You'd better get back to your apartment . . .' Greenberg was issuing an order, but he had the sense to be gentle about it.

'Who found him?'

'My man. No-one else knows yet.'

'Your man?'

'After our talk, I put Herron under surveillance. You get to spot the signs. He broke in and found him.'

'How?'

'Cut his wrists in the shower.'

'Oh, Christ! What have I done?'

'Cut that out! Get back here. We've got people to reach . . . Come on, Jim.'

133

'What can I tell Pat?' Matlock tried to find his mind but it kept wandering back to a helpless, frightened old man.

'As little as possible. But hurry.'

Matlock replaced the receiver and took several deep breaths. He searched his pockets for cigarettes and remembered that he'd left them at the table.

The table. Pat. He had to go back to the table and think of something to say.

The truth. Goddamn it, the *truth*.

He made his way around two antique pillars toward the far end of the room and the small side table by the window. In spite of his panic, he felt a degree of relief and knew it was because he had decided to be honest with Pat. God knew he had to have someone other than Greenberg and Kressel to talk to.

Kressel! He was supposed to have gone to Kressel's house at seven. He'd forgotten all about it!

But in an instant Sam Kressel went out of his thoughts. He saw the small side table by the window and there was no-one there.

Pat was gone.

Chapter 13

'No-one saw her leave?' Greenberg followed a frustrated Matlock into the living room from the foyer. Sam Kressel's voice could be heard from the bedroom, shouting excitedly into a telephone. Matlock took notice of it, his attention split in too many areas.

'That's Sam in there, isn't it?' he asked. 'Does he know about Herron?'

'Yes. I called him after I talked to you . . . What about the waitresses? Did you ask them?'

'Of course I did. None of them were sure. It was busy. One said she thought she might have gone to the ladies' room. Another hinted, s'help me, hinted, that she might have been the girl who left with a couple from another table.'

'Wouldn't they have had to pass you on the way out? Wouldn't you have seen her?'

'Not necessarily. We were in the back. There are two or three doors which lead to a terrace. In summer, especially when it's crowded, they put tables on the terrace.'

'You drove out in your car?'

'Naturally.'

'And you didn't see her outside, walking on the road, on the grounds?'

'No.'

'Did you recognize any of the other people there?'

'I didn't really look. I was . . . preoccupied.' Matlock lit a cigarette. His hand shook as he held the match.

'If you want my opinion, I think she spotted someone

135

she knew and asked for a lift home. A girl like that doesn't go anywhere she doesn't want to go without a fight.'

'I know. That's occurred to me.'

'Have a fight?'

'You might say it was diminishing but not over. The phone call probably set her off again. Old English teachers rarely get calls while out at restaurants.'

'I'm sorry.'

'It's not your fault. I told you, she's uptight. She keeps thinking about her father. I'll try her apartment when Sam gets off the phone.'

'*He's* a funny man. I tell him about Herron – naturally he goes off the deep end. He says he's got to talk privately with Sealfont so he goes into the bedroom and shouts so loud they can hear him in Poughkeepsie.'

Matlock's thoughts shifted quickly to Herron. 'His death – his *suicide* – is going to be the biggest shock this campus has had in twenty years. Men like Lucas simply don't die. They certainly don't die like *this* . . . Does Sam know I saw him?'

'He does. I couldn't withhold that. I told him pretty much what you told me – shorter version, of course. He refuses to believe it. The implications, I mean.'

'I don't blame him. They're not easy to believe. What do we do now?'

'We wait. I've made a report. Two lab men from the Hartford Bureau are out there now. The local police have been called in.'

At the mention of the police, Matlock suddenly remembered the patrolman out of uniform in the squash court corridor, who had walked rapidly away at the moment of recognition. He'd told Greenberg and Greenberg had never given him an explanation – if there was one. He asked again.

'What about the cop in the gym?'

'The story's reasonable. At least so far. The Carlyle police are assigned three mornings a week for limited use of the facilities. Town-gown relations. Coincidence.'

'You're settling for that?'

'I said, "so far." We're running a check on the man. Nothing's turned up but an excellent record.'

'He's a bigot, a nasty bastard.'

'This may surprise you, but that's no crime. It's guaranteed in the Bill of Rights.'

Sam Kressel walked through the bedroom door quickly, emphatically. Matlock saw that he was as close to pure fear as he'd ever seen a man. There was an uncomfortable similarity between Sam's face and the bloodless expression of Lucas Herron before the old man had raced into the woods.

'I heard you come in,' Kressel said. 'What are we going to *do*? What in hell are we *going to do*? . . . Adrian doesn't believe that absurd story any more than *I* do! *Lucas Herron! It's insane!*'

'Maybe. But it's true.'

'Because *you* say so? How can you be sure? You're no professional in these matters. As I understand it, Lucas admitted he was helping a student through a drug problem.'

'He . . . they aren't students.'

'I see.' Kressel stopped briefly and looked back and forth between Matlock and Greenberg. 'Under the circumstances, I demand to know the identities.'

'You'll get them,' said Greenberg quietly. 'Go on. I want to hear why Matlock's so wrong, the story so absurd.'

'Because Lucas Herron isn't . . . wasn't the only member of the faculty concerned with these problems. There are dozens of us giving aid, helping wherever we can!'

'I don't follow you.' Greenberg stared at Kressel. 'So you help. You don't go and kill yourself when a fellow member of the faculty finds out about it.'

Sam Kressel removed his glasses and looked momentarily reflective, sad. 'There's something else neither of you know about. I've been aware of it for some time but not so knowledgeably as Sealfont . . . Lucas Herron was a very sick man. One kidney was removed last summer. The other was also cancerous and he knew it. The pain must have been unbearable for him. He hadn't long.'

Greenberg watched closely as Kressel returned his glasses to his face. Matlock bent down and crushed out his cigarette in an ashtray on the coffee table. Finally, Greenberg spoke.

'Are you suggesting that there's no relationship between Herron's suicide and Matlock's seeing him this afternoon?'

'I'm not suggesting any such thing. I'm sure there's a relationship . . . But you didn't know Lucas. His whole life for nearly half a century, except for the war years, was Carlyle University. It's been his total, complete existence. He loved this place more than any man could love a woman, more than any parent a child. I'm sure Jim's told you. If he thought for a moment that his world here was going to be defaced, torn apart – that would be a greater pain than the physical torture his body gave him. What better time to take his own life?'

'*Goddamn you!*' roared Matlock. 'You're saying *I killed him!*'

'Perhaps I am,' Kressel said quietly. 'I hadn't thought of it in those terms. I'm sure Adrian didn't either.'

'But that's what you're *saying*! You're saying I went off half-cocked and killed him as much as if I'd slashed his wrists! . . . Well, you weren't there. *I was!*'

Kressel spoke gently. 'I didn't say you went off half-cocked. I said you were an amateur. A very well-intentioned amateur. I think Greenberg knows what I mean.'

Jason Greenberg looked at Matlock. 'There's an old Slovak proverb: "When the old men kill themselves, the cities are dying."'

The telephone bell suddenly pierced the air; its sound acted as a jolt to the three men. Matlock answered it, then turned to Greenberg. 'It's for you.'

'Thanks.' The federal agent took the phone from Matlock. 'Greenberg . . . OK I understand. When will you know? . . . I'll probably be on the road by then. I'll call you back. Talk later.' He replaced the telephone and stood by the desk, his back to Matlock and Kressel. The dean of colleges couldn't contain himself.

'What was it? What happened?'

Greenberg turned and faced them. Matlock thought his eyes seemed sadder than usual, which Matlock had learned was a sign of trouble in Greenberg.

'We're making a request of the police – the courts – for an autopsy.'

'*Why?!*' Kressel shouted as he approached the agent. 'For God's sake, *why*?! The man killed himself! He was in *pain*! . . . Jesus Christ, you can't do this! If news of it gets out . . .'

'We'll handle it quietly.'

'That can't be done and you know it! It'll leak out and all hell'll break loose around here! I won't *permit* it!'

'You can't stop it. Even I couldn't stop it. There's sufficient evidence to indicate that Herron didn't take his own life. That he was killed.' Greenberg smiled wryly at Matlock. 'And not by words.'

Kressel argued, threatened, made another call to Sealfont,

and finally, when it was obvious that all were to no avail, he left Matlock's apartment in fury.

No sooner had Kressel slammed the door than the telephone rang again. Greenberg saw that the sound disturbed Matlock – not merely annoyed him, but disturbed him; perhaps frightened him.

'I'm sorry . . . I'm afraid this place has to be a kind of patrol base for a while. Not long . . . Maybe it's the girl.'

Matlock picked up the phone, listened, but did not say anything into it. Instead, he turned to Greenberg. He said only one word.

'You.'

Greenberg took the telephone, uttered his name softly, and then spent the next minute staring straight ahead. Matlock watched Greenberg for half the time and then wandered into his kitchen. He didn't wish to stand awkwardly to one side while the agent listened to a superior's instructions.

The voice at the other end of the line had initially identified itself by saying, 'Washington calling.'

On the counter lay the empty envelope in which the brutally hypocritical statement had come from the Department of Justice. It had been one more sign that his worst fantasies were gradually becoming real. From that infinitesimal portion of the mind which concerns itself with the unthinkable, Matlock had begun to perceive that the land he had grown up in was changing into something ugly and destructive. It was far more than a political manifestation, it was a slow, all-embracing sense of morality by strategy. A corruption of intentions. Strong feelings were being replaced with surface anger, convictions and compromise. The land was becoming something other than its promise, its commitment. The grails were empty vessels of flat wine, impressive solely because they were possessed.

140

'I'm off the phone now. Would you like to try reaching Miss Ballantyne?'

Matlock looked up at Greenberg, standing in the frame of the kitchen door. Greenberg, the walking contradiction, the proverb-quoting agent deeply suspicious of the system for which he worked.

'Yes. Yes, I'd like to.' He started into the living room as Greenberg stepped aside to let him pass. Matlock reached the center of the room and stopped. 'That's one hell of a quotation. What was it? "When the old men kill themselves, the cities are dying."' He turned and looked at the agent. 'I think that's the saddest proverb I've ever heard.'

'You're not Hassidic. Of course, neither am I, but the Hassidim wouldn't think it sad . . . Come to think of it, no true philosopher would.'

'Why not? It *is* sad.'

'It's truth. Truth is neither joyful nor sad, neither good nor bad. It is simply truth.'

'Someday let's debate that, Jason.' Matlock picked up the telephone, dialed Pat's number, and let it ring a dozen times. There was no answer. Matlock thought of several of Pat's friends and wondered whether to call them or not. When angry or upset, Pat usually did one of two things. She either went off by herself for an hour or so, or, conversely, sought out one or two friends and drove off to a film in Hartford or an out-of-the-way bar. It was just over an hour. He'd give her another fifteen minutes before phoning around. It had, of course, occurred to him that she might have been taken involuntarily – that had been his first thought. But it wasn't logical. The Cheshire Cat had been filled with people, the tables close together. Greenberg was right. Wherever she went, she went because she wanted to go.

141

Greenberg stood by the kitchen door. He hadn't moved. He'd been watching Matlock.

'I'll try in a quarter of an hour. Then, if there's no answer, I'll call some friends of hers. As you said, she's one strong-willed young lady.'

'I hope you're not from the same cloth.'

'What does that mean?'

Greenberg took several steps into the living room. When he spoke, he looked directly into Matlock's eyes.

'You're out. Finished. Forget the letter, forget Loring, forget me . . . That's the way it's got to be. We understand you have reservations for St Thomas on Pan Am for Saturday. Enjoy it, because that's where you're going. Much better this way.'

Matlock returned the government man's look. 'Any decision like that will be made by me. I've got a gentle old man on my conscience; and you've got that stinkpot in your pocket. I signed it, remember?'

'The stinkpot doesn't count any more. DC wants you out. You go.'

'Why?'

'Because of the gentle old man. If he *was* killed, you could be, too. If that happened, certain records might be subpoenaed, certain men who had reservations about recruiting you might voice these reservations to the press. You were maneuvered. I don't have to tell you that.'

'So?'

'The directors at Justice have no wish to be called executioners.'

'I see.' Matlock took his eyes off Greenberg and wandered toward the coffee table. 'Suppose I refuse?'

'Then I remove you from the scene.'

'How?'

'I have you arrested on suspicion of murder one.'

'*What?*'

142

'You were the last person on record to see Lucas Herron alive. By your own admission, you went out to his house to threaten him.'

'To *warn* him!'

'That's subject to interpretation, isn't it?'

When the thunderous crash came, it was so ear-shattering both men threw themselves to the floor. It was as if the whole side of the building had collapsed in rubble. Dust was everywhere, furniture toppled, glass shattered, splinters of wood and plaster flew through the air, and the terrible stench of burning sulfur settled over the room. Matlock knew the smell of that kind of bomb, and his reflexes knew how to operate. He clung to the base of his couch waiting, waiting for a second explosion – a delayed detonator which would kill any who rose in panic. Through the mist, he saw Greenberg start to get up, and he leaped forward, tackling the agent at his knees.

'Get down! Stay . . .'

The second explosion came. Parts of the ceiling blackened. But Matlock knew it was not a killer explosive. It was something else, and he could not figure it out at the moment. It was an eye-grabber, a camouflage – not meant to kill, but to deflect all concentration. A huge firecracker.

Screams of panic could now be heard mounting from all parts of the building. The sounds of rushing feet pounded on the floor above his apartment.

And then a single screech of terror from outside Matlock's front door. It would not stop. The horror of it caused Matlock and Greenberg to struggle to their feet and race to the source. Matlock pulled the door open and looked down upon a sight no human being should ever see more than once in a lifetime, if his life must continue beyond that instant.

On his front step was Patricia Ballantyne wrapped in

143

a blood-soaked sheet. Holes were cut in the areas of her naked breasts, blood flowing from gashes beneath the nipples. The front of her head was shaved; blood poured out of lacerations where once had been the soft brown hair. Blood, too, came from the half-open mouth, her lips bruised and split. The eyes were blackened into deep crevasses of sore flesh – but they moved! The eyes moved!

Saliva began forming at the corners of her lips. The half-dead corpse was trying to speak.

'Jamie . . .' was the only word she managed and then her head slipped to one side.

Greenberg threw his whole weight against Matlock, sending him sprawling into the gathering crowd. He roared orders of 'Police!' and 'Ambulance!' until he saw enough people running to execute his commands. He put his mouth to the girl's mouth, to force air into the collapsing lungs, but he knew it wasn't really necessary. Patricia Ballantyne wasn't dead; she'd been tortured by experts, and the experts knew their business well. Every slash, every crack, every bruise meant utmost pain but did not mean death.

He started to pick the girl up but Matlock stopped him. The English professor's eyes were swollen with tears of hate. He gently removed Greenberg's hands and lifted Pat into his arms. He carried her inside and stretched her out on the half-destroyed sofa. Greenberg went into the bedroom and returned with a blanket. Then he brought a bowl of warm water from the kitchen and several towels. He lifted the blanket and held a towel beneath the bleeding breasts. Matlock, staring in horror at the brutally beaten face, then took the edge of another towel and began wiping away the blood around the shaven head and the mouth.

'She'll be all right, Jim. I've seen this before. She'll be all right.'

And as Greenberg heard the sounds of the sirens in the near distance, he wondered, really, if this girl would ever be right again.

Matlock, helpless, continued to wipe the girl's face, his tears now streaming down his cheeks, his eyes unblinking. He spoke through his controlled sobs.

'You know what this means, don't you? No-one pulls me out now. They try, I'll kill them.'

'I won't let them,' said Greenberg simply.

The screeching of brakes could be heard outside and the flashing lights of the police cars and the ambulances whipped in circles through the windows.

Matlock's face fell into the cushion beside the unconscious girl and he wept.

Chapter 14

Matlock awoke in the antiseptic whiteness of a hospital room. The shade was up, and the sun reflected harshly on the three walls he could see. At his feet a nurse was writing efficiently, emphatically, on top of a clipboard attached to the base of the bed by a thin keychain. He stretched his arms, then quickly brought his left back, aware of a sharp pain in his forearm.

'You feel those the next morning, Mr Matlock,' droned the nurse without looking up from the clipboard. 'Heavy intravenous sedations are murder, I can tell you. Not that I've ever had one, but Lord knows, I've seen enough who have.'

'Is Pat . . . Miss Ballantyne here?'

'Well, not in the same *room*! Lord, you campus types!'

'She's here?'

'Of course. Next room. Which I intend to keep *locked*! Lord, you people from the hill! . . . There! You're all accounted for.' The nurse let the clipboard crash down and vibrate back and forth. 'Now. *You've* got special privileges. *You're* allowed breakfast even though it's past breakfast time – *way* past! That's probably because they want you to pay your bill . . . You can be discharged any time after twelve.'

'What time is it? Someone took my watch.'

'It's eight minutes to nine,' said the nurse, glancing at her wrist. 'And no one *took* your watch. It's with any other valuables you had when you were admitted.'

'How *is* Miss Ballantyne?'

'We don't discuss other patients, Mr Matlock.'

146

'Where's her doctor?'

'He's the same as yours, I understand. Not one of *ours*.' The nurse made sure the statement was hardly complimentary. 'According to your chart, he'll be here at nine-thirty unless we phone for an emergency.'

'Call him. I want him here as soon as possible.'

'Now, really. There's no emergency . . .'

'Goddamn it, get him here!'

As Matlock raised his voice the door of his room opened. Jason Greenberg came in quickly. 'I could hear you in the corridor. That's a good sign.'

'How's Pat?!'

'Just a minute, sir. We have regulations . . .'

Greenberg took out his identification and showed it to the nurse. 'This man is in my custody, Miss. Check the front desk, if you like, but leave us alone.'

The nurse, ever professional, scrutinized the identification and walked rapidly out the door.

'How's Pat?'

'A mess, but with it. She had a bad night; she's going to have a worse morning when she asks for a mirror.'

'The hell with that! Is she *all right*?'

'Twenty-seven stitches – body, head, mouth, and, for variety, one on her left foot. But she's going to be fine. X-rays show only bone bruises. No fractures, no ruptures, no internal bleeding. The bastards did their usual professional job.'

'Was she able to talk?'

'Not really. And the doctor didn't advise it. She needs sleep more than anything else . . . You need a little rest, too. That's why we put you here last night.'

'Anyone hurt at the apartment?'

'Nope. It was a crazy bombing. We don't think it was intended to kill anyone. The first was a short two-inch stick taped below the window exterior; the second – activated

147

by the first – wasn't much more than a July Fourth rocket. You expected the second blast, didn't you?'

'Yes. I guess I did . . . Terror tactics, wasn't it?'

'That's what we figure.'

'Can I see Pat?'

'Rather you waited. The doctor thinks she'll sleep into the afternoon. There's a nurse in there with ice packs and stuff if localized pain bothers her. Let her rest.'

Matlock cautiously sat on the edge of the bed. He began flexing his legs, arms, neck, and hands, and found that he wasn't much below par. 'I feel sort of like a hangover without the headache.'

'The doctor gave you a heavy dose. You were . . . understandably . . . very emotional.'

'I remember everything. I'm calmer, but I don't retract one goddamned word . . . I have two classes today. One at ten and the other at two. I want to make them.'

'You don't have to. Sealfont wants to see you.'

'I'll talk to him after my last class . . . Then I'll see Pat.' Matlock stood on his feet and walked slowly to the large hospital window. It was a bright, sunlit morning; Connecticut had had a string of beautiful days. As he stared outside, Matlock remembered he'd looked out another window five days ago when he'd first met Jason Greenberg. He'd made a decision then as he was making one now. 'Last night you said you wouldn't let them pull me out. I hope you haven't changed your mind. I'm *not* going to be on that Pan Am flight tomorrow.'

'You won't be arrested. I promised you that.'

'Can you prevent it? You also said you were going to be replaced.'

'I can prevent it . . . I can morally object, an enigmatic phrase which is translated to mean I can embarrass people. However, I don't want to mislead you. If you create problems, you could be taken into protective custody.'

148

'They can if they can find me.'

'That's a condition I don't like.'

'Forget you heard it. Where are my clothes?' Matlock walked to the single closet door and opened it. His slacks, jacket, and shirt were hung on hangers; his loafers were on the floor with his socks carefully inserted. The lone bureau held his undershorts and a hospital-furnished toothbrush. 'Will you go down and see whoever you've got to see to get me out of here? Also, I'll need my wallet, cash, and watch. Will you do that, please?'

'What do you mean – if they could find you? What are you going to do?' Greenberg made no move to leave.

'Nothing earth-shattering. Merely continue making those enquiries . . . of a minor nature. That's the way the statement from your employers phrased it, wasn't it? Loring said it. Somewhere out there is the other half of that paper. I'm going to find it.'

'You listen to me first! I don't deny you have a right . . .'

'You don't *deny*!' Matlock turned on the federal agent. His voice was controlled but vicious. 'That's not good enough. That's *negative* approval! I've got several *big* rights! They include a kid brother in a sailboat, a black son of a bitch named Dunois or whatever you call him, a man by the name of Lucas Herron, and that girl in there! I suspect you and the doctor know the rest of what happened to her last night, and I can *guess*! Don't talk to me about a *right*!'

'In principle, we agree. I just don't want your "rights" to land you next to your brother. This is a job for professionals. Not an amateur! If you work at all, I want you to work with whoever takes my place. That's important. I want your word on it.'

Matlock took off the top of his pajamas and gave Greenberg a short, embarrassed smile. 'You have it. I don't really see myself as a one-man ranger team. Do you know who's taking your place?'

'Not yet. Probably someone from DC. They won't take a chance on using a Hartford or a New Haven man . . . The truth is . . . they don't know who's been bought. He'll be in touch. I'll have to brief him myself. No-one else can. I'll instruct him to identify himself with . . . what would you like?'

'Tell him to use your proverb. "When the old men kill themselves, the cities are dying."'

'You like that, don't you?'

'I don't like it or dislike it. It's simply the truth. Isn't that the way it should be?'

'And very applicable. I see what you mean.'

'Very.'

'Jim, before I go this afternoon, I'm going to write out a telephone number for you. It's a Bronx number – my parents. They won't know where I am, but I'll check with them every day. Use it if you have to.'

'Thanks, I will.'

'I want your word on it.'

'You have it.' Matlock laughed a short laugh of gratitude.

'Of course, under the circumstances, I may just be on the other end of the line if you do call.'

'Back in private practice?'

'The possibility is less remote than you think.'

Chapter 15

Between his two classes, Matlock drove to the small brokerage office in the town of Carlyle and emerged with a check for $7,312. It represented his total investment in the market, mostly from royalties. The broker had tried to dissuade him; it was no time to sell, especially at current prices. But Matlock had made up his mind. The cashier reluctantly issued the check.

From there Matlock went to his bank and transferred his entire savings into his checking account. He added the $7,312 to the slip and looked at the sum total of his immediate cash value.

It came to $11,501.72.

Matlock stared at the figure for several minutes. He had mixed feelings about it. On the one hand, it proved solvency; on the other, it was a little frightening to think that after thirty-three years of living he was able to pinpoint so accurately his net financial worth. There was no house, no land, no hidden investments anywhere. Only an automobile, a few possessions of minor value, and some published words of such a specialized nature that there would be no significant rewards.

Yet by many standards, it was a great deal of money.

Only nowhere *near* enough. He knew that. It was why Scarsdale, New York, was on the day's schedule.

The meeting with Sealfont had been unnerving, and Matlock wasn't sure how much more his shattered nerves could take. The cold fury of Carlyle's president was matched only by the depth of his anguish.

The bewildering shadow world of violence and corruption

was a world he could never come to grips with because it was not within the realm of his comprehension. Matlock had been startled to hear Sealfont say, as he sat in his chair staring out the bay window overlooking the most beautiful lawn on the Carlyle campus, that he might well resign.

'If this whole sordid, unbelievable business is true – and who can doubt it – I have no right to sit in this chair.'

'That's not so,' Matlock had answered. 'If it's true, this place is going to need you more than ever before.'

'A blind man? No-one needs a blind man. Not in this office.'

'Not blind. Unexposed.'

And then Sealfont had swung around in his chair and pounded on the top of his desk in an enormous display of strength.

'Why *here*?! *Why here*?!'

As he sat in front of Sealfont's desk, Matlock looked at the pained face of Carlyle's president. And for a second he thought the man might weep.

The trip down the Merritt Parkway was made at high speed. He had to race; it was necessary for him. It helped take his mind off the sight of Pat Ballantyne as he had seen her a few minutes before leaving. He had gone from Sealfont's to the hospital; still he hadn't been able to talk with her. No-one had yet.

She had awakened at noon, he'd been told. She'd gone into severe hysterics. The doctor from Litchfield had administered further sedatives. The doctor was worried, and Matlock knew it was Pat's mind he was worried about. The nightmare of terror inflicted upon her body had to touch her brain.

The first minutes with his parents at the huge Scarsdale house were awkward. His father, Jonathan Munro Matlock,

152

had spent decades in the highest spheres of his marketplace and knew instinctively when a man came to him without strength.

Without strength but with need.

Matlock told his father as simply and unemotionally as he could that he wanted to borrow a large sum of money; he could not guarantee its repayment. It would be used to help – ultimately help – young people like his dead brother.

The dead son.

'How?' asked Jonathan Matlock softly.

'I can't tell you that.' He looked into his father's eyes and the irrevocable truth of the son's statement was accepted by the father.

'Very well. Are you qualified for this undertaking?'

'Yes. I am.'

'Are there others involved?'

'By necessity, yes.'

'Do you trust them?'

'I do.'

'Have they asked for this money?'

'No. They don't know about it.'

Will it be at their disposal?'

'No. Not that I can foresee . . . I'll go further than that. It would be wrong for them to learn of it.'

'I'm not restricting you, I'm asking.'

'That's my answer.'

'And you believe that what you're doing will help, in some way, boys like David? Practical help, not theoretical, not dream stuff, not charity.'

'Yes. It has to.'

'How much do you want?'

Matlock took a deep breath silently. 'Fifteen thousand dollars.'

'Wait here.'

Several minutes later, the father came out of his study and gave the son an envelope.

The son knew better than to open it.

Ten minutes after the exchange – and Matlock knew it *was* an exchange – he left, feeling the eyes of his parents as they stood on the enormous porch and watched him drive out through the gates.

Matlock pulled into the apartment driveway, shut off the lights and the engine, and wearily climbed out. As he approached the old Tudor house, he saw that every light he owned was turned on. Jason Greenberg wasn't taking chances, and Matlock assumed that some part of Greenberg's silent, unseen army was watching his place from varying distances – none too far away.

He unlocked the door and pushed it open. There was no-one there. At least, not in sight. Not even his cat. 'Hello? Jason? . . . Anybody here? It's Matlock.'

There was no answer and Matlock was relieved. He wanted only to crawl into bed and sleep. He'd stopped at the hospital to see Pat, and the request had been denied. At least he'd learned that '. . . she is resting and her condition is deemed satisfactory.' That was a step up. That afternoon she'd still been on the critical list. He would see her at nine in the morning.

Now was the time for him to sleep – peaceably if possible. Sleep at all costs. There was a great deal to do in the morning.

He went into his bedroom, passing the still unrepaired sections of wall and window as he did so. Carpenter's and plasterer's tools were neatly stacked in corners. He removed his jacket and his shirt and then thought, with a degree of self-ridicule, that he was becoming far too confident. He walked rapidly out of the bedroom and into his bathroom. Once the door was shut, he reached down

154

to the litter box and lifted up the newspaper to the layer of canvas. The Corsican paper was there, the tarnished silver coating reflecting the light.

Back in the bedroom, Matlock removed his wallet, cash, and car keys, placing them on top of his bureau. As he did so, he remembered the envelope.

He hadn't been fooled. He knew his father, perhaps better than his father realized. He presumed there was a short note with the check stating clearly that the money was a gift, not a loan, and that no repayment was anticipated.

The note was there, folded inside the envelope, but the written words were not what Matlock expected.

> I believe in you. I always have.
> Love,
> Dad

On top of the note, clipped to the paper on the reverse side, was the check. Matlock slipped it off and read the figure.

It was for fifty thousand dollars.

Chapter 16

Much of the swelling on her face and around her eyes had subsided. He took her hand and held it tightly, putting his face once more next to hers.

'You're going to be fine,' were the innocuous words he summoned. He had to hold himself in check to stop himself from screaming out his anger and his guilt. That this could be done to a human being by other human beings was beyond his endurance. And he was responsible.

When she spoke, her voice was hardly audible, like a small child's, the words only partially formed through the immobile lips.

'Jamie . . . Jamie?'

'Shh . . . Don't talk if it hurts.'

'*Why?*'

'I don't know. But we'll find out.'

'No! . . . No, don't! They're . . . they're . . .' The girl had to swallow; it was nearly impossible for her. She pointed to a glass of water on the bedside table. Matlock quickly reached for it and held it to her lips, supporting her by the shoulders.

'How did it happen? Can you tell me?'

'Told . . . Greenberg. Man and woman . . . came to the table. Said you were . . . waiting . . . outside.'

'Never mind, I'll talk to Jason.'

'I . . . feel better. I hurt but . . . feel better, I . . . really do. . . . Am I going to be all right?'

'Of course you are. I spoke with the doctor. You're bruised, but nothing broken, nothing serious. He says you'll be out of bed in a few days, that's all.'

156

Patricia Ballantyne's eyes brightened, and Matlock saw the terrible attempt of a smile on her sutured lips. 'I fought . . . I fought and I fought . . . until I . . . couldn't remember any more.'

It took all of Matlock's strength not to burst into tears. 'I know you did. Now, no more talking. You rest, take it easy. I'll just sit here and we'll talk with our eyes. Remember? You said we always communicate around other people with our eyes . . . I'll tell you a dirty joke.'

When the smile came, it *was* from her eyes.

He stayed until a nurse forbade him to stay longer. Then he kissed her softly on the lips and left the room. He was a relieved man; he was an angry man.

'Mr Matlock?' The young doctor with the freshly scrubbed face of an intern approached him by the elevator.

'Yes?'

'There's a telephone call for you. You can take it at the second floor reception, if you'll follow me.'

The caller's voice was unknown. 'Mr Matlock, my name's Houston. I'm a friend of Jason Greenberg's. I'm to get in touch with you.'

'Oh? How's Jason?'

'Fine. I'd like to get together with you as soon as possible.'

Matlock was about to name a place, any place, after his first class. And then he stopped. 'Did Jason leave any message . . . where he is now, or anything?'

'No sir. Just that I was to make contact pronto.'

'I see.' Why didn't the man say it? Why didn't Houston identify himself? 'Greenberg definitely told me he'd leave word . . . a message . . . where he'd be. I'm sure he said that.'

'Against department regulations, Mr Matlock. He wouldn't be allowed to.'

'Oh? . . . Then he didn't leave any message at all?'

The voice on the other end of the line hesitated slightly, perceptively. 'He may have forgotten . . . As a matter of fact, I didn't speak to him myself. I received my orders directly from Washington. Where shall we meet?'

Matlock heard the anxiety in the man's voice. When he referred to Washington, his tone had risen in a small burst of nervous energy. 'Let me call you later. What's your number?'

'Now listen, Matlock. I'm in a telephone booth and we have to meet. I've got my orders!'

'Yes, I'll bet you do . . .'

'What?'

'Never mind. Are you downtown? In Carlyle?'

The man hesitated again. 'I'm in the area.'

'Tell me, Mr Houston . . . Is the city dying?'

'What? What are you talking about?'

'I'm going to be late for my class. Try me again. I'm sure you'll be able to reach me.' Matlock hung up the phone. His left hand shook and perspiration had formed on his brow.

Mr Houston was the enemy.

The enemy was closing in.

His first Saturday class was at eleven, which gave him just about an hour to make what he felt were the most logical arrangements for the money. He didn't want to think that he had to physically be in the town of Carlyle – at the Carlyle Bank – on Monday morning. He wasn't sure it would be possible. He wasn't sure where he would be on Monday.

Since, on the surface, Carlyle was a typical New England college town, it had a particular way of life common to such places. One knew, generally on a first-name basis, all the people whose jobs made day-to-day living the effortless,

158

unhurried existence that it was. The garage mechanic was 'Joe' or 'Mac,' the manager at J. Press was 'Al,' the dentist 'John' or 'Warren,' the girl at the dry cleaners 'Edith.' In Matlock's case, the banker was 'Alex.' Alex Anderson, a Carlyle graduate of forty, a local boy who'd made the jump from town to gown and then coordinated both. Matlock called him at home and explained his problem. He was carrying around a large check from his father. He was making some private family investments in his own name, and they were confidential. Since the robbery at his apartment, he wanted to divest himself of the check immediately. Could Alex suggest anything? Should he put it in the mail? How best to get it into his account, since he wasn't sure he would be in Carlyle on Monday, and he needed it cleared, the money available. Alex Anderson suggested the obvious. Matlock should endorse the check, put it in an envelope marked for Anderson's attention, and drop it in the night deposit box at the bank. Alex would take care of the rest first thing Monday morning.

And then Alex Anderson asked him the denomination and Matlock told him.

The account problem solved, Matlock concentrated on what he began to think of as his point of departure. There was no other phrase he could find, and he needed a phrase – he needed the discipline of a definition. He had to start precisely right, knowing that what might follow could be totally *undisciplined* – completely without plan or orthodoxy. For he had made up his mind.

He was going to enter the world of Nimrod. The builder of Babylon and Nineveh, the hunter of wild animals, the killer of children and old men, the beater of women.

He was going to find Nimrod.

As were most adults not wedded to the precept that all things enjoyable were immoral, Matlock was aware that

159

the state of Connecticut, like its sister states to the north, the south, and the west, was inhabited by a network of men only too eager to supply those divertissements frowned upon by the pulpits and the courts. What Hartford insurance executive in the upper brackets never heard of that string of 'Antique Shoppes' on New Britain Avenue where a lithe young girl's body could be had for a reasonable amount of petty cash? What commuter from Old Greenwich was oblivious to the large estates north of Green Farms where the gambling often rivaled the Vegas stakes? How many tired businessmen's wives from New Haven or Westport were really ignorant of the various 'escort' services operating out of Hamden and Fairfield? And over in the 'old country,' the Norfolks? Where the rambling mansions were fading apotheoses to the *real* money, the blooded first families who migrated just a little west to avoid the new rich? The 'old country' had the strangest diversions, it was rumored. Houses in shadows, lighted by candles, where the bored could become aroused by observation. Voyeurs of the sickest scenes. Female, male, animal – all types, all combinations.

Matlock knew that in this world Nimrod could be found. It had to be. For although narcotics were but one aspect of the services rendered within this network, they were available – as was everything else.

And of all these games of indulgence, none had the fire and ice, none had the magnetism, of the gambling houses. For those thousands who couldn't find time for the junkets to San Juan, London, or Paradise Island, there were the temporary excursions into the manic moments where daily boredom could be forgotten – a stone's throw from home. Reputations were made quickly over the green felt tables – with the roll of the dice or a turn of a card. It was here that Matlock would find his point of departure. It was in these places where a young man of thirty-three years was prepared to lose thousands – until someone asked who he was.

At twelve-thirty Matlock walked across the quadrangle toward his apartment. The time had come to initiate his first move. The vague outline of a plan was coming into focus.

He should have heard the footsteps, but he didn't. He only heard the cough, a smoker's cough, the cough of a man who'd been running.

'Mr Matlock?'

Matlock turned and saw a man in his middle thirties, like himself, perhaps a bit older and, indeed, out of breath.

'Yes?'

'Sorry, I keep missing you. I got to the hospital just as you'd left, then waited in the wrong damn building for you, after your class. There's a very confused biology teacher with a name similar to yours. Even looks a little like you. Same height, build, hair . . .'

'That's Murdock. Elliot Murdock. What's the matter?'

'He couldn't understand why I kept insisting that when "old men kill themselves, the cities are dying"!'

'You're from Greenberg!'

'That's it. Morbid code, if you don't mind my saying so. Keep walking. We'll separate at the end of the path. Meet me in twenty minutes at Bill's Bar & Grill by the freight depot. It's six blocks south of the railroad station. OK?'

'Never heard of it.'

'I was going to suggest you remove your necktie. I'll be in a leather jacket.'

'You pick classy spots.'

'Old habit. I cheat on the expense account.'

'Greenberg said I was to work with you.'

'You better believe it! He's up to his Kosher ass in boiling oil for you. I think they're shipping him out to

161

a job in Cairo . . . He's one hell of a guy. We field men like him. Don't louse him up.'

'All I wanted to ask was your name. I didn't expect a sermon.'

'It's Houston. Fred Houston. See you in twenty minutes. Get rid of the tie.'

Chapter 17

Bill's Bar & Grill was a part of Carlyle Matlock had never seen before. Railroad laborers and freight-yard drifters were its predominant clientele. He scanned the filthy room; Houston sat in a back booth.

'It's cocktail hour, Matlock. A little early by campus standards, but the effects aren't much different. Not even the clothes these days.'

'It's quite a place.'

'It serves the purpose. Go up to the bar and get yourself a drink. The bunnies don't come on till sundown.'

Matlock did as Houston instructed and brought back the best bourbon he could find. It was a brand he had given up when he reached a living wage.

'I think I should tell you right away. Someone using your name telephoned me at the hospital.'

It was as if Houston had been hit in the stomach. 'My God,' he said quietly. 'What did he say? How did you handle it?'

'I waited for him to identify himself . . . with Greenberg's proverb. I gave him a couple of chances but he didn't . . . So I told him to call me later and hung up.'

'He used *my* name?! *Houston*. You're sure?'

'Absolutely.'

'That doesn't make sense. He *couldn't*!'

'Believe me. He did.'

'No-one knew I was the replacement . . . I didn't know it until three this morning.'

'Someone found out.'

Houston took several swallows of his beer. 'If what you

163

say is true, I'll be out of here within a couple of hours. Incidentally, that was good thinking . . . Let me give you an extra hint, though. Never accept a contact made by telephone.'

'Why not?'

'If that *had* been me calling – how would *I* know it was *you* I was talking to?'

'I see what you mean . . .'

'Common sense. Most everything we do is common sense . . . We'll keep the same code. The "old men" and "the cities." Your next contact will be made tonight.'

'You're sure you'll be leaving?'

'I've been *spotted*. I'm not *about* to stick around. Maybe you forgot Ralph Loring . . . We gave big at the office.'

'All right. Have you talked to Jason? Did he brief you?'

'For two hours. From four till six this morning. My wife said he drank thirteen cups of coffee.'

'What can you tell me about Pat? Patricia Ballantyne. What happened?'

'You know the medical facts . . .'

'Not all of them.'

'I don't know *all* of them, either.'

'You're lying.'

Houston looked at Matlock without offense. When he replied, he did so compassionately. 'All right. There was evidence of rape. That's what you want to know, isn't it?'

Matlock gripped his glass. 'Yes,' he said softly.

'However, you should know this, too. The girl doesn't know it. Not at this stage of her recovery. I understand the mind plays tricks. It rejects things until it thinks – or something tells it – that the remembering can be handled.'

'Thanks for the lesson in psychology . . . . Animals. Filthy

164

animals . . .' Matlock pushed his glass away. The liquor was intolerable to him now. The thought of dulling his senses even slightly was abhorrent.

'I'm supposed to play this by ear, so if I read you wrong, all I can do is apologize . . . Be around when the puzzle gets put together for her. She's going to need you.'

Matlock looked up from the table, from the sight of his tensed hands. 'It was that bad?' he asked almost inaudibly.

'Preliminary lab tests – fingernails, hair, what have you – indicate that the assault was carried out by more than one person.'

Matlock's hatred could find only one expression. He closed his eyes and lashed out at the glass, sending it across the floor, where it smashed in front of the bar. The bartender dropped his soiled rag and started toward his latch, looking over at the man who threw the glass. Then he stopped. Houston held up a bill quickly, gesturing the man to stay away.

'Get hold of yourself!' Houston said. 'You're not going to do anyone any good like that. You're just calling attention to us . . . Now, listen. You're cleared to make further enquiries, but there are two stipulations. The first is to check with our man – it was supposed to be me – before approaching anyone. The second – keep your subjects to students and only students. No faculty, no staff, no-one outside – just students . . . Make your reports every night between ten and eleven. Your contact will reach you daily as to where. Have you got that?'

Matlock stared at the agent in disbelief. He understood what the man was saying – even why he said it – but he couldn't believe that anyone who'd been briefed by Jason Greenberg would think he could deliver such instructions. 'Are you serious?'

'The orders are explicit. No deviations. That's holy writ.'

It was there again for Matlock. Another sign, another compromise. Another plastic order from the unseen plastic leaders.

'I'm there but I'm *not* there, is that the idea? I'm consigned to the outer limits and that fulfills the bargain?'

'Frig that.'

Matlock's eyes wandered upward, at nothing. He was trying to buy a few seconds of sweet reason. 'Frigga is the Norse goddess of the sky. She shares the heavens with Odin. Don't insult the lady, Houston.'

'You're a nut!' said the agent. 'I'm not sorry I'm getting out of here . . . Look, it's for the best, take my word for it. And one last thing. I've got to take back the paper Loring gave you. That's a *must do*.'

'Is it, really?' Matlock slid across the filthy leatherette seat and started to get up. 'I don't see it that way. You go back to Washington and tell them I see it as a *must don't*. Take care of yourself, holy writ.'

'You're playing around with preventive custody!'

'We'll see who's playing,' said Matlock as he pushed himself away from the table, angling it to block the agent's exit, and started for the door. He could hear the screech of the table's legs as Houston moved it out of his way. He heard Houston call his name softly, intensely, as if he were confused, wanting to make Matlock come back, yet afraid of identifying him. Matlock reached the door, turned right on the sidewalk, and started running as fast as he could. He found a narrow alley and realized that it was, at least, in the right direction. He raced into it and stopped, pressing himself into a doorway. At the base of the alley, on the freight-yard thoroughfare, he saw Houston walking rapidly past the phlegmatic noonday laborers on their lunch breaks. Houston looked panicked; Matlock knew he couldn't return to his apartment.

*   *   *

It was a funny thing to do, he considered, as he sat in the booth of Bill's Bar & Grill. Returning to the place he couldn't wait to get out of twenty minutes ago. But it made vague sense to him – as much as anything made sense at the moment. He had to be by himself and think. He couldn't take the chance of wandering the streets where some part of the Greenberg-Houston unseen army might spot him. Ironically, the bar seemed safest.

He'd made his apologies to a wary bartender, offering to pay for the broken glass. He implied that the man he'd had words with before was a deadbeat – into him for a lot of money with no ability to pay. This explanation, given by the now-relaxed customer, was not only accepted by the bartender, it elevated him to a status not often seen in Bill's Bar & Grill.

He had to marshal his thoughts. There were checkpoints he'd mentally outlined which were to be passed before he began his journey to Nimrod. Now, there was another checkpoint. Houston had supplied it, although he'd never know. Pat had to be totally safe. He couldn't have that worry on his mind. All other items on his list were subservient to this. The clothes, the ready cash, the unfamiliar automobile, all would have to wait. He might have to alter his strategy now, Matlock thought. Nimrod's associates would be watched, his apartment would be watched, every name and location on the Justice list would be under surveillance.

But first, Pat. He'd have her guarded night and day, around the clock, every minute. Guarded openly, with no pretense of secrecy. Guarded in such a way as to be a signal to both the unseen armies, a warning that she was out of the game. Money was no problem now, none at all. And there were men in Hartford whose professions would fit his requirements. He knew that. The huge insurance companies used them incessantly.

He remembered an ex-faculty member from the math department who'd left Carlyle for the lucrative field of insurance actuaries. He worked for Aetna. He looked for a telephone inside the dingy bar.

Eleven minutes later, Matlock returned to the booth. The business was concluded with Blackstone Security, Incorporated, Bond Street, Hartford. There would be three men daily on eight-hour shifts, three hundred dollars for each twenty-four-hour period the subject was covered by Blackstone, Inc. There would, of course, be the additional charges for any expenses incurred and a fee attached for the use of a 'Tel-electronic' if it was required. The Tel-electronic was a small device which signaled the bearer with short beeps if the telephone number designated was called. Blackstone, of course, suggested a different telephone number from a resident phone – which, of course, they would have activated within twelve hours and for which, of course, there was an additional charge.

Matlock agreed to everything, was grateful *for* everything, and said he'd be in Hartford to sign the papers later in the afternoon. He wanted to meet Mr Blackstone – for another reason now. Blackstone, however, made it clear that since the head of Aetna's actuarial department had personally contacted him regarding Mr Matlock, the formalities were not pressing. He'd despatch his team to the Carlyle Hospital within the hour. And by any chance, was Mr Matlock related to Jonathan Munro Matlock . . . ? The head of Aetna's actuarial department had mentioned . . .

Matlock was relieved. Blackstone *could* be useful. The exfaculty member at Aetna had assured him that there was none better than Blackstone. Expensive, but the best. Blackstone's personnel for the most part were former officers of the Special Forces and Marine Intelligence teams. It was more than a business gimmick. They were smart, resourceful, and tough. They were also licensed and respected by the state and local police.

The next item on his list was clothes. He had planned to go to his apartment and pack a suit, several pairs of slacks, and a jacket or two. Now that was out. At least for the time being. He would buy clothes – what he needed – as he went along. The ready cash could prove more of a problem, considering the amount he wanted. It was Saturday – he wasn't going to waste a Saturday night. The banks were closed, the large money sources unavailable.

Alex Anderson would have to solve the problem. He'd lie to Alex Anderson, tell him Jonathan Munro Matlock would look kindly – financially kindly – on Anderson if the banker would make available a large sum of cash on a Saturday afternoon. It would be confidential on both sides, of course. There would be a gratuity rendered for a coveted favor on a Saturday afternoon. Nothing which could be construed remotely indelicate. And, of course, again, confidential.

Matlock rose from the ripped, stained, dirty leatherette seat and returned to the telephone.

Anderson had only fleeting doubts about accommodating Jonathan Munro Matlock's son, and they concerned not the act but the confidence of the act. Once that concern was allayed, the fact that he was giving aid in the best traditions of banking became clear. It was important for any bank to accommodate the better client. If a particular client wished to show gratitude . . . well, that was up to the client.

Alex Anderson would secure James Matlock five thousand dollars in cash on a Saturday afternoon. He would deliver it to him at three outside the Plaza Movie Theater, which was showing a revival of *A Knife in the Water* – with subtitles.

An automobile would be the least of his problems. There were two rent-a-car offices in the town, a Budget-National and a Luxor-Elite. The first for students, the second for affluent parents. He would rent a Luxor Cadillac or Lincoln and drive into Hartford to another Luxor lot and change cars. From Hartford he'd go to a Luxor branch in New Haven and do the same. With money, there would be the minimum of questions; with decent tips, there might even be cooperation.

He'd moved to his point of departure.

'Hey, mister. Your name Matlock?' The hairy bartender leaned over the table, the soiled bag rag squeezed in his right hand.

'Yes,' answered the startled Matlock with a short, violent intake of breath.

'Guy just came up t' me. Said for me to tell you you forgot something outside. On the curb, he said. You should hurry, he said.'

Matlock stared at the man. The pain in his stomach was the fear again, the panic. He reached into his pocket and pulled out several bills. Separating a five, he held it up to the bartender. 'Come to the door with me. Just to the window. Tell me if he's outside.'

'Sure . . . To the window.' The hairy bartender switched the soiled rag to his left hand and took the bill. Matlock got out of the booth and walked beside the man to the half-curtained, filthy glass looking out on the street 'No, he's not there. There's no-one there . . . Just a dead . . .'

'I see,' said Matlock, cutting the man off. He didn't have to go outside, it wasn't necessary.

Lying on the edge of the curb, its body draping down into the gutter, was Matlock's cat.

Its head was severed, held to the rest of its body by a small piece of flesh. The blood poured out, staining the sidewalk.

Chapter 18

The killing preyed on Matlock's mind as he approached the West Hartford town line. Was it another warning or had they found the paper? If they *had* found the paper, it didn't vitiate the warning, only reinforced it. He wondered whether to have a member of the Blackstone team check his apartment, check the litter box. He wasn't even sure why he hesitated. Why not have a Blackstone man find out? For three hundred dollars a day, plus charges, such an errand was hardly too much to ask. He was going to ask far more of Blackstone, Incorporated, but they didn't know it. Yet he kept balking. If the paper *was* secure, sending a man to check it might reveal its location.

He'd almost made up his mind to take the chance when he noticed the tan sedan in his rear-view mirror. It was there again. It had been there, off and on, since he'd entered Highway 72 a half hour ago. Whereas other cars turned off, passed him, or fell behind, this tan sedan was never really out of sight. Weaving in and around the traffic, it always managed to stay three or four cars behind him. There was one way to find out if it was coincidence. Off the next exit into West Hartford was a narrow street which wasn't a street at all but a cobblestone alley used almost exclusively for deliveries. He and Pat thought it was a shortcut one hectic afternoon and had been hemmed in for five minutes.

He swung off the exit and down the main street toward the alley. He made a sharp left and entered the narrow cobblestone lane. Since it was Saturday afternoon, there were no delivery trucks, and the alley was clear.

171

He raced through, emerging in a crowded A & P parking lot, which in turn led to a parallel main road. Matlock drove to an empty parking space, shut off his motor, and lowered himself on the seat. He angled his side-view mirror so that it reflected the entrance of the alley. In roughly thirty seconds, the tan sedan came into view.

The driver was obviously confused. He slowed down, looking at the dozens of automobiles. Suddenly, behind the tan sedan, another car began blowing its horn. The driver was impatient; the tan sedan was blocking his progress. Reluctantly, the driver of the tan sedan started up; but before he did, he turned his face, craning his neck over his right shoulder in such a way that Matlock, now looking directly at the automobile, recognized him.

It was the patrolman. The police officer who'd been in his demolished apartment after the Beeson episode, the man who had covered his face with a towel and raced down the corridor of squash alley two days ago.

Greenberg's 'coincidence.'

Matlock was perplexed. He was also frightened.

The patrolman in mufti drove the tan sedan haltingly toward a parking lot exit, still obviously searching. Matlock saw the car turn into the flow of traffic and drive away.

The offices of Blackstone Security, Incorporated, Bond Street, Hartford, looked more like a wealthy, sedate insurance company than an investigatory agency. The furniture was heavy colonial, the wallpaper a subdued, masculine stripe. Expensive hunting prints above the glow of brass table lamps. The effect was immediately one of strength, virility, and financial solidity. Why not? thought Matlock, as he sat in the Early American two-seater in the outer office. At three hundred dollars a day, Blackstone

172

Security, Incorporated, probably rivaled Prudential in ratio of investment to profits.

When he was at last ushered into the office, Michael Blackstone rose from his chair and walked around the cherrywood desk to greet him. Blackstone was a short, compact man, neatly dressed. He was in his early fifties, obviously a physical person, very active, probably very tough.

'Good afternoon,' he said. 'I hope you didn't drive down here just for the papers. They could have waited. Just because *we* work seven days a week, doesn't mean we expect the rest of the world to do so.'

'I had to be in Hartford, anyway. No problem.'

'Sit down, sit down. Can I offer you anything? A drink? Coffee?'

'No thanks.' Matlock sat in a huge black leather chair, the kind of chair usually found in the oldest, most venerated men's clubs. Blackstone returned to his desk. 'Actually, I'm in somewhat of a hurry. I'd like to sign our agreement, pay you, and leave.'

'Certainly. The file's right here.' Blackstone picked up a folder on his desk and smiled. 'As I mentioned on the phone, there are questions we'd like answered, of course. Beyond what you've instructed us to do. It would help us carry out your orders. Take just a few minutes.'

Matlock expected the request. It was part of his plan, why he wanted to see Blackstone. His assumption – once Blackstone entered the picture – was that Blackstone might be able to offer him shortcuts. Perhaps not willingly, but if it was a question of 'an additional charge.' . . . It was for this reason that he had to meet Blackstone face to face. If Blackstone could be bought, a great deal of time could be saved.

'I'll answer what I can. As I'm sure you've checked out, the girl was beaten severely.'

'We know that. What puzzles us is the reluctance of anyone to say why. No one's given that sort of beating for kicks. Oh, it's possible, but that kind of case is generally handled quickly and efficiently by the police. There's no need for us . . . Obviously you have information the police don't have.'

'That's true. I do.'

'May I ask why you haven't given it to them? Why you hired us? . . . The local police will gladly furnish protection if there's sufficient cause, and far less expensively.'

'You sound like you're turning away business.'

'We often do.' Blackstone smiled. 'It's never done happily, I can tell you that.'

'Then why . . .'

'You're a highly recommended client,' interrupted Blackstone, 'the son of a very prominent man. We want you to know your alternatives. That's our reasoning. What's yours?'

'You're plainspoken. I appreciate it. I assume what you're saying is that you don't want your reputation tarnished.'

'That's good enough.'

'Good. That's my reasoning, too. Only it's not *my* reputation. It's the girl's. Miss Ballantyne's . . . The simplest way to put it is that she showed bad judgment in her choice of friends. She's a brilliant girl with an exciting future, but unfortunately that intelligence didn't carry over into other areas.' Matlock purposely stopped and took out a pack of cigarettes. Unhurriedly, he removed one and lit it. The pause had its effect. Blackstone spoke.

'Did she profit financially from these associations?'

'Not at all. As I see it, she was used. But I can understand why you asked. There's a lot of money to be made on campuses these days, isn't there?'

'I wouldn't know. Campuses aren't our field.' Blackstone

174

smiled again, and Matlock knew he was lying. Professionally, of course.

'I guess not.'

'All right, Mr Matlock. Why was she beaten? And what do you intend to do about it?'

'It's my opinion she was beaten to frighten her from revealing information *she doesn't have*. I intend to find the parties involved and tell them that. Tell them to leave her alone.'

'And if you go to the police, her associations – past associations, I assume – become a matter of record and jeopardize this brilliant future of hers.'

'Exactly.'

'That's a tight story . . . Who are these parties involved?'

'I don't know them by name . . . However, I know their occupations. The main line of work seems to be gambling. I thought you might be able to help me here. Naturally, I would expect an additional charge for the service.'

'I see.' Blackstone got up and walked around his chair. For no particular reason, he fingered the dials on his inoperative air conditioner. 'I think you presume too much.'

'I wouldn't expect names. I'd like them, of course, and I'd pay well for them . . . But I'd settle for locations. I can find them myself, and you know I can. You'd be saving me time, though.'

'I gather you're interested in . . . private clubs. *Private* social organizations where members may meet to pursue activities of their choice.'

'Outside the eye of the law. Where private citizens can follow their perfectly natural inclinations to place bets. That's where I'd like to start.'

'Could I dissuade you? Is it possible I could convince you to go to the police, instead?'

'No.'

Blackstone walked to a file cabinet on the left wall, took

out a key, and opened it. 'As I said, a tight story. Very plausible. And I don't believe a word of it . . . However, you seem determined; that concerns me.' He took a thin metal case from the file cabinet and carried it back to the desk. Selecting another key from his chain, he unlocked it and withdrew a single sheet of paper. 'There's a Xerox machine over there,' he said, pointing to a large gray copier in the corner. 'To use it one places a page face down under the metal flap and dials the required duplicates. Records are kept of the numbers automatically. There's rarely a reason for more than one . . . If you'll excuse me for approximately two minutes, Mr Matlock, I must make a phone call in another office.'

Blackstone held up the single sheet of paper, then placed it face down on top of Matlock's file folder. He stood erect, and, with the fingers of both hands, tugged at the base of his jacket in the manner of a man used to displaying expensive suits. He smiled and walked around his desk toward the office door. He opened it and turned back.

'It may be what you're looking for, and then again, it may not. I wouldn't know. I've simply left a confidential memorandum on my desk. The charge will be listed on your billing as . . . additional surveillance.'

He went out the door, closing it firmly behind him. Matlock rose from the black leather chair and crossed behind the desk. He turned the paper over and read the typed heading.

FOR SURVEILLANCE: HARTFORD-NEW HAVEN AXIS

PRIVATE CLUBS: LOCATIONS AND CONTACTS (MANAGERS)

AS OF 3–15. NOT TO BE REMOVED FROM OFFICE

Beneath the short, capitalized paragraph were twenty-odd addresses and names.

Nimrod was closer now.

Chapter 19

The Luxor-Elite Rental Agency on Asylum Street, Hartford, had been cooperative. Matlock now drove a Cadillac convertible. The manager had accepted the explanation that the Lincoln was too funereal, and since the registration papers were in order, the switch was perfectly acceptable.

So was the twenty-dollar tip.

Matlock had analyzed Blackstone's list carefully. He decided to concentrate on the clubs northwest of Hartford for the simple reason that they were nearer the Carlyle area. They weren't the nearest, however. Two locations were within five and seven miles of Carlyle respectively – in opposite directions – but Matlock decided to hold them off for a day or so. By the time he reached them – if he did so – he wanted the managements to know he was a heavy plunger. Not a mark, just heavy. The network gossip would take care of that – if he handled himself properly.

He checked off his first location. It was a private swimming club west of Avon. The contact was a man named Jacopo Bartolozzi.

At nine-thirty Matlock drove up the winding driveway to a canopy extending from the entrance of the Avon Swim Club. A uniformed doorman signaled a parking attendant, who appeared out of nowhere and slid into the driver's seat the moment Matlock stepped on to the pavement. Obviously no parking ticket was to be given.

As he walked toward the entrance, he looked at the exterior of the club. The main building was a sprawling, one-story white brick structure with a tall stockade fence extending from both ends into the darkness. On the right, quite far behind the fence, was the iridescent glow of greenish blue light and the sound of water splashing. On the left was a huge tentlike canopy under which could be seen the shimmering light of dozens of patio torches. The former was obviously an enormous pool, the latter some kind of dining area. Soft music could be heard.

The Avon Swim Club appeared to be a very luxurious complex.

The interior did nothing to dispel this observation. The foyer was thickly carpeted and the various chairs and odd tables against the damask walls seemed genuine antiques. On the left was a large checkroom, and further down on the right was a white marble counter not unlike a hotel information desk. At the end of the narrow lobby was the only incongruous structure. It was a black, ornate wrought-iron gate, and it was closed, obviously locked. Beyond the grilled enclosure could be seen an open-air corridor, subtly lit, with an extended covering supported by a series of thin Ionic pillars. A large man in a tuxedo was standing at attention behind the iron gate.

Matlock approached him.

'Your membership card, sir?'

'I'm afraid I don't have one.'

'Sorry, sir, this is a private swimming club. Members only.'

'I was told to ask for Mr Bartolozzi.'

The man behind the grill stared at Matlock, frisking him with his eyes.

'You'd better check the front desk, sir. Right over there.'

Matlock walked back to the counter, to be greeted by a middle-aged, slightly paunchy desk clerk who had not been there when he first came in.

'May I help you?'

178

'You may. I'm fairly new in the area. I'd like to become a member.'

'We're sorry. Membership's full right now. However, if you'll fill out an application, we'll be glad to call you if there's an opening . . . Would that be a family application or individual, sir?' The clerk, very professionally, reached below the counter and brought up two application forms.

'Individual. I'm not married . . . I was told to ask for Mr Bartolozzi. I was told specifically to ask for him. Jacopo Bartolozzi.'

The clerk gave the name only the slightest indication of recognition. 'Here, fill out an application and I'll put it on Mr Bartolozzi's desk. He'll see it in the morning. Perhaps he'll call you, but I don't know what he can do. Membership's full and there's a waiting list.'

'Isn't he here now? On such a busy night?' Matlock said the words with a degree of incredulity.

'I doubt it, sir.'

'Why don't you find out? Tell him we have mutual friends in San Juan.' Matlock withdrew his money clip and removed a fifty-dollar bill. He placed it in front of the clerk, who looked at him sharply and slowly picked up the money.

'San Juan?'

'San Juan.'

Matlock leaned against the white marble counter and saw the man behind the wrought-iron gate watching him. If the San Juan story worked and he got through the gate, he realized that he would have to part with another large-sized bill. The San Juan story *should* work, thought Matlock. It was logical to the point of innocence. He had spent a winter vacation in Puerto Rico two years ago, and although no gambler, he'd traveled with a crowd – and a girl – who made the nightly rounds of the casinos. He'd met a number of people from the Hartford vicinity,

179

although he couldn't for the life of him remember a single name.

A foursome emerged from inside the grilled entrance, the girls giggling, the men laughing resignedly. The women had probably won twenty or thirty dollars, thought Matlock, while the men had probably lost several hundred. Fair exchange for the evening. The gate closed behind them; Matlock could hear the electric click of the latch. It was a very well-locked iron gate.

'Excuse me, sir?' It was the paunchy desk clerk, and Matlock turned around.

'Yes?'

'If you'll step inside, Mr Bartolozzi will see you.'

'Where? How?' There was no door except the wrought-iron gate and the clerk had gestured with his left hand, away from the gate.

'Over here, sir.'

Suddenly a knobless, frameless panel to the right of the counter swung open. The outline was barely discernible when the panel was flush against the damask wall; when shut, no border was in evidence. Matlock walked in and was taken by the clerk to the office of Jacopo Bartolozzi.

'We got mutual friends?' The obese Italian spoke hoarsely as he leaned back in his chair behind the desk. He made no attempt to rise, gave no gesture of welcome. Jacopo Bartolozzi was a short, squat caricature of himself. Matlock couldn't be sure, but he had the feeling that Bartolozzi's feet weren't touching the floor beneath his chair.

'It amounts to the same thing, Mr Bartolozzi.'

'What amounts? Who's in San Juan?'

'Several people. One fellow's a dentist in West Hartford. Another's got an accounting firm in Constitution Plaza.'

'Yeah . . . Yeah?' Bartolozzi was trying to associate people with the professions and locations Matlock described. 'What's the names? They members here?'

'I guess they are. They gave me *your* name.'

'This is a swim club. Private membership . . . Who are they?'

'Look, Mr Bartolozzi, it was a crazy night at the Condado casino. We all had a lot to drink and . . .'

'They don't drink in the Puerto Rican casinos. It's a law!' The Italian spoke sharply, proud of his incisive knowledge. He was pointing his fat finger at Matlock.

'More honored in the breach, believe me.'

'What?'

'We drank. Take my word for it. I'm just telling you I don't remember their names . . . Look, I can go downtown on Monday and stand all day outside the Plaza and I'll find the CPA. I could also go out to West Hartford and ring every dentist's doorbell. What difference does it make? I like to play and I've got the money.'

Bartolozzi smiled. 'This is a swim club. I don't know what the hell you're talking about.'

'OK,' said Matlock with a disgruntled edge to his voice. 'This place happened to be convenient, but if you want to show three lemons, there are others. My San Juan friends also told me about Jimmy Lacata's down in Middletown, and Sammy Sharpe's in Windsor Shoals . . . Keep your chips, fink.' He turned to the door.

'Hold it! Wait a minute!'

Matlock watched the fat Italian get out of the chair and stand up. He'd been right. Bartolozzi's feet couldn't have been touching the floor.

'What for? Maybe your limit's too small here.'

'You know Lacata? Sharpe?'

'Know *of* them, I told you . . . Look, forget it. You've got to be careful. I'll find my CPA on Monday and we'll

181

both come back some other time . . . I just felt like playing tonight.'

'OK. OK. Like you said, we gotta be careful.' Bartolozzi opened his top drawer and pulled out some papers. 'C'mere. Sign 'em. You got an itch. Maybe I'll take your money. Maybe you'll take mine.'

Matlock approached the desk. 'What am I signing?'

'Just a couple of forms. Initiation's five hundred. Cash. You got it? No checks, no credit.'

'I've got it. What are the forms?'

'The first is a statement that you understand that this is a non-profit corporation and that any games of chance are for charitable purposes . . . What are you laughing at? I built the Church of the Blessed Virgin down in Hamden.'

'What's this other? It's a long one.'

'That's for our files. A certificate of general partnership. For the five hundred you get a classy title. You're a partner. Everybody's a partner . . . Just in case.'

'In case?'

'In case anything good happens to us, it happens just as good to you. Especially in the newspapers.'

The Avon Swim Club was certainly a place for swimming, no doubt about it. The enormous pool curved back nearly two hundred feet, and scores of small, elegant cabanas bordered the far side. Beach chairs and tables were dotted about the grassy edges beyond the tiled deck of the pool, and the underwater floodlights made the setting inviting. All this was on the right of the open-air corridor. On the left, Matlock could see fully what was only hinted at from the outside. A huge green-and-white-striped tent rose above dozens of tables. Each table had a candled lantern in the center, and patio torches were safely placed about the whole enclosure. At the far end was a long table filled

182

with roasts, salads, and buffet food. A bar was adjacent to the long table; scores of couples were milling about.

The Avon Swim Club was a lovely place to bring the family.

The corridor led to the rear of the complex, where there was another sprawling, white-bricked structure similar to the main building. Above the large, black-enameled double doors was a wooden sign, in old English scroll:

The Avon Spa

This part of the Avon Swim Club was not a lovely place to bring the family.

Matlock thought he was back in a San Juan casino – his only experience in gambling rooms. The wall-to-wall carpet was sufficiently thick to muffle sound almost completely. Only the click of the chips and the low-keyed but intense mutterings of the players and the board men were heard. The craps tables were lined along the walls, the blackjack counters in the center. In between, in staggered positions to allow for the flow of traffic, were the roulette wheels. In the middle of the large room, raised on a platform, was the cashier's nest. All of the Avon Spa's employees were in tuxedos, neatly groomed and subservient. The players were less formal.

The gate man, pleased with Matlock's crisp fifty-dollar bill, led him to the half-circle counter in front of the cashier's platform. He spoke to a man counting out slips of paper.

'This is Mr Matlock. Treat him good, he's a personal friend.'

'No other way,' said the man with a smile.

'I'm sorry, Mr Matlock,' muttered the gate man quietly. 'No markers the first time around.'

'Naturally . . . Look, I'm going to wander about . . .'

'Sure. Get the feel of the action . . . I tell you, it ain't Vegas. Between you and me, it's Mickey Mouse most of the time. I mean for a guy like you, you know what I mean?'

Matlock knew exactly what the gate man meant. A fifty-dollar bill was not the ordinary gratuity in Avon, Connecticut.

It took him three hours and twelve minutes to lose $4,175. The only time he felt panic was when he had a streak at the craps table and had built up his reserves to nearly $5,000. He had begun the evening properly – for his purposes. He went to the cashier often enough to realize that the average purchase of chips was $200 to $300. Hardly 'Mickey Mouse' in his book. So his first purchase was $1,500. The second was $1,000; the third, $2,000.

By one in the morning, he was laughing with Jacopo Bartolozzi at the bar underneath the green-and-white-striped tent.

'You're a game one. Lots'a creeps would be screaming "ice pick" if they went for a bundle like you did. Right now I'd be showing them a few papers in my office.'

'Don't you worry, I'll get it back. I always do . . . You said it before. My itch was too much. Maybe I'll come back tomorrow.'

'Make it Monday. Tomorrow it's only swimming.'

'How come?'

'Sunday. Holy day.'

'Shit! I've got a friend coming in from London. He won't be here Monday. He's a big player.'

'Tell you what. I'll call Sharpe over in Windsor Shoals. He's a Jew. Holy days don't mean a fucking thing to him.'

'I'd appreciate that.'

184

'I may even drop over myself. The wife's got a Mothers of Madonna meeting, anyway.'

Matlock looked at his watch. The evening – his point of departure – had gone well. He wondered if he should press his luck. 'Only real problem coming into a territory is the time it takes to find the sources.'

'What's your problem?'

'I've got a girl over in the motel. She's sleeping, we traveled most of the day. She ran out of grass – no hard stuff – just grass. I told her I'd pick some up for her.'

'Can't help you, Matlock. I don't keep none here, what with the kids around during the day. It's not good for the image, see? A few pills, I got. No needle crap, though. You want some pills?'

'No, just grass. That's all I let her use.'

'Very smart of you . . . Which way you headed?'

'Back into Hartford.'

Bartolozzi snapped his fingers. A large bartender sprang into position instantly. Matlock thought there was something grotesque about the squat little Italian commandeering in such fashion. Bartolozzi asked the man for paper and pencil.

'Here. Here's an address. I'll make a phone call. It's an after-hours place right off the main drag. Down the street from G. Fox. Second floor. As for Rocco. What you couldn't use, he's got.'

'You're a prince.' And as Matlock took the paper, he meant it.

'For four grand the first night, you got privileges . . . Hey, y'know what? You never filled out an application! That's a gas, huh?'

'You don't need credit references. I play with cash.'

'Where the hell do you keep it?'

'In thirty-seven banks from here to Los Angeles.'

185

Matlock put down his glass and held out his hand to Bartolozzi. 'It's been fun. See you tomorrow?'

'Sure, sure. I'll walk you to the door. Don't forget now. Don't give Sammy all the action. Come on back here.'

'My word on it.'

The two men walked back to the open-air corridor, the short Italian placing his fat hand in the middle of Matlock's back, the gesture of a new friend. What neither man realized as they stepped on to the narrow causeway was that one well-dressed gentleman at a nearby table who kept punching at a fluidless lighter was watching them. As the two men passed his table, he put his lighter back into his pocket while the woman across from him lit his cigarette with a match. The woman spoke quietly through a smile.

'Did you get them?'

The man laughed softly. 'Karsh couldn't have done better. Even got close-ups.'

186

Chapter 20

If the Avon Swim Club was an advantageous point of departure, the Hartford Hunt Club – under the careful management of Rocco Aiello – was an enviable first lap. For Matlock now thought of his journey to Nimrod as a race, one which had to end within two weeks and one day. It would end with the convocation of the Nimrod forces and the Mafiosi somewhere in the Carlyle vicinity. It would be finished for him when someone, somewhere produced another silver Corsican paper.

Bartolozzi's telephone call was effective. Matlock entered the old red stone building – at first he thought he had the wrong address, for no light shone through the windows, and there was no sign of activity within – and found a freight elevator at the end of the hall-way with a lone Negro operator sitting in a chair in front of the door. No sooner had he come in than the black rose to his feet and indicated the elevator to Matlock.

In an upstairs hallway a man greeted him. 'Very nice to make your acquaintance. Name's Rocco. Rocco Aiello.' The man held out his hand and Matlock took it.

'Thanks . . . I was puzzled. I didn't hear anything. I thought maybe I was in the wrong place.'

'If you had heard, the construction boys would have taken me. The walls are eighteen inches thick, sound-proofed both sides; the windows are blinds. Very secure.'

'That's really something.'

Rocco reached into his pocket and withdrew a small wooden cigarette case. 'I got a box of joints for you. No charge. I'd like to show you around, but Jock-O said you might be in a hurry.'

'Jock-O's wrong. I'd like to have a drink.'

'Good! Come on in . . . Only one thing, Mr Matlock. I got a nice clientele, you know what I mean? Very rich, very cube. Some of them know about Jock-O's operation, most of them don't. You know what I mean?'

'I understand. I was never much for swimming anyway.'

'Good, good . . . Welcome to Hartford's finest.' He opened the thick steel door. 'I hear you went for a bundle tonight.'

Matlock laughed as he walked into the complex of dimly lit rooms crowded with tables and customers. 'Is that what it's called?'

'In Connecticut, that's what it's called . . . See? I got two floors – a duplex, like. Each floor's got five big rooms, a bar in each room. Very private, no bad behavior. Nice place to bring the wife, or somebody else, you know what I mean?'

'I think I do. It's quite something.'

'The waiters are mostly college boys. I like to help them make a few dollars for their education. I got niggers, spics, kikes – I got no discrimination. Just the hair, I don't go for the long hair, you know what I mean?'

'College kids! Isn't that dangerous? Kids talk.'

'Hey, what d'you think?! This place was originally started by a Joe College. It's like a fraternity home. Everybody's a bona fide, dues-paying member of a private organization. They can't getcha for that.'

'I see. What about the other part?'

'What other part?'

'What I came for.'

'What? A little grass? Try the corner newsstand.'

Matlock laughed. He didn't want to overdo it. 'Two

188

points, Rocco . . . Still, if I knew you better, maybe I'd like to make a purchase. Bartolozzi said what I couldn't use, you've got . . . Forget it, though. I'm bushed. I'll just get a drink and shove off. The girl's going to wonder where I've been.'

'Sometimes Bartolozzi talks too much.'

'I think you're right. By the way, he's joining me tomorrow night at Sharpe's over in Windsor Shoals. I've got a friend flying in from London. Care to join us?'

Aiello was obviously impressed. The players from London were beginning to take precedence over the Vegas and Caribbean boys. Sammy Sharpe's wasn't that well known, either.

'Maybe I'll do that . . . Look, you need something, you feel free to ask, right?'

'I'll do that. Only I don't mind telling you, the kids make me nervous.'

Aiello took Matlock's elbow with his left hand and walked him toward the bar. 'You got it wrong. These kids – they're not kids, you know what I mean?'

'No, I don't. Kids are kids. I like my action a little more subdued. No sweat. I'm not curious.' Matlock looked up at the bartender and withdrew what was left of his bankroll. He removed a twenty-dollar bill and placed it on the bar. 'Old Fitz and water, please.'

'Put your money away,' Rocco said.

'Mr Aiello?' A young man in a waiter's jacket approached them. He was perhaps twenty-two or twenty-three, Matlock thought.

'Yeah?'

'If you'll sign this tab. Table eleven. It's the Johnsons. From Canton. They're OK'

Aiello took the waiter's pad and scribbled his initials. The young man walked back toward the tables.

189

'See that kid? That's what I mean. He's a Yalie. He got back from Nam six months ago.'

'So?'

'He was a lieutenant. An officer. Now he's studying business administration . . . He fills in here maybe twice a week. Mostly for contacts. By the time he gets out, he'll have a real nest egg. Start his own business.'

'What?'

'He's a supplier . . . These kids, that's what I mean. You should hear their stories. Saigon, Da Nang. Hong Kong, even. Real peddling. Hey, these kids today, they're great! They know what's up. Smart, too. No worries, believe me!'

'I believe you.' Matlock took his drink and swallowed quickly. It wasn't that he was thirsty, he was trying to conceal his shock at Aiello's revelation. The graduates of Indochina were not the pink-cheeked, earnest, young-old veterans of Armentières, Anzio, or even Panmunjom. They were something else, something faster, sadder, infinitely more knowing. A hero in Indochina was the soldier who had contacts on the docks and in the warehouses. That man in Indochina was the giant among his peers. And such young-old men were almost all black.

Matlock drank the remainder of his bourbon and let Rocco show him the other rooms on the third floor. He displayed the controlled appreciation Aiello expected and promised he'd return. He said no more about Sammy Sharpe's in Windsor Shoals. He knew it wasn't necessary. Aiello's appetite had been whetted.

As he drove away, two thoughts occupied his mind. Two objectives had to be accomplished before Sunday afternoon was over. The first was that he had to produce an Englishman; the second was that he had to produce another large sum of money. It was imperative that he

190

have both. He had to be at Sharpe's in Windsor Shoals the next evening.

The Englishman he had in mind lived in Webster, an associate professor of mathematics at a small parochial campus, Madison University. He had been in the country less than two years; Matlock had met him – quite unprofessionally – at a boat show in Saybrook. The Britisher had lived on the Cornwall coast most of his life and was a sailing enthusiast. Matlock and Pat had liked him immediately. Now Matlock hoped to God that John Holden knew something about gambling.

The money was a more serious problem. Alex Anderson would have to be tapped again, and it was quite possible that he'd find enough excuses to put him off. Anderson was a cautious man, easily frightened. On the other hand, he had a nose for rewards. That instinct would have to be played upon.

Holden had seemed startled but not at all annoyed by Matlock's telephone call. If he was anything other than kind, it was curious. He repeated the directions to his apartment twice and Matlock thanked him, assuring him that he remembered the way.

'I'll be perfectly frank, Jim,' said Holden, admitting Matlock into his neat three-room apartment. 'I'm simply bursting. Is anything the matter? Is Patricia all right?'

'The answers are yes and no. I'll tell you everything I can, which won't be a hell of a lot . . . I want to ask you a favor, though. Two favors, actually. The first, can I stay here tonight?'

'Of course – you needn't ask. You look peaked. Come, sit down. Can I get you a drink?'

'No, no thanks.' Matlock sat on Holden's sofa. He remembered that it was one of those hide-a-beds and that it was comfortable. He and Pat had slept in it one

191

happy, alcoholic night several months ago. It seemed ages ago.

'What's the second favor? The first is my pleasure. If it's cash, I've something over a thousand. You're entirely welcome to it.'

'No, not money, thanks just the same . . . I'd like you to impersonate an Englishman for me.'

Holden laughed. He was a small-boned man of forty, but he laughed the way older, fatter men laughed.

'That shouldn't be too demanding, now should it? I suspect there's still a trace of Cornwall in my speech. Hardly noticeable, of course.'

'Hardly. With a little practice you may even lose the Yankee twang . . . There's something else, though, and it may not be so easy. Have you ever gambled?'

'Gambled? You mean horses, football matches?'

'Cards, dice, roulette?'

'Not substantially, no. Of course, as any reasonably imaginative mathematician, I went through a phase when I thought that by applying arithmetical principles – logarithmic averages – one could beat the gambling odds.'

'Did they work?'

'I said I went through the phase, I didn't stay there. If there's a mathematical system, it eluded me. Still does.'

'But you've played? You know the games.'

'Rather well, when you come right down to it. Laboratory research, you might say. Why?'

Matlock repeated the story he had told Blackstone. However, he minimized Pat's injuries and lightened the motives of those who assaulted her. When he finished, the Englishman, who'd lit his pipe, knocked the ashes out of the bowl into a large glass ashtray.

'It's right out of the cinema, isn't it? . . . You say Patricia's not seriously hurt. Frightened but nothing much more than that?'

'Right. If I went to the police it might louse up her scholarship money.'

'I see . . . Well, I don't really, but we'll let it go. And you'd rather I lost tomorrow night.'

'That doesn't matter. Just that you bet a great deal.'

'But you're *prepared* for heavy losses.'

'I am.'

Holden stood up. 'I'm perfectly willing to go through with this performance. It should prove rather a lark. However, there's a great deal you're not telling me and I wish you would. But I shan't insist upon it. I will tell you that your story is boggled with a large mathematical inconsistency.'

'What's that?'

'As I understand it, the money you are prepared to lose tomorrow evening is far in excess of any amount Patricia might realize in scholarship aid. The logical assumption, therefore, is that you do not wish to go to the police. Or perhaps, you can't.'

Matlock looked up at the Englishman and wondered at his own stupidity. He felt embarrassed and very inadequate. 'I'm sorry . . . I haven't consciously lied to you. You don't have to go through with it; maybe I shouldn't have asked.'

'I never implied that you lied – not that it matters. Only that there was much you haven't told me. Of course, I'll do it. I just want you to know I'm a willing audience when and if you decide to tell me everything that's happened . . . Now, it's late and you're tired. Why don't you take my room.'

'No, thanks. I'll sack out here. It has pleasant memories. A blanket's all I need. Also I have to make a phone call.'

'Anything you say. A blanket you'll get, and you know where the phone is.'

193

When Holden left, Matlock went to the phone. The Tel-electronic device he'd agreed to lease would not be ready until Monday morning.

'Blackstone.'

'This is James Matlock. I was told to call this number for any messages.'

'Yes, Mr Matlock. There is a message, if you'll hold on while I get the card . . . Here it is. From the Carlyle team. Everything is secure. The subject is responding nicely to medical treatment. The subject had three visitors. A Mr Samuel Kressel, a Mr Adrian Sealfont, and a Miss Lois Meyers. The subject received two telephone calls, neither of which the physician allowed to be taken. They were from the same individual, a Mr Jason Greenberg. The calls were placed from Wheeling, West Virginia. At no time was the subject separated from the Carlyle team . . . You can relax.'

'Thank you. I will. You're very thorough. Good night.' Matlock breathed deeply in relief and exhaustion. Lois Meyers lived across the hall from Pat in the graduate apartment house. The fact that Greenberg had called was comforting. He missed Greenberg.

He reached up and turned off the table lamp by the sofa. The bright April moon shone through the windows. The man from Blackstone's service was right – he could relax.

What he couldn't allow to relax were his thoughts about tomorrow – and after tomorrow. Everything had to remain accelerated; one productive day had to lead into another. There could be no letup, no sense of momentary satisfaction which might slow his thrust.

And after tomorrow. After Sammy Sharpe's in Windsor Shoals. If all went according to his calculations, it would be the time to head into the Carlyle area. Matlock closed his eyes and saw Blackstone's printed page in front of his mind.

CARMOUNT COUNTRY CLUB – CONTACT: HOWARD STOCKTON
WEST CARLYLE SAIL AND SKI RESORT –
CONTACT: ALAN CANTOR

Carmount was east of Carlyle near the border of Mount
Holly. The Sail and Ski was west, on Lake Derron – a
summer and winter resort area.

He'd find some reason to have Bartolozzi or Aiello, or,
perhaps, Sammy Sharpe, make the proper introductions.
And once in the Carlyle area, he would drop the hints.
Perhaps more than hints – commands, requirements,
necessities. This was the boldness he needed to use, this
was the way of Nimrod.

His eyes remained closed, the muscles in his body
sagged, and the pitch darkness of exhausted sleep came
over him. But before sleeping he remembered the paper.
The Corsican paper. He had to get the paper now. He
would need the silver paper. He would need the invitation
to Nimrod.

His invitation now. His paper.

The Matlock paper.

Chapter 21

If the elders at the Windsor Shoals Congregational Church had ever realized that Samuel Sharpe, attorney at law, the very bright Jewish lawyer who handled the church's finances, was referred to as Sammy the Runner by most of North Hartford and South Springfield, Massachusetts, vespers would have been canceled for a month. Fortunately, such a revelation had never been made to them and the Congregational Church looked favorably on him. He had done remarkable things for the church's portfolio and gave handsomely himself during fund drives. The Congregational Church of Windsor Shoals, as indeed most of the town, was nicely disposed toward Samuel Sharpe.

Matlock learned all of this in Sharpe's office inside the Windsor Valley Inn. The framed citations on the wall told half the story, and Jacopo Bartolozzi good-naturedly supplied the rest. Jacopo was actually making sure that Matlock and his English friend were aware that Sharpe's operation, as well as Sharpe himself, lacked the fine traditions of the Avon Swim Club.

Holden surpassed Matlock's expectations. Several times he nearly laughed out loud as he watched Holden take hundred-dollar bills – rushed into Webster by a harassed, nervous Alex Anderson – and flick them nonchalantly at a croupier, never bothering to count the chips but somehow letting everyone at whatever table he was at realize that he knew – to the dollar – the amount given him. Holden played intelligently, cautiously, and at one point was ahead of the house by nine thousand dollars. By the end of the evening, he had cut his winnings to several hundred and the

196

operators of the Windsor Valley breathed grateful sighs of relief.

James Matlock cursed his second night of terrible luck and took his twelve-hundred-dollar loss for what it meant to him – nothing.

At four in the morning Matlock and Holden, flanked by Aiello, Bartolozzi, Sharpe, and two of their cronies, sat at a large oak table in the colonial dining room. They were alone. A waiter and two busboys were cleaning up; the gambling rooms on the third floor of the inn had closed.

The husky Aiello and the short, fat Bartolozzi kept up a running commentary about their respective clientele, each trying to upstage the other with regard to their customers' status; each allowing that 'it might be nice' for the other to become 'acquainted' with a Mr and Mrs Johnson of Canton or a certain Dr Wadsworth. Sharpe, on the other hand, seemed more interested in Holden and the action in England. He told several funny, self-effacing stories about his visits to London clubs and his insurmountable difficulty with British currency in the heat of betting.

Matlock thought, as he watched Sammy Sharpe, that he was a very charming man. It wasn't hard to believe that Sharpe was considered a respectable asset to Windsor Shoals, Connecticut. He couldn't help comparing Sharpe to Jason Greenberg. And in the comparison, he found an essential difference. It was told in the eyes. Greenberg's were soft and compassionate, even in anger. Sharpe's were cold, hard, incessantly darting – strangely in conflict with the rest of his relaxed face.

He heard Bartolozzi ask Holden where he was off to next. Holden's offhand reply gave him the opportunity he was looking for. He waited for the right moment.

'I'm afraid I'm not at liberty to discuss my itinerary.'

'He means where he's going,' injected Rocco Aiello.

Bartolozzi shot Aiello a withering glance. 'I just thought

197

you should drop over to Avon. I got a real nice place I think you'd enjoy.'

'I'm sure I would. Perhaps another time.'

'Johnny'll be in touch with me next week,' Matlock said. 'We'll get together.' He reached for an ashtray and crushed out his cigarette. 'I have to be in . . . Carlyle, that's the name of the place.'

There was the slightest pause in the conversation. Sharpe, Aiello, and one of the other two men exchanged looks. Bartolozzi, however, seemed oblivious to any deep meaning.

'The college place?' asked the short Italian.

'That's right,' answered Matlock. 'I'll probably stay at Carmount or the Sail and Ski. I guess you fellows know where they are.'

'I guess we do.' Aiello laughed softly.

'What's your business in Carlyle?' The unidentified man – at least no-one had bothered to introduce him by name – drew deeply on a cigar as he spoke.

'*My* business,' said Matlock pleasantly.

'Just asking. No offense.'

'No offense taken . . . Hey, it's damned near four-thirty! You fellows are too hospitable.' Matlock pushed his chair back, prepared to stand.

The man with the cigar, however, had to ask another question.

'Is your friend going to Carlyle with you?'

Holden held up his hand playfully. 'Sorry, no itineraries. I'm simply a visitor to your pleasant shores and filled with a tourist's plans . . . We really must go.'

Both men rose from the table. Sharpe stood, too. Before the others could move, Sharpe spoke.

'I'll see the boys to their car and show them the road out. You fellows wait here – we'll settle accounts. I owe you money, Rocco. Frank owes me. Maybe I'll come out even.'

198

The man with the cigar, whose name was obviously Frank, laughed. Aiello looked momentarily perplexed but within seconds grasped the meaning of Sharpe's statement. The men at the table were to remain.

Matlock wasn't sure he'd handled the situation advantageously.

He had wanted to pursue the Carlyle discussion just enough to have someone offer to make the necessary calls to Carmount and the Sail and Ski. Holden's refusal to speak about his itinerary precluded it, and Matlock was afraid that it also implied that he and Holden were so important that further introductions were unnecessary. In addition, Matlock realized that as his journey progressed, he banked more and more on the dead Loring's guarantee that none of those invited to the Carlyle conference would discuss delegates among themselves. The meaning of 'Omerta' was supposedly so powerful that silence was inviolate. Yet Sharpe had just commanded those at the table to remain.

He had the feeling that perhaps he had gone too far with too little experience. Perhaps it was time to reach Greenberg – although he'd wanted to wait until he had more concrete knowledge before doing so. If he made contact with Greenberg now, the agent might force him – what was the idiotic phrase? – out of strategy. He wasn't prepared to face that problem.

Sharpe escorted them to the near-deserted parking lot. The Windsor Valley Inn wasn't crowded with overnight guests.

'We don't encourage sleeping accommodations,' Sharpe explained. 'We're known primarily as a fine restaurant.'

'I can understand that,' said Matlock.

'Gentlemen,' began Sharpe haltingly. 'May I make a request that might be considered impolite?'

'Go right ahead.'

'May I have a word with you, Mr Matlock? Privately.'

'Oh, don't concern yourself,' said Holden, moving off. 'I understand fully. I'll just walk around.'

'He's a very nice fellow, your English friend,' Sharpe said.

'The nicest. What is it, Sammy?'

'Several points of information, as we say in court.'

'What are they?'

'I'm a cautious man, but I'm also very curious. I run a fine organization, as you can see.'

'I can see.'

'I'm growing nicely – cautiously, but nicely.'

'I'll accept that.'

'I don't make mistakes. I've a trained legal mind and I'm proud that I don't make mistakes.'

'What are you driving at?'

'It strikes me – and I must be honest with you, it has also occurred to my partner Frank and to Rocco Aiello – that you may have been sent into the territory to make certain observations.'

'Why do you think that?'

'Why? . . . From nowhere comes a player like you. You got powerful friends in San Juan. You know our places like the back of your hand. Then you have a very rich, very nice associate from the London scene. That all adds up . . . But most important – and I think you know it – you mention this business in Carlyle. Let's be honest. That speaks a whole big book, doesn't it?'

'Does it?'

'I'm not foolhardy. I told you, I'm a cautious man. I understand the rules and I don't ask questions I'm not supposed to ask or talk about things I'm not privileged to know about . . . Still, I want the generals to realize they have a few intelligent, even ambitious, lieutenants in the organization. Anyone can tell you. I don't skim, I don't hold back.'

'Are you asking me to give you a good report?'

'That about sizes it up. I have value. I'm a respected attorney. My partner's a very successful insurance broker. We're naturals.'

'What about Aiello? It seems to me you're friendly with him.'

'Rocco's a good boy. Maybe not the quickest, but solid. He's a kind person, too. However, I don't believe he's in our league.'

'And Bartolozzi?'

'I have nothing to say about Bartolozzi. You'll have to make up your own mind about him.'

'By saying nothing, you're saying a lot, aren't you?'

'In my opinion, he talks too much. But that could be his personality. He rubs me the wrong way. Not Rocco, though.'

Matlock watched the methodical Sharpe in the predawn light of the parking lot and began to understand what had happened. It was logical; he, himself, had planned it, but now that it was taking place, he felt curiously objective. Observing himself; watching reacting puppets.

He had entered Nimrod's world a stranger; possibly suspect, certainly devious.

Yet suddenly, that suspicion, that deviousness, was not to be scorned but *honored*.

The suspect honored for his deviousness – because it *had* to come from a higher source. He was an emissary from the upper echelons now. He was feared.

What had Greenberg called it? The shadow world. Unseen armies positioning their troops in darkness, constantly on the alert for stray patrols, unfriendly scouts.

The thin line he had to tread was precarious. But it was his now.

'You're a good man, Sharpe. Goddamn smart, too . . . What do you know about Carlyle?'

'Nothing! Absolutely nothing.'

'Now you're lying, and that's *not* smart.'

'It's true. I don't *know anything*. Rumors I've heard. Knowledge and hearsay are two different kinds of testimony.' Sharpe held up his right hand, his two forefingers separated.

'What rumors? Give it straight, for your own sake.'

'Just rumors. A gathering of the clan, maybe. A meeting of very highly placed individuals. An agreement which has to be reached between certain people.'

'Nimrod?'

Sammy Sharpe closed his eyes for precisely three seconds. During those moments he spoke.

'Now you talk language I don't want to hear.'

'Then you didn't hear it, did you?'

'It's stricken from the record, I assure you.'

'OK You're doing fine. And when you go back inside, I don't think it would be such a good idea to discuss the rumors you've heard. That would be acting like a stupid lieutenant, wouldn't it?'

'Not only stupid – insane.'

'Why did you tell them to stay, then? It's late.'

'For real. I wanted to know what everybody thought of you and your English friend. I'll tell you now, though – since you have mentioned a certain name, no such discussion will take place. As I said, I understand the rules.'

'Good. I believe you. You've got possibilities. You'd better go back in . . . Oh, one last thing. I want you . . . *we* want you to call Stockton at Carmount and Cantor at the Sail and Ski. Just say I'm a personal friend and I'll be showing up. Nothing else. We don't want any guards up. That's important, Sammy. Nothing else.'

202

'It's my pleasure. And you won't forget to convey my regards to the others?'

'I won't forget. You're a good man.'

'I do my best. It's all a person can do . . .'

Just then, the quiet of the predawn was shattered by five loud reports. Glass smashed. The sounds of people running and screaming and furniture crashing came from within the inn. Matlock threw himself to the ground.

'John! John!'

'Over here! By the car! Are you all right?!'

'Yes. Stay there!'

Sharpe had run into the darkness by the base of the building. He crouched into a corner, pressing himself against the brick. Matlock could barely see the outline of his form, but he could see enough to watch Sharpe withdraw a revolver from inside his jacket.

Again there was a volley of shots from the rear of the building, followed once more by screams of terror. A busboy crashed through the side door and crawled on his hands and knees toward the edge of the parking lot. He shouted hysterically in a language Matlock could not understand.

Several seconds later, another of the inn's employees in a white jacket ran through the door pulling a second man behind him, this one obviously wounded, blood pouring from his shoulder, his right arm dangling, immobile.

Another shot rang out of nowhere and the waiter who had been screaming fell over. The wounded man behind him went pummeling forward, crashing face down into the gravel. Within the building, men were shouting.

'Let's go! Get *out*! Get to the *car*!'

He fully expected to see men come scrambling out of the side door into the parking lot, but no-one came. Instead, from another section of the property, he heard the gunning of an engine and, moments later, the screeching of tires as an automobile made a sharp turn. And then, to his left, about fifty yards away, a black sedan came racing out of the north driveway toward the main road. The car had to pass under a street light, and Matlock saw it clearly.

It was the same automobile that had plunged out of the darkness moments after Ralph Loring's murder.

Everything was still again. The grayish light of dawn was getting brighter.

'Jim! Jim, come here! I think they've gone!'

It was Holden. He had left the sanctuary of the automobile and was crouching over the man in the white jacket.

'Coming!' said Matlock, getting off the ground.

'This fellow's dead. He was shot between the shoulders . . . This one's still breathing. Better get an ambulance.' Holden had walked over to the unconscious busboy with the bloodied, immobile right arm.

'I don't hear anything. Where's Sharpe?'

'He just went inside. That door. He had a gun.'

The two men walked carefully to the side entrance of the inn. Matlock slowly opened the door and preceded Holden into the foyer. Furniture was overturned, chairs and tables on their sides; blood was glistening on the wooden floor.

'Sharpe? Where are you?' Matlock raised his voice cautiously. It was several seconds before the reply came. When it did, Sharpe could hardly be heard.

'In here. In the dining room.'

Matlock and Holden walked through the oak-framed arch. Nothing in either man's life had prepared him for what he saw.

The overpowering horror was the sight of the bodies literally covered with blood. What was left of Rocco Aiello was sprawled across the red-soaked tablecloth, most of his face blown off. Sharpe's partner, the unintroduced man named Frank, was on his knees, his torso twisted back over the seat of a chair, blood flowing out of his neck, his eyes wide open in death. Jacopo Bartolozzi was on the floor, his obese body arched around the leg of a table, the front of his shirt ripped up to the collar, revealing his bulging stomach, the flesh pierced with a score of bullet holes, blood still trickling out over the coarse black hair. Bartolozzi had tried to tear his shirt away from his battered chest, and a portion of cloth was clutched in his dead hand. The fourth man lay behind Bartolozzi, his head resting on Bartolozzi's right foot, his arms and legs extended in a spread-eagle pattern, his entire back covered with a thick layer of blood, portions of his intestines pushed through the skin.

'Oh, my God!' muttered Matlock, not fully believing what he saw. John Holden looked as though he might become sick. Sharpe spoke softly, rapidly, wearily.

'You'd better go. You and your English friend better leave quickly.'

'You'll have to call the police,' said Matlock, bewildered.

'There's a man outside, a boy. He's still alive.' Holden stuttered as he spoke.

Sharpe looked over at the two men, the revolver at his side, his eyes betraying only the slightest degree of suspicion. 'I have no doubt the lines have been cut. The nearest houses are farms at least half a mile from here . . . I'll take care of everything. You'd better get out of here.'

'Do you think we should?' asked Holden, looking at Matlock.

Sharpe replied. 'Listen, Englishman, personally I couldn't care less what either of you do. I've got enough to think about, enough to figure out . . . For your own good, get out of here. Less complications, less risk. Isn't that right?'

'Yes, you're right,' Matlock said.

'In case you're picked up, you left here a half hour ago. You were friends of Bartolozzi, that's all I know.'

'All right.'

Sharpe had to turn away from the sight of the murdered men. Matlock thought for a moment that the Windsor Shoals attorney was going to weep. Instead, he took a deep breath and spoke again.

'A trained legal mind, Mr Matlock. I'm valuable. You tell them that.'

'I will.'

'You also tell them I need protection, *deserve* protection. You tell them that, too.'

'Of course.'

'Now, get out.' Suddenly Sharpe threw his revolver on the floor in disgust. And then he screamed, as the tears came to his eyes, 'Get out for Christ's sake! *Get out!*'

Chapter 22

Matlock and Holden agreed to separate immediately. The English professor dropped off the mathematician at his apartment and then headed south to Fairfield. He wanted to register at a highway motel far enough away from Windsor Shoals to feel less panicked, yet near enough to Hartford so he could get to Blackstone's by two in the afternoon.

He was too exhausted, too frightened to think. He found a third-rate motel just west of Stratford and surprised the early morning clerk by being alone.

During the registration, he mumbled unpleasant criticisms about a suspicious wife in Westport, and with a ten-dollar bill convinced the clerk to enter his arrival at 2:00 A.M., single. He fell into bed by seven and left a call for twelve-thirty. If he slept for five hours, he thought, things had to become clearer.

Matlock slept for five hours and twenty minutes and nothing much had changed. Very little had cleared up for him. If anything, the massacre at Windsor Shoals now appeared more extraordinary than ever. Was it possible that he was meant to be a victim? Or were the killers waiting outside, waiting silently for him to leave before committing their executions?

Mistake or warning?

By one-fifteen he was on the Merritt Parkway. By one-thirty he entered the Berlin Turnpike, taking the back roads into Hartford. By five minutes past two he walked into Blackstone's office.

'Look,' said Michael Blackstone, leaning over his desk,

staring at Matlock, 'we ask a minimum of questions, but don't for one minute think that means we give our clients blank checks!'

'It seems to me you like that process reversed.'

'Then take your money and go somewhere else. We'll survive!'

'Just hold it! You were hired to protect a girl, that's all! That's what I'm paying three hundred dollars a day for! Anything else is marginal, and I'm paying for that, too, I expect.'

'There'll be no extra charges. I don't know what you're talking about.' Suddenly Blackstone bent his elbows, crouching forward. He whispered hoarsely. 'Christ, Matlock? *Two men!* Two men on that goddamn list were murdered last night! If you're a hopped-up maniac, I don't want anything to do with you! That's no part of any deal here! I don't care *who* your old man is or *how* much money you've got!'

'Now I don't know what *you're* talking about. Except what I read in the papers. I was at a motel in Fairfield last night. I was registered there at two this morning. According to the papers, those killings took place around five.'

Blackstone pushed himself off the desk and stood up. He looked at Matlock suspiciously. 'You can verify that?'

'Do you want the name and number of the motel? Give me a phone book, I'll get it for you.'

'No! . . . No. I don't want to know a thing. You were in Fairfield?'

'Get the phone book.'

'All right. All right, forget it. I think you're lying, but you've covered yourself. As you say, we're only hired to protect the girl.'

'Any change from Sunday afternoon? Is everything all right?'

'Yes . . . Yes.' Blackstone seemed preoccupied. 'I've

got your Tel-electronic. It's operative. It's an additional twenty dollars a day.'

'I see. Wholesale price.'

'We never implied we were cheap.'

'You couldn't.'

'We don't.' Blackstone remained standing, pushed a button on his office intercom, and spoke into it. 'Bring in Mr Matlock's Tel-electronic, please.'

Seconds later an attractive girl came into the office carrying a metal device no larger than a pack of cigarettes. She put it on Blackstone's desk and placed an index card beside it. She left as rapidly as she had entered.

'Here you are,' Blackstone said. 'Your code is Charger Three-zero. Meaning – Carlyle area, three-man team. The telephone number you call is five, five, five, six, eight, six, eight. We keep a list of numbers on reserve which we feel are easy to commit. The Tel-electronic will signal you by short beeps. You can shut it off by pushing this button here. When the signal is emitted, you are to call the number. A recording machine on that telephone will give you the message from the team. Often it will be to phone another number to make direct contact. Do you understand everything? It's really very simple.'

'I understand,' said Matlock, taking the small metal box. 'What confuses me is why you don't just have the men call this office and then you contact me. Outside of whatever profit there is, wouldn't it be easier?'

'No. Too much room for error. We handle a great many clients. We want our clients to be in direct contact with the men they're paying for.'

'I see.'

'Also, we respect the privacy of our clients. We don't think it's such a good idea for information to be transmitted through third and fourth parties. Incidentally, you can reach the team by the same procedures. Each one has a

209

machine. Just phone the number and record the message for them.'

'Commendable.'

'Professional.' And then Blackstone, for the first time since Matlock had entered the office, sat in his chair and leaned back. 'Now I'm going to tell you something, and if you want to take it as a threat, you'd be justified. Also, if you want to cancel our services on the strength of what I say, that's OK, too . . . We know that you're being actively sought by agents of the Justice Department. However, there are no charges leveled against you, no warrants for your arrest. You have certain rights which the federal men often overlook in their zealousness – it's one of the reasons we're in business. However, *again*, we want you to know that should your status change, should there *be* charges or a warrant for your arrest, our services are terminated immediately, and we won't hesitate to cooperate with the authorities regarding your whereabouts. Whatever information we possess will be held for your attorneys – it's privileged – but not your whereabouts, *Capiche?*'

'I do. That's fair.'

'We're more than fair. That's why I'm going to demand ten days' advance payment from you – unused portion returnable . . . In the event the situation changes and the federal men get a court order for you, you will receive – *only once* – the following message on the telephone recorder. Just *these words*.'

Blackstone paused for emphasis.

'What are they?'

'"*Charger Three-zero is canceled*"'

Out on Bond Street Matlock felt a sensation he knew wouldn't leave him until his journey, his race was over. He thought people were staring at him. He began to think strangers were watching him. He found himself involuntarily turning around, trying to find the unseen, observing eyes. Yet there were none.

None that he could distinguish.

The Corsican paper now had to be gotten out of his apartment. And considering Blackstone's statements, there was no point in his attempting to get it himself. His apartment would be under surveillance – from both camps, the seekers and the quarry.

He would use the Blackstone team, one of them, putting to the test the sartorial Blackstone's guarantee of privileged information. He would reach them – him – as soon as he placed one prior telephone call. A call that would make it clear whether the silver Corsican invitation was really necessary or not. A call to Samuel Sharpe, attorney at law, Windsor Shoals, Connecticut.

Matlock decided to show Sharpe a temporary, more compassionate side of his acquired personality. Sharpe himself had displayed a momentary lapse of control. Matlock thought it was the moment to indicate that even such men as himself – men who had influential friends in San Juan and London – had feelings beyond personal survival.

He walked into the lobby of the Americana Hotel and called him. Sharpe's secretary answered.

'Are you in an office where Mr Sharpe can return your call momentarily?'

'No, I'm in a telephone booth. I'm also in a hurry.'

There was silence, preceded by the click of a hold button. The wait was less than ten seconds.

'May I have the number you're calling from, Mr Matlock? Mr Sharpe will get back to you within five minutes.'

Matlock gave the girl the number and hung up.

As he sat in the plastic seat, his memory wandered back

211

to another telephone booth and another plastic seat. And a black sedan which raced past the dead man slouched in that booth, on that seat, with a bullet hole in his forehead.

The bell sounded; Matlock lifted the receiver.

'Matlock?'

'Sharpe?'

'You shouldn't call me at the office. You should know better. I had to go down to the lobby here, to a pay phone.'

'I didn't think a respected attorney's telephone would be any risk. I'm sorry.'

There was a pause at the other end of the line. Sharpe obviously never expected an apology. 'I'm a cautious man, I told you. What is it?'

'I just wanted to know how you were. How everything went. It was a terrible thing, last night.'

'I haven't had time for a reaction. There's so much to do. Police, funeral arrangements, reporters.'

'What are you saying? How are you handling it?'

'There won't be any major mistakes. In a nutshell – if it comes to that – I'm an innocent victim. Frank's a victim, too, only he's dead . . . I'm going to miss Frank. He was a very good fellow. I'll close down the upstairs, of course. The state police have been paid. By you people, I assume. It'll be what the papers say it was. A bunch of Italian hoodlums shot up in a nice country restaurant.'

'You're a cool operator.'

'I told you,' replied Sharpe sadly, 'I'm a cautious man. I'm prepared for contingencies.'

'Who did it?'

Sharpe did not answer the question. He did not speak at all.

'I asked you, who do you think did it?'

'I expect you people will find out before I do . . . Bartolozzi had enemies; he was an unpleasant person.

212

Rocco, too, I suppose . . . But why Frank? You tell me.'

'I don't know. I haven't been in touch with anyone.'

'Find out for me. Please. It wasn't right.'

'I'll try. That's a promise . . . And, Sammy, make those calls to Stockton and Cantor, don't forget.'

'I won't. I've got them listed on my afternoon calendar. I told you, I'm a methodical man.'

'Thanks. My sympathies about Frank. He seemed like a nice guy.'

'He was a prince.'

'I'm sure he was . . . I'll be in touch, Sammy. I haven't forgotten what I said I'd do for you. You've really impressed me. I'll . . .'

The sound of coins dropping into the telephone receptacle at Windsor Shoals interrupted Matlock. The time limit was up, and there was no point in prolonging the conversation. He had found out what he needed to know. He had to have the Corsican paper now. The horror of the dawn massacre had not caused the methodical Sharpe to forget the telephone calls he'd promised to make. Why it hadn't was a miracle to Matlock, but there it was. The cautious man had not panicked. He was ice.

The telephone booth was stuffy, close, uncomfortable, filled with smoke. He opened the door and walked rapidly across the hotel lobby to the front exit.

He rounded the corner of Asylum Street looking for an appropriate restaurant. One in which he could have lunch while awaiting the return call from Charger Three-zero. Blackstone had said that he should leave a number; what better than a restaurant?

He saw the sign: The Lobster House. The kind of place frequented by business executives.

He was given a booth to himself, not a table. It was nearly three; the luncheon crowd had thinned. He sat

213

down and ordered a bourbon on the rocks, asking the waitress the whereabouts of the nearest telephone. He was about to get out of the booth to make his call to 555–6868 when he heard the muted, sharp, terrifying sound of the Tel-electronic from within his jacket. At first it paralysed him. It was as if some part of his person, an hysterical organ perhaps, had gone mad and was trying to signal its distress. His hand shook as he reached inside his coat and withdrew the small metal device. He found the shut-off button and pressed it as hard as he could. He looked around, wondering if the sound had attracted attention.

It had not. No-one returned his looks. No-one had heard a thing.

He got out of his seat and walked quickly toward the telephone. His only thought was Pat – something had happened, something serious enough for Charger Three-zero to activate the terrible, insidious machine which had panicked him.

Matlock pulled the door shut and dialed 555–6868.

'Charger Three-zero reporting.' The voice had the once-removed quality of a taped recording. 'Please telephone five, five, five; one, nine, five, one. There is no need for alarm, sir. There's no emergency. We'll be at this number for the next hour. The number again is five, five, five; one, nine, five, one. Out.'

Matlock realized that Charger Three-zero took pains to allay his fears immediately, perhaps because it was his first experience with the Tel-electronic. He had the feeling that even if the town of Carlyle had gone up in thermonuclear smoke, Charger Three-zero's words would have a palliative quality about them. The other reasoning, perhaps, was that a man thought more clearly when unafraid. Whatever, Matlock knew that the method worked. He was calmer now. He reached into his pocket and took out some change, making a mental note as he did

214

so to convert some dollar bills into coins for future use. The pay telephone had become an important part of his life.

'Is this five, five, five; nineteen fifty-one?'

'Yes,' said the same voice he had heard on the recording. 'Mr Matlock?'

'Yes. Is Miss Ballantyne all right?'

'Doing very well, sir. That's a good doctor you've got. She sat up this morning. A lot of the swelling's gone down. The doctor's quite pleased. . . . She's asked for you a number of times.'

'What are you telling her?'

'The truth. That we've been hired by you to make sure she's not bothered.'

'I mean about where I am.'

'We've simply said you had to be away for several days. It might be a good idea to telephone her. She can take calls starting this afternoon. We'll screen them, of course.'

'Of course. Is that why you contacted me?'

'In part. The other reason is Greenberg. Jason Greenberg. He keeps calling for you. He insists that you get in touch with him.'

'What did he say? Who talked to him?'

'I did. Incidentally, my name's Cliff.'

'OK, Cliff, what did he say?'

'That I should tell you to call him the minute I reached you. It was imperative, critical. I've got a number. It's in Wheeling, West Virginia.'

'Give it to me.' Matlock withdrew his ballpoint pen and wrote the number on the wooden shelf under the telephone.

'Mr Matlock?'

'What?'

'Greenberg also said to tell you . . . that "the cities weren't dying, they were dead." Those were his words. "The cities were dead."'

215

Chapter 23

Cliff agreed without comment to retrieve the Corsican paper from Matlock's apartment. A rendezvous would be arranged later by telephone. In the event the paper was missing, Charger Three-zero would alert him immediately.

Matlock restricted himself to one drink. He picked at his lunch and left the Lobster House by three-thirty. It was time to regroup his forces, resupply his ammunition. He had parked the Cadillac in a lot several blocks south of Blackstone's office on Bond Street. It was one of those municipal parking areas, each slot with its own meter. It occurred to Matlock as he approached it that he hadn't returned to insert additional coins since going to Blackstone's. The meters were only good for an hour; he'd been there for nearly two. He wondered what rental-car businesses did with the slew of traffic violations which had to mount up with transients. He entered the lot and momentarily wondered if he was in the right aisle. Then he realized he was not. The Cadillac was two lanes over, in the fourth aisle. He started to sidle past the closely parked vehicles toward his own and then he stopped.

In between the automobiles, he saw the blue and white stripes of a Hartford patrol car. It was parked directly behind his Cadillac. One police officer was trying the Cadillac's door handle, a second patrolman was leaning against the police vehicle talking into a radio phone.

They'd found the car. It frightened him, but somehow it didn't surprise him.

He backed away cautiously, prepared to run if he was

216

spotted. His thoughts raced ahead to the problems to which this newest complication gave rise. First and most immediate was an automobile. Second was the fact that they knew he was in the Hartford vicinity. That ruled out other means of transportation. The rail-road stations, the bus terminals, even the hack bureaus would be alerted. It came back to finding another car.

And yet he wondered. Blackstone made it clear there were no charges against him, no warrants. If there were, he would have received the message from 555–6868. He would have heard the words: 'Charger Three-zero is canceled.'

He hadn't. There'd been no hint of it. For a moment he considered going back to the patrol car, accepting a ticket for overtime.

He dismissed the thought. These police were not meter maids. There had been a previous parking lot beyond an alley, at the rear of an A&P. And another policeman – in civilian clothes – following him. A pattern was there, though it eluded definition. Matlock walked swiftly up Bond Street away from the municipal lot. He turned into the first side street and found himself beginning to break into a run. Instantly he slowed down. There is nothing in a crowded street more noticeable than a man running – unless it is a woman. He resumed a pace equal to the afternoon shoppers, doing his best to melt into the flow of human traffic. He even paused now and then to stare blankly into store-front windows, not really seeing the displays of merchandise. And then he began to reflect on what was happening to him. The primitive instincts of the hunted were suddenly working inside his brain. The protective antennae of the would-be trapped animal were thrusting, parrying with their surroundings and, chameleonlike, the body did its best to conform to the environment.

Yet he wasn't the hunted! He was the hunter! Goddamn it, he was the *hunter*!

'Hello, Jim! How the hell are you? What are you doing in the big city?'

The shock of the greeting caused Matlock to lose his balance. To actually *lose his balance* and trip. He fell to the sidewalk and the man who had spoken to him reached down and helped him up.

'Oh! Oh, hello, Jeff! Christ, you startled me. Thanks.' Matlock got up and brushed himself off. He looked around wondering who else beside Jeff Kramer was watching him.

'A long lunch, buddy?' Kramer laughed. He was a Carlyle alumnus with a graduate degree in psychology that had been impressive enough for an expensive public relations firm.

'Lord, no! Just have something on my mind. My bumbling old professor bag.' And then Matlock looked at Jeff Kramer. Jeff Kramer was not only with an expensive firm, but he also had an expensive wife and two very expensive kids in extremely expensive prep schools. Matlock felt he should reemphasize his previous point. 'For a fact, I had one unfinished bourbon.'

'Why don't we rectify that,' said Kramer, pointing at the Hogshead Tavern across the street. 'I haven't seen you in months. I read in *The Courant* you got yourself robbed.'

'Goddamn, *did* I! The robbery I could take, but what they did to the apartment! And the *car*!' Matlock headed toward the Hogshead Tavern with Jeff Kramer. 'That's why I'm in town. Got the Triumph in a garage here. That's my problem, as a matter of fact.'

The hunted not only had antennae which served to warn the host of its enemies, but also the uncanny – if temporary – ability to turn disadvantage into advantage. Conceivable liabilities into positive assets.

218

Matlock sipped his bourbon and water while Kramer went through half his Scotch in several swallows. 'The idea of a bus down to Scarsdale, with changes at New Haven and Bridgeport, defeats me.'

'*Rent* a car, for Christ's sake.'

'Just tried two places. The first can't let me have one until tonight, the second not until tomorrow. Some kind of convention, I guess.'

'So wait until tonight.'

'Can't do it. Family business. My father called his council of economic advisers. For dinner – and if you think I'm going to Scarsdale without my own wheels, you're out of it!' Matlock laughed and ordered another round of drinks. He reached into his pocket and put a fifty-dollar bill on the bar. The bill had to attract the attention of Jeff Kramer, who had such an expensive wife.

'Never thought you could balance a checkbook, say nothing of being an economic adviser.'

'Ah, but I'm the prince royal. Can't forget that, can we?'

'Lucky bastard, that's what I can't forget. Lucky bastard.'

'Hey! I've got one hell of an idea. Your car in town?'

'Hey, wait a minute, good buddy . . .'

'No, listen.' Matlock took out his bills. 'The old man'll pay for it . . . Rent me *your* car. Four or five days . . . Here. I'll give you two, three hundred.'

'You're nuts!'

'No, I'm not. He wants me down. He'll pay!'

Matlock could sense Kramer's mind working. He was estimating the cost of a low-priced rent-a-car for a week. Seventy-nine-fifty and ten cents a mile with an average daily mileage of, perhaps, fifteen or twenty. Tops, $105, and maybe $110, for the week.

219

Kramer had that expensive wife and those two very expensive kids in extremely expensive prep schools.

'I wouldn't want to take you like that.'

'Not *me*! Christ, no. *Him!*'

'Well . . .'

'Here, let me write out a bill. I'll give it to him the minute I get there.' Matlock grabbed a cocktail napkin and turned it over to the unprinted side. He took out his ballpoint pen and began writing. 'Simple contract . . . "I, James B. Matlock, agree to pay Jeffrey Kramer three hundred" . . . what the hell, it's his money . . . "four hundred dollars for the rental of his . . ." – what's the make?'

'Ford wagon. A white Squire. Last year's.' Kramer's eyes alternately looked at the napkin and the roll of bills Matlock carelessly left next to Kramer's elbow on the bar.

'"Ford Wagon, for a period of" . . . let's say one week, OK?'

'Fine.' Kramer drank the remainder of his second Scotch.

'"One week . . . Signed, James B. Matlock!" There you are, friend. Countersign. And here's four hundred. Courtesy of Jonathan Munro. Where's the car?'

The hunted's instincts were infallible, thought Matlock, as Kramer pocketed the bills and wiped his chin, which had begun to perspire. Kramer removed the two car keys and the parking lot ticket from his pocket. True to Matlock's anticipation. Jeff Kramer wanted to part company. With his four hundred dollars.

Matlock said he would phone Kramer in less than a week and return the automobile. Kramer insisted on paying for the drinks and rapidly left the Hogshead Tavern. Matlock, alone, finished his drink and thought out his next move.

The hunted and the hunter were now one.

Chapter 24

He sped out Route 72 toward Mount Holly in Kramer's white station wagon. He knew that within the hour he would find another pay telephone and insert another coin and make another call. This time to one Howard Stockton, owner of the Carmount Country Club. He looked at his watch; it was nearly eight-thirty. Samuel Sharpe, attorney at law, should have reached Stockton several hours ago.

He wondered how Stockton had reacted. He wondered about Howard Stockton.

The station wagon's headlights caught the reflection of the road sign.

MOUNT HOLLY. INCORPORATED 1896

And just beyond it, a second reflection.

MOUNT HOLLY ROTARY
HARPER'S REST
TUESDAY NOON
ONE MILE

Why not? thought Matlock. There was nothing to lose. And possibly something to gain, even learn.

The hunter.

The white stucco front and the red Narragansett neons in the windows said all there was to say about Harper's cuisine. Matlock parked next to a pickup truck, got out,

221

and locked the car. His newly acquired suitcase with the newly acquired clothes lay on the back seat. He had spent several hundred dollars in Hartford; he wasn't about to take a chance.

He walked across the cheap, large gravel and entered the bar area of Harper's Restaurant.

'I'm on my way to Carmount,' said Matlock, paying for his drink with a twenty-dollar bill. 'Would you mind telling me where the hell it is?'

'About two and a half miles west. Take the right fork down the road. You got anything smaller than a twenty? I only got two fives and singles. I need my singles.'

'Give me the fives and we'll flip for the rest. Heads you keep it, tails I have one more and you still keep it.' Matlock took a coin from his pocket and threw it on the formica bar, covering it with his hand. He lifted his palm and picked up the coin without showing it to the bartender. 'It's your unlucky night. You owe me a drink – the ten's yours.'

His conversation did not go unheeded by the other customers – three men drinking draft beer. That was fine, thought Matlock, as he looked around for a telephone.

'Men's room's in the rear around the corner,' said a rustic-looking drinker in a chino jacket, wearing a baseball cap.

'Thanks. Telephone around?'

'Next to the men's room.'

'Thanks again.' Matlock took out a piece of paper on which he had written: Howard Stockton, Carmount C.C., # 203–421–1100. He gestured for the bartender, who came toward him like a shot. 'I'm supposed to phone this guy,' said Matlock quietly. 'I think I got the name wrong. I'm not sure whether it's Stackton or Stockton. Do you know him?'

The bartender looked at the paper and Matlock saw the instant reflex of recognition. 'Sure. You got it right. It's

222

Stockton. Mr Stockton. He's vice-president of the Rotary. Last term he was president. Right boys?' The bartender addressed this last to his other customers.

'Sure.'

'That's it. Stockton.'

'Nice fella.'

The man in the chino jacket and baseball cap felt the necessity of elaborating. 'He runs the country club. That's a real nice place. Real nice.'

'Country club?' Matlock implied the question with a trace of humor.

'That's right. Swimming pool, golf course, dancing on the weekends. Very nice.' It was the bartender who elaborated now.

'I'll say this, he's highly recommended. This Stockton, I mean.' Matlock drained his glass and looked toward the rear of the bar. 'Telephone back there, you say?'

'That's right, Mister. Around the corner.'

Matlock reached into his pocket for some change and walked to the narrow corridor where the rest rooms and telephone were located. The instant he rounded the corner, he stopped and pressed himself against the wall. He listened for the conversation he knew would be forthcoming.

'Big spender, huh?' The bartender spoke.

'They all are. Did I tell you? My kid caddied there a couple of weeks ago – some guy got a birdie and give the kid a fifty-dollar bill. Che-ryst! Fifty dollars!'

'My old woman says all them fancy dames there are *whoores*. Real whoores. She works a few parties there, my old woman does. Real whoores . . .'

'I'd like to get my hands on some of them. Jee-*sus*! I swear to Christ most of 'em got no brazzieres!'

'Real whoores . . .'

'Who gives a shit? That Stockton's OK. He's OK in

223

my book. Know what he did? The Kings. You know, Artie King who had a heart attack – dropped dead doin' the lawns up there. Old Stockton not only give the family a lotta dough – he set up a regular charge account for 'em at the A&P. No shit. He's OK.'

'Real whoores. They lay for money . . .'

'Stockton put most of the cash up for the grammar school extension, don't forget that. You're fuckin' right, he's OK. I got two kids in that school!'

'Not only – y'know what? He give a pocketful to the Memorial Day picnic.'

'Real, honest-to-Christ whoores . . .'

Matlock silently sidestepped his way against the wall to the telephone booth. He closed the door slowly with a minimum of noise. The men at the bar were getting louder in their appreciation of Howard Stockton, proprietor of the Carmount Country Club. He was not concerned that they might hear his delayed entrance into the booth.

What concerned him in an odd way was himself. If the *hunted* had instincts – protective in nature – the *hunter* had them also – aggressive by involvement. He understood now the necessity of tracking the scent, following the spoor, building a fabric of comprehensive habit. It meant that the hunter had abstract tools to complement his weapons. Tools which could build a base of entrapment, a pit in which the hunted might fall.

He ticked them off in his mind.

Howard Stockton: former president, current vice-president of the Mount Holly Rotary; a charitable man, a compassionate man. A man who took care of the family of a deceased employee named Artie King; who financed the extension of a grammar school. The proprietor of a luxurious country club in which men gave fifty-dollar tips to caddies and girls were available for members in good standing. Also a good American who made it possible for the town of Mount Holly to have a fine Memorial Day picnic.

It was enough to start with. Enough to shake up Howard Stockton if – as Sammy Sharpe had put it – 'it came to that.' Howard Stockton was not the formless man he was fifteen minutes ago. Matlock still didn't know the man's features, but other aspects, other factors were defined for him. Howard Stockton had become a *thing* in Mount Holly, Connecticut.

Matlock inserted the dime and dailed the number of the Carmount Country Club.

'It *suht*ainly is a pleasure, Mr Matlock!' exclaimed Howard Stockton, greeting Matlock on the marble steps of the Carmount Country Club. 'The boy'll take your car. Heah! Boy! Don't wrap it up, now!'

A Negro parking attendant laughed at his southern gentleman's command. Stockton flipped a half-dollar in the air and the black caught it with a grin.

'Thank you, suh!'

'Treat 'em good, they'll treat you good. That right, boy? Do I treat you good?'

'*Real* good, Mister Howard!'

Matlock thought for a moment that he was part of an odious television commercial until he saw that Howard Stockton was the real item. Right up to his grayish blond hair, which topped a sun-tanned face, which, in turn, set off his white moustache and deep blue eyes surrounded by crow's nests of wrinkles belonging to a man who lived well.

'Welcome to Carmount, Mr Matlock. It's not Richmond, but on the other hand, it ain't the Okefenokee.'

'Thank you. And the name is Jim.'

'Jim? Like that name. It's got a good, honest ring to it! My friends call me Howard. You call me Howard.'

225

The Carmount Country Club, what he could see of it, reminded Matlock of all those pictures of antebellum architecture. And why not, considering the owner? It was rife with potted palms and delicate chandeliers and light blue toile wallpaper depicting rococo scenes in which cavorted prettified figures in powdered wigs. Howard Stockton was a proselytizer of a way of life which had collapsed in 1865, but he wasn't going to admit it. Even the servants, mostly black, were in liveries – honest-to-god liveries, knickers and all. Soft, live music came from a large dining room, at the end of which was a string orchestra of perhaps eight instruments gracefully playing in a fashion long since abandoned. There was a slowly winding staircase in the center of the main hall which would have done honor to Jefferson Davis – or David O. Selznick. Attractive women were wandering around, linked with no-so-attractive men.

The effect was incredible, thought Matlock, as he walked by his host's side toward what his host modestly claimed was his private library.

The southerner closed the thick paneled door and strode to a well-stocked mahogany bar. He poured without asking a preference.

'Sam Sharpe says you drink sour mash. You're a man of taste, I tell you that. That's *my* drink.' He carried two glasses to Matlock. 'Take your pick. A Virginian has to disarm a northerner with his complete lack of bias these days.'

'Thank you,' said Matlock, taking a glass and sitting in the armchair indicated by Stockton.

'This Virginian,' continued Howard Stockton, sitting opposite Matlock, 'also has an unsouthern habit of getting to the point . . . I don't even know if it's wise for you to be in my place. I'll be honest. That's why I ushered you right in here.'

'I don't understand. You could have told me on the phone not to come. Why the game?'

'Maybe you can answer that better than I can. Sammy says you're a real big man. You're what they call . . . *international*. That's just dandy by me. I like a bright young fella who goes up the ladder of success. Very commendable, that's a fact . . . But I pay my bills. I pay every month on the line. I got the best combined operation north of Atlanta. I don't want trouble.'

'You won't get it from *me*. I'm a tired businessman making the rounds, that's all I am.'

'What happened at Sharpe's? The papers are full of it! I don't want *nothin'* like that!'

Matlock watched the southerner. The capillaries in the suntanned face were bloodred, which was probably why the man courted a year-round sunburn. It covered a multitude of blemishes.

'I don't think you understand.' Matlock measured his words as he lifted the glass to his lips. 'I've come a long way because I *have* to be here. I don't *want* to be here. Personal reasons got me into the area early, so I'm doing some sightseeing. But it's only that. I'm just looking around . . . Until my appointment.'

'What appointment?'

'An appointment in Carlyle, Connecticut.'

Stockton squinted his eyes and pulled at his perfectly groomed white moustache. 'You've got to be in Carlyle?'

'Yes. It's confidential, but I don't have to tell you that, do I?'

'You haven't told me anything.' Stockton kept watching Matlock's face, and Matlock knew the southerner was looking for a false note, a wrong word, a hesitant glance which might contradict his information.

'Good . . . By any chance, do you have an appointment in Carlyle, too? In about a week and a half?'

227

Stockton sipped his drink, smacking his lips and putting the glass on a side table as though it were some precious *objet d'art*. 'I'm just a southern cracker tryin' to make a dollar. Livin' the good life and makin' a dollar. That's all. I don't know about any appointments in Carlyle.'

'Sorry I brought it up. It's a . . . major mistake on my part. For both our sakes. I hope you won't mention it. Or *me*.'

'That's the *last* thing I'd do. Far as I'm concerned, you're a friend of Sammy's lookin' for a little action . . . and a little hospitality.' Suddenly Stockton leaned forward in his chair, his elbows on his knees, his hands folded. He looked like an earnest minister questioning a parishioner's sins. 'What in tarnation happened at Windsor Shoals? What in hell was it?'

'As far as I can see, it was a local vendetta. Bartolozzi had enemies. Some said he talked too goddamn much. Aiello, too, I suppose. They were show-offs. . . . Frank was just there, I think.'

'Goddamn *Eye*talians! Mess up everything! *That* level, of course, you know what I mean?'

There it was again. The dangling interrogative – but in this southerner's version, it wasn't really a question. It was a statement.

'I know what you mean,' said Matlock wearily.

'I'm afraid I got a little bad news for you, Jim. I closed the tables for a few days. Just plum scared as a jackrabbit after what happened at the Shoals.'

'That's not bad news for me. Not the way my streak's been going.'

'I heard. Sammy told me. But we got a couple of other diversions. You won't find Carmount lacking in hospitality, I promise you that.'

The two men finished their drinks, and Stockton, relieved, escorted his guest into the crowded, elegant

Carmount dining room. The food was extraordinary, served in a manner befitting the finest and wealthiest plantation of the antebellum South.

Although pleasant – even relaxing, in a way – the dinner was pointless to Matlock. Howard Stockton would not discuss his 'operation' except in the vaguest terms and with the constant reminder that he catered to the 'best class of Yankee.' His speech was peppered with descriptive anachronisms, he was a walking contradiction in time. Halfway through the meal, Stockton excused himself to say goodbye to an important member.

It was the first opportunity Matlock had to look at Stockton's 'best class of Yankee' clientele.

The term applied, thought Matlock, if the word *class* was interchangeable with *money*, which he wasn't willing to concede. Money screamed from every table. The first sign was the proliferation of sun tans in the beginning of a Connecticut May. These were people who jetted to the sun-drenched islands at will. Another was the easy, deep-throated laughter echoing throughout the room; also the glittering reflection of jewelry.

And the clothes – softly elegant suits, raw silk jackets, Dior ties. And the bottles of sparkling vintage wines, standing majestically in sterling silver stands upheld by cherrywood tripods.

But something was wrong, thought Matlock. Something was missing or out of place, and for several minutes he couldn't put his finger on what it was. And then he did.

The suntans, the laughter, the wrist jewelry, the jackets, the Dior ties – the money, the elegance, the aura was predominantly *male*.

The contradiction was the women – the girls. Not that there weren't some who matched their partners, but in the main, they didn't. They were younger. Much, much younger. And different.

229

He wasn't sure what the difference was at first. Then, abstractly, it came to him. For the most part, the girls – and they *were* girls – had a look about them he knew very well. He'd referred to it often in the past. It was the campus look – as differentiated from the office look, the secretary look. A slightly more intense expression around the eyes, a considerably more careless attitude in conversation. The look of girls not settling into routines, not welded to file cabinets or typewriters. It was definable because it was real. Matlock had been exposed to that look for over a decade – it was unmistakable.

Then he realized that within this contradiction there was another – minor – discrepancy. The clothes the girls wore. They weren't the clothes he expected to find on girls with the campus look. They were too precisely cut, too designed, if that was the word. In this day of unisex, simply too feminine.

They wore costumes!

Suddenly, in a single, hysterically spoken sentence from several tables away, he knew he was right.

'Honest, I mean it – it's too groovy!'

That voice! *Christ, he knew that voice!*

He wondered if he was meant to hear it.

He had his hand up to his face and slowly turned toward the direction of the giggling speaker. The girl was laughing and drinking champagne, while her escort – a much older man – stared with satisfaction at her enormous breasts.

The girl was Virginia Beeson. The 'pinky groovy' perennial undergraduate wife of Archer Beeson, Carlyle University's history instructor.

The man in an academic hurry.

Matlock tipped the black who carried his suitcase up the winding staircase to the large, ornate room Stockton had offered him. The floor was covered with a thick

230

wine-colored carpet, the bed canopied, the walls white with fluted moldings. He saw that on the bureau was an ice bucket, two bottles of Jack Daniels, and several glasses. He opened the suitcase, picked out his toilet articles, and put them on the bedside table. He then removed a suit, a light-weight jacket and two pairs of slacks, and carried them to the closet. He returned to the suitcase, lifted it from the bed, and laid it across the two wooden arms of a chair.

There was a soft tapping on his door. His first thought was that the caller was Howard Stockton, but he was wrong.

A girl, dressed in a provocative deep-red sheath, stood in the frame and smiled. She was in her late teens or very early twenties and terribly attractive.

And her smile was false.

'Yes?'

'Compliments of Mr Stockton.' She spoke the words and walked into the room past Matlock.

Matlock closed the door and stared at the girl, not so much bewildered as surprised.

'That's very thoughtful of Mr Stockton, isn't it?'

'I'm glad you approve. There's whiskey, ice, and glasses on your bureau. I'd like a short drink. Unless you're in a hurry.'

Matlock walked slowly to the bureau. 'I'm in no hurry. What would you like?'

'It doesn't matter. Whatever's there. Just ice, please.'

'I see.' Matlock poured the girl a drink and carried it over to her. 'Won't you sit down?'

'On the bed?'

The only other chair, besides the one on which the suitcase was placed, was across the room by a French window.

'I'm sorry.' He removed the suitcase and the girl sat

231

down. Howard Stockton, he thought, had good taste. The girl was adorable. 'What's your name?'

'Jeannie.' She drank a great deal of her drink in several swallows. The girl may not have perfected a selection in liquor, but she knew how to drink. And then, as the girl took the glass from her mouth, Matlock noticed the ring on her third right finger.

He knew that ring very well. It was sold in a campus bookstore several blocks from John Holden's apartment in Webster, Connecticut. It was the ring of Madison University.

'What would you say if I told you I wasn't interested?' asked Matlock, leaning against the thick pole of the bed's anachronistic canopy.

'I'd be surprised. You don't look like a fairy.'

'I'm not.'

The girl looked up at Matlock. Her pale blue eyes were warm – but professionally warm – meaning, yet not meaning at all. Her lips were young. And full; and taut.

'Maybe you just need a little encouragement.'

'You can provide that?'

'I'm good.' She made the statement with quiet arrogance.

She was so young, thought Matlock, yet there was age in her. And hate. The hate was camouflaged, but the cosmetic was inadequate. She was performing – the costume, the eyes, the lips. She may have detested the role, but she accepted it.

Professionally.

'Suppose I just want to talk?'

'Conversation's something else. There are no rules about that. I've equal rights in that department. Quid pro, Mister No-name.'

'You're facile with words. Should that tell me something?'

232

'I don't know why.'

'"Quid pro quo" isn't the language of your eight to three hooker.'

'This place – in case you missed it – isn't the Avenida de las Putas, either.'

'Tennessee Williams?'

'Who knows?'

'I think you do.'

'Fine. All right. We can discuss Proust in bed. I mean, that *is* where you want me, isn't it?'

'Perhaps I'd settle for the conversation.'

The girl suddenly, in alarm, whispered hoarsely, 'Are you a cop?'

'I'm the furthest thing from a cop,' laughed Matlock. 'You might say that some of the most important policemen in the area would like to find me. Although I'm no criminal . . . Or a nut, by the way.'

'Now *I'm* not interested. May I have another drink?'

'Surely.' Matlock got it for her. Neither spoke until he returned with her glass.

'Do you mind if I stay here awhile? Just long enough for you to have balled me.'

'You mean you don't want to lose the fee?'

'It's fifty dollars.'

'You'll probably have to use part of it to bribe the dormitory head. Madison University's a little old-fashioned. Some coed houses still have weekday check-ins. You'll be late.'

The shock on the girl's face was complete. 'You *are* a cop! You're a lousy *cop*!' She started to get out of the chair, but Matlock quickly stood in front of her, holding her shoulders. He eased her back into the chair.

'I'm not a cop, I told you that. And you're not interested, remember? But *I'm* interested. I'm *very* interested, and you're going to tell me what I want to know.'

The girl started to get up and Matlock grabbed her arms. She struggled; he pushed her back violently. 'Do you always get "balled" with your ring on? Is that to show whoever gets laid there's a little class to it?!'

'Oh, my God! Oh, Jesus!' She grabbed her ring and twisted her finger as if the pressure might make it disappear.

'Now, listen to me! You answer my questions or I'll be down in Webster tomorrow morning and I'll start asking them down there! Would you like that better?'

'Please. *Please!*' Tears came to the girl's eyes. Her hands shook and she gasped for breath.

'How did you get here?!'

'No! No . . .'

'*How?*'

'I was recruited . . .'

'By whom?'

'Others . . . Others. We recruit each other.'

'How many are there?'

'Not many. Not very many . . . It's quiet. We have to keep it quiet . . . Let me go, *please.* I want to go.'

'Oh, no. Not yet. I want to know how many and *why*!'

'I told you! Only a few, maybe seven or eight girls.'

'There must be thirty downstairs!'

'I don't *know* them. They're from other places. We don't ask each other's *names*!'

'But you know where they're from, don't you!'

'Some . . . Yes.'

'Other schools?'

'Yes . . .'

'*Why*, Jeannie? For Christ's sake, *why*?'

'Why do you *think*? *Money!*'

The girl's dress had long sleeves. He grabbed her right arm and ripped the fabric up past the elbow. She fought him back but he overpowered her.

There were no marks. No signs.

She kicked at him and he slapped her face, hard enough to shock her into momentary immobility. He took her left arm and tore the sleeve.

There they were. Faded. Not recent. But there.

The small purple dots of a needle.

'I'm not on it now! I haven't been in *months*!'

'But you need the money! You need fifty or a hundred dollars every time you come over here! . . . What is it *now*? Yellows? Reds? *Acid? Speed?* What the hell is it *now*? Grass isn't that expensive!'

The girl sobbed. Tears fell down her cheeks. She covered her face and spoke – moaned – through her sobs.

'There's so much trouble! So much . . . *trouble*! Let me *go, please*!'

Matlock knelt down and cradled the girl's head in his arms, against his chest.

'What trouble? tell me, please. What trouble?'

'They *make* you do it . . . You *have* to . . . So many need help. They won't help *anyone* if you don't do it. Please, whatever your name is, let me alone. Let me go. Don't say anything. Let me *go*! . . . *Please!*'

'I will, but you've got to clear something up for me. Then you can go and I won't say anything . . . Are you down here because they threatened you? Threatened the other kids?'

The girl nodded her head, gasping quietly, breathing heavily. Matlock continued. 'Threatened you with what? Turning you in? . . . Exposing a habit? That's not worth it. Not today . . .'

'Oh, you're outta sight!' The girl spoke through her tears. 'They can ruin you. For life. Ruin your family, your school, maybe later. Maybe . . . Some rotten prison. Somewhere! Habit, pushing, supplying . . . a boy you know's in trouble and *they* can get him off . . . Some

235

girl's in her third month, she needs a doctor . . . *they* can get one. No noise.'

'You don't need *them*! Where've you *been*?! There are agencies, counseling!'

'Oh, Jesus Christ, mister! Where have *you* been?! . . . The drug courts, the doctors, the judges! They run them *all*! . . . There's nothing *you* can do about it. Nothing *I* can do about it. So leave me alone, leave *us* alone. Too many people'll get hurt!'

'And you're just going to keep doing what they say! Frightened, spoiled little bastards who keep on whining! Afraid to wash your hands, or your *mouths*, or your *arms*!' He pulled at her left elbow and yanked it viciously.

The girl looked up at him, half in fear, half in contempt.

'That's right,' she said in a strangely calm voice. 'I don't think you'd understand. You don't know what it's all about . . . We're different from you. My friends are all I've got. All any of us have got. We help each other . . . I'm not interested in being a hero. I'm only interested in my friends. I don't have a flag decal in my car window and I don't like John Wayne. I think he's a shit. I think you all are. All shits.'

Matlock released the girl's arm. 'Just how long do you think you can keep it up?'

'Oh, I'm one of the lucky ones. In a month I'll have that scroll my parents paid for and I'm out of it. They hardly ever try to make contact with you later. They say they will, but they rarely do . . . You're just supposed to live with the possibility.'

He understood the implications of her muted testimony and turned away. 'I'm sorry. I'm very, very sorry.'

'Don't be. I'm one of the lucky ones. Two weeks after I pick up that piece of engraved crap my parents want so badly, I'll be on a plane. I'm leaving this goddamn country. And I'll never come back!'

Chapter 25

He had not been able to sleep, nor had he expected to. He had sent the girl away with money, for he had nothing else he could give her, neither hope nor courage. What he advocated was rejected, for it involved the risk of danger and pain to untold children committed to the well-being of each other. He could not demand; there was no trust, no threat equal to the burdens they carried. Ultimately, it was the children's own struggle. They wanted no help.

He remembered the Bagdhivi admonition: *Look ye to the children; look and behold. They grow tall and strong and hunt the tiger with greater cunning and stronger sinews than you. They shall save the flocks better than you. Ye are old and infirm. Look to the children. Beware of the children.*

Were the children hunting the tiger better? And even if they were, whose flocks would they save? And who was the tiger?

Was it the 'goddamn country'?

Had it come to that?

The questions burned into his mind. How many Jeannies were there? How extensive was Nimrod's recruiting?

He had to find out.

The girl admitted that Carmount was only one port of call; there were others, but she didn't know where. Friends of hers had been sent to New Haven, others to Boston, some north to the outskirts of Hanover.

Yale. Harvard. Dartmouth.

The most frightening aspect was Nimrod's threat of a thousand futures. What had she said?

'They hardly ever make contact . . . They say they will
. . . You live with the possibility.'

If such was the case, Bagdhivi was wrong. The children
had far less cunning, possessed weaker sinews; there was
no reason to beware. Only to pity.

Unless the children were subdivided, led by other,
stronger children.

Matlock made up his mind to go down to New Haven.
Maybe there were answers there. He had scores of friends
at Yale University. It would be a side trip, an unconsidered
excursion, but intrinsic to the journey itself. Part of the
Nimrod odyssey.

Short, high-pitched sounds interrupted Matlock's concentration. He froze, his eyes swollen in shock, his body
tense on top of the bed. It took him several seconds to
focus his attention on the source of the frightening sound.
It was the Tel-electronic, still in his jacket pocket. But
where had he put his jacket? It wasn't near his bed.

He turned on the bedside lamp and looked around,
the unrelenting, unceasing sounds causing his pulse to
hammer, his forehead to perspire. Then he saw his coat.
He had put it on top of the chair in front of the French
window, halfway across the room. He looked at his watch:
4:35 A.M. He ran to the jacket, pulled out the terrible
instrument, and shut it off.

The panic of the hunted returned. He picked up the
telephone on the bedside table. It was a direct line, no
switchboard.

The dial tone was like any other dial tone outside the
major utility areas. A little fuzzy, but steady. And if there
was a tap, he wouldn't be able to recognize it anyway. He
dialed 555–6868 and waited for the call to be completed.

'Charger Three-zero reporting,' said the mechanized
voice. 'Sorry to disturb you. There is no change with
the subject, everything is satisfactory. However, your

238

friend from Wheeling, West Virginia, is very insistent. He telephoned at four-fifteen and said it was imperative you call him at once. We're concerned. Out.'

Matlock hung up the telephone and forced his mind to go blank until he found a cigarette and lit it. He needed the precious moments to stop the hammering pulse.

He hated that goddamn machine! He hated what its terrifying little beeps did to him.

He drew heavily on the smoke and knew there was no alternative. He had to get out of the Carmount Country Club and reach a telephone booth. Greenberg wouldn't have phoned at four in the morning unless it was an emergency. He couldn't take the chance of calling Greenberg on the Carmount line.

He threw his clothes into the suitcase and dressed quickly.

He assumed there'd be a night watchman, or a parking attendant asleep in a booth, and he'd retrieve his, Kramer's, automobile. If not, he'd wake up someone, even if it was Stockton himself. Stockton was still frightened of trouble, Windsor Shoals trouble – he wouldn't try to detain him. Any story would do for the purveyor of young, adorable flesh. The sunburned southern flower of the Connecticut Valley. The stench of Nimrod.

Matlock closed the door quietly and walked down the silent corridor to the enormous staircase. Wall sconces were lighted, dimmed by rheostats to give a candlelight effect. Even in the dead of night, Howard Stockton couldn't forget his heritage. The interior of the Carmount Country Club looked more than ever like a sleeping great hall of a plantation house.

He started for the front entrance, and by the time he reached the storm carpet, he knew it was as far as he would go. At least for the moment.

Howard Stockton, clad in a flowing velour, nineteenth-century dressing gown, emerged from a glass door next to the entrance. He was accompanied by a large, Italian-looking man whose jet black eyes silently spoke generations of the Black Hand. Stockton's companion was a killer.

'Why, Mr Matlock! Are you leavin' us?'

He decided to be aggressive.

'Since you tapped my goddamn phone, I assume you gather I've got problems! They're *my business, not yours!* If you want to know, I resent your intrusion!'

The ploy worked. Stockton was startled by Matlock's hostility.

'There's no reason to be angry . . . I'm a businessman, like you. Any invasion of your privacy is for your protection. Goddamn! That's *true, boy*!'

'I'll accept the lousy explanation. Are my keys in the car?'

'Well, not in your *car*. My friend Mario here's got 'em. He's a real high-class Eyetalian, let me tell you.'

'I can see the family crest on his pocket. May I have my keys?'

Mario looked at Stockton, obviously confused.

'Now, just a minute,' Stockton said. 'Wait a bit, Mario. Let's not be impulsive . . . I'm a reasonable man. A very reasonable, rational person. I'm merely a Virginia . . .'

'*Cracker*, trying to make a dollar!' interrupted Matlock. 'I'll buy that! Now get the hell out of my way and give me the keys!'

'Good Lord, *you all* are downright *mean*! I mean, *mean*! Put yourself in my place! . . . Some crazy code like "Chargin' Three-zero" and an urgent call from Wheelin', West *Virginia*! And instead of usin' my perfectly good telephone, you gotta make space and get *outta* here! C'mon, Jim. What would *you* do?!'

Matlock kept his voice chillingly precise. 'I'd try to understand *who* I was dealing with . . . We've made a number of inquiries, Howard. My superiors are concerned about you.'

'What-do-you-mean?' Stockton's question was asked so swiftly the words had no separation.

'They think . . . we think you've called too much attention to yourself. President and vice-president of a *Rotary Club*! Jesus! A one-man fund-raiser for new school buildings; the big provider for widows and orphans – charge accounts included; Memorial Day picnics! Then hiring locals to spread rumors about the girls! Half the time the kids walk around half naked. You think the local citizens don't talk? *Christ*, Howard!'

'Who the hell are you?'

'Just a tired businessman who gets annoyed when he sees another businessman make an ass of himself. What the hell do you think you're running for? Santa Claus? Have you any idea how prominent that costume is?'

'Goddamn it, you got it in for me! I've got the finest combined operation north of Atlanta! I don't know who you people been talkin' to, but I tell you – this l'il old Mount Holly'd go to hell in a basket for me! Those things you people dug up – they're *good* things! *Real* good! . . . You twist 'em, make 'em sound bad! That ain't *right*!'

Stockton took out a handkerchief and patted his flushed, perspiring face. The southerner was so upset his sentences spilled over into one another, his voice strident. Matlock tried to think swiftly, cautiously. Perhaps the time was now – with Stockton. It had to be sometime. He had to send out his own particular invitation. He had to start the last lap of his journey to Nimrod.

'Calm down, Stockton. Relax. You may be right . . . I haven't time to think about it now. We've got a crisis. All of us. That phone call was serious.' Matlock paused, looking hard at the nervous Stockton, and then put his suitcase on the marble floor. 'Howard,' he said slowly, choosing his words carefully, 'I'm going to trust you with something and I hope to hell you're up to it. If you pull it off, no-one'll bother your operation – ever.'

'What's that?'

'Tell *him* to take a walk. Just down the hall, if you like.'

'You heard the man. Go smoke a cigar.'

Mario looked both hostile and confused as he trudged slowly toward the staircase. Stockton spoke.

'What do you want me to do? I told you, I don't want trouble.'

'We're *all* going to have trouble unless I reach a few delegates. That's what Wheeling was telling me.'

'What do you mean . . . delegates?'

'The meeting over at Carlyle. The conference with our people and the Nimrod organization.'

'That's not my affair!' Stockton spat out the words. 'I don't know a thing about that!'

'I'm sure you don't; you weren't meant to. But now it concerns all of us . . . Sometimes rules have to be broken; this is one of those times. Nimrod's gone too far, that's all I can tell you.'

'You tell *me*? I live with those *preachers*! I *parlay* with them, and when I complain, you know what our own people say? They say, "That's the way it is, old Howie, we all do business"! What kind of talk is that? Why do *I* have to do business with them?'

'Perhaps you won't much longer. That's why I have to reach some of the others. The delegates.'

'They don't include me in those meetings. I don't know anyone.'

'Of course you don't. Again, you weren't meant to. The conference is heavy; very heavy and very quiet. So quiet we may have screwed ourselves: we don't know who's in the area. From what organization; from what family? But I have my orders. We've got to get through to one or two.'

'I can't help you.'

Matlock looked harshly at the southerner. 'I think you can. Listen to me. In the morning, get on the phone and pass the word. *Carefully!* We don't want panic. Don't talk to anyone you don't know and don't use my name! Just say you've met someone who has the Corsican paper, the silver Corsican paper. He's *got* to meet quietly with someone else who has it, too. We'll start with one person if we have to. Have you got that?'

'I got it but I don't like it! It's none of *my business*!'

'Would you rather close down? Would you rather lose this magnificent relic of yours and stare out of a cell window for ten or twenty years? I understand prison funerals are very touching.'

'All right! . . . All right. I'll call my bag boy. I'll say I don't know nothin'! I'm just passin' along a message.'

'Good enough. If you make a contact, tell whoever it is that I'll be at the Sail and Ski tonight or tomorrow. Tell him to bring the paper. I won't talk to anyone without the paper!'

'Without the paper . . .'

'Now let me have my keys.'

Stockton called Mario back. Matlock got his keys.

He swung south on Route 72 out of Mount Holly. He didn't remember precisely where, but he knew he'd passed several highway telephone booths on his way up from Hartford. It was funny how he was beginning to notice public telephones, his only connecting link with solidity. Everything else was transient, hit or miss, unfamiliar and frightening. He'd phone Greenberg as Charger Three-zero

243

requested, but before he did, he was going to reach one of Blackstone's men.

A rendezvous would have to be arranged immediately. He now had to have the Corsican paper. He'd put out the word; he'd have to keep his end of the bargain or he would learn nothing. *If* Stockton's message got through and *if* someone *did* make contact, that someone would kill or be killed before breaking the oath of 'Omerta' unless Matlock produced the paper.

Or was it all for nothing? Was he the amateur Kressel and Greenberg said he was? He didn't know. He tried so hard to think things through, look at all sides of every action, use the tools of his trained, academic imagination. But was it enough? Or was it possible that his sense of commitment, his violent feelings of vengeance and disgust were only turning him into a Quixote?

It that were so, he'd live with it. He'd do his god-damnedest and live with it. He had good reasons – a brother named David; a girl named Pat; a gentle old man named Lucas; a nice fellow named Loring; a confused, terrified student from Madison named Jeannie. The sickening whole *scene*!

Matlock found a booth on a deserted stretch of Route 72 and called the inanimate receiver at the other end of 555–6868. He gave the number of the telephone booth and waited for Charger Three-zero to answer his call.

A milk truck lumbered by. The driver was singing and waved to Matlock. Several minutes later a huge Allied Van Lines sped past, and shortly after a produce truck. It was nearing five-thirty, and the day was brightening. Brightening to a dull gray, for there were rain clouds in the sky.

The telephone rang.

'Hello!'

'What's the problem, sir? Did you reach your friend in West Virginia? He said he's not kidding any more.'

244

'I'll call him in a few minutes. Are you the fellow named Cliff?' Matlock knew it was not; the voice was different.

'No, sir. I'm Jim. Same name as yours.'

'All right, Jim. Tell me, did the other fellow do what I asked him to? Did he get the paper for me?'

'Yes, sir. If it's the one on silver paper, written in Italian. I think it's Italian.'

'That's the one . . .'

Matlock arranged for the pickup in two hours. It was agreed that the Blackstone man named Cliff would meet him at an all-night diner on Scofield Avenue near the West Hartford town line. Charger Three-zero insisted that the delivery be made rapidly, in the parking lot. Matlock described the car he was driving and hung up the phone.

The next call would have to be Jason Greenberg in Wheeling. And Greenberg was furious.

'Schmuck! It isn't bad enough you break your word, you've got to hire your own army! What the hell do you think those clowns can do that the United States Government can't?'

'Those clowns are costing me three hundred dollars a day, Jason. They'd better be good.'

'You ran out! Why did you do that? You gave me your word you wouldn't. You said you'd work with our man!'

'Your man gave me an ultimatum I couldn't live with! And if it was your idea, I'll tell you the same thing I told Houston.'

'What does that mean? What ultimatum?'

'You know goddamn well! Don't play that game. And you listen to me . . .' Matlock took a break before plunging into the lie, giving it all the authority he could summon. 'There's a lawyer in Hartford who has a very precise letter signed by me. Along the same lines as the letter I signed for you. Only the information's a bit different: it's straight. It describes in detail the story of

245

my recruitment; how you bastards sucked me in and then how you let me hang. How you forced me to sign a lie . . . You try anything, he'll release it and there'll be a lot of embarrassed manipulators at the Justice Department . . . You gave me the idea, Jason. It was a damn good idea. It might even make a few militants decide to tear up the Carlyle campus. Maybe launch a string of riots, with luck, right across the country. The academic scene's ready to be primed out of its dormancy; isn't that what Sealfont said? Only this time it won't be the war or the draft or drugs. They'll find a better label: government infiltration, police state . . . *Gestapo* tactics. Are you prepared for that?'

'For Christ's sake, cut it out! It won't do you any good. You're not that important . . . Now, what the hell are you talking about? *I briefed him!* There weren't any conditions except that you keep him informed of what you were doing.'

'Bullshit! I wasn't to leave the campus; I wasn't to talk to anyone on the faculty or the staff. I was restricted to student inquiries, and I gathered those were to be cleared *first*! Outside of those minor restrictions, I was free as a bird! Come on! You *saw* Pat! You saw what they did to her. You know what else they did – the word is *rape*, Greenberg! Did you people expect me to *thank* Houston for being so *understanding*?'

'Believe me,' said Greenberg softly, in anger. 'Those conditions were added after the briefing. They should have told me, that's true. But they were added for your own protection. You can see that, can't you?'

'They weren't part of our bargain!'

'No, they weren't. And they should have told me . . .'

'Also, I wonder whose protection they were concerned with. Mine or theirs.'

'A good question. They should have told me. They can't

246

delegate responsibility and always take away the authority. It's not logical.'

'It's not *moral*. Let me tell you something. This little odyssey of mine is bringing me closer and closer to the sublime question of morality.'

'I'm glad for you, but I'm afraid your odyssey's coming to an end.'

'Try it!'

'They're going to. Statements in lawyers' offices won't mean a damn. I told them I'd try first . . . If you don't turn yourself over to protective custody within forty-eight hours, they'll issue a warrant.'

'On what grounds?!'

'You're a menace. You're mentally unbalanced. You're a nut. They'll cite your army record – two courts-martial, brig time, continuous instability under combat conditions. Your use of drugs. And alcohol – they've got witnesses. You're also a racist – they've got that Lumumba affidavit from Kressel. And now I understand, although I haven't the facts, you're consorting with known criminals. They have photographs – from a place in Avon . . . Turn yourself in, Jim. They'll ruin your life.'

Chapter 26

Forty-eight hours! Why forty-eight hours? Why not twenty-four or twelve or immediately? It didn't make sense! Then he understood and, alone in the booth, he started to laugh. He laughed out loud in a telephone booth at five-thirty in the morning on a deserted stretch of highway in Mount Holly, Connecticut.

The practical men were giving him just enough time to accomplish something – if he *could* accomplish something. If he couldn't, and anything happened, they were clean. It was on record that they considered him a mentally unbalanced addict with racist tendencies who consorted with known criminals, and they had given him warning. In deference to the delicate balance of dealing with such madmen, they allocated *time* in the hopes of reducing the danger. Oh, Christ! The manipulators!

He reached the West Hartford diner at six-forty-five and ate a large breakfast, somehow believing that the food would take the place of sleep and give him the energy he needed. He kept glancing at his watch, knowing that he'd have to be in the parking lot by seven-thirty.

He wondered what his contact at Charger Three-zero would look like.

The man was enormous, and Matlock had never considered himself small. Cliff of Charger Three-zero reminded Matlock of those old pictures of Primo Carnera. Except the face. The face was lean and intelligent and smiled broadly.

'Don't get out, Mr Matlock.' He reached in and shook

Matlock's hand. 'Here's the paper; I put it in an envelope. By the way, we had Miss Ballantyne laughing last night. She's feeling better. Encephalograph's steady, metabolism's coming back up to par, pupil dilation's receding. Thought you'd like to know.'

'I imagine that's good.'

'It is. We've made friends with the doctor. He levels.'

'How's the hospital taking your guard duty?'

'Mr Blackstone solves those problems in advance. We have rooms on either side of the subject.'

'For which, I'm sure, I'll be charged.'

'You know Mr Blackstone.'

'I'm getting to. He goes first class.'

'So do his clients. I'd better get back. Nice to meet you.' The Blackstone man walked rapidly away and got into a nondescript automobile several years old.

It was time for Matlock to drive to New Haven.

He had no set plan, no specific individuals in mind; he wasn't leading, he was being led. His information was, at best, nebulous, sketchy, far too incomplete to deal in absolutes. Yet perhaps there was enough for someone to make a connection. But whoever made it, or was capable of making it, had to be someone with an overall view of the university. Someone who dealt, as did Sam Kressel, with the general tensions of the campus.

However, Yale was five times the size of Carlyle; it was infinitely more diffuse, a section of the New Haven city, not really isolated from its surroundings as was Carlyle. There *was* a focal point, the Office of Student Affairs; but he didn't know anyone there. And to arrive off the street with an improbable story of college girls forming – or being formed into – a prostitution ring reaching, as so far determined, the states of Connecticut, Massachusetts, and New Hampshire, would create havoc if he was taken seriously. And he wasn't sure he *would* be taken seriously, in which case he'd learn nothing.

There was one possibility; a poor substitute for Student Affairs, but with its own general view of the campus: the Department of Admissions. He knew a man, Peter Daniels, who worked in Yale's admissions office. He and Daniels had shared a number of lecterns during prep school recruitment programs. He knew Daniels well enough to spell out the facts as he understood them; Daniels wasn't the sort to doubt him or to panic. He'd restrict his story to the girl, however.

He parked on Chappel Street near the intersection of York. On one side of the thoroughfare was an arch leading to the quadrangle of Silliman College, on the other a large expanse of lawn threaded with cement paths to the Administration Building. Daniels's office was on the second floor. Matlock got out of the car, locked it, and walked toward the old brick structure with the American flag masted next to the Yale banner.

'That's preposterous! This is the age of Aquarius and then some. You don't pay for sex; it's exchanged freely.'

'I know what I saw. I know what the girl told me; she wasn't lying.'

'I repeat. You can't be sure.'

'It's tied in with too many other things. I've seen them, too.'

'May I ask the obvious question? Why don't you go to the police?'

'Obvious answer. Colleges have been in enough trouble. What facts I have are isolated. I need more information. I don't want to be responsible for indiscriminate name-calling, any widespread panic. There's been enough of that.'

'All right, I'll buy it. But I can't help you.'

'Give me several names. Students *or* faculty. People you

know . . . you're certain are messed up, seriously messed up. Near the center. You've got those kinds of names, I know you do; we do . . . I swear, they'll never know who gave them to me.'

Daniels got out of his chair, lighting his pipe. 'You're being awfully general. Messed up how? Academically, politically . . . narcotics, alcohol? You're coving a wide territory.'

'Wait a minute.' Daniels's words evoked a memory. Matlock recalled a dimly lit, smoke-filled room inside a seemingly deserted building in Hartford. Rocco Aiello's Hunt Club. And a tall young man in a waiter's jacket who had brought over a tab for Aiello to sign. The veteran of Nam and Da Nang. The Yalie who was *making contacts, building up his nest egg . . . the business administration* major. 'I know who I want to see.'

'What's his name?'

'I don't know . . . But he's a veteran – Indochina, about twenty-two or three; he's pretty tall, light brown hair . . . majoring in business administration.'

'A description which might fit five hundred students. Except for premed, law, and engineering, it's all lumped under liberal arts. We'd have to go through every file.'

'Application photographs?'

'Not allowed any more, you know that.'

Matlock stared out the window, his eyebrows wrinkled in thought. He looked back at Daniels. 'Pete, it's May . . .'

'So? It could be November; that wouldn't change the Fair Practices law.'

'Graduation's in a month . . . Senior class photographs. Year-book portraits.'

Daniels understood instantly. He took his pipe from his mouth and started for the door.

'Come with me.'

*   *   *

251

His name was Alan Pace. He was a senior and his curriculum was not centered on business administration; he was a government major. He lived off campus on Church Street near the Hamden town line. According to his records, Alan Pace was an excellent student, consistent honors in all subjects, a fellowship in the offing at the Maxwell School of Political Science at Syracuse. He had spent twenty-eight months in the army, four more than was required of him. As with most veterans, his university extracurricular activities were minimal.

While Pace was in service, he was an officer attached to inventory and supply. He had volunteered for a four-month extended tour of duty in the Saigon Corps – a fact noted with emphasis on his reapplication form. Alan Pace had given four months of his life more than necessary to his country. Alan Pace was obviously an honorable man in these days of cynicism.

He was a winner, thought Matlock.

The drive out Church Street toward Hamden gave Matlock the chance to clear his mind. He had to take one thing at a time; one item crossed off – on to the next. He couldn't allow his imagination to interpret isolated facts beyond their meaning. He couldn't lump everything together and total a sum larger than the parts.

It was entirely possible that this Alan Pace played a solo game. Unattached, unencumbered.

But it wasn't logical.

Pace's apartment house was an undistinguished brown brick building, so common on the outskirts of cities. Once – forty or fifty years ago – it had been the proud symbol of a rising middle class extending themselves out beyond the cement confines toward the country, but not so courageous as to leave the city completely. It wasn't so much run down as it was . . . not spruced up. The most glaring aspect of the apartment house to Matlock,

252

however, was that it seemed to be a most unlikely place for a student to reside.

But he was there now; Peter Daniels had ascertained that.

Pace had not wanted to unlatch the door. It was only Matlock's strong emphasis on two points that made the student relent. The first point was that he wasn't from the police; the second, the name Rocco Aiello.

'What do you want? I've got a lot of work to do; I don't have time to talk. I've got comprehensives tomorrow.'

'May I sit down?'

'What for? I told you, I'm busy.' The tall, brown-haired student crossed back to his desk, piled with books and papers. The apartment was neat – except for the desk – and quite large. There were doors and short corridors leading to other doors. It was the sort of apartment that usually was shared by four or five students. But Alan Pace had no roommates.

'I'll sit down anyway. You owe that much to Rocco.'

'What does that mean?'

'Just that Rocco was my friend. I was the one with him the other night when you brought him a tab to sign. Remember? And he was good to you . . . He's dead.'

'I know. I read about it. I'm sorry. But I didn't owe him anything.'

'But you bought from him.'

'I don't know what you're talking about.'

'Come on, Pace. You don't have the time and neither do I. You're not connected to Aiello's death, I know that. But I've got to have information, and you're going to supply it.'

'You're talking to the wrong person. I don't know you. I don't know *anything*.'

'I know *you*. I've got a complete rundown on you.

253

Aiello and I were considering going into business together. Now, that's none of your concern, I realize that, but we exchanged . . . personnel information. I'm coming to you because, frankly, Rocco's gone and there are areas that need filling. I'm really asking a favor, and I'll pay for it.'

'I told you, I'm not your man. I hardly knew Aiello. I picked up a few dollars waiting tables. Sure, I heard rumors, but that's *all*. I don't know what you want, but you'd better go to someone else.'

Pace was sharp, thought Matlock. He was disengaging himself but not foolishly claiming complete innocence. On the other hand, perhaps he was telling the truth. There was only one way to find out.

'I'll try again . . . Fifteen months in Vietnam. Saigon, Da Nang; excursions to Hong Kong, Japan. I&S officer; the dullest, most exasperating kind of work for a young man with the potential that earns him honors at a very tough university.'

'I&S was good duty; no combat, no sweat. Everybody made the tourist hops. Check the R&R route sheets.'

'Then,' continued Matlock without acknowledging Pace's interruption, 'the dedicated officer returns to civilian life. After a four-month voluntary extension in Saigon – I'm surprised you weren't caught up on *that* one – he comes back with enough money to make the proper investments, and certainly not from his army pay. He's one of the biggest suppliers in New Haven. Do you want me to go on?'

Pace stood by the desk and seemed to stop breathing. He stared at Matlock, his face white. When he spoke, it was the voice of a frightened young man.

'You can't prove anything. I haven't done anything. My army record, my record here – they're both good. They're very good.'

'The best. Unblemished. They're records to be proud of;

254

I mean that sincerely. And I wouldn't want to do anything
to spoil them; I mean that, too.'

'You couldn't. I'm clean!'

'No, you're not. You're up to your fellowship neck.
Aiello made that *clear*. On *paper*.'

'You're lying!'

'You're stupid. You think Aiello would do business with
anyone he didn't run a check on? Do you think he'd be
allowed to? He kept very extensive books, Pace, and I've
got them. I told you; we were going into business together.
You don't form a partnership without audit disclosures,
you should know that.'

Pace spoke barely above a whisper. 'There are no books
like that. There never are. Cities, towns, codes. No names.
Never any names.'

'Then why am I here?'

'You saw me in Hartford; you're reaching for a connection.'

'You know better than that. Don't be foolish.'

Matlock's quickly put implications were too much for
the tall, shocked young man. 'Why did you come to me?
I'm not that important. You say you know about me; then
you know I'm not important.'

'I told you. I need information. I'm reluctant to go
to the high priests, anyone with real authority. I don't
want to be at a disadvantage. That's why I'm willing to
pay; why I'm prepared to tear up everything I've got
on you.'

The prospect of being cut free of the stranger's grip was
obviously all that was on Pace's mind. He replied quickly.

'Suppose I can't answer your questions? You'll think
I'm lying.'

'You can't be worse off. All you can do is try me.'

'Go ahead.'

'I met a girl . . . from a nearby college. I met her under

255

circumstances that can only be described as professional prostitution. Professional in every sense of the word. Appointments, set fees, no prior knowledge of clients, the works . . . What do you know about it?'

Pace took several steps toward Matlock. 'What do you mean, what do I know? I know it's there. What else is there to know?'

'How extensive?'

'All over. It's not news.'

'It is to me.'

'You don't know the scene. Take a walk around a few college towns.'

Matlock swallowed. Was he really that far out of touch? 'Suppose I were to tell you I'm familiar with a lot of . . . college towns?'

'I'd say your circles were cubed. Also, I'm no part of that action. What else?'

'Let's stick to this for a minute . . . Why?'

'Why what?'

'Why do the girls do it?'

'Bread, man. Why does anyone do anything?'

'You're too intelligent to believe that . . . Is it organized?'

'I guess so. I told you, I'm no part of it.'

'Watch it! I've got a lot of paper on you . . .'

'All right. Yes, it's organized. Everything's organized. If it's going to work.'

'Where *specifically* are the operations?'

'I *told* you! All *over*.'

'Inside the colleges?'

'No, not inside. On the outskirts. A couple of miles usually, if the campuses are rural. Old houses, away from the suburbs. If they're in cities – downtown hotels, private clubs, apartment houses. But not *here*.'

'Are we talking about . . . Columbia, Harvard, Radcliffe, Smith, Holyoke? And points south?'

256

'Everyone always forgets Princeton,' replied Pace with a wry smile. 'A lot of nice old estates in those back roads . . . Yes, we're talking about those places.'

'I never would have believed it . . .' Matlock spoke as much to himself as to Pace. 'But, *why*? Don't give me the "bread" routine . . .'

'Bread is *freedom*, man! For these kids it's freedom. They're not psyched-up freaks; they're not running around in black berets and field jackets. Very few of us are. We've *learned*. Get the money, fella, and the nice people will like you . . . Also, whether you've noticed it or not, the straight money's not as easy to come by as it once was. Most of these kids need it.'

'The girl I mentioned before; I gathered she was forced into it.'

'Oh, Jesus, nobody's *forced*! That's crap.'

'She was. She mentioned a few things . . . Controls is as good a word as any. Courts, doctors, even jobs . . .'

'I wouldn't know anything about that.'

'And afterward. Making contact later – perhaps a few years later. Plain old-fashioned blackmail. Just as I'm blackmailing you now.'

'Then she was in trouble before; this girl, I mean. If it's a bummer, she doesn't have to make the trip. Unless she's into somebody and owes what she can't pay for.'

'Who is Nimrod?' Matlock asked the question softly, without emphasis. But the question caused the young man to turn and walk away.

'I don't know that. I don't have that information.'

Matlock got out of the chair and stood motionless. 'I'll ask you just once more, and if I don't get an answer, I'll walk out the door and you'll be finished. A very promising life will be altered drastically – if you have a life . . . Who is Nimrod?'

The boy whipped around and Matlock saw the fear again. The fear he had seen on Lucas Herron's face, in Lucas Herron's eyes.

'So help me Christ, I can't answer that!'

'Can't or won't?'

'Can't. I *don't know*!'

'I think you do. But I said I'd only ask you once. That's it.' Matlock started for the apartment door without looking at the student.

'No! . . . Goddamn it, I *don't know*! . . . How *could* I know? You can't!' Pace ran to Matlock's side.

'Can't what?'

'Whatever you said you'd do . . . Listen to me! I don't know who they are! I don't have . . .'

'They?'

Pace looked puzzled. 'Yeah . . . I guess "they." I don't know. I don't have any contact. Others do; I don't. They haven't bothered me.'

'But you're aware of them.' A statement.

'Aware . . . Yes, I'm aware. But who, honest to God, *no*!'

Matlock turned and faced the student. 'We'll compromise. For now. Tell me what you *do* know.'

And the frightened young man did. And as the words came forth, the fear infected James Matlock.

Nimrod was an unseen master puppeteer. Faceless, formless, but with frightening, viable authority. It wasn't a *he* or a *they* – it was a *force*, according to Alan Pace. A complex abstraction that had its elusive tentacles in every major university in the Northeast, every municipality that served the academic landscape, all the financial pyramids that funded the complicated structures of New England's higher education. 'And points south,' if the rumors had foundation.

Narcotics was only one aspect, the craw in the throats

258

of the criminal legions – the immediate reason for the May conference, the Corsican letter.

Beyond drugs and their profits, the Nimrod imprimatur was stamped on scores of college administrations. Pace was convinced that curriculums were being shaped, university personnel hired and fired, degree and scholarship policies, all were expedited on the Nimrod organization's instructions. Matlock's memory flashed back to Carlyle. To Carlyle's assistant dean of admissions – a Nimrod appointee, according to the dead Loring. To Archer Beeson, rapidly rising in the history department; to a coach of varsity soccer; to a dozen other faculty and staff names on Loring's list.

How many more were there? How deep was the infiltration?

Why?

The prostitution rings were subsidiary accommodations. Recruitments were made by the child-whores among themselves; addresses were provided, fees established. Young flesh with ability and attractiveness could find its way to Nimrod and make the pact. And there was 'freedom,' there was 'bread' in the pact with Nimrod.

And 'no-one was hurt'; it was a victimless crime.

'No crime at all, just freedom, man. No pressures over the head. No screaming zonkers over scholarship points.'

Alan Pace saw a great deal of good in the elusive, practical Nimrod. More than good.

'You think it's all so different from the outside – straight? You're wrong, mister. It's mini-America: organized, computerized, and very heavy with the corporate structure. Hell, it's patterned on the American syndrome; it's company *policy*, man! It's GM, ITT, and Ma Bell – only someone was smart enough to organize the groovy groves of academe. And it's growing fast. Don't fight it. Join it.'

259

'Is that what you're going to do?' asked Matlock.

'It's the way, man. It's the faith. For all I know *you're* with it now. Could be, you're a recruiter. You guys are everywhere; I've been expecting you.'

'Suppose I'm not?'

'Then you're out of your head. And over it, too.'

Chapter 27

If one watched the white station wagon and its driver heading back toward the center of New Haven, one would have thought – if he thought at all – that it was a rich car, suitable to a wealthy suburb, the man at the wheel appropriately featured for the vehicle.

Such an observer would not know that the driver was barely cognizant of the traffic, numbed by the revelations he'd learned within the hour; an exhausted man who hadn't slept in forty-eight hours, who had the feeling that he was holding on to a thin rope above an infinite chasm, expecting any instant that his lifeline would be severed, plunging him into the infinite mist.

Matlock tried his best to suspend whatever thought processes he was capable of. The years, the specific months during which he'd run his academic race against self-imposed schedules had taught him that the mind – at least his mind – could not function properly when the forces of exhaustion and overexposure converged.

Above all, he had to function.

He was in uncharted waters. Seas where tiny islands were peopled by grotesque inhabitants. Julian Dunoises, Lucas Herrons; the Bartolozzis, the Aiellos, the Sharpes, the Stocktons, and the Paces. The poisoned and the poisoners.

Nimrod.

Uncharted waters?

No, they weren't uncharted, thought Matlock.

They were well traveled. And the travelers were the cynics of the planet.

261

He drove to the Sheraton Hotel and took a room.

He sat on the edge of the bed and placed a telephone call to Howard Stockton at Carmount. Stockton was out.

In brusque, officious tones, he told the Carmount switchboard that Stockton was to return his call – he looked at his watch; it was ten of two – in four hours. At six o'clock. He gave the Sheraton number and hung up.

He needed at least four hours' sleep. He wasn't sure when he would sleep again.

He picked up the telephone once more and requested a wake-up call at five-forty-five.

As his head sank to the pillow, he brought his arm up to his eyes. Through the cloth of his shirt he felt the stubble of his beard. He'd have to go to a barbershop; he'd left his suitcase in the white station wagon. He'd been too tired, too involved to remember to bring it to his room.

The short, sharp three rings of the telephone signified the Sheraton's adherence to his instructions. It was exactly quarter to six. Fifteen minutes later there was another ring, this one longer, more normal. It was precisely six, and the caller was Howard Stockton.

'I'll make this short, Matlock. You got a contact. Only he doesn't want to meet *inside* the Sail and Ski. You go to the East Gorge slope – they use it in spring and summer for tourists to look at the scenery – and take the lift up to the top. You be there at eight-thirty this evenin'. He'll have a man at the top. That's all I've got to say. It's none of *mah business*!'

Stockton slammed down the telephone and the echo rang in Matlock's ear.

But he'd made it! *He'd made it!* He had made the contact with Nimrod! With the conference.

He walked up the dark trail toward the ski lift. Ten

262

dollars made the attendant at the Sail and Ski parking lot understand his problem: the nice-looking fellow in the station wagon had an assignation. The husband wasn't expected till later – and, what the hell, that's life. The parking lot attendant was very cooperative.

When he reached the East Gorge slope, the rain, which had threatened all day, began to come down. In Connecticut, April showers were somehow always May thunderstorms, and Matlock was annoyed that he hadn't thought to buy a raincoat.

He looked around at the deserted lift, its high double lines silhouetted against the increasing rain, shining like thick strands of ship hemp in a fogged harbor. There was a tiny, almost invisible light in the shack which housed the complicated, hulking machines that made the lines ascend. Matlock approached the door and knocked. A small, wiry-looking man opened the door and peered at him.

'You the fella goin' up?'

'I guess I am.'

'What's your name?'

'Matlock.'

'Guess you are. Know how to catch a crossbar?'

'I've skied. Arm looped, tail on the slat, feet on the pipe.'

'Don't need no help from me. I'll start it, you get it.'

'Fine.'

'You're gonna get wet.'

'I know.'

Matlock positioned himself to the right of the entrance pit as the lumbering machinery started up. The lines creaked slowly and then began their halting countermoves, and a crossbar approached. He slid himself on to the lift, pressed his feet against the foottrail, and locked the bar in

263

front of his waist. He felt the swinging motion of the lines lifting him off the ground.

He was on his way to the top of the East Gorge, on his way to his contact with Nimrod. As he swung upward, ten feet above the ground, the rain became, instead of annoying, exhilarating. He was coming to the end of his journey, his race. Whoever met him at the top would be utterly confused. He counted on that, he'd planned it that way. If everything the murdered Loring and the very-much-alive Greenberg had told him was true, it couldn't be any other way. The total secrecy of the conference; the delegates, unknown to each other; the oath of 'Omerta,' the subculture's violent insistence on codes and countercodes to protect its inhabitants – it *was* all true. He'd seen it all in operation. And such complicated logistics – when sharply interrupted – inevitably led to suspicion and fear and ultimately confusion. It was the confusion Matlock counted on.

Lucas Herron had accused him of being influenced by plots and counterplots. Well, he wasn't *influenced* by them – he merely *understood* them. That was different. It was this understanding which had led him one step away from Nimrod.

The rain came harder now, whipped by the wind which was stronger off the ground than on it. Matlock's crossbar swayed and dipped, more so each time he reached a rung up the slope. The tiny light in the machine shack was now barely visible in the darkness and the rain. He judged that he was nearly halfway to the top.

There was a jolt; the machinery stopped. Matlock gripped the waist guard and peered above him through the rain trying to see what obstruction had hit the wheel or the rung. There was none.

He turned awkwardly in the narrow perch and squinted his eyes down the slope toward the shack. There was no light now, not even the slightest illumination. He held his hand up in front of his forehead, keeping the rain away as best he could. He had to be mistaken, the downpour was blurring his vision, perhaps the pole was in his line of sight. He leaned first to the right, then to the left. But still there was no light from the bottom of the hill.

Perhaps the fuses had blown. If so, they would have taken the bulb in the shack with them. Or a short. It was raining, and ski lifts did not ordinarily operate in the rain.

He looked beneath him. The ground was perhaps fifteen feet away. If he suspended himself from the footrail, the drop would only be eight or nine feet. He could handle that. He would walk the rest of the way up the slope. He had to do it quickly, however. It might take as long as twenty minutes to climb to the top, there was no way of telling. He couldn't take the chance of his contact's panicking, deciding to leave before he got to him.

'Stay right where you are! Don't unlatch that harness!'

The voice shot out of the darkness, cutting through the rain and wind. Its harsh command paralyzed Matlock as much from the shock of surprise as from fear. The man stood beneath him, to the right of the lines. He was dressed in a raincoat and some kind of cap. It was impossible to see his face or even determine his size.

'Who are you?! What do you want?!'

'I'm the man you came to meet. I want to see that paper in your pocket. Throw it down.'

'I'll show you the paper when I see *your* copy. That's the deal! That's the deal I made.'

'You don't understand, Matlock. Just throw the paper down. That's all.'

'What the hell are you talking about?!'

265

The glare of a powerful flashlight blinded him. He reached for the guard rail latch.

'Don't touch that! Keep your hands straight out or you're dead!'

The core of the high-intensity light shifted from his face to his chest, and for several seconds all Matlock saw were a thousand flashing spots inside his eyes. As his sight returned, he could see that the man below him was moving closer to the lines, swinging the flashlight toward the ground for a path. In the glow of the beam, he also saw that the man held a large, ugly automatic in his right hand. The blinding light returned to his face, now shining directly beneath him.

'Don't threaten me, punk!' yelled Matlock, remembering the effect his anger had on Stockton at four that morning. 'Put that goddamn gun away and help me down! We haven't much time and I don't like games!'

The effect now was not the same. Instead, the man beneath him began to laugh, and the laugh was sickening. It was, more than anything else, utterly genuine. The man on the ground was enjoying himself.

'You're very funny. You look funny sitting there on your ass in midair. You know what you look like? You look like one of those bobbing monkey targets in a shooting gallery! *You know what I mean?* Now, cut the bullshit and throw down the paper!'

He laughed again, and at the sound everything was suddenly clear to Matlock.

He hadn't made a contact. He hadn't cornered anyone. All his careful planning, all his thought-out actions. All for nothing. He was no nearer Nimrod now than he was before he knew Nimrod existed.

He'd been trapped.

Still, he had to try. It was all that was left him now.

'You're making the mistake of your life!'

266

'Oh, for Christ's sake, knock it off! Give me the paper! We've been looking for that fucking thing for a week! My orders are to get it *now*!'

'I can't give it to you.'

'I'll blow your head off!'

'I said I *can't*! I didn't say I *wouldn't*!'

'Don't shit me. You've got it on you! You wouldn't have come here without it!'

'It's in a packet strapped to the small of my back.'

'Get it out!'

'I told you, I can't! I'm sitting on a four-inch slat of wood with a footrail and I'm damn near twenty feet in the air!'

His words were half lost in the whipping rain. The man below was frustrated, impatient.

'*I said get it out!*'

'I'll have to drop down. I can't reach the straps!' Matlock yelled to be heard. 'I can't *do* anything! I haven't got a gun!'

The man with the large, ugly automatic moved back several feet from the lines. He pointed both the powerful beam and his weapon at Matlock.

'OK, come on down! You cough wrong and your head's blown off!'

Matlock undid the latch, feeling like a small boy on top of a ferris wheel wondering what could happen if the wheel stopped permanently and the safety bar fell off.

He held on to the footrail and let the rest of him swing beneath it. He dangled in the air, the rain soaking him, the beam of light blinding him. He had to think now, he had to create an instant strategy. His life was worth far less than the lives at Windsor Shoals to such men as the man on the ground.

'Shine the light down! I can't see!'

'Fuck that! Just drop!'

He dropped.

And the second he hit the earth, he let out a loud, painful scream and reached for his leg.

'Aaaahhh! My ankle, my foot! I broke my goddamn ankle!' He twisted and turned on the wet overgrowth, writhing in pain.

'Shut up! Get me that paper! *Now!*'

'*Jesus Christ!* What do you *want* from me? My ankle's turned *around*! It's *broken*!'

'Tough! Give me the paper!'

Matlock lay prostrate on the ground, his head moving back and forth, his neck straining to stand the pain. He spoke between short gasps.

'Strap's here. Undo the strap.' He tore at his shirt displaying part of the canvas belt.

'Undo it yourself. Hurry up!'

But the man came closer. He wasn't sure. And closer. The beam of light was just above Matlock now. Then it moved to his midsection and Matlock could see the large barrel of the ugly black automatic.

It was the second, the instant he'd waited for.

He whipped his right hand up towards the weapon, simultaneously springing his whole body against the legs of the man in the raincoat. He held the automatic's barrel, forcing it with all his strength toward the ground. The gun fired twice, the impact of the explosions nearly shattering Matlock's hand, the sounds partially muted by wet earth and the slashing rain.

The man was beneath him now, twisting on his side, thrashing with his legs and free arm against the heavier Matlock. Matlock flung himself on the pinned arm and sank his teeth into the wrist above the hand holding the weapon. He bit into the flesh until he could feel the blood spurting out, mingled with the cold rain.

The man released the automatic, screaming in anguish. Matlock grabbed for the gun, wrested it free, and smashed it repeatedly into the man's face. The powerful flashlight was in the tall grass, its beam directed at nothing but drenched foliage.

Matlock crouched over the half-conscious, bloody face of his former captor. He was out of breath, and the sickening taste of the man's blood was still in his mouth. He spat a half dozen times trying to cleanse his teeth, his throat.

'OK!' He grabbed the man's collar and yanked his head up. 'Now you tell me what happened! This was a trap, wasn't it?'

'The paper! I gotta get the paper.' The man was hardly audible.

'I was *trapped, wasn't I*! The whole last week was a trap!'

'Yeah . . . Yeah. The paper.'

'That paper's pretty important, isn't it?'

'They'll kill you . . . they'll kill you to get it! You stand no chance, mister . . . No chance . . .'

'Who's *they*?!'

'I don't know . . . don't know!'

'*Who's Nimrod?*'

'I don't know . . . "Omerta"! . . . "Omerta"!'

The man opened his eyes wide, and in the dim spill of the fallen flashlight, Matlock saw that something had happened to his victim. Some thought, some concept overpowered his tortured imagination. It was painful to watch. It was too close to the sight of the panicked Lucas Herron, the terrified Alan Pace.

'Come on, I'll get you down the slope . . .'

It was as far as he got. From the depths of his lost control, the man with the blood-soaked face lunged forward, making a last desperate attempt to reach the gun in Matlock's right hand. Matlock yanked back; instinctively he fired the weapon. Blood and pieces of flesh flew everywhere. Half the man's neck was blown off.

269

Matlock stood up slowly. The smoke of the automatic lingered above the dead man, the rain forcing it downward toward the earth.

He reached into the grass for the flashlight, and as he bent over he began to vomit.

Chapter 28

Ten minutes later he watched the parking lot below him
from the trunk of a huge maple tree fifty yards up the trail.
The new leaves partially protected him from the pouring
rain, but his clothes were filthy, covered with wet dirt and
blood. He saw the white station wagon near the front of
the area, next to the stone gate entrance of the Sail and Ski.
There wasn't much activity now; no automobiles entered,
and those drivers inside would wait until the deluge
stopped before venturing out on the roads. The parking
lot attendant he'd given the ten dollars to was talking
with a uniformed doorman under the carport roof of the
restaurant entrance. Matlock wanted to race to the station
wagon and drive away as fast as he could, but he knew
the sight of his clothes would alarm the two men, make
them wonder what had happened on the East Gorge slope.
There was nothing to do but wait, wait until someone came
out and distracted them, or both went inside.

He hated the waiting. More than hating it, he was
frightened by it. There'd been no-one he could see or
hear near the wheel shack, but that didn't mean no-one
was there. Nimrod's dead contact probably had a partner
somewhere, waiting as Matlock was waiting now. If the
dead man was found, they'd stop him, kill him – if not
for revenge, for the Corsican paper.

He had no choice now. He'd gone beyond his depth,
his abilities. He'd been manipulated by Nimrod as he'd
been maneuvered by the men of the Justice Department.
He would telephone Jason Greenberg and do whatever
Greenberg told him to do.

271

In a way, he was glad his part of it was over, or soon would be. He still felt the impulse of commitment, but there was nothing more he could do. He had failed.

Down below, the restaurant entrance opened and a waitress signaled the uniformed doorman. He and the attendant walked up the steps to speak with the girl.

Matlock ran down to the gravel and darted in front of the grills of the cars parked on the edge of the lot. Between automobiles he kept looking toward the restaurant door. The waitress had given the doorman a container of coffee. All three were smoking cigarettes, all three were laughing.

He rounded the circle and crouched in front of the station wagon. He crept to the door window and saw to his relief that the keys were in the ignition. He took a deep breath, opened the door as quietly as possible, and leaped inside. Instead of slamming it, he pulled the door shut quickly, silently, so as to extinguish the interior light without calling attention to the sound. The two men and the waitress were still talking, still laughing, oblivious.

He settled himself in the seat, switched on the ignition, threw the gears into reverse, and roared backward in front of the gate. He raced out between the stone posts and started down the long road to the highway.

Back under the roof, on the steps by the front door, the three employees were momentarily startled. Then, from being startled they became quickly bewildered – and even a little curious. For, from the rear of the parking lot, they could hear the deep-throated roar of a second, more powerful engine. Bright headlights flicked on, distorted by the downpour of rain, and a long black limousine rushed forward.

272

The wheels screeched as the ominous-looking automobile swerved toward the stone posts. The huge car went to full throttle and raced after the station wagon.

There wasn't much traffic on the highway, but he still felt he'd make better time taking the back roads into Carlyle. He decided to go straight to Kressel's house, despite Sam's proclivity toward hysteria. Together they could both call Greenberg. He had just brutally, horribly killed another human being, and whether it was justified or not, the shock was still with him. He suspected it would be with him for the reminder of his life. He wasn't sure Kressel was the man to see.

But there was no-one else. Unless he returned to his apartment and stayed there until a federal agent picked him up. And then again, instead of an agent, there might well be an emissary from Nimrod.

There was a winding S-curve in the road. He remembered that it came before a long stretch through farmland where he could make up time. The highway was straighter, but the back roads were shorter as long as there was no traffic to speak of. As he rounded the final half-circle, he realized that he was gripping the wheel so hard his forearms ached. It was the muscular defenses of his body taking over, controlling his shaking limbs, steadying the car with sheer unfeeling strength.

The flat stretch appeared; the rain had let up. He pushed the accelerator to the floor and felt the station wagon surge forward in overdrive.

He looked twice, then three times, up at his rear-view mirror, wary of patrol cars. He saw headlights behind him coming closer. He looked down at his speedometer. It read eighty-seven miles per hour and still the lights in the mirror gained on him.

The instincts of the hunted came swiftly to the surface;

273

he knew the automobile behind him was no police car. There was no siren penetrating the wet stillness, no flashing light heralding authority.

He pushed his right leg forward, pressing the accelerator beyond the point of achieving anything further from the engine. His speedometer reached ninety-four miles per hour – the wagon was not capable of greater speed.

The headlights were directly behind him now. The unknown pursuer was feet, inches from his rear bumper. Suddenly the headlights veered to the left, and the car came alongside the white station wagon.

It was the same black limousine he had seen after Loring's murder! The same huge automobile that had raced out of the darkened driveway minutes after the massacre at Windsor Shoals! Matlock tried to keep part of his mind on the road ahead, part on the single driver of the car, which was crowding him to the far right of the road. The station wagon vibrated under the impact of the enormous speed; he found it more and more difficult to hold the wheel.

And then he saw the barrel of the pistol pointed at him through the window of the adjacent automobile. He saw the look of desperation in the darting eyes behind the outstretched arm, trying to steady itself for a clean line of fire.

He heard the shots and felt the glass shattering into his face and over the front seat. He slammed his foot into the brake and spun the steering wheel to the right, jumping the shoulder of the road, careening violently into and through a barbed-wire fence and on to a rock-strewn field. The wagon lunged into the grass, perhaps fifty or sixty feet, and then slammed into a cluster of rocks, a property demarcation. The headlights smashed and went out, the grill buckled. He was thrown into the dashboard, only his upheld arms keeping his head from crashing into the windshield.

But he was conscious, and the instincts of the hunted would not leave him.

He heard a car door open and close, and he knew the killer was coming into the field after his quarry. After the Corsican paper. He felt a trickle of blood rolling down his forehead – whether it was the graze of a bullet or a laceration from the flying glass, he couldn't be sure – but he was grateful it was there. He'd need it now, he needed the sight of blood on his forehead. He remained slumped over the wheel, immobile, silent.

And under his jacket he held the ugly automatic he had taken from the dead man in the raincoat on the slope of East Gorge. It was pointed under his left arm at the door.

He could hear the mushed crunch of footsteps on the soft earth outside the station wagon. He could literally feel – as a blind man feels – the face peering through the shattered glass looking at him. He heard the click of the door button as it was pushed in and the creaking of the hinges as the heavy panel was pulled open.

A hand grabbed his shoulder. Matlock fired his weapon.

The roar was deafening; the scream of the wounded man pierced the drenched darkness. Matlock leaped out of the seat and slammed the full weight of his body against the killer, who had grabbed his left arm in pain. Wildly, inaccurately, Matlock pistol-whipped the man about his face and neck until he fell to the ground. The man's gun was nowhere to be seen, his hands were empty. Matlock put his foot on the man's throat and pressed.

'I'll stop when you signal you're going to talk to me, you son of a bitch! Otherwise I *don't* stop!'

The man sputtered, his eyes bulged. He raised his right hand in supplication.

Matlock took his foot away and knelt on the ground

over the man. He was heavy set, black-haired, with the blunt features of a brute killer.

'Who sent you after me? How did you know this car?'

The man raised his head slightly as though to answer. Instead, the killer whipped his right hand into his waist, pulled out a knife, and rolled sharply to his left, yanking his gorilla-like knee up into Matlock's groin. The knife slashed into Matlock's shirt, and he knew as he felt the steel point crease his flesh that he'd come as close as he would ever come to being killed.

He crashed the barrel of the heavy automatic into the man's temple. It was enough. The killer's head snapped back; blood matted itself around the hairline. Matlock stood up and placed his foot on the hand with the knife.

Soon the killer's eyes opened.

And during the next five minutes, Matlock did what he never thought he would be capable of doing – he tortured another man. He tortured the killer with the killer's own knife, penetrating the skin around and below the eyes, puncturing the lips with the same steel point that had scraped his own flesh. And when the man screamed, Matlock smashed his mouth with the barrel of the automatic and broke pieces of ivory off the killer's teeth.

It was not long.

'The paper!'

'What else?'

The writhing killer moaned and spat blood, but would not speak. Matlock did; quietly, in total conviction, in complete sincerity.

'You'll answer me or I'll push this blade down through your eyes. I don't care any more. Believe me.'

'The old man!' The guttural words came from deep inside the man's throat. 'He said he wrote it down . . . No-one knows . . . You talked to him . . ..'

'What old . . .' Matlock stopped as a terrifying thought

came into his mind. *'Lucas Herron?! Is that who you mean?!'*

'He said he wrote it down. They think you know. Maybe he lied . . . For Christ's sake, he could have lied . . .'

The killer fell into unconsciousness.

Matlock stood up slowly, his hands shaking, his whole body shivering. He looked up at the road, at the huge black limousine standing silently in the diminishing rain. It would be his last gamble, his ultimate effort.

But something was stirring in his brain, something elusive but palpable. He had to trust that feeling, as he had come to trust the instincts of the hunter and the hunted.

The old man!

The answer lay somewhere in Lucas Herron's house.

Chapter 29

He parked the limousine a quarter of a mile from Herron's Nest and walked toward the house on the side of the road, prepared to jump into the bordering woods should any cars approach.

None did.

He came upon one house, then another, and in each case he raced past, watching the lighted windows to see if anyone was looking out.

No-one was.

He reached the edge of Herron's property and crouched to the ground. Slowly, cautiously, silently he made his way to the driveway. The house was dark; there were no cars, no people, no signs of life. Only death.

He walked up the flagstone path and his eye caught sight of an official-looking document, barely visible in the darkness, tacked on to the front door. He approached it and lit a match. It was a sheriff's seal of closure.

One more crime, thought Matlock.

He went around to the back of the house, and as he stood in front of the patio door, he remembered vividly the sight of Herron racing across his manicured lawn into the forbidding green wall which he parted so deftly and into which he disappeared so completely.

There was another sheriff's seal on the back door. This one was glued to a pane of glass.

Matlock removed the automatic from his belt and as quietly as possible broke the small-paned window to the left of the seal. He opened the door and walked in.

The first thing that struck him was the darkness. Light

and dark were relative, as he'd come to understand during the past week. The night had light which the eyes could adjust to; the daylight was often deceptive, filled with shadows and misty blind spots. But inside Herron's house the darkness was complete. He lit a match and understood why.

The windows in the small kitchen was covered with shades. Only they weren't ordinary window shades, they were custom built. The cloth was heavy and attached to the frames with vertical runners, latched at the sills by large aluminum hasps. He approached the window over the sink and lit another match. Not only was the shade thicker than ordinary, but the runners and the stretch lock at the bottom insured that the shade would remain absolutely flat against the whole frame. It was doubtful that any light could go out or come in through the window.

Herron's desire – or need – for privacy had been extraordinary. And if all the windows in all the rooms were sealed, it would make his task easier.

Striking a third match, he walked into Herron's living room. What he saw in the flickering light caused him to stop in his tracks, his breath cut short.

The entire room was a shambles. Books were strewn on the floor, furniture overturned and ripped apart, rugs upended, even sections of the wall smashed. He could have been walking into his own apartment the night of the Beeson dinner. Herron's living room had been thoroughly, desperately searched.

He went back to the kitchen to see if his preoccupation with the window shades and the darkness had played tricks on his eyes. They had. Every drawer was pulled open, every cabinet ransacked. And then he saw on the floor of a broom closet two flashlights. One was a casement, the other a long-stemmed Sportsman. The first wouldn't light, the second did.

He walked rapidly back into the living room and tried to orient himself, checking the windows with the beam of the flashlight. Every window was covered, every shade latched at the sill.

Across the narrow hallway in front of the narrower stairs was an open door. It led to Herron's study, which was, if possible, more of a mess than his living room. Two file cabinets were lying on their sides, the backs torn off; the large leather-topped desk was pulled from the wall, splintered, smashed on every flat surface. Parts of the wall, as the living room, were broken into. Matlock assumed these were sections which had sounded hollow when tapped.

Upstairs, the two small bedrooms and the bath were equally dismantled, equally dissected.

He walked back down the stairs, even the steps had been pried loose from their treads.

Lucas Herron's home had been searched by professionals. What could he find that they hadn't? He wandered back into the living room and sat down on what was left of an armchair. He had the sinking feeling that his last effort would end in failure also. He lit a cigarette and tried to organize his thoughts.

Whoever had searched the house had not found what they were looking for. Or had they? There was no way to tell, really. Except that the brute killer in the field had screamed that the old man 'had written it down.' As if the fact was almost as important as the desperately coveted Corsican document. Yet he had added: '. . . maybe he lied, he could have lied.' *Lied?* Why would a man in the last extremity of terror add that qualification to something so vital?

The assumption had to be that in the intricate delicacy of a mind foundering on the brink of madness, the worst evil was rejected. Had to be rejected so as to hold on to what was left of sanity.

No . . . No, they had not found whatever it was they *had to find*. And since they hadn't found it after such exhaustive, extraordinary labors – it didn't *exist*.

But he knew it did.

Herron may have been involved with Nimrod's world, but he was not born of it. His was not a comfortable relationship – it was a tortured one. Somewhere, someplace he had left an indictment. He was too good a man not to. There had been a great decency in Lucas Herron. Somewhere . . . someplace.

But where?

He got out of the chair and paced in the darkness of the room, flicking the flashlight on and off, more as a nervous gesture than for illumination.

He re-examined minutely every word, every expression used by Lucas that early evening four days ago. He was the hunter again, tracking the spoor, testing the wind for the scent. And he was close; goddamn it, he was close! . . . Herron had *known* from the second he'd opened his front door what Matlock was after. That instantaneous, fleeting moment of recognition had been in his eyes. It had been unmistakable to Matlock. He'd even said as much to the old man, and the old man had laughed and accused him of being influenced by plots and counterplots.

But there'd been something else. Before the plots and counterplots . . . Something *inside*. In this room. Before Herron suggested sitting *outside* . . . Only he hadn't *suggested*, he'd made a statement, given a command.

And just before he'd given the command to rear-march toward the backyard patio, he'd walked in silently, *walked in silently*, and startled Matlock. He had opened the swinging door, *carrying* two filled glasses, and Matlock *hadn't heard* him. Matlock pushed the button on the flashlight and shot the beam to the base of the kitchen door. There was no rug, nothing to muffle footsteps – it was

281

a hardwood floor. He crossed to the open swing-hinged door, walked through the frame, and shut it. Then he pushed it swiftly open in the same direction Lucas Herron had pushed it carrying the two drinks. The hinges clicked as such hinges do if they are old and the door is pushed quickly – *normally*. He let the door swing shut and then he pressed against it slowly, inch by inch.

It was silent.

Lucas Herron had made the drinks and then *silently* had eased himself back into the living room so he wouldn't be heard. So he could observe Matlock without Matlock's knowing it. And then he'd given his firm command for the two of them to go outside.

Matlock forced his memory to recall *precisely* what Lucas Herron said and did at that *precise* moment.

'. . . we'll go out on the patio. It's too nice a day to stay inside. Let's go.'

Then, *without waiting for an answer*, even a mildly enthusiastic agreement, Herron had walked *rapidly* back through the kitchen door. No surface politeness, none of the courtly manners one expected from Lucas.

He had given an order, the firm command of an officer and a gentleman.

By Act of Congress.

That was *it*! Matlock swung the beam of light over the writing desk.

The photograph! The photograph of the marine officer holding the map and the Thompson automatic in some tiny section of jungle on an insignificant island in the South Pacific.

'I keep that old photograph to remind myself that time wasn't always so devastating.'

At the precise moment Herron walked through the door, Matlock had been looking closely at the photograph! The fact that he was doing so disturbed the old man, disturbed him enough for him to insist that they go outside instantly. In a curt, abrupt manner so unlike him.

Matlock walked rapidly to the desk. The small cellophane-topped photograph was still where it had been – on the lower right wall above the desk. Several larger glass-framed pictures had been smashed; this one was intact. It was small, not at all imposing.

He grabbed the cardboard frame and pulled the photo off the single thumbtack which held it to the wall. He looked at it carefully, turning it over, inspecting the thin edges.

The close, harsh glare of the flashlight revealed scratches at the upper corner of the cardboard. Fingernail scratches? Perhaps. He pointed the light down on the desk top. There were unsharpened pencils, scraps of note paper, and a pair of scissors. He took the scissors and inserted the point of one blade between the thin layers of cardboard until he could rip the photograph out of the frame.

And in that way he found it.

On the back of the small photograph was a diagram drawn with a broad-tipped fountain pen. It was in the shape of a rectangle, the bottom and top lines filled in with dots. On the top were two small lines with arrows, one straight, the other pointing to the right. Above each arrowhead was the numeral 30. Two 30s.

Thirty.

On the sides, bordering the lines, were childishly drawn trees.

On the top, above the numbers, was another simplified sketch. Billowy half-circles connected to one another with a wavy line beneath. A cloud. Underneath, more trees.

It was a map, and what it represented was all too apparent. It was Herron's back yard; the lines on three sides represented Herron's forbidding green wall.

The numerals, the 30s, were measurements – but

they were also something else. They were contemporary symbols.

For Lucas Herron, chairman for decades of Romance Languages, had an insatiable love for words and their odd usages. What was more appropriate than the symbol '30' to indicate finality?

As any first year journalism student would confirm, the number 30 at the bottom of any news copy meant the story was finished. It was over.

There was no more to be said.

Matlock held the photograph upside down in his left hand, his right gripping the flashlight. He entered the woods at mid-section – slightly to the left – as indicated on the diagram. The figure 30 could be feet, yards, meters, paces – certainly not inches.

He marked off thirty twelve-inch spaces. Thirty feet straight, thirty feet to the right.

Nothing.

Nothing but the drenched, full overgrowth and under-brush which clawed at his feet.

He returned to the green wall's entrance and decided to combine yards and paces, realizing that paces in such a dense, jungle-like environment might vary considerably.

He marked off the spot thirty paces directly ahead and continued until he estimated the point of yardage. Then he returned to the bent branches where he had figured thirty paces to be and began the lateral trek.

Again nothing. An old rotted maple stood near one spot Matlock estimated was thirty steps. There was nothing else unusual. He went back to the bent branches and proceeded to his second mark.

Thirty yards straight out. Ninety feet, give or take a foot or two. Then the slow process of thirty yards through the soaking wet foliage to his next mark. Another ninety feet. Altogether, one hundred and eighty feet. Nearly two-thirds of a football field.

The going was slower now, the foliage thicker, or so it seemed. Matlock wished he had a machete or at least some kind of implement to force the wet branches out of his way. Once he lost count and had to keep in mind the variation as he proceeded – was it twenty-one or twenty-three large steps? Did it matter? Would the difference of three to six feet really matter?

He reached the spot. It was either twenty-eight or thirty. Close enough if there was anything to be seen. He pointed the flashlight to the ground and began slowly moving it back and forth laterally.

Nothing. Only the sight of a thousand glistening weeds and the deep-brown color of soaked earth. He kept swinging the beam of light, inching forward as he did so, straining his eyes, wondering every other second if he had just covered that particular section or not – everything looked so alike.

The chances of failure grew. He could go back and begin again, he thought. Perhaps the 30s connoted some other form of measurement. Meters, perhaps, or multiples of another number buried somewhere in the diagram. The dots? Should he count the dots on the bottom and top of the rectangle? Why were the dots there?

He had covered the six-foot variation and several feet beyond.

Nothing.

His mind returned to the dots, and he withdrew the photograph from his inside pocket. As he positioned himself to stand up straight, to stretch the muscles at the base of his spine – pained by crouching – his foot touched a hard, unyielding surface. At first he thought it was a fallen limb, or perhaps a rock. At first he thought it was a fallen limb, or perhaps a rock.

And then he knew it was neither.

285

He couldn't see it – whatever it was, was underneath a clump of overgrown weeds. But he could feel the outline of the object with his foot. It was straight, precisely tooled. It was no part of a forest.

He held the light over the cluster of weeds and saw that they weren't weeds. They were some kind of small-budded flower in partial bloom. A flower which did not need sunlight or space.

A jungle flower. Out of place, purchased, replanted.

He pushed them out of the way and bent down. Underneath was a thick, heavily varnished slab of wood about two feet wide and perhaps a foot and a half long. It had sunk an inch or two into the ground; the surface had been sanded and varnished so often that the layers of protective coating reached a high gloss, reflecting the beam of the flashlight as though it were glass.

Matlock dug his fingers into the earth and lifted up the slab. Beneath it was a weathered metal plaque, bronze perhaps.

For Major Lucas N. Herron, USMCR
In Gratitude from the Officers and Men of Bravo Company,
Fourteenth Raider Battalion, First Marine Division
Solomon Islands – South Pacific
May 1943

Seeing it set in the ground under the glare of light, Matlock had the feeling he was looking at a grave.

He pushed away the surrounding mud and dug a tiny trench around the metal. On his hands and knees, he slowly, awkwardly lifted the plaque up and carefully placed it to one side.

He had found it.

Buried in earth was a metal container – the type used

286

in library archives for valuable manuscripts. Airtight, weather-proofed, vacuumed, a receptacle for the ages.

A coffin, Matlock thought.

He picked it up and inserted his cold, wet fingers under the lever of the coiled hasp. It took considerable strength to pull it up, but finally it was released. There was the rush of air one hears upon opening a tin of coffee. The rubber edges parted. Inside Matlock could see an oilcloth packet in the shape of a notebook.

He knew he'd found the indictment.

Chapter 30

The notebook was thick, over three hundred pages, and every word was handwritten in ink. It was in the form of a diary, but the lengthy entries varied enormously. There was no consistency regarding dates. Often days followed one another; at other times entries were separated by weeks, even months. The writing also varied. There were stretches of lucid narrative followed by incoherent, disjointed rambling. In the latter sections the hand had shaken, the words were often illegible.

Lucas Herron's diary was a cry of anguish, an outpouring of pain. A confessional of a man beyond hope.

As he sat on the cold wet ground, mesmerized by Herron's words, Matlock understood the motives behind Herron's Nest, the forbidding green wall, the window shades, the total isolation.

Lucas Herron had been a drug addict for a quarter of a century. Without the drugs, his pain was unendurable. And there was absolutely nothing anyone could do for him except confine him to a ward in a Veterans' Hospital for the remainder of his unnatural life.

It was the rejection of this living death that had plunged Lucas Herron into another.

Major Lucas Nathaniel Herron, USMCR, attached to Amphibious Assault Troops, Raider Battalions, Fleet Marine Force, Pacific, had led numerous companies of the Fourteenth Battalion, First Marine Division, in ranger assaults on various islands throughout the Japanese-held Solomons and Carolinas.

And Major Lucas Herron had been carried off the tiny

288

island of Peleliu in the Carolinas on a stretcher, having brought two companies back to the beach through jungle fire. None thought he could survive.

Major Lucas Herron had a Japanese bullet imbedded at the base of his neck, lodged in a section of his nervous system. He was not expected to live. The doctors, first in Brisbane, then San Diego, and finally at Bethesda, considered further operations unfeasible. The patient could not survive them; he would be reduced to a vegetable should even the slightest complication set in. No-one wished to be responsible for that.

They put the patient under heavy medication to relieve the discomfort of his wounds. And he lay there in the Maryland hospital for over two years.

The stages of healing – partial recovery – were slow and painful. First, there were the neck braces and the pills; then the braces and the metal frames for walking, and still the pills. At last the crutches, along with the braces and always the pills. Lucas Herron came back to the land of the living – but not without the pills. And in moments of torment – the needle of morphine at night.

There were hundreds, perhaps thousands, like Lucas Herron, but few had his extraordinary qualifications – for those who sought him out. An authentic hero of the Pacific war, a brilliant scholar, a man above reproach.

He was perfect. He could be used perfectly.

On the one hand, he could not live, could not endure, without the relief afforded him by the narcotics – the pills and the increasingly frequent needles. On the other hand, if the degree of his dependence was known medically, he would be returned to a hospital ward.

These alternatives were gradually, subtly made clear to him. Gradually in the sense that his sources of supply needed favors now and then – a contact to be made in Boston, men to be paid in New York. Subtly in that when Herron questioned the involvement, he was told it was really quite harmless. Harmless but *necessary*.

As the years went by, he became enormously valuable to the men he needed so badly. The contact in Boston, the men to be paid in New York, became more and more frequent, more and more *necessary*. Then Lucas was sent farther and farther afield. Winter vacations, spring midterms, summers: Canada, Mexico, France . . . the Mediterranean.

He became a courier.

And always the thought of the hospital ward on his tortured body and brain.

They had manipulated him brilliantly. He was never exposed to the results of his work, never specifically aware of the growing network of destruction he was helping to build. And when finally he learned of it all, it was too late. The network had been built.

Nimrod had his power.

'*April 22, 1951*. At midterm they're sending me back to Mexico. I'll stop at the U. of M. – as usual – and on the way back at Baylor. A touch of irony: the bursar here called me in, saying Carlyle would be pleased to help defray my "research" expenses. I declined, and told him the *disability allowance* was sufficient. Perhaps I should have accepted . . .

'*June 13, 1956*. To Lisbon for three weeks. A routing map, I'm told, for a small ship. Touching the Azores, through Cuba (a mess!), finally into Panama. Stops – for me – at the Sorbonne, U. of Toledo, U. of Madrid. I'm becoming an academic gadfly! I'm not happy about methods – who could be? – but neither am I responsible for the archaic laws. So many, many can be helped. They need help! I've been in touch with scores on the telephone – they put me in touch – men like myself who couldn't face another day without help . . . Still, I

290

worry . . . Still, what can I do? Others would do it, if not me . . .

'*February 24, 1957.* I'm alarmed but calm and reasonable (I hope!) about my concerns. I'm told now that when they send me to make contacts I am the *messenger* from "*Nimrod*"! The name is a code – a meaningless artifice, they say – and will be honored. It's all so foolish – like the intelligence information we'd receive from MacArthur's HQ in So-Pac. *They* had *all* the codes and *none* of the *facts* . . . The pain is worse, the medics said it would get worse. But . . . "Nimrod's" considerate . . . As I am . . .

'*March 10, 1957.* They were angry with me! They withheld my dosage for two days – I thought I would kill myself! I started out in my car for the VA hospital in Hartford, but they stopped me on the highway. They were in a Carlyle *patrol car* – I should have known they had the police here! . . . It was either *compromise* or the *ward*! . . . They were right! . . . I'm off to Canada and the job is to bring in a man from North Africa . . . I *must* do it! The calls to me are constant. This evening a man – Army, 27th – Naha casualty – from East Orange, NJ, said that he and six others *depended* on me! There are so many like ourselves! Why? Why, for God's sake, are we *despised*? We need *help* and all that's offered to us are the *wards*! . . .

'*August 19, 1960.* I've made my position clear! They go too far! . . . "Nimrod" is not just a code name for a location, it's also a *man*! The geography doesn't change but the man does. They're not helping men like me any longer – well, maybe they are – but it's more than *us*! They're reaching out – they're *attracting* people – for a great deal of money! . . .

'*August 20, 1960.* Now they're threatening me. They say I'll have no more once my cabinet's empty . . . I don't care! I've enough for a week – with luck – a week and a half . . . I wish I liked alcohol more, or that it didn't make me sick . . .

'*August 28, 1960*. I shook to my ankles but I went to the Carlyle Police Station. I wasn't thinking. I asked to speak with the highest man in authority and they said it was after five o'clock – he had gone home. So I said I had information about narcotics and within ten minutes the chief of police showed up . . . By now I was obvious – I couldn't control myself – I urinated through my trousers. The chief of police took me into a small room and opened his kit and administered a needle. He was from Nimrod! . . .

'*October 7, 1965*. This Nimrod is displeased with me. I've always gotten along with the Nimrods – the two I've met, but this one is sterner, more concerned with my accomplishments. I refuse to touch *students*, he accepts that, but he says I am getting silly in my classroom lectures, I'm not bearing down. He doesn't care that I don't *solicit* – he doesn't want me to – but he tells me that I should be – well, be more conservative in my outlook . . . It's strange. His name is Matthew Orton and he's an insignificant aide to the lieutenant governor in Hartford. But he's Nimrod. And I'll obey . . .

'*November 14, 1967*. The back is intolerable now – the doctors said it would *disintegrate* – that was *their* word – but not like *this*! I can get through forty minutes of a lecture and then I *must* excuse myself! . . . I ask always – is it worth it? . . . It must be or I wouldn't go on . . . Or am I simply too great an egoist – or too much a coward – to take my life? . . . Nimrod sees me tonight. In a week it's *Thanksgiving* – I wonder where I will go . . .

'*January 27, 1970*. *It has* to be the end now. In C. Fry's beautiful words, the "seraphic strawberry, beaming in its bed" must turn and show its nettles. There's nothing more for me and Nimrod has infected too many, too completely.

I will take my life – as painlessly as possible – there's been so much pain . . .

'*January 28, 1970*. I've tried to kill myself! I can't do it! I bring the gun, then the knife to the point, but it *will not happen*! Am I *really* so infused, so infected that I cannot accomplish that which is most to be desired? . . . Nimrod will kill me. I know that and he knows it better.

'*January 29, 1970. Nimrod* – he's now *Arthur Latona*! Unbelievable! The same *Arthur Latona* who built the middle-income housing projects in Mount Holly! – At any rate, he's given me an unacceptable order. I've *told* him it's *unacceptable*. I'm far too valuable to be discarded and I've told him that, *too* . . . He wants me to carry a great deal of money to Toros Daglari in Turkey! . . . Why, oh why, can't my life be *ended*? . . .

'*April 18, 1971*. It's a wondrously strange world. To survive, to exist and breathe the air, one does so much one comes to loathe. The total is frightening . . . the excuses and the rationalizations are worse . . . Then something happens which suspends – or at least postpones – all necessity of judgment . . . The pains shifted from the neck and spine to the lower sides. I knew it had to be something else. Something *more* . . . I went to Nimrod's doctor – as I must – always. My weight has dropped, my reflexes are pathetic. He's worried and tomorrow I enter the private hospital in Southbury. He says for an exploratory . . . I know they'll do their best for me. They have other trips – very important trips, Nimrod says. I'll be traveling throughout most of the summer, he tells me . . . If it wasn't me, it would be someone else. The pains are terrible.

'*May 22, 1971*. The old, tired soldier is home. Herron's Nest is my salvation! I'm minus a kidney. No telling yet about the other, the doctor says. But I know better. I'm dying . . . Oh, God, I welcome it! There'll be no more

293

trips, no more threats. Nimrod can do no more . . . They'll keep me alive, too. As long as they can. *They have to now!* . . . I hinted to the doctor that I've kept a record over the years. He just stared at me speechless. I've never seen a man so frightened . . .

'*May 23, 1971*. Latona – Nimrod – dropped by this morning. Before he could discuss anything, I told him I knew I was dying. That nothing mattered to me now – the decision to end my life was made, not by me. I even told him that I was prepared – relieved; that I had tried to end it myself but couldn't. He asked about "*what you told the doctor*." He wasn't able to say the *words*! His *fear* blanketed the living room like a heavy mist . . . I answered calmly, with great authority, I think. I told him that whatever records there were would be given to him – *if my last days or months were made easier for me*. He was furious but he knew there wasn't anything he could do. What can a person do with an old man in pain who knows he's going to die? What arguments are left?

'*August 14, 1971*. Nimrod is dead! Latona died of a coronary! Before *me*, and there's irony in that! . . . Still the business continues without change. Still I'm brought my supplies every week and every week the frightened messengers ask the questions – where are they? Where are the records? – they come close to threatening me but I remind them that Nimrod had the word of a dying old man. Why would I change that? . . . They retreat into their fear . . . A new Nimrod will be chosen soon . . . I've said I didn't want to know – and I don't!

'*September 20, 1971*. A new year begins for Carlyle. My last year, I know that – what responsibilities I can assume, that is . . . Nimrod's death has given me courage. Or is it the knowledge of my own? God knows I can't undo much but I can try! . . . I'm reaching out, I'm finding a few who've been hurt badly, and if nothing else I offer help.

It may only be words, or advice, but just the knowledge that *I've been there* seems to be comforting. It's always such a shock to those I speak with! Imagine! The "grand old bird"! The pains and the numbness are nearly intolerable. I may not be able to wait . . .

'*December 23, 1971*. Two days before my last Christmas. I've said to so many who've asked me to their homes that I was going into New York. Of course, it's not so. I'll spend the days here at the Nest . . . A disturbing note. The messengers tell me that the new Nimrod is the sternest, strongest one of all. They say he's ruthless. He orders executions as easily as his predecessors issued simple requests. Or are they telling me these things to frighten me? That can't frighten me!

'*February 18, 1972*. The doctor told me that he'd prescribe heavier "medication" but warned me not to overdose. He, too, spoke of the new Nimrod. Even he's worried – he implied that the man was mad. I told him I didn't want to know anything. I was out of it.

'*February 26, 1972*. I can't believe it! Nimrod *is a monster*! He's got to be *insane*! He's demanded that all those who've been working here over three years be cut off – sent out of the country – and if they refuse – be killed! The doctor's leaving next week. Wife, family, practice . . . Latona's widow was murdered in an "automobile accident"! One of the messengers – Pollizzi – was shot to death in New Haven. Another – Capalbo – OD'd and the rumor is that the dose was administered!

'*April 5, 1972*. From Nimrod to me – deliver to the messengers any and all records or he'll shut off my supplies. My house will be watched around the clock. I'll be followed wherever I go. I'll not be allowed to get any medical attention whatsoever. The combined effects of the cancer and the withdrawal will be beyond anything I can imagine. What Nimrod doesn't know is that before

295

he left the doctor gave me enough for several months. He frankly didn't believe I'd last that long . . . For the first time in this terrible, horrible life, I'm dealing from a position of strength. My life is firmer than ever because of death.

'*April 10, 1972.* Nimrod is near the point of hysterics with me. He's threatened to expose me – which is meaningless. I've let him know that through the messengers. He's said that he'll destroy the whole Carlyle campus, but if he does that he'll destroy himself as well. The rumor is that he's calling together a conference. An important meeting of powerful men . . . My house is now watched – as Nimrod said it would be – around the clock. By the Carlyle police, of course. Nimrod's private army!

'*April 22, 1972.* Nimrod has won! It's horrifying, but he's won! He sent me two newspaper clippings. In each a student was killed by an overdose. The first a girl in Cambridge, the second a boy from Trinity. He says that he'll keep adding to the list for every week I withhold the records . . . Hostages are executed! – He's got to be *stopped*! But how? What can I *do*? . . . I've got a plan but I don't know if I can do it – I'm going to try to *manufacture* records. Leave them intact. It will be difficult – my hands shake so sometimes! Can I possibly get through it? – I have to. I said I'd deliver a *few* at a time. For my *own* protection. I wonder if he'll agree to that?

'*April 24, 1972.* Nimrod's unbelievably evil, but he's a realist. He knows he can do nothing else! We both are racing against the time of my death. Stalemate! I'm alternating between a typewriter and different fountain pens and various types of paper. The killings are suspended but I'm told they will resume if I miss *one* delivery! Nimrod's hostages are in my hands! Their executions can be prevented only by me!

'*April 27, 1972.* Something strange is happening! The

296

Beeson boy phoned our contact at Admissions. Jim Matlock was there and Beeson suspects him. He asked questions, made an ass of himself with Beeson's wife . . . Matlock isn't on any list! He's no part of Nimrod – on either side. He's never purchased a thing, never sold . . . The Carlyle patrol cars are always outside now. Nimrod's army is alerted. What is it?

'*April 27, 1972 – P.M.* The messengers came – two of them – and what they led me to believe is so incredible I cannot write it here . . . I've never asked the identity of Nimrod, I never wanted to know. But panic's rampant now, something is happening beyond even Nimrod's control. And the messengers told me who Nimrod is . . . They *lie*! *I cannot, will not believe it!* If it is true we are all in hell!'

Matlock stared at the last entry helplessly. The handwriting was hardly readable; most of the words were connected with one another as if the writer could not stop the pencil from racing ahead.

'*April 28.* Matlock was here. He knows! Others know! He says the government men are involved now . . . It's over! But what they can't understand is what will happen – a bloodbath, killings – executions! Nimrod can do *no less*! There will be so much *pain*. There will be mass killing and it will be provoked by an insignificant teacher of the Elizabethans . . . A messenger called. Nimrod *himself* is coming out. It is a confrontation. Now I'll know the truth – who he really is . . . If he's who I've been led to believe – somehow I'll get this record out – somehow. It's all that's left. It's my turn to threaten . . . It's over now. The pain will soon be over, too . . . There's been so much pain . . . I'll make one final entry when I'm sure . . .'

Matlock closed the notebook. What had the girl named Jeannie said? *They* have the *courts*, the *police*, the *doctors*. And Alan Pace. He'd added the major university

297

administrations – all over the Northeast. Whole academic policies; employments, deployments, curriculums – sources of enormous financing. *They* have it *all*.

But Matlock had the indictment.

It was enough. Enough to stop Nimrod – whoever he was. Enough to stop the bloodbath, the executions.

Now he *had* to reach Jason Greenberg.

Alone.

Chapter 31

Carrying the oilcoth packet, he began walking toward the town of Carlyle, traveling the back roads on which there was rarely any night traffic. He knew it would be too dangerous to drive. The man in the field had probably recovered sufficiently to reach someone – reach Nimrod. An alarm would be sent out for him. The unseen armies would be after him now. His only chance was to reach Greenberg. Jason Greenberg would tell him what to do.

There was blood on his shirt, mud caked on his trousers and jacket. His appearance brought to mind the outcasts of Bill's Bar & Grill by the railroad freight yards. It was nearly two-thirty in the morning, but such places stayed open most of the night. The blue laws were only conveniences for them, not edicts. He reached College Parkway and descended the hill to the yards.

He brushed his damp clothes as best he could and covered the bloodstained shirt with his jacket. He walked into the filthy bar; the layers of cheap smoke were suspended above the disheveled customers. A jukebox was playing some Slovak music, men were yelling, a stand-up shuffleboard was being abused. Matlock knew he melted into the atmosphere. He would find a few precious moments of relief.

He sat down at a back booth.

'What the hell happened to *you*?'

It was the bartender, the same suspicious bartender whom he'd finally befriended several days ago. Years . . . ages ago.

'Caught in the rainstorm. Fell a couple of times. Lousy whisky . . . Have you got anything to eat?'

'Cheese sandwiches. The meat I wouldn't give you. Bread's not too fresh either.'

'I don't care. Bring me a couple of sandwiches. And a glass of beer. Would you do that?'

'Sure. Sure, mister . . . You sure you want to eat here? I mean, I can tell, this ain't your kind of place, you know what I mean?'

There it was again. The incessant, irrelevant question; the dangling interrogative. *You know what I mean . . . ?* Not a question at all. Even in his few moments of relief he had to hear it once more.

'I know what you mean . . . but I'm sure.'

'It's your stomach.' The bartender trudged back to his station.

Matlock found Greenberg's number and went to the foul-smelling pay phone on the wall. He inserted a coin and dialed.

'I'm sorry, sir,' the operator said, 'the telephone is disconnected. Do you have another number where the party can be reached?'

'Try it again! I'm sure you're wrong.'

She did and she wasn't. The supervisor in Wheeling, West Virginia, finally informed the operator in Carlyle, Connecticut, that any calls to a Mr Greenberg were to be routed to Washington, DC. It was assumed that whoever was calling would know where in Washington.

'But Mr Greenberg isn't expected at the Washington number until early A.M.,' she said. 'Please inform the party on the line.'

He tried to think. Could he trust calling Washington, the Department of Justice, Narcotics Division? Under the circumstances, might not Washington – for the sake of speed – alert someone in the Hartford vicinity to get to him? And Greenberg had made it clear – he didn't trust the Hartford office, the Hartford agents.

He understood Greenberg's concern far better now. He had only to think of the Carlyle police – Nimrod's private army.

No, he wouldn't call Washington. He'd call Sealfont. His last hope was the university president. He dialed Sealfont's number.

'James! Good Lord, James! Are you all right?! Where in heaven's name have you *been*?!'

'To places I never knew were there. Never knew existed.'

'But you're all right? That's all that matters! Are you all right?!'

'Yes, sir. And I've got everything. I've got it all. Herron wrote everything down. It's a record of twenty-three years.'

'Then he *was* part of it?'

'Very much so.'

'Poor, *sick* man . . . I don't understand. However, that's not important now. That's for the authorities. Where are you? I'll send a car . . . No, I'll come myself. We've all been so worried. I've been in constant touch with the men at the Justice Department.'

'Stay where you are,' Matlock said quickly. 'I'll get to you myself – everyone knows your car. It'll be less dangerous this way. I know they're looking for me. I'll have a man here call me a taxi. I just wanted to make sure you were home.'

'Whatever you say. I must tell you I'm relieved. I'll call Kressel. Whatever you have to say, he should know about it. That's the way it's to be.'

'I agree, sir. See you shortly.'

He went back to the booth and began to eat the unappetizing sandwiches. He had swallowed half the beer when from inside his damp jacket, the short, hysterical beeps of

301

Blackstone's Tel-electronic seared into his ears. He pulled out the machine and pressed the button. Without thinking of anything but the number 555–6868 he jumped up from the seat and walked rapidly back to the telephone. His hand trembling, he awkwardly manipulated the coin and dialed.

The recorded words were like the lash of a whip across his face.

'Charger Three-zero is canceled.'

Then there was silence. As Blackstone had promised, there was nothing else but the single sentence – stated but once. There was no-one to speak to, no appeal. Nothing.

But there had to be! He would not, *could not*, be cut off like this! If Blackstone was canceling him, he had a right to know *why*! He had a right to know that Pat was *safe*!

It took several minutes and a number of threats before he reached Blackstone himself.

'I don't have to talk to you!' The sleepy voice was belligerent. 'I made that clear! . . . But I don't mind because if I can put a trace on this call I'll tell them where to find you the second you hang up!'

'Don't threaten me! You've got too much of my money to threaten me . . . Why am I canceled? I've got a right to know that.'

'Because you stink! You stink like garbage!'

'That's not good enough! That doesn't *mean* anything!'

'I'll give you the rundown then. A warrant is out for you. Signed by the court and . . .'

'For *what*, goddamn it?! Protective custody?! *Preventive detention?!*'

'For *murder*, Matlock! For conspiracy to distribute *narcotics*! For aiding and abetting known narcotics *distributors*! . . . You sold *out*! Like I said, you *smell*! And I hate the business you're in!'

302

Matlock was stunned. Murder? Conspiracy! What was Blackstone talking about?

'I don't know what you've been told, but it's not true. None of it's *true*! I risked my life, my *life*, do you *hear* me! To bring what I've got . . .'

'You're a good talker,' interrupted Blackstone, 'but you're careless! You're also a ghoulish bastard! There's a guy in a field outside of Carlyle with his throat slit. It didn't take the government boys ten minutes to trace that Ford wagon to its owner!'

'I didn't *kill* that man! I swear to Christ I *didn't kill him!*'

'No, of course not! And you didn't even *see* the fellow whose head you shot off at East Gorge, did you? Except that there's a parking lot attendant and a couple of others who've got you on the scene! . . . I forgot. You're also stupid. You left the parking ticket under your windshield wiper!'

'No, wait a minute! *Wait a minute!* This is all *crazy*! The man at East Gorge asked to meet me there! He tried to *murder me!*'

'Tell that to your lawyer. We got the whole thing – straight – from the Justice boys! I demanded that. I've got a damned good reputation . . . I'll say this. When you sell out, you sell *high*! Over sixty thousand dollars in a *checking* account. Like I said, you *smell*, Matlock!'

He was so shocked he could not raise his voice. When he spoke, he was out of breath, hardly audible. 'Listen to me. You've *got* to listen to me. Everything you say . . . there are explanations. Except the man in the field. I don't understand that. But I don't care if you believe me or not. It doesn't matter. I'm holding in my hand all the vindication I'll ever need . . . What *does* matter is that you watch *that girl*! Don't cancel me out! *Watch her!*'

'Apparently you don't understand English very well. You *are* canceled! Charger Three-zero is *canceled!*'

'What about the girl?'

'We're not irresponsible,' said Blackstone bitterly. 'She's perfectly safe. She's under the protection of the Carlyle police.'

There was a general commotion at the bar. The bartender was closing up and his customers resented it. Obscenities were shouted back and forth over the beer-soaked, filthy mahogany, while cooler or more drunken heads slowly weaved their way toward the front door.

Paralyzed, Matlock stood by the foul-smelling telephone. The roaring at the bar reached a crescendo but he heard nothing; the figures in front of his eyes were only blurs. He felt sick to his stomach, and so he held the front of his trousers, the oilcloth packet with Lucas Herron's notebook between his hands and his belt. He thought he was going to be sick as he had been sick beside the corpse on the East Gorge slope.

But – there was no time. Pat was held by Nimrod's private army. He had to act *now*. And when he acted, the spring would be sprung. There would be no rewinding.

The horrible truth was that he didn't know where to begin.

'What's the matter, mister? The sandwiches?'

'What?'

'Ya look like you're gonna throw up.'

'Oh? . . . No.' Matlock saw for the first time that almost everyone had left the place.

The notebook! The notebook would be the ransom! There would be no tortured decision – not for the plastic men! Not for the *manipulators*! Nimrod could have the notebook! The indictment!

But then what? Would Nimrod let her live? Let him live?!

304

. . . What had Lucas Herron written: 'The new Nimrod is a monster . . . ruthless. He orders executions . . .'

Nimrod had murdered with far less motive than someone's knowledge of Lucas Herron's diaries.

'Look, mister. I'm sorry, but I gotta close up.'

'Will you call a taxi for me, please?'

'A taxi? It's after three o'clock. Even if there was one, he wouldn't come down *here* at three o'clock in the morning.'

'Have you got a car?'

'Now wait a minute, mister. I gotta clean up and ring out. I had some action tonight. The register'll take me twenty minutes.'

Matlock withdrew his bills. The smallest denomination was a hundred. 'I've got to have a car – right away. How much do you want? I'll bring it back in an hour – maybe less.'

The bartender looked at Matlock's money. It wasn't a normal sight. 'It's a pretty old heap. You might have trouble driving it.'

'I can drive *anything*! Here! Here's a hundred! If I wreck it you can have the whole roll. Here! Take it, for Christ's sake!'

'Sure. Sure, mister.' The bartender reached under his apron and took out his car keys. 'The square one's the ignition. It's parked in the rear. Sixty-two Chevy. Go out the back door.'

'Thanks.' Matlock started for the door indicated by the bartender.

'Hey, mister!'

'What?'

'What's your name again? . . . Something "rock"? I forgot. I mean, for Christ's sake, I give you the car, I don't even know your name!'

Matlock thought for a second. 'Rod. Nimrod. The name's Nimrod.'

'That's no name, mister.' The burly man started toward Matlock. 'That's a spin fly for catchin' trout. Now, what's your name? You got my car, I gotta know your name.'

Matlock still held the money in his hand. He peeled off three additional hundreds and threw them on the floor. It seemed right. He had given Kramer four hundred dollars for his station wagon. There should be symmetry somewhere. Or, at least, meaningless logic.

'That's four hundred dollars. You couldn't get four hundred dollars for a '62 Chevy. I'll bring it back!' He ran for the door. The last words he heard were those of the grateful but confused manager of Bill's Bar & Grill.

'Nimrod. Fuckin' joker!'

The car was a heap, as its owner had said. But it moved, and that was all that mattered. Sealfont would help him analyze the facts, the alternatives. Two opinions were better than one; he was afraid of assuming the total responsibility – he wasn't capable of it. And Sealfont would have people in high places he could contact. Sam Kressel, the liaison, would listen and object and be terrified for his domain. No matter; he'd be dismissed. Pat's safety was uppermost. Sealfont would see that.

Perhaps it was time to threaten – as Herron ultimately had threatened. Nimrod had Pat; he had Herron's indictment. The life of one human being for the protection of hundreds, perhaps thousands. Even Nimrod had to see their bargaining position. It was irrefutable, the odds were on their side.

He realized as he neared the railroad depot that this kind of thinking, by itself, made him a manipulator, too. Pat had been reduced to *quantity X*, Herron's diaries, *quantity Y*. The equation would then be postulated and the mathematical observers would make their decisions based on the data presented. It was the ice-cold logic of

306

survival; emotional factors were disregarded, consciously despised.

Frightening!

He turned right at the station and started to drive up College Parkway. Sealfont's mansion stood at the end. He went as fast as the '62 Chevy would go, which wasn't much above thirty miles an hour on the hill. The streets were deserted, washed clean by the storm. The store fronts, the houses, and finally the campus were dark and silent.

He remembered that Kressel's house was just a half block off College Parkway on High Street. The detour would take him no more than thirty seconds. It was worth it, he thought. If Kressel hadn't left for Sealfont's, he would pick him up and they could talk on the way over. Matlock *had* to talk, *had* to begin. He couldn't stand the isolation any longer.

He swung the car to the left at the corner of High Street. Kressel's house was a large gray colonial set back from the street by a wide front lawn bordered by rhododendrons. There were lights on downstairs. With luck, Kressel was still home. There were two cars, one in the driveway; Matlock slowed down.

His eyes were drawn to a dull reflection at the rear of the driveway. Kressel's kitchen light was on; the spill from the window illuminated the hood of a third car, and the Kressels were a two-car family.

He looked again at the car in front of the house. It was a Carlyle patrol car. The Carlyle police were in Kressel's house!

Nimrod's private army was with *Kressel*!

Or was Nimrod's private army with *Nimrod*?

He swerved to the left, narrowly missing the patrol car, and sped down the street to the next corner. He turned right and pressed the accelerator to the floor. He was confused, frightened, bewildered. If Sealfont had called

307

Kressel – which he had obviously done – and Kressel worked with Nimrod, or *was* Nimrod, there'd be other patrol cars, other soldiers of the private army waiting for him.

His mind went back to the Carlyle Police Station – a century ago, capsuled in little over a week – the night of Loring's murder. Kressel had disturbed him then. And even before that – with Loring and Greenberg – Kressel's hostility to the federal agents had been outside the bounds of reason.

Oh, Christ! It was so clear now! His instincts had been right. The instincts which had served him as the *hunted* as well as the *hunter* had been true! He'd been watched *too* thoroughly, his every action anticipated. Kressel, the *liaison*, was, in fact, Kressel the tracker, the seeker, the supreme killer.

Nothing was ever as it appeared to be – only what one sensed behind the appearance. Trust the senses.

Somehow he had to get to Sealfont. Warn Sealfont that the Judas was Kressel. Now they *both* had to protect themselves, establish some base from which they could strike back.

Otherwise the girl he loved was lost.

There couldn't be a second wasted. Sealfont had certainly told Kressel that he, Matlock, had Lucas Herron's diaries, and that was all Kressel would need to know. All Nimrod needed to know.

Nimrod had to get possession of both the Corsican paper *and* the diaries; now he knew where they were. His private army would be told that this was its moment of triumph or disaster. They would be waiting for him at Sealfont's; Sealfont's mansion was the trap they expected him to enter.

Matlock swung west at the next corner. In his trouser pocket were his keys, and among them was the key to Pat's apartment. To the best of his knowledge, no-one knew he had such a key, certainly no-one would expect him to go there. He had to chance it; he couldn't risk going to a public telephone, risk being seen under a street lamp. The patrol cars would be searching everywhere.

He heard the roar of an engine behind him and felt the sharp pain in his stomach. A car was following him – closing in on him. And the '62 Chevrolet was no match for it.

His right leg throbbed from the pressure he exerted on the pedal. His hands gripped the steering wheel as he turned wildly into a side street, the muscles in his arms tensed and aching. Another turn. He spun the wheel to the left, careening off the edge of the curb back into the middle of the road. The car behind him maintained a steady pace, never more than ten feet away, the headlights blinding in the rear-view mirror.

His pursuer was *not* going to close the gap between them! Not then. Not at that moment. He could have done so a hundred, two hundred yards ago. He was waiting. Waiting for something. But what?

There was so *much* he couldn't understand! So much he'd miscalculated, misread. He'd been outmaneuvered at every important juncture. He was what they said – an amateur! He'd been beyond his depth from the beginning. And now, at the last, his final assault was ending in ambush. They would kill him, take the Corsican paper, the diaries of indictment. They would kill the girl he loved, the innocent child whose life he'd thrown away so brutally. Sealfont would be finished – he knew too much now! God knew how many others would be destroyed.

So be it.

If it had to be this way, if hope really had been taken from him, he'd end it all with a gesture, at least. He reached into his belt for the automatic.

The streets they now traveled – the pursuer and the pursued – ran through the outskirts of the campus, consisting mainly of the science buildings and a number of large parking lots. There were no houses to speak of.

He swerved the Chevrolet as far to the right as possible, thrusting his right arm across his chest, the barrel of the pistol outside the car window, pointed at the pursuing automobile.

He fired twice, the car behind him accelerated; he felt the repeated jarring of contact, the metal against metal as the car behind hammered into the Chevrolet's left rear chassis. He pulled again at the trigger of the automatic. Instead of a loud report, he heard and felt only the single click of the firing pin against an unloaded chamber.

Even his last gesture was futile.

His pursuer crashed into him once more. He lost control; the wheel spun, tearing his arm, and the Chevrolet reeled off the road. Frantic, he reached for the door handle, desperately trying to steady the car, prepared to jump if need be.

He stopped all thought; all instincts of survival were arrested. Within those split seconds, time ceased. For the car behind him had drawn parallel and he saw the face of his pursuer.

There were bandages and gauze around the eyes, beneath the glasses, but they could not hide the face of the black revolutionary, Julian Dunois.

It was the last thing he remembered before the Chevrolet swerved to the right and skidded violently off the road's incline.

Blackness.

Chapter 32

Pain roused him. It seemed to be all through his left side. He rolled his head, feeling the pillow beneath him.

The room was dimly lit; what light there was came from a table lamp on the other side. He shifted his head and tried to raise himself on his right shoulder. He pushed his elbow into the mattress, his immobile left arm following the turn of his body like a dead weight.

He stopped abruptly.

Across the room, directly in line with the foot of the bed, sat a man in a chair. At first Matlock couldn't distinguish the features. The light was poor and his eyes were blurred with pain and exhaustion.

Then the man came into focus. He was black and his dark eyes stared at Matlock beneath the perfectly cut semicircle of an Afro haircut. It was Adam Williams, Carlyle University's firebrand of the Black Left.

When Williams spoke, he spoke softly and, unless Matlock misunderstood – once again – there was compassion in the black's voice.

'I'll tell Brother Julian you're awake. He'll come in to see you.' Williams got out of the chair and went to the door. 'You've banged up your left shoulder. Don't try to get out of bed. There are no windows in here. The hallway is guarded. Relax. You need rest.'

'I don't have *time* to rest, you *goddamn fool!*' Matlock tried to raise himself further but the pain was too great. He hadn't adjusted to it.

'You don't have a choice.' Williams opened the door and walked rapidly out, closing it firmly behind him.

311

Matlock fell back on the pillow . . . Brother Julian
. . . He remembered now. The sight of Julian Dunois's
bandaged face watching him through the speeding car
window, seemingly inches away from him. And his ears
had picked up Dunois's words, his commands to his driver.
They had been shouted in his Caribbean dialect.

'Hit him, mon! Hit him again! Drive him *off*, mon!'

And then everything had become dark and the darkness
had been filled with violent noise, crashing metal, and
he had felt his body twisting, turning, spiraling into the
black void.

Oh, God! How long ago was it? He tried to lift up his
left hand to look at his watch, but the arm barely moved;
the pain was sharp and lingering. He reached over with
his right hand to pull the stretch band off his wrist, but it
wasn't there. His watch was gone.

He struggled to get up and finally managed to perch on
the edge of the bed, his legs touching the floor. He pressed
his feet against the wood, thankful that he could sit up . . .
He had to put the pieces together, to reconstruct what had
happened, where he was going.

He'd been on his way to Pat's. To find a secluded
telephone on which to reach Adrian Sealfont. To warn
him that Kressel was the enemy, Kressel was Nimrod.
And he'd made up his mind that Herron's diaries would
be Pat's ransom. Then the chase had begun, only it wasn't a
chase. The car behind him, commanded by Julian Dunois,
had played a furious game of terror. It had toyed with him
as a lethal mountain cat might play with a wounded goat.
Finally it had attacked – steel against steel – and driven
him to darkness.

Matlock knew he had to escape. But *from where* and *to
whom*?

The door of the windowless room opened. Dunois
entered, followed by Williams.

'Good morning,' said the attorney. 'I see you've managed to sit up. That's good. It augurs well for your very abused body.'

'What time is it? Where am I?'

'It's nearly four-thirty. You are in a room at Lumumba Hall. You see? I withhold nothing from you . . . Now, you must reciprocate. You must withhold nothing from me.'

'Listen to me!' Matlock kept his voice steady. 'I have no fight with you, with *any* of you! I've got . . .'

'Oh, I disagree,' Dunois smiled. 'Look at my face. It's only through enormous good fortune that I wasn't blinded by you. You tried to crush the lenses of my glasses into my eyes. Can you imagine how my work would suffer if I were blind?'

'Goddamn it! You filled me with acid!'

'And you provoked it! You were actively engaged in pursuits inimicable to our brothers! Pursuits you had no *right* to engage in! . . . But this is concentric debate. It will get us nowhere . . . We *do* appreciate what you've brought us. Beyond our most optimistic ambitions.'

'You've got the notebook . . .'

'*And* the Corsican document. The Italian invitation we knew existed. The notebook was only a rumor. A rumor which was fast being ascribed to fiction until tonight – this morning. You should feel proud. You've accomplished what scores of your more experienced betters failed to accomplish. You found the treasure. The *real* treasure.'

'I've got to have it back!'

'Fat chance!' said Williams, leaning against the wall, watching.

'If I don't get it back, a girl will *die*! Do whatever you goddamn well please with me, but let me *use* it to get her back. Christ! Please, *please*!'

'You feel deeply, don't you? I see tears in your eyes . . .'

'Oh, *Jesus*! You're an *educated man*! You can't *do* this!

313

. . . *Listen*! Take whatever information you want out of it! Then give it to me and let me go! . . . I swear to you I'll come back. Give her a chance. Just give her a *chance*!'

Dunois walked slowly to the chair by the wall, the chair in which Adam Williams sat when Matlock awoke. He pulled it forward, closer to the bed, and sat down, crossing his knees gracefully. 'You feel helpless, don't you? Perhaps . . . even without hope.'

'I've been through a great deal!'

'I'm sure you have. And you appeal to my reason . . . as an *educated man*. You realize that it is within my scope to help you and therefore I am superior to you. You would not make such an appeal if it were not so.'

'Oh, Christ! Cut that out!'

'Now you know what it's like. You are helpless. Without hope. You wonder if your appeal will be lost on a deaf ear . . . Do you really, for one second, think that I care for the life of Miss Ballantyne? Do you honestly believe she has any priority for me? Any more than the lives of *our* children, *our* loved ones mean anything to you!'

Matlock knew he had to answer Dunois. The black would offer nothing if he evaded him. It was another game – and he had to play, if only briefly.

'I don't deserve this and you know it. I loathe the people who won't do anything for them. You know me – you've made that clear. So you must know that.'

'Ahh, but I *don't* know it! You're the one who made the choice, the decision to work for the superior mon! The *Washington* mon! For decades, two *centuries, my* people have appealed to the *superior Washington mon*! "Help us," they cry. "Don't leave us without hope!" they scream. But nobody listens. Now, you expect me to listen to you?'

'Yes, I *do*! Because I'm not your enemy. I may not be everything you want me to be, but I'm not your enemy. If you turn me – and men like me – into objects of hatred,

314

you're *finished*. You're out-numbered, don't forget that, Dunois. We won't storm the barricades every time you yell "foul," but we hear you. We're willing to help; we want to help.'

Dunois looked coldly at Matlock. 'Prove it.'

Matlock returned the black's stare. 'Use me as your bait, your hostage. Kill me if you have to. But get the girl out.'

'We can do that – the hostaging, the killing – without your consent. Brave but hardly proof.'

Matlock refused to allow Dunois to disengage the stare between them. He spoke softly. 'I'll give you a statement. Written, verbal – on tape; freely, without force or coercion. I'll spell it all out. How I was used, what I did. Everything. You'll have your Washington men as well as Nimrod.'

Dunois folded his arms and matched Matlock's quiet voice. 'You realize you would put an end to your professional life; this life you love so much. No university administration worthy of its name would consider you for a position. You'd never be trusted again. By any factions. You'd become a pariah.'

'You asked for proof. It's all I can offer you.'

Dunois sat immobile in the chair. Williams had straightened up from his slouching position against the wall. No one spoke for several moments. Finally Dunois smiled gently. His eyes, surrounded by the gauze, were compassionate.

'You're a good man. Inept, perhaps, but persevering. You shall have the help you need. We won't leave you without hope. Do you agree, Adam?'

'Agreed.'

Dunois got out of the chair and approached Matlock.

'You've heard the old cliché, that politics make strange bedfellows. Conversely, practical objectives often make for strange political alliances. History bears this out . . .

315

We want this Nimrod as much as you do. As well as the Mafiosi he tries to make peace with. It is they and their kind who prey upon the children. An example must be made. An example which will instill terror in other Nimrods, other Mafiosi . . . You shall have help, but this is the condition we demand.'

'What do you mean?'

'The disposition of Nimrod and the others will be left to us. We don't trust your judges and your juries. Your courts are corrupt, your legalistics no more than financial manipulations . . . The barrio addict is thrown into jail. The rich gangsters appeal . . . No, the disposition must be left to us.'

'I don't care about that. You can do whatever you like.'

'Your not caring is insufficient. We demand more than that. We must have our guarantee.'

'How can I give a guarantee?'

'By your silence. By not acknowledging our presence. We will take the Corsican paper and somehow we will find the conference and be admitted. We will extract what we want from the diaries – that's being done now, incidentally . . . But your *silence* is the paramount issue. We will help you now – on a best-efforts basis, of course – but you must never mention our involvement. Irrespective of what may happen, you must not, directly or indirectly, allude to our participation. Should you do so, we will take your life and the life of the girl. Is this understood?'

'It is.'

'Then we are in agreement?'

'We are.'

'Thank you,' said Dunois, smiling.

Chapter 33

As Julian Dunois outlined their alternatives and began to formulate strategy, it became clearer to Matlock why the blacks had sought him out with such concentration – and why Dunois was willing to offer help. He, Matlock, had the basic information they needed. Who were his contacts? Both inside and without the university? Who and where were the government men? How were communications expedited?

In other words – whom should Julian Dunois *avoid* in his march to Nimrod?

'I must say, you were extraordinarily unprepared for contingencies,' Dunois said. 'Very slipshod.'

'That occurred to me, too. But I think I was only partially to blame.'

'I dare say you were!' Dunois laughed, joined by Williams. The three men remained in the windowless room. A card table had been brought in along with several yellow pads. Dunois had begun writing down every bit of information Matlock supplied. He double-checked the spelling of names, the accuracy of addresses – a professional at work; Matlock once again experienced the feeling of inadequacy he had felt when talking with Greenberg.

Dunois stapled a number of pages together and started on a fresh pad. 'What are you doing?' asked Matlock.

'These will be duplicated by a copier downstairs. The information will be sent to my office in New York . . . As will a photostat of every page in Professor Herron's notebook.'

317

'You don't fool around, do you?'

'In a word – no.'

'It's all I've got to give you. Now, what do we do? What do *I* do? I'm frightened, I don't have to tell you that. I can't even let myself think what might happen to her.'

'*Nothing* will happen. Believe me when I tell you that. At the moment, your Miss Ballantyne is as safe as if she were in her mother's arms. Or yours. She's the bait, not you. The bait will be kept fresh and unspoiled. For you have what they want. They can't survive without it.'

'Then let's make the offer. The sooner the better.'

'Don't worry. It will be made. But we must decide carefully – aware of the nuances – how we do it. So far, we have two alternatives, we agreed upon that. The first is Kressel, himself. The direct confrontation. The second, to use the police department, to let your message to Nimrod be delivered through it.'

'Why do that? Use the police?'

'I'm only listing alternatives . . . Why the police? I'm not sure. Except that the Herron diaries state clearly that Nimrod was replaced in the past. This current Nimrod is the third since the position's inception, is that not correct?'

'Yes. The first was a man named Orton in the lieutenant governor's office. The second, Angelo Latona, a builder. The third, obviously, Kressel. What's your point?'

'I'm speculating. Whoever assumes the position of Nimrod has authoritarian powers. Therefore, it is the position, not the man. The man can make whatever he can of the office.'

'But the office,' interrupted Williams, 'is given and taken away. Nimrod isn't the last voice.'

'Exactly. Therefore, it might be to Matlock's advantage to let the word leak out very specifically that it is *he* who

318

possesses the weapon. That Kressel – Nimrod – must exercise great caution. For everyone's sake.'

'Wouldn't that mean that more people would be after me?'

'Possibly. Conversely, it could mean that there'd be a legion of anxious criminals protecting you. Until the threat you impose is eliminated. No-one will act rashly until that threat is taken away. No-one will want Nimrod to act rashly.'

Matlock lit a cigarette, listening intently. 'What you're trying to do then is to partially separate Nimrod from his own organization.'

Dunois snapped the fingers of both hands, the sound of castanets, applause. He smiled as he spoke.

'You're a quick student. It's the first lesson of insurgency. One of the prime objectives of infiltration. Divide. Divide!'

The door opened; an excited black entered. Without saying a word, he handed Dunois a note. Dunois read it and closed his eyes for several moments. It was his way of showing dismay. He thanked the black messenger calmly and dismissed him politely. He looked at Matlock but handed the note to Williams.

'Our stratagems may have historic precedence, but I'm afraid for us they're empty words. Kressel and his wife are dead. Dr Sealfont has been taken forcibly from his house under guard. He was driven away in a Carlyle patrol car.'

'What? Kressel! I don't believe it! It's not true!'

'I'm afraid it is. Our men report that the two bodies were carried out not more than fifteen minutes ago. The word is murder and suicide. Naturally. It would fit perfectly.'

'Oh, Christ! Oh, Jesus Christ! It's my fault! I made them do it! I *forced* them! Sealfont! Where did they take him?'

319

'We don't know. The brothers on watch didn't dare follow the patrol car.'

He had no words. The paralysis, the fear, was there again. He reeled blindly into the bed and sank down on it, sitting, staring at nothing. The sense of futility, of inadequacy, of defeat was now overwhelming. He had caused so much pain, so much death.

'It's a severe complication,' said Dunois, his elbows on the card table. 'Nimrod has removed your only contacts. In so doing, he's answered a vital question, prevented us from making an enormous error – I refer to Kressel, of course. Nevertheless, to look at it from another direction, Nimrod has reduced our alternatives. You have no choice now. You must deal through his private army, the Carlyle police.'

Matlock looked numbly across at Julian Dunois. 'Is that all you can *do*? Sit there and coolly decide a next move? . . . Kressel's *dead*. His *wife* is *dead*. Adrian Sealfont's probably killed by now. These were my *friends*!'

'And you have my sympathies, but let me be honest; I don't regret the loss of the three individuals. Frankly, Adrian Sealfont is the only *real* casualty – we might have worked with him, he was brilliant – but this loss does not break my heart. We lose thousands in the barrios every month. I weep for them more readily . . . However, to the issue at hand. You really don't have a choice. You must make your contact through the police.'

'But that's where you're wrong.' Matlock felt suddenly stronger. 'I *do* have a choice . . . Greenberg left West Virginia early this morning. He'll be in Washington by now. I have a number in New York that can put me in touch with him. I'm getting hold of Greenberg.' He'd done enough, caused enough anguish. He couldn't take the chance with Pat's life. Not any longer. He wasn't capable.

320

Dunois leaned back in his chair, removing his arms from the card table. He stared at Matlock. 'I said a little while ago that you were an apt student. I amend that observation. You are quick but obviously superficial . . . You will *not* reach Greenberg. He was not part of our agreement and you *will not* violate that agreement. You will carry through on the basis we agree upon or you will be subject to the penalties I outlined.'

'Goddamn it, don't threaten me! I'm sick of threats!' Matlock stood up. Dunois reached under his jacket and took out a gun. Matlock saw that it was the black automatic he had taken from the dead man on the East Gorge slope. Dunois, too, rose to his feet.

'The medical report will no doubt estimate your death to be at dawn.'

'For God's sake! The girl is being held by killers!'

'So are you,' Dunois said quietly. 'Can't you *see* that? Our motives are different, but make no mistake about it. We are *killers*. We *have* to be.'

'You wouldn't go that far!'

'Oh, but we would. We have. And much, much further. We would drop your insignificant corpse in front of the police station with a note pinned to your bloodstained shirt. We would *demand* the death of the girl prior to any negotiations. They would readily agree, for neither of us can take the chance of her living. Once she, too, is dead, the giants are left to do battle by themselves.'

'You're a monster.'

'I am what I have to be.'

No-one spoke for several moments. Matlock shut his eyes, his voice a whisper. 'What do I do?'

'That's much better.' Dunois sat down, looking up at the nervous Adam Williams. Briefly, Matlock felt a kinship with the campus radical. He, too, was frightened, unsure. As Matlock, he was ill-equipped to deal with the world

321

of Julian Dunois or Nimrod. The Haitian seemed to read Matlock's thoughts.

'You must have confidence in yourself. Remember, you've accomplished far more than anyone else. With far less resources. And you have extraordinary courage.'

'I don't feel very courageous.'

'A brave man rarely does. Isn't that remarkable? Come, sit down.' Matlock obeyed. 'You know, you and I are not so different. In another time, we might even be allies. Except, as many of my brothers have noted, I look for saints.'

'There aren't any,' Matlock said.

'Perhaps not. And then again, perhaps . . . we'll debate it some other time. Right now, we must plan. Nimrod will be expecting you. We can't disappoint him. Yet we must be sure to guard ourselves on all flanks.' He pulled closer to the table, a half-smile on his lips, his eyes shining.

The black revolutionary's strategy, if nothing else, was a complex series of moves designed to protect Matlock and the girl. Matlock grudgingly had to acknowledge it.

'I have a double motive,' Dunois explained. 'The second is, frankly, more important to me. Nimrod will not appear himself unless he has no other choice, and I want Nimrod. I will not settle for a substitute, a camouflage.'

The essence of the plan was Herron's notebook itself, the last entries in the diary.

The identity of Nimrod.

'Herron states explicitly that he *would* not write the name intimated by the messengers. Not that he couldn't. His feeling obviously was that he could not implicate that man if the information was incorrect. Guilt by innuendo would be abhorrent to him. Like yourself, Matlock; you refused to offer up Herron on the basis of an hysterical phone call. He knew that he might die at any given moment; his body had taken about as much abuse as it could endure . . . He had to be positive.' Dunois, by now, was drawing meaningless geometric shapes on a blank page of yellow paper.

'And then he was murdered,' said Matlock. 'Made to look like suicide.'

'Yes. If nothing else, the diaries confirm that. Once Herron had proved to himself who Nimrod was, he would have moved heaven and earth to include it in the notebook. Our enemy cannot know that he did not. That is our Damocletian sword.'

Matlock's first line of protection was to let the chief of the Carlyle police understand that he, Matlock, knew the identity of Nimrod. He would reach an accommodation solely with Nimrod. This accommodation was the lesser of two evils. He was a hunted man. There was a warrant out for his arrest of which the Carlyle police surely were aware. He might conceivably be exonerated from the lesser indictments, but he would not escape the charge of murder. Possibly, two murders. For he had killed, the evidence was overwhelming, and he had no tangible alibis. He did not know the men he had killed. There were no witnesses to corroborate self-defense; the manner of each killing was grotesque to the point of removing the killer from society. The best he could hope for was a number of years in prison.

And then he would spell out his terms for an accommodation with Nimrod. Lucas Herron's diaries for his life – and the life of the girl. Certainly the diaries were worth a sum of money sufficient for both of them to start again somewhere.

Nimrod could do this. Nimrod *had* to do it.

'The key to this . . . let's call it phase one . . . is the amount of conviction you display.' Dunois spoke carefully. 'Remember, you are in panic. You have taken lives, killed

323

other human beings. You are not a violent man but you've been forced, coerced into frightening crimes.'

'It's the truth. More than you know.'

'Good. Convey that feeling. All a panicked man wants is to get away from the scene of his panic. Nimrod must believe this. It guarantees your immediate safety.'

A second telephone call would then be made by Matlock – to confirm Nimrod's acceptance of a meeting. The location, at this point, could be chosen by Nimrod. Matlock would call again to learn where. But the meeting must take place before ten o'clock in the morning.

'By now, you, the fugitive, seeing freedom in sight, suddenly possess doubts,' said Dunois. 'In your gathering hysteria, you need a guarantee factor.'

'Which is?'

'A third party; a mythical third party . . .'

Matlock was to inform the contact at the Carlyle Police Headquarters that he had written up a complete statement about the Nimrod operation; Herron's diaries, identities, everything. This statement had been sealed in an envelope and given to a friend. It would be mailed to the Justice Department at ten in the morning unless Matlock instructed otherwise.

'Here, phase two depends again on conviction, but of another sort. Watch a caged animal whose captors suddenly open the gate. He's wary, suspicious; he approaches his escape with caution. So, too, must our fugitive. It will be expected. You have been most resourceful during the past week. By logic you should have been dead by now, but you survived. You must continue that cunning.'

'I understand.'

The last phase was created by Julian Dunois to guarantee – as much as was possible in a 'best-efforts situation' – the reclaiming of the girl and the safety of Matlock. It would be engineered by a third and final telephone call to

324

Nimrod's contact. The object of the call was to ascertain the specific location of the meeting and the precise time.

When informed of both, Matlock was to accept without hesitation.

At first.

Then moments later – seemingly with no other reason that the last extremity of panic and suspicion – he was to reject Nimrod's choice.

Not the time – the location.

He was to hesitate, to stutter, to behave as close to irrationality as he could muster. And then, suddenly, he was to blurt out a second location of his *own* choice. As if it had just come to mind with no thoughts of it before that moment. He was then to restate the existence of the nonexistent statement which a mythical friend would mail to Washington at ten in the morning. He was then to hang up without listening further.

'The most important factor in phase three is the recognizable consistency of your panic. Nimrod must see that your reactions are now primitive. The act itself is about to happen. You lash out, recoil, set up barriers to avoid his net, should that net exist. In your hysteria, you are as dangerous to him as a wounded cobra is deadly to the tiger. For rationality doesn't exist, only survival. He now must meet you himself, he now must bring the girl. He will, of course, arrive with his palace guard. His intentions won't change. He'll take the diaries, perhaps discuss elaborate plans for your accommodation, and when he learns that there is no written statement, no friend about to mail it, he'll expect to kill you both . . . However, none of his intentions will be carried out. For we'll be waiting for him.'

'How? How will you be waiting for him?'

'With my own palace guard . . . We shall now, you and I, decide on that hysterically arrived at second location.

It should be in an area you know well, perhaps frequent often. Not too far away, for it is presumed you have no automobile. Secluded, because you are hunted by the law. Yet accessible, for you must travel fast, most likely on back roads.'

'You're describing Herron's Nest. Herron's house.'

'I may be, but we can't use it. It's psychologically inconsistent. It would be a break in our fugitive's pattern of behavior. Herron's Nest is the root of his fear. He wouldn't go back there . . . Someplace else.'

Williams started to speak. He was still unsure, still wary of joining Dunois's world. 'I think, perhaps . . .'

'What, Brother Williams? What do you think?'

'Professor Matlock often dines at a restaurant called the Cheshire Cat.'

Matlock snapped his head up at the black radical. 'You too? You've had me followed.'

'Quite often. We don't enter such places. We'd be conspicuous.'

'Go on, brother,' broke in Dunois.

'The Cheshire Cat is about four miles outside Carlyle. It's set back from the highway, which is the normal way to get there, about half a mile, but it also can be reached by taking several back roads. Behind and to the sides of the restaurant are patios and gardens used in the summer for dining. Beyond these are woods.'

'Anyone on the premises?'

'A single night watchman, I believe. It doesn't open until one. I don't imagine cleanup crews or kitchen help get there before nine-thirty or ten.'

'Excellent.' Dunois looked at his wristwatch. 'It's now ten past five. Say we allow fifteen minutes between phases one, two, and three and an additional twenty minutes for traveling between stations, that would make it approximately six-fifteen. Say six-thirty for contingencies.

326

We'll set the rendezvous for seven. Behind the Cheshire Cat. Get the notebook, brother. I'll alert the men.'

Williams rose from his chair and walked to the door. He turned and addressed Dunois. 'You won't change your mind? You won't let me come with the rest of you?'

Dunois didn't bother to look up. He answered curtly. 'Don't annoy me. I've a great deal to think about.'

Williams left the room quickly.

Matlock watched Dunois. He was still sketching his meaningless figures on the yellow pad, only now he bore down on the pencil, causing deep ridges on the paper. Matlock saw the diagram emerging. It was a series of jagged lines, all converging.

They were bolts of lightning.

'Listen to me,' he said. 'It's not too late. Call in the authorities. Please, for Christ's sake, you can't risk the lives of these kids.'

From behind his glasses, surrounded by the gauze bandages, Dunois's eyes bore into Matlock. He spoke with contempt. 'Do you for one minute think I would allow these children to tread in waters I don't even know *I* can survive? We're not your Joint Chiefs of Staff, Matlock. We have greater respect, greater love for our young.'

Matlock recalled Adam Williams' protestations at the door. 'That's what Williams meant then? About coming with you.'

'Come with me.'

Dunois led Matlock out of the small, windowless room and down the corridor to a staircase. There were a few students milling about, but only a few. The rest of Lumumba Hall was asleep. They proceeded down two flights to a door Matlock remembered as leading to the cellars, to the old, high-ceilinged chapter room in which he'd witnessed the frightening performance of the African tribal rite. They descended the stairs and,

327

as Matlock suspected, went to the rear of the cellars, to the thick oak door of the chapter room. Dunois had not spoken a word since he'd bade Matlock follow him.

Inside the chapter room were eight blacks, each well over six feet tall. They were dressed alike: dark, tight-fitting khakis with open shirts and black, soft leather ankle boots with thick rubber soles. Several were sitting, playing cards; others were reading, some talking quietly among themselves. Matlock noticed that a few had their shirt sleeves rolled up. The arms displayed were tautly muscular, veins close to the skin. They all nodded informally to Dunois and his guest. Two or three smiled intelligently at Matlock, as if to put him at ease. Dunois spoke softly.

'The palace guard.'

'My God!'

'The élite corps. Each man is trained over a period of three years. There is not a weapon he cannot fire or fix, a vehicle he cannot repair . . . or a philosophy he cannot debate. Each is familiar with the most brutal forms of combat, traditional as well as guerrilla. Each is committed until death.

'The terror brigade, is that it? It's not new, you know.'

'Not with that description, no, it wouldn't be. Don't forget, I grew up with such dogs at my heels. Duvalier's Ton Ton Macoute were a pack of hyenas; I witnessed their work. These men are no such animals.'

'I wasn't thinking of Duvalier.'

'On the other hand, I acknowledge the debt to Papa Doc. The Ton Ton's concept was exciting to me. Only I realized it had to be restructured. Such units are springing up all over the country.'

'They sprung up once before,' Matlock said. 'They were called "élite" then, too. They were also called "units" – SS units.'

Dunois looked at Matlock and Matlock saw the hurt in

his eyes. 'To reach for such parallels is painful. Nor is it justified. We do what we have to do. What is right for us to do.'

'*Ein Volk, Ein Reich, Ein Fuehrer,*' said Matlock softly.

Chapter 34

Everything happened so fast. Two of Dunois's élite guard were assigned to him, the rest left for the rendezvous with Nimrod, to prepare themselves to meet another élite guard – the selected few of Nimrod's private army who undoubtedly would accompany him. Matlock was ushered across the campus by the two huge blacks after the word came back from scouts that the path was clear. He was taken to a telephone booth in the basement of a freshman dormitory, where he made his first call.

He found that his fear, his profound fear, aided the impression Dunois wanted to convey. It wasn't difficult for him to pour out his panicked emotions, pleading for sanctuary, for, in truth, he *felt* panicked. As he spoke hysterically into the phone, he wasn't sure which was the reality and which the fantasy. He wanted to be free. He wanted Pat to live and be free with him. If Nimrod could bring it all about, why not deal with Nimrod in good faith?

It was a nightmare for him. He was afraid for a moment that he might yell out the truth and throw himself on the mercy of Nimrod.

The sight of Dunois's own Ton Ton Macoute kept bringing him back to his failing senses, and he ended the first telephone call without breaking. The Carlyle police 'superintendent' would forward the information, receive an answer, and await Matlock's next call.

The blacks received word from their scouts that the second public telephone wasn't clear. It was on a street corner, and a patrol car had been spotted in the area.

Dunois knew that even public phones could be traced, although it took longer, and so he had alternate sites for each of the calls, the last one to be made on the highway. Matlock was rushed to the first alternate telephone booth. It was on the back steps of the Student Union.

The second call went more easily, although whether that was an advantage was not clear. Matlock was emphatic in his reference to the mythical statement that was to be mailed at ten in the morning. His strength had its effect, and he was grateful for it. The 'superintendent' was frightened now, and he didn't bother to conceal it. Was Nimrod's private army beginning to have its doubts? The troops were, perhaps, picturing their own stomachs blown out by the enemy's shells. Therefore, the generals had to be more alert, more aware of the danger.

He was raced to a waiting automobile. It was an old Buick, tarnished, dented, inconspicuous. The exterior, however, belied the inside. The interior was as precisely tooled as a tank. Under the dashboard was a powerful radio; the windows were at least a half-inch thick, paned, Matlock realized, with bulletproof glass. Clipped to the sides were high-powered, short-barreled rifles, and dotted about the body were rubber-flapped holes into which these barrels were to be inserted. The sound of the engine impressed Matlock instantly. It was as powerful a motor as he'd ever heard.

They followed an automobile in front of them at moderate speed; Matlock realized that another car had taken up the rear position. Dunois had meant it when he said they were to cover themselves on all flanks. Dunois was, indeed, a professional.

And it disturbed James Matlock when he thought about the profession.

It was black. It was also *Ein Volk, Ein Reich, Ein Fuehrer*.

As was Nimrod and all he stood for.

The words came back to him.

'. . . *I'm getting out of this goddamn country, mister* . . .'

Had it come to that?

And: '. . . *You think it's all so different?* . . . *It's mini-America!* . . . *It's company policy, man!*'

The land was sick. Where was the cure?

'Here we are. Phase three.' The black revolutionary in command tapped him lightly on the arm, smiling reassuringly as he did so. Matlock got out of the car. They were on the highway south of Carlyle. The car in front had pulled up perhaps a hundred yards ahead of them and parked off the road, its lights extinguished. The automobile behind had done the same.

In front of him stood two aluminum-framed telephone booths, placed on a concrete platform. The second black walked to the right booth, pushed the door open – which turned on the dull overhead light – and quickly slid back the pane of glass under the light, exposing the bulb. This he rapidly unscrewed so that the booth returned to darkness. It struck Matlock – impressed him, really – that the Negro giant had eliminated the light this way. It would have been easier, quicker, simply to have smashed the glass.

The objective of the third and final call, as Dunois had instructed, was to reject Nimrod's meeting place. Reject it in a manner that left Nimrod no alternative but to accept Matlock's panicked substitute: the Cheshire Cat.

The voice over the telephone from the Carlyle police was wary, precise.

'Our mutual friend understands your concerns, Matlock. He'd feel the same way you do. He'll meet you with the girl at the south entrance of the athletic field, to the left of the rear bleachers. It's a small stadium, not far from the gym and the dormitories. Night watchmen are on; no harm could come to you . . .'

'All right. All right, that's OK.' Matlock did his best to sound quietly frantic, laying the groundwork for his ultimate refusal. 'There are people around; if any of you tried anything, I could scream my head off. And I *will*!'

'Of course. But you won't have to. Nobody wants anyone hurt. It's a simple transaction; that's what our friend told me to tell you. He admires you . . .'

'How can I be sure he'll bring Pat? I have to be sure!'

'The *transaction*, Matlock.' The voice was oily, there was a hint of desperation. Dunois's 'cobra' was unpredictable. 'That's what it's all about. Our friend wants what you found, remember?'

'I remember . . .' Matlock's mind raced. He realized he had to maintain his hysteria, his unpredictability. But he had to switch the location. Change it without being suspect. If Nimrod became suspicious, Dunois had sentenced Pat to death. 'And you tell our *friend* to remember that there's a statement in an envelope addressed to men in Washington!'

'He knows that, for Christ's sake. I mean . . . he's concerned, you know what I mean? Now, we'll see you at the field, OK? In an hour, OK?'

This was the moment. There might not come another.

'No! Wait a minute . . . I'm not going on that campus! The Washington people, they've got the whole place watched! They're all around! They'll put me away!'

'No, they won't . . .'

'How the hell do you know?'

'There's nobody. So help me, it's *OK*. Calm down, please.'

'That's easy for you, not me! No, I'll tell you where . . .'

He spoke rapidly, disjointedly, as if thinking desperately while talking. First he mentioned Herron's house, and before the voice could either agree or disagree, he rejected it himself. He then pinpointed the freight yards, and immediately found irrational reasons why he could not go there.

'Now, don't get so excited,' said the voice. 'It's a simple transaction . . .'

'That restaurant! Outside of town. The Cheshire Cat! Behind the restaurant, there's a garden . . .'

The voice was confused trying to keep up with him, and Matlock knew he was carrying off the ploy. He made last references to the diaries and the incriminating affidavit and slammed the telephone receiver into its cradle.

He stood in the booth, exhausted. Perspiration was dripping down his face, yet the early morning air was cool.

'That was handled very nicely,' said the black man in command. 'Your adversary chose a place within the college, I gather. An intelligent move on his part. Very nicely done, sir.'

Matlock looked at the uniformed Negro, grateful for his praise and not a little astonished at his own resourcefulness. 'I don't know if I could do it again.'

'Of course you could,' answered the black, leading Matlock toward the car. 'Extreme stress activates a memory bank, not unlike a computer. Probing, rejecting, accepting – all instantaneously. Until panic, of course. There are interesting studies being made regarding the varying thresholds.'

'Really?' said Matlock as they reached the car door. The Negro motioned him inside. The car lurched forward and they sped off down the highway flanked by the two other automobiles.

'We'll take a diagonal route to the restaurant using the roads set back in the farm country,' said the black behind the wheel. 'We'll approach it from the southwest and let you off about a hundred yards from a path used by employees to reach the rear of the building. We'll point it out to you. Walk directly to the section of the gardens

334

where there's a large white arbor and a circle of flagstones surrounding a goldfish pond. Do you know it?'

'Yes, I do. I'm wondering how *you* do, though.'

The driver smiled. 'I'm not clairvoyant. While you were in the telephone booth, I was in touch with our men by radio. Everything's ready now. We're prepared. Remember, the white arbor and the goldfish pond . . . And here. Here's the notebook and the envelope.' The driver reached down to a flap pocket on the side of his door and pulled out the oilcloth package. The envelope was attached to it by a thick elastic band.

'We'll be there in less than ten minutes,' said the man in command, shifting his weight to get comfortable. Matlock looked at him. Strapped to his leg – sewn into the tight-fitting khaki, actually – was a leather scabbard. He hadn't noticed it before and knew why. The bone-handled knife it contained had only recently been inserted. The scabbard housed a blade at least ten inches long.

Dunois's élite corps was now, indeed, prepared.

Chapter 35

He stood at the side of the tall white arbor. The sun had risen over the eastern curve, the woods behind him still heavy with mist, dully reflecting the light of the early morning. In front of him the newly filled trees formed corridors for the old brick paths that converged into this restful flagstone haven. There were a number of marble benches placed around the circle, all glistening with morning moisture. From the center of the large patio, the bubbling sounds of the man-made goldfish pond continued incessantly with no break in the sound pattern. Birds could be heard activating their myriad signals, greeting the sun, starting the day's foraging.

Matlock's memory wandered back to Herron's Nest, to the forbidding green wall which isolated the old man from the outside world. There were similarities, he thought. Perhaps it was fitting that it should all end in such a place.

He lit a cigarette, extinguishing it after two intakes of smoke. He clutched the notebook, holding it in front of his chest as though it were some impenetrable shield, his head snapping in the direction of every sound, a portion of his life suspended with each movement.

He wondered where Dunois's men were. Where had the élite guard hidden itself? Were they watching him, laughing quietly among themselves at his nervous gestures – his so obvious fear? Or were they spread out, guerrilla fashion? Crouched next to the earth or in the low limbs of the trees, ready to spring, prepared to kill?

And who would they kill? In what numbers and how

armed would be Nimrod's forces? Would Nimrod come? Would Nimrod bring the girl he loved safely back to him? And if Nimrod did, if he finally saw Pat again, would the two of them be caught in the massacre which surely had to follow?

Who *was* Nimrod?

His breathing stopped. The muscles in his arms and legs contorted spastically, stiffened with fear. He closed his eyes tightly – to listen or to pray, he'd never really know, except that his beliefs excluded the existence of God. And so he listened with his eyes shut tight until he was sure.

First one, then two automobiles had turned off the highway and had entered the side road leading to the entrance of the Cheshire Cat. Both vehicles were traveling at enormous speeds, their tires screeching as they rounded the front circle leading into the restaurant parking area.

And then everything was still again. Even the birds were silent; no sound came from anywhere.

Matlock stepped back under the arbor, pressing himself against its lattice frame. He strained to hear – anything.

Silence. Yet not silence! Yet, again, a sound so blended with stillness as to be dismissed as a rustling leaf is dismissed.

It was a scraping. A hesitant, halting scraping from one of the paths in front of him, one of the paths hidden amongst the trees, one of the old brick lanes leading to the flagstone retreat.

At first it was barely audible. Dismissible. Then it became slightly clearer, less hesitant, less unsure.

Then he heard the quiet, tortured moan. It pierced into his brain.

'Jamie . . . Jamie? Please, Jamie . . .'

The single plea, his name, broke off into a sob. He felt a rage he had never felt before in his life. He threw down the oilcloth packet, his eyes blinded by tears and fury.

337

He lunged out of the protective frame of the white arbor and yelled, roared so that his voice startled the birds, who screeched out of the trees, out of their silent sanctuary.

'Pat! Pat! Where are you? Pat, my God, where? *Where!*'

The sobbing – half relief, half pain – became louder.

'Here . . . Here, Jamie! Can't see.'

He traced the sound and raced up the middle brick path. Halfway to the building, against the trunk of a tree, sunk to the ground, he saw her. She was on her knees, her bandaged head against the earth. She had fallen. Rivulets of blood were on the back of her neck; the sutures in her head had broken.

He rushed to her and gently lifted up her head.

Under the bandages on her forehead were layers of three-inch adhesive tape, pushed brutally against the lids of her eyes, stretched tight to her temples – as secure and unmovable as a steel plate covering her face. To try and remove them would be a torture devised in hell.

He held her close and kept repeating her name over and over again.

'Everything will be all right now . . . Everything will be all right . . .'

He lifted her gently off the ground, pressing her face against his own. He kept repeating those words of comfort which came to him in the midst of his rage.

Suddenly, without warning, without any warning at all, the blinded girl screamed, stretching her bruised body, her lacerated head.

'Let them have it, for God's sake! Whatever it is, *give it to them*!'

He stumbled down the brick path back to the flagstone circle.

'I will, I will, my darling . . .'

'Please, Jamie! Don't let them touch me again! *Ever again!*'

'No, my darling. Not ever, not ever . . .'

He slowly lowered the girl on to the ground, on to the soft earth beyond the flagstones.

'Take the tape off! Please take the tape off.'

'I can't now, darling. It would hurt too much. In a little . . .'

'I don't *care*! I can't stand it any longer!'

What could he do? What was he supposed to *do*? Oh, God! Oh, God, you son-of-a-bitching God! *Tell me! Tell me!*

He looked over at the arbor. The oilcloth packet lay on the ground where he had thrown it.

He had no choice now. He did not care now.

'*Nimrod! . . . Nimrod! Come to me now, Nimrod! Bring your goddamn army! Come on and get it, Nimrod! I've got it here!*'

Through the following silence, he heard the footsteps.

Precise, surefooted, emphatic.

On the middle path, Nimrod came into view.

Adrian Sealfont stood on the edge of the flagstone circle.

'I'm sorry, James.'

Matlock lowered the girl's head to the ground. His mind was incapable of functioning. His shock was so total that no words came, he couldn't assimilate the terrible, unbelievable fact in front of him. He rose slowly to his feet.

'Give it to me, James. You have your agreement. We'll take care of you.'

'No . . . No. No, I don't, I *won't believe* you! This isn't so. This isn't the way it can be . . .'

'I'm afraid it is.' Sealfont snapped the fingers of his right hand. It was a signal.

'No . . . No! No! No!' Matlock found that he was screaming. The girl, too, cried out. He turned to Sealfont.

'They said you were taken away! I thought you were dead! I blamed myself for your death!'

'I wasn't taken, I was escorted. Give me the diaries.' Sealfont, annoyed, snapped his fingers again. 'And the Corsican paper. I trust you have both with you.'

There was the slightest sound of a muffled cough, a rasp, an interrupted exclamation. Sealfont looked quickly behind him and spoke sharply to his unseen forces.

'Get out here!'

'Why?'

'Because we *had* to. *I* had to. There was no alternative.'

'No alternative?' Matlock couldn't believe he had heard the words. 'No alternative to *what*?'

'Collapse! We were financially exhausted! Our last reserves were committed; there was no-one left to appeal to. The moral corruption was complete: the pleas of higher education became an unprofitable, national bore. There was no other answer but to assert our own leadership . . . over the corruptors. We did so, and we survived!'

In the agonizing bewilderment of the moment, the pieces of the puzzle fell into place for Matlock. The unknown tumblers of the unfamiliar vault locked into gear and the heavy steel door was opened . . . Carlyle's extraordinary endowment . . . But it was more than Carlyle; Sealfont had just said it. The *pleas* had become a *bore*! It was subtle, but it was there!

Everywhere!

The raising of funds throughout all the campuses continued but there were no cries of panic these days; no threats of financial collapse that had been the themes of a hundred past campaigns in scores of colleges and universities.

The general assumption to be made – if one bothered to

340

make it – was that the crises had been averted. Normality had returned.

But it *hadn't*. The norm had become a monster.

'Oh, my God,' said Matlock softly, in terrified consternation.

'He was no help, I can assure you,' replied Sealfont. 'Our accomplishments are extremely human. Look at us now. *Independent!* Our strength growing systematically. Within five years every major university in the Northeast will be part of a self-sustaining federation!'

'You're diseased . . . You're a *cancer!*'

'We *survive!* The choice was never really that difficult. No-one was going to stop the way things were. Least of all ourselves . . . We simply made the decision ten years ago to alter the principal players.'

'But *you* of all people . . .'

'Yes. I was a good choice, wasn't I?' Sealfont turned once again in the direction of the restaurant, toward the sleeping hill with the old brick paths. He shouted. 'I told you to come out here! There's nothing to worry about. Our friend doesn't care who you are. He'll soon be on his way . . . Won't you, James?'

'You're *insane*. You're . . .'

'Not for a *minute!* There's no-one saner. Or more practical . . . History repeats, you should know that. The fabric is torn, society divided into viciously opposing camps. Don't be fooled by the dormancy; scratch the surface – it bleeds profusely.'

'You're *making* it bleed!' Matlock screamed. There was nothing left; the spring had sprung.

'On the contrary! You pompous, self-righteous *ass!*' Sealfont's eyes stared at him in cold fury, his voice scathing. 'Who gave you the right to make pronouncements? Where were you when men like myself – in *every institution* – faced the very real prospects of closing our doors! You

341

were safe; we *sheltered* you . . . And our appeals went unanswered. There wasn't room for our needs . . .'

'You didn't try! Not hard enough . . .'

'Liar! *Fool!*' Sealfont roared now. He was a man possessed, thought Matlock. Or a man tormented. 'What was *left*? Endowments? Dwindling? There are other, more *viable tax incentives!* . . . Foundations? Small-minded tyrants – smaller allocations! . . . The Government? *Blind! Obscene!* Its priorities are bought! Or returned in kind at the ballot box! We had no funds; we bought no votes! For us, the system had collapsed! It was finished! . . . And no-one knew it better than I did. For years . . . begging, pleading; palms outstretched to the ignorant men and their pompous *committees* . . . It was hopeless; we were killing ourselves. Still no-one listened. And always . . . *always* – behind the excuses and the delays – there was the snickering, the veiled reference to our common God-given frailty. After all . . . we were *teachers*. Not *doers* . . .'

Sealfont's voice was suddenly low. And hard. And utterly convincing as he finished. 'Well, young man, we're *doers now*. The system's damned and rightly so. The leaders never learn. Look to the children. They saw. They understood . . . And we've enrolled them. Our alliance is no coincidence.'

Matlock could do no more than stare at Sealfont. Sealfont had said it: *Look to the children . . . Look, and behold. Look and beware.* The leaders never learn . . . Oh, God! Was it so? Was it really the way things were? The Nimrods and the Dunoises. The 'federations,' the 'élite guards.' Was it happening all over again?

'Now James. Where is the letter you spoke of? Who has it?'

'Letter? What?'

'The letter that is to be mailed this morning. We'll stop it now, won't we?'

'I don't understand.' Matlock was trying, trying *desperately* to make contact with his senses.

'Who has the letter!'

'The letter?' Matlock knew as he spoke that he was saying the wrong words, but he couldn't help himself. He couldn't stop to think, for he was incapable of thought.

'The letter! . . . There *is no letter, is there*?! There's . . . no "incriminating statement" typed and ready to be mailed at ten o'clock in the morning! You were lying!'

'I was lying . . . Lying.' His reserves had been used up. There was nothing now but what was so.

Sealfont laughed softly. It wasn't the laugh Matlock was used to hearing from him. There was a cruelty he'd not heard before.

'Weren't you clever? But you're ultimately weak. I knew that from the beginning. You were the government's perfect choice, for you have no really firm commitments. They called it mobility. I knew it to be unconcerned flexibility. You talk but that's all you do. It's meaningless . . . You're very representative, you know.' Sealfont spoke over his shoulder toward the paths. 'All right, *all* of you! Dr Matlock won't be in a position to reveal any names, any identities. Come out of your hutches, you rabbits!'

'Augh . . .'

The guttural cry was short, punctuating the stillness. Sealfont whipped around.

Then there was another gasp, this the unmistakable sound of a human windpipe expunging its last draft of air.

And another, this coupled with the beginnings of a scream.

'Who is it? Who's up there?' Sealfont rushed to the path from which the last cry came.

He was stopped by the sound of a terrifying shout – cut short – from another part of the sanctuary. He

343

raced back; the beginnings of panic were jarring his control.

'Who's up there?! Where are all of you? *Come down here!*'

The silence returned. Sealfont stared at Matlock.

'What have you done? What have you done, you unimportant little man? Whom have you brought with you? *Who is up there? Answer me!*'

Even if he'd been capable, there was no need for Matlock to reply. From a path at the far end of the garden, Julian Dunois walked into view.

'Good morning, Nimrod.'

Sealfont's eyes bulged. 'Who *are* you? Where are my men?!'

'The name is Jacques Devereaux, Heysoú Daumier, Julian Dunois – take your choice. You were no match for us. You had a complement of ten, I had eight. No match. Your men are dead and how their bodies are disposed of is no concern of yours.'

'Who *are* you?'

'Your enemy.'

Sealfont ripped open his coat with his left hand, plunging his right inside. Dunois shouted a warning. Matlock found himself lurching forward toward the man he'd revered for a decade. Lunging at him with only one thought, one final objective, if it had to be the end of his own life.

To kill.

The face was next to his. The Lincoln-like face now contorted with fear and panic. He brought his right hand down on it like the claw of a terrified animal. He ripped into the flesh and felt the blood spew out of the distorted mouth.

He heard the shattering explosion and felt a sharp, electric pain in his left shoulder. But still he couldn't stop.

'Get off, Matlock! For God's sake, get off!'

He was being pulled away. Pulled away by huge black muscular arms. He was thrown to the ground, the heavy arms holding him down. And through it all he heard the cries, the terrible cries of pain and his name being repeated over and over again.

'Jamie . . . Jamie . . . Jamie . . .'

He lurched upward, using every ounce of strength his violence could summon. The muscular black arms were taken by surprise; he brought his legs up in crushing blows against the ribs and spines above him.

For a few brief seconds, he was free.

He threw himself forward on the hard surface, pounding his arms and knees against the stone. Whatever had happened to him, whatever was meant by the stinging pain, now spreading throughout the whole left side of his body, he had to reach the girl on the ground. The girl who had been through such terror for him.

'Pat!'

The pain was more than he could bear. He fell once more, but he had reached her hand. They held each other's hands, each trying desperately to give comfort to the other, fully aware that both might die at that moment.

Suddenly Matlock's hand went limp.

All was darkness for him.

He opened his eyes and saw the large black kneeling in front of him. He had been propped up into a sitting position at the side of a marble bench. His shirt had been removed, his left shoulder throbbed.

'The pain, I'm sure, is far more serious than the wound,' said the black. 'The upper left section of your body was badly bruised in the automobile, and the bullet penetrated below your left shoulder cartilage. Compounded that way, the pain would be severe.'

'We gave you a local anesthetic. It should help.' The

345

speaker was Julian Dunois, standing to his right. 'Miss Ballantyne has been taken to a doctor. He'll remove the tapes. He's black and sympathetic, but not so much so to treat a man with a bullet wound. We've radioed our own doctor in Torrington. He should be here in twenty minutes.'

'Why didn't you wait for him to help Pat?'

'Frankly, we have to talk. Briefly, but in confidence. Secondly, for her own sake, those tapes had to be removed as quickly as possible.'

'Where's Sealfont?'

'He's disappeared. That's all you know, all you'll ever know. It's important that you understand that. Because, you see, if we must, we will carry out our threat against you and Miss Ballantyne. We don't wish to do that . . . You and I, we are not enemies.'

'You're wrong. We are.'

'Ultimately, perhaps. That would seem inevitable. Right now, however, we've served each other in a moment of great need. We acknowledge it. We trust you do also.'

'I do.'

'Perhaps we've even learned from each other.'

Matlock looked into the eyes of the black revolutionary. 'I understand things better. I don't know what you could have learned from me.'

The revolutionary laughed gently. 'That an individual, by his actions – his courage, if you like – rises above the stigma of labels.'

'I don't understand you.'

'Ponder it. It'll come to you.'

'What happens now? To Pat? To me? I'll be arrested the minute I'm seen.'

'I doubt that sincerely. Within the hour, Greenberg will be reading a document prepared by my organization. By me, to be precise. I suspect the contents will become part

346

of a file buried in the archives. It's most embarrassing. Morally, legally, and certainly politically. Too many profound errors were made . . . We'll act this morning as your intermediary. Perhaps it would be a good time for you to use some of your well-advertised money and go with Miss Ballantyne on a long, recuperative journey . . . I believe that will be agreed upon with alacrity. I'm sure it will.'

'And Sealfont? What happens to him. Are you going to kill him?'

'Does Nimrod deserve to die? Don't bother to answer; we'll not discuss the subject. Suffice it to say he'll remain alive until certain questions are answered.'

'Have you any idea what's going to happen when he's found to be missing?'

'There will be explosions, ugly rumors. About a great many things. When icons are shattered, the believers panic. So be it. Carlyle will have to live with it . . . Rest, now. The doctor will be here soon.' Dunois turned .is attention to a uniformed Negro who had come up to him and spoken softly. The kneeling black who had bandaged his wound stood up. Matlock watched the tall, slender figure of Julian Dunois, quietly, confidently issuing his instructions, and felt the pain of gratitude. It was made worse because Dunois suddenly took on another image.

It was the figure of death.

'Dunois?'

'Yes?'

'Be careful.'

Epilogue

The blue green waters of the Caribbean mirrored the hot afternoon sun in countless thousands of swelling, blinding reflections. The sand was warm to the touch, soft under the feet. This isolated stretch of the island was at peace with itself and with a world beyond that it did not really acknowledge.

Matlock walked down to the edge of the water and let the miniature waves wash over his ankles. Like the sand on the beach, the water was warm.

He carried a newspaper sent to him by Greenberg. Part of a newspaper, actually.

KILLINGS IN CARLYLE, CONN.

23 SLAIN, BLACKS AND WHITES, TOWN
STUNNED, FOLLOWS DISAPPEARANCE
OF UNIVERSITY PRESIDENT

CARLYLE, MAY 10 – On the outskirts of this small university town, in a section housing large, old estates, a bizarre mass killing took place yesterday. Twenty-three men were slain; the federal authorities have speculated the killings were the result of an ambush that claimed many lives of both the attackers and the attacked . . .

There followed a cold recitation of identities, short summaries of police file associations.

348

Julian Dunois was among them.

The spectre of death had not been false; Dunois hadn't escaped. The violence he engendered had to be the violence that would take his life.

The remainder of the article contained complicated speculations on the meaning and the motives of the massacre's strange cast of characters. And the possible connection to the disappearance of Adrian Sealfont.

Speculations only. No mention of Nimrod, nothing of himself; no word of any long-standing federal investigations. Not the truth; nothing of the truth.

Matlock heard his cottage door open, and he turned around. Pat was standing on the small veranda fifty yards away over the dune. She waved and started down the steps toward him.

She was dressed in shorts and a light silk blouse; she was barefoot and smiling. The bandages had been removed from her legs and arms, and the Caribbean sun had tanned her skin to a lovely bronze. She had devised a wide orange headband to cover the wounds above her forehead.

She would not marry him. She said there would be no marriage out of pity, out of debt – real or imagined. But Matlock knew there would be a marriage. Or there would be no marriages for either of them. Julian Dunois had made it so.

'Did you bring cigarettes?' he asked.

'No. No cigarettes,' she replied. 'I brought matches.'

'That's cryptic.'

'I used that word – cryptic – with Jason. Do you remember?'

'I do. You were mad as hell.'

'You were spaced out . . . In hell. Let's walk down to the jetty.'

'Why did you bring matches?' He took her hand, putting the newspaper under his arm.

'A funeral pyre. Archeologists place great significance in funeral pyres.'

'What?'

'You've been carrying around that damned paper all day. I want to burn it.' She smiled at him, gently.

'Burning it won't change what's in it.'

Pat ignored his observation. 'Why do you think Jason sent it to you? I thought the whole idea was several weeks of nothing. No newspapers, no radios, no contact with anything but warm water and white sand. He made the rules and he broke them.'

'He *recommended* the rules and knew they were difficult to live by.'

'He should have let someone else break them. He's not as good a friend as I thought he was.'

'Maybe he's a better one.'

'That's sophistry.' She squeezed his hand. A single, over-extended wave lapped across their bare feet. A silent gull swooped down from the sky into the water offshore; its wings flapped against the surface, its neck shook violently. The bird ascended screeching, no quarry in its beak.

'Greenberg knows I've got a very unpleasant decision to make.'

'You've made it. He knows that, too.'

Matlock looked at her. Of course Greenberg knew; she knew, too, he thought. 'There'll be a lot more pain; perhaps more than justified.'

'That's what they'll tell you. They'll tell you to let them do it their way. Quietly, efficiently, with as little embarrassment as possible. For everyone.'

'Maybe it's best; maybe they're right.'

'You don't believe that for a second.'

'No, I don't.'

They walked in silence for a while. The jetty was in

front of them, its rocks placed decades, perhaps centuries ago, to restrain a long-forgotten current. It was a natural fixture now.

As Nimrod had become a natural fixture, a logical extension of the anticipated; undesirable but nevertheless expected. To be fought in deep cover.

Mini-America . . . just below the surface.

Company policy, man.

Everywhere.

The hunters, builders. The killers and their quarry were making alliances.

Look to the children. They understand . . . We've enrolled them.

The leaders never learn.

A microcosm of the inevitable? Made unavoidable because the needs were real? Had been real for years?

And still the leaders would not learn.

'Jason said once that truth is neither good nor bad. Simply truth. That's why he sent me this.' Matlock sat down on a large flat rock; Pat stood beside him. The tide was coming in and the sprays of the small waves splashed upward. Pat reached over and took the two pages of the newspaper.

'This is the truth then.' A statement.

'Their truth. Their judgment. Assign obvious labels and continue the game. The good guys and the bad guys and the posse will reach the pass on time. Just in time. This time.'

'What's your truth?'

'Go back and tell the story. All of it.'

'They'll disagree. They'll give you reasons why you shouldn't. Hundreds of them.'

'They won't convince me.'

'Then they'll be against you. They've threatened; they won't accept interference. That's what Jason wants you to know.'

351

'That's what he wants me to think about.'

Pat held the pages of the newspaper in front of her and struck a wooden island match on the dry surface of a rock.

The paper burned haltingly, retarded by the Caribbean spray.

But it burned.

'That's not a very impressive funeral pyre,' said Matlock.

'It'll do until we get back.'

ROBERT LUDLUM

THE CRY OF THE HALIDON

ROBERT LUDLUM

THE CRY OF THE HALIDON

HarperCollinsPublishers

For all those who in strictest confidence
helped me research this novel so
many years ago – you know who you
are, and I remain forever grateful.

INTRODUCTION

A number of years ago – a quarter of a century to be precise – an author barely in his forties was so exuberant about the fact that he had actually *published* two novels that, like an addict, he relentlessly pursued the source of his addiction. Fortunately, it was the narcotic of writing, chemically not dangerous, mentally an obsession. That obsessed author, me, is now far older and only slightly wiser, and I *was* exhilarated until I was given a gentle lecture by a cadre of well-meaning publishing executives. I was stunned – wall-eyed and speechless.

Apparently, it was the conventional wisdom of the time that no author who sold more than a dozen or so books to his immediate family and very close friends should write more than one novel a year! If he did, he would automatically be considered a 'hack' by 'readers and critics alike'. (I loved this last dual-personae, as expressed.) Such writing giants of the past came to mind, like Dickens, Trollope and Thackeray, fellows who thought nothing of filling up reams of copy for monthly and weekly magazines, much of said copy excerpts from their novels in progress. Perhaps, I thought silently, 'hack' had a different meaning then, as in 'he can't hack it', which implies that to 'hack' is good, as opposed to 'he's a hack', obviously pejorative. It was all too confusing, and, as I mentioned, I was speechless anyway. So I said nothing.

Nevertheless, I was the new kid on the block, more precisely on Publishers Row. I listened to my more experienced betters, and submitted *The Cry of the Halidon*, as written by someone called 'Jonathan Ryder', actually the first name of one of our sons and a contraction of my wife's stage name when she was a popular actress in New York and its environs.

I'd be foolish to deny the influence this novel had on subsequent books, for it was the first time I actively forced myself to research obscure history along with the roots of myth, as opposed to well-documented, if difficult to unearth, historical records. For me, it was terrific. My wife, Mary, and I flew to Jamaica, where most of the novel was to take place. I was like a kid in a giant toy store. There was so much to absorb, to study! I even stole real names before I learned you weren't supposed to do that without permission. For example, 'Timothy Durell', the first character we meet in the book, actually was the youngest and brightest manager of a large international resort that I'd ever met; 'Robert Hanley' is a pilot in the novel and was, as well, in everyday life. Among other detours, Bob ferried Howard Hughes around the Caribbean, and was on Errol Flynn's payroll as his private pilot when the motion-picture star lived in Jamaica. (Other liberties I really should not reveal – on advice of counsel.)

Of course, research is that *antipasto* before an entrée, or the succulent shrimp cocktail before the hearty prime rib, the appetizer leading to serious dining. It is also both a trap and a springboard. A trap, for it ensnares one in a world of geometric probabilities that an author resists leaving, and a springboard, for it fires one's imagination to get on with the infinite possibilities a writer finds irresistible.

The first inkling I had regarding the crosscurrents of deeply felt Jamaican religiosity and myth came when my wife and I took our daughter, along with the regal lady who ran the kitchen at our rented house, to a native village market in Port Antonio. Our young daughter was a very blonde child and very beautiful (still is). She became the instant centre of attention, for this was, indeed, a remote thoroughfare and the inhabitants were not used to the sight of a very blonde white child. The natives were delightful, as most Jamaicans are: they're gentle, filled with laughter and kindness and intelligent concern for the guests on their island. One man, however, was none of these. He was large, abusive, and kept making remarks that any parent would find revolting. The people around him admonished him; many shouted, but he simply became more abusive, bordering on the physical. I'd had enough.

Having been trained as a Marine – and far younger than I am now – I approached this offensive individual, spun him around, hammerlocked his right arm, and marched him across the dirt road to the edge of a ravine. I sat him down on a rock, and vented my parental spleen.

Suddenly, he became docile, trancelike, then started to chant in a sing-song manner words to the effect of: 'The Hollydawn, the Hollydawn, all is for the Hollydawn!' I asked him what he was talking about. 'You can never know, mon! It is not for you to know. It is the holy church of the Hollydawn! *Obeah, Obeah.* Give me money for the magic of the Hollydawn!'

I realized he was high on something – grass, alcohol, who knows? I gave him a few dollars and sent him on his way. An elderly Jamaican subsequently came up to me, his dark eyes sad, knowing. 'I'm sorry, young man,' he said. 'We watched closely and would have rushed to your assistance should you have been in danger.'

'You mean he might have had a gun, a weapon?'

'No, never a gun, no one allows those people to have guns, but a weapon, yes. He frequently carries a machete in his trousers.'

I swallowed several times, and no doubt turned considerably paler than I had been. But the episode did ignite the fuses of my imagination. From there, and courtesy of Bob Hanley and his plane, I crisscrossed the infamous Cock Pit jungles, flying low and seeing things no one in a commercial airliner could ever see. I travelled to Kingston, to waterfronts Bob thought I was nuts to visit. (Remember, I was much, much younger.) I explored the coves, the bays and the harbours of the north coast, questioning, always questioning, frequently met by laughter and dancing eyes, but never once hostility. I even went so far as to initiate negotiations to purchase Errol Flynn's old estate, but, as I recall, Hanley hammerlocked *me* and dragged me back to the plane under sentence of bodily harm. (Much younger!)

I was having so much fun that one evening, while sipping cocktails in the glorious glow of a Jamaican sunset, Mary turned to me and, in her delightfully understated way, said, 'You were actually going to *buy* the Flynn estate?'

'Well, there are a series of natural waterfalls leading to a pool, and –'

'Bob Hanley has my permission to severely wound you. Your right hand excepted.' (I write in longhand.) 'Do you think you'll ever start the novel?'

'What novel?'

'I rest my case. I think it's time we go home.'

'What home . . . ?'

'The other children, our sons.'

'*I* know *them*! Big fellas!'

Do you get the picture? Call it island fever, a mad dog in the noonday sun, or a mentally impaired author obsessed with *Research*. But my bride was right. It was time to go home and begin the hearty prime rib.

While re-reading this novel for editorial considerations, I was struck by how much I'd forgotten, and the memories came flooding back. Not regarding the quality of the book – that's for others to comment on one way or another – but the things I experienced that gave rise to whole scenes, composite characters, back-country roads dotted with the great houses and their skeletons of bygone eras, the *cocoruru* peddlers on the white sandy beaches with their machetes decapitating the fruit into which was poured the rum – above all, the countless hundreds of large dark eyes that held the secrets of centuries.

It was a beautiful time, and I thank all those who made it possible. I hope you enjoy the novel, for I truly enjoyed working on it.

Robert Ludlum
Naples, Florida

ONE

Port Antonio/London

1

Port Antonio, Jamaica

The white sheet of ocean spray burst up from the coral rock and appeared suspended, the pitch-blue waters of the Caribbean serving as a backdrop. The spray cascaded forward and downward and asserted itself over thousands of tiny, sharp, ragged crevices that were the coral overlay. It became ocean again, at one with its source.

Timothy Durell walked out on the far edge of the huge free-form pool deck, imposed over the surrounding coral, and watched the increasing combat between water and rock. This isolated section of the Jamaican north coast was a compromise between man and natural phenomenon. Trident Villas were built on top of a coral sheet, surrounded by it on three sides, with a single drive that led to the roads in front. The villas were miniature replicas of their name: guest houses that fronted the sea and the fields of coral. Each an entity in itself; each isolated from the others, as the entire resort complex was isolated from the adjoining territory of Port Antonio.

Durell was the young English manager of Trident Villas, a graduate of London's College of Hotel Management, with a series of letters after his name indicating more knowledge and experience than his youthful appearance would seem to support. But Durell was good; he knew it, the Trident's owners knew it. He never stopped looking for the unexpected – that, along with routine smoothness, was the essence of superior management.

He had found the unexpected now. And it troubled him.

It was a mathematical impossibility. Or, if not impossible, certainly improbable in the extreme.

3

It simply did not make sense.

'Mr Durell?'

He turned. His Jamaican secretary, brown, her skin and features bespeaking the age-old coalition of Africa and Empire, had walked out on the deck with a message.

'Yes?'

'Lufthansa flight 16 from Munich will be late getting into Montego.'

'That's the Keppler reservation, isn't it?'

'Yes. They'll miss the in-island connection.'

'They should have come into Kingston . . .'

'They didn't,' said the girl, her voice carrying the same disapproval as Durell's statement, but not so sternly. 'They obviously don't wish to spend the night in Montego; they had Lufthansa radio ahead. You're to get them a charter . . .'

'On three hours' notice? Let the Germans do it! It's their equipment that's late . . .'

'They tried. None available in Mo'Bay.'

'Of course, there isn't . . . I'll ask Hanley. He'll be back from Kingston with the Warfields by five o'clock.'

'He may not wish to . . .'

'He will. We're in a spot. I trust it's not indicative of the week.'

'Why do you say that? What bothers you?'

Durell turned back to the railing overlooking the fields and cliffs of coral. He lighted a cigarette, cupping the flame against the bursts of warm breeze. 'Several things. I'm not sure I can put my finger on them all. One I *do* know.' He looked at the girl, but his eyes were remembering. 'A little over twelve months ago, the reservations for this particular week began coming in. Eleven months ago they were complete. All the villas were booked . . . for this particular week.'

'Trident's popular. What is so unusual?'

'You don't understand. Since eleven months ago, every one of those reservations has stood firm. Not a single cancellation, or even a minor change of dates. Not even a day.'

4

'Less bother for you. I'd think you'd be pleased.'

'Don't you see? It's a mathematical imp – well, inconsistency, to say the least. Twenty villas. Assuming couples, that's forty families, really – mothers, fathers, aunts, uncles, cousins . . . For eleven months nothing has happened to change anyone's plans. None of the principals died – and at our rates we don't cater exclusively to the young. No misfortunes of consequence, no simple business interferences, or measles or mumps or weddings or funerals or lingering illness. Yet we're not the Queen's coronation; we're just a week-in-Jamaica.'

The girl laughed. 'You're playing with numbers, Mr Durell. You're put out because your well-organized waiting list hasn't been used.'

'And the way they're all arriving,' continued the young manager, his words coming faster. 'This Keppler, he's the only one with a problem, and how does he solve it? Having an aircraft radio ahead from somewhere over the Atlantic. Now, you'll grant *that's* a bit much . . . The others? No one asks for a car to meet them, no in-island confirmations required, no concerns about luggage or distances. Or anything. They'll just be here.'

'Not the Warfields. Captain Hanley flew his plane to Kingston for the Warfields.'

'But *we* didn't know that. Hanley assumed that we did, but we didn't. The arrangements were made privately from London. He thought we'd given them his name; we hadn't. *I* hadn't.'

'No one else would . . .' The girl stopped. 'But everyone's . . . from all over.'

'Yes. Almost evenly divided. The States, England, France, Germany, and . . . Haiti.'

'What's your point?' asked the girl, seeing the concern on Durell's face.

'I have a strange feeling that all our guests for the week are acquainted. But they don't want us to know it.'

London, England

The tall, light-haired American in the unbuttoned Burberry trench coat walked out the Strand entrance of the Savoy Hotel. He stopped for an instant and looked up at the English sky between the buildings of the courtyard. It was a perfectly normal thing to do – to observe the sky, to check the elements after emerging from shelter – but this man did not give the normally cursory glance and form a judgment based primarily on the chill factor.

He looked.

Any geologist who made his living developing geophysical surveys for governments, companies and foundations knew that the weather was income; it connoted progress or delay.

Habit.

His clear grey eyes were deeply set beneath wide eyebrows, darker than the light brown hair that fell with irritating regularity over his forehead. His face was the colour of a man's exposed to the weather, the tone permanently stained by the sun, but not burned. The lines at the sides and below his eyes seemed stamped more from his work than from age; again a face in constant conflict with the elements. The cheekbones were high, the mouth full, the jaw casually slack; for there was a softness also about the man . . . in abstract contrast to the hard, professional look.

This softness, too, was in his eyes. Not weak, but inquisitive; the eyes of a man who probed . . . perhaps because he had not probed sufficiently in the past.

Things . . . things . . . had happened to this man.

The instant of observation over, he greeted the uniformed doorman with a smile, and a brief shake of his head, indicating a negative.

'No taxi, Mr McAuliff?'

'Thanks, no, Jack. I'll walk.'

'A bit nippy, sir.'

'It's refreshing – only going a few blocks.'

The doorman tipped his cap and turned his attention to an

6

incoming Jaguar. Alexander McAuliff continued across the courtyard, past the theatre and the American Express office to the Strand. He crossed the pavement and entered the flow of human traffic heading north towards Waterloo Bridge. He buttoned his raincoat, pulling the lapels up to ward off London's February chill.

It was nearly one o'clock; he was to be at the Waterloo intersection by one. He would make it with only minutes to spare.

He had agreed to meet the Dunstone company man this way, but he hoped his tone of voice had conveyed his annoyance. He had been perfectly willing to take a taxi, or rent a car, or hire a chauffeur . . . if any or all were necessary; but if Dunstone was sending a car for him, why not send it to the Savoy? It wasn't that he minded the walk; he just hated to meet people in vehicles in the middle of congested streets. It was a goddamn nuisance.

The Dunstone man had had a short, succinct explanation that was, for the Dunstone man, the only reason necessary – for all things:

'Mr Julian Warfield prefers it this way.'

He spotted the car immediately. It had to be Dunstone's – and/or Warfield's. A St James Rolls-Royce, its glistening black, hand-tooled body breaking space majestically, anachronistically, among the petrol-conscious Austins, MGs and European imports. He waited on the kerb, ten feet from the crossing onto the bridge. He would not gesture or acknowledge the slowly approaching Rolls. He waited until the car stopped directly in front of him, a chauffeur driving, the rear window open.

'Mr McAuliff?' said the eager, young-old face in the frame.

'Mr Warfield?' asked McAuliff, knowing that this fiftyish, precise-looking executive was not.

'Good heavens, no. The name's Preston. Do hop in; I think we're holding up the traffic.'

'Yes, you are.' Alex got into the back seat as Preston moved over. The Englishman extended his hand.

7

'It's a pleasure. I'm the one you've been talking to on the telephone.'

'Yes . . . Mr Preston.'

'I'm really very sorry for the inconvenience, meeting like this. Old Julian has his quirks, I'll grant you that.'

McAuliff decided he might have misjudged the Dunstone man. 'It was a little confusing, that's all. If the object was precautionary – for what reason I can't imagine – he picked a hell of a car to send.'

Preston laughed. 'True. But then, I've learned over the years that Warfield, like God, moves in mysterious ways that basically are quite logical. He's really all right. You're having lunch with him, you know.'

'Fine. Where?'

'Belgravia.'

'Aren't we going the wrong way?'

'Julian and God – basically logical, old chap.'

The Rolls crossed the Waterloo Bridge, proceeded south to The Cut, turned left until Blackfriars Road, then left again, over Blackfriars Bridge and north into Holborn. It was a confusing route.

Ten minutes later the car pulled up to the entrance canopy of a white stone building with a brass plate to the right of the glass double doors that read SHAFTESBURY ARMS. The doorman pulled at the handle and spoke jovially.

'Good afternoon, Mr Preston.'

'Good afternoon, Ralph.'

McAuliff followed Preston into the building, to a bank of three elevators in the well-appointed hallway. 'Is this Warfield's place?' he asked, more to pass the moment than for inquiry.

'No, actually. It's mine. Although I won't be joining you for lunch. However, I trust Cook implicitly; you'll be well taken care of.'

'I won't try to follow that . . . "Julian and God".'

Preston smiled noncommittally as the lift door opened.

Julian Warfield was talking on the telephone when Preston

ushered McAuliff into the tastefully – elegantly – decorated living room. The old man was standing by an antique table in front of a tall window overlooking Belgrave Square. The size of the window, flanked by long white curtains, emphasized Warfield's shortness. He is really quite a small man, thought Alex as he acknowledged Warfield's wave with a nod and a smile.

'You'll send the accrual statistics on to Macintosh, then,' said Warfield deliberately into the telephone; he was not asking a question. 'I'm sure he'll disagree, and you can both hammer it out. Goodbye.' The diminutive old man replaced the receiver and looked over at Alex. 'Mr McAuliff, is it?' Then he chuckled. 'That was a prime lesson in business. Employ experts who disagree on just about everything and take the best arguments from both for compromise.'

'Good advice generally, I'd say,' replied McAuliff. 'As long as the experts disagree on the subject matter and not just chemically.'

'You're quick. I like that . . . Good to see you.' Warfield crossed to Preston. His walk was like his speech: deliberate, paced slowly. Mentally confident, physically unsure. 'Thank you for the use of your flat, Clive. And Virginia, of course. From experience, I know the lunch will be splendid.'

'Not at all, Julian. I'll be off.'

McAuliff turned his head sharply, without subtlety, and looked at Preston. The man's first-name familiarity with old Warfield was the last thing he expected. Clive Preston smiled and walked rapidly out of the room as Alex watched him, bewildered.

'To answer your unspoken questions,' said Warfield, 'although you have been speaking with Preston on the telephone, he is not with Dunstone plc, Mr McAuliff.'

Alexander turned back to the diminutive businessman. 'Whenever I phoned the Dunstone offices for you, I had to give a number for someone to return the call –'

'Always within a few minutes,' interrupted Warfield. 'We never kept you waiting; that would have been rude. Whenever

9

you telephoned – four times, I believe – my secretary informed Mr Preston. At his offices.'

'And the Rolls at Waterloo was Preston's,' said Alex.

'Yes.'

'So if anyone was following me, my business is with Preston. Has been since I've been in London.'

'That was the object.'

'Why?'

'Self-evident, I should think. We'd rather not have anyone know we're discussing a contract with you. Our initial call to you in New York stressed that point, I believe.'

'You said it was confidential. Everyone says that. If you meant it to this degree, why did you even use the name of Dunstone?'

'Would you have flown over otherwise?'

McAuliff thought for a moment. A week of skiing in Aspen notwithstanding, there *had* been several other projects. But Dunstone *was* Dunstone, one of the largest corporations in the international market. 'No. I probably wouldn't have.'

'We were convinced of that. We knew you were about to negotiate with ITT about a little matter in southern Germany.'

Alex stared at the old man. He couldn't help but smile. 'That, Mr Warfield, was supposed to be as confidential as anything you might be considering.'

Warfield returned the good humour. 'Then we know who deals best in confidence, don't we? ITT is patently obvious . . . Come, we'll have a drink, then lunch. I know your preference: Scotch with ice. Somewhat more ice than I think is good for the system.'

The old man laughed softly and led McAuliff to a mahogany bar across the room. He made drinks rapidly, his ancient hands moving deftly, in counterpoint to his walk. He offered Alex a glass and indicated that they should sit down. 'I've learned quite a bit about you. Mr McAuliff. Rather fascinating.'

'I heard someone was asking around.'

They were across from one another, in armchairs. At McAuliff's statement, Warfield took his eyes off his glass and

10

looked sharply, almost angrily, at Alex. 'I find that hard to believe.'

'Names weren't used, but the information reached me. Eight sources. Five American, two Canadian, one French.'

'*Not* traceable to Dunstone.' Warfield's short body seemed to stiffen; McAuliff understood that he had touched an exposed nerve.

'I said names weren't mentioned.'

'Did *you* use the Dunstone name in any ensuing conversations? Tell me the truth, Mr McAuliff.'

'There'd be no reason not to tell you the truth,' answered Alex, a touch disagreeably. 'No, I did not.'

'I believe you.'

'You should.'

'If I didn't, I'd pay you handsomely for your time and suggest you return to America and take up with ITT.'

'I may do that anyway, mightn't I? I *do* have that option.'

'You like money.'

'Very much.'

Julian Warfield placed his glass down and brought his thin, small hands together. 'Alexander T. McAuliff. The "T" is for Tarquin, rarely, if ever, used. It's not even on your stationery; rumour is you don't care for it . . .'

'True. I'm not violent about it.'

'Alexander Tarquin McAuliff, thirty-eight years old. BS, MS, PhD, but the title of Doctor is used as rarely as his middle name. The geology departments of several leading American universities, including California Tech and Columbia, lost an excellent research fellow when Dr McAuliff decided to put his expertise to more commercial pursuits.' The man smiled, his expression one of how-am-I-doing; but, again, not a question.

'Faculty and laboratory pressures are no less aggravating than those outside. Why not get paid for them?'

'Yes. We agreed you like money.'

'Don't you?'

Warfield laughed, and his laugh was genuine and loud. His

thin, short body fairly shook with pleasure as he brought Alex his glass. 'Excellent reply. Really quite fine.'

'It wasn't that good . . .'

'But you're interrupting me,' said Warfield as he returned to his chair. 'It's my intention to impress you.'

'Not about myself, I hope.'

'No. Our thoroughness . . . You are from a close-knit family, secure academic surroundings –'

'Is this necessary?' asked McAuliff, fingering his glass, interrupting the old man.

'Yes, it is,' replied Warfield simply, continuing as though his line of thought were unbroken. 'Your father was – and is, in retirement – a highly regarded agro-scientist; your mother, unfortunately deceased, a delightfully romantic soul adored by all. It was she who gave you the "Tarquin", and until she died you never denied the initial or the name. You had an older brother, a pilot, shot down in the last days of the World War; you yourself made a splendid record in Vietnam . . . Upon receipt of your doctorate, it was assumed that you would continue the family's academic tradition. Until personal tragedy propelled you out of the laboratory. A young woman – your fiancée – was killed on the streets of New York. At night. You blamed yourself . . . and others. You were to have met her. Instead, a hastily called, quite unnecessary research meeting prohibited it . . . Alexander Tarquin McAuliff fled the university. Am I drawing an accurate picture?'

'You're invading my privacy. You're repeating information that may be personal but hardly classified. Easy to piece together. You're also extremely obnoxious. I don't think I want to have lunch with you.'

'A few more minutes. Then it is your decision.'

'It's my decision right now.'

'Of course. Just a bit more . . . Dr McAuliff embarked on a new career with extraordinary precision. He hired out to several established geological-survey firms, where his work was outstanding; then left the companies and underbid them on upcoming contracts. Industrial construction knows no national boundaries: Fiat builds in Moscow; General Motors in Berlin; British Petroleum in Buenos Aires; Volkswagen in New Jersey, USA; Renault in Madrid – I could go on for hours. And everything begins with a single file folder profuse with complicated technical paragraphs describing what is and what is not possible in terms of construction upon the land. Such a simple, taken-for-granted exercise. But without that file, nothing else is possible.'

'Your few minutes are about up, Warfield. And, speaking for the community of surveyors, we thank you for acknowledging our necessity. As you say, we're so often taken for granted.' McAuliff put his glass down on the table next to his armchair and started to get up.

Warfield spoke quietly, precisely. 'You have twenty-three bank accounts, including four in Switzerland; I can supply the code numbers if you like. Others in Prague, Tel Aviv, Montreal, Brisbane, São Paulo, Kingston, Los Angeles, and, of course, New York, among others.'

Alexander remained immobile at the edge of his chair and stared at the little old man. 'You've been busy.'

'Thorough . . . Nothing patently illegal; none of the accounts is enormous. Altogether they total two million four hundred-odd US dollars, as of several days ago when you flew from New York. Unfortunately, the figure is meaningless. Due to international tax agreements regarding financial transfers, the money cannot be centralized.'

'Now I know I don't want to have lunch with you.'

'Perhaps not. But how would you like another two million dollars? Free and clear, all American taxes paid. Deposited in the bank of your choice.'

McAuliff continued to stare at Warfield. It was several moments before he spoke.

'You're serious, aren't you?'

'Utterly.'

'For a *survey*?'

'Yes.'

'There are five good houses right here in London. For that kind of money, why call on me? Why not use them?'

'We don't want a firm. We want an individual. A man we have investigated thoroughly; a man we believe will honour the most important aspect of the contract. Secrecy.'

'That sounds ominous.'

'Not at all. A financial necessity. If word got out, the speculators would move in. Land prices would skyrocket, the project would become untenable. It would be abandoned.'

'What is it? Before I give you my answer, I have to know that.'

'We're planning to build a city. In Jamaica.'

2

McAuliff politely rejected Warfield's offer to have Preston's car brought back to Belgravia for him. Alex wanted to walk, to think in the cold winter air. It helped him to sort out his thoughts while in motion: the brisk, chilling winds somehow forced his concentration inward.

Not that there was so much to think about as to absorb. In a sense, the hunt was over. The end of the intricate maze was in sight, after eleven years of complicated wandering. Not for the money *per se*. But for money as the conveyor belt to independence.

Complete. Total. Never having to do what he did not wish to do.

Ann's death – murder – had been the springboard. Certainly the rationalization, he understood that. But the rationalization had solid roots, beyond the emotional explosion. The research meeting – accurately described by Warfield as 'quite unnecessary' – was symptomatic of the academic system.

All laboratory activities were geared to justify whatever grants were in the offing. God! How much useless activity! How many pointless meetings! How often useful work went unfinished because a research grant did not materialize or a department administrator shifted priorities to achieve more obvious *progress* for *progress*-oriented foundations.

He could not fight the academic system; he was too angry to join its politics. So he left it.

He could not stand the companies, either. *Jesus!* A different set of priorities, leading to only one objective: profit. Only profit. Projects that didn't produce the most favourable 'profit picture' were abandoned without a backward glance.

15

Stick to business. Don't waste time.

So he left the companies and went out on his own. Where a man could decide for himself the price of immediate values. And whether they were worth it.

All things considered, everything ... everything Warfield proposed was not only correct and acceptable, it was glorious. An unencumbered, legitimate two million dollars for a survey Alex knew he could handle.

He knew vaguely the area in Jamaica to be surveyed: east and south of Falmouth, on the coast as far as Duncan's Bay; in the interior into the Cock Pit. It was actually the Cock Pit territory that Dunstone seemed most interested in: vast sections of uninhabited – in some cases, unmapped – mountains and jungles. Undeveloped miles ten minutes by air to the sophistication of Montego Bay, fifteen to the expanding, exploding New Kingston.

Dunstone would deliver him the specific degree marks within the next three weeks, during which time he was to assemble his team.

He was back on the Strand now, the Savoy several blocks away. He hadn't resolved anything, really; there was nothing to resolve, except perhaps the decision to start looking for people at the university. He was sure there would be no lack of interested applicants; he only hoped he could find the level of qualification he needed.

Everything was fine. Really *fine*.

He walked down the alley into the courtyard, smiled at the doorman, and passed the thick glass doors of the Savoy. He crossed to the reservations desk on the right and asked for any messages.

There were none.

But there was something else. The tuxedoed clerk behind the counter asked him a question.

'Will you be going upstairs, Mr McAuliff?'

'Yes ... yes, I'll be going upstairs,' answered Alex, bewildered at the inquiry. 'Why?'

'I beg your pardon?'

'Why do you ask?' McAuliff smiled.

'Floor service, sir,' replied the man, with intelligence in his eyes, assurance in his soft British voice. 'In the event of any cleaning or pressing. These are frightfully busy hours.'

'Of course. Thank you.' Alex smiled again, nodded his appreciation, and started for the small brass-grilled elevator. He had tried to pry something else from the Savoy man's eyes, but he could not. Yet he knew something else was there. In the six years he had been staying at the hotel, no one had ever asked him if he was 'going upstairs'. Considering English . . . Savoy propriety, it was an unlikely question.

Or were his cautions, his Dunstone cautions, asserting themselves too quickly, too strongly?

Inside his room, McAuliff stripped to shorts, put on a bathrobe, and ordered ice from the floor steward. He still had most of a bottle of Scotch on the bureau. He sat in an armchair next to the window and opened a newspaper, considerately left by room service.

With the swiftness for which the Savoy stewards were known, there was a knock on his corridor door. McAuliff got out of the chair and then stopped.

The Savoy stewards did not knock on hallway doors – they let themselves into the foyers. Room privacy was obtained by locking the bedroom doors, which opened onto the foyers.

Alex walked rapidly to the door and opened it. There was no steward. Instead, there was a tall, pleasant-looking middle-aged man in a tweed overcoat.

'Mr McAuliff?'

'Yes?'

'My name is Hammond. May I speak to you, sir?'

'Oh? Sure . . . certainly.' Alex looked down the hallway as he gestured the man to pass him. 'I rang for ice; I thought you were the steward.'

'Then may I step into your . . . excuse me, your lavatory, sir? I'd rather not be seen.'

'What? Are you from Warfield?'

'No, Mr McAuliff, British Intelligence.'

3

'That was a sorry introduction, Mr McAuliff. Do you mind if I begin again?' Hammond walked into the bedroom-sitting room. Alex dropped ice cubes into a glass.

'No need to. I've never had anyone knock on my hotel door, say he's with British Intelligence, and ask to use the bathroom. Has kind of a quaint ring to it . . . Drink?'

'Thank you. Short, if you please; a touch of soda will be fine.'

McAuliff poured as requested and handed Hammond his glass. 'Take off your coat. Sit down.'

'You're most hospitable. Thank you.' The Englishman removed his tweed overcoat and placed it carefully on the back of a chair.

'I'm most curious, that's what I am, Mr Hammond.' McAuliff sat by the window, the visitor across from him. 'The clerk at the desk; he asked if I was going upstairs. That was for you, wasn't it?'

'Yes, it was. He knows nothing, however. He thinks the managers wished to see you unobtrusively. It's often done that way. Over financial matters, usually.'

'Thanks very much.'

'We'll set it right, if it disturbs you.'

'It doesn't.'

'I was in the cellar. When word reached me, I came up in the service lift.'

'Rather elaborate –'

'Rather necessary,' interrupted the Englishman. 'For the past few days, you've been under continuous surveillance. I don't mean to alarm you.'

18

McAuliff paused, his glass halfway to his lips. 'You just have. I gather the surveillance wasn't yours.'

'Well, you could say we observed – from a distance – both the followers and their subject.' Hammond sipped his whisky and smiled.

'I'm not sure I like this game,' said McAuliff quietly.

'Neither do we. May I introduce myself more completely?'

'Please do.'

Hammond removed a black leather identification case from his jacket pocket, rose from the chair, and crossed to McAuliff. He held out the flat case and flipped it open. 'There is a telephone number below the seal. I'd appreciate it if you would place a call for verification, Mr McAuliff.'

'It's not necessary, Mr Hammond. You haven't asked me for anything.'

'I may.'

'If you do, I'll call.'

'Yes, I see ... Very well.' Hammond returned to his chair. 'As my credentials state, I'm with Military Intelligence. What they do not say is that I have been assigned to the Foreign Office and Inland Revenue. I'm a financial analyst.'

'In the Intelligence Service?' Alex got out of his chair and went to the ice bucket and the whisky. He gestured at them; Hammond shook his head. 'That's unusual, isn't it? I can understand a bank or a brokerage office, not the cloak-and-dagger business.'

'The vast majority of intelligence gathering is allied with finance, Mr McAuliff. In greater or lesser degrees of subtlety, of course.'

'I stand corrected.' Alex replenished his drink and realized that the ensuing silence was Hammond's waiting for him to return to his chair. 'When I think about it, I see what you mean,' he said, sitting down.

'A few minutes ago, you asked if I were with Dunstone plc.'

'I don't think I said that.'

'Very well. Julian Warfield – same thing.'

'It was a mistake on my part. I'm afraid I don't remember asking you anything.'

'Yes, of course. That's an essential part of your agreement. There can be no reference whatsoever to Mr Warfield or Dunstone or any *one* or *thing* related. We understand. Quite frankly, at this juncture we approve wholeheartedly. Among other reasons, should you violate the demands of secrecy, we think you'd be killed instantly.'

McAuliff lowered his glass and stared at the Englishman, who spoke so calmly, precisely. 'That's preposterous,' he said simply.

'That's Dunstone plc,' replied Hammond softly.

'Then I think you'd better explain.'

'I shall do my best. To begin with, the geophysical survey that you've contracted for is the second such team to be sent out –'

'I wasn't told that,' interrupted Alex.

'With good reason. They're dead. I should say, "disappeared and dead". No one's been able to trace the Jamaican members; the whites are dead, of that we are sure.'

'How so? I mean, how can you be sure?'

'The best of all reasons, Mr McAuliff. One of the men was a British agent.'

McAuliff found himself mesmerized by the soft-spoken Intelligence man's narrative. Hammond might have been an Oxford don going over the blurred complexities of a dark Elizabethan drama, patiently clarifying each twist of an essentially inexplicable plot. He supplied conjectures where knowledge failed, making sure that McAuliff understood that they were conjectures.

Dunstone plc was not simply an industrial-development company; that was to say, its objectives went far beyond those of a conglomerate. And it was not solely British, as its listed board of directors implied. In actuality, Dunstone plc, London, was the 'corporate' headquarters of an organization of international financiers dedicated to building global cartels beyond the interferences and controls of the European union and its trade alliances. *That* was to say – by conjecture – eliminating the economic intervention of governments: Washington, London, Bonn, Paris, The Hague, and all other points of the financial compass. Ultimately, these were to be reduced to the status of clients, not origins of resource or negotiation.'

'You're saying, in essence, that Dunstone is in the process of setting up its own government.'

'Precisely. A government based solely on economic trade factors. A concentration of financial resources unheard of since the pharaohs. Along with this economic catastrophe, and no less important, is the absorption of the government of Jamaica by Dunstone plc. Jamaica is Dunstone's projected base of operations. They can succeed, Mr McAuliff.'

Alex put his glass on the wide windowsill. He began slowly, trying to find words, looking out at the slate rooftops converging into the Savoy courtyard. 'Let me try to understand . . . from what you've told me and from what I know. Dunstone anticipates investing heavily in Jamaican development. All right, we agree on that, and the figures *are* astronomical. Now, in exchange for this investment, they expect to be awarded a lot of clout from a grateful Kingston government. At least, that's what I'd expect if I were Dunstone. The normal tax credits, importing concessions, employment breaks, real estate . . . general incentives. Nothing new.' McAuliff turned his head and looked at Hammond. 'I'm not sure I see any financial catastrophe . . . except, maybe, an English financial catastrophe.'

'You stand corrected; I stand rebuked,' said Hammond. 'But only in a minor way. You're quite perceptive; it's true that our concerns were – at *first* – UK-oriented. English perversity, if you will. Dunstone is an important factor in Britain's balance of trade. We'd hate to lose it.'

'So you build a conspiracy –'

'Now, just a minute. Mr McAuliff,' the agent broke in, without raising his voice. 'The highest echelons of the British government do not *invent* conspiracies. If Dunstone were what it is purported to be, those responsible in Downing Street would fight openly for our interests. I'm afraid that is not the case. Dunstone reaches into extremely sensitive areas in London, Bonn, Paris, Rome . . . and, most assuredly, in Washington. But I shall return to that . . . I'd like to concentrate on Jamaica for the moment. You used the terms "concessions", "tax breaks" . . . "clout" and "incentives". I say "absorption".'

'Words.'

'*Laws*, Mr McAuliff. Sovereign; sanctioned by prime ministers and cabinets and parliaments. Think for a minute, Mr McAuliff. An existing, viable government in a strategically located independent nation controlled by a huge industrial monopoly with world markets. It's not outlandish. It's around the corner.'

Alex did think about it. For more than a minute. Prodded by Hammond's gently spoken, authoritatively phrased 'clarifications'.

Without disclosing MI5's method of discovery, the Englishman explained Dunstone's *modus operandi*. Enormous sums of capital had been transferred from Swiss banks to Kingston's King Street, that short stretch of the block that housed major international banking institutions. But the massive cash flow was not deposited in British, American or Canadian banks. Those went begging, while the less secure Jamaican banks were stunned by an influx of hard money unheard of in their histories.

Few knew that the vast new Jamaican riches were solely Dunstone's. But for these few, proof was supplied by the revolving transfers of a thousand accounts within an eight-hour business day.

Heads spun in astonishment. A few heads. Selected men in extraordinarily high places were shown incontrovertibly that a new force had invaded Kingston, a force so powerful that Wall Street and Whitehall would tremble at its presence.

'If you know this much, why don't you move in? Stop them.'

'Not possible,' answered Hammond. 'All transactions are covered; there's no one to accuse. It's too complex a web of financing. Dunstone is masterminded by Warfield. He operates on the premise that a closed society is efficient only when its various arms have little or no knowledge of each other.'

'In other words, you can't prove your case and –'

'We cannot expose what we cannot prove,' interrupted Hammond. 'That is correct.'

'You could threaten. I mean, on the basis of what you know damn well is true, you could raise one hell of a cry . . . But you can't chance it. It goes back to those "sensitive" areas in Bonn, Washington, Paris, et cetera. Am I correct about that, too?'

'You are.'

'They must be goddamn sensitive.'

'We believe they comprise an international cross-section of extraordinarily powerful men.'

'In governments?'

'Allied with major industries.'

'For instance?'

Hammond held Alex's eyes with his own. His message was clear. 'You understand that what I say is merely . . . conjecture.'

'All right. And my memory is short.'

'Very well.' Hammond got out of the chair and walked around it. His voice remained quiet, but there was no lack of precision. 'Your own country: conceivably the Vice-President of the United States or someone in his office and, certainly, unknown members of the Senate and the President's cabinet. England: prominent figures in the House of Commons and undoubtedly various department directors at Inland Revenue. Germany: ranking *Vorsitzenden* in the Bundestag. France: members of the élite right wing . . . Such men as I have described *must* be working with Warfield. The progress made by Dunstone would have been impossible without influence in such places. Of that we are certain.'

'But you don't know who, specifically.'

'No.'

'And you think, somehow, I can help you?'

'We do, Mr McAuliff.'

23

'With all the resources you have, you come to me? I've been contracted for a Dunstone field survey, nothing else.'

'The *second* Dunstone survey, Mr McAuliff.'

Alexander stared at the Englishman.

'And you say the first team is dead.'

Hammond returned to his chair and sat down once more. 'Yes, Mr McAuliff. Which means Dunstone has an adversary. One that's as deadly and powerful as Warfield's forces. And we haven't the slightest idea what it is . . . who they are. Only that it exists, *they* exist. We wish to make contact with those who want the same thing as we do. We can guarantee the safety of your expedition. You are the key. Without you, we're stymied. Without us, you and your people might well be in extreme jeopardy.'

McAuliff shot out of the chair and stood above the British agent. He took several short, deep breaths and walked purposefully away from Hammond; then he aimlessly paced the Savoy room. The Englishman seemed to understand Alex's action. He let the moment subside; he said nothing.

'*Jesus!* You're something, Hammond!' McAuliff returned to his chair, but he did not sit down. He reached for his drink on the windowsill, not so much for the whisky as to hold the glass. 'You come in here, build a case against Warfield by way of an economics lecture, and then calmly tell me that I've signed what amounts to my last contract if I don't cooperate with you.'

'That's rather black and white, old chap . . .'

'That's rather exactly what you just said! Suppose you're mistaken?'

'We're not.'

'You know goddamn well I can't prove *that* either. If I go back to Warfield and tell him about this little informal chat, I'll lose the contract the second I open my mouth. And the largest fee any surveyor was ever offered.'

'May I ask the amount? Just academic interest.'

McAuliff looked at Hammond. 'What would you say to two million dollars?'

24

'I'd say I'm surprised he didn't offer three. Or four . . . Why not? You wouldn't live to spend it.'

Alex held the Englishman's eyes. 'Translated, that means if Dunstone's enemies don't kill me, Dunstone will?'

'It's what we believe. There's no other logical conclusion. Once your work is finished.'

'I see . . .' McAuliff walked slowly to the whisky and poured deliberately, as if measuring. He did not offer anything to Hammond. 'If I confront Warfield with what you've told me, you're really saying that he'd . . .'

'Kill you? Are those the words that stick, Mr McAuliff?'

'I don't have much cause to employ those kind of words, Mr Hammond.'

'Naturally. No one ever gets used to them . . . Yes, we think he would kill you. Have you killed, of course. After picking your brains.'

McAuliff leaned against the wall, staring at the whisky in his glass, but not drinking. 'You're not giving me an alternative, are you?'

'Of course we are. I can leave these rooms; we never met.'

'Suppose someone sees you? That surveillance you spoke of.'

'They won't see me; you will have to take my word for that.' Hammond leaned back in the chair. He brought his fingers together pensively. 'Of course, under the circumstances, we'd be in no position to offer protection. From either faction –'

'Protection from the unprovable,' interjected Alex softly.

'Yes.'

'No alternative . . .' McAuliff pushed himself away from the wall and took several swallows of whisky. 'Except one, Hammond. Suppose I cooperate, on the basis that there *may* be substance to your charges . . . or theories, or whatever you call them. But I'm not accountable to you.'

'I'm not sure I understand.'

'I don't accept orders blindly. No puppet strings. I want that condition – on the record. If that's the phrase.'

'It must be. I've used it frequently.'

McAuliff crossed in front of the Englishman to the arm of his chair. 'Now, put it in simple words. What am I supposed to do?'

Hammond's voice was calm and precise. 'There are two objectives. The first, and most vital, is Dunstone's opposition. Those knowledgeable enough and fanatical enough to have killed the first survey team. If uncovered, it is conceivable that they will lead you to the second and equally important objective: the names of Dunstone's unknown hierarchy. The faceless men in London, Paris, Bonn, Washington . . . even one or two. We'd be grateful for anything specific.'

'How do I begin?'

'With very little, I'm afraid. But we do have something. It's only a word, a name, perhaps. We don't know. But we have every reason to think it's terribly important.'

'A word?'

'Yes . . . "Halidon".'

4

It was like working in two distinct spheres of reality, neither completely real. During the days, McAuliff conferred with the men and women in the University of London's geophysics laboratories, gathering personnel data for his survey team. The university was Dunstone's cover – along with the Royal Historical Society – and neither was aware that Dunstone's finances were behind the expedition.

During the nights, into the early morning hours, he met with R. C. Hammond, British Intelligence, in small, guarded houses on dimly lit streets in Kensington and Chelsea. These locations were reached by two changes of vehicles – taxis driven by MI5. And for each meeting Alex was provided with a cover story regarding his whereabouts: a dinner party, a girl, a crowded restaurant he was familiar with; nothing out of the ordinary, everything easily explained and verifiable.

The sessions with Hammond were divided into areas of instruction: the political and financial climate of Jamaica, MI5 contacts throughout the island, and basic skills – with instruments – in communication and countersurveillance.

At several sessions, Hammond brought in West Indian 'specialists' – black agents who were capable of answering just about any question McAuliff might raise. He had few questions; he had surveyed for the Kaiser bauxite interests near Oracabessa a little over a year ago, a fact he suspected had led Julian Warfield to him.

When they were alone, R. C. Hammond droned on about the attitudes and reactions Alex should foster.

*Always build on part of the truth ... keeping it simple ...
the basics easily confirmed ...*

*You'll find it quite acceptable to operate on different levels
... naturally, instinctively. Your concentration will separate
independently ...*

*Very rapidly your personal antennae will be activated ...
second nature. You'll fall into a rhythm ... the connecting link
between your divided objectives ...*

The British agent was never emphatic, simply redundant.
Over and over again, he repeated the phrases, with minor
variations in the words.

Alex understood. Hammond was providing him with fundamentals: tools and confidence.

'Your contact in Kingston will be given you in a few days;
we're still refining. Kingston's a mess; trust isn't easily come
by there.'

'Whose trust?' asked McAuliff.

'Good point,' replied the agent. 'Don't dwell on it. That's our
job. Memorize everyone else.'

Alex looked at the typewritten names on the paper that was
not to be removed from the house in Kensington. 'You've got
a lot of people on your payroll.'

'A few too many. Those that are crossed out were on double
rosters. Ours and the CIA's. Your Central Intelligence Agency
has become too political in recent years.'

'Are you concerned about leaks?'

'Yes. Dunstone plc is alive in Washington. Elusive, but very
much alive.'

The mornings found him entering Dunstone's sphere of reality,
the University of London. He discovered that it was easier than
he'd thought to shut out the previous night's concerns. Hammond's theory of divided objectives was borne out; he did fall
into a rhythm. His concentration was now limited to professional
concerns – the building of his survey team.

It was agreed that the number should not exceed eight,

28

preferably fewer. The areas of expertise would be the normal ones: shale, limestone, and bedrock stratification; water and gas-pocket analyses; vegetation – soil and botanical research; and finally, because the survey extended into the interior regions of the Cock Pit country, someone familiar with the various dialects and outback customs. Warfield had thought this last was superfluous; Alex knew better. Resentments ran high in Jamaica.

McAuliff had made up his mind about one member of the team, a soil analyst from California named Sam Tucker. Sam was an immense, burly man in his fifties, given to whatever excesses could be found in any immediate vicinity, but a top professional in his field. He was also the most reliable man Alex had ever known, a strong friend who had worked surveys with him from Alaska to last year's Kaiser job in Oracabessa. McAuliff implied that if Julian Warfield withheld approval from Sam, he might have to find himself another surveyor.

It was a hollow threat, all things considered, but it was worth the risk of having to back down. Alex wanted Sam with him in Jamaica. The others would be new, unproven; Tucker had worn well over the years. He could be trusted.

Warfield ran a Dunstone check on Sam Tucker and agreed there was nothing prejudicial beyond certain minor idiosyncrasies. But Sam was to be no different from any other member; none was to be informed of Dunstone's interests. Obviously.

None would be. Alex meant it. More than Warfield realized. If there was *any* truth to R. C. Hammond's astonishing pronouncements. Everyone on the survey would be told the same story. Given a set of facts engineered by Dunstone plc. Even the organizations involved accepted the facts as truth; there was no reason not to. Financial grants were not questioned; they were academic holy writ. Coveted, revered, never debated.

The geological survey had been made possible through a grant from the Royal Historical Society, encouraged by the Commonwealth Activities Committee, House of Lords. The expedition was to be a joint endeavour of the University of London and the Jamaican Ministry of Education. All salaries, expenses, disbursements of any kind were to be made through the bursar's office at the university. The Royal Society would establish lines of bank credit, and the university was to draw on these funds.

The reason for the survey was compatible with the endeavours of the Commonwealth Committee, whose members peopled and paid for most royal societies. It was a patrimonial gift to the new, independent nation – another not-to-be-forgotten link with Britannia. A study which would be acknowledged in textbooks for years to come. For, according to the Jamaican Ministry, there were no records of this particular territory having been subjected to a geophysical survey of any dimensions.

Obviously.

And if there were, certainly no one was going to bring them up.

Academic holy writ.

The university rip-off. One did not question.

The selection of Alexander McAuliff for the post of survey director was acknowledged to be an embarrassment to both the society and the university. But the American was the Jamaican Ministry's choice. One suffered such insults from the colonies.

One took the money; one did not debate.

Holy writ.

Everything was just complicated enough to be academically viable, thought McAuliff. Julian Warfield understood the environs through which he manoeuvred.

As did R. C. Hammond of British Intelligence.

And Alex began to realize that he would have to catch up. Both Dunstone and MI5 were committed to specific objectives. He could get lost in those commitments. In some ways, he had lost already. But choosing the team was his immediate concern.

McAuliff's personnel approach was one he had used often enough to know it worked. He would not interview anyone whose work he had not read thoroughly; anyone he did

30

interview had already proven himself on paper. Beyond the specific areas of expertise, he cared about adaptability to the physical and climatic requirements, and to the give-and-take of close-quarters association.

He had done his work. He was ready.

'My secretary said you wanted to see me, Dr McAuliff.' The speaker at the door was the chairman of the geophysics department, a bespectacled, gaunt academician who tried not to betray his resentment of Alex. It was obvious that the man felt cheated by both the Royal Society and Kingston for not having been chosen for McAuliff's job. He had recently completed an excellent survey in Anguilla; there were too many similarities between that assignment and the Jamaican grant for comfort.

'Good Lord,' said Alex. 'I expected to come to your office.' He crossed to his desk and smiled awkwardly. He had been standing by the single window, looking out over a miniature quadrangle, watching students carrying books, thankful that he was no longer part of that world. 'I think I'll be ready to start the interviews this afternoon.'

'So soon?'

'Thanks mainly to you, Professor Ralston. Your recommendations were excellent.' McAuliff wasn't being polite; the academic candidates were good – on paper. Of the ten final prospects, exactly half were from Ralston; the remaining five were free-lancers highly thought of by two London survey firms. 'I'm inclined just to take your people without seeing any others,' continued Alex, now being polite. 'But the Kingston Ministry is adamant that I interview these.' McAuliff handed Ralston a sheet of paper with the five non-university names.

'Oh, yes. I recognize several,' said Ralston, his voice now pleasantly acknowledging Alex's compliment. 'A couple here are . . . a couple, you know.'

'What?'

'Man-and-wife team. The Jensens.'

'There's one Jensen. Who's the woman?'

'R. L. Wells. That's Ruth Wells, Jensen's wife.'

31

'I didn't realize . . . I can't say that fact is in their favour.'

'Why not?'

'I'm not sure,' answered Alex sincerely. 'I've never had a married couple on a survey. Silly reaction, isn't it? Do you know anybody else there?'

'One fellow. I'd rather not comment.'

'Then I wish you would.'

'Ferguson. James Ferguson. He was a student of mine. Very outspoken chap. Quite opinionated, if you know what I mean.'

'But he's a botanist, a plant specialist, not a geology man.'

'Survey training; geophysics was his second subject. Of course, it was a number of years ago.'

McAuliff sorted out some papers on the desk. 'It couldn't have been too many. He's only been on three tours, all in the past four years.'

'It wasn't, actually. And you should see him. He's considered quite good, I'm told.'

'Here are your people,' said Alex, offering a second page to Ralston. 'I chose five out of the eight you submitted. Any more surprises there? Incidentally, I hope you approve.'

Ralston read the list, adjusting his spectacles and pursing his lips as he did so. 'Yes, I thought you'd select these. You realize, of course, that this Whitehall chap is not one of us. He was recommended by the West Indies Studies. Brilliant fellow apparently. Never met him myself. Makes quite a lot of money on the lecture circuits.'

'He's black, isn't he?'

'Oh, certainly. He knows every tongue, every dialect, every cultural normality and aberration in the Antilles. His doctoral thesis traced no fewer than twenty-seven African tribes to the islands. From the Bushwadie to the Coromantees. His research on Indian–African integration is the standard reference. He's quite a dandy, too, I believe.'

'Anyone else you want to talk about?'

'No, not actually. You'll have a difficult time deciding between your shale-bedrock experts. You've two very decent ones here.

32

Unless your . . . immediate reactions take precedence. One way or the other.'

'I don't understand.'

Ralston smiled. 'It would be presumptuous of me to comment further.' And then the professor added quickly, 'Shall I ask one of our girls to set up the appointments?'

'Thanks, I'd appreciate it. If schedules can be organized with all ten. I'd like an hour apiece over the next few days; whatever order is convenient for everyone.'

'An hour . . .'

'I'll call back those I want to talk with further – no sense in wasting everyone's time.'

'Yes, of course.'

One applicant disqualified himself the moment he walked into McAuliff's cubicle. The fact that he was more drunk than sober at one o'clock in the afternoon might have been explained, but, instead, it was used as the excuse to eliminate him for a larger problem: He was crippled in his right leg. Three men were crossed off for identical conditions: Each was obviously hostile to West Indians – a spreading English virus, Britain's parallel to *Americus Redneckus*.

The Jensens – Peter Jensen and Ruth Wells – were delightful surprises, singly and together. They were in their early fifties, bright, confident, and good-natured. A childless couple, they were financially secure and genuinely interested both in each other and in their work. His expertise was ore minerals; hers, the sister science of palaeontology – fossils. His had direct application, hers was removed but academically justifiable.

'Might I ask you some questions, Dr McAuliff?' Peter Jensen packed his pipe, his voice pleasant.

'By all means.'

'Can't say that I know much about Jamaica, but this seems like a damned curious trip. I'm not sure I understand – what's the point?'

Alex was grateful for the opportunity to recite the explanation created by Dunstone plc. He watched the ore man closely as he spoke, relieved to see the light of recognition in the geologist's eyes. When he finished, he paused and added, 'I don't know if that clears up anything.'

'Oh, my word, it certainly does, old chap. *Burke's Peerage* strikes again!' Peter Jensen chuckled, glancing at his wife. 'The royal H has been hard pressed to find something to do. Its members at the House of Lords simply provided it. Good show . . . I trust the university will make a pound or two.'

'I'm afraid the budget's not that loose.'

'Really?' Peter Jensen held his pipe as he looked at McAuliff. 'Then perhaps I *don't* understand. You'll forgive me, but you're not known in the field as a particularly inexpensive director . . . quite rightfully, let me add; your reputation precedes you.'

'From the Balkans to Australia,' added Ruth Wells Jensen, her expression showing minor irritation with her husband. 'And if you have a separate arrangement, it's none of Peter's bloody business.'

Alex laughed softly. 'You're kind, both of you. But there's nothing special. I got caught, it's as simple as that. I've worked for companies on the island; I hope to again. Often. All geophysical certificates are issued by Kingston, and Kingston asked for me. Let's call it an investment.'

Again McAuliff watched Peter Jensen closely; he had rehearsed the answer. The Englishman looked once more at his wife. Briefly. Then he chuckled, as he had done seconds before.

'I'd do the same, old chap. But God help the survey *I* was director on.'

'It's one I'd avoid like the plague,' said Ruth, matching her husband's quiet laugh. 'Who have you picked, if it's proper to ask? Anyone we might know?'

'Nobody yet. I've really just started –'

'Well,' interrupted Peter Jensen, his eyes alive with humour, 'since you suffer from inadequate freight charges, I should tell you we'd rather not be separated. Somewhat used to each other by now. If you're interested in one of us, the other would take half pay to tag along.'

Whatever doubts remained for Alex were dispelled by Ruth Wells Jensen's words. She mimicked her husband's professorial tones with good-natured accuracy. 'Half pay, old chap, can be negotiated. Our flat's damned cold this time of year.'

The Jensens would be hired.

The third non-university name, James Ferguson, had been accurately described by Ralston as outspoken and opinionated. These traits, however, were the results of energy and impatience, it seemed to McAuliff. Ferguson was young – twenty-six – and was not the sort to survive, much less thrive, in an academic environment. Alex recognized in Ferguson much of his younger self: consummate interest in his subject, intolerance of the research world in which it was studied. A contradiction, if not a conflict of objectives. Ferguson freelanced for agro-industry companies, and his best recommendation was that he was rarely out of work in a market not famous for excessive employment. James Ferguson was one of the best vegetation specialists around.

'I'd love to get back to Jamaica,' said the young man seconds after the preliminary interview began. 'I was in Port Maria for the Craft Foundation two years ago. It's my judgment the whole bloody island is a gold mine if the fruit and synthetic industries would allow development.'

'What's the gold?' asked McAuliff.

'The baracoa fibres. In the second growth stages. A banana strain could be developed that would send the nylon and the polyester boys into panic, to say nothing of the fruit shippers.'

'Can you prove it?'

'Damn near did, *I* think. That's why I was thrown out by the foundation.'

'You were thrown out?'

'Quite unceremoniously. No sense hiding the fact; don't care to, really. They told me to stick to business. Can you imagine? You'll probably run across a few negatives about me, if you're interested.'

35

'I'm interested, Mr Ferguson.'

The interview with Charles Whitehall disturbed McAuliff. That was to say, the man disturbed him, not the quality of information received. Whitehall was a black cynic, a now-Londoner whose roots and expertise were in the West Indies but whose outlook was aggressively self-perpetuating. His appearance startled McAuliff. For a man who had written three volumes of Caribbean history, whose work was, in Ralston's words, 'the standard reference', Charles Whitehall looked barely as old as James Ferguson.

'Don't let my appearance fool you, Mr McAuliff,' said Whitehall, upon entering the cubicle and extending his hand to Alex. 'My tropic hue covers the years better than paler skin. I'm forty-two years old.'

'You read my thoughts.'

'Not necessarily. I'm used to the reaction,' replied Whitehall, sitting down, smoothing his expensive blazer, and crossing his legs, which were encased in pin-striped trousers.

'Since you don't waste words, Dr Whitehall, neither will I. Why are you interested in this survey? As I gather, you can make a great deal more money on the lecture circuit. A geophysical survey isn't the most lucrative employment.'

'Let's say the financial aspects are secondary: one of the few times in my life that they will be, perhaps.' Whitehall spoke while removing a silver cigarette case from his pocket. 'To tell you the truth, Mr McAuliff, there's a certain ego fulfilment in returning to one's country as an expert under the aegis of the Royal Historical Society. It's really as simple as that.'

Alex believed the man. For, as he read him, Whitehall was a scholar far more honoured abroad than at home. It seemed that Charles Whitehall wanted to achieve an acceptance commensurate with his scholarship that had been denied him in the intellectual – or was it social? – houses of Kingston.

'Are you familiar with the Cock Pit country?'

'As much as anyone who isn't a runner. Historically and culturally, much more so, of course.'

'What's a runner?'

'Runners are hill people. From the mountain communities. They act as guides ... when you can find one. They're primitives, really. Who have you hired for the survey?'

'What?' Alex's thoughts were on runners.

'I asked who was going with you. On the survey team. I'd be interested.'

'Well ... not all the posts have been filled. There's a couple named Jensen – ores and palaeo; a young botanist, Ferguson. An American friend of mine, a soil analyst, name of Sam Tucker.'

'I've heard of Jensen, I believe. I'm not sure, but I think so. I don't know the others.'

'Did you expect to?'

'Frankly, yes. Royal Society projects generally attract very high-calibre people.' Whitehall delicately tapped his cigarette on the rim of an ashtray.

'Such as yourself?' asked McAuliff, smiling.

'I'm not modest,' replied the black scholar, returning Alex's smile with an open grin. 'And I'm very much interested. I think I could be of service to you.'

So did McAuliff.

The second shale-bedrock analyst was listed as A. Gerrard Booth. Booth was a university applicant personally recommended by Ralston in the following manner:

'I promised Booth I'd bring these papers and articles to your attention. I do believe Booth would be a fine asset to the survey.'

Ralston had given McAuliff a folder filled with A. Gerrard Booth's studies of sheet strata in such diverse locations as Turkey, Corsica, Zaire and Australia. Alex recalled having read several of the articles in the *National Geologist*, and remembered them as lucid and professional. Booth was good; Booth was better than good.

Booth was also a woman. A. Gerrard Booth was known to her colleagues as Alison Booth; no one bothered with the middle name.

37

She had one of the most genuine smiles McAuliff had ever seen. It was more a half laugh – one might even say masculine, but the word was loudly denied by her complete femininity. Her eyes were blue and alive and level – the eyes of a professional. Her handshake was firm, again professional. Her light brown hair was long and soft and slightly waved – brushed repeatedly, thought Alex, for the interview. Her age was anywhere from late twenties to middle thirties; there was no way to tell by observation, except that there were laugh lines at the corners of her eyes.

Alison Booth was not only good and a woman; she was also, at least on first meeting, a very attractive, outgoing person. The term 'professional' kept recurring to McAuliff as they spoke.

'I made Rolly – Dr Ralston – promise to omit the fact that I was a woman. Don't hold him responsible.'

'Were you so convinced I was anti-feminist?'

The girl raised her hand and brushed her long, soft hair away from the side of her lovely face. 'No preformed hostility, Dr McAuliff. I just understand the practical obstacles. It's part of my job to convince you I'm qualified.' And then, as if she were aware of the possible double-entendre, Alison Booth stopped smiling and smoothed her skirt . . . professionally.

'In field work and the laboratory, I'm sure you *are* qualified . . .'

'Any other considerations would be extraneous, I should think,' said the girl, with a slight trace of English aloofness.

'Not necessarily. There are environmental problems, degrees of physical discomfort, if not hardship.'

'I can't conceive of Jamaica being in that league with Zaire or the Aussie Outback. I've surveyed in those places.'

'I know –'

'Rolly told me,' interrupted Alison Booth, 'that you would not accept tour references until you had interviewed us.'

'Group isolation tends to create fallible judgments. Insupportable relationships. I've lost good men in the past because other good men reacted negatively to them for the wrong reasons.'

38

'What about women?'

'I used the term inclusively, not exclusively.'

'I have very good references, Dr McAuliff. For the right reasons.'

'I'll request them.'

'I have them with me.' Alison unbuckled the large leather bag on her lap, extracted two business envelopes, and placed them on the edge of McAuliff's desk. 'My references, Dr McAuliff.'

Alex laughed as he reached for the envelopes. He looked over at the girl, her eyes locked with his. There was both a good-humoured challenge and a degree of supplication in her expression. 'Why is this survey so important to you, Miss Booth?'

'Because I'm good and I can do the job,' she answered simply.

'You're employed by the university, aren't you?'

'On a part-time basis, lecture and laboratory. I'm not permanent . . . by choice, incidentally.'

'Then it's not money.' McAuliff made a statement.

'I could use it; I'm not desperate, however.'

'I can't imagine your being desperate anywhere,' he said, with a partial smile. And then Alex saw – or thought he saw – a trace of a cloud across the girl's eyes, an instant of concern that left as rapidly as it had come. He instinctively pressed further. 'But why *this* tour? With your qualifications, I'm sure there are others. Probably more interesting, certainly more money.'

'The timing is propitious,' she replied softly, with precise hesitation. 'For personal reasons that have absolutely nothing to do with my qualifications.'

'Are there reasons why you want to spend a prolonged period in Jamaica?'

'Jamaica has nothing to do with it. You could be surveying Outer Mongolia for all that it matters.'

'I see.' Alex replaced the two envelopes on the desk. He intentionally conveyed a trace of indifference. The girl reacted.

'Very well, Dr McAuliff. It's no secret among my friends.' The girl held her bag on her lap. She did not grip it; there was no intensity about her whatsoever. When she spoke her voice was steady, as were her eyes. She was the total professional again. 'You called me "Miss Booth"; that's incorrect. "Booth" is my married name. I regret to say the marriage was not successful; it was terminated recently. The solicitousness of well-meaning people during such times can be boring. I'd prefer to be out of touch.'

McAuliff returned her steady gaze, trying to evoke something beyond her words. There *was* something, but she would not allow his prying further; her expression told him that . . . professionally.

'It's not relevant. I apologize. But I appreciate your telling me.'

'Is your . . . responsibility satisfied?'

'Well, my curiosity, at any rate.' Alex leaned forward, elbows on the desk, his hands folded under his chin. 'Beyond that, and I hope it's not improper, you've made it possible for me to ask you to have dinner with me.'

'I think that would depend on the degree of relevance you ascribed to my acceptance.' Alison's voice was polite but not cold. And there was that lovely humour in her eyes.

'In all honesty, I *do* make it a point to have dinner or a long lunch . . . even a fair amount of drinks with those I'm thinking about hiring. But right now, I'm reluctant to admit it.'

'That's a very disarming reply, Dr McAuliff,' said the girl, her lips parted, laughing her half laugh. 'I'd be delighted to have dinner with you.'

'I'll do my damnedest not to be solicitous. I don't think it's necessary at all.'

'And I'm sure you're never boring.'

'Not relevantly.'

5

McAuliff stood on the corner of High Holborn and Chancery Lane and looked at his watch. The hands glowed in the mist-laden London darkness; it was 11:40. Preston's Rolls-Royce was ten minutes late. Or perhaps it would not appear at all. His instructions were that if the car did not arrive by midnight, he was to return to the Savoy. Another meeting would be scheduled.

There were times when he had to remind himself whose furtive commands he was following, wondering whether he in turn was being followed. It was a degrading way to live, he reflected: the constant awareness that locked a man into a pocket of fear. All the fictions about the shadow world of conspiracy omitted the fundamental indignity intrinsic to that world. There was no essential independence; it was strangling.

This particular evening's rendezvous with Warfield had necessitated a near-panic call to Hammond, for the British agent had scheduled a meeting himself, for one in the morning. That is, McAuliff had requested it, and Hammond had set the time and the place. And at 10:20 that night the call had come from Dunstone: Be at High Holborn and Chancery at 11:30, an hour and ten minutes from then.

Hammond could not, at first, be found. His highly secret, private telephone at MI5 simply did not answer. Alex had been given no other number, and Hammond had told him repeatedly never to call the office and leave his name. Nor was he ever to place a call to the agent from his rooms at the Savoy. Hammond did not trust the switchboards at either establishment. Nor the open frequencies of cellular phones.

41

So Alex had to go out onto the Strand, into succeeding pubs and public telephones until Hammond's line answered. He was sure he was being observed – by someone – and thus he had to pretend annoyance each time he hung up after an unanswered call. He found that he had built the fabric of a lie, should Warfield question him. His lie was that he was trying to reach Alison Booth and cancel a lunch date they had for the following day. They did have a lunch date which he had no intention of cancelling, but the story possessed sufficient truth to be valid.

Build on part of the truth . . . Attitude and reaction. MI5.

Finally, Hammond's telephone was answered, by a man who stated casually that he had gone out for a late supper.

A late supper! Good God! . . . Global cartels, international collusion in the highest places, financial conspiracies, and a late supper.

In reasoned tones, as opposed to McAuliff's anxiety, the man told him that Hammond would be alerted. Alex was not satisfied; he insisted that Hammond be at his telephone – if he had to wait all night – until he, Alex, made contact after the Warfield appointment.

It was 11:45. Still no St James Rolls-Royce. He looked around at the few pedestrians on High Holborn, walking through the heavy mist. He wondered which, if any, was concerned with him.

The pocket of fear.

He wondered, too, about Alison. They had had dinner for the third night in succession; she had claimed she had a lecture to prepare, and so the evening was cut short. Considering the complications that followed, it was a good thing.

Alison was a strange girl. The professional who covered her vulnerability well; who never strayed far from that circle of quiet humour that protected her. The half laugh, the warm blue eyes, the slow, graceful movement of her hands . . . these were her shields, somehow.

There was no problem in selecting her as his first choice . . . professionally. She was far and away the best applicant for the

42

team. Alex considered himself one of the finest rock-strata specialists on both continents, yet he wasn't sure he wanted to pit his expertise against hers. Alison Gerrard Booth was really good.

And lovely.

And he wanted her in Jamaica.

He had prepared an argument for Warfield, should Dunstone's goddamn security computers reject her. The final clearance of his selections was the object of the night's conference.

Where *was* that goddamned black ship of an automobile? It was ten minutes to midnight.

'Excuse me, sir,' said a deep, almost guttural voice behind McAuliff. He turned, and saw a man about his own age, in a heavy brown jacket; he looked like a longshoreman or a construction worker.

'Yes?'

'It's m' first time in London, sir, and I think I'm lost.'

The man then pointed up at the street sign, barely visible in the spill of the lamp through the mist. 'This says Chancery Lane, which is *supposed* to be near a place called Hatton Garden, which is where I'm supposed to meet m' friends. I can't *find* it, sir.'

Alex gestured to his left. 'It's up there two or three blocks.'

The man pointed again, as a simpleton might point, in the direction of McAuliff's gesture. 'Up there?'

'That's right.'

The man shook his arm several times, as if emphasizing. 'You're sure, sir?' And then the man lowered his voice and spoke rapidly. 'Please don't react, Mr McAuliff. Continue as though you are explaining. Mr Hammond will meet you in Soho; there's an all-night club called The Owl of Saint George. He'll be waiting. Stay at the bar, he'll contact you. Don't worry about the time ... He doesn't want you to make any more telephone calls. You're being watched.'

McAuliff swallowed, blanched, and waved his hand – a little too obviously, he felt – in the direction of Hatton Garden. He,

43

too, spoke quietly, rapidly. *'Jesus!* If *I'm* being watched, so are *you!'*

'We calculate these things –'

'I don't like your addition! What am I supposed to tell War-field? To let me off in *Soho!'*

'Why not? Say you feel like a night out. You've nothing scheduled in the morning. Americans like Soho; it's perfectly natural. You're not a heavy gambler, but you place a bet now and then.'

'Christ! Would you care to describe my sex life?'

'I could, but I won't.' The guttural, loud voice returned. 'Thank you, sir. You're very kind, sir. I'm sure I'll find m' friends.'

The man walked swiftly away into the night mist towards Hatton Garden. McAuliff felt his whole body shiver; his hands trembled. To still them, he reached into his pocket for cigarettes. He was grateful for the opportunity to grip the metal of his lighter.

It was five minutes to twelve. He would wait several minutes past midnight and then leave. His instructions were to 'return to the Savoy'; another meeting would be set. Did that mean it was to be scheduled later that night? In the morning hours? Or did 'return to the Savoy' simply mean that he was no longer required to remain at the corner of High Holborn and Chancery Lane? He was free for the evening?

The words were clear, but the alternate interpretation was entirely feasible. If he chose, he could – with a number of stops – make his way into Soho, to Hammond. The network of surveillance would establish the fact that Warfield had not appeared for the appointment. The option was open.

My God! thought Alex. *What's happening to me? Words and meanings . . . options and alternates. Interpretations of . . . orders!*

Who the hell *gave him orders!*

He was *not* a man to be commanded!

But when his hand shook as he raised his cigarette to his lips, he knew that he was . . . for an indeterminate period of time. Time in a hell he could not stand; he was not free.

The hands on his wristwatch converged. It was midnight. To goddamn hell with all of them! He *would* leave! He would call Alison and tell her he wanted to come over for a drink . . . ask her if she would let him. Hammond could wait all night in Soho. Where was it? The Owl of Saint George. Silly fucking name!

To hell with him!

The Rolls-Royce sped out of the fog from the direction of Newgate, its deep-throated engine racing, a powerful intrusion on the otherwise still street. It swung alongside the kerb in front of McAuliff and stopped abruptly. The chauffeur got out of his seat, raced around the long bonnet of the car, and opened the rear door for Alex.

It all happened so quickly that McAuliff threw away his cigarette and climbed in, bewildered; he had not adjusted to the swift change of plans. Julian Warfield sat in the far right corner of the huge rear seat, his tiny frame dwarfed by the vehicle's expansive interior.

'I'm sorry to have kept you waiting until the last minute, Mr McAuliff. I was detained.'

'Do you always do business with one eye on secrecy, the other on shock effect?' asked Alex, settling back in the seat, relieved to feel he could speak with confidence.

Warfield replied by laughing his hard, old-man's laugh. 'Compared to Ross Perot, I'm a used-car salesman.'

'You're still damned unsettling.'

'Would you care for a drink? Preston has a bar built in right there.' Warfield pointed to the felt back of the front seat. 'Just pull on that strap.'

'No, thank you. I may do a little drinking later, not now.' *Easy. Easy, McAuliff,* he thought to himself. *For Christ's sake, don't be obvious. Hammond can wait all night. Two minutes ago, you were going to let him do just that!*

The old man took an envelope from his jacket pocket. 'I'll

give you the good news straight off. There's no one we objected to strenuously, subject to minor questions. On the contrary, we think you finalized your selections rather ingeniously . . .'

According to Warfield, the initial reaction at Dunstone to his list of first choices was negative. Not from security – subject to those minor questions; nor in quality – McAuliff had done his homework. But from a conceptual viewpoint. The idea of female members on a geological survey expedition was rejected out of hand, the central issue being that of less strength, not necessarily weakness. Any project entailing travel had, by tradition, a masculine identification; the intrusion of the female was a disquieting component. It could only lead to complications – any number of them.

'So we crossed off two of your first choices, realizing that by eliminating the Wells woman, you would also lose her husband, Jensen . . . Three out of the first five rejected; knew you'd be unhappy, but then, you *did* understand . . . Later, it came to me. By George, you'd out-thought the lot of us!'

'I wasn't concerned with any strategies, Warfield. I was putting together the best team I could.' McAuliff felt he had to interject the statement.

'Perhaps not consciously, and qualitatively you have a splendid group. But the inclusion of the two ladies, one a wife and both superior in their fields, was a profound improvement.'

'Why?'

'It provides – they provide – a unique ingredient of innocence. A patina of scholarship, actually; an aspect we had overlooked. A dedicated team of men and women – on a grant from the Royal Society . . . so different somehow from an all-male survey expedition. Really, most remarkable.'

'That wasn't my intention. I hate to disabuse you.'

'No disabusement whatsoever. The result is the same. Needless to say, I pointed out this consideration to the others, and they agreed instantly.'

'I have an idea that whatever you might "point out" would be instantly agreed to. What are the minor questions?'

46

'"Incidental information you might wish to consider" is a better description.' The old man reached up and snapped on a reading lamp. He then removed several pages from his overcoat, unfolded them, and placed them in front of the envelope. He adjusted his glasses and scanned the top paper. 'The husband and wife, this Jensen and Wells. They're quite active in leftish political circles. Peace marches, demonstrations, that sort of thing.'

'That doesn't have any bearing on their work. I doubt they'll be organizing the natives.' McAuliff spoke wearily – on purpose. If Warfield intended to raise such 'questions', he wanted the financier to know he thought them irrelevant.

'There is a great deal of political instability in Jamaica; unrest, to be precise. It would not be in our interests for any of your people to be outspoken on such matters.'

McAuliff shifted in his seat and looked at the little old man – tiny lips pursed, the papers held in his thin, bony fingers under the pin spot of yellow light, giving his ancient flesh a sallow colour. 'Should the occasion arise – and I can't conceive of it – when the Jensens make political noises, I'll quieten them . . . On the other hand, the inclusion of such people might be an asset to you. They'd hardly, knowingly, work for Dunstone.'

'Yes,' said Warfield quietly. 'That, too, occurred to us . . . This chap, Ferguson. He ran into trouble with the Craft Foundation.'

'He ran into a potentially vital discovery concerning baracoa fibres, that's what he ran into. It scared the hell out of Craft and Craft's funding resources.'

'*We* have no fight with Craft. We don't want one. The fact that he's with you could raise eyebrows. Craft's well thought of in Jamaica.'

'There's no one as good as Ferguson, certainly not the alternate, and *he* was the best of those remaining. I'll keep Ferguson away from Craft.'

'That is essential. We cannot permit him otherwise.'

Charles Whitehall, the black scholar-dandy, was a psychological mess, according to Dunstone's data banks. Politically he

47

was a conservative, a black conservative who might have led the Kingston reactionaries had he remained on the island. But his future was not in Jamaica, and he had recognized it early. He was bitter over the fact. Warfield hastened to add, however, that this negative information was balanced – and more so – by Whitehall's academic standing. His interest in the survey was ultimately a positive factor; his inclusion tended to remove any commercial stain from the project. To compound the complications of this very complex man, Whitehall was a Class Triple A Black Belt practitioner of Jukato, a more intricate and deadly development of Judo.

'Our contacts in Kingston are quite impressed with his being with you. I suspect they'll offer him a chair at the West Indies University. I think he'll probably accept, if they pay him enough ... Now, we come to the last submission.' Warfield removed his glasses, placed them on his lap with the papers, and rubbed the bridge of his thin, bony nose. 'Mrs Booth ... Mrs Alison Gerrard Booth.'

Alex felt the stirrings of resentment. Warfield had already told him that Alison was acceptable; he did not want to hear intimate, private information dredged up by Dunstone's faceless men or whirring machines.

'What about her?' asked McAuliff, his voice careful. 'Her record speaks for itself.'

'Unquestionably. She's extremely qualified ... And extremely anxious to leave England.'

'She's explained that. I buy it. She's just been divorced, and the circumstances, I gather, are not too pleasant ... socially.'

'Is that what she told you?'

'Yes. I believe her.'

Warfield replaced his glasses and flipped the page in front of him. 'I'm afraid there's a bit more to it than that, Mr McAuliff. Did she tell you who her husband was? What he did for a living?'

'No. And I didn't ask her.'

'Yes ... Well, I think you should know. David Booth is from

a socially prominent family – the peerage, actually – that hasn't had the cash flow of a pound sterling for a generation. He is a partner in an export–import firm whose books indicate a barely passable subsistence ... Yet Mr Booth lives extremely well. Several homes – here and on the Continent – drives expensive cars, belongs to the better clubs. Contradictory, isn't it?'

'I'd say so. How does he do it?'

'Narcotics,' said Julian Warfield, as if he had just given the time of day. 'David Booth is a courier for Franco-American interests operating out of Corsica and Marseilles.'

For the next few moments both men were silent. McAuliff understood the implication, and finally spoke. 'Mrs Booth was on surveys in Corsica, Zaire and Turkey. You're suggesting that she's involved.'

'Possibly; not likely. If so, unwittingly. After all, she did divorce the chap. What we are saying is that she undoubtedly learned of her husband's involvement; she's afraid to remain in England. We don't think she plans to return.'

Again, there was silence, until McAuliff broke it.

'When you said "afraid", I presume you mean she's been threatened.'

'Quite possibly. Whatever she knows could be damaging. Booth didn't take the divorce action very well. Not from the point of view of affection – he's quite a womanizer – but, we suspect, for reasons related to his travels.' Warfield refolded the pages and put them back into his overcoat pocket.

'Well,' said Alex, 'that's quite a ... minor explosion. I'm not sure I'm ready for it.'

'I gave you this information on Mrs Booth because we thought you'd find out for yourself. We wanted to prepare you ... not to dissuade you.'

McAuliff turned sharply and looked at Warfield. 'You want her along because she might ... might possibly be valuable to you. And not for geological reasons.' *Easy, McAuliff. Easy!*

'Anything is conceivable in these complicated times.'

'I don't like it!'

49

'You haven't thought about it. It is our opinion that she's infinitely safer in Jamaica than in London . . . You are concerned, aren't you? You've seen her frequently during the past week.'

'I don't like being followed, either.' It was all Alex could think to say.

'Whatever was done was minimal and for your protection,' replied Warfield quickly.

'Against what? For Christ's sake, protection from whom?' McAuliff stared at the little old man, realizing how much he disliked him. He wondered if Warfield would be any more explicit than Hammond on the subject of protection. Or would he admit the existence of a prior Jamaican survey? 'I think I have a right to be told,' he added angrily.

'You shall be. First, however, I should like to show you these papers. I trust everything will be to your satisfaction.' Warfield lifted the flap of the unsealed envelope and withdrew several thin pages stapled together on top of a single page of stationery. They were onionskin carbons of his lengthy Letter of Agreement signed in Belgrave Square over a week ago. He reached above, snapped on his own reading lamp, took the papers from Warfield and flipped over the carbons to the thicker page of stationery. Only it wasn't stationery; it was a Xerox copy of a Letter Deposit Transfer from the Chase Bank in New York. The figures were clear: On the left was the amount paid into his account by a Swiss concern; on the right, the maximum taxes on that amount, designated as income, to the Swiss authorities and the United States Internal Revenue Service.

The net figure was $1,270,000.

He looked over at Warfield. 'My first payment was to have been twenty-five per cent of the total contract upon principal work of the survey. We agreed that would be the team's arrival in Kingston. Prior to that date, you're responsible only for my expenses and, if we terminate, five hundred a day for my time. Why the change?'

'We're very pleased with your preliminary labours. We wanted to indicate our good faith.'

'I don't believe you –'

'Besides,' continued Warfield, raising his voice over Alex's objection, 'there's been no contractual change.'

'I know what I signed.'

'Not too well, apparently ... Go on, read the agreement. It states clearly that you will be paid a *minimum* of twenty-five per cent, *no later* than the end of the business day we determined to be the start of the survey. It says nothing about an excess of twenty-five per cent; no prohibitions as to an earlier date ... We thought you'd be pleased.' The old man folded his small hands like some kind of Gandhi The Non-Violent in Savile Row clothes.

McAuliff reread the transfer letter from Chase. 'This bank transfer describes the money as payment for services rendered as of today's date. That's past tense, free and clear. You'd have a hard time recouping if I didn't go to Jamaica. And considering your paranoia over secrecy, I doubt you'd try too hard ... No, Mr Warfield, this is out of character.'

'Faith, Mr McAuliff. Your generation overlooks it.' The financier smiled benignly.

'I don't wish to be rude, but I don't think you ever had it. Not that way. You're a manipulator, not an ideologue ... I repeat: out of character.'

'Very well.' Warfield unfolded his delicate hands, still retaining the Gandhi pose under the yellow light. 'It leads to the protection of which I spoke and which, rightly, you question ... You are one of us, Alexander Tarquin McAuliff. A very important and essential part of Dunstone's plans. In recognition of your contribution, we have recommended to our Directors that you be elevated – in confidence – to their status. Ergo, the payments made to you are the initial monies due one of our own. As you say, it would be out of character for such excessive payments to be made otherwise.'

'What the hell are you driving at?'

'In rather abrupt words, don't ever try to deny us. You are a consenting participant in our work. Should you at any time,

51

for whatever motive, decide you do not approve of Dunstone, don't try to separate yourself. You'd never be believed.'

McAuliff stared at the now smiling old man. 'Why would I do that?' he asked softly.

'Because we have reason to believe there are ... elements most anxious to stop our progress. They may try to contact you; perhaps they have already. Your future is with us. No one else. Financially, perhaps ideologically ... certainly, legally.'

Alex looked away from Warfield. The Rolls had proceeded west into New Oxford Street, south down Charing Cross Road, and west again on Shaftesbury Avenue. They were approaching the outer lights of Piccadilly Circus, the gaudy colours diffused by the heavy mist.

'Who were you trying to call so frantically this evening?' The old man was not smiling now.

McAuliff turned from the window. 'Not that it's any of your damned business, but I was calling – not frantically – Mrs Booth. We're having lunch tomorrow. Any irritation was due to your hastily scheduled meeting and the fact that I didn't want to disturb her after midnight. Who do you think?'

'You shouldn't be hostile –'

'I forgot,' interrupted Alex. 'You're only trying to protect me. From ... elements.'

'I can be somewhat more precise.' Julian Warfield's eyes bore into Alex's, with an intensity he had not seen before. 'There would be no point in your lying to me, so I expect the truth. What does the word "Halidon" mean to you, Mr McAuliff?'

6

The screaming, hysterical cacophony of the acid-rock music caused a sensation of actual pain in the ears. The eyes were attacked next, by tear-provoking layers of heavy smoke, thick and translucent – the nostrils reacting immediately to the pungent sweetness of tobacco laced with grass and hashish.

McAuliff made his way through the tangled network of soft flesh, separating thrusting arms and protruding shoulders gently but firmly, finally reaching the rear of the bar area.

The Owl of Saint George was at its undulating peak. The psychedelic lights exploded against the walls and ceiling in rhythmic crescendos; bodies were concave and convex, none seemingly upright, all swaying, writhing violently.

Hammond was seated in a circular booth with five others: two men and three women. Alex paused, concealed by drinkers and dancers, and looked at Hammond's gathering. It was funny; not sardonically funny, humorously funny. Hammond and his middle-aged counterpart across the table were dressed in the 'straight' fashion, as were two of the three women, straight and past forty. The remaining couple was young, relaxed and casual in the fashion of the hour. The picture was instantly recognizable: parents indulging the generation gap, uncomfortable but game.

McAuliff remembered the man's words on High Holborn. *Stay at the bar, he'll reach you.* He manoeuvred his way to within arm's length of the mahogany and managed to shout his order to the black Soho bartender with an Afro haircut. He wondered when Hammond would make his move; he did not want to wait long. He had a great deal to say to the British agent.

53

'Pardon, but you *are* a chap named McAuliff, aren't you?' The shouted question caused Alex to spill part of his drink. The shouter was the young man from Hammond's table. Hammond was not wasting time.

'Yes. Why?'

'My girl's parents recognized you. Asked me to invite you over.'

The following moments, McAuliff felt, were like a play within a play. A brief, staged exercise with acutely familiar dialogue, acted out in front of a bored audience of other, more energetic actors. But with a surprise that made Alex consider Hammond's skill in a very favourable light.

He *did* know the middle-aged man across from Hammond. And his wife. Not well, of course, but they were acquaintances. He'd met them two or three times before, on previous London trips. They weren't the sort of memorable people one recognized on the street, or in The Owl of Saint George – unless the circumstances were recalled.

Hammond was introduced by his correct name, and McAuliff was seated next to him.

'How the hell did you arrange this?' asked Alex after five excruciating minutes remembering the unmemorable with the acquaintances. 'Do they know who you are?'

'Laugh occasionally,' answered Hammond with a calm, precise smile. 'They believe I'm somewhere in that great government pyramid, juggling figures in poorly lit rooms ... The arrangements were necessary. Warfield has doubled his teams on you. We're not happy about it: he may have spotted us, but, of course, it's unlikely.'

'He's spotted something, I guarantee it.' Alex bared his teeth, but the smile was false. 'I've got a lot to talk to you about. Where can we meet?'

'Here. Now,' was the Britisher's reply. 'Speak occasionally to the others, but it's perfectly acceptable that we strike up a conversation. We might use it as a basis for lunch or drinks in a day or two.'

'No way. I leave for Kingston the day after tomorrow in the morning.'

Hammond paused, his glass halfway to his lips. 'So soon? We didn't expect that.'

'It's insignificant compared to something else ... Warfield knows about Halidon. That is, he asked me what *I* knew about it.'

'*What?*'

'Mr McAuliff?' came the shouted inquiry from across the table. 'Surely you know the Bensons, from Kent ...'

The timing was right, thought Alex. Hammond's reaction to his news was one of astonishment. Shock that changed swiftly to angered acceptance. The ensuing conversation about the unremembered Bensons would give Hammond time to think. And Alex wanted him to think.

'What *exactly* did he say?' asked Hammond. The revolving psychedelic lights now projected their sharp patterns on the table, giving the agent a grotesque appearance. 'The exact words.'

'"What does the word 'Halidon' mean to you?" That's what he said.'

'Your answer?'

'What answer? I didn't have one. I told him it was a town in New Jersey.'

'I beg your pardon?'

'Halidon, New Jersey. It's a town.'

'Different spelling, I believe. And pronunciation ... Did he accept your ignorance?'

'Why wouldn't he? I'm ignorant.'

'Did you conceal the fact that you'd heard the word? It's terribly important!'

'Yes ... yes, I think I did. As a matter of fact, I was thinking about something else. Several other things –'

'Did he bring it up later?' broke in the agent.

'No, he didn't. He stared hard, but he didn't mention it again ... What do you think it means?'

Suddenly a gyrating, spaced-out dancer careened against the

table, his eyes half focused, his lips parted without control. 'Well, if it ain't old Mums and Dadsies!' he said, slurring his words with rough Yorkshire. 'Enjoying the kiddie's show-and-tell, Mums?'

'Damn!' Hammond had spilled part of his drink.

'Ring for the butler, Pops! Charge it to old Edinburgh. He's a personal friend! Good old Edinburgh.'

The solo, freaked-out dancer bolted away as quickly as he had intruded. The other middle-aged straights were appropriately solicitous of Hammond, simultaneously scathing of The Owl's patrons; the youngsters did their best to mollify.

'It's all right, nothing to be concerned about,' said the agent goodnaturedly. 'Just a bit damp, nothing to it.' Hammond removed his handkerchief and began blotting his front. The table returned to its prior and individual conversations. The Englishman turned to McAuliff, his resigned smiling belying his words. 'I have less than a minute; you'll be contacted tomorrow if necessary.'

'You mean that . . . collision was a signal?'

'Yes. Now, listen and commit. I haven't time to repeat myself. When you reach Kingston, you'll be on your own for a while. Quite frankly, we weren't prepared for you so soon –'

'Just a minute!' interrupted McAuliff, his voice low, angry. 'Goddamn you! *You* listen . . . and commit! You guaranteed complete safety, contacts twenty-four hours a day. It was on that basis I agreed –'

'Nothing has changed.' Hammond cut in swiftly, smiling paternalistically – in contradiction to the quiet hostility between them. 'You *have* contacts; you've memorized eighteen, twenty names –'

'In the north country, not Kingston! You're supposed to deliver the Kingston names!'

'We'll do our best for tomorrow.'

'That's not good enough!'

'It will have to be, Mr McAuliff,' said Hammond coldly. 'In Kingston, east of Victoria Park on Duke Street, there is a fish store called Tallon's. In the last extremity – and only then – should you wish to transmit information, see the owner. He's quite arthritic in his right hand. But, mind you, all he can do is transmit. He's of no other use to you ... Now, I really must go.'

'I've got a few other things to say.' Alex put his hand on Hammond's arm.

'They'll have to wait –'

'One thing ... Alison Booth. You knew, didn't you?'

'About her husband?'

'Yes.'

'We did, Frankly, at first, we thought she was a Dunstone plant. We haven't ruled it out ... Oh, you asked about Warfield's mention of Halidon; what he meant. In my judgment, he knows no more than we do. And he's trying just as hard to find out.'

With the swiftness associated with a much younger man, Hammond lifted himself up from the booth, sidled past McAuliff, and excused himself from the group. McAuliff found himself seated next to the middle-aged woman he presumed had come with Hammond. He had not listened to her name during the introductions, but as he looked at her now, he did not have to be told. The concern – the fear – was in her eyes; she tried to conceal it, but she could not. Her smile was hesitant, taut.

'So you're the young man ...' Mrs Hammond stopped and brought the glass to her lips.

'Young and not so young,' said McAuliff, noting that the woman's hand shook, as his had shaken an hour ago with Warfield. 'It's difficult to talk in here with all the blaring. And those godawful lights.'

Mrs Hammond seemed not to hear or be concerned with his words. The psychedelic oranges and yellows and sickening greens played a visual tattoo on her frightened features. It was strange, thought Alex, but he had not considered Hammond as a private man with personal possessions or a wife, or even a private, personal life.

57

And as he thought about these unconsidered realities, the woman suddenly gripped his forearm and leaned against him. Under the maddening sounds and through the wild, blinding lights, she whispered in McAuliff's ear: 'For God's sake, go after him!'

The undulating bodies formed a violently writhing wall. He lunged through, pushing, pulling, shoving, finally shouldering a path for himself amid the shouted obscenities. He tried looking around for the spaced-out intruder who had signalled Hammond by crashing into the table. He was nowhere to be found.

Then, at the rear of the crowded, flashing dance floor, he could see the interrupted movements of several men pushing a single figure back into a narrow corridor. It was Hammond!

He crashed through the writhing wall again, towards the back of the room. A tall black man objected to Alex's assault.

'Hey, mon! Stop it! You own The Owl, I think not!'

'Get out of my way! Goddamnit, take your hands off me!'

'With pleasure, mon!' The black removed his hands from McAuliff's coat, pulled back a tight fist, and hammered it into Alex's stomach. The force of the blow, along with the shock of its utter surprise, caused McAuliff to double up.

He rose as fast as he could, the pain sharp, and lurched for the man. As he did so, the black twisted his wrist somehow, and McAuliff fell into the surrounding, nearly oblivious dancers. When he got to his feet, the black was gone.

It was a curious and very painful moment.

The smoke and its accompanying odours made him dizzy; then he understood. He was breathing deep breaths; he was out of breath. With less strength but no less intensity, he continued through the dancers to the narrow corridor.

It was a passageway to the rest-rooms, 'Chicks' to the right, 'Roosters' to the left. At the end of the narrow hallway was a door with a very large lock, an outsized padlock, that was meant, apparently, to remind patrons that the door was no egress; The Owl of Saint George expected tabs to be paid before departure.

The lock had been prised open. Prised open and then reset in the round hasps, its curving steel arm half an inch from insertion.

McAuliff ripped it off and opened the door.

He walked out into a dark, very dark, alleyway filled with garbage cans and refuse. There was literally no light but the night sky, dulled by fog, and a minimum spill from the windows in the surrounding ghettolike apartment buildings. In front of him was a high brick wall; to the right the alley continued past other rear doorways, ending in a cul-de-sac formed by the sharply angled wall. To his left, there was a break between The Owl's building and the brick; it was a passageway to the street. It was also lined with garbage cans, and the stench that had to accompany their presence.

McAuliff started down the cement corridor, the light from the street lamps illuminating the narrow confines. He was within twenty feet of the pavement when he saw it. Them: small pools of deep red fluid.

He raced out into the street. The crowds were thinning out; Soho was approaching its own witching hour. Its business was inside now: the private clubs, the illegal all-night gambling houses, the profitable beds where sex was found in varying ways and prices. He looked up and down the sidewalk, trying to find a break in the pattern of human traffic: a resistance, an eruption.

There was none.

He stared down at the pavement; the rivulets of blood had been streaked and blotted by passing feet, the red drops stopping abruptly at the kerb. Hammond had been taken away in a car.

Without warning, McAuliff felt the impact of lunging hands against his back. He had turned sideways at the last instant, his eyes drawn by the flickering of a neon light, and that small motion kept him from being hurled into the street. Instead, his attacker – a huge black man – plunged over the kerb, into the path of an onrushing Bentley, travelling at extraordinary speed. McAuliff felt a stinging pain on his face. Then man and vehicle collided; the anguished scream was the scream at the moment

59

of death; the screeching wheels signified the incredible to McAuliff. The Bentley raced forward, crushing its victim, and sped off. It reached the corner and whipped violently to the left, its tyres spinning above the kerb, whirring as they touched stone again, propelling the car out of sight. Pedestrians screamed, men ran, whores disappeared into doorways, pimps gripped their pockets, and McAuliff stood above the bloody, mangled corpse in the street and knew it was meant to be him.

He ran down the Soho street; he did not know where, just away. Away from the gathering crowds on the pavement behind. There would be questions, witnesses ... people placing him at the scene – *involved*, not placed, he reflected. He had no answers, and instinctively he knew he could not allow himself to be identified – not until he had some answers.

The dead black was the man in The Owl of Saint George, of that he was certain: the man who had stunned him with a savage blow to the stomach on the dance floor and twisted his wrist, throwing him onto the surrounding gyrating bodies. The man who had stopped him from reaching Hammond in the narrow corridor that led past the *'Chicks'* and the *'Roosters'* into the dark alleyway beyond.

Why had the black stopped him? Why for Christ Almighty's sake had he tried to kill him?

Where was Hammond?

He had to get to a telephone. He had to call Hammond's number and speak to someone, anyone who could give him some answers.

Suddenly, Alex was aware that people in the street were staring at him. Why? ... Of course. He was running – well, walking too rapidly. A man walking rapidly at this hour on a misty Soho street was conspicuous. He could not be conspicuous; he slowed his walk, his aimless walk, and aimlessly crossed unfamiliar streets.

Still they stared. He tried not to panic. What *was* it?

And then he knew. He could feel the warm blood trickling

down his cheek. He remembered now: the sting on his face as the huge black hands went crashing past him over the kerb. A ring, perhaps. A fingernail ... what difference? He had been cut, and he was bleeding. He reached into his coat pocket for a handkerchief. The whole side of his jacket had been ripped.

He had been too stunned to notice or feel the jacket ripping, or the blood.

Christ! What a sight! A man in a torn jacket with blood on his face running away from a dead black in Soho.

Dead? Deceased? Life spent?

No. Murdered.

By the method meant for him: a violent thrust into the street, timed to meet the heavy steel on an onrushing, racing Bentley.

In the middle of the next block – what block? – there was a telephone booth. An English telephone booth, wider and darker than its American cousin. He quickened his pace as he withdrew coins from his pocket. He went inside; it was dark, too dark. Why was it so dark? He took out his metal cigarette lighter, gripping it as though it were a handle that, if released, would send him plunging into an abyss. He pressed the lever, breathed deeply, and dialled by the light of the flame.

'We know what's happened, Mr McAuliff,' said the clipped, cool British voice. 'Where precisely are you calling from?'

'I don't know. I ran ... I crossed a number of streets.'

'It's urgent we know where you are ... When you left The Owl, which way did you walk?'

'I ran, goddamnit! I *ran*. Someone tried to *kill* me!'

'Which *way* did you run, Mr McAuliff?'

'To the right ... four or five blocks. Then right again; then left, I think, two blocks later.'

'All right. Relax, now ... You're phoning from a call box?'

'Yes. No, damn it, I'm *calling* from a *phone* booth! ... Yes. For Christ's sake, tell me what's happening! There aren't any street signs; I'm in the middle of the block.'

'Calm down, please.' The Englishman was maddening:

61

imperviously condescending. 'What are the structures outside the booth? Describe anything you like, anything that catches your eye.'

McAuliff complained about the fog and described as best he could the darkened shops and buildings. 'Christ, that's the best I can do . . . I'm going to get out of here. I'll grab a taxi somehow; and then I want to see one of you! Where do I go?'

'You will *not* go *anywhere*, Mr McAuliff!' The cold British tones were suddenly loud and harsh. 'Stay right where you are. If there is a light in the booth, smash it. We know your position. We'll pick you up in minutes.'

Alex hung up the receiver. There was no light bulb in the booth, of course. The tribes of Soho had removed it . . . He tried to think. He hadn't got any answers. Only orders. More commands.

It was insane. The last half hour was madness. What was he *doing*? Why was he in a darkened telephone booth with a bloody face and a torn jacket, trembling and afraid to light a cigarette?

Madness!

There was a man outside the booth, jingling coins in his hand and pointedly shifting his weight from foot to foot in irritation. The command over the telephone had instructed Alex to wait inside, but to do so under the circumstances might cause the man on the pavement to object vocally, drawing attention. He could call someone else, he thought. But who? . . . Alison? No . . . He had to think about Alison now, not talk to her.

He was behaving like a terrified child! With terrifying justification, perhaps. He was actually afraid to move, to walk outside a telephone booth and let an impatient man jingling coins go in. No, he could not behave like that. He could not freeze. He had learned that lesson years ago – centuries ago – in the hills of Che San. To freeze was to become a target. One had to be flexible within the perimeters of common sense. One had to, above all, use one's natural antennae and stay intensely alert. Staying alert, retaining the ability and capacity to move swiftly, these were the important things.

Jesus! He was correlating the murderous fury of Vietnam with a back street in Soho. He was actually drawing a parallel and forcing himself to adjust to it. Too goddamn much!

He opened the door, blotted his cheek, and mumbled apologies to the man jingling coins. He walked to a recessed doorway opposite the booth and waited.

The man on Hammond's telephone was true to his word. The wait wasn't long, and the car recognizable as one of those Alex and the agent had used several times. It came down the street at a steady pace and stopped by the booth, its motor running.

McAuliff left the darkness of the recessed doorway and walked rapidly to the car. The rear door was flung open for him, and he climbed in.

And he froze again.

The man in the back seat was black. The man in the back seat was supposed to be dead, a mangled corpse in the street in front of The Owl of Saint George!

'Yes, Mr McAuliff. It is I,' said the black who was supposed to be dead. 'I apologize for having struck you, but then, you were intruding. Are you all right?'

'Oh, my God!' Alex was rigid on the edge of the seat as the car lurched forward and sped off down the street. 'I thought . . . I mean, I *saw* . . .'

'We're on our way to Hammond. You'll understand better then. Sit back. You've had a very strenuous past hour . . . Quite unexpectedly, incidentally.'

'*I saw you killed!*' McAuliff blurted out the words involuntarily.

'You saw a black man killed; a large black man like myself. We *do* weary of the bromide that we all look alike. It's both unflattering and untrue. By the way, my name is Tallon.'

McAuliff stared at the man. 'No, it's not. Tallon is the name of a fish store near Victoria Park. In Kingston.'

The black laughed softly. 'Very good, Mr McAuliff. I was testing you. Smoke?'

Alex took the offered cigarette gratefully. 'Tallon' held a

63

match for him, and McAuliff inhaled deeply, trying to find a brief moment of sanity.

He looked at his hands. He was both astonished and disturbed.

He was cupping the glow of the cigarette as he had done . . . centuries ago as an infantry officer in the hills of Vietnam.

They drove for nearly twenty minutes, travelling swiftly through the London streets to the outskirts. McAuliff did not try to follow their route out of the window; he did not really care. He was consumed with the decision he had to make. In a profound way it was related to the sight of his hands – no longer trembling – cupping the cigarette. From the non-existent wind? From betraying his position? From enemy snipers?

No. He was not a soldier, had never been one really. He had performed because it was the only way to survive. He had no motive other than survival; no war was his or ever would be his. Certainly not Hammond's.

'Here we are, Mr McAuliff,' said the black who called himself 'Tallon'. 'Rather deserted place, isn't it?'

The car had entered a road by a field – a field, but not grass-covered. It was a levelled expanse of ground, perhaps five acres, that looked as though it was being prepared for construction. Beyond the field was a river bank; Alex presumed it was the Thames, it had to be. In the distance were large square structures that looked like warehouses. Warehouses along a river bank. He had no idea where they were.

The driver made a sharp left turn, and the car bounced as it rolled over a primitive track on the rough ground. Through the windscreen, McAuliff saw in the glare of the headlamps two vehicles about a hundred yards away, both sedans. The one on the right had its inside lights on. Within seconds, the driver had pulled up parallel with the second car.

McAuliff got out and followed 'Tallon' to the lighted car. What he saw bewildered him., angered him, perhaps, and un-questionably reaffirmed his decision to remove himself from Hammond's war.

The British agent was sitting stiffly in the rear seat, his shirt and overcoat draped over his shoulders, an open expanse of flesh at his midsection revealing wide, white bandages. His eyes were squinting slightly, betraying the fact that the pain was not negligible. Alex knew the reason; he had seen the sight before – centuries ago – usually after a bayonet encounter.

Hammond had been stabbed.

'I had you brought here for two reasons, McAuliff. And I warrant you, it was a gamble,' said the agent as Alex stood by the open door. 'Leave us alone, please,' he added to the black.

'Shouldn't you be in a hospital?'

'No, it's not a severe penetration.'

'You got cut, Hammond,' interrupted McAuliff. 'That's severe enough.'

'You're melodramatic; it's unimportant. You'll notice, I trust, that I am very much alive.'

'You're lucky.'

'Luck, sir, had nothing whatsoever to do with it! That's part of what I want you to understand.'

'All right. You're Captain Marvel, indestructible nemesis of the evil people.'

'I am a fifty-year-old veteran of Her Majesty's Service who was never very good at football . . . soccer, to you.' Hammond winced and leaned forward. 'And it's quite possible I would not be in these extremely tight bandages had you followed my instructions and not made a scene on the dance floor.'

'*What?*'

'But you provoke me into straying. First things first. The instant it was apparent that I was in danger, that danger was removed. At no time, no moment, was my life in jeopardy.'

'Because you say so? With a ten-inch bandage straddling your stomach? Don't try to sell water in the Sahara.'

'This wound was delivered in panic caused by you! I was in the process of making the most vital contact on our schedule, the contact we sought *you* out to make.'

'Halidon?'

'It's what we believed. Unfortunately, there's no way to verify. Come with me.' Hammond gripped the side strap, and with his right hand supported himself on the front seat as he climbed painfully out of the car. Alex made a minor gesture of assistance, knowing that it would be refused. The agent led McAuliff to the forward car, awkwardly removing a flashlight from his draped overcoat as they approached. There were several other men in shadows: they stepped away, obviously under orders.

Inside the car were two lifeless figures: one sprawled over the wheel, the other slumped across the rear seat. Hammond shot the beam of light successively on both corpses. Each was male, black, in his mid-thirties, perhaps, and dressed in conservative, though not expensive, business suits. McAuliff was confused: There were no signs of violence, no shattered glass, no blood. The interior of the car was neat, clean, even peaceful. The two dead men might have been a pair of young executives taking a brief rest off the highway in the middle of a long business trip. Alex's bewilderment was ended with Hammond's next word.

'Cyanide.'

'Why?'

'Fanatics, obviously. It was preferable to revealing information . . . unwillingly, of course. They misread us. It began when you made such an obvious attempt to follow me out of The Owl of Saint George. That was their first panic; when they inflicted . . . this.' Hammond waved his hand just once at his midsection.

McAuliff did not bother to conceal his anger. 'I've about had it with your goddamn caustic deductions!'

'I told you it was a gamble bringing you here –'

'Stop *telling* me things!'

'Please bear in mind that without us you had a life expectancy of four months – at the outside.'

'Your version.' But the agent's version had more substance than McAuliff cared to think about at the moment.

Alex turned away from the unpleasant sight. For no particular reason, he ripped the torn lining from the base of his jacket and leaned against the bonnet of the car. 'Since you hold me responsible for so much tonight, what happened?'

Hammond told him. Several days ago, MI5's surveillance had picked up a second 'force' involved with Dunstone's movements. Three, possibly four, unidentifiable subjects who kept reappearing. The subjects were black. Photographs were taken, fingerprints obtained by way of restaurants, discarded objects – cigarette packs, newspapers, and the like – and all the data fed into the computers at New Scotland Yard and Emigration. There were no records; the subjects were in the country illegally. Hammond had been elated; the connection was so possible. It was obvious that the subjects were 'negative' insofar as Dunstone was concerned. Obvious . . . then proven without doubt earlier in the evening, when one of the subjects killed a Dunstone man who spotted him.

'We knew then,' said Hammond, 'that we had centred in; the target was accurate. It remained to make positive contact, *sympathetic* contact. I even toyed with the idea of bringing these men and you together in short order, perhaps this morning. So much resolved so damned quickly . . .'

A cautious preliminary contact was made with the subjects: 'so harmless and promising, we damn near offered what was left of the Empire. They were concerned, of course, about a trap.'

A rendezvous was arranged at The Owl of Saint George, a racially integrated club that offered a comfortable environment. It was scheduled for 2:30 in the morning, after Hammond's meeting with McAuliff.

When Alex made his panicked – and threatening – call to Hammond's number, insisting that they meet regardless of time, the agent left his options open. And then made his decision. Why not The Owl of Saint George? Bring the American into Soho, to the club, and if it proved the wrong decision, McAuliff could be stopped once inside. If the decision was the right one, the circumstances would be optimal – all parties present.

'What about Warfield's men?' asked Alex. 'You said he doubled his teams on me.'

'I lied. I wanted you to remain where you were. Warfield had a single man on you. We diverted him. The Dunstone people had their own anxieties: One of their men had been killed. You couldn't be held responsible for that.'

The night progressed as Hammond had anticipated: without incident. The agent made arrangements for the table – 'we know just about everyone you've met in London, old chap' – and awaited the compatible merging of elements.

And then, in rapid succession, each component fell apart. First was Alex's statement that the survey team was leaving in two days – MI5 and its counterpart overseas, MI6, were not ready for them in Kingston. Then the information that Warfield had spoken the name of 'Halidon'; it was to be expected, of course. Dunstone would be working furiously to find the killers of the first survey team. But, again, MI5 had not expected Dunstone to have made such progress. The next breakdown was the spaced-out agent who crashed into the table and used the word 'Edinburgh' – used it twice.

'Each twenty-four-hour period we circulate an unusual word that has but one connotation: "abort, extreme prejudice". If it's repeated, that simply compounds the meaning: Our cover is blown. Or misread. Weapons should be ready.'

At that moment, Hammond saw clearly the massive error that had been made. His agents had diverted Warfield's men away from Alex, but not one of the blacks. McAuliff had been observed in Warfield's company at midnight for a considerable length of time. Within minutes after he had walked into The Owl, his black surveillance had followed, panicked that his colleagues had been led into a trap.

The confrontation had begun within the gyrating, psychedelic madness that was The Owl of Saint George.

Hammond tried to stop the final collapse.

He broke the rules. It was not yet 2:30, but since Alexander McAuliff had been seen with him, he dared not wait. He tried to establish a bridge, to explain, to calm the raging outburst.

He had nearly succeeded when one of the blacks – now dead behind the wheel – saw McAuliff leap from his seat in the booth and plunge into the crowds, whipping people out of his way, looking frantically – obviously – for Hammond.

This sight triggered the panic. Hammond was cut, used as a shield, and propelled out the rear door into the alley by two of the subjects while the third fled through the crowds in front to alert the car for escape.

'What happened during the next few minutes was as distressing as it was comforting,' said Hammond. 'My people would not allow my physical danger, so the instant my captors and I emerged on the pavement, they were taken. We put them in this car and drove off, still hoping to re-establish good will. But we purposely allowed the third man to disappear – an article of faith on our part.'

The MI5 had driven out to the deserted field. A doctor was summoned to patch up Hammond. And the two subjects – relieved of weapons, car key removed unobtrusively – were left alone to talk by themselves, hopefully to resolve their doubts, while Hammond was being bandaged.

'They made a last attempt to get away but, of course, there were no keys in the vehicle. So they took their deadly little vials or tablets and, with them, their lives. Ultimately, they could not trust us.'

McAuliff said nothing for several moments. Hammond did not interrupt the silence.

'And your "article of faith" tried to kill me.'

'Apparently. Leaving one man in England we must try to find: the driver ... You understand that we cannot be held accountable; you completely disregarded our instructions –'

'We'll get to that,' broke in McAuliff. 'You said you brought me out here for two reasons. I get the first: Your people are quick, safety guaranteed ... if instructions aren't "disregarded".' Alex mimicked Hammond's reading of the word. 'What's the second reason?'

The agent walked directly in front of McAuliff and, through the night light, Alex could see the intensity in his eyes. 'To tell you you have no choice but to continue now. Too much has happened. You're too involved.'

'That's what Warfield said.'

'He's right.'

'Suppose I refuse? Suppose I just pack up and leave?'

'You'd be suspect, and expendable. You'd be hunted down. Take my word for that, I've been here before.'

'That's quite a statement from a ... what was it, a financial analyst?'

'Labels, Mr McAuliff. Titles. Quite meaningless.'

'Not to your wife.'

'I beg your –' Hammond inhaled deeply, audibly. When he continued, he did not ask a question. He made a quiet, painful statement. 'She sent you after me.'

'Yes.'

It was Hammond's turn to remain silent. And Alex's option not to break that silence. Instead, McAuliff watched the fifty-year-old agent struggle to regain his composure.

'The fact remains, you disregarded my instructions.'

'You must be a lovely man to live with.'

'Get used to it,' replied Hammond with cold precision. 'For the next several months, our association will be very close. And you'll do exactly as I say. Or you'll be dead.'

TWO

Kingston

7

The red-orange sun burned a hole in the streaked blue tapestry that was the evening sky. Arcs of yellow rimmed the lower clouds; a purplish-black void was above. The soft Caribbean night would soon envelope this section of the world. It would be dark when the plane landed at Port Royal.

McAuliff started out at the horizon through the tinted glass of the aircraft's window. Alison Booth was in the seat beside him, asleep.

The Jensens were across the 747's aisle, and for a couple whose political persuasions were left of centre, they adapted to British Airways' first-class accommodation with a remarkable lack of guilt, thought Alex. They ordered the best wine, the foie gras, duck à l'orange, and Charlotte Malakof as if they had been used to them for years. And Alex wondered if Warfield was wrong. All the left-oriented he knew, outside the Soviet bloc, were humourless; the Jensens were not.

Young James Ferguson was alone in a forward seat. Initially, Charles Whitehall had sat with him, but Whitehall had gone up to the lounge early in the flight, found an acquaintance from Savanna-La-Mar, and stayed. Ferguson used the unoccupied seat for a leather bag containing photographic equipment. He was currently changing lens filters, snapping shots of the sky outside.

McAuliff and Alison had joined Charles Whitehall and his friend for several drinks in the lounge. The friend was white, rich, and a heavy drinker. He was also a vacuous inheritor of old south-west Jamaican money, and Alex found it contradictory that Whitehall would care to spend much time with him; and

73

it was a little disturbing to watch Whitehall respond with such alacrity to his friend's alcoholic, unbright, unfunny observations.

Alison had touched McAuliff's arm after the second drink. It had been a signal to return to their seats; she had had enough. So had he.

Alison?

During the last two days in London there had been so much to do that he had not spent the time with her he had wanted to, intended to. He was involved with all-day problems of logistics: equipment purchases and rentals, clearing passports, ascertaining whether inoculations were required (none was), establishing bank accounts in Montego, Kingston and Ocho Rios, and scores of additional items necessary for a long geological survey. Dunstone stayed out of the picture but was of enormous help behind the scenes. The Dunstone people told him precisely whom to contact where; the tangled webs of bureaucracy – governmental and commercial – were untangled.

He had spent one evening bringing everyone together – everyone but Sam Tucker, who would join them in Kingston. Dinner at Simpsons. It was sufficiently agreeable; all were professionals. Each sized up the others and made flattering comments where work was known. Whitehall received the most recognition – as was appropriate. He was an authentic celebrity of sorts. Ruth Jensen and Alison seemed genuinely to like each other, which McAuliff had thought would happen. Ruth's husband, Peter, assumed a paternalistic attitude towards Ferguson, laughing gently, continuously at the young man's incessant banter. And Charles Whitehall had the best manners, slightly aloof and very proper, with just the right traces of scholarly wit and unfelt humility.

But Alison.

He had kept their luncheon date after the madness at The Owl of Saint George and the insanity that followed in the deserted field on London's outskirts. He had approached her with ambiguous feelings. He was annoyed that she had not

74

brought up the questionable activities of her recent husband. But he did not accept Hammond's vague concern that Alison was a Warfield plant. It was senseless. She was nothing if not independent – as he was. To be a silent emissary from Warfield meant losing independence – as he knew. Alison could not do that, not without showing it.

Still, he tried to provoke her into talking about her husband. She responded with humorously 'civilized' clichés such as leaving sleeping dogs lie, which he had. Often. She would not, at this point, discuss David Booth with him.

It was not relevant.

'Ladies and gentlemen,' said the very masculine, in-charge tones over the aircraft's speaker. 'This is Captain Thomas. We are nearing the north-east coast of Jamaica; in several minutes we shall be over Port Antonio, descending for our approach to Palisados Airport, Port Royal. May we suggest that all passengers return to their seats. There may be minor turbulence over the Blue Mountain range. Time of arrival is now anticipated at 8:20, Jamaican. The temperature in Kingston is seventy-eight degrees, weather and visibility clear . . .'

As the calm, strong voice finished the announcement, McAuliff thought of Hammond. If the British agent spoke over a loudspeaker, he would sound very much like Captain Thomas.

Hammond.

McAuliff had not ended their temporary disassociation – as Hammond phrased it – too pleasantly. He had countered the agent's caustic pronouncement that Alex should do as Hammond instructed with a volatile provision of his own: He had a million dollars coming to him from Dunstone and he expected to collect it. From Dunstone or some other source.

Hammond had exploded. What good were two million dollars to a dead geologist? Alex should be paying for the warnings and the protection afforded him. But, in the final analysis, Hammond recognized the necessity for something to motivate Alexander's cooperation. Survival was too abstract; lack of survival could not be experienced.

75

In the early morning hours, a Letter of Agreement was brought to McAuliff by a temporary Savoy floor steward; Alex recognized him as the man in the brown jacket on High Holborn. The letter covered the conditions of reimbursement in the event of 'loss of fees' with a *very* clear ceiling of one million dollars.

If he remained in one piece – and he had every expectation of so doing – he would collect. He mailed the agreement to New York.

Hammond.

He wondered what the explanation was; what could explain a wife whose whispered voice could hold such fear? He wondered about the private, personal Hammond, yet knew instinctively that whatever private questions he had would never be answered.

Hammond was like that. Perhaps all the people who did what Hammond did were like that. Men in shadows; their women in unending tunnels of fear. Pockets of fear.

And then there was . . .

Halidon.

What did it mean? What was it?

Was it black?

Possibly. Probably not, however, Hammond had said. At least, not exclusively. It had too many informational resources, too much apparent influence in powerful sectors. Too much money.

The word had surfaced under strange and horrible circumstances. The British agent attached to the previous Dunstone survey had been one of two men killed in a bush fire that began inside a bamboo camp on the banks of the Martha Brae River, deep within the Cock Pit country. Evidence indicated that the two dead members of the survey had tried to salvage equipment within the fire, collapsed from the smoke, and burned in the bamboo inferno.

But there was something more; something so appalling that even Hammond found it difficult to recite it.

The two men had been bound by bamboo shoots to separate trees, each next to valuable survey equipment. They had been consumed in the conflagration, for the simple reason that neither could run from it. But the agent had left a message, a single word scratched on the metal casing of a geoscope.

Halidon.

Inspection under a microscope gave the remainder of the horror story: particles of human tooth enamel. The agent had scratched the letters with broken teeth.

Halidon . . . holly-dawn.

No known definition. A word? A name? A man? A three-beat sound?

What did it mean?

'It's beautiful, isn't it,' said Alison, looking beyond him through the window.

'You're awake.'

'Someone turned on a speaker and a man spoke . . . endlessly.' She smiled and stretched her long legs. She then inhaled in a deep yawn, which caused her breasts to swell against the soft white silk of her blouse. McAuliff watched. And she saw him watching, and smiled again – in humour, not provocation. 'Relevancy, Dr McAuliff. Remember?'

'That word's going to get you into trouble, Ms Booth.'

'I'll stop saying it instantly. Come to think, I don't believe I used it much until I met you.'

'I like the connection; don't stop.'

She laughed, and reached for her bag, on the deck between them.

There was a sudden series of rise-and-fall motions as the plane entered air turbulence. It was over quickly, but during it Alison's open bag landed on its side – on Alex's lap. Lipstick, compact, matches and a short thick tube fell out, wedging themselves between McAuliff's legs. It was one of those brief, indecisive moments. Pocketbooks were unfair vantage points, somehow unguarded extensions of the private self. And Alison was not the type to reach swiftly between a man's legs to retrieve property.

'Nothing fell on the floor,' said Alex awkwardly, handing Alison the bag. 'Here.'

He picked out the lipstick and the compact with his left hand, his right on the thick tube, which, at first, seemed to have a very personal connotation. As his eyes were drawn to the casing, however, the connotation became something else. The tube was a weapon, a compressor. On the cylinder's side were printed words:

312 GAS CONTENTS
FOR MILITARY AND/OR POLICE USE ONLY
AUTHORIZATION NUMBER 4316
RECORDED: 1–6

The authorization number and the date had been handwritten in indelible ink. The gas compressor had been issued by British authorities a month ago.

Alison took the tube from his hand. 'Thank you' was all she said.

'You planning to hijack the plane? That's quite a lethal-looking object.'

'London has its problems for girls ... women these days. There were incidents in my building. May I have a cigarette? I seem to have run out.'

'Sure.' McAuliff reached into his shirt pocket and withdrew his cigarettes, shaking one up for her. He lighted it, then spoke softly, very gently. 'Why are you lying to me, Alison?'

'I'm not. I think it's presumptuous of you to think so.'

'Oh, come on.' He smiled, reducing the earnestness of his inquiry. 'The police, especially the London police, do not issue compressors of gas because of "incidents". And you don't look like a colonel in the Women's Auxiliary Army.' As he said the words, Alex suddenly had the feeling that perhaps he was wrong. Was Alison Booth an emissary from Hammond? Not Warfield, but British Intelligence?

'Exceptions are made. They really are, Alex.' She locked her eyes with his; she was not lying.

'May I venture a suggestion? A reason?'

'If you like.'

'David Booth?'

She looked away, inhaling deeply on her cigarette. 'You know about him. That's why you kept asking questions the other night.'

'Yes. Did you think I wouldn't find out?'

'I didn't care . . . no, that's not right; I think I wanted you to find out if it helped me get the job. But I couldn't tell you.'

'Why not?'

'Oh Lord, Alex! Your own words; you wanted the best professionals, not personal problems! For all I knew, you'd have scratched me instantly.' Her smile was gone now. There was only anxiety.

'This Booth must be quite a fellow.'

'He's a very sick, very vicious man . . . But I can handle David. I was always able to handle him. He's an extraordinary coward.'

'Most vicious people are.'

'I'm not sure I subscribe to that. But it wasn't David. It was someone else. The man he worked for.'

'Who?'

'A Frenchman. A marquis. Chatellerault is his name.'

The team took separate taxis into Kingston. Alison remained behind with McAuliff while he commandeered the equipment with the help of the Jamaican government people attached to the Ministry of Education. Alex could feel the same vague resentment from the Jamaicans that he had felt with the academicians in London; only added now was the aspect of pigmentation. Were there no black geologists? they seemed to be thinking.

The point was emphasized by the Customs men, their khaki uniforms creased into steel. They insisted on examining each box, each carton, as though each contained the most dangerous contraband imaginable. They decided to be officially thorough as McAuliff stood helplessly by long after the aircraft had taxied into a Palisados berth. Alison remained ten yards away, sitting on a luggage dolly.

An hour and a half later, the equipment had been processed and marked for in-island transport to Boscobel Airfield, in Ocho Rios. McAuliff's temper was stretched to the point of gritted teeth and a great deal of swallowing. He grabbed Alison's arm and marched them both towards the terminal.

'For heaven's sake, Alex, you're bruising my elbow!' said Alison under her breath, trying to hold back her laughter.

'Sorry . . . I'm *sorry*. Those goddamned messiahs think they inherited the earth! The *bastards*!'

'They recently inherited their own island —'

'I'm in no mood for anti-colonial lectures,' he interrupted. 'I'm in the mood for a drink. Let's stop at the lounge.'

'What about our bags?'

'Oh, Christ! I forgot . . . it's this way, if I remember,' said Alex, pointing to a gate entrance on the right.

'Yes,' replied Alison. ' "Incoming Flights" usually means that.'

'Be quiet. My first order to you as a subordinate is not to say another word until we get our bags and I have a drink in my hand.'

But McAuliff's command, by necessity, was rescinded. Their luggage was nowhere in sight. And apparently no one knew where it might be; all passenger baggage stored on Flight 640 from London had been picked up. An hour ago.

'*We* were on that flight. We did *not* pick up our bags. So, you see, you're mistaken,' said Alex curtly to the luggage manager.

'Then you look-see, mon,' answered the Jamaican, irritated by the American's implication that he was less than efficient. 'Every suitcase taken – nothing left. Flight 640 all *here*, mon! No place other.'

'Let me talk to the British Airways representative. Where is he?'

'Who?'

'Your boss, goddamnit!'

'I top mon!' replied the black angrily.

Alex held himself in check. 'Look, there's been a mix-up. The airline's responsible, that's all I'm trying to say.'

'I think not, mon,' interjected the luggage manager defensively as he turned to a telephone on the counter. 'I will call British Airways.'

McAuliff spoke softly to Alison. 'Our bags are probably on the way to Buenos Aires.' The waited while the man spoke briefly on the phone.

'Here, mon.' The manager held the phone out for Alex. 'You talk, please.'

'Hello?'

'Dr McAuliff?' said the British voice.

'Yes. McAuliff.'

'We merely followed the instructions in your note, sir.'

'What note?'

'To First Class Accommodations. The driver brought it to us. The taxi. Mrs Booth's and your luggage was taken to Courtleigh Manor. That *is* what you wished, is it not, sir?' The voice was laced with a trace of over-clarification, as if the speaker were addressing someone who had had an extra drink he could not handle.

'I see . . . Yes, that's fine,' said Alex quietly. He hung up the telephone and turned to Alison. 'Our bags were taken to the hotel.'

'Really? Wasn't that nice.' A statement.

'No, I don't think it was,' answered McAuliff. 'Come on, let's find that bar.'

They sat at a corner table in the Palisados observation lounge. The red-jacketed waiter brought their drinks while humming a Jamaican folk tune softly. Alex wondered if the island's tourist bureau instructed all those who served visitors to hum tunes and move rhythmically. He reached for his glass and drank a large portion of his double Scotch. He noticed that Alison, who was not much of a drinker, seemed as anxious as he was to put some alcohol into her system.

All things considered – all things – it was conceivable that his luggage might be stolen. Not hers. But the note had specified his and Mrs Booth's.

'You didn't have any more artillery, did you?' asked Alex quickly. 'Like that compressor?'

'No. It would have set off bells in the airline X-ray. I declared this prior to boarding.' Alison pointed to her purse.

'Yes, of course,' he mumbled.

'I must say, you're remarkably calm. I should think you'd be telephoning the hotel, see if the bags got there . . . oh, not for me. I don't travel with the Crown jewels.'

'Oh, Lord, I'm sorry, Alison.' He pushed his chair back. 'I'll call right away.'

'No, please.' She reached out and put her hand over his. 'I think you're doing what you're doing for a reason. You don't want to appear upset. I think you're right. If they're gone, there's nothing I can't replace in the morning.'

'You're very understanding. Thanks.'

She withdrew her hand and drank again. He pulled his chair back and shifted his position slightly, towards the interior of the lounge. Unobtrusively, he began scanning the other tables.

The observation lounge was half filled, no more than that. From his position – their position – in the far west corner of the room, Alex could see nearly every table. And he slowly riveted his attention on every table, wondering, as he had wondered two nights ago on High Holborn, who might be concerned with *him*.

There was movement in the dimly lighted entrance. Mc-Auliff's eyes were drawn to it: the figure of a stocky man in a white shirt and no jacket standing in the wide frame. He spoke to the lounge's hostess, shaking his head slowly, negatively, as he looked inside. Suddenly, Alex blinked and focused on the man.

He knew him.

A man he had last seen in Australia, in the fields of Kimberly Plateau. He had been told the man had retired to Jamaica.

Robert Hanley, a pilot.

Hanley was standing in the entranceway of the lounge,

looking for someone inside. And Alex knew instinctively that Hanley was looking for him.

'Excuse me,' he said to Alison. 'There's a fellow I know. Unless I'm mistaken, he's trying to find me.'

McAuliff thought, as he threaded his way around the tables and through the subdued shadows of the room, that it was somehow right that Robert Hanley, of all the men in the Caribbean, would be involved. Hanley, the open man who dealt with a covert world because he was, above all, a man to be trusted. A laughing man, a tough man, a professional with expertise far beyond that required by those employing him. Someone who had miraculously survived six decades when all the odds indicated nearer to four. But then, Robert Hanley did not look much over forty-five. Even his close-cropped, reddish-blond hair was devoid of grey.

'Robert!'

'Alexander!'

The two men clasped hands and held each other's shoulders.

'I said to the lady sitting with me that I thought you were looking for me. I'll be honest, I hope I'm wrong.'

'I wish you were, lad.'

'That's what I was afraid of. What is it? Come on in.'

'In a minute. Let me tell you the news first. I wouldn't want the lady to see you uncork your temper.' Hanley led Alex away from the door; they stood alone by the wall. 'It's Sam Tucker.'

'Sam? Where is he?'

'That's the point, lad. I don't know. Sam flew into Mo'Bay three days ago and called me at Port Antone'; the boys in Los Angeles told him I was here. I hopped over, naturally, and it was a grand reunion. I won't go into the details. The next morning, Sam went down to the lobby to get a paper, I think. He never came back.'

8

Robert Hanley was flying back to Port Antonio in an hour. He and McAuliff agreed not to mention Sam Tucker to Alison. Hanley also agreed to keep looking for Sam; he and Alex would stay in touch.

The three of them took a taxi from Port Royal into Kingston, to the Courtleigh. Hanley remained in the cab and took it on to the small Tinson Pen Airfield, where he kept his plane.

At the hotel desk, Alex inquired nonchalantly, feeling no casualness whatsoever, 'I assume our luggage arrived?'

'Indeed, yes, Mr McAuliff,' replied the clerk, stamping both registration forms and signalling a bellhop. 'Only minutes ago. We had them taken to your rooms. They're adjoining.'

'How thoughtful,' said Alex softly, wondering if Alison had heard the man behind the desk. The clerk did not speak loudly, and Alison was at the end of the counter, looking at tourist brochures. She glanced over at McAuliff; she had heard. The expression on her face was noncommittal. He wondered.

Five minutes later, she opened the door between their two rooms, and Alex knew there was no point speculating further.

'I did as you ordered, Mister Bossman,' said Alison, walking in. 'I didn't touch the –'

McAuliff held up his hand quickly, signalling her to be quiet. 'The *bed*, bless your heart! You're all heart, luv!'

The expression now on Alison's face was definitely committal. Not pleasantly. It was an awkward moment, which he was not prepared for; he had not expected her to walk deliberately into

84

his room. Still, there was no point standing immobile, looking foolish.

He reached into his jacket pocket and withdrew a small, square-shaped metal instrument the size of a cigarette pack. It was one of several items given him by Hammond. (Hammond had cleared his boarding pass with British Airways in London, eliminating the necessity of declaring whatever metallic objects were on his person.)

The small metal box was an electronic scanner with a miniaturized high-voltage battery. Its function was simple, its mechanism complex, and Hammond claimed it was in very common use these days. It detected the presence of electronic listening devices within a nine-by-nine-foot area. Alex had intended to use it the minute he entered the room. Instead, he absentmindedly had opened the doors to his small balcony and gazed for a brief time at the dark, majestic rise of the Blue Mountains beyond in the clear Kingston night.

Alison Booth stared at the scanner and then at McAuliff. Both anger and fear were in her eyes, but she had the presence of mind to say nothing.

As he had been taught, Alex switched on the instrument and made half circles laterally and vertically, starting from the far corner of the room. This pattern was to be followed in the other three corners. He felt embarrassed, almost ludicrous, as he waved his arm slowly, as though administering some occult benediction. He did not care to look at Alison as he went through the motions.

Then, suddenly, he was not embarrassed at all. Instead, he felt a pain in the centre of his upper stomach, a sharp sting as his breath stopped and his eyes riveted on the inch-long, narrow bar in the dial of the scanner. He had seen that bar move often during the practice sessions with Hammond; he had been curious, even fascinated at its wavering, stuttering movements. He was not fascinated now. He was afraid.

This was not a training session in an out-of-the-way, safe practice room with Hammond patiently, thoroughly explaining

85

the importance of overlapping areas. It was actually happening; he had not really thought that it *would* happen. It all had been . . . well, basically *insincere*, somehow so improbable.

Yet now, in front of him, the thin, inch-long bar was vibrating, oscillating with a miniature violence of its own. The tiny sensors were responding to an intruder.

Somewhere within the immediate area of his position was a foreign object whose function was to transmit everything being said in this room.

He motioned to Alison; she approached him warily. He gestured and realized that his gestures were those of an unimaginative charade contestant. He pointed to the scanner and then to his lips. When she spoke he felt like a goddamned idiot.

'You promised me a drink in that lovely garden downstairs. Other considerations will have to wait . . . *luv*.' She said the words quietly, simply. She was very believable.

'You're right,' he answered, deciding instantly that he was no actor. 'Just let me wash up.'

He walked swiftly into the bathroom and turned the taps on in the basin. He pulled the door to within several inches of closing; the sound of the rushing water was discernible, not obvious. He returned to where he had been standing and continued to operate the scanner, reducing the semicircles as the narrow bar reacted, centring in on the location of the object as he had been taught to do by Hammond.

The only non-stunning surprise was the fact that the scanner's tiny red light went on directly above his suitcase, against the wall on a baggage rack.

The red light indicated that the object was within twelve inches of the instrument.

He handed Alison the scanner and opened the case cautiously. He separated his clothes, removing shirts, socks and underwear, and placing them – throwing them – on the bed. When the suitcase was more empty than full, he stretched the elasticized liner and ran his fingers against the leather wall.

86

McAuliff knew what to feel for; Hammond had showed him dozens of bugs of varying sizes and shapes.

He found it.

It was attached to the outer lining: a small bulge the size of a leather-covered button. He let it stay and, as Hammond had instructed, continued to examine the remainder of the suitcase for a second, back-up device.

It was there, too. On the opposite side.

He took the scanner from Alison, walked away from the area, and rapidly 'half circled' the rest of the room. As Hammond had told him to expect, there was no further movement on the scanner's dial. For, if a transmitter was planted on a movable host, it usually indicated that it was the only source available.

The rest of the room was clean. 'Sterile' was the word Hammond used.

McAuliff went into the bathroom; it, too, was safe. He turned off the taps and called out to Alison.

'Are you unpacked?' *Now why the hell did he say that? Of all the stupid . . .*

'I'm an old hand at geo trips,' came the relaxed reply. 'All my garments are mostly polyester; they can wait. I really want to see that *lovely* garden. Do hurry.'

He pulled the door open and saw that she was closing the balcony door, drawing the curtains across the floor-to-ceiling glass. Alison Booth was doing the right thing, he reflected. Hammond had often repeated the command: *When you find a transmitter, check outside sightlines; assume visual surveillance.*

He came out of the bathroom; she looked across at him . . . No, he thought, she did not look at him, she stared at him.

'Good,' she said. 'You're ready. I think you missed most of your beard, but you're presentable. Let's go . . . *luv.*'

Outside the room, in the hotel corridor, Alison took his arm, and they walked to the elevator. Several times he began to speak, but each time he did so, she interrupted him.

'Wait till we're downstairs,' she kept repeating softly.

In the patio garden, it was Alison who, after they had been seated, requested another table. One on the opposite side of the open area; a table, Alex realized, that had no palms or plants in its vicinity. There were no more than a dozen other couples, no single men or unescorted women. McAuliff had the feeling that Alison had observed each couple closely.

Their drinks arrived; the waiter departed, and Alison Booth spoke.

'I think it's time we talked to each other . . . about things we haven't talked about.'

Alex offered her a cigarette. She declined, and so he lighted one for himself. He was buying a few seconds of time before answering her, and both of them knew it.

'I'm sorry you saw what you did upstairs. I don't want you to give it undue importance.'

'That would be funny, darling, except that *you* were halfway to hysterics.'

'That's nice.'

'What?'

'You said "darling".'

'Please. May we stay professional?'

'Good Lord! Are you? Professional, I mean?'

'I'm a geologist. What are you?'

McAuliff ignored her. 'You said I was . . . excited upstairs. You were right. But it struck me that you weren't. You did all the correct things while I was fumbling.'

'I agree. You were fumbling . . . Alex, were you told to hire me?'

'No. I was told to think twice or three times before accepting you.'

'That could have been a ploy. I wanted the job badly; I would have gone to bed with you to get it . . . Thank you for not demanding that.'

'There was no pressure one way or the other about you. Only a warning. And that was because of your recent husband's sideline occupation, which, incidentally, apparently accounts for

88

most of his money. I say money because it's not considered income, I gather.'

'It accounts for *all* of his money, and is not reported as income. And I don't for a minute believe the Geophysics Department of London University would have access to such information. Much less the Royal Society.'

'Then you'd be wrong. A lot of the money for this survey is a grant from the government funnelled through the society and the university. When governments spend money, they're concerned about personnel *and* payrolls.' McAuliff was pleasantly surprised at himself. He was responding as Hammond said he would: creating instant, logical replies. *Build on part of the truth, keep it simple* ... Those had been Hammond's words.

'We'll let that dubious, American-oriented assessment pass,' said Alison, now reaching for his cigarettes. 'Surely you'll explain what happened upstairs.'

The moment had come, thought Alex, wondering if he could carry it off the way Hammond said: *Reduce any explanation to very few words, rooted in common sense and simplicity, and do not vary.* He lighted her cigarette and spoke as casually as possible.

'There's a lot of political jockeying in Kingston. Most of it's petty, but some of it gets rough. This survey has controversial overtones. Resentment of origin, jealousies, that sort of thing. You saw it at Customs ... There are people who would like to discredit us. I was given that goddamned scanner to use in case I thought something very unusual happened. I thought it had, and I was right.' Alex drank the remainder of his drink and watched the girl's reaction. He did his best to convey only sincerity.

'Our bags, you mean,' said Alison.

'Yes. That note didn't make sense, and the clerk at the desk said they got here just before we did. But they were picked up at Palisados over two hours ago.'

'I see. And a geological survey would drive people to those extremes? That's hard to swallow, Alex.'

'Not if you think about it. Why are surveys made? What's

generally the purpose? Isn't it usually because someone – some people – expect to build something?'

'Not one like ours, no. It's too spread out over too great an area. I'd say it's patently, *obviously* academic. Anything else would –' Alison stopped as her eyes met McAuliff's. 'Good Lord! If it *was* anything else, it's unbelievable!'

'Perhaps there are those who *do* believe it. If they did, what do you think they'd do?' Alex signalled the waiter by holding up two fingers for refills. Alison Booth's lips were parted in astonishment.

'Millions and millions *and millions*,' she said quietly. 'My God, they'd buy up everything in sight.'

'Only if they were convinced they were right.'

Alison forced him to look at her. When, at first, he refused, and glanced over at the waiter, who was dawdling, she put her hand on top of his and made him pay attention. 'They *are* right, aren't they, Alex?'

'I wouldn't have any proof of it. My contract's with London University, with countersigned approvals from the Society and the Jamaican Ministry. What they do with the results is their business.' It was pointless to issue a flat denial. He was a professional surveyor, not a clairvoyant.

'I don't believe you. You've been primed.'

'Not primed. Told to be on guard, that's all.'

'Those . . . deadly little instruments aren't given to people who've only been told to be on guard.'

'That's what I thought. But you know something? You and I are wrong, Alison. Scanners are in common use these days. Nothing out of the ordinary. Especially if you're working outside home territory. Not a very nice comment on the state of trust, is it?'

The waiter brought their drinks. He was humming and moving rhythmically to the beat of his own tune. Alison continued to stare at McAuliff. He wasn't sure, but he began to think she believed him. When the waiter left, she leaned forward, anxious to speak.

'And what are you supposed to do now? You found those awful things. What are you going to do about them?'

'Nothing. Report them to the Ministry in the morning, that's all.'

'You mean you're not going to take them out and step on them or something? You're just going to leave them there?'

It was not a pleasant prospect, thought Alex, but Hammond had been clear: If a bug was found, let it remain intact and *use* it. It could be invaluable. Before eliminating any such device, he was to report it and await instructions. A fish store named Tallon's, near Victoria Park.

'They're paying me . . . paying us. I suppose they'll want to quietly investigate. What difference does it make? I don't have any secrets.'

'And you *won't* have,' Alison said softly but pointedly, removing her hand from his.

McAuliff suddenly realized the preposterousness of his position. It was at once ridiculous and sublime, funny and not funny at all.

'May I change my mind and call someone now?' he asked.

Alison slowly – very slowly – began to smile her lovely smile. 'No, I was being unfair . . . And I *do* believe you. You're the most maddeningly unconcerned man I've ever known. You are either supremely innocent or superbly ulterior. I can't accept the latter; you were far too nervous upstairs.' She put her hand back on top of his free one. With his other, he finished the second drink.

'May I ask why you weren't? Nervous.'

'Yes. It's time I told you. I owe you that . . . I shan't be returning to England, Alex. Not for many years, if ever. I can't. I spent several months cooperating with Interpol. I've had experience with those horrid little buggers. That's what we called them. Buggers.'

McAuliff felt the stinging pain in his stomach again. It was fear, and more than fear. Hammond had said British Intelligence doubted she would return to England. Julian Warfield suggested that she might be of value for abstract reasons having nothing to do with her contributions to the survey.

He was not sure how – or why – but Alison was being used. Just as he was being used.

'How did *that* happen?' he asked with appropriate astonishment.

Alison touched on the highlights of her involvement. The marriage was sour before the first anniversary. Succinctly put. Alison Booth came to the conclusion very early that her husband had pursued and married her for reasons having more to do with her professional travels than for anything else.

'... it was as though he had been ordered to take me, use me, absorb me ...'

The strain came soon after they were married: Booth was inordinately interested in her prospects. And, from seemingly nowhere, survey offers came out of the blue, from little-known but good-paying firms, for operations remarkably exotic.

'... among them, of course, Zaire, Turkey, Corsica. He joined me each time. For days, weeks at a time ...'

The first confrontation with David Booth came about in Corsica. The survey was a coastal-offshore expedition in the Capo Senetosa area. David arrived during the middle stages for his usual two- to three-week stay, and during this period a series of strange telephone calls and unexplained conferences took place, which seemed to disturb him beyond his limited abilities to cope. Men flew into Ajaccio in small, fast planes; others came by sea in trawlers and small ocean-going craft. David would disappear for hours, then for days at a time. Alison's field work was such that she returned nightly to the team's seacoast hotel; her husband could not conceal his behaviour, nor the fact that his presence in Corsica was not an act of devotion to her.

She forced the issue, enumerating the undeniable, and brutally labelling David's explanations for what they were: amateurish lies. He had broken down, wept, pleaded, and told his wife the truth.

In order to maintain a life style David Booth was incapable

92

of earning in the marketplace, he had moved into international narcotics. He was primarily a courier. His partnership in a small importing–exporting business was ideal for the work. The firm had no real identity; indeed, it was rather nondescript, catering – as befitted the owners – to a social rather than a commercial clientele, dealing in art objects on the decorating level. He was able to travel extensively without raising official eyebrows. His introduction to the world of the contrabandists was banal: gambling debts compounded by an excess of alcohol and embarrassing female alliances. On the one hand, he had no choice; on the other, he was well paid and had no moral compunctions.

But Alison did. The geological surveys were legitimate, testimonials to David's employers' abilities to ferret out unsuspecting collaborators. David was given the names of survey teams in selected Mediterranean sites and told to contact them, offering the services of his very respected wife, adding further that he would confidentially contribute to her salary if she was hired. A rich, devoted husband only interested in keeping an active wife happy. The offers were invariably accepted. And, by finding her 'situations', his travels were given a twofold legitimacy. His courier activities had grown beyond the dilettante horizons of his business.

Alison threatened to leave the Corsican job.

David was hysterical. He insisted he would be killed, and Alison as well. He painted a picture of such widespread, powerful corruption-without-conscience that Alison, fearing for both their lives, relented. She agreed to finish the work in Corsica, but made it clear their marriage was finished. Nothing would alter *that* decision.

So she believed at the time.

But one late afternoon in the field – on the water, actually – Alison was taking bore samples from the ocean floor several hundred yards offshore. In the small cabin cruiser were two men. They were agents of Interpol. They had been following her husband for a number of months. Interpol was gathering massive documentation of criminal evidence. It was closing in.

'Needless to say, they were prepared for his arrival. My room was as private as yours was intended to be this evening...'

The case they presented was strong and clear. Where her husband had described a powerful network of corruption, the Interpol men told of another world of pain and suffering and needless, horrible death.

'Oh, they were experts,' said Alison, her eyes remembering, her smile compassionately sad. 'They brought photographs, dozens of them. Children in agony; young men, girls destroyed. I shall never forget those pictures. As they intended I would not...'

Their appeal was the classic recruiting approach: Mrs David Booth was in a unique position; there was no one like her. She could do *so* much, provide *so* much. And if she walked away in the manner she had described to her husband – abruptly, without explanation – there was the very real question of whether she would be allowed to do so.

My God, thought McAuliff as he listened, *the more things change... The Interpol men might have been Hammond speaking in a room at the Savoy Hotel.*

The arrangements were made, schedules created, a reasonable period of time specified for the 'deterioration' of the marriage. She told a relieved Booth that she would try to save their relationship, on the condition that he never again speak to her of his outside activities.

For half a year Alison Gerrard Booth reported the activities of her husband, identified photographs, planted dozens of tiny listening devices in hotel rooms, cars, their own apartment. She did so with the understanding that David Booth – whatever the eventual charges against him – would be protected from physical harm. To the best of Interpol's ability.

Nothing was guaranteed.

'When did it all come to an end?' asked Alex.

Alison looked away, briefly, at the dark, ominous panorama of the Blue Mountains, rising in blackness several miles to the north. 'When I listened to a very painful recording. Painful to hear; more painful because I had made the recording possible.'

One morning after a lecture at the university, an Interpol man arrived at her office in the geology department. In his briefcase he had a cassette machine and a cartridge that was a duplicate of a conversation recorded between her husband and a liaison from the Marquis de Chatellerault, the man identified as the overlord of the narcotics operation. Alison sat and listened to the voice of a broken man drunkenly describing the collapse of his marriage to a woman he loved very much. She heard him rage and weep, blaming himself for the inadequate man that he was. He spoke of his refused entreaties for the bed, her total rejection of him. And at the last, he made it clear beyond doubt that he loathed using her; that if she ever found out, he would kill himself. What he had done, almost too perfectly, was to exonerate her from any knowledge whatsoever of Chatellerault's operation. He had done it superbly.

'Interpol reached a conclusion that was as painful as the recording. David had somehow learned what I was doing. He was sending a message. It was time to get out.'

A forty-eight hour divorce in far-off Haiti was arranged. Alison Booth was free.

And, of course, not free at all.

'. . . within a year, it will all close in on Chatellerault, on David . . . on all of them. And somewhere, someone will put it together: Booth's wife . . .'

Alison reached for her drink and drank and tried to smile.

'That's it?' said Alex, not sure it was at all.

'That's it, Mr McAuliff. Now, tell me honestly, would you have hired me had you known?'

'No, I would not. I wonder why I didn't know.'

'It's not the sort of information the university, or Emigration, or just about anyone else would have.'

'Alison?' McAuliff tried to conceal the sudden fear he felt. 'You *did* hear about this job from the university people, didn't you?'

The girl laughed and raised her lovely eyebrows in mock

protest. 'Oh, Lord, it's tell-all time! ... No, I admit to having a jump; it gave me time to compile that *very* impressive portfolio for you.'

'How did you learn of it?'

'Interpol. They'd been looking for months. They called me about ten or twelve days before the interview.'

McAuliff did not have to indulge in any rapid calculations. Ten or twelve days before the interview would place the date within reasonable approximation of the afternoon he had met with Julian Warfield in Belgravia.

And later with a man named Hammond from British Intelligence.

The stinging pain returned to McAuliff's stomach. Only it was sharper now, more defined. But he could not dwell on it. Across the dark-shadowed patio, a man was approaching. He was walking to their table unsteadily. He was drunk, thought Alex.

'Well, for God's sake, *there* you are! We wondered where the hell you were! We're all in the bar inside. Whitehall's an absolute riot on the piano! A bloody black Noël Coward! ... Oh, by the way, I trust your luggage got here. I saw you were having problems, so I scribbled a note for the bastards to send it along. If they could read my whisky slant.'

Young James Ferguson dropped into an empty chair and smiled alcoholically at Alison. He then turned and looked at McAuliff, his smile fading as he was met by Alex's stare.

'That was very kind of you,' said McAuliff quietly.

And then Alexander saw it in Ferguson's eyes. The focused consciousness behind the supposedly glazed eyes.

James Ferguson was nowhere near as drunk as he pretended to be.

9

They expected to stay up most of the night. It was their silent, hostile answer to the 'horrid little buggers'. They joined the others in the bar and, as a good captain should, McAuliff was seen talking to the maître d'; all knew the evening was being paid for by their director.

Charles Whitehall lived up to Ferguson's judgment. His talent was professional; his island patter songs – filled with Caribbean idiom and Jamaican black wit – were funny, brittle, cold, and episodically hot. His voice had the clear, high-pitched thrust of a Kingston balladeer; only his eyes remained remote. He was entertaining and amusing, but he was neither entertained nor amused himself, thought Alex.

He was performing.

And finally, after nearly two hours, he wearied of the chore, accepted the cheers of the half-drunken room, and wandered to the table. After receiving individual shakes, claps and hugs from Ferguson, the Jensens, Alison Booth, and Alex, he opted for a chair next to McAuliff. Ferguson had been sitting there – encouraged by Alex – but the young botanist was only too happy to move. Unsteadily.

'That was remarkable!' said Alison, leaning across McAuliff, reaching for Whitehall's hand. Alex watched as the Jamaican responded; the dark Caribbean hand – fingernails manicured, gold ring glistening – curled delicately over Alison's as another woman's might. And then, in contradiction, Whitehall raised the girl's wrist and kissed her fingers.

A waiter brought over a bottle of white wine for Whitehall's inspection. He read the label in the nightclub light, looked up at the smiling attendant, and nodded. He turned back to McAuliff; Alison was now chatting with Ruth Jensen across the table. 'I should like to speak with you privately,' said the Jamaican casually. 'Meet me in my room, say, twenty minutes after I leave.'

'Alone?'

'Alone.'

'Can't it wait until morning?'

Whitehall levelled his dark eyes at McAuliff and spoke softly but sharply. 'No, it cannot.'

James Ferguson suddenly lurched up from his chair at the end of the table and raised his glass to Whitehall. He weaved and gripped the edge with his free hand; he was the picture of a very drunk young man. 'Here's to Charles the First of Kingston! The bloody black Sir Noel! You're simply fan*test*ic, Charles!'

There was an embarrassing instant of silence as the word 'black' was absorbed. The waiter hurriedly poured Whitehall's wine; it was no moment for sampling.

'Thank you,' said Whitehall politely. 'I take that as a high compliment, indeed . . . Jimbo-mon.'

'*Jimbo-mon!*' shouted Ferguson with delight. 'I love it! You shall call me *Jimbo-mon!* And now, I should like –' Ferguson's words were cut short, replaced by an agonizing grimace on his pale young face. It was suddenly abundantly clear that his alcoholic capacity had been reached. He set his glass down with wavering precision, staggered backwards and, in a slow motion of his own, collapsed to the floor.

The table rose *en masse;* surrounding couples turned. The waiter put the bottle down quickly and started towards Ferguson; he was joined by Peter Jensen, who was nearest.

'Oh, Lord,' said Jensen, kneeling down. 'I think the poor fellow's going to be sick. Ruth, come help . . . You there, waiter. Give me a hand, old chap!'

The Jensens, aided by two waiters now, gently lifted the young botanist into a sitting position, loosened his tie, and generally tried to reinstate some form of consciousness. And Charles Whitehall, standing beside McAuliff, smiled, picked up two napkins, and lobbed them across the table onto the floor near those administering aid. Alex watched the Jamaican's action; it was not pleasant. Ferguson's head was nodding back and forth; moans of impending illness came from his lips.

'I think this is as good a time as any for me to leave,' said Whitehall. 'Twenty minutes?'

McAuliff nodded. 'Or thereabouts.'

The Jamaican turned to Alison, delicately took her hand, kissed it, and smiled. 'Good night, my dear.'

With minor annoyance, Alex sidestepped the two of them and walked over to the Jensens, who, with the waiters' help, were getting Ferguson to his feet.

'We'll bring him to his room,' said Ruth. 'I warned him about the rum; it doesn't go with whisky. I don't think he listened.' She smiled and shook her head.

McAuliff kept his eyes on Ferguson's face. He wondered if he would see what he saw before. What he had been watching for for over an hour.

And then he did. Or thought he did.

As Ferguson's arms went limp around the shoulders of a waiter and Peter Jensen, he opened his eyes. Eyes that seemingly swum in their sockets. But for the briefest of moments, they were steady, focused, devoid of glaze. Ferguson was doing a perfectly natural thing any person would do in a dimly lit room. He was checking his path to avoid obstacles.

And he was – for that instant – quite sober.

Why was James Ferguson putting on such a splendidly embarrassing performance? McAuliff would have a talk with the young man in the morning. About several things, including a 'whisky-slanted' note that resulted in a suitcase that triggered the dial of an electronic scanner.

'Poor lamb. He'll feel miserable in the morning.' Alison had come alongside Alex. Together they watched the Jensens take Ferguson out the door.

'I hope he's just a poor lamb who went astray for the night and doesn't make a habit of it.'

'Oh, come on, Alex, don't be old-auntie. He's a perfectly nice young man who's had a pint too many.' Alison turned and looked at the deserted table. 'Well, it seems the party's over, doesn't it?'

'I thought we agreed to keep it going.'

'I'm fading fast, darling; my resolve is weakening. We also agreed to check my luggage with your little magic box. Shall we?'

'Sure.' McAuliff signalled the waiter.

They walked down the hotel corridor; McAuliff took Alison's key as they approached her door. 'I have to see Whitehall in a few minutes.'

'Oh? How come? It's awfully late.'

'He said he wanted to speak to me. Privately. I have no idea why. I'll make it quick.' He inserted the key, opened the door, and found himself instinctively barring Alison in the frame until he had switched on the lights and looked inside.

The single room was empty, the connecting door to his still open, as it had been when they left hours ago.

'I'm impressed,' whispered Alison, resting her chin playfully on the outstretched, forbidding arm that formed a bar across the entrance.

'What?' He removed his arm and walked towards the connecting door. The lights in his room were on – as he had left them. He closed the door quietly, withdrew the scanner from his jacket, and crossed to the bed, where Alison's two suitcases lay alongside each other. He held the instrument above them; there was no movement on the dial. He walked rapidly about the room, laterally and vertically blessing it from all corners. The room was clean. 'What did you say?' he asked softly.

'You're protective. That's nice.'

'Why were the lights off in this room and not in mine?' He had not heard her words.

'Because I turned them off. I came in here, got my purse, used some lipstick, and went back into your room. There's a switch by the door. I used it.'

'I don't remember.'

'You were upset at the time. I gather my room isn't the centre of attention that yours is.' Alison walked in and closed the corridor door.

'No, it's not, but keep your voice low . . . Can those goddamn things listen through doors and walls?'

'No, I don't think so.' She watched him take her suitcases from the bed and carry them across the room. He stood by the closet, looking for a luggage rack. There was none. 'Aren't you being a little obvious?'

'What?'

'What are you doing with my bags? I haven't unpacked.'

'Oh.' McAuliff could feel the flush on his face. He felt like a goddamn idiot. 'I'm sorry. I suppose I could say I'm compulsively neat.'

'Or just compulsive.'

He carried the bags back to the bed and turned to look at her, the suitcases still in his hands. He was so terribly tired. 'It's been a rotten day . . . a very confusing day,' he said. 'The fact that it's not over yet is discouraging as hell; there's still Whitehall to go . . . And in the next room, if I snore or talk in my sleep or go to the bathroom with the door open, everything is recorded somewhere on a tape. I can say it doesn't bother me, but it doesn't make me feel any better, either . . . I'll tell you something else, too, while I'm rambling. You are a lovely, lovely girl, and you're right, I'm compulsive . . . for example, at this moment I have the strongest compulsion to hold you and kiss you and feel your arms around me, and . . . you are so goddamn desirable . . . and you have such a beautiful smile and laugh . . . when you laugh I just want to watch you and touch your face . . . and all I want to do is hold you and forget everything else . . . Now, I'm finished rambling, and you can tell me to go to hell because I'm not relevant.'

Alison Booth stood silently, looking at McAuliff for what seemed to him far too long. Then she walked slowly, deliberately, to him.

'Do you know how silly you look holding those suitcases?' she whispered as she leaned forward and kissed him on the lips.

He dropped the bags; the noise of their contact with the floor made them both smile. He pulled her to him and the comfort was splendid, the warm, growing excitement a special thing. And as he kissed her, their mouths moistly exploring, pressing, widening, he realized Alison was trembling, gripping him with a strength that was more than a desire to be taken. Yet it was not fear; there was no hesitancy, no holding back, only anxiety.

He lowered her gently to the bed; as he did so, she unbuttoned the silk blouse and guided his hand to her breasts. She closed her eyes as he caressed her and whispered.

'It's been a terribly long time, Alex. Do you think Whitehall could wait a while longer? You see, I don't think I can.'

They lay beside each other, naked, under the soft covers. She rose on her elbow, her hair falling over her face, and looked at him. She traced his lips with her fingers and bent down, kissing him, outlining his lips now with her tongue.

'I'm absolutely shameless,' she said, laughing softly. 'I want to make love to you all night long. And most of the day . . . I'm parched and I've been to the well and I want to stay here.'

He reached up and let her hair fall through his fingers. He followed the strands downward to the swell of her body and cupped her left breast. 'We'll take the minimum time out for food and sleep.'

There was the faint ring of a telephone. It came from the direction of the connecting door. From his room.

'You're late for Charles Whitehall,' said Alison. 'You'd better go answer it.'

'Our goddamn Sir Noel.' He climbed out of the bed, walked

rapidly to the door, opened it, and went into the room. As he picked up the telephone, he looked at the drawn curtains of his balcony doors; he was grateful for Alison's experience. Except for his socks – why his socks? – he was naked.

'I said twenty minutes, Mr McAuliff. It's nearly an hour.' Whitehall's voice was quietly furious.

'I'm sorry. I told you "thereabouts". For me, an hour is "thereabouts". Especially when someone gives me orders at this time of night and he's not bleeding.'

'Let's not argue. Will you be here soon?'

'Yes.'

'When?'

'Twenty minutes.' Alex hung up the telephone a bit harder than was necessary and looked over at his suitcase. Whoever was on the other end of *that* line knew he was going out of the room to meet someone who had tried to issue him orders at three o'clock in the morning. He would think about it later.

'Do you know how positively handsome you are? All over,' said Alison as he came back into the room.

'You're right, you're shameless.'

'Why do you have your knee socks on? It looks peculiar.' She sat up, pulling the sheet over her breasts, and reached for the cigarettes on the night table.

'Light me one, will you, please? I've got to get dressed.' McAuliff looked around the bed for the clothing he had removed in such haste a half hour ago.

'Was he upset?' She handed him a cigarette as he pulled on his trousers and picked up his shirt from the floor.

'He was upset. He's also an arrogant son of a bitch.'

'I think Charles Whitehall wants to strike back at someone, or something,' said Alison, watching him absently. 'He's angry.'

'Maybe it's recognition. Not granted to the extent he thinks it should be.' McAuliff buttoned his shirt.

'Perhaps. That would account for his dismissing the compliments.'

'The what?' he asked.

103

'His little entertainment downstairs tonight was frighteningly thought out. It wasn't prepared for a nightclub. It was created for Covent Garden. Or the grand hall of the United Nations.'

He tapped gently on Whitehall's door, and when it opened, McAuliff found the Jamaican dressed in an embroidered Japanese *hopi* coat. Beneath the flowery garment, Whitehall wore his pin-stripe trousers and velvet slippers.

'Come in, please. This time you're early. It's not yet fifteen minutes.'

'You're obsessed with time. It's after three in the morning; I'd rather not look at my watch.' Alex closed the door behind him. 'I hope you have something important to tell me. Because if you don't, I'm going to be damned angry.'

The black had crossed to the bureau; he picked up a folded piece of paper from the top and indicated a chair for McAuliff. 'Sit down, please. I, too, am quite exhausted, but we must talk.'

Alex walked to the armchair and sat down. 'Go ahead.'

'I think it's time we had an understanding. It will in no way affect my contributions to the survey.'

'I'm relieved to hear that. I didn't hire you to entertain the troops downstairs.'

'A dividend,' said Whitehall coldly. 'Don't knock it; I'm very good.'

'I know you are. What else is new?'

The scholar tapped the paper in his hands. 'There'll be periods when it will be necessary for me to be absent. Never more than a day or two at a time. Naturally, I'll give you advance notice, and if there are problems – where *possible* – I shall rearrange my schedule.'

'You'll *what*?' McAuliff sat forward in the chair. 'Where . . . *possible* . . . you'll fit your time to *mine*? That's goddamn nice of you. I hope the survey won't be a burden.'

Whitehall laughed, impersonally. 'Not at all. It was just what I was looking for. And you'll see, you'll be quite pleased . . . although I'm not sure why I should be terribly concerned. You

104

see, I cannot accept the stated reasons for this survey. And I suspect there are one or two others, if they spoke their thoughts, who share my doubts.'

'Are you suggesting that I hired you under false pretences?'

'Oh, come now,' replied the black scholar, his eyes narrowing in irritation. 'Alexander McAuliff, a highly confidential, one-man survey company whose work takes him throughout the world ... for very large fees, abruptly decides to become academically *charitable*? To take from four to six months away from a lucrative practice to head up a *university survey*?' Whitehall laughed like a nervous jackal, walked rapidly to the curtains of the room's balcony doors, and flipped one side partially open. He twisted the latch and pulled the glass panel several inches inward; the curtain billowed in the night breeze.

'You don't know the specifics of my contract,' said Alex noncommittally.

'I know what universities and royal societies *and* ministries of education pay. It's not your league, McAuliff.' The Jamaican returned to the bed and sat down on the edge. He brought the folded paper to his chin and stared at Alex.

McAuliff hesitated, then spoke slowly. 'In a way, aren't you describing your own situation? There were several people in London who didn't think you'd take the job. It was quite a drop in income for you.'

'Precisely. Our positions are similar; I'm sure for very different reasons ... Part of *my* reasoning takes me to Savanna-la-Mar in the morning.'

'Your friend on the plane?'

'A bore. Merely a messenger.' Whitehall held up the folded piece of paper. 'He brought me an invitation. Would you care to read it?'

'You wouldn't offer unless it was pertinent.'

'I have no idea whether it is or not. Perhaps *you* can tell *me*.'

Alex took the paper extended to him and unfolded it. It was hotel stationery. The George V, Paris. The handwriting was slanted, the strokes rapid, words joined in speed.

My dear Whitehall –

Forgive this hastily written note but I have just learned that we are both en route to Jamaica. I for a welcome rest and you, I understand, for more worthwhile pursuits.

I should deem it an honour and a pleasure to meet with you. Our mutual friend will give you the details. I shall be staying in Savanna-la-Mar, albeit incognito. He will explain.

I do believe our coming together at the earliest would be mutually beneficial. I have long admired your past (?) island activities. I ask only that our meeting and my presence in Jamaica remain confidential. Since I so admire your endeavours, I know you will understand.

Chatellerault

Chatellerault . . . ?

The Marquis de Chatellerault.

David Booth's 'employer'. The man behind a narcotics network that spread throughout most of Europe and the Mediterranean. The man Alison feared so terribly that she carried a lethal-looking cylinder of gas with her at all times!

McAuliff knew that Whitehall was observing him. He forced himself to remain immobile, betraying only numbness on his face and in his eyes.

'Who is he?' asked McAuliff blandly. 'Who's this Chatel . . . Chatellerault?'

'You don't know?'

'Oh, for Christ's *sake*, Whitehall,' said Alex in weary exasperation. 'Stop playing games. I've never heard of him.'

'I thought you might have.' The scholar was once again staring at McAuliff. 'I thought the connection was rather evident.'

'What connection?'

'To whatever *your* reasons are for being in Jamaica. Chatellerault is . . . among other things . . . a financier with considerable resources. The coincidence is startling, wouldn't you agree?'

'I don't know what you're talking about.' McAuliff glanced down at Chatellerault's note. 'What does he mean by your past question mark island activities?'

106

Whitehall paused before replying. When he did, he spoke quietly, thus lending emphasis to his words. 'Fifteen years ago I left my homeland because the political faction for which I worked . . . devotedly, and in secret . . . was forced underground. Farther underground, I should say. For a decade we have remained dormant – on the surface. But only on the surface . . . I have returned now. Kingston knows nothing. It never associated me with the movement. But Chatellerault knows, and therefore demands confidentiality. I have, with considerable risk, broken this confidence as an article of faith. For you . . . please. Why are you here, McAuliff? Perhaps it will tell me why such a man as Chatellerault wishes a conference.'

Alex got out of the chair and walked aimlessly towards the balcony doors. He moved because it helped him concentrate. His mind was racing; some abstract thoughts signalling a warning that Alison was in danger . . . others balking, not convinced.

He crossed to the back of the chair facing Whitehall's bed and gripped the cloth firmly. 'All right, I'll make a deal with you. I'll tell you why I'm here, if you'll spell out this . . . activity of yours.'

'I will tell you what I can,' replied Charles, his eyes devoid of deceit. 'It will be sufficient, you will see. I cannot tell you everything. It would not be good for you.'

'That's a condition I'm not sure I like.'

'*Please*. Trust me.'

The man was not lying, that much was clear to Alex. 'Okay . . . I know the north coast; I worked for Kaiser's bauxite. I'm considered very pro – that is, I've put together some good teams and I've got a decent reputation –'

'Yes, yes. To the point, please.'

'By heading up this job, the Jamaican government has guaranteed me first refusal on twenty per cent of any industrial development for the next six years. That could mean millions of dollars. It's as simple as that.'

Whitehall sat motionless, his hands still folded beneath his chin, an elegant little boy in a concerned man's body. 'Yes, that is plausible,' he said finally. 'In much of Kingston, everything's for sale. It could be a motive for Chatellerault.'

Alex remained behind the chair. 'All right. Now, that's why *I'm* here. Why are you?'

'It is good you told me of your arrangement . . . I shall do my best to see that it is lived up to. You deserve that.'

'What the hell does that mean?'

'It means I am here in a political capacity. A solely Jamaican concern. You must respect that condition . . . and my confidence. I'd deny it anyway, and you would soil your foreigner's hands in things Jamaican. Ultimately, however, we will control Kingston.'

'Oh, Christ! Comes the goddamn revolution!'

'Of a different sort, Mr McAuliff. Put plainly, I'm a fascist. Fascism is the only hope for my island.'

10

McAuliff opened his eyes, raised his wrist from beneath the covers, and saw that it was 10:25. He had intended to get up by 8:30–9:00 at the latest.

He had a man to see. A man with arthritis at a fish store called Tallon's.

He looked over at Alison. She was curled up away from him, her hair sprayed over the sheets, her face buried in the pillow. She had been magnificent, he thought. No, he thought again, *they* had been magnificent together. She had been . . . what was the word she used? Parched. She had said: 'I've been parched and I've been to the well . . .' And she had been.

Magnificent. And warm, meaningful.

Yet still the thoughts came back.

A name that meant nothing to him twenty-four hours ago was suddenly an unknown force to be reckoned with, separately put forward by two people who were strangers a week ago.

Chatellerault. The Marquis de Chatellerault.

Currently in Savanna-la-Mar, on the south-west coast of Jamaica.

Charles Whitehall would be seeing him shortly, if they had not met by now. The black fascist and the French financier. It sounded like a vaudeville act.

But Alison Booth carried a deadly cylinder in her handbag, in the event she ever had occasion to meet him. Or meet with those who worked for him.

What was the connection? Certainly there had to be one.

He stretched, taking care not to wake her. Although he wanted to wake her and hold her and run his hands over her body and make love to her in the morning.

He couldn't. There was too much to do. Too much to think about.

He wondered what his instructions would be. And how long it would take to receive them. And what the man with arthritis at a fish store named Tallon's would be like. And, no less important, where in God's name was Sam Tucker? He was to be in Kingston by tomorrow. It wasn't like Sam to just take his leave without a word; he was too kind a man. And yet, there had been times . . .

When would they get the word to fly north and begin the actual work on the survey?

He was not going to get the answers staring up at the ceiling from Alison Booth's bed. And he was not going to make any telephone calls from his room.

He smiled as he thought about the 'horrid little buggers' in his suitcase. Were there horrid little men crouched over dials in dark rooms waiting for sounds that never came? There was a certain comfort in that.

'I can hear you thinking.' Alison's voice was muffled in the pillow. 'Isn't that remarkable.'

'It's frightening.'

She rolled over, her eyes shut, and smiled and reached under the blankets for him. 'You also stretch quite sensually.' She caressed the flatness of his stomach, and then his thighs, and then McAuliff knew the answers would have to wait. He pulled her to him; she opened her eyes and raised the covers so there was nothing between them.

The taxi let him off at Victoria's South Parade. The thoroughfare was aptly named, in the nineteenth-century sense. The throngs of people flowing in and out of the park's entrance were like crowds of brightly coloured peacocks, strutting, half acknowledging, quickening steps only to stop and gape.

McAuliff walked into the park, doing his best to look like a strolling tourist. Intermittently he could feel the hostile, questioning glances as he made his way up the gravel path to the centre of the park. It occurred to him that he had not seen a single other white person; he had not expected that. He had the distinct feeling that he was an object, to be tolerated but watched. Not essentially to be trusted.

He was a strange-toned outsider who had invaded the heart of this Man's playground. He nearly laughed when a young Jamaican mother guided a smiling child to the opposite side of the path as he approached. The child obviously had been fascinated by the tall, pinkish figure; the mother, quietly, efficiently, knew better. With dignity.

He saw the rectangular white sign with the brown lettering: QUEEN STREET, EAST. The arrow pointed to the right, at another, narrower gravel path. He started down it.

He recalled Hammond's words: *Don't be in a hurry. Ever, if possible. And never when you are making a contact. There's nothing so obvious as a man in a rush in a crowd that's not; except a woman. Or that same man stopping every five feet to light the same cigarette over and over again, so he can peer around at everyone. Do the natural things, depending on the day, the climate, the surroundings.*

It was a warm morning . . . noon. The Jamaican sun was hot, but there were breezes from the harbour, less than a mile away. It would be perfectly natural for a tourist to sit down and take the sun and the breeze; to unbutton his collar, remove his jacket, perhaps. To look about with pleasant tourist curiosity.

There was a bench on the left; a couple had just got up. It was empty. He took off his jacket, pulled at his tie, and sat down. He stretched his legs and behaved as he thought was appropriate.

But it was not appropriate. For the most self-conscious of reasons: He was too free, too relaxed in this Man's playground. He felt it instantly, unmistakably. The discomfort was heightened by an old man with a cane who walked by and hesitated in front of him. He was a touch drunk, thought Alex; the head swayed slightly, the legs a bit unsteady. But the eyes were not unsteady. They conveyed mild surprise mixed with disapproval.

McAuliff rose from the bench and swung his jacket under his arm. He smiled blankly at the old man and was about to proceed down the path when he saw another man, difficult to miss. He was white – the only other white man in Victoria Park. At least, the only one he could see. He was quite far away, diagonally across the lawns, on the north–south path, about a hundred and fifty yards in the distance.

A young man with a slouch and a shock of untrained dark hair. And he had turned away. He had been watching him, Alex was sure of that. Following him.

It was James Ferguson. The young man who had put on the second-best performance of the night at the Courtleigh Manor last evening. The drunk who had the presence of mind to keep sharp eyes open for obstacles in a dimly lit room.

McAuliff took advantage of the moment and walked rapidly down the path, then cut across the grass to the trunk of a large palm. He was nearly two hundred yards from Ferguson now. He peered around the tree, keeping his body out of sight. He was aware that a number of Jamaicans sitting about on the lawn were looking at him; he was sure, disapprovingly.

Ferguson, as he expected, was alarmed that he had lost the subject of his surveillance. (It was funny, thought Alex. He could think the word 'surveillance' now. He doubted he had used the word a dozen times in his life before three weeks ago.) The young botanist began walking rapidly past the brown-skinned strollers. Hammond was right, thought McAuliff. A man in a hurry in a crowd that wasn't was obvious.

Ferguson reached the intersection of the Queen Street path and stopped. He was less than forty yards from Alex now; he hesitated, as if not sure whether to retreat back to the South Parade or go on.

McAuliff pressed himself against the palm trunk. Ferguson thrust forward, as rapidly as possible. He had decided to keep going, if only to get out of the park. The bustling crowds on

Queen Street East signified sanctuary. The park had become unsafe.

If these conclusions were right – and the nervous expression on Ferguson's face seemed to confirm them – McAuliff realized that he had learned something else about this strange young man. He was doing what he was doing under duress and with very little experience.

Look for the small things, Hammond had said. *They'll be there; you'll learn to spot them. Signs that tell you there is valid strength or real weakness . . .*

Ferguson reached the East Parade gate, obviously relieved. He stopped and looked carefully in all directions. The unsafe field was behind him. The young man checked his watch while waiting for the uniformed policeman to halt the traffic for pedestrians. The whistle blew, cars stopped with varying levels of screeches, and Ferguson continued down Queen Street. Concealing himself as best he could in the crowd, Alex followed. The young man seemed more relaxed now. He wasn't so aggressive in his walk, in his darting glances. It was as though, having lost the enemy, he was more concerned with explanations than with re-establishing contact.

But McAuliff wanted that contact re-established. It was as good a time as any to ask young Ferguson those questions he needed answered.

Alex started across the street, dodging the traffic, and jumped over the kerb out of the way of a Kingston taxi. He made his way through the stream of shoppers to the far side of the walk.

There was a side street between Mark Lane and Duke Street. Ferguson hesitated, looked around, and apparently decided it was worth trying. He abruptly turned and entered.

McAuliff realized that he knew that street. It was a free-port strip interspersed with bars. He and Sam Tucker had been there late one afternoon a year ago, following a Kaiser conference at the Sheraton. He remembered, too, that there was a diagonally connecting alley that intersected the strip from Duke Street. He'd remembered because Sam had thought there might be native saloons in the moist, dark brick corridor, only to discover it was used for deliveries. Sam had been upset; he was fond of back-street native saloons.

Alex broke into a run. Hammond's warning about drawing attention would have to be disregarded. Tallon's could wait; the man with arthritis could wait. This was the moment to reach James Ferguson.

He crossed Queen Street again, now paying no attention to the disturbance he caused, or the angry whistle from the harassed Kingston policeman. He raced down the block; there was the diagonally connecting alley. It seemed even narrower than he remembered. He entered and pushed his way past a half a dozen Jamaicans, muttering apologies, trying to avoid the hard stares of those walking in the opposite direction towards him – silent challenges, grown-up children playing king-of-the-road. He reached the end of the passageway and stopped. He pressed his back against the brick and peered around the edge, up the side street. His timing was right.

James Ferguson, his expression ferret-like, was only ten yards away. Then five. And then McAuliff walked out of the alley and confronted him.

The young man's face paled to a deathly white. Alex gestured him against the stucco wall; the strollers passed in both directions, several complaining.

Ferguson's smile was false, his voice strained. 'Well, hello, Alex . . . Mr McAuliff. Doing a bit of shopping? This is the place for it.'

'*Have* I been shopping, Jimbo-mon? You'd know if I had, wouldn't you?'

'I don't know what you . . . I wouldn't –'

'Maybe you're still drunk,' interrupted Alex. 'You had a lot to drink last night.'

'Made a bloody fool of myself, I expect. Please accept my apologies.'

'No apologies necessary. You stayed just within the lines. You were very convincing.'

'Really, Alex, you're a bit much.' Ferguson moved back. A Jamaican woman, basket balanced on her head, hurried past. 'I said I was sorry. I'm sure you've had occasion to overindulge.'

'Very often. As a matter of fact, I was a hell of a lot drunker than you last night.'

'I don't know what you're implying, old chap, and frankly, my head's too painful to play anagrams. Now, for the last time, I apologize.'

'For the wrong sins, Jimbo-mon. Let's go back and find some real ones. Because I have some questions.'

Ferguson awkwardly straightened his perennial slouch and whisked away the shock of hair on his forehead. 'You're really quite abusive. I have shopping to do.'

The young man started to walk around McAuliff. Alex grabbed his arm and slammed him back into the stucco wall. 'Save your money. Do it in London.'

'No!' Ferguson's body stiffened; the taut flesh around his eyes stretched farther. 'No, please,' he whispered.

'Then let's start with the suitcases.' McAuliff released the arm, holding Ferguson against the wall with his stare.

'I told you,' the young man whined. 'You were having trouble. I tried to help.'

'You bet your ass I had trouble! And not only with Customs. Where did my luggage go? Our luggage? Who took it?'

'I don't know. I swear I don't!'

'Who told you to write that note?'

'No one told me! For God's sake, you're crazy!'

'Why did you put on that act last night?'

'What act?'

'You weren't drunk – you were sober.'

'Oh, Christ Almighty, I wish you had my hangover. Really –'

'Not good enough, Jimbo-mon. Let's try again. Who told you to write that note?'

'You won't listen to me –'

'I'm listening. Why are you following me? Who told you to follow me this morning?'

'By God, you're insane!'

'By God, *you're fired*!'

'No! ... You *can't. Please.*' Ferguson's voice was frightened again, a whisper.

'What did you say?' McAuliff placed his right hand against the wall, over Ferguson's frail shoulder. He leaned into the strange young man. 'I'd like to hear you say that again. What can't I do?'

'Please ... don't send me back. I beg you.' Ferguson was breathing through his mouth; spots of saliva had formed on his thin lips. 'Not now.'

'Send you back? I don't give a goddamn where you go! I'm not your keeper, little boy.' Alex removed his hand from the wall and yanked his jacket from under his left arm. 'You're entitled to return-trip air fare. I'll draw it for you this afternoon, and pay for one more night at the Courtleigh. After that, you're on your own. Go wherever the hell you please. But not with me; not with the survey.'

McAuliff turned and abruptly walked away. He entered the narrow alleyway and took up his position in the line of laconic strollers. He knew the stunned Ferguson would follow. It wasn't long before he heard him. The whining voice had the quality of controlled hysteria. Alex did not stop or look back.

'McAuliff! Mr McAuliff! *Please!*' The English tones echoed in the narrow brick confines, creating a dissonant counterpoint to the lilting hum of a dozen Jamaican conversations. 'Please, *wait* ... Excuse me, excuse me, please. I'm sorry, let me pass, please ...'

'What you do, mon?! Don't push you.'

The verbal objections did not deter Ferguson; the bodily obstructions were somewhat more successful. Alex kept moving, hearing and sensing the young man closing the gap slowly. It was eerily comic: a white man chasing another white man in a dark, crowded passageway that was exclusively – by civilized cautions – a native thoroughfare. McAuliff was within feet of the exit to Duke Street when he felt Ferguson's hand gripping his arm.

'*Please*. We have to talk . . . not here.'

'Where?'

They emerged on the sidewalk. A long, horse-drawn wagon filled with fruits and country vegetables was in front of them at the kerb. The sombreroed owner was arguing with customers by a set of ancient scales; several ragged children stole bananas from the rear of the vehicle. Ferguson still held McAuliff's arm.

'Go to the Devon House. It's a tourist –'

'I know.'

'There's an outside restaurant.'

'When?'

'Fifteen minutes.'

The taxi drove into the long entrance of Devon House, a Georgian monument to an era of English supremacy and white, European money. Circular floral gardens fronted the spotless columns; rinsed gravelled paths wove patterns around an immense fountain. The small outdoor restaurant was off to the side, the tables behind tall hedges, the diners obscured from the front. There were only six tables, McAuliff realized. A very small restaurant; a difficult place in which to follow someone without being observed. Perhaps Ferguson was not as inexperienced as he appeared to be.

'Well, hello, old chap!'

Alex turned. James Ferguson had yelled from the central path to the fountain; he now carried his camera and the cases and straps and meters that went with it. 'Hi,' said McAuliff, wondering what role the young man intended to play now.

'I've got some wonderful shots. This place has quite a history, you know.' Ferguson approached him, taking a second to snap Alex's picture.

'This is ridiculous,' replied McAuliff quietly. 'Who the hell are you trying to fool?'

'I know *exactly* what I'm doing. Please cooperate.' And then

Ferguson returned to his play-acting, raising his voice and his camera simultaneously. 'Did you know that this old brick area was the original courtyard? It leads to the rear of the house, where the soldiers were housed in rows of brick cubicles.'

'I'm fascinated.'

'It's well past elevenses, old man,' continued an enthusiastic, loud Ferguson. 'What say to a pint? Or a rum punch? Perhaps a spot of lunch.'

There were only two other separate couples within the small courtyard restaurant. The men's straw hats and bulging walking shorts complemented the women's rhinestone sunglasses; they were tourists, obviously unimpressed by Kingston's Devon House. They would soon be talking with each other, thought McAuliff, making happier plans to return to the bar of the cruise ship or, at least, to a free-port strip. They were not interested in Ferguson or himself, and that was all that mattered.

The Jamaican rum punches were delivered by a bored waiter in a dirty white jacket. He did not hum or move with any rhythmic punctuation, observed Alex. The Devon House restaurant was a place of inactivity. Kingston was not Montego Bay.

'I'll tell you exactly what happened,' said Ferguson suddenly, very nervously; his voice once more a panicked whisper. 'And it's everything I know. I worked for the Craft Foundation, you knew all about that. Right.'

'Obviously,' answered McAuliff. 'I made it a condition of your employment that you stay away from Craft. You agreed.'

'I didn't have a choice. When we got off the plane, you and Alison stayed behind; Whitehall and the Jensens went on ahead to the luggage pick-up. I was taking some infrared photographs of the airport ... I was in between, you might say. I walked through the arrival gate, and the first person I saw was Craft himself; the son, of course, not the old fellow. The son runs the foundation now. I tried to avoid him. I had every reason to; after all, he sacked me. But I couldn't. And I was amazed – he was positively effusive. Filled with apologies; what outstanding work I had done, how he personally had come to the airport to meet me when he heard I was with the survey.' Ferguson swallowed a portion of his punch, darting his eyes around the brick courtyard. He seemed to have reached a block, as if uncertain how to continue.

'Go on,' said Alex. 'All you've described is an unexpected welcome wagon.'

'You've *got to understand*. It was all so strange ... as you say, unexpected. And as he was talking, this chap in uniform comes through the gate and asks me if I'm Ferguson. I say yes and he tells me you'll be delayed, you're tied up; that *you* want me to have your bags sent on to the hotel. I should write a note to that effect so British Airways will release them. Craft offered to help, of course. It all seemed minor, quite plausible, really, and everything happened so fast. I wrote the note and this chap said he'd take care of it. Craft tipped him. Generously, I believe.'

'What kind of uniform was it?'

'I don't know. I didn't think. Uniforms all look alike when you're out of your own country.'

'Go on.'

'Craft asked me for a drink. I said I really couldn't. But he was adamant, and I didn't care to cause a scene, and you were delayed. You *do* see why I agreed, don't you?'

'Go on.'

'We went to the lounge upstairs ... the one that looks out over the field. It's got a name ...'

'"Observation."'

'What?'

'It's called the "Observation Lounge". Please, go on.'

'Yes. Well, I was concerned. I mean, I told him there were my own suitcases and Whitehall, the Jensens. And you, of course. I didn't want you wondering where I was ... especially under the circumstances.' Ferguson drank again; McAuliff held his temper and spoke simply.

'I think you'd better get to the point, Jimbo-mon.'

'I hope that name doesn't stick. It was a bad evening.'

'It'll be a worse afternoon if you don't go on.'

'Yes . . . Craft told me you'd be in Customs for another hour and the chap in uniform would tell the others I was taking pictures; I was to go on to the Courtleigh. I mean, it was strange. Then he changed the subject – completely. He talked about the foundation. He said they were close to a major breakthrough in the baracoa fibres; that much of the progress was due to my work. And, for reasons ranging from the legal to the moral, they wanted me to come back to Craft. I was actually to be given a percentage of the market development . . . Do you realize what that could mean?'

'If this is what you had to tell me, you can join them today.'

'Millions!' continued Ferguson, oblivious to Alex's interruption. 'Actually *millions* . . . over the years, of course. I've never had any money. Stony, most of the time. Had to borrow the cash for my camera equipment, did you know that?'

'It wasn't something I dwelled on. But that's all over with. You're with Craft now . . .'

'*No.* Not yet. That's the point. After the survey. I *must* stay with the survey – stay with *you*.' Ferguson finished his rum punch and looked around for the waiter.

'Merely stay with the survey? With me? I think you've left out something.'

'Yes. Actually.' The young man hunched his shoulders over the table; he avoided McAuliff's eyes. 'Craft said it was harmless, completely harmless. They only want to know the people you deal with in the government . . . which is just about everyone you deal with, because most everyone's *in* the government. I am to keep a log. That's all: simply a diary.' Ferguson looked up at Alex, his eyes pleading. 'You *do* see, don't you? It *is* harmless.'

McAuliff returned the young man's stare. 'That's why you followed me this morning?'

'Yes. But I didn't mean to do it this way. Craft suggested that I could accomplish a great deal by just . . . tagging along with you. Asking if I could join you when you went about survey business. He said I was embarrassingly curious and talked a lot anyway; it would be normal.'

'Two points for Craft.'

'What?'

'An obsolete American expression . . . Nevertheless, you followed me.'

'I didn't mean to. I rang your room. Several times. There was no answer. Then I called Alison . . . I'm sorry. I think she was upset.'

'What did she say?'

'That she thought she heard you leave your room only minutes ago. I ran down to the lobby. And outside. You were driving away in a taxi. *Then* I followed you, in another cab.'

McAuliff put his glass aside. 'Why didn't you come up to me in Victoria Park? I saw you and you turned away.'

'I was confused . . . and frightened. I mean, instead of asking to tag along, there I was, really following you.'

'Why did you pretend you were so drunk last night?'

Ferguson took a long nervous intake of breath. 'Because when I got to the hotel, I asked if your luggage had arrived. It hadn't. I panicked, I'm afraid . . . You see, before Craft left, he told me about your suitcases –'

'The bugs?' interrupted Alex angrily.

'The what?' Instantly, James understood. 'No. *No!* I swear to you, *nothing* like that. Oh, God, how *awful.*' Ferguson paused, his expression suddenly pensive. 'Yet, of course, it makes sense . . .'

No one could have rehearsed such a reversal of reactions, thought Alex. It was pointless to explode. 'What about the suitcases?'

'What? . . . Oh, yes, Craft. At the very end of the conversation, he said they were checking your luggage – *checking,* that's all he said. He suggested, if anyone asked, that I say I'd taken it upon myself to write the note; that I saw you were having trouble. But I wasn't to worry, your bags would get to the hotel. But they weren't *there,* you see.'

McAuliff did not see. He sighed wearily. 'So you pretended to be smashed?'

'Naturally. I realized you'd have to know about the note; you'd ask me about it, of course, and be terribly angry if the luggage was lost: blame me for it . . . Well, it's a bit unsporting to be hard on a fellow who's squiffed and tried to do you a good turn. I mean, it is, really.'

'You've got a very active imagination, Jimbo-mon. I'd go so far as to say convoluted.'

'Perhaps. But you didn't get angry, did you? And here we are and nothing has changed. That's the irony: Nothing has changed.'

'Nothing changed? What do you mean?'

Ferguson nervously smiled. 'Well . . . I'm tagging along.'

'I think something very basic has changed. You've told me about Craft.'

'Yes. I would have anyway; that was my purpose this morning. Craft need never know; no way he could find out. I'll just tag along with you. I'll give you a portion of the money that's coming to me. I promise you that. I'll write it out, if you like. I've never had any money. It's simply a marvellous opportunity. You do see that, don't you?'

11

He left Ferguson at the Devon House and took a cab into Old Kingston. If he was being followed, he didn't give a damn. It was a time for sorting out thoughts again, not worrying about surveillance. He wasn't going anywhere.

He had conditionally agreed to cooperate with Ferguson. The condition was that theirs was a two-way street; the botanist could keep his log – freely supplied with controlled names – and McAuliff would be kept informed of this Craft's inquiries.

He looked up at the street signs; he was at the corner of Tower and Matthew, two blocks from the harbour. There was a coin telephone on a stanchion halfway down the sidewalk. He hoped it was operable. It was.

'Has a Mr Sam Tucker checked in?' he asked the clerk on the other end of the line.

'No, Mr McAuliff. As a matter of fact, we were going over the reservations list a few minutes ago. Check-in time is three o'clock.'

'Hold the room. It's paid for.'

'I'm afraid it isn't, sir. Our instructions are only that you're responsible; we're trying to be of service.'

'You're very kind. Hold it, nevertheless. Are there any messages for me?'

'Just one minute, sir. I believe there are.'

The silence that ensued gave Alex the time to wonder about Sam. Where the hell *was* he? McAuliff had not been as alarmed as Robert Hanley over Tucker's disappearance. Sam's eccentricities included sudden wanderings, impulsive treks through native areas. There had been a time in Australia when Tucker stayed four weeks with an outback aborigine community, travelling daily in a Land Rover to the Kimberly survey site twenty-six miles away. Old Tuck was always looking for the unusual – generally associated with the customs and life styles of whatever country he was in. But his deadline was drawing near in Kingston.

'Sorry for the delay,' said the Jamaican, his lilt denying the sincerity of the statement. 'There are several messages. I was putting them in the order of their sequence.'

'Thank you. What are –'

'They're all marked urgent, sir,' interrupted the clerk. 'Eleven fifteen is the first; from the Ministry of Education. Contact Mr Latham as soon as possible. The next at 11:20 is from a Mr Piersall at the Sheraton. Room 51. Then a Mr Hanley called from Montego Bay at 12:06; he stressed the importance of your reaching him. His number is –'

'Wait a minute,' said Alex, removing a pencil and a notebook from his pocket. He wrote down the names 'Latham', 'Piersall', 'Hanley'. 'Go ahead.'

'Montego exchange, 8227. Until five o'clock. Mr Hanley said to call him in Port Antonio after 6:30.'

'Did he leave that number?'

'No, sir. Mrs Booth left word at 1:35 that she would be back in her room at 2:30. She asked that you ring through if you telephoned from outside. That's everything, Mr McAuliff.'

'All right. Thank you. Let me go back, please.' Alex repeated the names, the gists of the messages, and asked for the Sheraton's telephone number. He had no idea who 'Mr Piersall' was. He mentally scanned the twelve contact names provided by Hammond; there was no Piersall.

'Will that be all, sir?'

'Yes. Put me through to Mrs Booth, if you please.'

Alison's phone rang several times before she answered. 'I was taking a shower,' she said, out of breath. 'Rather hoping you were here.'

'Is there a towel around you?'

124

'Yes. I left it on the knob with the door open, if you must know. So I could hear the telephone.'

'If I was there, I'd remove it. The towel, not the phone.'

'I should think it appropriate to remove both.' Alison laughed, and McAuliff could see the lovely half smile in the haze of the afternoon sun on Tower Street.

'You're right, you're parched. But your note said it was urgent. Is anything the matter?' There was a click within the interior of the telephone box; his time was nearly up. Alison heard it, too.

'Where are you? I'll call you right back,' she said quickly.

The number had been deliberately, maliciously scratched off the dial's centre. 'No way to tell. How urgent? I've got another call to make.'

'It can wait. Just don't speak to a man named Piersall until we talk. 'Bye now, darling.'

McAuliff was tempted to call Alison right back; who is Piersall? But it was more important to reach Hanley in Montego. It would be necessary to call collect; he didn't have enough change.

It took the better part of five minutes before Hanley's phone rang and another three while Hanley convinced a switchboard operator at a less-than-chic hotel that he would pay for the call.

'I'm sorry, Robert,' said Alex. 'I'm at a coin box in Kingston.'

'It's all right, lad. Have you heard from Tucker?' There was an urgency in Hanley's rapidly asked question.

'No. He hasn't checked in. I thought you might have something.'

'I have, indeed, and I don't like it at all . . . I flew back to Mo'Bay a couple of hours ago, and these damn fools here tell me that two blacks picked up Sam's belongings, paid the bill, and walked out without a word.'

'Can they do that?'

'This isn't the Hilton, lad. They had the money and they did it.'

'Then where are you?'

'Goddamn it, I took the same room for the afternoon. In case

Sam tries to get in touch. He'll start here, I figured. In the meantime, I've got some friends asking around town. You still don't want the police?'

McAuliff hesitated. He had agreed to Hammond's command not to go to the Jamaican police for anything until he had checked with a contact and received clearance. 'Not yet, Bob.'

'We're talking about an old friend!'

'He's still not overdue, Robert. I can't legitimately report him missing. And, knowing our old friend, I wouldn't want him embarrassed.'

'I'd sure as hell raise a stink over two strangers picking up his belongings!' Hanley was angry, and McAuliff could not fault him for it.

'We're not sure they're strangers. You know Tuck; he hires attendants like he's the court of Eric the Red. Especially if he's got some money and he can spread it around the outback. Remember Kimberly, Bob.' A statement. 'Sam blew two months' wages setting up an agricultural commune, for Christ's sake.'

Hanley chuckled. 'Aye, lad, I do. He was going to put the hairy bastards in the wine business. He's a one-man Peace Corps with a vibrating crotch . . . All right, Alex. We'll wait until tomorrow. I have to get back to Port Antone'. I'll phone you in the morning.'

'If he's not here by then, I'll call the police and you can activate your subterranean network – which I'm sure you've developed by now.'

'Goddamn right. We old travellers have to protect ourselves. And stick together.'

The blinding sun on the hot, dirty Caribbean street and the stench of the telephone mouthpiece were enough to persuade McAuliff to return to Courtleigh Manor.

Later, perhaps early this evening, he would find the fish store called Tallon's and his arthritic contact.

He walked north on Matthew Lane and found a taxi on Barry Street; a half-demolished touring car of indeterminate make, and certainly not of this decade, or the last. As he stepped in, the odour of vanilla assaulted his nostrils. Vanilla and bay rum, the scents of Jamaica: delightful in the evening, oppressive during the day under the fiery equatorial sun.

As the cab headed out of Old Kingston – harbour-front Kingston – where man-made decay and cascading tropical flora struggled to coexist, Alex found himself staring with uncomfortable wonder at the suddenly emerging new buildings of New Kingston. There was something obscene about the proximity of such bland, clean structures of stone and tinted glass to the rows of filthy, tin, corrugated shacks – the houses of gaunt children who played slowly, without energy, with bony dogs, and of pregnant young-old women hanging rags on ropes salvaged from the waterfront, their eyes filled with the bleak, hated prospects of getting through another day. And the new, bland, scrubbed obscenities were less than two hundred yards from even more terrible places of human habitation: rotted, rat-infested barges, housing those who had reached the last cellars of dignity. Two hundred yards.

McAuliff suddenly realized what these buildings were: banks. Three, four, five ... six banks. Next to, and across from one another, all within an easy throw of a safe-deposit box.

Banks.

Clean, bland, tinted glass.

Two hundred yards.

Eight minutes later, the odd, ancient touring car entered the palm-lined drive of Courtleigh Manor. Ten yards in from the gates, the driver stopped, briefly, with a jerk. Alex, who was sitting forward, taking out his wallet, braced himself against the front seat as the driver quickly apologized. Then McAuliff saw what the Jamaican was doing. He was removing a lethal, thirty-inch machete from the worn felt next to him, and putting it under the seat. The driver grinned.

'I take a fare into old town, mon. Shack town. I keep long knife by me alla time there.'

'Is it necessary?'

'Oh, mon! True, mon. Bad people; dirty people. Not Kingston, mon. Better to shoot alla dirty people. No good, mon. Put 'em in boats back to Africa. Sink boats; yes, mon!'

'That's quite a solution.' The car pulled up to the kerb, and McAuliff got out. The driver smiled obsequiously as he stated an inflated charge. Alex handed him the precise amount. 'I'm sure you included the tip,' he said as he dropped the bills through the window.

At the front desk, McAuliff took the messages handed to him: there was an addition. Mr Latham of the Ministry of Education had telephoned again.

Alison was on the small balcony, taking the afternoon sun in her bathing suit. McAuliff entered the room from his connecting door.

She reached out and he took her hand. 'Have you any idea what a lovely lady you are, lovely lady?'

'Thank you, lovely man.'

He gently released her hand. 'Tell me about Piersall,' he said.

'He's at the Sheraton.'

'I know. Room 51.'

'You spoke to him.' Alison obviously was concerned.

'No. That was his message. Phone him in room 51. Very urgent.'

'He may be there now; he wasn't when you called.'

'Oh? I got the message just before I talked to you.'

'Then he must have left it downstairs. Or used a pay phone in the lobby. Within minutes.'

'Why?'

'Because he was here. I talked with him.'

'Do tell.'

She did.

Alison had finished sorting out research notes she had prepared for the north coast, and was about to take her shower when she heard a rapid knocking from Alex's room. Thinking it was one of their party, Alison opened her own door and looked

128

out in the corridor. A tall, thin man in a white Palm Beach suit seemed startled at her appearance. It was an awkward moment for both. Alison volunteered that she had heard the knocking and knew McAuliff was out; would the gentleman care to leave a message?

'He seemed very nervous. He stuttered slightly, and said he'd been trying to reach you since eleven o'clock. He asked if he could trust me. Would I speak only to you? He was really quite upset. I invited him into my room, but he said no, he was in a hurry. Then he blurted it out. He had news of a man named Sam Tucker. Isn't he the American who's to join us here?'

Alex did not bother to conceal his alarm. He bolted from his reclining position and stood up. 'What about Tucker?'

'He didn't go into it. Just that he had word *from* him or *about* him. He wasn't really clear.'

'Why didn't you tell me on the phone?'

'He asked me not to. He said I was to tell you when I saw you, *not* over the telephone. He implied that you'd be angry, but you should get in touch with him before you went to anyone else. Then he left . . . Alex, what the hell was he talking about?'

McAuliff did not answer; he was on his way to her telephone. He picked up the receiver, glanced at the connecting door, and quickly replaced the phone. He walked rapidly to the open door, closed it, and returned to the telephone. He gave the Sheraton's number and waited.

'Mr Piersall, room 51, please.'

The interim of silence was infuriating to McAuliff. It was broken by the soothing tones of a subdued English voice, asking first the identity of the caller and then whether the caller was a friend or, perhaps, a relative of Dr Piersall's. Upon hearing Alex's replies, the unctuous voice continued, and as it did so, McAuliff remembered a cold night on a Soho street outside The Owl of Saint George. And the flickering of a neon light that saved his life and condemned his would-be killer to death.

Dr Walter Piersall had been involved in a terrible, tragic accident.

He had been run down by a speeding automobile in a Kingston street.

He was dead.

12

Walter Piersall, American, PhD, anthropologist, student of the Caribbean, author of a definitive study on Jamaica's first known inhabitants, the Arawak Indians, and the owner of a house called 'High Hill' near Carrick Foyle in the parish of Trelawny.

That was the essence of the information supplied by the Ministry's Mr Latham.

'A tragedy, Mr McAuliff. He was an honoured man, a titled man. Jamaica will miss him greatly.'

'*Miss* him! Who killed him, Mr Latham?'

'As I understand it, there is very little to go on: the vehicle sped away, the description is contradictory.'

'It was broad daylight, Mr Latham.'

There was a pause on Latham's part. 'I know, Mr McAuliff. What can I say? You are an American; he was an American. I am Jamaican, and the terrible thing took place on a Kingston street. I grieve deeply for several reasons. And I did not know the man.'

Latham's sincerity carried over the wire. Alex lowered his voice. 'You say "the terrible thing". Do you mean more than an accident?'

'No. There was no robbery, no mugging. It was an accident. No doubt brought on by rum and inactivity. There is a great deal of both in Kingston, Mr McAuliff. The men – or children – who committed the crime are undoubtedly well into the hills now. When the rum wears off, the fear will take its place; they will hide. The Kingston police are not gentle.'

'I see.' McAuliff was tempted to bring up the name 'Sam Tucker', but he held himself in check. He had told Latham only that Piersall had left a message for him. He would say no more for the time being. 'Well, if there's anything I can do ...'

'Piersall was a widower, he lived alone in Carrick Foyle. The police said they were getting in touch with a brother in Cambridge, Massachusetts ... Do you know why he was calling you?'

'No idea.'

'A great deal of your survey will take place in Trelawny Parish. Perhaps he had heard and was offering you hospitality.'

'Perhaps ... Mr Latham, is it logical that he would know about the survey?' Alex listened intently to Latham's reply. Again, Hammond: *Learn to spot the small things.*

'Logical? What is logical in Jamaica, Mr McAuliff? It is a poorly kept secret that the Ministry – with the gracious help of our recent mother country – is undertaking an overdue scientific evaluation. A secret poorly kept is not really much of a secret. Perhaps it is not logical that Dr Piersall knew; it is certainly possible, however.'

No hesitations, no over-quick responses, no rehearsed words.

'Then I guess that's what he was calling about. I'm sorry.'

'I grieve.' Again Latham paused; it was not for effect. 'Although it may seem improper, Mr McAuliff, I should like to discuss the business between us.'

'Of course. Go ahead.'

'All of the survey permits came in late this morning ... less than twenty-four hours. It generally takes the best part of a week ...'

The processing was unusual, but Alex had come to expect the unusual with Dunstone plc. The normal barriers fell with abnormal ease. Unseen expeditors were everywhere, doing the bidding of Julian Warfield.

Latham said that the Ministry had anticipated more, rather than less, difficulty, as the survey team would be entering the territory of the Cock Pit, miles of uninhabited country – jungle, really. Escorts were required, guides trained in the treacherous environs. And arrangements had to be made with the recognized descendants of the Maroon people, who, by a treaty of 1739, controlled much of the territory. An arrogant, warlike people, brought to the islands as slaves, the Maroons knew the jungles far better than their white captors. The British sovereign, George I, had offered the Maroons their independence with a treaty that guaranteed the Cock Pit territories in perpetuity. It was a wiser course than continuing bloodshed. Besides, the territory was considered unfit for colonial habitation.

For more than 250 years that treaty was scoffed at but never violated, said Latham. Formal permission was still sought by Kingston from the 'Colonel of the Maroons' for all those who wished to enter their lands. The Ministry was no exception.

Yet the Ministry, thought McAuliff, was in reality Dunstone plc. So permissions were granted, permits obtained with alacrity.

'Your equipment was air-freighted to Boscobel,' said Latham. 'Trucks will transport it to the initial point of the survey.'

'Then I'll leave tomorrow afternoon or, at the latest, early the next day. I'll be hiring out of Ocho Rios; the others can follow when I'm finished. It shouldn't take more than a couple of days.'

'Your escort-guides, we call them "runners", will be available in two weeks. You will not have any need for them until then, will you? I assume you will be working the coast to begin with.'

'Two weeks'll be fine . . . I'd like a choice of runners, please.'

'There are not that many to choose from, Mr McAuliff. It is not a career that appeals to many young people; the ranks are thinning. But I shall do what I can.'

'Thank you. May I have the approved maps in the morning?'

'They will be sent to your hotel by ten o'clock. Good-bye, Mr McAuliff. And again, my deeply felt regrets over Dr Piersall.'

'I didn't know him either, Mr Latham,' said Alex. 'Good-bye.'

He did not know Piersall, thought McAuliff, but he *had* heard the name 'Carrick Foyle', Piersall's village. He could not remember where he had heard it, only that it was familiar.

Alex replaced the telephone and looked over at Alison, on the small balcony. She had been watching him, listening, and she could not conceal her fear. A thin, nervous man in a white Palm Beach suit had told her – less than two hours ago – that he had confidential information, and now he was dead.

The late afternoon sun was a Caribbean orange, the shadows shafts of black across the miniature balcony. Behind her was the near deep green of the high palms, behind them the awesome rise of the mountain range. Alison Booth seemed to be framed within a tableau of chiaroscuro tropic colours. As though she were a target.

'He said it was an accident.' Alex walked slowly to the balcony doors. 'Everyone's upset. Piersall was liked on the island. Apparently, there's a lot of drunken hit-and-runs in Kingston.'

'And you don't believe him for an instant.'

'I didn't say that.' He lighted a cigarette; he did not want to look at her.

'You don't have to. You didn't say one word about your friend Tucker, either. Why not?'

'Common sense. I want to talk to the police, not an associate director of the Ministry. All he can do is babble and create confusion.'

'Then let's go to the police.' Alison rose from the deck chair. 'I'll get dressed.'

'*No!*' McAuliff realized as he said the word that he was too emphatic. 'I mean, I'll go. I don't want you involved.'

'I spoke to the man. You didn't.'

'I'll relay the information.'

'They won't accept it from you. Why should they hear it secondhand?'

'Because I say so.' Alex turned away, ostensibly to find an ashtray. He was not convincing, and he knew it. 'Listen to me, Alison.' He turned back. 'Our permits came in. Tomorrow I'm going to Ocho Rios to hire drivers and carriers; you people will follow in a couple of days. While I'm gone I don't want you – or any member of the team – involved with the police or anybody else. Our job here is the survey. That's my responsibility; you're my responsibility. I don't want delays.'

She walked down the single step, out of the frame of colour, and stood in front of him. 'You're a dreadful liar, Alex. Dreadful in the sense that you're quite poor at it.'

'I'm going to the police now. Afterwards, if it's not too late, I may drop over to the Ministry and see Latham. I was a little rough with him.'

'I thought you ended on a very polite note.'

It was Alison who spotted Hammond's small things, thought McAuliff. She was better than he was. 'You only heard me. You didn't hear him . . . If I'm not back by seven, why not call the Jensens and have dinner with them? I'll join you as soon as I can.'

'The Jensens aren't here.'

'What?'

'Relax. I called them for lunch. They left word at the desk that since it was a day off, they were touring. Port Royal, Spanish Town, Old Harbour. The manager set up their tour.'

'I hope they enjoy themselves.'

He told the driver that he wanted a half-hour's tour of the city. He had thirty minutes to kill before cocktails in Duke Street – he'd spot the restaurant; he didn't know the specific address – so the driver could do his imaginative best within the time span.

The driver protested: Thirty minutes was barely sufficient to reach Duke Street from the Courtleigh in the afternoon traffic. McAuliff shrugged and replied that the time was not absolute.

It was precisely what the driver wanted to hear. He drove out onto Trafalgar, south on Lady Musgrave, into Old Hope Road. He extolled the commercial virtues of New Kingston, likening the progress to Olympian feats of master planning. The words droned on, filled with idiomatic exaggerations of the 'alla time big American millions' that were turning the tropical and human overgrowth that was Kingston into a Caribbean financial mecca. It was understood that the millions would be German or English or French, depending on the accent of the passenger.

It didn't matter. Within minutes, McAuliff knew that the

driver knew he was not listening. He was staring out the rear window, watching the traffic behind them.

It was there.

A green Chevrolet sedan, several years old. It stayed two to three cars behind, but whenever the taxi turned or sped ahead of other vehicles, the green Chevrolet did the same.

The driver saw it, too.

'You got trouble, mon?'

There was no point in lying. 'I don't know.'

'*I* know, mon. Lousy green car be'n d'ere alla time. It stay in big parking lot at Courtleigh Manor. Two block son of a bitch drivin'.'

McAuliff looked at the driver. The Jamaican's last statement triggered his memory of Robert Hanley's words from Montego Bay. *Two blacks picked up Sam's things.* Alex knew the connection was far-fetched, coincidental at best in a black country, but it was all he had to go on. 'You can earn twenty dollars, friend,' he said quickly to the driver. 'If you can do two things.'

'You tell me, mon!'

'First, let the green car get close enough so I can read the licence plate, and when I've got it, lose them. Can you do that?'

'You watch, mon!' The Jamaican swung the wheel to the right; the taxi veered briefly into the right lane, narrowly missing an oncoming bus, then lurched back into the left, behind a Volkswagen. McAuliff crouched against the seat, his head pressed to the right of the rear window. The green Chevrolet duplicated the taxi's movements, taking up a position two cars behind.

Suddenly the cab driver accelerated again, passing the Volks and speeding ahead to a traffic light that flashed the yellow caution signal. He swung the car into the left intersection: Alex read the street sign and the wording on the large shield-shaped sign beneath:

TORRINGTON ROAD
ENTRANCE
GEORGE VI MEMORIAL PARK

136

'We head into race course, mon!' shouted the driver. 'Green son of a bitch have to stop at Snipe Street light. He come out'a d'ere fast. You watch good now!'

The cab sped down Torrington, swerving twice out of the left lane to pass three vehicles, and through the wide-gated entrance into the park. Once inside, the driver slammed on the brakes, backed the taxi into what looked like a bridle path, spun the wheel, and lurched forward into the exit side of the street.

'You catch 'em good now, mon!' yelled the Jamaican as he slowed the car down and entered the flow of traffic leaving the George VI Memorial Park.

Within seconds the green Chevrolet came into view, hemmed between automobiles entering the park. And then McAuliff realized precisely what the driver had done. It was early track time; George VI Memorial Park housed the sport of kings. Gambling Kingston was on the way to the races.

Alex wrote down the licence number, keeping himself out of sight but seeing clearly enough to know that the two blacks in the Chevrolet did not realize that they had passed within feet of the car they were following.

'Them sons of bitches got to drive alla way 'round, mon! Them dumb block sons of bitches! ... Where you want to go, mon? Plenty of time, now. They don't catch us.'

McAuliff smiled. He wondered if the Jamaican's talents were listed in Hammond's manual somewhere. 'You just earned yourself an extra five dollars. Take me to the corner of Queen and Hanover streets, please. No sense wasting time, now.'

'Hey, mon! You hire my taxi alla time in Kingston. I do what you say. I don't ask questions, mon.'

Alex looked at the identification behind the dirty plastic frame above the dashboard. 'This isn't a private cab ... Rodney.'

'You make a deal with me, mon; I make a deal with the taxi boss.' The driver grinned in the rear-view mirror.

'I'll think about it. Do you have a telephone number?'

The Jamaican quickly produced an outsized business card and handed it back to McAuliff. It was the taxi company's card, the type that was left on hotel counters. Rodney's name was printed childishly in ink across the bottom. 'You telephone company number, say you gotta have Rodney. Only Rodney, mon. I get the message real quick. All'a time they know where Rodney is. I work hotels and Palisados. Them get me quick.'

'Suppose I don't care to leave my name –'

'No name, mon!' broke in the Jamaican, grinning in the mirror. 'I got lousy son-of-a-bitch memory. Don't want no name! You tell taxi phone ... you the fella at the race course. Give place; I get to you, mon.'

Rodney accelerated south to North Street, left to Duke, and south against past the Gordon House, the huge new complex of the Kingston legislature.

Out on the sidewalk, McAuliff straightened his jacket and his tie and tried to assume the image of an average white business-man not entirely sure of which government entrance he should use. Tallon's was not listed in any telephone or shopping direc-tory; Hammond had indicated that it was below the row of government houses, which meant below Queen Street, but he was not specific.

As he looked for the fish store, he checked the people around him, across the street, and in the automobiles that seemed to go slower than the traffic allowed.

For a few minutes he felt himself in the pocket of fear again; afraid that the unseen had their eyes on him.

He reached Queen Street and hurried across with the last contingent making the light. On the kerb he turned swiftly to watch those behind on the other side.

The orange sun was low on the horizon, throwing a corridor of blinding light from the area of Victoria Park several hundred yards to the west. The rest of the street was in dark, sharply defined shadows cast from the structures of stone and wood all around. Cars passed east and west, blocking a clear vision of those on the north corner. Corners.

He could tell nothing. He turned and proceeded down the block.

He saw the sign first. It was filthy, streaked with runny print that had not been touched up in months, if not years:

TALLON'S
FINE FISH & NATIVE DELICACIES
311-½ QUEEN'S ALLEY
1 BLOCK – DUKE ST. WEST

He walked the block. The entrance to Queen's Alley was barely ten feet high, cut off by grillwork covered with tropical flowers. The cobblestone passage did not go through to the next street. It was a dead end, a lightless cul-de-sac; the sort of hidden back street common to Paris and Rome and Greenwich Village. Although it was in the middle of a commercial market area, there was a personal quality about its appearance, as though an unwritten sign proclaimed this section private: residents only, keys required, not for public usage. All that was needed, thought McAuliff, was a gate.

In Paris and Rome and Greenwich Village, such wide alleys held some of the best restaurants in the world, known only to those who cared.

In Shenzen and Macao and Hong Kong, they were the recesses where anything could be had for a price.

In Kingston, this one housed a man with arthritis who worked for British Intelligence.

Queen's Alley was no more than fifty feet long. On the right was a bookstore with subdued lighting in the windows, illuminating a variety of wares from heavy academic leather to non-glossy pornography. On the left was Tallon's.

He had pictured casements of crushed ice supporting rows of wide-eyed dead fish, and men in soiled, cheap white aprons running around scales, arguing with customers.

The crushed ice was in the window; so were several rows of glassy-eyed fish. But what impressed him was the other forms of ocean merchandise placed artistically: squid, octopus, shark, and exotic shellfish.

Tallon's was no Fulton Market.

As if to add confirmation to his thoughts, a uniformed chauffeur emerged from Tallon's entrance carrying a plastic shopping bag, insulated, Alex was sure, with crushed ice.

The double doors were thick, difficult to open. Inside, the counters were spotless; the sawdust on the floor was white. The two attendants were just that: attendants, not countermen. Their full-length aprons were striped blue and white and made of expensive linen. The scales behind the chrome-framed glass cases had shiny brass trimmings. Around the shop, stacked on shelves lighted by tiny spotlights in the ceiling, were hundreds of tins of important delicacies from all parts of the world.

It was not quite real.

There were three other customers: a couple and a single woman. The couple was at the far end of the store, studying labels on the shelves: the woman was ordering from a list, being overly precise, arrogant.

McAuliff approached the counter and spoke the words he had been instructed to speak.

'A friend in Santo Domingo told me you had north-coast trout.'

The light-skinned black behind the white wall barely looked at Alex, but within that instant there was recognition. He bent down, separating shellfish inside the case, and answered casually. Correctly. 'We have some fresh-water trout from Martha Brae, sir.'

'I prefer salt-water trout. Are you sure you can't help me?'

'I'll see, sir.' The man shut the case, turned, and walked down a corridor in the wall behind the counter, a passageway Alex assumed led to large refrigerated rooms.

When a man emerged from a side door within the corridor, McAuliff caught his breath, trying to suppress his astonishment. The man was black and slight and old; he walked with a cane, his right forearm stiff, and his head trembled slightly with age.

It was the man in Victoria Park: the old man who had stared at him disapprovingly in front of the bench on the Queen Street path.

He walked to the counter and spoke, his voice apparently stronger than his body. 'A fellow salt-water trout lover,' he said, in an accent more British than Jamaican, but not devoid of the Caribbean. 'What are we to do with those fresh-water aficionados who cost me so much money? Come, it is nearly closing. You shall have your choice from my own selection.'

A hinged panel of the butcher-block counter was lifted by the light-skinned black in the striped apron. Alex followed the arthritic old man down the short corridor and through a narrow door into a small office that was a miniature extension of the expensive outer design. The walls were panelled in fruitwood; the furniture was a single mahogany desk with a functional antique swivel chair, a soft leather couch against the wall, and an armchair in front of the desk. The lighting was indirect, from a lone china lamp on the desk. With the door closed, Alex saw oak filing cabinets lined against the inner wall. Although the room was confining in size, it was eminently comfortable – the isolated quarters of a contemplative man.

'Sit, Mr McAuliff,' said the proprietor of Tallon's, indicating the armchair as he hobbled around the desk and sat down, placing his cane against the wall. 'I've been expecting you.'

'You were in Victoria Park this morning.'

'I did not expect you then. To be quite frank, you startled me. I'd been looking at your photograph minutes before I took my stroll. From nowhere the face of this photograph was in front of my eyes in Victoria.' The old man smiled and gestured with his palms up, signifying unexpected coincidence. 'Incidentally, my name is "Tallon". Westmore Tallon. We're a fine old Jamaican family, as I'm sure you've been told.'

'I hadn't, but one look at your . . . fish store would seem to confirm it.'

'Oh, yes. We're frightfully expensive, very exclusive. Private telephone number. We cater only to the wealthiest on the island. From Savanna to Montego to Antonio and Kingston. We have our own delivery service – by private plane, of course . . . It's most convenient.'

141

'I should think so. Considering your extracurricular activities.'

'Which, of course, we must never consider to the point of discussion, Mr McAuliff,' replied Tallon quickly.

'I've got several things to tell you. I expect you'll transmit the information and let Hammond do what he wants.'

'You sound angry.'

'On one issue, I am. Goddamned angry . . . Mrs Booth. Alison Booth. She was manipulated here through Interpol. I think that smells. She made one painful – and dangerous – contribution. I should think you people would let her alone.'

Tallon pushed his foot against the floor, turning the silent antique swivel to his right. He aimlessly reached over for his cane and fingered it. 'I am merely a . . . liaison, Mr McAuliff, but from what I understand, no pressure was exerted on you to employ Mrs Booth. You did so freely. Where was the manipulation?'

Alex watched the small, arthritic man toy with the handle of the cane. He was struck by the thought that in some strange way Westmore Tallon was like an artist's composite of Julian Warfield and Charles Whitehall. The communion of elements was disturbing. 'You people are very professional,' he said quietly, a touch bitterly. 'You're ingenious when it comes to presenting alternatives.'

'She can't go home, Mr McAuliff. Take my word for that.'

'From a certain point of view, she might as well . . . The Marquis de Chatellerault is in Jamaica.'

Tallon spun in the antique chair to face McAuliff. For an instant he seemed frozen. He stared at Alex, and when he blinked it was as though he silently rejected McAuliff's statement. 'This is impossible,' he said simply.

'It's not only possible, I don't even think it's a secret. Or if it is, it's poorly kept; and as somebody said about an hour ago, that's not much of a secret.'

'Who gave you this information?' Tallon held onto his cane, his grasp visibly firmer.

'Charles Whitehall. At three o'clock this morning. He was invited to Savanna-la-Mar to meet Chatellerault.'

'What were the circumstances?'

'The circumstances aren't important. The important fact is that Chatellerault is in Savanna-la-Mar. He is the houseguest of a family named Wakefield. They're white and rich.'

'We know them,' said Tallon, writing a note awkwardly with his arthritic hand. 'They're customers. What else do you have?'

'A couple of items. One is extremely important to me, and I warn you, I won't leave here until something's done about it.'

Tallon looked up from his notepaper. 'You make pronouncements without regard for realistic appraisal. I have no idea whether I can do anything about anything. Your camping here would not change that. Please continue.'

Alex described James Ferguson's unexpected meeting with Craft at the Palisados Airport and the manipulation that resulted in the electronic devices in his luggage. He detailed Craft's offer of money in exchange for information about the survey.

'It's not surprising. The Craft people are notoriously curious,' said Tallon, writing painfully on his notepaper. 'Shall we get to the item you say is so vital?'

'I want to summarize first.'

'Summarize what?' Tallon put down his pencil.

'What I've told you.'

Tallon smiled. 'It's not necessary, Mr McAuliff. I take notes slowly, but my mind is quite alert.'

'I'd like us to understand each other ... British Intelligence wants the Halidon. That was the purpose – the only purpose – of my recruitment. Once the Halidon could be reached, I was finished. Complete protection still guaranteed to the survey team.'

'And so?'

'I think you've got the Halidon. It's Chatellerault and Craft.'

Tallon continued to stare at McAuliff. His expression was totally neutral. 'You have arrived at this conclusion?'

'Hammond said this Halidon would interfere. Eventually try to stop the survey. Diagrams aren't necessary. The marquis and Craft fit the prints. Go get them.'

'I see . . .' Tallon reached once more for his cane. His personal sceptre, his sword Excalibur. 'So, in one extraordinary simplification, the American geologist has solved the riddle of the Halidon.'

Neither man spoke for several moments. McAuliff broke the silence with equally quiet anger. 'I could get to dislike you, Mr Tallon. You're a very arrogant man.'

'My concerns do not include your approval, Mr McAuliff. Jamaica is my passion – yes, my *passion*, sir. What you think is not important to me . . . except when you make absurd pronouncements that could affect my work . . . Arthur Craft, *père et fils*, have been raping this island for half a century. They subscribe to the belief that theirs is a mandate from God. They can accomplish too much in the name of Craft; they would not hide behind a symbol. And Halidon *is* a symbol, Mr McAuliff . . . The Marquis de Chatellerault? You were quite correct, Mrs Booth *was* manipulated – brilliantly, I think – into your survey. It was cross-pollination, if you like; the circumstances were optimum. Two kling-klings in a hibiscus, one inexorably forcing the other to reveal himself. She was bait, pure and simple, Mr McAuliff. Chatellerault has long been suspected of being an associate of Julian Warfield. The marquis is with Dunstone plc.' Tallon lifted his cane up laterally, placed it across his desk, and continued to gaze blankly at Alex.

McAuliff said finally, 'You withheld information; you didn't tell me things I should have been told. Yet you expect me to function as one of you. That smells, Tallon.'

'You exaggerate. There is no point in complicating further an already complicated picture.'

'I should have been told about Chatellerault, instead of hearing his name from Mrs Booth.'

Tallon shrugged. 'An oversight. Shall we proceed?'

'All right. There's a man named Tucker. Sam Tucker.'

'Your friend from California? The soil analyst?'

'Yes.'

McAuliff told Hanley's story without using Hanley's name.

144

He emphasized the coincidence of the two blacks who had removed Tucker's belongings and the two Jamaicans who had followed his taxi in the green Chevrolet sedan. He described briefly the taxi owner's feats of driving skills in the racetrack park, and gave Tallon the licence-plate number of the Chevrolet.

Tallon reached for his telephone and dialled without speaking to Alex. 'This is Tallon,' he said quietly into the phone. 'I want MV information. It is urgent. The licence is KYB-448. Call me back on this line.' He hung up and shifted his eyes to McAuliff. 'It should take no longer than five minutes.'

'Was that the police?'

'Not in any way the police would know ... I understand the Ministry received your permits today. Dunstone does facilitate things, doesn't it?'

'I told Latham I was leaving for Ocho Rios tomorrow afternoon. I won't if Tucker doesn't show up. That's what I want you to know.'

Once again, Westmore Tallon reached for his cane, but not with the aggressiveness he had displayed previously. He was suddenly a rather thoughtful, even gentle, man. 'If your friend was taken against his will, it would be kidnapping. A very serious crime, and insofar as he's American, the sort of headline attraction that would be an anathema. It doesn't make sense, Mr McAuliff ... You say he's due today, which could be extended to this evening, I presume?'

'Yes.'

'Then I suggest we wait ... I cannot believe the parties involved could – or would – commit such a gargantuan mistake. If Mr Tucker is not heard from by ... say ten o'clock, call me.' Tallon wrote a number on a piece of paper and handed it to Alex. 'Commit this to memory, please; leave the paper here.'

'What are you going to do if Tucker doesn't show?'

'I will use perfectly legitimate connections and have the matter directed to the most authoritative officials in the Jamaican police. I will alert highly placed people in the government: the Governor-General, if necessary. St Croix has had its murders;

145

tourism is only now coming back. Jamaica could not tolerate an American kidnapping . . . Does that satisfy you?'

'I'm satisfied.' Alex crushed out his cigarette in the ashtray, and as he did so, he remembered Tallon's reaction to Chatellerault's appearance in Savanna-la-Mar. 'You were surprised that Chatellerault was on the island. Why?'

'Two days ago, he was registered at the George V in Paris. There's been no word of his leaving, which means he flew here clandestinely, probably by way of Mexico. It is disturbing. You must keep a close watch on Mrs Booth . . . You have a weapon, I assume?'

'Two rifles in the equipment. An .030 Remington telescopic and a long-power .22 automatic. Nothing else.'

Tallon seemed to debate with himself, then make his decision. He took a key ring from his pocket, selected a key, and opened a lower drawer of his desk. He removed a bulky manila envelope, opened the flap, and shook a pistol onto his blotter. A number of cartridges fell out with the gun. 'This is a .38 Smith and Wesson, short barrel. All markings have been destroyed. It's untraceable. Take it, please; it's wiped clean. The only finger-prints will be yours. Be careful.'

McAuliff looked at the weapon for several seconds before reaching out and slowly picking it up. He did not want it; there was a finality of commitment somehow attached to his having it. But again, there was the question of alternatives: Not having it might possibly be foolish, though he did not expect to use it for anything more than a show of force.

'Your dossier includes your military service and experience in small-arms fire. But that was a long time ago. Would you care to refresh yourself at a pistol range? We have several, within minutes by plane.'

'No, thank you,' replied Alex. 'Not too long ago, in Australia, it was the only diversion we had.'

The telephone rang with a muted bell. Tallon picked it up and acknowledged with a simple 'Yes?'

He listened without speaking to the party on the other end

of the line. When he terminated the call, he looked at McAuliff.

'The green Chevrolet sedan is registered to a dead man. The vehicle's licence is in the name of Walter Piersall. Residence: High Hill, Carrick Foyle, parish of Trelawny.'

13

McAuliff spent another hour with Westmore Tallon, as the old Jamaican aristocrat activated his informational network. He had sources all over the island.

Before the hour was up, one important fact had been uncovered: The deceased, Walter Piersall of Carrick Foyle, parish of Trelawny, had in his employ two black assistants with whom he invariably travelled. The coincidence of the two men who had removed Sam Tucker's belongings from the hotel in Montego Bay and the two men who followed Alex in the green Chevrolet was no longer far-fetched. And since Piersall had brought up Sam's name with Alison Booth, the conclusion was now to be assumed.

Tallon ordered his own people to pick up Piersall's men. He would telephone McAuliff when they had done so.

Alex returned to Courtleigh Manor. He stopped at the desk for messages. Alison was at dinner; she hoped he would join her. There was nothing else.

No word from Sam Tucker.

'If there are any calls for me, I'll be in the dining room,' he said to the clerk.

Alison sat alone in the middle of the crowded room, which was profuse with tropical plants and open-grilled windows. In the centre of each table was a candle within a lantern; these were the only sources of light. Shadows flickered against the dark red and green and yellow foliage; the hum was the hum of contentment, rising but still quiet crescendos of laughter; perfectly groomed, perfectly dressed manikins in slow motion, all seemingly waiting for the nocturnal games to begin.

This was the manikins' good hour. When manners and studied grace and minor subtleties were important. Later it would be different; other things would become important ... and too often ugly. Which is why James Ferguson knew his drunken pretence had been plausible last night.

And why Charles Whitehall arrogantly, quietly, had thrown the napkin across the table onto the floor. To clean up the foreigner's mess.

'You look pensive. Or disagreeable,' said Alison as Alex pulled out the chair to sit down.

'Not really.'

'What happened? What did the police say? I half expected a call from them.'

McAuliff had rehearsed his reply, but before delivering it he gestured at the cup of coffee and the brandy glass in front of Alison. 'You've had dinner, I guess.'

'Yes. I was famished. Haven't you?'

'No. Keep me company?'

'Of course. I'll dismiss the eunuchs.'

He ordered a drink. 'You have a lovely smile. It's sort of a laugh.'

'No sidetracking. What happened?'

McAuliff lied quite well, he thought. Certainly better – at least more persuasively – than before. He told Alison he had spent nearly two hours with the police. Westmore Tallon had furnished him with the address and even described the interior of the main headquarters; it had been Tallon's idea for him to know the general details. One could never tell when they were important.

'They backed up Latham's theory. They say it's hit-and-run. They also hinted that Piersall had a diversion or two that was closeted. He was run down in a very rough section.'

'That sounds suspiciously pat to me. They're covering themselves.' Alison's eyebrows furrowed, her expression one of disbelief.

'They may be,' answered Alex casually, sincerely. 'But they

149

can't tie him to Sam Tucker, and that's my only concern.'

'He *is* tied. He told me.'

'And *I* told *them*. They've sent men to Carrick Foyle, that's where Piersall lived. In Trelawny. Others are going over his things at the Sheraton. If they find anything, they'll call me.' McAuliff felt that he was carrying off the lie. He was, after all, only bending the truth. The arthritic Westmore Tallon was doing these things.

'And you're satisfied with that? You're just going to take their word for it? You were awfully troubled about Mr Tucker a few hours ago.'

'I still am,' said Alex, putting down his glass and looking at her. He had no need to lie now. 'If I don't hear from Sam by late tonight . . . or tomorrow morning, I'm going to go to the American Embassy and yell like hell.'

'Oh . . . all right. Did you mention the little buggers this morning? You never told me.'

'The what?'

'Those bugs in your luggage. You said you were supposed to report them.'

Again McAuliff felt a wave of inadequacy; it irked him that he wasn't keeping track of things. Of course, he hadn't seen Tallon earlier, had not received his instructions, but that was no explanation. 'I should have listened to you last night. I can just get rid of them; step on them, I guess.'

'There's a better way.'

'What's that?'

'Put them someplace else.'

'For instance?'

'Oh, somewhere harmless but with lots of traffic. It keeps the tapes rolling and people occupied.'

McAuliff laughed; it was not a false laugh. 'That's very funny. And very practical. Where would they be, listening, I mean?'

Alison brought her hands to her chin; a mischievous little girl thinking mischievously. 'It should be within a hundred yards or so – that's usually the range tolerance between bugs and the receivers. And where there's a great deal of activity ... Let's see. I complimented the headwaiter on the red snapper. I'll bet he'd take me to the chef for the recipe.'

'They love that sort of thing,' added Alex. 'It's perfect. Don't go away. I'll be right back.'

Alison Booth, former liaison to Interpol, reported that two electronic devices were securely attached to the permanent laundry hamper under the salad table in the Courtleigh Manor kitchen. She had slipped them inside – and pushed them down – along with a soiled napkin, as an enthusiastic chef described the ingredients of his Jamaican red snapper sauce.

'The hamper was long, not deep,' she explained as McAuliff finished the last of his dinner. 'I pressed rather hard; the adhesive will hold quite well, I think.'

'You're incredible,' said Alex, meaning it.

'No, just experienced,' she replied, without much humour. 'You were only taught one side of the game, my darling.'

'It doesn't sound much like tennis.'

'Oh, there are compensations. For example, do you have any idea how limitless the possibilities are? In that kitchen, for the next three hours or so, until it's tracked?'

'I'm not sure I know what you mean.'

'Depending upon who's on the tapes, there'll be a mad scramble writing down words and phrases. Kitchen talk has its own contractions, its own language, really. It will be assumed you've taken your suitcase to a scheduled destination, for reasons of departure, naturally. There'll be quite a bit of confusion.' Alison smiled, her eyes again mischievous, as they had been before he had gone upstairs to pry loose the bugs.

'You mean "Sauce Béarnaise" is really a code for sub-machine gun? "BLT" stands for "hit the beaches"?'

'Something like that. It's quite possible, you know.'

'I thought that sort of thing only happened in World War Two movies. With Nazis screaming at each other, sending panzer divisions in the wrong directions.' McAuliff looked at his watch. It was 9:15. 'I have a phone call to make, and I want to go over a list of supplies with Ferguson. He's going to –'

He stopped. Alison had reached over, her hands suddenly on his arm. 'Don't turn your head,' she commanded softly, 'but I think your little buggers provoked a reaction. A man just came through the dining room entrance very rapidly, obviously looking for someone.'

'For us?'

'For you, to be precise, I'd say.'

'The kitchen codes didn't fool them very long.'

'Perhaps not. On the other hand, it's quite possible they've been keeping loose tabs on you and were double checking. It's too small a hotel for round-the-clock –'

'Describe him,' interrupted McAuliff. 'As completely as you can. Is he still facing this way?'

'He saw you and stopped. He's apologizing to the man on the reservations book, I think. He's white; he's dressed in light trousers, a dark jacket, and a white – no, a yellow shirt. He's shorter than you by a bit; fairly chunky –'

'What?'

'You know, bulky. And middle-young, thirties, I'd say. His hair is long, not extreme, but long. It's dark blond or light brown; it's hard to tell in this candlelight.'

'You've done fine. Now I've got to get to a telephone.'

'Wait till he leaves; he's looking over again,' said Alison, feigning interested, intimate laughter. 'Why don't you leer a little and signal for the bill. Very casually, my darling.'

'I feel like I'm in some kind of nursery school. With the prettiest teacher in town.' Alex held up his hand, spotted the waiter, and made the customary scribble in the air. 'I'll take you to your room, then come back downstairs and call.'

'Why? Use the phone in the room. The buggers aren't there.'

Damn! Goddamn! It had happened again; he wasn't prepared. The little things, always the little things. They were the traps.

Hammond said it over and over again ... Hammond. The Savoy. Don't make calls on the Savoy phone.

'I was told to use a pay telephone. They must have their reasons.'

'Who?'

'The Ministry. Latham ... the police, of course.'

'Of course. The police.' Alison withdrew her hand from his arms as the waiter presented the bill for Alex to sign. She didn't believe him; she made not pretence of believing him. Why should she? He was a rotten actor; he was caught ... But it was preferable to an ill-phrased statement or an awkward response to Westmore Tallon over the phone while Alison watched him. And listened. He had to feel free in his conversation with the arthritic liaison; he could not have one eye, one ear on Alison as he talked. He could not take the chance that the name Chatellerault, or even a hint of the man, was heard. Alison was too quick.

'Has he left yet?'

'As you signed the bill. He saw we were leaving.' Her reply was neither angry nor warm, merely neutral.

They walked out of the candlelit dining room, past the cascading arcs of green foliage into the lobby, towards the bank of elevators. Neither spoke. The ride up to their floor continued in silence, made bearable by other guests in the small enclosure.

He opened the door and repeated the precautions he had taken the previous evening – minus the scanner. He was in a hurry now; if he remembered, he would bless the room with electronic benediction later. He checked his own room and locked the connecting door from her side. He looked out on the balcony and in the bathroom. Alison stood in the corridor doorway, watching him.

He approached her. 'Will you stay here until I get back?'

'Yes,' she answered simply.

He kissed her on the lips, staying close to her, he knew, longer than she expected him to; it was his message to her. 'You are a lovely lady.'

'Alex?' She placed her hands carefully on his arms and looked up at him. 'I know the symptoms. Believe me, I do. They're not easy to forget . . . There are things you're not telling me and I won't ask. I'll wait.'

'You're overdramatizing, Alison.'

'That's funny.'

'What is?'

'What you just said. I used those words with David. In Malaga. He was nervous, frightened. He was so unsure of himself. And of me. And I said to him: David, you're being over dramatic . . . I know now that it was at that moment he knew.'

McAuliff held her eyes with his own. 'You're not David and I'm not you. That's as straight as I can put it. Now, I have to get to a telephone. I'll see you later. Use the latch.'

He kissed her again, went out the door, and closed it behind him. He waited until he heard the metallic sounds of the inserted bolt, then turned towards the elevators.

The doors closed; the elevator descended. The soft music was piped over the heads of assorted businessmen and tourists; the cubicle was full. McAuliff's thoughts were on his imminent telephone call to Westmore Tallon, his concerns about Sam Tucker.

The elevator stopped at an intermediate floor. Alex looked up at the lighted digits absently, vaguely wondering how another person could fit in the cramped enclosure. There was no need to think about the problem; the two men who waited by the parting doors saw the situation, smiled, and gestured that they would wait for the next lift.

And then McAuliff saw him. Beyond the slowly closing panels, far down in the corridor. A stocky man in a dark jacket and light trousers. He had unlocked a door and was about to enter a room; as he did so, he pulled back his jacket to replace the key in his pocket. The shirt was yellow.

The door closed.

'Excuse me! Excuse me, please!' said McAuliff rapidly as he

154

reached across a tuxedoed man near the panel of buttons and pushed the one marked 2, the next number in descent. 'I forgot my floor. I'm terribly sorry.'

The elevator, its thrust suddenly, electrically interrupted, jerked slightly as it mindlessly prepared for the unexpected stop. The panels opened and Alex sidled past the irritated but accommodating passengers.

He stood in the corridor in front of the bank of elevators and immediately pushed the *Up* button. Then he reconsidered. Where were the stairs?

The EXIT—STAIRCASE sign was blue with white letters. That seemed peculiar to him; exit signs were always red. It was at the far end of the hallway. He walked rapidly down the heavily carpeted corridor, nervously smiling at a couple who emerged from a doorway at midpoint. The man was in his fifties and drunk; the girl was barely in her twenties, sober and mulatto. Her clothes were the costume of a high-priced whore. She smiled at Alex; another sort of message. He acknowledged, his eyes telling her he wasn't interested but good luck, take the company drunk for all she could.

He pushed the crossbar on the exit door. Its sound was too loud; he closed it carefully, quietly, relieved to see there was a knob on the inside of the door.

He ran up the concrete stairs on the balls of his feet, minimizing the sound of his footsteps. The steel panel had the Roman numeral *III* stencilled in black over the beige paint. He twisted the knob slowly and opened the door onto the third-floor corridor.

It was empty. The nocturnal games had begun below; the players would remain in the competitive arenas until the prizes had been won or lost or forgotten in alcoholic oblivion. He had only to be alert for stragglers, or the over-anxious, like the pigeon on the second floor who was being manoeuvred with such precision by the child-woman mulatto. He had been quite far down the hallway, but not at the end. Not by the staircase; two-thirds of the way, perhaps. On the right; he had pulled back his jacket with his right hand, revealing the yellow shirt. That meant he was now inside a door on Alex's left. Reversing the viewpoint, he focused on three . . . no, four doors on his left that were possible. Beginning with the second door from the staircase, one-third the distance to the elevators.

Which one?

McAuliff began walking noiselessly on the thick carpet down the corridor, hugging the left wall. He paused before each door as he passed, his head constantly turning, his eyes alert, his ears listening for the sound of voices, the tinkling of glasses. For anything.

Nothing.

Silence. Everywhere.

He looked at the brass numbers – 218, 216, 214, 212. Even 210. Any farther would be incompatible with what he remembered.

He stopped at the halfway point and turned. Perhaps he knew enough. Enough to tell Westmore Tallon. Alison had said that the tolerance range for the electronic bugs was one hundred yards from first positioning to the receiving equipment. This floor, this section of the hotel, was well within that limit. Behind one of those doors was a tape recorder activated by a man in front of a speaker or with earphones clamped over his head.

Perhaps it was enough to report those numbers. Why should he look further?

Yet he knew he would. Someone had seen fit to intrude on his life in a way that filled him with revulsion. Few things caused him to react violently, but one of them was the actual, intended invasion of his privacy. And greed. Greed, too, infuriated him. Individual, academic, corporate.

Someone named Craft – because of his greed – had instructed his minions to invade Alex's personal moments.

Alexander Tarquin McAuliff was a very angry man.

He started back towards the staircase, retracing his steps, close to the wall, closer to each door, where he stopped and stood immobile. Listening.

Two-twelve. 214. 216. 218 . . .

And back once again. It was a question of patience. Behind one of those doors was a man in a yellow shirt. He wanted to find that man.

He heard it.

Room 214.

It was a radio. Or a television set. Someone had turned up the volume of a television set. He could not distinguish the words, but he could hear the excitement behind the rapid bursts of dialogue from a clouded speaker, too loud to avoid distortion.

Suddenly, there was the sound of a harsh, metallic crack of a door latch. Inches away from McAuliff someone had pulled back the bolt and was about to open the door.

Alex raced to the staircase. He could not avoid noise, he could only reduce it as much as possible as he lurched into the dimly lit concrete foyer. He whipped around, pushing the heavy steel door closed as fast and as quietly as he could; he pressed the fingers of his left hand around the edge, preventing the door from shutting completely, stopping the sound of metal against metal at the last half second.

He peered through the crack. The man in the yellow shirt came out of the room, his attention still within it. He was no more than fifty feet away in the silent corridor – silent except for the sound of the television set. He seemed angry, and before he closed the door he looked inside and spoke harshly in a Southern drawl.

'Turn that fuckin' thing down, you goddamn ape!'

The man in the yellow shirt then slammed the door and walked rapidly towards the elevators. He remained at the end of the corridor, nervously checking his watch, straightening his tie, rubbing his shoes over the back of his trousers until a red light, accompanied by a soft, echoing bell, signalled the approach of an elevator. McAuliff watched from the stairwell two hundred feet away.

The elevator doors closed, and Alex walked out into the

corridor. He crossed to Room 214 and stood motionless for a few moments. It was a decision he could abandon, he knew that. He could walk away, call Tallon, tell him the room number, and that would be that.

But it would not be very satisfying. It would not be satisfying at all. He had a better idea: He would take whoever was in that room to Tallon himself. If Tallon didn't like it, he could go to hell. The same for Hammond. Since it was established that the electronic devices were planted by a man named Craft, who was in no way connected with the elusive Halidon, Arthur Craft could be taught a lesson. Alex's arrangements with Hammond did not include abuses from third and fourth parties.

It seemed perfectly logical to get Craft out of the chess game. Craft clouded the issues, confused the pursuit.

McAuliff had learned two physical facts about Arthur Craft: He was the son of Craft the elder and he was American. He was also an unpleasant man. It would have to do.

He knocked on the door beneath the numerals 214.

'Yes, mon? Who is it, mon?' came the muffled reply from within.

Alex waited and knocked again. The voice inside came nearer the door.

'Who is it, please, mon?'

'Arthur Craft, you idiot!'

'Oh! Yes sir, Mr Craft, mon!' The voice was clearly frightened. The knob turned; the bolt had not been inserted.

The door had opened no more than three inches when McAuliff slammed his shoulder against it with the full impact of his near two hundred pounds. The door crashed against the medium-sized Jamaican inside, sending him reeling into the centre of the room. Alex gripped the edge of the vibrating door and swung it back into place, the slam of the heavy wood echoing throughout the corridor.

The Jamaican steadied himself, in his eyes a combination of fury and fear. He whipped around to the room's writing desk:

there were boxed speakers on each side. Between them was a pistol.

McAuliff lurched forward, his left hand aiming for the gun, his right grabbing any part of the man it could reach. Their hands met above the warm steel of the pistol; Alex gripped the black's throat and dug his fingers into the man's flesh.

The man shook loose; the gun went careening off the surface of the desk onto the floor. McAuliff lashed out with the back of his fist at the black's face, instantaneously opening his hand and yanking forward, pulling the man's head down by the hair. As the head went down, Alex brought his left knee crashing up into the man's chest, then into his face.

Voices from a millennium ago came back to him: *Use your knees! Your feet! Grab! Hold! Slash at the eyes! The blind can't fight! . . . Rupture!*

It was over. The voices subsided. The man collapsed at his feet.

McAuliff stepped back. He was frightened; something had happened to him. For a few terrifying seconds, he had been back in the Vietnam hills. He looked down at the motionless Jamaican beneath him. The head was turned, flat against the carpet; blood was oozing from the pink lips.

Thank God the man was breathing.

It was the gun. The goddamned *gun*! He had not expected a gun. A fight, yes. His anger justified that. But he had thought of it as a scuffle – intense, over quickly. He would confront, embarrass, forcibly make whoever was monitoring the tapes go with him. To embarrass; to teach an avaricious employer a lesson.

But not this.

This was deadly. This was the violence of survival.

The tapes. The *voices*. The excited voices kept coming out of the speakers on the desk.

It was not a television set he had heard. The sounds were the sounds of the Courtleigh Manor kitchen. Men shouting, other men responding angrily; the commands of superiors, the whining complaints of subordinates. All frantic, agitated . . . mostly unintelligible. They must have driven those listening furious.

Then Alex saw the revolving reels of the tape deck. For some reason, it was on the floor, to the right of the desk. A small, compact Wollensak recorder, spinning as if nothing had happened.

McAuliff grabbed the two speakers and crashed them repeatedly against each other until the wood splintered and the cases cracked open. He tore out the black shells and the wires and threw them across the room. He crossed to the right of the desk and crushed his heel into the Wollensak, grinding the numerous flat switches until a puff of smoke emerged from the interior and the reels stopped their movement. He reached down and ripped off the tape; he could burn it, but there was nothing of consequence recorded. He rolled the two reels across the floor, the thin strand of tape forming a narrow *V* on the carpet.

The Jamaican groaned; his eyes blinked as he swallowed and coughed.

Alex picked up the pistol on the floor, and squeezed it into his belt. He went into the bathroom, turned on the cold water, and threw a towel into the basin.

He pulled the drenched towel from the sink and walked back to the coughing, injured Jamaican. He knelt down, helped the man into a sitting position, and blotted his face. The water flowed down on the man's shirt and trousers . . . water mingled with blood.

'I'm sorry,' said Alex. 'I didn't mean to hurt you. I wouldn't have if you hadn't reached for that goddamned pistol.'

'*Mon!*' The Jamaican coughed his interruption. 'You *crazy-mon!*' The Jamaican held his chest and winced painfully as he struggled to his feet. 'You break up . . . everyt'ing, mon!' said the injured man, looking at the smashed equipment.

'I certainly did! Maybe your Mr Craft will get the message. If he wants to play industrial espionage, let him play in somebody else's backyard. I resent the intrusion . . . Come on, let's go.' Alex took the man by the arm and began leading him to the door.

'No, mon!' shouted the black, resisting.

'*Yes,* mon,' said McAuliff quietly. 'You're coming with me.'

'Where, mon?'

'To see a little old man who runs a fish store, that's all.' Alex shoved him; the Negro gripped his side. His ribs were broken, thought McAuliff.

'Please, mon! No *police,* mon! I lose everyt'ing!' The Jamaican's dark eyes were pleading as he held his ribs.

'You went for a gun, mon! That's a very serious thing to do.'

'Them not my gun. Them gun got no bullets, mon.'

'*What?*'

'Look-see, mon! Please! I got good job . . . I don't hurt nobody . . .'

Alex wasn't listening. He reached into his belt for the pistol.

It was no weapon at all.

It was a starter's gun; the kind held up by referees at track meets.

'Oh, for Christ's sake . . .' Arthur Craft, Junior, played games – little boys' games with little boys' toys.

McAuliff looked at the panicked Jamaican.

'Okay, mon. You just tell your employer what I said. The next time, I'll haul him into court.'

It was a silly thing to say, thought Alex, as he walked out into the corridor, slamming the door behind him. There'd be no courts; Julian Warfield or his adversary, R. C. Hammond, were far preferable. Alongside Dunstone plc and British Intelligence, Arthur Craft was a cipher. An unimportant intrusion that in all likelihood was no more.

He walked out of the elevator and tried to recall the location of the telephone booths. They were to the left of the entrance, past the front desk, he remembered.

He nodded to the clerks while thinking of Westmore Tallon's private number.

'Mr McAuliff, sir?' The speaker was a tall Jamaican with very broad shoulders, emphasized by a tight nylon jacket.

'Yes?'

'Would you come with me, please?'

Alex looked at the man. He was neat, the trousers pressed, a white shirt and a tie in evidence beneath the jacket. 'No . . . why should I?'

'Please, we have very little time. A man is waiting for you outside. A Mr Tucker.'

'What? How did –'

'*Please*, Mr McAuliff. I cannot stay here.'

Alex followed the Jamaican out the glass doors of the entrance. As they reached the driveway, he saw the man in the yellow shirt – Craft's man – walking on the path from the parking lot: the man stopped and stared at him, as if unsure what to do.

'Hurry, please,' said the Jamaican several steps in front of McAuliff, breaking into a run. 'Down past the gates. The car is waiting!'

They ran down the drive, past the stone gateposts.

The green Chevrolet was on the side of the road, its motor running. The Jamaican opened the back door for Alex.

'Get in!'

McAuliff did so.

Sam Tucker, his massive frame taking up most of the back seat, his shock of red hair reflecting the outside lights, extended his hand.

'Good to see you, boy!'

'Sam!'

The car lurched forward, throwing Alex into the felt. In the front seat, McAuliff saw that there were three men. The driver wore a baseball cap; the third man – nearly as large as Sam Tucker – was squeezed between the driver and the Jamaican who had met him inside the Courtleigh lobby. Alex turned back to Tucker.

'What *is* all this, Sam? Where the hell have you been?'

The answer, however, did not come from Sam Tucker. Instead, the black by the window, the man who had led Alex down the driveway, turned and spoke quietly.

'Mr Tucker has been with us, Mr McAuliff . . . If events can be controlled, we are your link to the Halidon.'

14

They drove for nearly an hour. Always climbing, higher and higher, it seemed to McAuliff. The winding roads snaked upward, the turns sudden, the curves hidden by sweeping waterfalls of tropic greenery. There were stretches of unpaved road. The car took them poorly; the whining of the low gear was proof of the strain.

McAuliff and Sam Tucker spoke quietly, knowing their conversation was overheard by those in front. That knowledge did not seem to bother Tucker.

Sam's story was totally logical, considering his habits and life-style. Sam Tucker had friends, or acquaintances, in many parts of the world no one knew about. Not that he intentionally concealed their identities, only that they were part of his personal, not professional, life.

One of these people had been Walter Piersall.

'I mentioned him to you last year, Alexander,' said Tucker in the darkness of the back seat. 'In Ocho Rios.'

'I don't remember.'

'I told you I'd met an academic fellow in Carrick Foyle. I was going to spend a couple of weekends with him.'

That was it, thought McAuliff. The name 'Carrick Foyle', he *had* heard it before. 'I remember now. Something about a lecture series at the Kingston Institute.'

'That's right. Walter was a very classy type – an anthro man who didn't bore you to death. I cabled him I was coming back.'

'You also got in touch with Hanley. He's the one who set off the alarms.'

'I called Bob after I got into Montego. For a little sporting life. There was no way I could reach him later. We travelled fast, and when we got where we were going, there was no telephone. I figured he'd be mad as hell.'

'He was worried, not mad. It was quite a disappearing act.'

'He should know better. I have friends on this island, not enemies. At least, none either of us knows about.'

'What happened? Where did you go?'

Tucker told him.

When Sam arrived in Montego Bay, there was a message from Piersall at the arrivals desk. He was to call the anthropologist in Carrick Foyle after he was settled. He did, but was told by a servant in Carrick Foyle that Piersall might not return until late that night.

Tucker then phoned his old friend Hanley, and the two men got drunk, as was their established custom at reunions.

In the morning, while Hanley was still sleeping, Sam left the hotel to pick up cigars.

'It's not the sort of place that's large on room service, boy.'

'I gathered that,' said Alex.

'Out on the street, our friends here –' Tucker gestured towards the front seat – 'were waiting in a station wagon –'

'Mr Tucker was being followed,' interrupted the black by the window. 'Word of this reached Dr Piersall. He sent us to Mo'Bay to look after his friend. Mr Tucker gets up early.'

Sam grinned. 'You know me. Even with the juice, I can't sleep long.'

'I know,' said Alex, remembering too many hotel rooms and survey campsites in which Tucker had wandered about at the first light of dawn.

'There was a little misunderstanding,' continued Sam. 'The boys here said Piersall was waiting for me. I figured, what the hell, the lads thought enough of me to stick out the night, I'd go with 'em straight off. Old Hanley wouldn't be up for an hour or so . . . I'd call him from Piersall's house. But, goddamnit, we

165

didn't go to Carrick Foyle. We headed for a bamboo camp down the Martha Brae. It took us damn near two hours to get there, a godforsaken place, Alexander.'

When they arrived at the bamboo camp, Walter Piersall greeted Sam warmly. But within minutes Tucker realized that something had happened to the man. He was not the same person that Sam had known a year ago. There was a zealousness, an intensity not in evidence twelve months before.

Walter Piersall was caught up in things Jamaican. The quiet anthropologist had become a fierce partisan in the battles being waged between social and political factions within Jamaica. He was suddenly a jealous guardian of the islanders' rights, an enemy of the outside exploiters.

'I've seen it happen dozens of times, Alexander,' said Sam. 'From the Tasman to the Caribbean; it's a kind of island fever. Possession . . . oneness, I think. Men migrate for taxes or climate or whatever the hell and they turn into self-proclaimed protectors of their sanctuaries . . . the Catholic convert telling the pope he's not with it . . .'

In his cross-island proselytizing, Piersall began to hear whispers of an enormous land conspiracy. In his own backyard in the parish of Trelawny. At first he dismissed them; they involved men with whom one might disagree, but whose integrity was not debated. Men of extraordinary stature.

The conspiratorial syndrome was an ever-present nuisance in any infant, growing government; Piersall understood that. In Jamaica it was given credence by the influx of foreign capital looking for tax havens, by a parliament ordering more reform programmes than it could possibly control, and by a small, wealthy island aristocracy trying to protect itself – the bribe was an all-too-prevalent way of life.

Piersall had decided, once and for all, to put the whispered rumours to rest. Four months ago he'd gone to the Ministry of Territories and filed a Resolution of Intent to purchase by way of syndication twenty square miles of land on the north border of the Cock Pit. It was a harmless gesture, really. Such a purchase would take years in the courts and involve the satisfactory settling of historic island treaties; his point was merely to prove Kingston's willingness to accept the filing. That the land was not controlled by outsiders.

'Since that day, Alexander, Piersall's life was made a hell.' Sam Tucker lit a thin native cigar; the aromatic smoke whipped out the open window into the onrushing darkness. 'He was harassed by the police, pulled into the parish courts dozens of times for nonsense; his lectures were cancelled at the university and the Institute; his telephone tapped – conversations repeated by government attorneys . . . Finally, the whispers he tried to silence killed him.'

McAuliff said nothing for several moments. 'Why was Piersall so anxious to contact you?' he asked Tucker.

'In my cable I told him I was doing a big survey in Trelawny. A project out of London by way of Kingston. I didn't want him to think I was travelling six thousand miles to be his guest; he was a busy man, Alexander.'

'But you were in Kingston tonight. Not in a bamboo camp on the Martha Brae. Two of these men' – McAuliff gestured front – 'followed me this afternoon. In this car.'

'Let me answer you, Mr McAuliff,' said the Jamaican by the window, turning and placing his arm over the seat. 'Kingston intercepted Mr Tuck's cable; they made kling-kling addition, mon. They thought Mr Tuck was mixed up with Dr Piersall in bad ways. Bad ways for them, mon. They sent dangerous men to Mo'Bay. To find out what Mr Tuck was doing –'

'How do you know this?' broke in Alex.

For the briefest instant, the black by the window glanced at the driver. It was difficult to tell in the dim light and rushing shadows, but McAuliff thought the driver nodded imperceptibly.

'We took the men who came to Mo'Bay after Mr Tuck. That is all you need to know, mon. What was learned caused Dr Piersall much concern. So much, mon, that we flew to Kingston. To reach you, mon . . . Dr Piersall was killed for that.'

'Who killed him?'

'If we knew, there would be dead men hanging in Victoria Park.'

'What did you learn . . . from the men in Montego?'

Again, the black who spoke seemed to glance at the driver. In seconds he replied, 'That people in Kingston believed Dr Piersall would interfere further. When he went to find you, mon, it was their proof. By killing him they took a big sea urchin out of their foot.'

'And you don't know who did it –'

'Hired niggers, mon,' interrupted the black.

'It's insane!' McAuliff spoke to himself as much as to Sam Tucker. 'People killing people . . . men following other men. It's goddamn crazy!'

'Why is it crazy to a man who visits Tallon's Fish Market?' asked the black suddenly.

'How did –' McAuliff stopped. He was confused; he had been so careful. 'How did you know that? I lost you at the racetrack!'

The Jamaican smiled, his bright teeth catching the light from the careening reflections through the windshield. 'Ocean trout is not really preferable to the fresh-water variety, *mon.*'

The counterman! The nonchalant counterman in the striped linen apron. 'The man behind the counter is one of you. That's pretty good,' said McAuliff quietly.

'We're *very* good. Westmore Tallon is a British agent . . . So like the English: Enlist the clandestine help of the vested interests. And so fundamentally stupid. Tallon's senile Etonian classmates might trust him; his countrymen do not.'

The Jamaican removed his arm from the seat and turned front. The answer was over.

Sam Tucker spoke pensively, openly. 'Alexander . . . now tell me what the hell is going on. What have you done, boy?'

McAuliff turned to Sam. The huge, vital, capable old friend was staring at him in the darkness, the rapid flashes of light bouncing across his face. Tucker's eyes held confusion and hurt. And anger.

What in hell *had* he done, thought Alex.

'Here we are, mon,' said the driver in the baseball cap, who had not spoken throughout the trip.

McAuliff looked out the windows. The ground was flat now, but high in the hills and surrounded by them. Everything was sporadically illuminated by a Jamaican moon filtering through the low-flying clouds of the Blue Mountains. They were on a dirt road; in the distance, perhaps a quarter of a mile away, was a structure, a small cabin-like building. A dim light could be seen through a single window. On the right were two other . . . structures. Not buildings, not houses or cabins, nothing really definable; just free-form, sagging silhouettes . . . translucent? Yes . . . wires, cloth. Or netting . . . They were large tent-like covers, supported by numerous poles. And then Alex under- stood: beyond the tents the ground was matted flat and along the border, spaced every thirty or forty feet apart, were unlit cradle torches. The tents were camouflaged hangars; the ground a landing strip.

They were at an unmarked airfield in the mountains.

The Chevrolet slowed down as it approached what turned out to be a small farmhouse. There was an ancient tractor beyond the edge of the building; field tools – ploughs, shoulder yokes, pitchforks – were scattered about carelessly. In the moonlight the equipment looked like stationary relics. Unused, dead re- membrances only.

Camouflage.

As the hangers were camouflaged.

An airfield no map would indicate.

'Mr McAuliff? Mr Tucker? If you would come with me, please.' The black spokesman by the window opened the door and stepped out. Sam and Alex did the same. The driver and the third Jamaican remained inside, and when the disembarked passengers stepped away from the car, the driver accelerated the motor and sped off down the dirt road.

'Where are they going?' asked McAuliff anxiously.

'To conceal the automobile,' answered the black. 'Kingston sends out ganja air patrols at night, hoping to find such fields as these. With luck to spot light aircraft on narcotics runs.'

'This ganja country? I thought it was north,' said Tucker.

The Jamaican laughed. 'Ganja, weed, poppy . . . north, west, east. It is a healthy export industry, mon. But not ours . . . Come, let us go inside.'

The door of the miniature farmhouse opened as the three of them approached. In the frame stood the light-skinned black whom Alex had first seen in a striped apron behind the counter at Tallon's.

The interior of the small house was primitive: wooden chairs, a thick round table in the centre of the single room, an army cot against the wall. The jarring contradiction was a complicated radio set on a table to the right of the door. The light in the window was from the shaded lamp in front of the machinery; a generator could be heard providing what electricity was necessary.

All this McAuliff observed within seconds of entering. Then he saw a second man, standing in shadows across the room, his back towards the others. The body – the cut of the coat, the shoulders, the tapered waist, the tailored trousers – was familiar.

The man turned around; the light from the table lamp illuminated his features.

Charles Whitehall stared at McAuliff and then nodded once, slowly.

The door opened, and the driver of the Chevrolet entered with the third black. He walked to the round table in the centre of the room and sat down. He removed his baseball cap, revealing a large shaven head.

'My name is Moore. Barak Moore, Mr McAuliff. To ease your concerns, the woman, Alison Booth, has been called. She was told that you went down to the Ministry for a conference.'

'She won't believe that,' replied Alex.

'If she cares to check further, she will be informed that you are with Latham at a warehouse. There is nothing to worry about, mon.'

170

Sam Tucker stood by the door; he was relaxed but curious. And strong; his thick arms were folded across his chest, his lined features – tanned by the California sun – showed his age and accentuated his leathery strength. Charles Whitehall stood by the window in the left wall, his elegant, arrogant face exuding contempt.

The light-skinned black from Tallon's Fish Market and the two Jamaican 'guerrillas' had pulled their chairs back against the far right wall, away from the centre of attention. They were telegraphing the fact that Barak Moore was their superior.

'Please, sit down.' Barak Moore indicated the chairs around the table. There were three. Tucker and McAuliff looked at each other; there was no point in refusing. They walked to the table and sat down. Charles Whitehall remained standing by the window. Moore glanced up at him. 'Will you join us?'

'If I feel like sitting,' answered Whitehall.

Moore smiled and spoke while looking at Whitehall. 'Charley-mon finds it difficult to be in the same room with me, much less at the same table.'

'Then why is he here?' asked Sam Tucker.

'He had no idea he was going to be until a few minutes before landing. We switched pilots in Savanna-la-Mar.'

'His name is Charles Whitehall,' said Alex, speaking to Sam. 'He's part of the survey. I didn't know he was going to be here either.'

'What's your field, boy?' Tucker leaned back in his chair and spoke to Whitehall.

'Jamaica . . . *boy*.'

'I meant no offence, son.'

'You are offensive,' was Whitehall's simple reply.

'Charley and me,' continued Barak Moore, 'we are at the opposite poles of the politic. In your country, you have the term "white trash"; he considers me "black garbage". For roughly the same reasons: He thinks I'm too crude, too loud, too unwashed. I am an uncouth revolutionary in Charley-mon's eyes . . . he is a graceful rebel, you see.' Moore swept his hand

171

in front of him, balletically, insultingly. 'But our rebellions are different, *very* different, mon. I want Jamaica for *all* the people. He wants it for only a few.'

Whitehall stood motionless as he replied. 'You are as blind now as you were a decade ago. The only thing that has changed is your name, Bramwell Moore.' Whitehall sneered vocally as he continued. '*Barak* ... as childish and meaningless as the social philosophy you espouse; the sound of a jungle toad.'

Moore swallowed before he answered. 'I'd as soon kill you, I think you know that. But it would be as counterproductive as the solutions you seek to impose on our homeland. We have a common enemy, you and I. Make the best of it, *fascistimon.*'

'The vocabulary of your mentors. Did you learn it by rote, or did they make you read?'

'*Look!*' McAuliff interrupted angrily. 'You can fight or call names, or kill each other for all I give a damn, but I want to get back to the hotel!' He turned to Barak Moore. 'Whatever you have to say, get it over with.'

'He has a point, Charley-mon,' said Moore. 'We come later ... I will, as they say, summarize. It is a brief summary, mon ... That there are development plans for a large area of the island – plans that exclude the people – is now established. Dr Piersall's death confirms it. That your geological survey is tied to those plans, we logically assume; therefore, the Ministry and the Royal Society are – knowingly or unknowingly – concealing the identity of the financial interests. Furthermore, Mr McAuliff here is not unaware of these facts, because he deals with British Intelligence through the despicable Westmore Tallon ... That is the summary. Where do we go?' Moore stared at Alex, his eyes small black craters in a huge mountain of dark skin. 'We have a right to go somewhere, Mr McAuliff.'

'Before you shove him against the wall, boy,' interjected Sam Tucker, to Alex's surprise, 'remember, I'm no part of you. I don't say I won't be, but I'm not now.'

'I should think you'd be as interested as we are, Tucker.' The absence of the 'Mister', McAuliff thought, was Moore's hostile response to Sam's use of the word 'boy'. Moore did not realize that Tucker used the term for everyone.

'Don't mistake me,' added Sam. 'I'm interested. Just don't go running off too fast at the mouth ... I think you should say what you know, Alex.'

McAuliff looked at Tucker, then Moore, then over at Whitehall. Nothing in Hammond's instructions included such a confrontation. Except the admonition to *keep it simple; build on part of the truth.*

'The people in British Intelligence – and everything they represent – want to stop this development as much as you do. But they need information. They think the Halidon has it. They want to make contact with the Halidon. I'm supposed to try and make that contact.'

Alex wasn't sure what to expect from his statement, but certainly not what happened. Barak Moore's blunt features, grotesque under the immense shaven head, slowly changed from immobility to amusement, from amusement to the pinched flesh of outright mirth; it was a humour based on cruelty, however. His large mouth opened, and a coughing, malevolent laugh emerged.

From the window there was another sound, another laugh: higher and jackal-like. Charles Whitehall's elegant neck was stretched back, his head tilted towards the ceiling, his arms folded across his tailored jacket. He looked like some thin, black Oriental priest finding amusement in a novice's ignorance.

The three Jamaicans in the row of chairs, their white teeth gleaming in the shadows, were smiling, their bodies shaking slightly in silent laughter.

'What's so goddamn funny?' asked McAuliff, annoyed by the undefined humiliation.

'Funny, mon? Many times more than *funny*. The mongoose chases the deadly snake, so the snake wants to make friends?' Moore laughed his hideous laugh once again. 'It is not in any law of nature, mon!'

173

'What Moore is telling you, Mr McAuliff,' broke in White-hall, approaching the table, 'is that it's preposterous to think the Halidon would cooperate with the English. It is inconceivable. It is the Halidons of this island who drove the British from Jamaica. Put simply, MI6 is not to be trusted.'

'What *is* the Halidon?' Alex watched the black scholar, who stood motionless, his eyes on Barak Moore.

'It is a force,' said Whitehall quietly.

McAuliff looked at Moore; he was returning Whitehall's stare. 'That doesn't say very much, does it?'

'There is no one in this room who can tell you more, mon.' Barak Moore shifted his gaze to Alex.

Charles Whitehall spoke. 'There are no identities, McAuliff. The Halidon is an unseen curia, a court that has no chambers. No one is lying to you. Not about this . . . This small contingent here, these three men; Moore's élite corps, as it were –'

'Your words, Charley-mon! We don't use them! *Elite!*' Barak spat out the word.

'Immaterial,' continued Whitehall. 'I venture to say there are no more than five hundred people in all Jamaica who have heard of the Halidon. Less than fifty who know for certain any of its members. Those who do would rather face the pains of Obeah than reveal identities.'

'*Obeah!*' Sam Tucker's comment was in his voice. He had no use for the jingoistic diabolism that filled thousands upon thousands of native minds with terror – Jamaica's counterpart of the Haitian voodoo. 'Obeah's horsehit, boy! The sooner your hill and village people learn that, the better off they'll be!'

'If you think it's restricted to the hills and the villages, you are sadly mistaken,' said Whitehall. 'We in Jamaica do not offer Obeah as a tourist attraction. We have too much respect for it.'

Alex looked up at Whitehall. 'Do *you* have respect for it? Are *you* a believer?'

Whitehall levelled his gaze at McAuliff, his eyes knowing – with a trace of humour. 'Yes, Mr McAuliff, I have respect for Obeah. I have traced its strains to its origins in Mother Africa.

I have seen what it's done to the veldt, in the jungles. Respect; I do not say commitment or belief.'

'Then the Halidon is an organization.' McAuliff took out his cigarettes. Barak Moore reached over to accept one; Sam Tucker leaned forward in his chair. Alex continued. 'A secret society that has a lot of clout. Why? . . . Obeah?'

'Partly, mon,' answered Moore, lighting his cigarette like a man who does not smoke often. 'It is also very rich. It is whispered that it possesses wealth beyond anyone's thinking, mon.'

Suddenly, McAuliff realized the obvious. He looked back and forth between Charles Whitehall and Barak Moore.

'Christ Almighty! You're as anxious to reach the Halidon as I am! As British Intelligence is!'

'That is so, mon.' Moore crushed out his barely smoked cigarette on the surface of the table.

'Why?' asked Alex.

Charles Whitehall replied. 'We are dealing with two giants, Mr McAuliff. One black, one white. The Halidon must win.'

15

The meeting in the isolated farmhouse high in the hills of the Blue Mountains lasted until two o'clock in the morning.

The common objective was agreed to: contact with the Halidon.

And since Barak Moore's and Charles Whitehall's judgment that the Halidon would not deal directly with British Intelligence was convincing, McAuliff further agreed to cooperate with the two black antagonists. Barak and his 'élite' guerrillas would provide additional safety for the survey team. Two of the three men sitting against the wall of the farmhouse would fly to Ocho Rios and be hired as carriers.

If the Jamaicans suspected he knew more than he was telling them, they did not press him, thought Alex. They accepted his story – now told twice to Whitehall – that initially he had taken the survey as an investment for future work. From Kingston, MI6 was a complication thrust upon him.

It was as if they understood he had his own concerns, unrelated to theirs. And only when he was sure those concerns were not in conflict would he be completely open. Insane circumstances had forced him into a war he wanted no part of, but one thing was clear above all other considerations: the safety of those he had brought to the island.

Two things. Two million dollars.

From either enemy, Dunstone plc or British Intelligence.

'MI6 in London did not tell you, then, who is behind this land rape,' said Barak Moore – not asking a question – continuing immediately. 'It goes beyond their Kingston flunkies, mon.'

'If the British reach the Halidon, they'll tell them what they know,' said McAuliff. 'I'm sure of that. They want to pool their information, that much they've told me.'

'Which means the English assume the Halidon know a great deal,' added Whitehall pensively. 'I wonder if that is so.'

'They have their reasons,' said Alex cautiously. 'There was a previous survey team.'

The Jamaicans knew of it. Its disappearance was either proof of the Halidon's opposition or an isolated act of theft and murder by a roving band of primitive hill people in the Cock Pit. There was no way to tell.

Circles within circles.

What of the Marquis de Chatellerault? Why had he insisted upon meeting with Whitehall in Savanna-la-Mar?

'The marquis is a nervous man,' said Whitehall. 'He claims to have widespread interests on the island. He smells bad fish with this survey.'

'Has it occurred to you that Chatellerault is himself involved?' McAuliff spoke directly to the black scholar. 'MI5 and 6 think so. Tallon told me that this afternoon.'

'If so, the marquis does not trust his colleagues.'

'Did Chatellerault mention anyone else on the team?' asked Alex, afraid of the answer.

Whitehall looked at McAuliff and replied simply, 'He made several allusions, and I told him that I wasn't interested in side issues. They were not pertinent; I made that clear.'

'Thank you.'

'You're welcome.'

Sam Tucker raised his scraggy eyebrows, his expression dubious. 'What the hell *was* pertinent? What did he want?'

'To be kept informed of the survey's progress. Report all developments.'

'Why did he think you'd do that?' Sam leaned forward in the chair.

'I would be paid handsomely, to begin with. And there could be other areas of interest, which, frankly, there are not.'

'*Ha*, mon!' interjected Moore. 'You see, they believe Charley-mon can be bought! They know better with Barak Moore!'

Whitehall looked at the revolutionary, dismissing him. 'There is little to pay you for.' He opened his silver cigarette case; Moore grinned at the sight of it. Whitehall closed it slowly, placed it at his right, and lighted his cigarette with a match. 'Let's get on. I'd rather not be here all night.'

'Okay, mon.' Barak glanced at each man quickly. 'We want the same as the English. To reach the Halidon.' Moore pronounced the word in the Jamaican dialect: *hollydawn*. 'But the Halidon must come to us. There must be a strong reason. We cannot cry out for them. They will not come into the open.'

'I don't understand a damn thing about any of this,' said Tucker, lighting a thin cigar, 'but if you wait for them, you could be sitting on your asses a long goddamn time.'

'We think there is a way. We think Dr Piersall provided it.' Moore hunched his shoulders, conveying a sense of uncertainty, as if he was not sure how to choose his words. 'For months Dr Piersall tried to . . . define the Halidon. To seek it out, to understand. He went back into Caribe history, to the Arawak, to Africa. To find meaning.' Moore paused and looked at Whitehall. 'He read your books, Charley-mon. I told him you were a bad liar, a diseased goat. He said you did not lie in your books . . . From many small things, Dr Piersall put together pieces of the puzzle, he called it. His papers are in Carrick Foyle.'

'Just a minute.' Sam Tucker was irritated. 'Walter talked a goddamned streak for two days. On the Martha Brae, in the plane, at the Sheraton. He never mentioned any of this. Why didn't he?' Tucker looked over at the Jamaicans against the wall, at the two who had been with him since Montego Bay.

The black who had spoken in the Chevrolet replied. 'He would have, mon. It was agreed to wait until McAuliff was with you. It is not a story one repeats often.'

'What did the puzzle tell him?' asked Alex.

'Only part, mon,' said Barak Moore. 'Only part of the puzzle was complete. But Dr Piersall arrived at several theories. To begin with, Halidon is an offshoot from the Coromanteen tribe. They isolated themselves after the Maroon wars, for they would not agree to the treaties that called upon the Maroon nation – the Coromantees – to run down and capture runaway slaves for the English. The Halidon would not become bounty hunters of brother Africans. For decades they were nomadic. Then, perhaps two hundred, two hundred and fifty years ago, they settled in one location. Unknown, inaccessible to the outside world. But they did not divorce themselves from the outside world. Selected males were sent out to accomplish what the elders believed should be accomplished. To this day it is so. Women are brought in to bear children so that the pains of inbreedings are avoided ... And two final points: The Halidon community is high in the mountains where the winds are strong, of that Piersall was certain. And last, the Halidon has great riches ... These are the pieces of the puzzle; there are many missing.'

No one spoke for a while. Then Tucker broke the silence.

'It's a hell of a story,' said Sam 'but I'm not sure where it gets us. Our knowing it won't bring them out. And you said we can't go after them. Goddamn! If this ... tribe has been in the mountains for two hundred years and nobody's found them, we're not likely to, boy! Where is "the way" Walter provided?'

Charles Whitehall answered. 'If Dr Piersall's conclusions are true, the *way* is in the knowledge of them, Mr Tucker.'

'Would you explain that?' asked Alex.

In an unexpected show of deference, the erudite scholar turned to the rough-hewn guerrilla. 'I think ... Barak Moore should amplify. I believe the key is in what he said a few minutes ago. That the Halidon must have a strong reason to contact us.'

'You are not mistaken, mon. Dr Piersall was certain that if word got to the Halidon that their existence – and their great wealth – had been confirmed by a small band of responsible men, they would send an emissary. They guard their wealth

179

above all things, Piersall believed. But they have to be convinced beyond doubt . . . That is the way.'

'Who do you convince?' asked Alex.

'Someone must travel to Maroon Town, on the border of the Cock Pit. This person should ask for an audience with the Colonel of the Maroon people, offer to pay much, much money. It was Dr Piersall's belief that this man, whose title is passed from one generation to the next within the same tribal family, is the only link to the Halidon.'

'The story is told him, then?'

'No, McAuliff, mon! Not even the Colonel of the Maroons is to be so trusted. At any rate, it would be meaningless to him. Dr Piersall's studies hinted that the Halidon kept open one perpetual line to the African brothers. It was called "nagarro" –'

'The Akwamu tongue,' broke in Whitehall. 'The language is extinct, but derivations exist in the Ashanti and Mossai-Grusso dialects. "Nagarro" is an abstraction, best translated to mean "a spirit materialized".'

'A spirit . . .' Alex began to repeat the phrase, then stopped. 'Proof . . . proof of something real.'

'Yes,' replied Whitehall.

'Where is it?' asked McAuliff.

'The proof is in the meaning of another word,' said Barak Moore. 'The meaning of the word "Halidon".'

'What is it?'

'I do not know –'

'Goddamn!' Sam Tucker exploded. Barak Moore held up his hand, silencing him.

'Piersall found it. It is to be delivered to the Colonel of the Maroon people. For him to take up into the mountains.'

McAuliff's jaws were tense; he controlled himself as best he could. 'We can't deliver what we don't have.'

'You will have it, mon.' Barak settled his gaze on Alexander. 'A month ago Dr Piersall took me to his home in Carrick Foyle. He gave me my instructions. Should anything happen to him, I was to go to a place in the forests of his property. I have committed this place to memory, mon. There, deep under the ground, is an oilcloth packet. Inside the packet is a paper; on it is written the meaning of the Halidon.'

The driver on the ride back to Kingston was the Jamaican who was obviously Barak Moore's second-in-command, the black who had done the talking on the trip out to the airfield. His name was Floyd. Charles Whitehall sat in the front seat with him; Alex and Sam Tucker sat in the back.

'If you need stories to say where you were,' said Floyd to all of them, 'there was a long equipment meeting at a Ministry warehouse. On Crawford Street, near the docks. It can be verified.'

'Who were we meeting with?' asked Sam.

'A man named Latham. He is in charge –'

'Latham?' broke in Alex, recalling all too vividly his telephone conversation with the Ministry man that afternoon. 'He's the one –'

'We know,' interrupted Floyd, grinning in the rear-view mirror at McAuliff. 'He's one of us, mon.'

He let himself into the room as quietly as possible. It was nearly 3:30: the Courtleigh Manor was quiet, the nocturnal games concluded. He closed the door silently and started across the soft carpet. A light was on in Alison's room, the door open perhaps a foot. His own room was dark. Alison had turned off all the lamps; they had been on when he left her five hours ago.

Why had she done that?

He approached the slightly open door, removing his jacket as he did so.

There was a click behind him. He turned. A second later, the bedside lamp was snapped on, flooding the room with its dim light, harsh only at the source.

Alison was sitting up in his bed. He could see that her right hand gripped the small deadly weapon 'issued by the London police'; she was placing it at her side, obscuring it with the covers.

181

'Hello, Alex.'

'Hello.' It was an awkward moment.

'I stayed here because I thought your friend Tucker might call. I wouldn't have heard the telephone.'

'I could think of better reasons.' He smiled and approached the bed. She picked up the cylinder and twisted it. There was the same click he had heard seconds ago. She placed the strange weapon on the night table.

'Also, I wanted to talk.'

'You sound ominous.' He sat down. 'I wasn't able to call you . . . everything happened so fast. Sam showed up; he just walked through the goddamn lobby doors and wondered why I was so upset . . . Then, as he was registering, the call came from Latham. He was really in a hurry. I think I threw him with Ocho Rios tomorrow. There was a lot of equipment that hadn't been shipped to Boscobel –'

'Your phone didn't ring,' interrupted Alison quietly.

'What?'

'Mr Latham didn't ring through to your room.'

McAuliff was prepared; he had remembered *a little thing*. 'Because I'd left word we were having dinner. They were sending a page to the dining room.'

'That's very good, Alex.'

'What's the matter with you? I told the clerk to call you and explain. We *were* in a hurry; Latham said we had to get to the warehouse . . . down on Crawford Street, by the docks . . . before they closed the check-in books for the night.'

'That's not very good. You can do better.'

McAuliff saw that Alison was deadly serious. And angry. 'Why do you say that?'

'The front desk did not call me; there was no explaining *clerk* . . .' Alison pronounced the word 'clerk' in the American fashion, exaggerating the difference from English speech. It was insulting. 'An "assistant" of Mr Latham's telephoned. He wasn't very good, either. He didn't know what to say when I asked to speak to Latham; he didn't expect that . . . Did you know that

Gerald Latham lives in the Barbican district of Kingston? He's listed in the telephone book.'

Alison stopped; the silence was strained. Alex spoke softly as he made the statement. 'He was home.'

'He was home,' replied Alison. 'Don't worry. He didn't know who called him. I spoke to a woman first, and when he got on the phone I hung up.'

McAuliff inhaled a deep breath and reached into his shirt pocket for his pack of cigarettes. He wasn't sure there was anything to say. 'I'm sorry.'

'So am I,' she said quietly. 'I'll write you out a proper letter of resignation in the morning. You'll have to accept a promissory note for the air fare and whatever other expenses I'm liable for. I'll need what money I have for a while. I'm sure I'll find a situation.'

'You can't do that.' McAuliff found himself saying the words with strength, in utter conviction. And he knew why. Alison was perfectly willing to leave the survey: she was *going* to leave it. If her motive – or motives – for coming to Jamaica were not what she had said they were, she would not do that. 'For Christ's sake, you can't resign because I lied about a few hours! Damn it, Alison, I'm not accountable to you!'

'Oh, stop behaving like a pompous, wounded ass! You don't do that very well, either . . . I will *not* go through the labyrinth again; I'm sick to death of it. No more, do you hear!' Suddenly her voice fell and she caught her breath – and the fear was in her eyes. 'I can't stand it any longer.'

He stared at her. 'What do you mean?'

'You elaborately described a long interview with the Jamaican police this afternoon. The station, the district, the officers . . . very detailed, Alex. I called them after I hung up on Latham. They'd never heard of you.'

16

He knew he had to go back to the beginning – to the very beginning of the insanity. He had to tell her the truth. There was relief in sharing it.

All of it. So it made sense, what sense there was to make.

He did.

And as he told the story, he found himself trying to understand all over again. He spoke slowly, in a monotone actually; it was the drone of a man speaking through the mists of confusion.

Of the strange message from Dunstone plc that brought him to London from New York, and a man named 'Julian Warfield'. Of a 'financial analyst' at the Savoy Hotel whose plastic card identified him as 'R. C. Hammond, British Intelligence'. The pressurized days of living in two worlds that denied their own realities – the covert training, the secret meetings, the vehicle transfers, the hiring of survey personnel under basically false pretences. Of a panicked, weak James Ferguson, hired to spy on the survey by a man named 'Arthur Craft the Younger', who was not satisfied being one of the richest men in Jamaica. Of an arrogant Charles Whitehall, whose brilliance and scholarship could not lift him above a fanatic devotion to an outworn, outdated, dishonoured concept. Of an arthritic little islander, whose French and African blood had strained its way into the Jamaican aristocracy and MI6 by way of Eton and Oxford.

Of Sam Tucker's odd tale of the transformation of Walter Piersall, anthropologist, converted by 'island fever' into a self-professed guardian of his tropic sanctuary.

And finally of a shaven-headed guerrilla revolutionary named

'Barak Moore'. And everyone's search for an 'unseen curia' called 'the Halidon'.

Insanity. But all very, very real.

The sun sprayed its shafts of early light into the billowing grey clouds above the Blue Mountains. McAuliff sat in the frame of the balcony door; the wet scents of the Jamaican dawn came up from the moist grounds and down from the tall palms, cooling his nostrils and so his skin.

He was nearly finished now. They had talked – he had talked – for an hour and forty-five minutes. There remained only the Marquis de Chatellerault.

Alison was still in the bed, sitting up against the pillows. Her eyes were tired, but she did not take them off him.

He wondered what she would say – or do – when he mentioned Chatellerault. He was afraid.

'You're tired; so am I. Why don't I finish in the morning?'

'It is morning.'

'Later, then.'

'I don't think so. I'd rather hear it all at once.'

'There isn't much more.'

'Then I'd say you saved the best for last. Am I right?' She could not conceal the silent alarm she felt. She looked away from him, at the light coming through the balcony doors. It was brighter now, that strange admixture of pastel yellow and hot orange that is peculiar to the Jamaican dawn.

'You know it concerns you . . .'

'Of course I know it. I knew it last night.' She returned her eyes to him. 'I didn't want to admit it to myself . . . but I knew it. It was all too tidy.'

'Chatellerault,' he said softly. 'He's here.'

'Oh, *God*,' she whispered.

'He can't touch you. Believe me.'

'He followed me. Oh my God . . .'

McAuliff got up and crossed to the bed. He sat on the edge and gently stroked her hair. 'If I thought he could harm you, I never would have told you. I'd simply have him . . . removed.'

Oh, Christ, thought Alex. How easily the new words came. Would he soon be using *killed* or *eliminated*?

'Right from the very start, it was all programmed. *I* was programmed.' She stared at the balcony, allowing his hand to caress the side of her face, as if oblivious to it. 'I should have realized; they don't let you go that easily.'

'Who?'

'All of them, my darling,' she answered, taking his hand, holding it to her lips. 'Whatever names you want to give them, it's not important. The letters, the numbers, the official-sounding nonsense . . . I was warned, I can't say I wasn't.'

'How?' He pulled her hand down, forcing her to look at him. 'How were you warned? Who warned you?'

'In Paris one night. Barely three months ago. I'd finished the last of my interviews at the . . . underground carnival, we called it.'

'Interpol?'

'Yes. I met a chap and his wife. In a waiting room, actually. It's not supposed to happen; isolation is terribly important, but someone got their rooms mixed up . . . They were English. We agreed to have a late supper together . . . He was a Porsche dealer from Macclesfield. He and his wife were at the end of their tethers. He'd been recruited because his dealership – the cars, you see – were being used to transport stolen stock certificates from European exchanges. Every time he thought he was finished, they found reasons for him to continue – more often than not, without telling him. It was almost three years; he was about out of his mind. They were going to leave England. Go to Buenos Aires.'

'He could always say no. They couldn't force him.'

'Don't be naive, darling. Every name you learn is another hook, each new method of operation you report is an additional notch in your expertise.' Alison laughed sadly. 'You've travelled to the land of the informer. You've got a stigmata all your own.'

'I'll tell you again: Chatellerault can't touch you.'

She paused before acknowledging his words, his anxiety. 'This may sound strange to you, Alex. I mean, I'm not a brave person – no brimfuls of courage for me – but I have no great fear of him. The appalling thing ... the fear, is *them*. They wouldn't let me go. No matter the promises, the agreements, the guarantees. They couldn't resist. A file somewhere, or a computer, was activated and came up with *his* name; automatically mine appeared in a data bank. That was it: factor X plus factor Y, subtotal – your life is not your own. It never stops. You live with the fear all over again.'

Alex took her by the shoulders. 'There's no law, Alison. We can pack; we can leave.'

'My darling, my darling ... You *can't*. Don't you see? Not that way. It's what's behind you: the agreements, the countless files filled with words, your words ... you can't deny them. You cross borders, you need papers; you work, you need references. You drive a car or take a plane or put money in a bank ... They have all the weapons. You can't hide. Not from them.'

McAuliff let go of her and stood up. He picked up the smooth, shiny cylinder of gas from the bedside table and looked at the printing and the inked date of issue. He walked aimlessly to the balcony doors and instinctively breathed deeply; there was the faint, very faint, aroma of vanilla with the slightest trace of a spice.

Bay rum and vanilla.

Jamaica.

'You're wrong, Alison. We don't have to hide. For a lot of reasons, we have to finish what we've started; you're right about that. But you're wrong about the conclusion. It does stop. It will stop.' He turned back to her. 'Take my word for it.'

'I'd like to. I really would. I don't see how.'

'An old infantry game. Do unto others before they can do unto you. The Hammonds and the Interpols of this world use us because we're afraid. We know what they can do to what we think are our well-ordered lives. That's legitimate; they're

187

bastards. And they'll admit it . . . But have you ever thought about the magnitude of disaster we can cause *them*? That's also legitimate, because we can be bastards, too. We'll play this out – with armed guards on all our flanks. And when we're finished, we'll *be* finished. With them.'

Charles Whitehall sat in the chair, the tiny glass of Pernod on the table beside him. It was six o'clock in the morning; he had not been to bed. There was no point in trying to sleep; sleep would not come.

Two days on the island and the sores of a decade ago were disturbed. He had not expected it; he had expected to control everything. Not *be* controlled.

His enemy now was not the enemy – enemies – he had waited ten years to fight: the rulers in Kingston; worse, perhaps, the radicals like Barak Moore. It was a new enemy, every bit as despicable, and infinitely more powerful, because it had the means to control his beloved Jamaica.

Control by corruption; ultimately own . . . by possession.

He had lied to Alexander McAuliff. In Savanna-la-Mar, Chatellerault openly admitted that he was part of the Trelawny Parish conspiracy. British Intelligence was right. The marquis's wealth was intrinsic to the development of the raw acreage on the north coast and in the Cock Pit, and he intended to see that his investment was protected. Charles Whitehall was his first line of protection, and if Charles Whitehall failed, he would be destroyed. It was as simple as that. Chatellerault was not the least obscure about it. He had sat opposite him and smiled his thin Gallic smile and recited the facts . . . and names . . . of the covert network Whitehall had developed on the island over the past decade.

He had capped his narrative with the most damaging information of all: the timetable and the methods Charles and his political party expected to follow on their road to power in Kingston.

The establishment of a military dictatorship with one non-military leader to whom all were subservient – the Praetorian of Jamaica was the title, Charles Whitehall the man.

If Kingston knew these things . . . well, Kingston would react.

But Chatellerault made it clear that their individual objectives were not necessarily in conflict. There were areas – philosophical, political, financial – in which their interests might easily be merged. But first came the activity on the north coast. That was immediate; it was the springboard to everything else.

The marquis did not name his partners – Whitehall got the distinct impression that Chatellerault was not entirely sure who they all were – but it was manifestly clear that he did not trust them. On one level he seemed to question motives, on another it was a matter of abilities. He spoke briefly about previous interference and/or bungling, but did not dwell on the facts.

The facts obviously concerned the first survey.

What had happened?

Was the Halidon responsible?

Was the Halidon *capable* of interference?

Did the Halidon really exist?

The Halidon.

He would have to analyse the anthropologist Piersall's papers; separate a foreigner's exotic fantasies from island reality. There was a time, ten years ago, when the Rastafarians were symbols of African terror, before they were revealed to be children stoned on grass with mud-caked hair and a collective desire to avoid work. And there were the Pocomanians, with their bearded high priests inserting the sexual orgy into the abstract generosities of the Christian ethic: a socio-religious excuse for promiscuity. Or the Anansi sects – inheritors of the long-forgotten Ashanti belief in the cunning of the spider, on which all progress in life was patterned.

There were so many. So often metaphysically paranoid; so fragmented, so obscure.

Was the Halidon – Hollydawn – any different?

At this juncture, for Charles Whitehall it didn't really matter. What mattered was his own survival and the survival of his

189

plans. His aims would be accomplished by keeping Chatellerault at bay and infiltrating the structure of Chatellerault's financial hierarchy.

And working with his first enemy, Barak Moore.

Working with both enemies.

Jamaica's enemies.

James Ferguson fumbled for the light switch on the bedside lamp. His thrusts caused an ashtray and a glass to collide, sending both crashing to the floor. Light was coming through the drawn curtains: he was conscious of it in spite of the terrible pain in his eyes and through his head, from temple to temple. Pain that caused flashes of darkness to envelop his inner eye. He looked at his watch as he shaded his face from the dim spill of the lamp. It was 6:15.

Oh, Christ! His head hurt so, tears welled in the far corners of his eyes. Shafts of pain – sharp, immobilizing – shot down into his neck and seemed to constrict his shoulders, even his arms. His stomach was in a state of tense, muscular suspension; if he thought about it, he knew he would be sick and vomit.

There was no pretence regarding the amount of alcohol he had consumed last night. McAuliff could not accuse him of play-acting now. He had got drunk. Very drunk. And with damn good reason.

He had been elated.

Arthur Craft had telephoned him in panic. In *panic*!

Craft the Younger had been caught. McAuliff had found the room where the taping was being done and beaten someone up, *physically beaten* him *up*! Craft had yelled over the telephone, demanding where McAuliff had got his name.

Not from him! Certainly not from Jimbo-mon. He had said nothing.

Craft had roared, swearing at the 'goddamned nigger on the tape machine', convinced the 'black fucker' had confessed to McAuliff, adding that the bastard would never get near a courtroom. 'If it came to that.'

If it came to that.

'You never *saw* me,' Craft the Younger had screamed. 'We never talked! We didn't meet! You get that absolutely clear, you shaky son of a bitch!'

'Of course . . . of course, Mr Craft,' he had replied. 'But then, sir . . . we *did* talk, didn't we? This doesn't have to change anything.'

He had been petrified, but he had said the words. Quietly, with no great emphasis. But his message had been clear.

Arthur Craft, Junior, was in an awkward position. Craft the Younger should not be yelling; he should be polite. Perhaps even solicitous.

After all, they *had* talked . . .

Craft understood. The understanding was first indicated by his silence, then confirmed by his next statement.

'We'll be in touch.'

It had been so simple. And if Craft the Younger wanted it different, wanted things as they were not, well, Craft controlled an enormously wealthy foundation. Certainly he could find something for a very, *very* talented botanist.

When he hung up the telephone last night, James had felt a wave of calm come over him. The sort of quiet confidence he experienced in a laboratory, where his eye and mind were very sure indeed.

He would have to be cautious, but he could do it.

He had got drunk when he realized that.

And now his head and stomach were in pain. But he could stand them; they were bearable now. Things were going to be different.

He looked at his watch. His goddamn Timex. It was 6:25. A cheap watch, but accurate.

Instead of a Timex there might be a Breitling Chronometer in his future. And new, very expensive camera equipment. And a real bank balance.

And a new life.

If he was cautious.

*   *   *

The telephone rang on Peter Jensen's side of the bed, but his wife heard it first.

'Peter ... Peter! For heaven's sake, the *phone*.'

'What? ... What, old girl?' Peter Jensen blinked his eyes; the room was dark, but there was daylight beyond the drawn curtains.

The telephone rang again. Short bursts of bell; the kind of rapid blasts hotel switchboards practise. Nimble fingers, irritated guests.

Peter Jensen reached over and switched on the light. The travelling clock read ten minutes to eight. Again the shrill bell, now steady.

'Damn!' sputtered Peter as he realized the instrument was beyond the lamp, requiring him to reach farther. 'Yes, *yes*? Hello?'

'Mr Peter Jensen, please?' said the unfamiliar male voice.

'Yes. What is it? This is Jensen.'

'Cable-International, Mr Jensen. A wire arrived for you several minutes ago. From London. Shall I read it? It's marked urgent, sir.'

'No!' replied Peter quickly, firmly. 'No, don't do that. I've been expecting it; it's rather long, I should think.'

'Yes, sir, it is.'

'Just send it over right away, if you please. Can you do that? The Courtleigh Manor. Room 401. It won't be necessary to stop at the desk.'

'I understand, Mr Jensen. Right away. There'll be a charge for an unscheduled –'

'Of course, of course,' interrupted Peter. 'Just send it over, please.'

'Yes, sir.'

Twenty-five minutes later, the messenger from Cable-International arrived. Moments before, room service had wheeled in a breakfast of melon, tea, and scones. Peter Jensen opened the two-page cablegram and spread it out over the linen cloth on his side of the table. There was a pencil in his hand.

Across from him, Ruth held up a page of paper, scanning it over the rim of her cup. She, too, had a pencil, at the side of the saucer.

'The company name is "Parkhurst",' said Peter.

'Check,' said Ruth, putting down her tea. She placed the paper alongside, picked up the pencil, and made a mark on the page.

'The address is "Sheffield by the Glen".' Peter looked over at her.

'Go ahead,' replied Ruth, making a second notation.

'The equipment to be inspected is microscopes.'

'Very well.' Ruth made a third mark on the left of the page, went back to her previous notes, and then darted her eyes to the bottom right. 'Are you ready?'

'Yes.'

Ruth Wells Jensen, palaeontologist, proceeded to recite a series of numbers. Her husband started at the top of the body of the cablegram and began circling words with his pencil. Several times he asked his wife to repeat a number. As she did so, he counted from the previous circle and circled another word.

Three minutes later, they had finished the exercise. Peter Jensen swallowed some tea and reread the cablegram to himself. His wife spread jam on two scones and covered the teapot with the cosy.

'Warfield is flying over next week. He agrees. McAuliff has been reached.'

THREE

The North Coast

17

Hammond's words kept coming back to McAuliff: *You'll find it quite acceptable to operate on different levels. Actually, it evolves rather naturally, even instinctively. You'll discover that you tend to separate your concentrations.*

The British Intelligence agent had been right. The survey was in its ninth day, and Alex found that for hours at a time he had no other thoughts but the immediate work at hand.

The equipment had been trucked from Boscobel Airfield straight through to Puerto Seco, on Discovery Bay. Alex, Sam Tucker and Alison Booth flew into Ocho Rios ahead of the others and allowed themselves three days of luxury at the Sans Souci while McAuliff ostensibly hired a crew – two of the five of which had been agreed upon in an isolated farmhouse high in the hills of the Blue Mountains. Alex found – as he'd expected – that Sam and Alison got along extremely well. Neither was difficult to like; each possessed an easy humour; both were professionals. And there was no reason to conceal from Sam the fact that they were lovers. As Tucker phrased it: 'I'd be shocked if you weren't, Alexander.'

Sam's approval was important to McAuliff. For at no time was Alison to be left alone when he was away. Under no circumstances. Ever.

Sam Tucker was the ideal protective escort. Far superior to himself, Alex realized. Tuck was the most resourceful man he had ever known, and just about the hardest. He had within him an aggressiveness that when called upon was savage. He was not a man to have as an enemy. Alison was as safe as a human being could be in his care.

197

The fourth day had been the first day of the survey work. The team was housed halfway between Puerto Seco and Rio Bueno Harbour, in a pleasant beach motel called Bengal Court. Work began shortly after six in the morning. The initial objective of the survey was to plot the coastline definitively. Alex and Sam Tucker operated the equipment.

Azimuths were shot along the shoreline, recorded by transit cameras. The angular degree demarcations were correlated with the coastal charts provided by the Jamaican Institute. By and large, these charts were sectional and imperfect, acceptable for the details of road maps and small-craft navigation, but inadequate for geophysical purposes. To set up accurate perimeters, McAuliff employed sonic geodometers which bounced sound waves back and forth between instruments, giving what amounted to perfect bearings. Each contour, each elevation was recorded on both sonic graphs and transit cameras.

These chores were dull, laborious, and sweat-provoking under the hot sun. The single relief was the constant presence of Alison, much as she herself objected to it. Alex was adamant, however. He instructed Barak Moore's two men to stay within a hundred feet of her at all times, and then commanded Alison not to stroll out of his sight.

It was an impossible demand, and McAuliff realized he could not prolong it more than a few days. Alison had work to do; minor over the coastal area, a great deal once they started inland. But all beginnings were awkward under pressure; he could not separate this particular concentration that easily, nor did he wish to.

Very rapidly your own personal antennae will be activated automatically. Their function will be second nature, as it were. You will fall into a rhythm, actually. It is the connecting link between your divided objectives. You will recognize it and build a degree of confidence in the process.

Hammond.

But not during the first few days; there was no confidence to speak of. He did grant, however, that the fear was lessening . . .

partially, imperceptibly. He thought this was due to the constant physical activity and the fact that he *could* require such men as Sam and Barak Moore's 'special forces' to take up posts around Alison. And at any given moment he could turn his head and there she was – on the beach, in a small boat – chipping rocks, instructing one of the crew in the manipulation of a drill bore.

But, again, were not all these his antennae? And was not the lessening of fear the beginnings of confidence? *R. C. Hammond. Supercilious son of a bitch. Manipulator. Speaker of truths.*

But not the whole truth.

The areas bordering Braco beach were hazardous. Sheets of coral overlay extended hundreds of yards out into the surf. McAuliff and Sam Tucker crawled over the razor-sharp minia-ture hills of ocean polyps and set up their geodometers and cameras. Both men incurred scores of minor cuts, sore muscles, and sorer backs.

That was the third day, marked by the special relief of Alison's somehow commandeering a fisherman's flat-bottom boat and, with her two 'escorts', bringing a picnic lunch of cold chicken out to the reef. It was a comfortable hour on the most uncom-fortable picnic ground imaginable.

The black revolutionary, Floyd, who had guided the boat into its precarious coral mooring, succinctly observed that the beach was flatter and far less wet.

'But then they'd have to crawl all the way out here again,' Alison had replied, holding onto her wide-brimmed cloth sun hat.

'Mon, you have a good woman!' This observation came from Floyd's companion, the huge, quiet Jamaican named Lawrence.

The five of them perched – there was no other description – on the highest ridges of the coral jetty, the spray cascading up from the base of the reef, creating faint rainbow prisms of colour in its mist. Far out on the water two freighters were passing each other, one heading for the open sea, the second aiming for the bauxite docks east of Runaway Bay. A luxurious cabin cruiser rigged for deep-sea fishing sliced through the swell several hundred yards in front of them, the passengers pointing in astonishment at the strange sight of five humans picnicking on a reef.

McAuliff watched the others respond to the cruiser's surprised riders. Sam Tucker stood up, gestured at the coral, and yelled, 'Diamonds!'

Floyd and Lawrence, their black, muscular bodies bared to the waist, roared at Sam's antics. Lawrence pried loose a coral stone and held it up, then chucked it to Tucker, who caught it and shouted again. 'Twenty carats!'

Alison, her blue jeans and light field blouse drenched with the spray, joined in the foolish game. She elaborately accepted the coral stone, presented by Sam, and held it on top of her outstretched hand as though it were a jewelled ring of great value. A short burst of breeze whipped across the reef; Alison dropped the stone in an effort to hold her hat, whose brim had caught the wind. She was not successful; the hat glided off and disappeared over a small mound of coral. Before Alex could rise and go after it, Lawrence was on his feet, dashing sure-footedly over the rocks and down towards the water. Within seconds he had the hat, now soaked, and effortlessly leaped back up from the water's edge and handed it to Alison.

The incident had taken less than ten seconds.

'You keep the hat on the head, Miss *Aleesawn*. Them sun very hot; roast skin like cooked chicken, mon.'

'Thank you, Lawrence,' said Alison gratefully, securing the wet hat over her head. 'You run across this reef as though it were a golf green!'

'Lawrence is a fine caddy, Miss Alison,' said Floyd smiling, still sitting. 'At the Negril Golf Club he is a favourite, is that not so, Lawrence?'

Lawrence grinned and glanced at McAuliff knowingly. 'Eh, mon. At Negril they alla time ask for me. I cheat good, mon. Alla time I move them golf balls out of bad places to the smooth grass. I think everybody know. Alla time ask for Lawrence.'

Sam Tucker chuckled as he sat down again. 'Alla time big goddamn tips, I'd say.'

'Plenty good tips, mon,' agreed Lawrence.

'And probably something more,' added McAuliff, looking at Floyd and remembering the exclusive reputation of the Negril Golf Club. 'Alla time plenty of information.'

'Yes, mon.' Floyd smiled conspiratorially. 'It is as they say: The rich Westmorelanders talk a great deal during their games of golf.'

Alex fell silent. It seemed strange, the whole scene. Here they were, the five of them, eating cold chicken on a coral reef three hundred yards from shore, playing children's games with passing cabin cruisers and joking casually about the surreptitious gathering of information on a golf course.

Two black revolutionaries – recruits from a band of hill country guerrillas. A late middle-aged 'soldier of fortune'. (Sam Tucker would object to the cliché, but if it was ever applicable, he was the applicant.) A strikingly handsome . . . lovely English divorcée whose background just happened to include undercover work for an international police organization. And one thirty-eight-year-old ex-infantry man who six weeks ago flew to London thinking he was going to negotiate a geological survey contract.

The five of them. Each knowing that he was not what he appeared to be; each doing what he was doing . . . she was doing . . . because there were no alternatives. Not really.

It wasn't strange; it was insane. And it struck McAuliff once again that he was the least qualified among these people, under these circumstances. Yet because of the circumstances – having nothing to do with qualifications – he was their leader.

Insanity.

By the seventh day, working long hours with few breaks, Alex and Sam had charted the coastline as far as Burwood, five miles from the mouth of the Martha Brae, their western perimeter. The Jensens and James Ferguson kept a leisurely parallel pace, setting up tables with microscopes, burners, vials, scales and chemicals as they went about their work. None found anything exceptional, nor did they expect to in the coastal regions. The areas had been studied fairly extensively for industrial and resort purposes; there was nothing of consequence not previously recorded. And since Ferguson's botanical analyses were closely allied with Sam Tucker's soil evaluations, Ferguson volunteered to make the soil tests, freeing Tucker to finish the topographics with Alex.

These were the geophysical concerns. There was something else, and none could explain it. It was first reported by the Jensens.

A sound. Only a sound. A low wail or cry that seemed to follow them throughout an entire afternoon.

When they first heard it, it came from the underbrush beyond the dunes. They thought that perhaps it was an animal in pain. Or a small child in some horrible anguish, an agony that went beyond a child's tears. In a very real sense, it was terrifying.

So the Jensens raced beyond the dunes into the underbrush, thrashing at the tangled foliage to find the source of the dreadful, frightening cry.

They had found nothing.

The animal, or the child, or whatever it was, had fled.

Shortly thereafter – late in the same afternoon – James Ferguson came running down to the beach, his face an expression of bewildered panic. He had been tracing a giant mollusc fern to its root source; the trek had taken him up into a rocky precipice above the shore. He had been in the centre of the overhanging vines and macca-fats when a vibration – at first a vibration – caused his whole body to tremble. There followed a wild, piercing screech, both high-pitched yet full, that pained his ears beyond – he said – endurance.

He had gripped the vines to keep from plummeting off the precipice.

Terrified, he had scrambled down hysterically to firmer ground and raced back to the others.

James had not been more than a few hundred yards away.

Yet none but he had heard the terrible thing.

Whitehall had another version of the madness. The black scholar had been walking along the shoreline, half sand, half forest, of Bengal Bay. It was an aimless morning constitutional; he had no destination other than the point, perhaps.

About a mile east of the motel's beach, he rested briefly on a large rock overlooking the water. He heard a noise from behind, and so he turned, expecting to see a bird or a mongoose fluttering or scampering in the woods.

There was nothing.

He turned back to the lapping water beneath him, when suddenly there was an explosion of sound – substained, hollow-like, a dissonant cacophony of wind. And then it stopped.

Whitehall had gripped the rock and stared into the forest. At nothing, aware only that he was afflicted with a terrible pain in his temples.

But Charles was a scholar, and a scholar was a sceptic. He had concluded that, somewhere in the forest, an enormous unseen tree had collapsed from the natural weight of ages. In its death fall, the tons of ripping, scraping wood-against-wood within the huge trunk had caused the phenomenon.

And none was convinced.

As Whitehall told his story, McAuliff watched him. He did not think Charles believed it himself. Things not explicable had occurred, and they were all – if nothing else – scientists of the physical. The explainable. Perhaps they all took comfort in Whitehall's theory of sonics. Alexander thought so; they could not dwell on it. There was work to do.

Divided objectives.

Alison thought she had found something, and with Floyd's and Lawrence's help she made a series of deep bores arcing the beaches and coral jetties. Her samplings showed that there were strata of soft lignite interspersed throughout the limestone beds on the ocean floor. Geologically it was easily explained: Hundreds of thousands of years ago, volcanic disturbances swallowed

203

whole land masses of wood and pulp. Regardless of explanations, however, if there were plans to sink pilings for piers or even extended docks, the construction firms were going to have to add to their base supports.

Alison's concentrations were a relief to McAuliff. She was absorbed, and so complained less about his restrictions, and, more important, he was able to observe Floyd and Lawrence as they went about the business of watching over her. The two blacks were extremely thorough. And gracefully subtle. Whenever Alison wandered along the beach or up into the shore grass, one or both had her flanked or preceded or followed. They were like stalking panthers prepared to spring, yet they did not in their tracking call attention to themselves. They seemed to become natural appendages, always carrying something – binoculars, sampling boxes, clipboards . . . whatever was handy – to divert any zeroing in on their real function.

And during the nights, McAuliff found a protective bonus he had neither asked for nor expected: Floyd and Lawrence alternated patrols around the lawns and in the corridors of the Bengal Court motel. Alex discovered this on the night of the eighth day, when he got up at four in the morning to get himself a plastic bucket of ice from the machine down the hall. He wanted ice water.

As he turned the corner into the outside alcove where the machine was situated, he was suddenly aware of a figure behind the latticework that fronted the lawn. The figure had moved quickly; there had been no sound of footsteps.

McAuliff rapidly scooped the cubes into the small bucket, closed the metal door, and walked back around the corner into the hallway. The instant he was out of sight, he silently placed the ice at his feet and pressed his back against the wall's edge.

There was movement.

McAuliff whipped around the corner, with every intention of hurling himself at whoever came into view. His fists were clenched, his spring accurate; he lunged into the figure of Lawrence. It was too late to regain his footing.

'Eh, *mon*!' cried the black softly as he recoiled and fell back under Alex's weight. Both men rolled out of the alcove onto the lawn.

'Christ!' whispered McAuliff, next to Lawrence on the ground. 'What the hell are you doing here?'

Lawrence smiled in the darkness; he shook his hand, which had been pinned by Alex under his back. 'You're a big fella, mon! You pretty quick, too.'

'I was pretty damned excited ... What *are* you doing out here?'

Lawrence explained briefly, apologetically. He and Floyd had made an arrangement with the night watchman, an old fisherman who prowled around at night with a shotgun neither guerrilla believed he knew how to use. Barak Moore had ordered them to stand evening patrols; they would have done so whether commanded to or not, said Lawrence.

'When do you sleep?'

'Sleep *good*, mon,' replied Lawrence. 'We take turns alla time.'

Alex returned to his room. Alison sat up in bed when he closed the door.

'Is everything all right?' she asked apprehensively.

'Better than I expected. We've got our own miniature army. We're fine.'

On the afternoon of the ninth day, McAuliff and Tucker reached the Martha Brae River. The geodometer charts and transit photographs were sealed hermetically and stored in the cool vaults of the equipment truck. Peter Jensen gave his summary of the coastal ore and mineral deposits; his wife, Ruth, had found traces of plant fossils embedded in the coral, but her findings were of little value, and James Ferguson, covering double duty in soil and flora, presented his unstartling analyses. Only Alison's discovery of the lignite strata was unexpected.

All reports were to be driven into Ocho Rios for duplication. McAuliff said he would do this himself; it had been a difficult nine days, and the tenth was a day off. Those who wanted to go into Ochee could come with him; the others could go to

Montego or laze around the Bengal Court beach, as they preferred. The survey would resume on the morning of the eleventh day.

They made their respective plans on the river bank, with the inevitable picnic lunches put up by the motel. Only Charles Whitehall, who had done little *but* lie around the beach, knew precisely what he wanted to do, and he could not state it publicly. He spoke to Alex alone.

'I really *must* see Piersall's papers. Quite honestly, McAuliff, it's been driving me crazy.'

'We wait for Moore. We agreed to that.'

'When? For heaven's sake, when will he show up? It will be ten days tomorrow; he said ten days.'

'There were no guarantees. I'm as anxious as you. There's an oilcloth packet buried somewhere on his property, remember?'

'I haven't forgotten for an instant.'

Separation of concentrations; divided objectives.

Hammond.

Charles Whitehall was as concerned academically as he was conspiratorially. Perhaps more so, thought Alex. The black scholar's curiosity was rooted in a lifetime of research.

The Jensens remained at Bengal Court. Ferguson requested an advance from McAuliff and hired a taxi to drive him into Montego Bay. McAuliff, Sam Tucker and Alison Booth drove the truck to Ocho Rios. Charles Whitehall followed in an old station wagon with Floyd and Lawrence: the guerrillas insisted that the arrangements be thus.

Barak Moore lay in the tall grass, binoculars to his eyes. It was sundown: rays of orange and yellow light filtered through the green trees above him and bounced off the white stone of Walter Piersall's house, four hundred yards away. Through the grass he saw the figures of the Trelawny Parish police circling the house, checking the windows and the doors; they would leave at least one man on watch. As usual.

The police had finished the day's investigation, the longest

206

investigation, thought Barak, in the history of the parish. They had been at it nearly two weeks. Teams of civilians had come up from Kingston: men in pressed clothes, which meant they were more than police.

They would find nothing, of that Barak Moore was certain. If Walter Piersall had accurately described his caches.

And Barak could not wait any longer. It would be a simple matter to retrieve the oilcloth packet – he was within a hundred and fifty yards of it at the moment – but it was not that simple. He needed Charles Whitehall's total cooperation – more than Whitehall realized – and that meant he had to get inside Piersall's house and bring out the rest of Piersall's legacy. The anthropologist's papers.

The papers. They were cemented in the wall of an old, unused cistern in Piersall's basement.

Walter Piersall had carefully removed several cistern blocks, dug recesses in the earth beyond and replaced the stones. It was in one of these recesses that he had buried his studies of the Halidon.

Charles Whitehall would not help unless he saw those papers. Barak needed Charley-mon's help.

The Trelawny police got into their vehicles; a single uniformed guard waved as the patrol cars started down the road.

He, Barak, the people's revolutionary, had to work with Whitehall, the political criminal. Their own war – perhaps a civil war – would come later, as it had in so many new lands.

First, there was the white man. And his money and his companies and his unending thirst for the sweat of the black man. That was first, very much first, mon!

Barak's thoughts had caused him to stare blindly into the binoculars. The guard was nowhere in sight now. Moore scanned the area, refocusing the Zeiss Ikon lenses as he covered the sides and the sloping back lawn of Piersall's house. It was a comfortable white man's home, thought Barak.

It was on top of a hill, the entrance road a long climb from

George's Valley to the west and the Martha Brae to the east. Mango trees, palms, hibiscus and orchids lined the entrance and surrounded the one-and-a-half-storeyed white stone structure. The house was long, most of the wide, spacious rooms on the first floor. There was black iron grillwork everywhere, across the windows and over the door entrances. The only glass was in the first-floor bedrooms; all the windows had teak shutters.

The rear of High Hill, as the house was called, was the most striking. To the east of the old pasture of high grass, where Barak lay, the gently sloping back lawn had been carved out of the forests and the fields, seeded with a Caribbean fescue that was as smooth as a golf course; the rocks, painted a shiny white, gave the appearance of whitecaps in a green sea.

In the centre of the area was a medium-sized pool, installed by Piersall, with blue and white tiles that reflected the sun as sharply as the blue-green water in it. Around the pool and spreading out over the grass were tables and chairs – white wrought iron – delicate in appearance, sturdy in design.

The guard came into view again, and Moore caught his breath, as much in astonishment as in anger. The guard was playing with a dog, a vicious-looking Doberman. There had been no dogs before. It was a bad thing, thought Barak . . . yet, perhaps, not so bad. The presence of the dog probably meant that this policeman would stay alone at his post longer than the normal time span. It was a police custom to leave dogs with men for two reasons: because the district they patrolled was dangerous, or because the men would remain for a relatively long time at their watches. Dogs served several purposes; they were alarms, they protected, and they helped pass the hours.

The guard threw a stick; the Doberman raced beyond the pool, nearly crashing into a wrought-iron table, and snatched it up in his mouth. Before the dog could bring it back the policeman threw another stick, bewildering the Doberman, who dropped the first retrieval and went after the second.

He is a stupid man, thought Barak, watching the laughing

guard. He did not know animals, and a man who did not know animals was a man who could be trapped.

He would be trapped tonight.

18

It was a clear night. The Jamaican moon – three-quarters of it – shone brightly between the high banks of the river. They had poled a stolen bamboo raft down the rushing waters of the Martha Brae until they had reached the point of shortest distance to the house in Carrick Foyle. They manoeuvred the raft into a pitch-black recess and pulled it out of the water, hiding it under cascading umbrellas of full-leaved mangroves and maiden palms.

They were the raiding party: Barak, Alex, Floyd and White-hall. Sam Tucker and Lawrence had stayed at Bengal Court to protect Alison.

They crept up the slope through the dense, ensnaring foliage. The slope was steep, the travelling slow and painfully difficult. The distance to the High Hill property was no more than a mile – perhaps a mile and a quarter – but it took the four of them nearly an hour to reach it. Charles Whitehall thought the route was foolish. If there was one guard and one dog, why not drive to the road below the winding, half-mile entrance and simply walk up to the outer gates?

Barak's reasoning held more sophistication than Whitehall conceded to the Trelawny police. Moore thought it possible that the parish authorities had set up electronic tripwires along the entrance drive. Barak knew that such instruments had been in use in Montego Bay, Kingston and Port Antonio hotels for months. They could not take the chance of setting one off.

Breathing heavily, they stood at the southern border of Piersall's sloping lawn and looked up at the house called High

Hill. The moon's illumination on the white stone made the house stand out like an alabaster monument, still, peaceful, graceful and solid. Light spilled out of the teak shutters in two areas of the house: the downstairs back room opening onto the lawn and the centre bedroom on the first floor. All else was in darkness.

Except the underwater spotlights in the pool. A slight breeze caused ripples on the water; the bluish light danced from underneath.

'We must draw him out,' said Barak. 'Him and the dog, mon.'

'Why? What's the point?' asked McAuliff, the sweat from the climb rolling down into his eyes. 'He's one, we're four.'

'Moore is right,' answered Charles Whitehall. 'If there are electronic devices outside, then certainly he has the equivalent within.'

'He would have a police radio, at any rate, mon,' interjected Floyd. 'I know those doors; by the time we broke one down, he would have time – easy to reach others.'

'It's a half hour from Falmouth; the police are in Falmouth,' pressed Alex. 'We'd be in and out by then.'

'Not so, mon,' argued Barak. 'It will take us a while to select and pry loose the cistern stones . . . We'll dig up the oilcloth packet first. Come!'

Barak Moore led them around the edge of wooded property, to the opposite side, into the old grazing field. He shielded the glass of his flashlight with his fingers and raced to a cluster of breadfruit trees at the northern end of the rock-strewn pasture. He crouched at the trunk of the farthest tree; the others did the same. Barak spoke – whispered.

'Talk quietly. These hill winds carry voices. The packet is buried in the earth forty-four paces to the right of the fourth large rock on a north-west diagonal from this tree.'

'He was a man who knew Jamaica,' said Whitehall softly.

'How do you mean?' McAuliff saw the grim smile on the scholar's face in the moonlight.

'The Arawak symbols for a warrior's death march were in units of four, always to the right of the setting sun.'

'That's not very comforting,' said Alex.

'Like your American Indians,' replied Whitehall, 'the Arawaks were not comforted by the white man.'

'Neither were the Africans, Charley-mon.' Barak locked eyes with Whitehall in the moonlight. 'Sometimes I think you forget that.' He addressed McAuliff and Floyd. 'Follow me. In a line.'

They ran in crouched positions through the tall grass behind the black revolutionary, each man slapping a large prominent rock as he came upon it. One, two, three, four.

At the fourth rock, roughly a hundred and fifty yards from the base of the breadfruit tree, they knelt around the stone. Barak cupped his flashlight and shone it on the top. There was a chiselled marking, barely visible. Whitehall bent over it.

'Your Dr Piersall had a progressive imagination; progressive in the historical sense. He's jumped from Arawak to Coromantee. See?' Whitehall traced his index finger over the marking under the beam of the flashlight and continued softly. 'This twisted crescent is an Ashanti moon the Coromantees used to leave as a trail for members of the tribe perhaps two or three days behind in a hunt. The chips on the convex side of the crescent determine the direction: one – to the left; two – to the right. Their placement on the rim shows the angle. Here: two chips, dead centre; therefore, directly to the right of the stone facing the base of the crescent.' Whitehall gestured with his right hand north-east.

'As Piersall instructed.' Barak nodded his head: he did not bother to conceal his pique at Charley-mon's explanation. Yet there was respect in that pique, thought McAuliff, as he watched Moore begin pacing off the forty-four steps.

Piersall had disguised the spot chosen for burial. There was a thicket of mollusc ferns spreading out in a free-form spray within the paced-off area of the grass. They had been rerooted expertly; it was illogical to assume any sort of digging had taken place there in years.

Floyd took a knapsack shovel from his belt, unfolded the stem, and began removing the earth. Charles Whitehall bent down on his knees and joined the revolutionary, clawing at the dirt with his bare hands.

The rectangular black box was deep in the ground. Had not the instructions been so precise, the digging might have stopped before reaching it. The depth was over three feet. Whitehall suspected it was exactly four feet when deposited. The Arawak unit of four.

The instant Floyd's small shovel struck the metal casing, Whitehall lashed his right hand down, snatched the box out of the earth, and fingered the edges, trying to pry it apart. It was not possible, and Whitehall realized it within seconds. He had used this type of receptacle perhaps a thousand times: It was a hermetically sealed archive case whose soft, rubberized edges created a vacuum within. It had two locks, one at each end, with separate keys; once the keys were inserted and turned, air was allowed in, and after a period of minutes the box could be forced open. It was the sort of repository used in the most heavily endowed libraries to house old manuscripts, manuscripts that were studied by scholars no more than once every five years or so and thus preserved with great care. The name 'archive case' was well suited for documents in archives for a millennium.

'Give me the keys!' whispered Charles urgently to Barak.

'I have no keys, mon. Piersall said nothing about keys.'

'*Damn!*'

'Keep quiet!' ordered McAuliff.

'Put that dirt back,' said Moore to Floyd. 'So it is not so obvious, mon. Push back the ferns.'

Floyd did as he was told; McAuliff helped him. Whitehall stared at the rectangular box in his hands; he was furious.

'He was paranoid!' whispered the scholar, turning to Barak. 'You said it was a packet. An oilcloth packet! Not this. This will take a blowtorch to open!'

'Charley's got a point,' said Alex, shovelling in dirt with his hands, realizing that he had just called Whitehall 'Charley'.

'Why did he go to this trouble? Why didn't he just put the box with the rest of the papers in the cistern?'

'You ask questions I cannot answer, mon. He was very concerned, that's all I can tell you.'

The dirt was back in the hole. Floyd smoothed out the surface and pushed the roots of the mollusc ferns into the soft earth. 'That will do, I think, mon,' he said, folding the stem of the shovel and replacing it in his belt.

'How are we going to get inside?' asked McAuliff. 'Or get the guard outside?'

'I have thought of this for several hours,' replied Barak. 'Wild pigs, I think.'

'Very *good*, mon!' interrupted Floyd.

'In the pool?' added Whitehall knowingly.

'Yes.'

'What the hell are you talking about?' Alex watched the faces of the three blacks in the moonlight.

Barak answered. 'In the Cock Pit there are many wild pigs. They are vicious and troublesome. We are perhaps ten miles from the Cock Pit's borders. It is not unusual for pigs to stray this far . . . Floyd and I will imitate the sounds. You and Charley-mon throw rocks into the pool.'

'What about the dog?' asked Whitehall. 'You'd better shoot it.'

'No shooting, mon! Gunfire would be heard for miles. I will take care of the dog.' Moore withdrew a small anaesthetizing dart gun from his pocket. 'Our arsenal contains many of these. Come.'

Five minutes later McAuliff thought he was part of some demonic children's charade. Barak and Floyd had crept to the edge of the tall grass bordering the elegant lawn. On the assumption that the Doberman would head directly to the first human smell, Alex and Whitehall were in parallel positions ten feet to the right of the revolutionaries, a pile of stones between them. They were to throw the rocks as accurately as possible into the lighted pool sixty feet away at the first sounds emanating from Moore and his comrade.

It began.

The shrieks intruded on the stillness of the night with terrible authenticity. They were the bellows of panicked beasts, shrill and somehow horrible.

'*Eeeowahhee . . . gnnrahha, gnnrahhaaa . . . eeaww, eeaww . . . eewahhee . . .*'

McAuliff and Whitehall lobbed rocks into the pool; the splashes were interspersed with the monstrous shrieks. A weird cacophony filled the air.

The shutters from the ground-floor room were thrown open. The guard could be seen behind the grillwork, a rifle in his hand.

Suddenly a stone hit Alex's cheek. The blow was gentle, not stunning. He whipped his head towards the direction of the throw. Floyd was waving his arm in the tall grass, commanding McAuliff to stop hurling the rocks. Alex grabbed Whitehall's hand. They stopped.

The shrieks then became louder, accompanied by blunt thuds of pounding earth. Alex could see Barak and Floyd in the moonlight. They were slapping the ground like crazed animals; the horrible noises coming from their shaking heads reached a crescendo.

Wild pigs fighting in the high grass.

The door of Piersall's house crashed open. The guard, rifle in hand, released the dog at his side. The animal lurched out onto the lawn and raced towards the hysterical sounds and all-too-human odours.

McAuliff knelt, hypnotized by what followed in the Jamaican moonlight. Barak and Floyd scrambled back into the field without raising their bodies above the grass and without diminishing the pitch of their animal screams. The Doberman streaked across the lawn and sprang headlong over the border of the field and into the tall grass.

The continuing shrieks and guttural roars were joined by the savage barking of the vicious dog. And, amid the terrible sounds, Alex could distinguish a series of spits; the dart gun was being fired repeatedly.

A yelping howl suddenly drowned out the man-made

bellowing; the guard ran to the edge of the lawn, his rifle raised to fire. And before McAuliff could absorb or understand the action, Charles Whitehall grabbed a handful of rocks and threw them towards the lighted pool. And then a second handful hard upon the first.

The guard spun around to the water; Whitehall slammed Alex out of the way, raced along the edge of the grass, and suddenly leaped out on the lawn at the black patrol.

McAuliff watched, stunned.

Whitehall, the elegant academic – the delicately boned Charley-mon – lashed his arm out into the base of the guard's neck, crashed his foot savagely into the man's midsection, and seized a wrist, twisting it violently so that the rifle flew out of the guard's hands; the man jerked off his feet, spun into the air, and whipped to the ground. As the guard vibrated off the grass, Whitehall took swift aim and crashed his heel into the man's skull below his forehead.

The body contorted, then lay still.

The shrieking stopped: all was silent.

It was over.

Barak and Floyd raced out from the high grass onto the lawn. Barak spoke. 'Thank you, Charley-mon. Indiscriminate gunfire might have found us.'

'It was necessary,' replied Whitehall simply. 'I must see those papers.'

'Then let us go,' said Barak Moore. 'Floyd, take this real pig inside; tie him up somewhere.'

'Don't waste time,' countered Whitehall, starting for the house, the receptacle under his arm. 'Just throw him into the grass. He's dead.'

Inside, Floyd led them to the cellar stairs and down into Piersall's basement. The cistern was in the west section, about six feet deep and five wide. The walls were dry; cobwebs laced the sides and the top. Barak brushed aside the filmy obstructions and lowered himself into the pit.

'How do you know which are the blocks?' asked Whitehall urgently, the black rectangular box clasped in his hand.

'There is a way; the doctor explained,' replied Moore, taking out a small box of safety matches. He struck one and started at the north centre line, revolving slowly clockwise, holding the lighted match against the cracks in the blocks on the lower half of the pit.

'Ground phosphorus,' stated Whitehall quietly. 'Packed into the concrete edges.'

'Yes, mon. Not much; enough to give a little flame, or a sputter, perhaps.'

'You're wasting time!' Whitehall spat out the words. 'Swing to your *left*, towards the north-west point! Not to your right.'

The three men looked abruptly at the scholar. '*What*, Charley-mon?' Barak was bewildered.

'Do as I say! . . . Please.'

'The Arawak symbols?' asked McAuliff. 'The . . . odyssey to death, or whatever you called it? To the right of the setting sun?'

'I'm glad you find it amusing.'

'I don't, Charley. Not one goddamn bit,' answered Alex softly.

'Ayee . . .' Barak whistled as tiny spits of flame burst out of the cistern's cracks. 'Charley, you got brains, mon! Here they are . . . Floyd, mon, give me the tools.'

Floyd reached into his field jacket and produced a five-inch stone chisel and an all-metal folding hammer. He handed them down to his superior. 'You want help?' he asked.

'There is not room for two,' replied Barak as he started hammering along the cracks.

Three minutes later Moore had managed to dislodge the first block from its surrounding adhesive; he tugged at it, pulling it slowly out of the cistern wall. Whitehall held the flashlight now, his eyes intent on Moore's manipulations. The block came loose; Floyd reached down and took it from Barak's hands.

'What's behind?' Whitehall pierced the beam of light into the gaping hole.

'Space, mon. Red dirt and space,' said Moore. 'And I think the top of another box. A larger box.'

'For God's sake, *hurry*!'

'Okay, Charley-mon. There is no dinner engagement at the Mo'Bay Hilton, mon.' Barak chuckled. 'Nothing will be re-written by a hidden mongoose.'

'Relax.' McAuliff did not look at Whitehall when he spoke. He did not want to. 'We have all night, don't we? You killed a man out there. He was the only one who could have interfered. And you decided he had to die for that.'

Whitehall turned his head and stared at McAuliff. 'I killed him because it was necessary.' Whitehall transferred his attention back to Barak Moore. The second block came loose with far less effort than the first. Barak reached into the space and rocked the stone until the cracks widened and it slid out. Floyd took the block and placed it carefully to one side.

Whitehall crouched opposite the hole, shining the flashlight into it. 'It's an archive case. Let me have it.' He handed Floyd the flashlight and reached across the pit as Barak pulled the receptacle out of the dirt and gave it to him. 'Extraordinary!' said Charles, fingering the oblong box, his knee pressed against the top of the first receptacle on the floor beside him. Whitehall was not going to let either out of his possession.

'The case you mean, mon?' asked Moore.

'Yes.' Whitehall turned the box over, then held it up as Floyd shone the beam of light on it. 'I don't think any of you understand. Without the keys or proper equipment, these bloody things take hours to open. Watertight, airtight, vacuumed, and crushproof. Even a starbit drill could not penetrate the metal . . . Here! See.' The scholar pointed to some lettering on the bottom surface. 'Hitchcock Vault Company, Indianapolis. The finest in the world. Museums, libraries . . . government archives everywhere use Hitchcock. Simply extraordinary.'

When the sound came, it had the impact of an earth-shattering explosion, although the noise was distant – that of the whining low gear of a car racing up the long entrance drive from the road below.

And then another.

The four men looked back and forth at one another. They were stunned. Outside there was an intrusion that was not to be. *Could* not be.

'Oh my *God, Jesus, mon!*' Barak jumped out of the pit.

'Take those tools, you damn fool!' cried Whitehall. 'Your fingerprints!'

Floyd, rather than Barak, leaped into the cistern, grabbed the hammer and chisel, and put them into the pockets of his field jacket. 'There is only the staircase, mon! No other way!'

Barak ran to the stairs. McAuliff reached down for the first receptacle at Whitehall's side; simultaneously, Whitehall's hand was on it.

'You can't carry both, Charley,' said Alex in answer to White-hall's manic stare. 'This one's mine!' He grabbed the box, jerked it out from under Whitehall's grip, and followed Moore to the stairs. The cars, in grinding counterpoint, were getting nearer.

The four men leaped up the stairs in single file and raced through the short corridor into the darkened, rugless living room. The beams of headlights could be seen shining through the slits in the teak shutters. The first car had reached the compact parking area; the sounds of doors opening could be heard. The second vehicle roared in only seconds behind. In the corner of the room could be seen, in the strips of light, the cause of the intrusion: an open-line portable radio. Barak ran to it and, with a single blow of his fist into the metal, smashed the front and then tore off the back antennae.

Men outside began shouting. Predominantly one name:

'*Raymond!*'

'*Raymond!*'

'Raymond! Where you at, mon!'

Floyd assumed the lead and raced to the rear centre door. 'This way! Quick, mon!' he whispered to the others. He yanked the door open and held it as they all gathered. McAuliff could see in the reflection of the pool's light that Floyd held a pistol in his free hand. Floyd spoke to Barak. 'I will deflect them, mon. To the west. I know the property good, mon!'

'Be careful! You two,' said Barak to Whitehall and McAuliff. 'Go straight into the woods; we'll meet at the raft. Half an hour from now. No more. Whoever is there, leave. Pole down, mon. The Martha Brae is no good without a raft, mon. *Go!*' He shoved Alex through the door.

Outside, McAuliff started across the strangely peaceful lawn, with the blue-green light of the pool illuminating the stately wrought-iron furniture. He could hear the shouts from behind. Men had raced up from the entrance drive to the sides of the house. Alex wondered if they could see him; he was running as fast as he could towards the seemingly impenetrable wall of forest beyond the sloping lawn. He gripped the oblong receptacle under his right arm.

He got his answer instantly.

The insanity had started.

Gunshots!

Bullets cracked above him; abrupt detonations spaced erratically behind him.

Men were firing pistols indiscriminately.

Oh, Jesus; he was back there again!

Long-forgotten instructions returned once more. Diagonals; make diagonals. *Short, quick spurts; but not too short. Just enough to give the enemy a half second to assume zero aim.*

He had given those instructions. To scores of men in the Che San hills.

The shouting became an overslapping chorus of hysteria; and then a single scream pierced the symphony.

McAuliff hurled himself into the air, into the sudden growth of dense foliage that bordered the lawn. He fell into a thicket and rolled to his left.

On the ground, out of sightlines, roll! Roll for all you're worth into a second position!

Basics.

Fundamentals.

He was positive he would see men coming after him down the hill.

There weren't.

Instead, what he saw hypnotized him, as he had been hypnotized watching the two black revolutionaries in the high grass pretending to be wild pigs.

Up by the house – to the west of it, actually – Floyd was reeling around and around, the light of the pool catching the dull green of his field jacket. He was allowing himself to be an open target, firing a pistol, pinning the police to the sides of the house. He ran out of ammunition, reached into his pocket, withdrew another gun, and started firing again – now racing to the edge of the pool, in full sacrificial view.

He had been hit. Repeatedly. Blood was spreading throughout the cloth of the field jacket and all over the trousers covering his legs. The man had at least a half dozen bullets in him, ebbing away his life, leaving him only moments to live.

'McAuliff!' The whispered shout was from his right. Barak Moore, his grotesque shaven head glistening with sweat in the filtered moonlight, threw himself down beside Alex. 'We get out of here, mon! Come!' He tugged at McAuliff's drenched shirt.

'For God's sake! Can't you see what's happening up there? That man's dying!'

Barak glanced up through the tangled overgrowth. He spoke calmly. 'We are committed till death. In its way, it is a luxury. Floyd knows that.'

'For *what*, for Christ's sake? For goddamn stinking *what*? You're goddamn madmen!'

'Let us *go*!' commanded Moore. 'They will follow us in seconds. Floyd is giving us this chance, you white shit, mon!'

Alex grabbed Barak's hand, which was still gripping his shirt, and threw it off. 'That's it, isn't it? I'm a white shit. And Floyd has to die because you think so. And that guard had to die because Whitehall thinks so! . . . You're sick.'

Barak Moore paused. 'You are what you are, mon. And you will not take this island. Many, many will die, but this island will not be yours . . . You will be dead, too, if you do not run with me.' Moore suddenly stood up and ran into the forest darkness.

McAuliff looked after him, holding the black oblong box to his chest. Then he rose from the ground and followed the black revolutionary.

They waited at the water's edge, the raft bobbing up and down in the onrushing current. They were waist deep in the river, Barak checking his wristwatch, Alex shifting his feet in the soft mud to hold the bamboo sides of the raft more firmly.

'We cannot wait much longer, mon,' said Barak. 'I can hear them in the hills. They come closer!'

McAuliff could not hear anything but the sounds of the rushing river and the slapping of water against the raft. And Barak. 'We can't leave him here!'

'No choice. You want your head blown off, mon?'

'No. And it *won't* be. We stole papers from a dead man. At his instructions. That's no call for being shot at. Enough's enough, goddamnit!'

Barak laughed. 'You have a short memory, mon! Up in the tall grass there is a dead policeman. Without doubt, Floyd took at least one other life with him; Floyd was an expert shot . . . Your head will be blown off; the Falmouth police will not hesitate.'

Barak Moore was right. *Where the hell was Whitehall?*

'Was he shot? Do you know if he was wounded?'

'I think not, mon. I cannot be sure . . . Charley-mon did not do as I told him. He ran south-west into the field.'

A single shaft of light was seen a hundred yards upstream, streaking down through the overgrown banks.

'Look!' cried Alex. Moore turned.

There was a second, then a third beam. Three dancing columns of light, wavering towards the river below.

'No time now, mon! Get in and pole fast!'

The two of them shoved the raft towards the centre current and jumped onto the bamboo-rodded surface.

'I get in front, mon!' yelled Moore, scrambling over the plat-formed, high-backed seat used by tourists viewing the beauty of the Martha Brae. 'You stay in the rear, mon! Use the pole and when I tell you, stop and put your legs over the backside!'

McAuliff focused his eyes in the moonlight, trying to distinguish which was the loose pole among the strapped cylinders of bamboo. It was wedged between the low railing and the deck; he picked it up and plunged it into the waters, into the mud below.

The raft entered the rapids and began careening downstream. Moore stood up in the bow and used his pole as a deflector, warding the racing bamboo float off the treacherous series of flesh-cutting rocks that broke the surface of the water. They were approaching a bend in the river. Barak shouted.

'Sit on the backside, mon! Put your feet into the water. *Quick, mon!*'

Alex did as he was ordered; he soon understood. The drag created by his weight and his feet gave Moore the slightly slower speed he needed to navigate the raft through a miniature archipelago of hazardous rocks. The bamboo sides crashed back and forth, into and over the mounds of jagged stone; twice McAuliff thought the raft would list right out of the water.

It was the sound of the harsh scrapings and his concentration on the rapids that caused Alex to delay his realization of the gunshots. And then that realization was complete with the stinging, searing pain in his left arm. A bullet had grazed his flesh: the blood trickled down his sleeve in the moonlight.

There was a staccato burst of gunfire.

'You get down, mon!' yelled Barak. 'Get flat! They cannot follow us; we get around the bend, there is a grotto. Many caves. They lead up to the Brae Road, mon . . . *Ayeee!*'

Moore buckled; he let go of the pole, grabbed his stomach, and fell onto the bamboo deck. Alex reached down for the oblong archive case, crammed it into his belt, and crawled as fast as he could to the front of the raft. Barak Moore was writhing; he was alive.

'How bad are you hurt?'

'Pretty bad, mon! . . . Stay *down*! If we get stuck, jump out and push us off . . . Around bend, mon.'

Barak was unconscious. The bamboo raft plunged over a shallow, gravelled surface and then into the final curve of the bend, where the water was deep, the current powerful and faster than before. The sounds of gunfire stopped; they were out of sight of the Trelawny police.

McAuliff raised his shoulders; the archive case was cutting into his skin beneath his belt, his left arm stung with pain. The river now became a huge flat pool, the waters rushing under the surface. There were stone cliffs diagonally across, rising sharply out of the river bank.

Suddenly Alex saw the beam of a lone flashlight, and the terrible pain of fear pierced his stomach. The enemy was not behind – he was waiting.

Involuntarily, he reached into his pocket for his gun. The Smith & Wesson given him by Westmore Tallon. He raised it as the raft steered itself towards the stone cliffs and the flashlight.

He lowered himself over the unconscious body of Barak Moore and waited, his arm outstretched, the pistol aimed at the body beyond the flashlight.

He was within forty yards of the silent figure. He was about to squeeze the trigger and take a life.

'*Barak, mon!*' came the words.

The man on the river bank was Lawrence.

Charles Whitehall waited in the high grass by the cluster of breadfruit trees. The archive case was securely under his arm; he knelt immobile in the moonlight and watched Piersall's house and grounds two hundred yards away. The body of the dead guard had not been found. Floyd's corpse had been carried into the house for the light necessary for a complete search of the dead body.

One man remained behind. The others had all raced into the eastern forests and down to the Martha Brae in pursuit of Moore and McAuliff.

That was precisely what Charles Whitehall thought would happen. And why he had not done as Barak Moore commanded.

There was a better way. If one acted alone.

The single Trelawny policeman was fat. He waddled back and forth by the wooded border of the lawn; he was pacing nervously, as if afraid to be alone. He carried a rifle in his hands, jerking it towards every sound he heard or thought he heard.

Suddenly there was gunfire far below in the distance, down at the river. It was full, rapid. Either much ammunition was being wasted, or Moore and McAuliff were having a bad time of it.

But it was *his* moment to move. The patrolman was hugging the edge of the forest, peering down. The gunfire was both his protection and the source of his fear. He cradled his rifle and nervously lighted a cigarette.

Charles got up and, clutching the archive case, raced through the tall grass behind the west flank of the field. He then turned right and ran towards Piersall's house, through the diminishing woods to the border of the entrance drive.

The two patrol cars stood peacefully in the moonlight, in front of the wide stone steps to High Hill. Whitehall emerged from the woods and crossed to the first vehicle. One door was open – the driver's door. The dim interior light shone over the black leather.

The keys were in the ignition. He removed them and then reached under the dashboard radio and ripped every wire out of the panel. He closed the door silently, ran to the second car, and saw that its keys were also in place. He walked rapidly back to the first car and as quietly as possible unlatched the bonnet.

225

He yanked off the distributor cap and tugged at the rubber lid until it sprang loose from the wires.

He returned to the second vehicle, got in, and placed the archive case beside him. He pressed the accelerator several times. He checked the gear shift mechanism and was satisfied.

He turned the key in the ignition. The motor started instantly.

Charles Whitehall backed the patrol car out of the parking area, swung the wheel, and sped off down the drive.

19

The doctor closed the patio door and walked out onto the Bengal Court's terrace that connected Alison's and McAuliff's rooms. Barak Moore was in Alison's bed. She had insisted; no comments were offered, the decision was not debated.

Alex's upper left arm was bandaged; the wound was surface, painful, and not serious. He sat with Alison on the waist-high terrace sea wall. He did not elaborate on the night raid: there would be time later. Sam Tucker and Lawrence had taken positions at each end of the patio in order to keep any wanderers from coming into the small area.

The doctor from Falmouth whom Lawrence had contacted at midnight, approached McAuliff. 'I have done what I can. I wish I felt more confident.'

'Shouldn't he be in a hospital?' Alison's words were as much a rebuke as a question.

'He should be,' agreed the doctor wearily. 'I discussed it with him; he concluded it was not feasible. There is only a government clinic in Falmouth. I think this is cleaner.'

'Barak is wanted,' explained Alex quietly. 'He'd be put in prison before they got the bullet out.'

'I sincerely doubt they would take the trouble to remove the bullet, Mr McAuliff.'

'What do you think?' asked Alex, lighting a cigarette.

'He will have a chance if he remains absolutely still. But only a chance. I have cauterized the abdominal wall; it could easily rerupture. I have replaced blood . . . yes, my office has a discreet file of certain individuals' blood classifications. He is extremely weak. If he survives two or three days, there is hope.'

'But you don't think he will,' stated McAuliff.

'No. There was too much internal bleeding. My . . . portable operating kit is not that good. Oh, my man is cleaning up. He will take out the sheets, clothing, anything that has been soiled. Unfortunately, the odour of ether and disinfectant will remain. Keep the outside doors open when you can. Lawrence will make sure no one enters.'

Alex slid off the wall and leaned against it. 'Doctor? I gather you're part of Barak's organization, if that's the word.'

'It is too precise at this juncture.'

'But you know what's going on.'

'Not specifically. Nor do I wish to. My function is to be available for medical purposes. The less involvement otherwise, the better for everyone.'

'You can get word to people, though, can't you?'

The doctor smiled. 'By "people" I assume you mean Barak's followers.'

'Yes.'

'There are telephone numbers . . . public telephones, and specific hours. The answer is yes.'

'We're going to need at least one other man. Floyd was killed.'

Alison Booth gasped. Her eyes riveted on Alex; her hand reached out for his arm. He covered it gently. 'Oh my God,' she whispered.

The doctor looked at Alison but did not comment on her reaction. He turned back to McAuliff. 'Barak told me. There may be a problem; we do not know yet. The survey is being watched. Floyd was part of it, and the police will find out. You will be questioned, of course. Naturally, you know absolutely nothing; wear long sleeves for a while – a few days, until the wound can be covered with a large plaster. To replace Floyd now with one of our men could be a self-induced trap.'

Reluctantly, Alex nodded. 'I see,' he said softly. 'But I need another man. Lawrence can't do triple duty . . .'

'May I make a suggestion?' asked the doctor with a thin smile and a knowing look in his eyes.

228

'What's that?'

'Use British Intelligence. You really should not ignore them.'

'Get some sleep, Sam. Lawrence, you do the same,' said Alex to the two men on the terrace. The doctor had left; his assistant remained with Barak Moore. Alison had gone into McAuliff's room and shut the door. 'Nothing will happen tonight, except possibly the police ... to ask me questions about a crewman I haven't seen since early afternoon.'

'You know what to say, mon?' Lawrence asked the question with authority, as he would provide the answer.

'The doctor explained; Barak told him.'

'You must be angry, mon! Floyd alla time a no good thief from Ochee. Now you know; supplies stolen. You drum-drum angry, mon!'

'It doesn't seem fair, does it?' said Alex sadly.

'Do as he says, lad,' countered Sam Tucker. 'He knows what he's talking about ... I'll nap out here. Hate the goddamn bed, anyway.'

'It isn't necessary, Sam.'

'Has it occurred to you, boy, that the police may just come here without announcing themselves? I'd hate like hell for them to get the rooms mixed up.'

'Oh Lord ...' McAuliff spoke with weariness. It was the exhaustion of inadequacy, the pressure of continually being made aware of it. 'I didn't think about that.'

'Neither did the goddamn doctor,' replied Sam. 'Lawrence and I have, which is why we'll stand turns.'

'Then I'll join you.'

'You do enough tonight, mon,' said Lawrence firmly. 'You have been hurt ... Maybe policemen do not come so quick. Floyd carry no papers. Early morning Sam Tuck and me take Barak away.'

'The doctor said he was to stay where he is.'

'The doctor is a kling-kling, mon! Two, three hours Barak will sleep. If he is not dead, we take him to Braco Beach. The ocean is still before sunrise; a flat-bottom is very gentle, mon. We take him away.'

'He makes sense again, Alex.' Tucker gave his approval without regret. 'Our medical friend notwithstanding, it's a question of alternatives. And we both know most wounded men can travel gentle if you give 'em a couple of hours.'

'What'll we do if the police come tonight? And search?'

Lawrence answered, again with authority. 'I tell Tuck, mon. The person in that room has Indie Fever. The bad smell helps us. Falmouth police plenty scared of Indie Fever.'

'So is everybody else,' added Sam, chuckling.

'You're inventive,' said McAuliff. And he meant it. 'Indie Fever' was the polite term for a particularly nasty offshoot of encephalitis, infrequent but nevertheless very much a reality, usually found in the hill country. It could swell a man's testicles many times their size and render him impotent as well as a figure of grotesque ridicule.

'You go get sleep now, McAuliff, mon . . . please.'

'Yes. Yes, I will. See you in a few hours.' Alex looked at Lawrence for a moment before turning to go inside. It was amazing. Floyd was dead, Barak barely alive, and the grinning, previously carefree youngster who had seemed so naive and playful in comparison to his obvious superiors was no longer the innocent. He had, in a matter of hours, become the leader of his faction, lord of his pack. A hard authority had been swiftly developed, although he still felt the need to qualify that authority.

Get sleep now . . . please.

In a day or two the 'please' would be omitted. The command would be all.

So for ever the office made the man.

Sam Tucker smiled at McAuliff in the bright Jamaican moonlight. He seemed to be reading Alex's thoughts. Or was Sam remembering McAuliff's first independent survey? Tucker had been there. It had been in the Aleutians, in springtime, and a man had died because Alex had not been firm enough in

230

disciplining the team regarding the probing of ice fissures. Alexander Tarquin McAuliff had matured quickly that springtime in the Aleutians.

'See you later, Sam.'

Inside the room, Alison lay in bed, the table lamp on. By her side was the archive case he had carried out of Carrick Foyle. She was outwardly calm, but there was no mistaking the intensity beneath the surface. McAuliff removed his shirt, threw it on a chair, and crossed to the dial on the wall that regulated the overhead fan. He turned it up; the four blades suspended from the ceiling accelerated, the whirr matching the sound of the distant surf outside. He walked to the bureau, where the bucket of ice had melted halfway. Cubes were bunched together in the water, enough for drinks.

'Would you like a Scotch?' he asked without looking at her.

'No thank you,' she replied in her soft British accent. Soft, but laced – as all British speech was laced – with that core of understated, superior rationality.

'I would.'

'I should think so.'

He poured the whisky into a hotel glass, threw in two ice cubes, and turned around. 'To answer you before you ask, I had no idea tonight would turn out the way it did.'

'Would you have gone had you known?'

'Of course not . . . But it's over. We have what we need now.'

'This?' Alison touched the archive case.

'Yes.'

'From what you've told me . . . on the word of a dying primitive. Told to him by a dead fanatic.'

'I think those descriptions are a little harsh.' McAuliff went to the chair by the bed and sat down facing her. 'But I won't defend either one yet. I'll wait. I'll find out what's in here, do what they say I should do, and see what happens.'

'You sound positively confident, and I can't imagine why. You've been shot at. A bullet came within five inches of killing you. Now you sit here calmly and tell me you'll simply bide

231

your time and see what happens? Alex, for God's sake, what are you *doing?*'

McAuliff smiled and swallowed a good deal of whisky. 'What I never thought was possible,' he said slowly, abruptly serious. 'I mean that . . . And I've just seen a boy grow up into a man. In one hour. The act cost a terrible price, but it happened . . . and I'm not sure I can understand it, but I saw it. That transformation had something to do with belief. We haven't got it. We act out of fear or greed or both . . . all of us. He doesn't. He does what he does, becomes what he becomes, because he believes . . . And, strangely enough, so does Charley Whitehall.'

'What in heaven's name are you talking about?'

McAuliff lowered his glass and looked at her. 'I have an idea we're about to turn this war over to the people who should be fighting it.'

Charles Whitehall exhaled slowly, extinguished the acetylene flame, and removed his goggles. He put the torch down on the long narrow table and took off the asbestos gloves. He noted with satisfaction that his every movement was controlled; he was like a confident surgeon. No motion wasted, his mind ahead of his every muscle.

He rose from the stool and stretched. He turned to see that the door of the small room was still bolted. A foolish thing to do, he thought; he had bolted the door. He was alone.

He had driven over back roads nearly forty miles away from Carrick Foyle, to the border of Saint Anne's. He had left the police car in a field and walked the last mile into the town.

Ten years ago St Anne's was a meeting place for those of the Movement between Falmouth and Ocho Rios. The 'nigger rich', they had called themselves, with good-sized fields in Drax Hall, Chalky Hill and Davis Town. Men of property and certain wealth, which they had forced from the earth and were not about to turn over to the Commonwealth sycophants in Kingston. Whitehall remembered names, as he remembered most things

– a necessary discipline – and within fifteen minutes after he reached St Anne's he was picked up by a man in a new Pontiac who cried at seeing him.

When his needs were made known, he was driven to the house of another man in Drax Hall, whose hobby was machinery. The introductions were brief; this second man embraced him, held on to him for such a length of time – silently – that Charles found it necessary to disengage him.

He was taken to a tool shack at the side of the house, where everything he had requested was laid out on the long narrow table that butted the wall, a sink at midpoint. Besides the overhead light, there was a gooseneck lamp, whose bright illumination could be directed at a small area. Charles was amused to see that along with these requirements was a bowl of fresh fruit and a huge pewter tankard filled with ice.

A messiah had returned.

And now the archive case was open. He stared down at the severed end, the metal edges still glowing with dying orange, then yellow – lingering – soon to be black again. Inside he could see the brown folds of a document roll – the usual encasement for folded papers, each sheet against the imperceptibly moist surface of the enveloping shield.

In the earth a living vault. Precise for a thousand years.

Walter Piersall had buried a rock for many ages in the event his own overlooked it. He was a professional.

As a physician might with a difficult birth, Charles reached in and pulled the priceless child from its womb. He unravelled the document and began reading.

Acquaba.

The tribe of Acquaba.

Walter Piersall had gone back into the Jamaican archives and found the brief allusion in the records pertaining to the Maroon Wars.

On January 2, 1739, a descendant of the Coromanteen tribal chieftains, one Acquaba, led his followers into the mountains. The tribe of Acquaba would not be a party to the Cudjoe treaty

233

with the British, insofar as said treaty called upon the Africans to recapture slaves for the white garrisons ...

There was the name of an obscure army officer who had supplied the information to His Majesty's Recorder in Spanish Town, the colony's capital.

Middlejohn, Robt. Maj. W. I. Reg. 641.

What made the name of 'Middlejohn, Robt.' significant was Piersall's discovery of the following.

His Majesty's Recorder, Spanish Town. February 9–1739. [*Docm'ts. recalled. Middlejohn. W. I. Reg. 641.*]

And ...

His Majesty's Recorder. Spanish Town. April 20–1739. [*Docm'ts. recalled. R.M. W. I. Reg 641.*]

Robert Middlejohn. Major. West Indian Regiment 641, in the Year of Our Lord 1739, had been significant to someone.

Who?

Why?

It took Walter Piersall weeks at the Institute to find the next clue. A second name.

But not in the eighteenth century; instead, 144 years later, in the year 1883.

Fowler, Jeremy. Clerk. Foreign Service.

One Jeremy Fowler had removed several documents from the archives in the new capital of Kingston on *the instructions of Her Majesty's Foreign Office, June 7, 1883. Victoria Regina.*

The colonial documents in question were labelled simply 'Middlejohn papers'. 1739.

Walter Piersall speculated. Was it possible that the *Middlejohn papers* continued to speak of the Tribe of Acquaba, as the first document had done? Was the retention of that first document in the archives an oversight? An omission committed by one Jeremy Fowler on 7 June 1883?

Piersall had flown to London and used his academic credentials to gain access to the Foreign Office's West Indian Records. Since he was dealing in matters of research over a hundred years old, the FO had no objections. The archivists were most helpful.

And there were no transferred documents from Kingston in the year 1883.

Jeremy Fowler, clerk of the Foreign Service, had stolen the *Middlejohn papers!*

If there was a related answer, Walter Piersall now had two specifics to go on: the name 'Fowler' and the year 1883 in the colony of Jamaica.

Since he was in London, he traced the descendants of Jeremy Fowler. It was not a difficult task.

The Fowlers – sons and uncles – were proprietors of their own brokerage house on the London Stock Exchange. The patriarch was Gordon Fowler, Esquire, great-great-grandson of Jeremy Fowler, clerk, Foreign Service, colony of Jamaica.

Walter Piersall interviewed old Fowler on the premise that he was researching the last two decades of Victoria's rule in Jamaica; the Fowler name was prominent. Flattered, the old gentleman gave him access to all papers, albums and documents relative to Jeremy Fowler.

These materials told a not unfamiliar story of the times: a young man of 'middle breeding' entering the Colonial Service, spending a number of years in a distant outpost, only to return to England far richer than when he left.

Sufficiently rich to be able to buy heavily into the Exchange during the last decade of the nineteenth century. A propitious time; the source of the current Fowler wealth.

One part of the answer.

Jeremy Fowler had made his connection in the Colonial Service.

Walter Piersall had returned to Jamaica to look for the second part.

He studied, day by day, week by week, the recorded history of Jamaica for the year 1883. It was laborious.

And then he found it. 25 May 1883.

A disappearance that was not given much attention insofar as small groups of Englishmen – hunting parties – were constantly getting lost in the Blue Mountains and tropic jungles, usually to be found by scouting parties of blacks led by other Englishmen.

As this lone man had been found.

Not a clerk, but the official Crown Recorder.

Her Majesty's Recorder, Jeremy Fowler.

Not a clerk, but the official Crown Recorder.

Which was why his absence justified the space in the papers. The Crown Recorder was not insignificant. Not landed gentry, of course, but a person of substance.

The ancient newspaper accounts were short, imprecise, and strange.

A Mr Fowler had last been observed in his government office on the evening of 25 May, a Saturday. He did not return on Monday and was not seen for the rest of the workweek. Nor had his quarters been slept in.

Six days later, Mr Fowler turned up in the garrison of Fleet-course, south of the impenetrable Cock Pit, escorted by several Maroon 'Negroes'. He had gone on horseback . . . alone . . . for a Sunday ride. His horse had bolted, he had got lost and wandered for days until found by the Maroons.

It was illogical. In those years, Walter Piersall knew, men did not ride alone into such territories. And if one did, a man who was sufficiently intelligent to be Her Majesty's Recorder would certainly know enough to take a left angle from the sun and reach the south coast in a matter of hours, at best a day.

And one week later Jeremy Fowler stole the *Middlejohn papers* from the archives. The documents concerning a sect led by a Coromanteen chieftain named Acquaba . . . that had disappeared into the mountains 144 years before.

And six months later he left the Foreign – Colonial – Service and returned to England a very, very wealthy man.

He had discovered the Tribe of Acquaba.

It was the only logical answer. And if that were so, there was a second, logical speculation: Was the Tribe of Acquaba . . . the Halidon?

Piersall was convinced it was. He needed only current proof. Proof that there was substance to the whispers of the incredibly wealthy sect high in the Cock Pit mountains. An isolated community that sent its members out into the world, into Kingston, to exert influence.

Piersall tested five men in the Kingston government, all in positions of trust, all with obscure backgrounds. Did any of them belong to the Halidon?

He went to each, telling each that he alone was the recipient of his startling information: *the Tribe of Acquaba.*

The Halidon.

Three of the five were fascinated but bewildered. They did not understand.

Two of the five disappeared.

Disappeared in the sense of being removed from Kingston. Piersall was told one man had retired suddenly to an island in the Martinique chain. The other was transferred out of Jamaica to a remote post.

Piersall had his current proof.

The Halidon was the Tribe of Acquaba.

It existed.

If he needed further confirmation, final proof, the growing harassment against him was it. The harassment now included the selected rifling and theft of his files and untraceable university inquiries into his current academic studies. Someone beyond the Kingston government was concentrating on him. These acts were not those of concerned bureaucrats.

The Tribe of Acquaba . . . Halidon.

What was left was to reach the leaders. A staggeringly difficult thing to do. For throughout the Cock Pit there were scores of insulated sects who kept to themselves: most of them poverty-stricken, scraping an existence off the land. The Halidon would not proclaim its self-sufficiency; which one was it?

The anthropologist returned once again to the volumes of African minutiae, specifically seventeenth- and eighteenth-century Coromanteen. The key had to be there.

Piersall had found the key: he had not footnoted its source.

Each tribe, each offshoot of a tribe, had a *single sound*

applicable to it only. A whistle, a slap, a word. This symbol was known only within the highest tribal councils, understood by only a few, who communicated it to their out-tribal counterparts.

The symbol, the sound, the word . . . was 'Halidon'.

Its meaning.

It took him nearly a month of sleepless days and nights, using logarithmic charts of phonetics, hieroglyphs and African symbols of daily survival.

When he was finished, he was satisfied. He had broken the ancient code.

It was too dangerous to include it in this summary. For in the event of his death – or murder – this summary might fall into the wrong hands. Therefore, there was a second archive case containing the secret.

The second without the first was meaningless.

Instructions were left with one man. To be acted upon in the event he was no longer capable of doing so himself.

Charles Whitehall turned over the last page. His face and neck were drenched with sweat. Yet it was cool in the shack. Two partially opened windows in the south wall let in the breezes from the hills of Drax Hall, but they could not put out the nervous fires of his anxiety.

Truths had been learned. A greater, overwhelming truth was yet to be revealed.

That it would be now, he was certain.

The scholar and the patriot were one again.

The Praetorian of Jamaica would enlist the Halidon.

20

James Ferguson, at the fashionable bar in Montego Bay, was exhilarated. It was the feeling he had when momentous things happened in the lens of a microscope and he knew he was the first observer – or, at least, the first witness who recognized a causal effect for what it was.

Like the baracoa fibre.

He was capable of great imagination when studying the shapes and densities of microscopic particles. A giant manipulating a hundred million infinitesimal subjects. It was a form of total control.

He had control now. Over a man who did not know what it was like to have to protest too loudly over the inconsequential because no one paid attention: to be for ever down to his last few quid in the bank because none paid him the value of his work.

All that was changing. He could think about a great many things that were preposterous fantasies only yesterday: his own laboratories with the most expensive equipment – electronic, computerized, data-banked; throwing away the little budget pads that told him whom he had last borrowed from.

A Maserati. He would buy a Maserati. Arthur Craft had one, why shouldn't he?

Arthur Craft was paying for it.

Ferguson looked at his watch – his too inexpensive Timex – and signalled the bartender to total his bill.

When the bartender did not come over in thirty seconds, Ferguson reached for the tab in front of him and turned it over. It was simple enough to add: a dollar and fifty cents, twice.

239

James Ferguson then did what he had never done in his life. He took out a five-dollar bill, crumpled it up in his hand, got off the bar stool, and threw the wadded bill towards the cash register several yards in front of him. The bill bounced off the bottles on the lighted shelf and arced to the floor.

He started for the entrance.

There was *machismo* in his gesture; that was the word, that was the feeling.

In twenty minutes, he would meet the emissary from Craft the Younger. Down off Harbour Street, near Parish Wharf, on Pier Number Six. The man would be obsequious – he had no choice – and give him an envelope containing one thousand dollars.

One thousand dollars.

In a single envelope; not saved in bits and pieces over months of budgeting, nor with the tentacles of Inland Revenue or debtors-past reaching out to cut it in half. It was his to do with as he pleased. To squander, to throw away on silly things, to pay a girl to get undressed and undress him and do things to him that were fantasies . . . only yesterday.

He had borrowed – taken a salary advance, actually – from McAuliff. Two hundred dollars. There was no reason to repay it. Not now. He would simply tell McAuliff . . . 'Alex'; from now on it would be 'Alex' or perhaps 'Lex' – very informal, very sure . . . to deduct the silly money from his pay cheque. All at once, if he felt like it. It was inconsequential; it didn't really matter.

And it certainly didn't, thought Ferguson.

Every month Arthur Craft would give him an envelope. The agreed-upon amount was a thousand dollars in each envelope, but that was subject to change. Related to the increased cost of living, as it were. Increased as his appetites and comforts increased. Just the beginning.

Ferguson crossed St James Square and proceeded towards the waterfront. It was a warm night, with no breeze, and humid. Fat clouds, flying low and threatening rain, blocked the moon;

the antiquated street lamps threw a subdued light in counter-point to the gaudy neons of white and orange that announced the diversions of Montego Bay night life.

Ferguson reached Harbour Street and turned left. He stopped under a street lamp and checked his watch again. It was ten minutes past midnight; Craft had specified 12:15. In five minutes, he would have a thousand dollars.

Pier Six was directly ahead on his right, across the street. There was no ship in the dock, no activity within the huge loading area beyond the high linked fence; only a large naked bulb inside a wire casing that lit up the sign:

PIER SIX
MONTEGO LINES

He was to stand under the lamp, in front of the sign, and wait for a man to drive up in a Triumph sports car. The man would ask him for identification. Ferguson would show him his passport and the man would give him the envelope.

So simple. The entire transaction would take less than thirty seconds. And change his life.

Craft had been stunned: speechless, actually, until he had found his voice and screamed a torrent of abuse . . . until, again, he realized the futility of his position. Craft the Younger had gone too far. He had broken laws and would be an object of scorn and embarrassment. James Ferguson could tell a story of airport meetings and luggage and telephone calls and industrial espionage . . . and promises.

Such promises.

But his silence could be purchased. Craft could buy his confidence for a first payment of one thousand dollars. If Craft did not care to do so, Ferguson was sure the Kingston authorities would display avid interest in the details of his story.

No, he had not spoken to anyone yet. But things had been written down. (Lies Craft could not trace, of course.) That did not mean he was incapable of finding the spoken words: such capability was very much within his province . . . as the first

241

payment was within Craft's province. One cancelled the other: which would it be?

And so it was.

Ferguson crossed Harbour Street and approached the wire-encased light and the sign. A block and a half away, crowds of tourists swelled into the street, a one-way flow towards the huge passenger terminal and the gangplanks of a cruise ship. Taxis emerged out of side streets and alleys from the centre of Montego Bay, blowing their horns anxiously, haltingly making their way to the dock. Three bass-toned whistles filled the air, vibrating the night, signifying that the ship was giving a warning: All passengers were to be on board.

He heard the Triumph before he saw it. There was the gunning of an engine from the darkness of a narrow side street diagonally across from Pier Six. The shiny, red, low-slung sports car sped out of the dark recess and coasted to a stop in front of Ferguson. The driver was another Craft employee, one he recognized from a year ago. He did not recall the man's name; only that he was a quick, physical person, given to arrogance. He would not be arrogant now.

He wasn't. He smiled in the open car and gestured Ferguson to come over. 'Hello, *Fergy*! It's been a long time.'

Ferguson hated the nickname 'Fergy'; it had dogged him for most of his life. Just when he had come to think it was part of a schoolboy past, someone – always someone unpleasant, he reflected – used it. He felt like correcting the man, reminding him of his messenger status, but he did not. He simply ignored the greeting.

'Since you recognize me, I assume there's no need to show you my identification,' said James, approaching the Triumph.

'Christ, no! How've you been?'

'Well, thank you. Do you have the envelope? I'm in a hurry.'

'Sure. Sure, I do, Fergy . . . Hey, you're a pistol, buddy! Our friend is pissing rocks! He's half out of his skull, you know what I mean?'

'I know what you mean. He should be. The envelope, please.'

'Sure.' The driver reached into his jacket and withdrew an envelope. He then leaned over and handed it to Ferguson. 'You're supposed to count it. If it's all there, just give me back the envelope ... make any kind of mark on it you like. Oh, here's a pen.' The man opened the glove compartment and took out a ballpoint pen and held it up for Ferguson.

'That's not necessary. He wouldn't try to cheat me.'

'Hey, come on, Fergy! It's my ass that'll be in a sling! Count it, mark it; what's the difference?'

Ferguson opened the bulky envelope. The denominations were all tens and fives, dozens of bills. He had not asked for small denominations; it was convenient, though, he had to admit that. Less suspicious than hundreds or fifties or even twenties.

He started counting the bills.

Twice Craft's man interrupted him with insignificant questions, causing James to lose his count. He had to start over again both times.

When he had finished, the driver suddenly handed him a wrapped package. 'Oh, because our friend wants to show there's no bad feeling – he's a sport, you know what I mean? – he sent you one of those new Yashica .35 millimetres. He remembered you're crazy about photography.'

Ferguson saw the Yashica label on the top of the package. A seven-hundred-dollar instrument! One of the very best! Craft the Younger was indeed a frightened man. 'Thank ... Arthur for me. But tell him this isn't deductible from any future payments.'

'Oh, I'll tell him ... Now, I'm going to tell you something, Fergy-baby. You're on fuckin' *Candid Camera*.' The driver spoke quietly.

'What are you talking about?

'Right behind you, Fergy-baby.'

Ferguson whipped around towards the high linked fence and the deserted area beyond. There were two men in the shadows of a doorway. They came out slowly, perhaps thirty yards away from him. And one of the men carried a camcorder. 'What have you done?'

'Just a little insurance, Fergy-baby. Our friend is contract-conscious, you know what I mean? Infrared tape, babe. I think you know what that is. And you just gave a terrific performance counting out money and taking Christ knows what from a guy who hasn't been seen in public north of Caracas for over six months. You see, our friend flew me out of Rio just to get my picture taken . . . with you.'

'You can't do this! Nobody would believe this!'

'Why not, babe? You're a hungry little prick, you know what I mean? Hungry little pricks like you get hung easy . . . Now, you listen to me, asshole. You and Arthur, you're one on one. Only his one is a little heavier. That tape would raise a lot of questions you couldn't find any answers for. I'm a very unpopular man, Fergy. You'd get thrown off the island . . . but probably you'd get thrown into the can first. You wouldn't last fifteen minutes with those social rejects, you know what I mean? They'd peel your white skin, babe, layer by layer . . . Now, you be a good boy, Fergy. Arthur says for you to keep the thousand. You'll probably earn it.' The man held up the empty envelope. 'Two sets of prints on this. Yours and mine . . . Ciao, baby. I've got to get out of here and back to non-extradition country.'

The driver gunned the engine twice and slapped the gearshift effortlessly. He swung the Triumph expertly in a semicircle and roared off into the darkness of Harbour Street.

Julian Warfield was in Kingston now. He had flown in three days ago and used all of Dunstone's resources to uncover the strange activities of Alexander McAuliff. Peter Jensen had followed instructions to the letter; he had kept McAuliff under the closest scrutiny, paying desk clerks and doormen and taxi drivers to keep him informed of the American's every move.

And always he and his wife were out of sight, in no way associated with that scrutiny.

It was the least he could do for Julian Warfield . . . He would do anything Julian asked, anything Dunstone plc demanded. He would deliver nothing but his best to the man and the organization that had taken him and his wife out of the valley of despair and given them a world with which they could cope and in which they could function.

Work they loved, money and security beyond the reach of most academic couples. Enough to forget.

Julian had found them nearly twenty years ago, beaten, finished, destroyed by events ... impoverished, with nowhere and no one to return to. He and Ruth had been caught; it was a time of madness, of agents and double agents, of convictions born of misplaced zeal. He and his wife had supplemented their academic income by working for the government on covert geological operations – oil, gold, minerals of value. And they had willingly turned over everything in the classified files to a contact at the Soviet Embassy.

Another blow for equality and justice. And they were caught.

But Julian Warfield came to see them.

Julian Warfield offered them their lives again ... in exchange for certain assignments he might find for them. Inside the government and out; on the temporary staffs of companies ... within England and without; always in the highest professional capacities, pursuing their professional labours.

All charges were dropped by the Crown. Terrible mistakes had been made against most respected members of the academic community. Scotland Yard had apologized. Actually *apologized*.

Peter and Ruth never refused Julian; their loyalty was unquestioned. Which was why Peter was now on his stomach in the cold, damp sand while the light of a Caribbean dawn broke over the eastern horizon. He was behind a mound of coral rock with a perfect view of McAuliff's oceanside terrace. Julian's last instructions had been specific.

Find out who comes to see him. Who's important to him. Get identities, if you can. But for God's sake, stay in the background. We'll need you both in the interior.

Julian had agreed that McAuliff's disappearances – into Kingston, into taxis, into an unknown car at the gates of the

245

Courtleigh Manor – all meant that he had interests in Jamaica other than Dunstone plc.

It had to be assumed that he had broken the primary article of faith. Secrecy.

If so, McAuliff could be transferred . . . forgotten without difficulty. But before that happened, it was essential to discover the identity of Dunstone's island enemy. Or enemies.

In a very real sense, the survey itself was secondary to that objective. Definitely secondary. If it came down to it, the survey could be sacrificed if, by that sacrifice, identities were revealed.

And Peter Jensen knew he was nearer those identities now . . . in this early dawn on the beach of Bengal Court. It had begun three hours ago.

Peter and Ruth had retired a little past midnight. Their room was in the east wing of the motel, along with Ferguson's and Charles Whitehall's. McAuliff, Alison and Sam Tucker were in the west wing, the division signifying only old friends, new lovers and late drinkers.

They heard it around one o'clock: a car swerving into the front drive, its wheels screeching, then silent, as if the driver had heard the noise and suddenly become alarmed by it.

It had been strange. Bengal Court was no kind of nightclub, no 'drum-drum' watering hole that catered to the swinging and/or younger tourist crowds. It was quiet, with very little to recommend it to the image of fast drivers. As a matter of fact, Peter Jensen could not remember having heard *any* cars drive into Bengal Court after nine o'clock in the evening since they had been there.

He had risen from the bed and walked out on the terrace, and had seen nothing. He had walked around the east end of the motel to the edge of the front parking lot, where he did see something; something extremely alarming, barely visible.

In the far section of the lot, in shadows, a large black man – he believed he was black – was lifting the unconscious figure of another man out of the rear seat of a car. Then, farther beyond, a white man ran across the lawn from around the corner of the

246

west wing. It was Sam Tucker. He approached the black carrying the unconscious form, gave instructions – pointing to the direction from which he had come – and continued to the car, silently closing the rear door.

Sam Tucker was supposed to be in Ocho Rios with McAuliff. It seemed unlikely that he would have returned to Bengal Court alone.

And as Jensen pondered this, there was the outline of another figure on the west lawn. It was Alison Booth. She gestured to the black man; she was obviously excited, trying to remain in control of herself. She led the large black man into the darkness around the far corner.

Peter Jensen suddenly had a sinking feeling. Was the unconscious figure Alexander McAuliff? Then he rethought the immediate visual picture. He could not be sure – he could barely see, and everything was happening so rapidly – but as the black passed under the dim spill of a parking light, the bobbing head of his charge extended beyond his arms. Peter had been struck by the oddness of it. The head appeared to be completely bald . . . as if shaven.

Sam Tucker looked inside the car, seemed satisfied, then raced back across the west lawn after the others.

Peter remained crouched in his concealed position after the figure had disappeared. It was extraordinary. Tucker and Alison Booth were not in Ocho Rios; a man had been hurt, apparently quite seriously, and instead of taking him directly inside the motel's front entrance, they furtively carried him in, smuggled him in. And it might be conceivable that Sam Tucker would come back to Bengal Court without McAuliff; it was inconceivable that Alison Booth would do so.

What were they doing? What in heaven's name had happened . . . was happening?

The simplest way to find out, thought Peter, was to get dressed, return to the tiny bar, and, for reasons he had not yet created, call McAuliff for a drink.

He would do this alone. Ruth would remain in their room.

But first Peter would walk down to the beach, to the water's edge, where he would have a full view of the motel and the oceanside terraces.

Once in the miniature lounge, Peter invented his reason to phone McAuliff. It was simple to the point of absurdity. He had been unable to sleep, taken a stroll on the beach, seen a light beyond the drawn curtains in Alexander's room, and gathered he had returned from Ocho Rios. Would he and Alison be his guests for a nightcap?

Jensen went to the house phone at the end of the bar. When McAuliff answered, his voice was laced with the frustration of a man forced to be civil in the most undesirable of circumstances. And McAuliff's lie was apparent.

'Oh, Jesus, Peter, thanks but we're *beat*. We just got settled at the Sans Souci when Latham called from the Ministry. Some damned bureaucratic problem with our interior permits; we had to drive all the way back for some kind of goddamned . . . inspection first thing in the morning . . . inoculation records, medical stuff. Crew, mainly.'

'Terribly inconsiderate, old boy. Nasty bastards, I'd say.'

'They are . . . We'll take a rain check, though. Perhaps tomorrow.'

Peter had wanted to keep McAuliff on the phone a bit longer. The man was breathing audibly; each additional moment meant the possibility of Jensen's learning something. 'Ruth and I thought we'd hire a car and go to Dunn's Falls around noon tomorrow. Surely you'll be finished by then. Care to come along?'

'Frankly, Peter,' said McAuliff haltingly, 'we were hoping to get back to Ochee, if we could.'

'Then that would rule out Dunn's Falls, of course. You've seen it, though, haven't you? Is it all they say?'

'Yes . . . yes, it certainly is. Enjoy yourselves – '

'You *will* be back tomorrow night, then?' interjected Jensen.

'Sure . . . Why?'

'Our rain check, old boy.'

'Yes,' said McAuliff slowly, carefully. 'We'll be back to-morrow night. Of course we'll be back tomorrow night . . . Good night, Peter.'

'Good night, old chap. Sleep well.' Jensen hung up the house phone. He carried his drink slowly back to a table in the corner, nodding pleasantly to the other guests, giving the impression he was waiting for someone, probably his wife. He had no wish to join anyone; he had to think out his moves.

Which was why he was now lying in the sand behind a small mound of surfaced coral on the beach, watching Lawrence and Sam Tucker talking.

He had been there for nearly three hours. He had seen things he knew he was not supposed to see: two men arriving – one obviously a doctor with the inevitable bag, the other some sort of assistant carrying a large trunk-like case and odd-shaped paraphernalia.

There had been quiet conferences between McAuliff, Alison and the doctor, later joined by Sam Tucker and the black crew-man, Lawrence.

Finally, all left the terrace but Tucker and the black. They stayed outside.

On guard.

Guarding not only Alexander and the girl, but also whoever was in that adjoining room. The injured man with the oddly shaped head who had been carried from the automobile. Who was he?

The two men had stayed at their posts for three hours now. No one had come or gone. But Peter knew he could not leave the beach. Not yet.

Suddenly, Jensen saw the black crewman, Lawrence, walk down the terrace steps and start across the dunes towards the beach. Simultaneously, Tucker made his way over the grass to the corner of the building. He stood immobile on the lawn; he was waiting for someone. Or watching.

Lawrence reached the surf, and Jensen lay transfixed as the huge black man did a strange thing. He looked at his watch and then proceeded to light two matches, one after the other, holding each aloft in the breezeless dawn air for several seconds and throwing each into the lapping water.

Moments later, the action was explained. Lawrence cupped his hand over his eyes to block the blinding, head-on light of the sun as it broke the space above the horizon, and Peter followed his line of sight.

Across the calm ocean surface, in the massive land shadows by the point, there were two corresponding flickers of light. A small boat had rounded the waters of the cove's entrance, its grey-black hull slowly emerging in the early sunlight.

Its destination was that section of the beach where Lawrence stood.

Several minutes later, Lawrence struck another match and held it up until there was an acknowledgment from the approaching craft, at which instant both were extinguished and the black crewman started running back over the sand towards Bengal Court.

On the lawn, by the corner of the building, Sam Tucker turned and saw the racing Lawrence. He walked to the stairs in the sea wall and waited for him. The black man reached the steps; he and Tucker spoke briefly, and together they approached the terrace doors of the adjoining room – Alison Booth's room. Tucker opened them, and the two men went inside, leaving the double doors ajar.

Peter kept shifting his eyes from the motel to the beach. There was no visible activity from the terrace; the small boat plodded its way over the remarkably still waters towards the beach, now only three or four hundred yards from shore. It was a long, flat-bottom fishing boat, propelled by a muffled engine. Sitting in the stern was a black man in what appeared to be ragged clothes and a wide straw sun hat. Hook poles shot up from the small deck, nets were draped over the sides of the hull; the effect was that of a perfectly normal Jamaican fisherman out for the dawn catch.

When the boat came within several hundred feet of the shore, the skipper lit a match, then extinguished it quickly. Jensen looked up at the terrace. In seconds, the figure of Sam Tucker emerged from the darkness beyond the open doors. He held one end of a stretcher on which a man lay wrapped in blankets; Lawrence followed, holding the other end.

Gently but swiftly, the two men ran – glided – the stretcher across the terrace, down the sea-wall steps, over the sand, and towards the beach. The timing was precise, not a moment wasted. It seemed to Jensen that the instant the boat hit shallow water, Tucker and Lawrence waded into the calm surf with the stretcher and placed it carefully over the sides onto the deck. The nets were swung over on top of the blanketed man and the fishing boat was immediately pushed back into the water by Sam Tucker as Lawrence slid onto the bow slat. Seconds later, Lawrence had removed his shirt and from some recess in the boat lifted out a torn, dishevelled straw hat, clamped it on his head, and yanked a hook pole from its clasp. The transformation was complete. Lawrence the conspirator was now a lethargic native fisherman.

The small flat-bottom craft turned, rippling the glass-like surface of the water, and headed out. The motor chugged a bit louder than before; the skipper wanted to get away from the beach with his concealed human cargo.

Sam Tucker waved; Lawrence nodded and dipped the hook pole. Tucker came out of the miniature surf and walked swiftly back towards Bengal Court.

Peter Jensen watched as the fishing boat veered in open water towards the point. Several times Lawrence leaned forward and down, fingering nets but obviously checking the condition of the man on the stretcher. Intermittently, he seemed to be issuing quiet commands to the man at the engine tiller. The sun had now cleared the edge of the Jamaican horizon. It would be a hot day.

Up at the terrace Peter saw that the double doors of Alison Booth's room remained open. With the additional light, he could also see that there was new activity inside. Sam Tucker came

251

out twice, carrying tan plastic bags, which he left on the patio. Then a second man – the doctor's assistant, Peter realized – emerged, holding a large cylinder by its neck and a huge black suitcase in his other hand. He placed them on the stone, bent down below them on the sea wall, and stood up moments later with two elongated cans – aerosol cans, thought Jensen – and handed one to Tucker as he came through the door. The two men talked briefly and then went back inside the room.

No more than three minutes had elapsed when Tucker and the doctor's aide were seen again, this time somewhat comically as they backed into the door frame simultaneously. Each held his arm outstretched; in each hand was an aerosol can, clouds of mist spewing from both.

Tucker and the black aide had systematically sprayed the interior of the room.

Once finished, they crossed to the plastic bags, the case and the large cylinder. They picked up the objects, spoke briefly again, and started for the lawn.

Out on the water, the fishing boat was halfway to the point of the cove. But something had happened. It had stopped; it bobbed gently on the calm surface, no longer travelling forward. Peter could see the now tiny figure of Lawrence standing up in the bow, then crouching, then standing up again. The skipper was gesturing, his movements excited.

The boat pushed forward once more, only to turn slowly and change direction. It did not continue on its course – if the point was, indeed, its course. Instead, it headed for the open sea.

Jensen lay on the moist sand for the next fifteen minutes, watching the small craft progressively become a black dot within a grey-black ocean splashed with orange sunlight. He could not read the thoughts of the two Jamaicans; he could not see the things that were happening on that boat so illogically far out on the water. But his knowledge of tides and currents, his observations during the last three hours, led his conclusions to one end.

The man on the stretcher had died. His corpse would soon be

stripped of identification, weighted down with net lead, and thrown into the water, eventually to be carried by floor currents far away from the island of Jamaica. Perhaps to be washed ashore weeks or months from now on some Cayan reef or, more fortuitously, torn apart and devoured by the predators of the deep.

Peter knew it was time to call Warfield, meet with Julian Warfield.

Immediately.

McAuliff rolled over on his side, the sharp pain in his shoulder suddenly surging through his chest. He sat up quickly, momentarily bewildered. He focused his thoughts; it was morning; the night before had been a series of terrifying confusions. The pieces would have to be put back together, plans made.

He looked down at Alison, beside him. She was breathing deeply, steadily, in complete sleep. If the evening had been a nightmare for him, it had been no less a torment for her. Perhaps worse. At least he had been in motion, constant, unceasing movement. She had been waiting, thinking; he had had no time for thoughts. It was worse to wait. In some ways.

Slowly, as silently as he could, he swung his legs over the side of the bed and stood up. His whole body was stiff; his joints pained him, especially his kneecaps.

It was understandable. The muscles he had used last night were dormant strings of an unused instrument, called into play by a panicked conductor. The allusion was proper, thought Alex – about his thoughts. He nearly smiled as he conjured up the phrase: so out of tune. Everything was out of tune.

But the notes *were* forming recognizable chords ... somewhere. In the distance. There was a melody of sorts that could be vaguely distinguished.

Yet not *distinguished*. Hardly noble. Not yet.

An odour assaulted his nostrils. It was not the illusion of spice and vanilla, but nevertheless sweet. If there was an association, it was south Oriental ... Java, the Sunda Trench, pungent, a big sickening. He crossed quietly to the terrace door, about to

253

open it, when he realized he was naked. He walked silently to a chair by the curtained window, where he had thrown a pair of swimming trunks several days ago. He removed them from the wooden rim and put them on.

'I hope they're not wet,' said Alison from the bed. 'The maid service here is a touch lacking, and I didn't hang them up.'

'Go back to sleep.' Alex replied. 'You were asleep a moment ago. Very much asleep.'

'I'm very much awake now . . . Good heavens, it's a quarter past eight.'

'And?'

'Nothing, really . . . I just didn't think we'd sleep this long.'

'It's not long. We didn't get to bed until after three. Considering everything that happened, noon would have been too early.'

'How's your arm? The shoulder?'

'A little sore . . . like most of me. Not crippling.'

'What *is* that terrible smell?' Alison sat up: the sheet fell away, revealing a curiously prim nightgown, opaque cotton with buttons. She saw Alex's gaze, the beginning of a smile on his lips. She glanced down and laughed. 'My granny nightshirt. I put it on after you fell asleep. It was chilly, and you hadn't the slightest interest in anything but philosophical discourse.'

He walked to the edge of the bed and sat down beside her. 'I was long-winded, wasn't I?'

'I couldn't shut you up; there was simply no way. You drank a great deal of Scotch – how's your head, incidentally?'

'Fine. As though I'd had Ovaltine . . .'

'. . . straight alcohol couldn't have stayed with you. I've seen that before, too . . . Sorry. I forgot you object to my British pronouncements.'

'I made a few myself last night. I withdraw my objections.'

'Do you still believe them? Your pronouncements? As they say . . . in the cold logic of the morning?'

'I think I do; the thrust of my argument being that no one fights better for his own turf than he who lives on it, depends on it . . . Yes, I believe it. I'd feel more confident if Barak hadn't been hurt.'

'Strange name, Barak.'

'Strange man. And very strong. He's needed, Alison. Boys can become men quickly, but they're still not seasoned. His ken is needed.'

'By whom?'

McAuliff looked at her, at the lovely way her eyebrows rose quizzically above her clear, light blue eyes. 'By his own side,' he answered simply.

'Which is not Charles Whitehall's side.' There was no question implied.

'No. They're very different. And I think it's necessary . . . at this point, under these circumstances . . . that Barak's faction be as viable as Charley-mon's.'

'That concern strikes me as dangerously close to interference, darling.'

'I know. It's just that everything seems so complicated to me. But it doesn't to Whitehall. And it doesn't to Barak Moore. They see a simple division muddled up by second and third parties . . . Don't you see? They're not distracted. They first go after one objective, then another, and another; knowing ultimately they'll have to deal with each other. Neither one loses sight of that. Each stores his apples as he goes along.'

'What?' Alison leaned back on the pillow, watching McAuliff as he stared blankly at the wall. 'I don't follow that.'

'I'm not sure I can explain it. A wolf pack surrounds its victims, who huddle in the centre. The dogs set up an erratic rhythm of attack, taking turns lunging in and out around the circle until the quarry's confused to the point of exhaustion. Then the wolves close in.' Alex stopped; he was uncertain.

'I gather Charles and this Barak are the victims,' said Alison, trying to help him.

'Jamaica's the victim, and they're Jamaica. The wolves – the enemies – are Dunstone and all it represents: Warfield and his crowd of . . . global manipulators – the Chatelleraults of this world; British Intelligence, with its élitists, like Tallon and *his* crowd of colonial opportunists; the Crafts of this island . . . internal bleeders, you could call them. Finally, maybe even this Halidon, because you can't control what you can't find; and even if you find it, it may not be controllable . . . There are a lot of wolves.'

'There's a lot of confusion,' added Alison.

McAuliff turned and looked at her. 'For *us*. Not for *them*. That's what's remarkable. The victims have worked out a strategy: Take each wolf as it lunges. Destroy it.'

'What's that got to do with . . . apples?'

'I jumped out of the circle and went into a straight line.'

'Aren't we abstract,' stated Alison Booth.

'It's valid. As any army – and don't kid yourself, Charles Whitehall and Barak Moore have their armies – as any army moves forward, it maintains its lines of supply. In this case, support. Remember. When all the wolves have been killed, they face each other. Whitehall and Moore both are piling up apples . . . support.' McAuliff stopped again and got up from the bed. He walked to the window to the right of the terrace doors, pulled the curtain, and looked out at the beach. 'Does any of this make sense to you?' he asked softly.

'It's very political, I think, and I'm not much good at that sort of thing. But you're describing a rather familiar pattern, I'd say –'

'You bet your *life* I am,' interrupted Alex, speaking slowly and turning from the windows. 'Historical precedents unlimited . . . and *I'm* no goddamn historian. Hell, where do you want to start? Caesar's Gaul? Rome's Ferrara? China in the thirties? The Koreas, the Vietnams, the Cambodias? Half a dozen African countries? The words are there, over and over again. Exploitation from outside, inside revolt – insurgence and counterinsurgence. Chaos, bloodbath, expulsion. Ultimately reconstruction in so-called compromise. That's the pattern. That's what Barak and Charley expect to play out. And each knows that while he's joining the other to kill a wolf, he's got to entrench himself further in the turf at the same time. Because when the compromise comes . . . as it must . . . he wants it more *his* way than less.'

'What you're saying – getting away from circles and straight lines – is that you don't approve of Barak's "army" being weakened. Is that it?'

'Not *now*. Not at this moment.'

'Then you *are* interfering. You're an outsider taking an inside position. It's not your . . . turf, my darling.'

'But I brought Charley here. I gave him his respectability, his cover. Charley's a son of a bitch.'

'Is Barak Moore a saint?'

'Not for a second. He's a son of a bitch, too. And it's important that he is.' McAuliff returned to the window. The morning sun was striking the panes of glass, causing tiny modules of condensation. It was going to be a hot day.

'What are you going to do?' Alison sat forward, prepared to get up as she looked over at Alex.

'Do? he asked quietly, his eyes concentrating on something outside the window. 'What I was sent here to do; what I'm being paid two million dollars to do. Complete the survey or find this Halidon. Whichever comes first. Then get us out of here . . . on our terms.'

'That sounds reasonable,' said Alison, rising from the bed. 'What *is* that sickening smell?'

'Oh, I forgot to tell you. They were going to spray down your room, get rid of the medicine smells.' McAuliff stepped closer to the window and shaded his eyes from the rays of the morning sun.

'The ether or disinfectant or whatever it was was far more palatable. My bathing suit's in there. May I get it?'

'What?' Alex was not listening, his attention on the object of his gaze outside.

'My bathing suit, darling. It's in my room.'

McAuliff turned from the window, oblivious to her words. 'Wait here. I'll be right back.' He walked rapidly to the terrace door, opened it and ran out.

257

Alison looked after him, bewildered. She crossed to the window to see what Alex had seen. It took several seconds to understand; she was helped by watching McAuliff run across the sand towards the water.

In the distance, down at the beach, was the lone figure of a large black man staring out at the ocean. It was Lawrence.

Alex approached the tall Jamaican, wondering if he should call out. Instinctively, he did not. Instead, he cleared his throat when he was within ten yards; cleared it loud enough to be heard over the sound of the lapping small waves.

Lawrence turned around. Tears were in his eyes, but he did not blink or change the muscles of his face. He was a child-man accepting the agonies of a very personal torment.

'What happened?' asked McAuliff softly, walking up to the shirtless boy-giant.

'I should have listened to you, mon. Not to him. He was wrong, mon.'

'Tell me what happened,' repeated Alex.

'Barak is dead. I did what he ordered me to do and he is dead. I listened to him and he is dead, mon.'

'He knew the risk; he had to take it. I think he was probably right.'

'No ... He was wrong because he is dead. That makes him wrong, mon.'

'Floyd's gone ... Barak. Who is there now?'

Lawrence's eyes bore into McAuliff's; they were red from silent weeping, and beyond the pride and summoned strength, there was the anguish of a child. And the pleading of a boy. 'You and me, mon. There is no one else ... You will help me, mon?'

Alex returned the rebel's stare; he did not speak.

Welcome to the seat of revolution, McAuliff thought to himself.

21

The Trelawny police made Floyd's identification at 7:02 in the morning. The delay was caused by the lack of any print facilities in Falmouth and the further lack of cooperation on the part of several dozen residents who were systematically routed from their beds during the night to observe the corpse. The captain was convinced that any number of them recognized the bullet-pierced body, but it was not until two minutes past seven when one old man – a gardener from Carrick Foyle – had reacted sufficiently to the face of the bloody mess on the table for the captain to decide to apply sterner methods. He held a lighted cigarette millimetres in front of the old man's left eye, which he stretched open with his free hand. He told the trembling black that he would burn the gelatine of his eyeball unless he told the truth.

The ancient gardener screamed and told the truth. The man who was the corpse on the table had worked for Walter Piersall. His name was Floyd Cotter.

The captain then telephoned several parish precincts for further information on one Cotter, Floyd. There was nothing; they had never heard of him. But the captain had persisted; Kingston's interest in Dr Walter Piersall, before and after his death, was all-inclusive. Even to the point of around-the-clock patrols at the house on the hill in Carrick Foyle. The captain did not know why; it was not his province to question, much less analyse, Kingston's commands. That they were was enough. Whatever the motives that resulted in the harassment of the white scholar before his death, and the continued concern about his residence after, was Kingston's bailiwick, not his. He simply followed orders. He followed them well, even enthusiastically. That was why he was the prefect captain of the parish police in Falmouth.

And that was why he kept making telephone calls about one Floyd Cotter, deceased, whose corpse lay on the table and whose blood would not stop oozing out of the punctures on his face and in his chest and stomach and legs; blood that dried on the pages of *The Gleaner*, hastily scattered about the floor.

At five minutes to eight, as the captain was about to lift the receiver off its base and call the precinct in Sherwood Content, the telephone rang. It was his counterpart in Puerto Seco, near Discovery Bay, whom he had contacted twenty minutes ago. The man said that after their conversation he had talked with his deputies on the early shift. One of the men reported that there was a Floyd with a survey team, headed by an American named McAuliff, who had begun work about ten days ago on the shoreline. The survey had hired a carrier crew out of Ocho Rios. The Government Employment Office had been involved.

The captain then woke up the director of the GEO in Ochee. The man was thoroughly awake by the time he got on the line because he had no telephone and consequently had had to leave his house and walk to a Johnny Canoe store, where he – and most of the neighbourhood – took calls. The employment chief recalled that among the crewmen hired by the American named McAuliff, there *had* been a Floyd, but he did not remember the last name. This Floyd had simply shown up with other applicants who had heard of the available work from the Ochee grapevine. He had not been listed in the employment files: neither had one or two others eventually hired.

The captain listened to the director, thanked him, and said nothing to contradict or enlighten him. But after hanging up the phone, he put in a call to Gordon House in Kingston. To the inspector who headed the search teams that had meticulously gone over Piersall's house in Carrick Foyle.

The inspector's conclusion was the same as the captain's: The deceased Floyd Cotter – former employee of Walter Piersall – had returned with friends to loot the house and been interrupted.

Was anything missing?

Digging in the cellar? In an old cistern out of use for years?

The inspector would fly back to Falmouth by noon. In the meantime, the captain might discreetly interrogate Mr Mc-Auliff. If nothing else, ascertain his whereabouts.

At twenty minutes past nine, the captain and his first deputy drove through the gates of Bengal Court.

Alexander was convincingly agitated. He was appalled – and naturally sorry – that Floyd Cotter had lost his life, but god-damnit, the episode answered several questions. Some very expensive equipment was missing from the supply truck, equipment that could bring high prices in a thieves' market. This Floyd Cotter obviously had been the perpetrator; he was a thief, had been the thief.

Did the captain want a list of the missing items? There was a geodometer, a water scope, half a dozen jewelled compasses, three Polaroid filter screens, five brand-new medicine kits in Royal Society cases, a Rolleiflex camera, and a number of other things of lesser value – but not inexpensive. The captain's deputy wrote as rapidly as he could on a notepad as Alex rattled off the 'missing' items. Twice he asked for spellings; once the point of his pencil broke. It was a harried few minutes.

After the interview was over, the captain and his deputy shook hands with the American geologist and thanked him for his cooperation. McAuliff watched them get into the police car and waved a friendly good-bye as the vehicle sped out of the parking lot through the gates.

A quarter of a mile down the road, the captain braked the patrol car to a stop. He spoke quietly to his deputy.

'Go back through the woods to the beach, mon. Find out who he is with, who comes to see him.'

The deputy removed his visor cap and the creased khaki shirt of his uniform with the yellow insignias of his rank, and reached into the back for a green T-shirt. He slipped it over his head and got out of the car. He stood on the tarred pavement, unbuckled his belt, and slid his holster off the leather strip. He handed it through the window to the captain.

The captain reached down below the dashboard and pulled out a rumpled black baseball cap that was discoloured with age and human sweat. He gave it to the deputy and laughed.

'We all look alike, mon. Aren't you the fella who alla time sell *cocoruru*?'

'Alla time John Crow, mon. Mongoose him not.'

The deputy grinned and started towards the woods beyond the bank of the pavement, where there was a rusty, torn wire fence. It was the demarcation of the Bengal Court property.

The patrol car roared off down the road. The prefect captain of the Falmouth police was in a hurry. He had to drive to Halfmoon Bay and meet a seaplane that was flying in from Kingston.

Charles Whitehall stood in the tall grass on a ridge overlooking the road from Priory-on-the-Sea. Under his arm was the black archive case, clamped shut and held together with three-inch strips of adhesive. It was shortly after twelve noon, and McAuliff would be driving up the road soon.

Alone.

Charles had insisted on it. That is, he had insisted before he had heard McAuliff's words – spoken curtly, defensively – that Barak Moore was dead.

Barak dead.

Bramwell Moore, schoolboy chum from so many years ago in Savanna-la-Mar, dead from Jamaican bullets.

Jamaican bullets.

Jamaican *police* bullets. That was better. In adding the establishmentarian, there was a touch of compassionate logic – a contradiction in terms, thought Whitehall; logic was neither good nor evil, merely logic. Still, words defined logic and words could be interpreted – thus the mendacity of all official statistics: self-serving logic.

His mind was wandering, and he was annoyed with himself.

Barak had known, as he knew, that they were not playing chicken-in-de-kitchen any longer. There was no bandana-headed mother wielding a straw broom, chasing child and fowl out into the yard, laughing and scolding simultaneously. This was a different sort of insurgence. Bandana-headed mothers were replaced by visor-capped men of the state; straw brooms became high-powered rifles. The chickens were ideas . . . far more deadly to the uniformed servants of the state than the loose feathers were to the bandana-headed servants of the family.

Barak dead.

It seemed incredible. Yet not without its positive effect. Barak had not understood the problems of their island; therefore, he had not understood the proper solutions. Barak's solutions were decades away.

First there had to be strength. The many led by a very strong, militant few.

Perhaps one.

In the downhill distance there was a billow of dust; a station wagon was travelling much too fast over the old dirt road.

McAuliff was anxious too.

Charles started back across the field to the entrance drive of the house. He had requested that his Drax Hall host be absent between the hours of twelve and three. No explanations were given, and no questions were asked.

A messiah had returned. That was enough.

'Here it is,' said McAuliff, standing in front of Whitehall in the cool toolshed, holding the smaller archive case in his left hand. 'But before you start fiddling around, I want a couple of things clear.'

Charles Whitehall stared at the American. 'Conditions are superfluous. We both know what must be done.'

'What's not superfluous,' countered Alex, 'is that you understand there'll be no . . . unilateral decisions. This isn't your private war, *Charley-mon*.'

'Are you trying to sound like Barak?'

'Let's say I'm looking after his interests. And mine.'

263

'Yours I can comprehend. Why his? They're not compatible, you know.'

'They're not even connected.'

'So why concern yourself?' Whitehall shifted his eyes to the archive case. He realized that his breathing had become audible; his anxiety was showing, and again he was annoyed with himself. 'Let me have that, please.'

'You asked me a question. I'm going to answer it first,' replied McAuliff. 'I don't trust you, Charlie. You'll use anyone. Anything. Your kind always does. You make pacts and agreements with anything that moves, and you do it very well. You're so flexible you meet yourself around corners. But all the time it's *Sturm und Drang*, and I'm not much for that.'

'Oh, I see. You subscribe to Barak's canefield paratroopers. The chaos of the Fidelisti, where the corporals spit and chew cigars and rape the generals' daughters so society is balanced. Three-year plans and five-year plans and crude uneducated bullies managing the affairs of state. Into disaster, I might add. Don't be a fool, McAuliff. You're better than that.'

'Cut it out, Charley. You're not on a podium addressing your chiefs of staff,' said Alex wearily. 'I don't believe in that over-simplification any more than I believe in your two-plus-two solutions. Pull in your hardware. I'm still the head of this survey. I can fire you in a minute. Very publicly. Now, that might not get you off the island, but your situation won't be the same.'

'What guarantee do I have that you won't force me out?'

'Not much of one. You'll just have to take my word that I want those bastards off my back as badly as you do. For entirely different reasons.'

'Somehow I think you're lying.'

'I wouldn't gamble on that.'

Whitehall searched McAuliff's eyes. 'I won't. I said this conversation was superfluous, and it is. Your conditions are accepted because of what must be done . . . Now, may I have that case, please?'

*   *   *

264

Sam Tucker sat on the terrace, alternately reading the newspaper and glancing over the sea wall to the beach, where Alison and James Ferguson were in deck chairs near the water. Every now and then, when the dazzling Caribbean sun had heated their skin temperatures sufficiently, Alison and the young botanist waded into the water. They did not splash or jump or dive; they simply fell onto the calm surface, as though exhausted. It seemed to be an exercise of weariness for both of them.

There was no joy *sur la plage*, thought Sam, who nevertheless picked up a pair of binoculars whenever Alison began paddling about and scanned the immediate vicinity around where she swam. He focused on any swimmer who came near her; there were not many, and all were recognizable as guests of Bengal Court.

None was a threat, and that's what Sam Tucker was looking for.

Ferguson had returned from Montego Bay a little before noon, just after Alex had driven off to Drax Hall. He had wandered onto the connecting terraces, startling Sam and the temporarily disoriented Lawrence, who had been sitting on the sea wall talking quietly about the dead Barak Moore. They had been stunned because Ferguson had been expansive about his day-off plans in Mo'Bay.

Ferguson arrived looking haggard, a nervous wreck. The assumption was that he had overindulged and was hung to his fuzzy-cheeked gills; the jokes were along this line, and he accepted them with a singular lack of humour. But Sam Tucker did not subscribe to the explanation. James Ferguson was not ravaged by the whisky input of the night before; he was a frightened young man who had not slept. His fear, thought Sam, was not anything he cared to discuss; indeed, he would not even talk about his night in Montego, brushing it off as a dull, unrewarding interlude. He appeared only to want company, as if there was immediate security in the familiar. He seemed to cling to the presence of Alison Booth, offering to fetch and carry . . . A schoolboy's crush or a gay's devotion? Neither fit, for he was neither.

He was afraid.

Very inconsistent behaviour, concluded Sam Tucker.

Tucker suddenly heard the quiet, rapid footsteps behind him and turned. Lawrence, fully clothed now, came across the terrace from the west lawn. The black revolutionary walked over to Sam and knelt – not in fealty, but in a conscious attempt to conceal his large frame behind the sea wall. He spoke urgently.

'I don't like what I see and hear, mon.'

'What's the matter?'

'John Crow hide wid' block chicken!'

'We're being watched?' Tucker put down the newspaper and sat forward.

'Yes, mon. Three, four hours now.'

'Who?'

'A digger been walking on the sand since morning. Him keep circling the west-cove beach too long for tourist leave-behinds. I watch him good. His trouser pants rolled up, look too new, mon. I go behind in the woods and find his shoes. Then I know the trouser pants, mon. Him policeman.'

Sam's gnarled features creased in thought. 'Alex spoke with the Falmouth police around 9:30. In the lobby . . . He said there were two: a chief and an Indian.'

'What, mon?'

'Nothing . . . That's what you saw. What did you hear?'

'Not all I saw.' Lawrence looked over the sea wall, east towards the centre beach. Satisfied, he returned his attention to Sam. 'I follow the digger to the kitchen alley, where he waits for a man to come outside to speak with him. It is the clerk from the lobby desk. Him shake his head many times. The policeman angry, mon.'

'But what did you *hear*, boy?'

'A porter-fella was plenty near, cleaning snapper in his buckets. When the digger-policeman left I ask him hard, mon. He tell me this digger kep' asking where the American fella went, who had telephoned him.'

'And the clerk didn't know.'

'That's right, mon. The policeman was angry.'

'Where is he now?'

'Him wait down at the east shore.' Lawrence pointed over the sea wall, across the dunes to a point on the other side of the central beach. 'See? In front of the sunfish boats, mon.'

Tucker picked up the binoculars and focused on the figure near the shallow-bottomed sailboats by the water. The man and boats were about four hundred yards away. The man was in a torn green T-shirt and rumpled baseball cap; the trousers *were* a contradiction. They were rolled up to the knees, like most scavengers of the beach wore them, but Lawrence was right, they were creased, too clean. The man was chatting with a *cocoruru* peddler, a thin, very dark Jamaican who rolled a wheelbarrow filled with coconuts up and down the beach, selling them to the bathers, cracking them open with a murderous-looking machete. From time to time the man glanced over towards the west-wing terraces, directly into the binoculars, thought Sam. Tucker knew the man did not realize he was being observed; if he did, the reaction would appear on his face. The only reaction was one of irritation, nothing else.

'We'd better supply him with the proper information, son,' said Sam, putting down the binoculars.

'What, mon?'

'Give him something to soothe that anger . . . So he won't think about it too much.'

Lawrence grinned. 'We make up a story, eh, mon?'

'Eh, mon,' replied Sam smiling. 'A casual, very believable kind of story.'

'McAuliff went shopping at Ochee, maybe? Ochee is six, seven miles from Drax Hall, mon. Same road.'

'Why didn't Mrs Booth . . . Alison go with him?'

'Him buy the lady a present. Why not, mon?'

Sam looked at Lawrence, then down at the beach, where Alison was standing up, prepared to go back into the water. 'It's possible, boy. We should make it a little festive, though.' Tucker got out of the chair and walked to the sea wall. 'I think Alison should have a birthday.'

The telephone rang in McAuliff's room. The doors were closed against the heat, and the harsh bell echoed from beyond the slatted panels. Tucker and Lawrence looked at each other, each knowing the other's thoughts. Although McAuliff had not elaborated on his late-morning departure from Bengal Court, neither had he concealed it. Actually, he had asked the desk for a road map, explaining only that he was going for a drive. Therefore the front desk knew that he was not in his room.

Tucker crossed rapidly to the double doors, opened them, and went inside to the telephone.

'Mr McAuliff?' The soft, precise Jamaican voice answered Sam's question with the obvious explanation. It was that of the switchboard operator.

'No, Mr McAuliff is out. May I give him a message?'

'Please, sir, I have a call from Kingston. From a Mr Latham. Will you hold the line, please?'

'Certainly. Tell Mr Latham you've got Sam Tucker on the phone. He may want to speak with me.'

Sam held the telephone under his wrinkled chin as he struck a match to a thin cigar. He had barely drawn the first smoke when he heard the double click of the connecting line. The voice was now Latham's. Latham, the proper bureaucrat from the Ministry who was also committed to the cause of Barak Moore. As Latham spoke, Tucker made the decision not to tell him of Barak's death.

'Mr Tucker?'

'Yes, Mr Latham. Alex drove into Ocho Rios.'

'Very well. You can handle this, I'm sure. We were able to comply with McAuliff's request. He's got his interior runners several days early. They're in Duanvale and will be driving on Route 11 into Queenhythe later this afternoon.'

'Queenhythe's near here, isn't it?'

'Three or four miles from your motel, that's all. They'll telephone when they get in.'

268

'What are their names?'

'They're brothers. Marcus and Justice Hedrik. They're Maroons, of course. Two of the best runners in Jamaica; they know the Cock Pit extremely well, and they're trustworthy.'

'That's good to hear. Alexander will be delighted.'

Latham paused but obviously was not finished. 'Mr Tucker . . . ?'

'Yes, Mr Latham?'

'McAuliff's altered the survey's schedule, it would appear. I'm not sure we understand . . .'

'Nothing to understand, Mr Latham. Alex decided to work from a geographical midpoint. Less room for error that way; like bisecting a triangle from semicircular coordinates. I agree with him.' Tucker inhaled on his thin cigar while Latham's silence conveyed his bewilderment. 'Also,' continued Sam, 'it gives everyone a lot more to do.'

'I see . . . The reasons, then, are quite compatible with . . . let us say, professional techniques?'

'Very professional, Mr Latham.' Tucker realized that Latham would not speak freely on the telephone. Or felt he could not. 'Beyond criticism, if you're worried about the Ministry's concerns. Actually, Alexander could be saving you considerable sums of money. You'll get a lot more data much quicker.'

Latham paused again, as though to telegraph the importance of the following statement. 'Naturally, we're always interested in conserving funds . . . And I assume you *all* agree with the decision to go in so quickly. Into the Cock Pit, that is.'

Sam knew that Latham's statement could be translated into the question: *Does Barak Moore agree?*

'We *all* agree, Mr Latham. We're all professionals.'

'Yes . . . Well, that's splendid. One last item, Mr Tucker.'

'Yes, Mr Latham?'

'We want Mr McAuliff to use all the resources provided him. He's not to stint in an effort to save money; the survey's too important for that.'

Tucker again translated Latham's code easily: *Alex was to*

maintain contact with British Intelligence liaisons. If he avoided them, suspicions would be aroused.

'I'll tell him that, Mr Latham, but I'm sure he's aware of it. These past two weeks have been very routine, very dull – simple coastline geodometrics. Not much call for equipment. Or resources.'

'As long as he knows our feelings,' said Latham rapidly, now anxious to terminate the conversation. 'Goodbye, Mr Tucker.'

'Goodbye, Mr Latham.' Sam held his finger down on the telephone button for several moments, then released it and waited for the switchboard. When the operator came on the line, Tucker asked for the front desk.

'Bengal Court, good afternoon.'

'This is Mr Tucker, west wing 6, Royal Society survey.'

'Yes, Mr Tucker?'

'Mr McAuliff asked me to make arrangements for tonight. He didn't have time this morning; besides, it was awkward. Mrs Booth was with him.' Sam paused, letting his words register.

The clerk automatically responded. 'Yes, Mr Tucker. What can we do for you?'

'It's Mrs Booth's birthday. Do you think the kitchen could whip up a little cake? Nothing elaborate, you understand.'

'Of course! We'd be *delighted*, sir.' The clerk was effusive. 'Our pleasure, Mr Tucker.'

'Fine. That's very kind of you. Just put it on Mr McAuliff's bill –'

'There'll be no charge,' interrupted the clerk, fluidly subservient.

'Very kind indeed. We'll be dining around 8:30, I guess. Our usual table.'

'We'll take care of everything . . .'

'That is, it'll be 8:30,' continued Sam, 'if Mr McAuliff finds his way *back* in time . . .' Tucker paused again, listening for the clerk's appropriate response.

'Oh? Is there a problem, Mr Tucker?'

'Well, the damn fool drove south of Ocho Rios, around Fern Gully, I think, to locate some stalactite sculpture. He told me there were natives who did that sort of thing down there.'

'That's true, Mr Tucker. There are a number of stalactite craftsmen in the Gully. However, there are government restrictions –'

'Oh Lord, son!' interrupted Sam defensively. 'He's just going to find Mrs Booth a little present, that's all.'

The clerk laughed, softly and obsequiously. 'Please don't mistake me, Mr Tucker. Government interference is often most unwarranted. I only meant that I hope Mr McAuliff is successful. When he asked for the petrol map, he should have mentioned where he was going. I might have helped him.'

'Well . . .' drawled Sam conspiratorially, 'he was probably embarrassed, if you know what I mean. I wouldn't mention it; he'd be mad as hell at me.'

'Of course.'

'And thanks for the cake tonight. That's really very nice of you, son.'

'Not at all, sir.'

The goodbyes were rapid, more so on the clerk's part. Sam replaced the telephone and walked back out onto the terrace. Lawrence turned from peering over the wall and sat on the flagstone deck, his back against the sea wall, his body hidden from the beach.

'Mrs Booth and Jimbo-mon are out of water,' said the black revolutionary. 'They are in chairs again.'

'Latham called. The runners will be here this afternoon . . . And I talked with the front desk. Let's see if our information gets transmitted properly.' Tucker lowered himself on the chair slowly and reached for the binoculars on the table. He picked up the newspaper and held it next to the binoculars as he focused on the swimming-pool patio fronting the central beach of Bengal Court.

Within ten seconds he saw the figure of a man dressed in a coat and tie come out of the rear entrance of the motel. It was the front-desk clerk. He walked around the edge of the pool, past a group of wooden, padded sun chairs, nodding to guests, chatting with several. He reached the stone steps leading to the sand and stood there several moments, surveying the beach. Then he started down the steps and across the white, soft sand. He walked diagonally to the right, to the row of sunfish sailboats.

Sam watched as the clerk approached the digger-policeman in the sloppy baseball cap and the *cocoruru* peddler. The *cocoruru* man saw him coming, picked up the handles of his wheelbarrow, and rolled it on the hard sand near the water to get away. The digger-policeman stayed where he was and acknowledged the clerk.

The magnified features in the glass conveyed all that was necessary to Sam Tucker. The policeman's features contorted with irritation. The man was apparently lamenting his waste of time and effort, commodities not easily expended on such a hot day.

The clerk turned and started back across the sand towards the patio. The digger-policeman began walking west, near the water's edge. His gait was swifter now; gone was the stooped posture indigenous to a scavenger of the beach.

He wasn't much of an undercover man, thought Sam Tucker as he watched the man's progress towards the woods of Bengal Court's west property. On his way to his shoes and the egress to the shore road, he never once looked down at the sand for tourist leave-behinds.

McAuliff stood looking over Charles Whitehall's left shoulder as the black scholar ridged the flame of the acetylene torch across the seamed edge of the archive case. The hot point of flame bordered no more than an eighth of an inch behind the seam, at the end of the case.

The top edge of the archive case cracked. Charles extinguished the flame quickly and thrust the end of the case under the tap in the sink. The thin stream of water sizzled into vapour as it touched the hot steel. Whitehall removed his tinted goggles, picked up a miniature hammer, and tapped the steaming end.

It fell off, cracking and sizzling, into the metal sink. Within the case could be seen the oilcloth of a packet. His hands trembling slightly, Charles Whitehall pulled it out. He got off the stool, carrying the rolled-up oilcloth to a deserted area of the bench, and untied the nylon laces. He unwound the packet until it was flat, unzipped the inner lining, and withdrew two sheets of single-spaced typing. As he reached for the bench lamp, he looked at McAuliff.

Alex was fascinated by what he saw. Whitehall's eyes shone with a strange intensity. It was a fever. A messianic fever. A kind of victory rooted in the absolute.

A fanatic's victory, thought McAuliff.

Without speaking, Whitehall began to read. As he finished the first page, he slid it across the bench to Alex.

The word 'Halidon' was in reality three words – or sounds – from the African Ashanti, so corrupted by later phonetics as to be hardly traceable. (Here Piersall included hieroglyphs that were meaningless to Alex.) The root word, again a hieroglyph, was in the sound *leedaw*, translated to convey the picture of a hollowed-out piece of wood that could be held in the hand. The *leedaw* was a primitive instrument of sound, a means of communication over distances in the jungles and hills. The pitch of its wail was controlled by the breath of the blower and the placement of his hand over slits carved through the surface – the basic principle of the woodwind.

The historical parallel had been obvious to Walter Piersall. Whereas the Maroon tribes, living in settlements, used an *abeng* – a type of bugle made from the horns of cattle – to signal their warriors or spread the alarm of an approaching white enemy, the followers of Acquaba were nomadic and could not rely on animal products with any certainty. They returned to the African custom of utilizing the most prolific material of their surroundings: wood.

Once having established the root symbol as the primitive horn, it remained for Piersall to specify the modification of

273

the accompanying sounds. He went back to the Ashanti-Coromanteen studies to extract compatible noun roots. He found the final syllable, or sound, first. It was in the hieroglyph depicting a deep river current, or undertow, that imperilled man or animal in the water. Its sonic equivalent was a bass-toned wail or cry. The phonetic spelling was *nwa*.

The pieces of the primitive puzzle were nearly joined.

The initial sound was the symbol *hayee*, the Coromanteen word meaning the council of their tribal gods.

Hayee – leedaw – nwa.

The low cry of a jungle horn signifying peril, a supplication to the council of the gods.

Acquaba's code. The hidden key that would admit an outsider into the primitive tribal sect.

Primitive and not primitive at all.

Halidon. Hollydawn. A wailing instrument whose cry was carried by the wind to the gods.

This, then, was Dr Walter Piersall's last gift to his island sanctuary. The means to reach, enlist and release a powerful force for the good of Jamaica. To convince 'it' to accept its responsibility.

There remained only to determine which of the isolated communities in the Cock Pit mountains was the Halidon. Which would respond to the code of Acquaba?

Finally, the basic scepticism of the scholar inserted itself into Piersall's document. He did not question the existence of the Halidon; what he did speculate on was its rumoured wealth and commitment. Were these more myth than current fact? Had the myth grown out of proportion to the conceivably diminished resources?

The answer was in the Cock Pit.

McAuliff finished the second page and looked over at Charles Whitehall. The black fascist had walked from the workbench to the small window overlooking the Drax Hall fields. Without turning, he spoke quietly, as though he knew Alex was staring at him, expecting him to speak.

'Now we know what must be done. But we must proceed cautiously, sure of every step. A wrong move on our part and the cry of the Halidon will vanish with the wind.'

22

The Caravel prop plane descended on its western approach to the small Boscobel airfield in Oracabessa. The motors revved in short bursts to counteract the harsh wind and rain of the sudden downpour, forcing the aircraft to enter the strip cleanly. It taxied to the far end, turned awkwardly, and rolled back towards the small, one-level concrete passenger terminal.

Two Jamaican porters ran through the low gates to the aircraft, both holding umbrellas. Together they pushed the metal step unit to the side of the plane, under the door; the man on the left then knocked rapidly on the fuselage.

The door was slapped open by a large white man who immediately stepped out, waving aside the offer of the two umbrellas. He jumped from the top level to the ground and looked around in the rain.

His right hand was in his jacket pocket.

He turned up to the aircraft door and nodded. A second large white man disembarked and ran across the muddy space towards the concrete terminal. His right hand, too, was in his pocket. He entered the building, glanced around, and proceeded out the exit to the parking area.

Sixty seconds later the gate by the luggage depot was swung open by the second man and a Mercedes 660 limousine drove through towards the Caravel, its wheels spinning frequently in the drenched earth.

The two Jamaicans remained by the step unit, their umbrellas waiting.

The Mercedes pulled alongside the plane, and the tiny, ancient figure of Julian Warfield was helped down the steps, his head and body shielded by the blacks. The second white man held the door of the Mercedes; his large companion was in front of the car, scanning the distance and the few passengers who had come out of the terminal.

When Warfield was enclosed in the back seat, the Jamaican driver stepped out and the second white man got behind the wheel. He honked the horn once; his companion turned and raced around to the left front door and climbed in.

The Mercedes's deep-throated engine roared as the limousine backed up beyond the tail assembly of the Caravel, then belched forward and sped through the gate.

With Julian Warfield in the back seat were Peter Jensen and his wife, Ruth.

'We'll drive to Peale Court, it's not far from here,' said the small, gaunt financier, his eyes alive and controlled. 'How long do you have? With reasonable caution.'

'We rented a car for a trip to Dunn's Falls,' replied Peter. 'We left it in the lot and met the Mercedes outside. Several hours, at least.'

'Did you make it clear you were going to the Falls?'

'Yes. I invited McAuliff.'

Warfield smiled. 'Nicely done, Peter.'

The car raced over the Oracabessa road for several miles and turned into a gravel drive flanked by two white stone posts. On both were identical brass plaques reading PEALE COURT They were polished to a high gloss, a rich mixture of gold and black.

At the end of the drive was a long parking area in front of a longer, one-storey white stucco house with expensive wood in the doors and many windows. It was perched on top of a steep incline above the beach.

Warfield and the Jensens were admitted by a passive, elderly black woman in a white uniform, and Julian led the way to a veranda overlooking the waters of Golden Head Bay.

The three of them settled in chairs, and Warfield politely asked the Jamaican servant to bring refreshments. Perhaps a light rum punch.

The rain was letting up; streaks of yellow and orange could be seen beyond the grey sheets in the sky.

'I've always been fond of Peale Court,' said Warfield. 'It's so peaceful.'

'The view is breathtaking,' added Ruth. 'Do you own it, Julian?'

'No, my dear. But I don't believe it would be difficult to acquire. Look around, if you like. Perhaps you and Peter might be interested.'

Ruth smiled and, as if on cue, rose from her chair. 'I think I shall.'

She walked back through the veranda doors into the larger living room with the light brown marble floor. Peter watched her, then looked over at Julian. 'Are things that serious?'

'I don't want her upset,' replied Warfield.

'Which, of course, gives me my answer.'

'Possibly. Not necessarily. We've come upon disturbing news. MI5 and over here its brother, MI6.'

Peter reacted as though he'd been jolted unnecessarily. 'I thought we had that area covered. *Completely*. It was passive.'

'On the island, perhaps. Sufficient for our purposes. Not in London. Obviously.' Warfield paused and took a deep breath, pursing his narrow, wrinkled lips. 'Naturally, we'll take steps immediately to intercede, but it may have gone too far. Ultimately, we can control the Service . . . if we must, right out of the Foreign Office. What bothers me now is the current activity.'

Peter Jensen looked out over the veranda railing. The afternoon sun was breaking through the clouds. The rain had stopped.

'Then we have two adversaries. This Halidon – whatever in blazes it is. And British Intelligence.'

'Precisely. What is of paramount importance, however, is to keep the two separate. Do you see?'

Jensen returned his gaze to the old man. 'Of course. Assuming they haven't already joined forces.'

'They have not.'

'You're sure of that, Julian?'

'Yes. Don't forget, we first learned of this Halidon through MI5 personnel – specialist level. Dunstone's payrolls are diverse. If contact had been made, we'd know it.'

Again Jensen looked out at the waters of the bay, his expression pensive and questioning. 'Why? *Why?* The man was offered two million dollars ... There is nothing, *nothing* in his dossier that would give an *inkling* of this. McAuliff is suspect of *all* government interference ... quite rabid on the subject, actually. It was one of the reasons I proposed him.'

'Yes,' said Warfield noncommittally. 'McAuliff was your idea, Peter ... Don't mistake me, I am not holding you responsible, I concurred with your choice ... Describe what happened last night. This morning.'

Jensen did so, ending with the description of the fishing boat veering off into open water and the removal of the medical equipment from the motel room. 'If it was an MI6 operation, it was crude, Julian. Intelligence has too many facilities available to be reduced to motels and fishing boats. If we only knew what happened.'

'We do. At least, I think we do,' replied Warfield. 'Late last night the house of a dead white man, an anthropologist named Piersall, was broken into; ten, twelve miles from the coast. There was a skirmish. Two men were killed that we know of: others could have been wounded. They officially called it a robbery, which, of course, it wasn't really. Not in the sense of larceny.'

'I know the name "Piersall" –'

'You should. He was the university radical who filed that insane Letter of Intent with the Department of Territories.'

'Of course! He was going to purchase half the Cock Pit! That was months ago. He was a lunatic.' Jensen lighted his pipe; he gripped the bowl as he did so, he did not merely hold it. 'So there is a third intruder,' he said, his words drifting off quietly, nervously.

'Or one of the first two, Peter.'

'How? What do you mean?'

'You just ruled out MI6. It could be the Halidon.'

Jensen stared at Warfield. 'If so, it would mean McAuliff is working with both camps. And if Intelligence has not made contact, it's because McAuliff has not permitted it.'

'A very complicated young man.' The old financier placed his glass down carefully on a tiled table next to his chair. He turned slightly to look through the veranda doors; the voice of Ruth Jensen could be heard chatting with the Jamaican maid inside the house. Warfield looked back at Peter. He pointed his thin, bony finger to a brown leather case on a white wicker table across the open porch. 'That is for you, Peter. Please get it.'

Jensen rose from his chair, walked to the table, and stood by the case. It was smaller than the attaché variety. And thicker. Its two hasps were secured by combination locks. 'What are the numbers?'

'The left lock is three zeros. The right, three fives. You may alter the combinations as you wish.' Peter bent down and began manipulating the tiny vertical dials. Warfield continued. 'To-morrow you will start into the interior. Learn everything you can. Find out who comes to see him, for certainly he will have visitors. And the minute you establish the fact that he is in actual contact, and whom with, send out Ruth on some medical pretext with the information . . . Then, Peter, you must kill him. McAuliff is a keystone. His death will panic both camps, and we shall know all we need to know.'

Jensen lifted the top of the leather case. Inside, recessed in the green felt, was a brand-new Luger pistol. Its steel glistened, except for a dull space below the trigger housing where the serial number had been removed. Below the weapon was a five-inch cylinder, one end grooved.

A silence.

'You've never asked this of me, Julian. Never . . . You mustn't.' Jensen turned and stared at Warfield.

'I am not asking, Peter. I am demanding. Dunstone plc has given you everything. And now it needs you in a way it has not needed you before. You must, you see.'

FOUR

The Cock Pit

23

They began at midpoint of the western perimeter, two and a half miles south of Weston Favel, on the edge of the Cock Pit range. They made base camp on the bank of a narrow offshoot of the Martha Brae. All but the runners, Marcus and Justice Hedrik, were stunned by the seemingly impenetrable walls of jungle that surrounded them.

Strange, contradictory forests that were filled with the wet verdancy of tropic growth and the cold massiveness of sky-reaching black and green associated with northern climates. Dense macca-fat palms stood next to silk-cotton, or ceiba, trees that soared out of sight, their tops obscured by the midgrowth. Mountain cabbage and bull thatch, orchid and moss, fungi and eucalyptus battled for their individual rights to coexist in the Oz-like jungle primaeval.

The ground was covered with ensnaring spreads of fern and pteridophyte, soft, wet and treacherous. Pools of swamp-like mud were hidden in the thick, crowded sprays of underbrush. Sudden hills rose out of nowhere, remembrances of Oligocene upheavals, never to be settled back into the cradle of the earth.

The sounds of the screeching bat and parrot and tanager intruded on the forest's undertones; jungle rats and the mongoose could be heard intermittently in their unseen games of death. Every now and then there was the scream of a wild pig, pursuing or in panic.

And far in the distance, in the clearing of the river bank, were the mountains, preceded by sudden stretches of untamed grassland. Strangely grey with streaks of deep green and blue and yellow – rain and hot sunlight in an unceasing interchange.

All this fifteen minutes by air from the gaudy strips of Montego.

Unbelievable.

McAuliff had made contact with the north-coast contacts of British Intelligence. There were five, and he had reached each one.

They had given him another reason to consign R. C. Hammond to the despised realm of the manipulator. For the Intelligence people were of small comfort. They stated perfunctorily their relief at his reporting, accepted his explanations of routine geographic chores that kept him occupied, and assured him – with more sound than conviction – that they were at his beck and call.

One man, the MI6 contact from Port Maria, drove down the coast to Bengal Court to meet Alex. He was a portly black merchant who limited his identification to the single name of 'Garvey'. He insisted on a late-night rendezvous in the tiny bar of the motel, where he was known as a liquor distributor.

It did not take McAuliff long to realize that Garvey, ostensibly there to assure him of total cooperation and safety, was actually interrogating him for a report that would be sent back to London. Garvey had the stench and sight of a practised informer about him. The stench was actual: The man suffered from body odour, which could not be concealed by liberal applications of bay rum. The sight was in his eyes – ferret-like, and a touch bloodshot. Garvey was a man who sought out opportunities and enjoyed the fruits thereof.

His questions were precise, McAuliff's answers apparently not satisfactory. And all questions led to the one question, the only one that mattered: Any progress concerning the Halidon?

Anything?

Unknown observers, strangers in the distance . . . a signal, a sign – no matter how remote or subtle?

Anything?

'Absolutely nothing' was a hard reply for Garvey to accept.

What about the men in the green Chevrolet who had followed him in Kingston? Tallon had traced them to the anthropologist Walter Piersall. Piersall had been a white agitator . . . common knowledge. Piersall had telephoned McAuliff . . . the Courtleigh switchboard cooperated with MI6. What did Piersall want?

Alex claimed he did not – could not – know, as Piersall had never reached him. An agitator, white *or* black, was an unpredictable bearer of unpredictable news. Predictably, this agitator had had an accident. It might be presumed – from what little McAuliff had been told by Tallon and others – that Piersall had been closing in on Dunstone; without a name, of course. If so, he, McAuliff, was a logical person to reach. But this was conjecture; there was no way to confirm it as fact.

What had happened to the late-arriving Samuel Tucker? Where had he been?

Drinking and whoring in Montego Bay. Alex was sorry he had caused so much trouble about Sam; he should have known better. Sam Tucker was an incorrigible wanderer, albeit the best soil analyst in the business.

The perspiring Garvey was bewildered, frustrated by his confusion. There was too much activity for McAuliff to remain so insulated.

Alex reminded the liaison in short, coarse words that there was far too much survey activity – logistical, employment, above all government paperwork – for him not to be insulated. What the hell did Garvey think he had been doing?

The interview lasted until 1:30 in the morning. Before leaving, the MI6 contact reached into his filthy briefcase and withdrew a metallic object the size of a pen-and-pencil case, with its approximate thickness. It was a miniaturized radio-signal transmitter, set to a specific frequency. There were three thick, tiny glass lights across the top of the small panel. The first, explained Garvey, was a white light that indicated sufficient power for sending when turned on – not unlike the illuminated filigree of a strobe light. The second, a red light, informed the operator that his signal was being transmitted. The third, a green light, confirmed the reception of the signal by a corresponding device within a radius of twenty-five miles. There would be two simple codes, one for normal conditions, one for emergency. Code One was to be transmitted twice daily, once every twelve hours. Code Two, when aid was needed.

The receiving set, said Garvey, was capable of defining the signal within a diameter of one thousand yards by means of an attached radarscope with terrain coordinates. Nothing was left to chance. Unbelievable.

The incredible assumption, therefore, was that the Intelligence men would never be more than twenty-five miles away, and Hammond's 'guaranteed' safety factor was the even more ridiculous assumption that the jungle distance could be traversed and the exact location pinpointed within a time period that precluded danger.

R. C. Hammond was a winner, thought McAuliff.

'Is this everything?' McAuliff asked the sweating Garvey. 'This goddamn metal box is our protection?'

'There are additional precautions,' Garvey replied enigmatically. 'I told you, nothing is left to chance –'

'What the hell does that mean?'

'It means you are protected. I am not authorized to speak further. As a matter of fact, mon, I do not *know* anything further. I am, like you, merely an employee. I do what I am told to do, say what I am told to say . . . And now I have said enough. I have an uncomfortable drive back to Port Maria.'

The man named Garvey rose from the table, picked up his tattered briefcase, and waddled towards the door of the dimly lit room. Before leaving, however, he could not help himself. He stopped at the bar, where one of the motel's managers was standing, and solicited an order of liquor.

McAuliff shook his thoughts loose as he heard the voices of Ruth and Peter Jensen behind him. He was sitting on a dried mud flat above the river bank; the Jensens were talking as they walked across the clearing from their bivouac tent. It amazed

286

Alex – *they* amazed him. They walked so casually, so normally, over the chopped Cock Pit ground cover; one might think they had entered Regent's Park for a stroll.

'Majestic place in its way, rather,' said Peter, removing the ever present pipe from between his teeth.

'It is the odd combination of colour and substance, don't you think, Alex?' Ruth had her arm linked through her husband's. A noonday walk down the Strand. 'One is so very sensuous, the other so massive and intricate.'

'You make the terms sound contradictory, darling. They're not, you know.' Peter chuckled as his wife feigned minor exasperation.

'He has an incorrigibly pornographic mind, Alex. Pay no attention. Still, he's right. It is majestic. And positively *dense*. Where's Alison?'

'With Ferguson and Sam. They're testing the water.'

'Jimbo-mon's going to use up all of his film, I dare say,' muttered Peter as he helped his wife to sit down next to McAuliff. 'That new camera he brought back from Montego has consumed him.'

'Frightfully expensive, I should think.' Ruth smoothed the unsmoothable cloth of her bivouac slacks, like a woman not used to being without a skirt. Or a woman who was nervous. 'For a boy who's always saying he's bone-stony, quite an extravagance.'

'He didn't buy it; he borrowed it,' said Alex. 'From a friend he knew last year in Port Antonio.'

'That's right, I forgot.' Peter relit his pipe as he spoke. 'You were all here last year, weren't you?'

'Not all, Peter. Just Sam and me; we worked for Kaiser. And Ferguson. He was with the Craft Foundation. No one else.'

'Well, Charles is Jamaican,' intruded Ruth nervously. 'Surely he flies back and forth. Heaven knows, he must be rich enough.'

'That's a rather brass speculation, luv.'

'Oh, come off it, Peter. Alex knows what I mean.'

McAuliff laughed. 'I don't think he worries about money.

He's yet to submit his bills for the survey outfits. I have an idea they're the most expensive in Harrod's Safari Shop.'

'Perhaps he's embarrassed,' said Peter, smiling. 'He looks as though he had jumped right off the cinema screen. The black hunter; very impressive image, if somewhat contrived.'

'Now you're the one who's talking brass, luv. Charles *is* impressive.' Ruth turned to Alex. 'My over-age Lochinvar is green with envy.'

'That camera's damn well new . . . not the sort of thing one lends, I shouldn't think.' Peter looked at McAuliff as he spoke the *non sequitur.*

'Depends on the friend, I guess,' replied Alex, aware that Peter was implying something beyond his words. 'Ferguson can be a likeable guy.'

'*Very,*' added Ruth. 'And so helpless, somehow. Except when he's over his equipment. Then he's positively a whiz.'

'Which is all I really care about.' McAuliff addressed this judgment to Peter. 'But then, you're all whizzes, cameras and fancy clothes and aromatic pipes notwithstanding.' Alex laughed.

'Got me there, old chap.' Peter removed his pipe and shook his head. 'Dreadful habit.'

'Not at all,' said McAuliff. 'I like the smell, I really do. I'd smoke one myself but my tongue burns. Then stings.'

'There are preventive measures, but it's a dull subject . . . What's fascinating is this jungle laboratory we're in. Have you decided on crew assignments?'

'Vaguely,' answered Alex. 'Doesn't make an awful lot of difference. Who do you want?'

'One of those brothers for me,' said Ruth. 'They seem to know *exactly* where they are. I'd be lost in half a mo'! . . . Of course, that's selfish; my work is least important . . .'

'We still don't want to lose you, do we, Peter?' McAuliff leaned forward.

'Not as long as she behaves.'

'Take your pick,' said Alex. 'Marcus or Justice?'

'What marvellously dotty names!' cried Ruth. 'I choose Justice.' She looked at her husband. 'Always justice.'

'Yes, of course, my dear.'

'All right,' agreed McAuliff. 'Then Marcus'll be with me. One of them has to. And Alison asked for Lawrence, if you don't mind, Peter.'

'Not at all, old chap. Sorry his friend . . . what was his name? Floyd? Yes, Floyd. Sorry he jumped ship, as it were. Did you ever find out what happened to him?'

'No,' replied Alex. 'He just disappeared. Unreliable guy. Something of a thief, too, according to Lawrence.'

'Pity . . . He seemed rather intelligent.'

'*That's* condescending, darling. Worse than brassy.' Ruth Jensen picked up a tiny stone and chucked it into the narrow river offshoot.

'Then just pick out a stout fellow who'll promise to lead me back to camp for meals and sleep.'

'Fine. I'll do that. We'll work four-hour field sessions, staying in touch by radio. I don't want anyone going beyond a sonic mile from camp for the first few days.'

'*Beyond!*' Ruth looked at McAuliff, her voice having risen an octave. '*Dear* Alex, if I stumble more than twenty feet into that maze of overgrowth, commit me!'

'Rubbish,' countered her husband, 'when you start cracking rocks, you lose time *and* distance . . . Speaking of which, Alex, old boy, I presume there'll be a fairly steady flow of visitors. To observe our progress; that sort of thing.'

'Why?' McAuliff was now aware that both husband and wife were sending out abstract, perhaps unconscious, signals. Peter less than Ruth. He was subtler, surer of himself than she was. But not completely sure. 'We'll bring out field reports every ten days or so. Rotate days off that way. That'll be good enough.'

'Well, we're not exactly at the end of nowhere; although I grant you, it looks like it. I should think the moneymen would want to check up on what they're paying for.'

Peter Jensen had just made a mistake, and McAuliff was suddenly alarmed. 'What moneymen?'

Ruth Jensen had picked up another stone, about to throw it into the brackish river. Arm poised, she froze for a second before hurling it. The moment was not lost on any of them. Peter tried to minimize it.

'Oh . . . some Royal Society titans or perhaps a few of these buggers from the Ministry. I know the RS boys, and God knows the Jamaicans have been less than cordial. I just thought . . . Oh, well, perhaps I'm off-centre.'

'Perhaps,' said Alex quietly, 'you're ahead of me. On-site inspectors aren't unusual. I was thinking about the convenience. Or lack of it. It took us nearly a day to get here. Of course, we had the truck and the equipment . . . Still, it seems like a lot of trouble.'

'Not really.' Peter Jensen tapped his pipe on his boots. 'I've been checking the maps, looking about from the river clearing. The grasslands are nearer than we think. Less than a couple of miles, I'd say. Light planes or helicopters could easily land.'

'That's a good point. I hadn't thought of it.' McAuliff leaned forward once again to engage Peter, but Peter did not look at him now. 'I mean if we needed . . . equipment or supplies, we could get them much quicker than I'd anticipated. Thanks, Peter.'

'Oh, don't *thank* him.' Ruth spoke with a nervous giggle. 'Don't *cater* to him.' She looked briefly at her husband; McAuliff wished he could have seen her eyes. 'Peter just wants to convince himself he's a hop-skip from a pub.'

'Rubbish. Just idle conversation, old girl . . .'

'I think he's bored with us, Ruth,' said Alex laughing softly, almost intimately. 'I think he wants to see new faces.'

'As long as it's not new bodies, my dear, the tolerance is possible,' retorted Ruth Jensen with throated caricature.

The three of them laughed out loud.

McAuliff knew the humour was forced. Mistakes had been made, and the Jensens were afraid.

Peter *was* looking for new faces . . . or a new face. A face he believed Alex expected.

Who was it?

Was it possible . . . remotely possible that the Jensens were not what they seemed?

There was the sound of whistling from a path in the north bush. Charles Whitehall emerged into the clearing, his safari uniform pressed and clean, in counterpoint to the rumpled clothes of Marcus Hedrik, the older brother of the two Cock Pit runners. Marcus remained a respectful distance behind Whitehall, his passive black face inscrutable.

McAuliff rose from the ground and spoke to the Jensens. 'It's Charley. There's a hill community several miles west of the river; he was going to try to hire a couple of hands.'

Ruth and Peter took their cue, because they very much wanted to. 'Well, we've still got some equipment sorting to do,' said the husband, rising quickly.

'Indeed we do! Help me up, luv.'

The Jensens waved to Charles Whitehall and rapidly started for their tent.

McAuliff met Whitehall at the midpoint of the clearing. The black scholar dismissed Marcus Hedrik, instructing him to issue preparation orders to the rest of the crew about the evening patrols. Alex was fascinated to watch and listen to Charley-mon speaking to the runner. He fell easily into the hill country patois – damn near indecipherable to McAuliff – and used his hands and eyes in gestures and looks that were absolutely compatible with the obtuse speech.

'You do that very well,' said Alex as the runner trudged out of hearing.

'I should. It's what you hired me for. I am the best there is.'

'That's one of the things I like about you, Charley. You take compliments so gracefully.'

'You did not hire me for my graces. They are a bonus you don't deserve.' Whitehall allowed himself a slight smile. 'You enjoy calling me "Charley", McAuliff?' added the elegant black.

'Do you object?'

'Not really. Because I understand. It is a defence mechanism; you Americans are rife with them. "Charley" is an idiomatic leveller, peculiarly indigenous to the sixties and seventies. The Vietcong were "Charleys", so too the Cambodians and the Laotians; so too your man on the American street. It makes you feel superior. Strange that the name should be Charley, is it not?'

'It happens to be *your* name.'

'Yes, of course, but I think that is almost beside the point.' The black looked away briefly, then back at Alex. 'The name "Charles" is Germanic in origin, actually. Its root meaning is "full grown" or possibly – here scholars differ – "great size". Is it not interesting that you Americans take just such a name and reverse its connotation?'

McAuliff exhaled audibly and spoke wearily. 'I accept the lesson for the day and all its subtle anti-colonialism. I gather you'd prefer I call you "Charles", or "Whitehall", or perhaps "Great Black Leader".'

'Not for a moment. "Charley" is perfectly fine. Even amusing. And, after all, it is better than "Rufus".'

'Then what the hell is this all about?'

Whitehall smiled – again, only slightly – and lowered his voice. 'Until ten seconds ago, Marcus Hedrik's brother has been standing behind the lean-to on our left. He was trying to listen to us. He is gone now.'

Alex whipped his head around. Beyond the large tarpaulin lean-to, erected to cover some camp furniture against a forest shower, Justice Hedrik could be seen walking slowly towards two other crewmen across the clearing. Justice was younger than his brother Marcus, perhaps in his late twenties, and stockily muscular.

'Are you sure? I mean, that he was listening to us?'

'He was carving a piece of ceiba wood. There is too much to do to waste time carving artefacts. He was listening. Until I looked over at him.'

'I'll remember that.'

'Yes. Do. But do not give it under emphasis. Runners are splendid fellows when they are taking in tourist groups; the tips are generous. I suspect neither brother is too pleased to be with us. Our trip is professional – worse, academically professional. There is not much in it for them. So there will be some hostility.'

McAuliff started to speak, then hesitated. He was bewildered. 'I . . . I may have missed something. What's that got to do with his listening?'

Whitehall blinked slowly, as if patiently explaining to an inept pupil – which, obviously, he felt was the case. 'In the primitive intelligence, hostility is usually preceded by an overt, blunt curiosity.'

'Thank you, Dr Strangelove.' Alex did not hide his irritation. 'Let's get off this. What happened over in the hill community?'

'I sent a messenger to Maroon Town. I asked for a very private meeting with the Colonel of the Maroons. He will listen; he will accept.'

'I wasn't aware a meeting was that tough to get. If I remember what Barak said, and I do, we just offer money.'

'We do not want a tourist audience, McAuliff. No tribal artefacts or Afro-Carib beads bought for an extra two-dollah-Jamaican. Our business is more serious than tourist trade. I want to prepare the Colonel psychologically; make him think.'

Alex paused; Whitehall was probably right. If what Barak Moore had said had validity. If the Colonel of the Maroons was the sole contact with the Halidon, the decision to make that contact would not be lightly arrived at; a degree of psychological preparation would be preferable to none at all. But not so much as to make him run, avoid the decision.

'How do you think you accomplished that?' asked McAuliff.

'I hired the leader of the community to act as courier. I gave him one hundred dollars, which is like offering either of us roughly a quarter of a million. The message requests a meeting in four days, four hours after the sun descends over the mountains –'

293

'The Arawak symbols?' interrupted Alex.

'Precisely. Completed by specifying that the meeting should take place to the right of the Coromanteen crescent, which I would presume to be the Colonel's residence. The Colonel was to send back the exact location with our courier ... Remember, the Colonel of the Maroon Tribes is an ancestral position; he is a descendant and, like all princes of the realm, schooled in its traditions. We shall know soon enough if he perceives us to be quite out of the ordinary.'

'How?'

'If the location he chooses is in some unit of four. Obviously.'

'Obviously ... so for the next few days we wait.'

'Not just wait, McAuliff. We will be watched, observed very closely. We must take extreme care that we do not appear as a threat. We must go about our business quite professionally.'

'I'm glad to hear that. We're being paid to make a geological survey.'

24

With the first penetration into the Cock Pit, the work of the survey consumed each member of the team. Whatever their private fears or foreign objectives, they were professionals, and the incredible laboratory that was the Cock Pit demanded their professional attentions.

Portable tables, elaborately cased microscopes, geoscopes, platinum drills, sediment prisms and depository vials were transported by scientist and carrier alike into the barely penetrable jungles and into the grasslands. The four-hour field sessions were more honoured in the breach; none cared to interrupt his experiments or analyses for such inconveniences as meals and routine communications. The disciplines of basic precautions were swiftly consigned to aggravating nuisances. It took less than a full working day for the novelty of the ever-humming, ever-irritating walkie-talkies to wear off. McAuliff found it necessary to remind Peter Jensen and James Ferguson angrily that it was mandatory to leave the radio receiving switches on, regardless of the intermittent chatter between stations.

The first evenings lent credence to the wisdom of Charles Whitehall's purchases at Harrod's Safari Shop: The team sat around the fires in canvas chairs, as though recuperating from the day's hunt. But instead of talk of cat, horn, spore and bird, other words flew around, spoken with no less enthusiasm. *Zinc, manganese* and *bauxite; ochres, gypsum and phosphate . . . Cretaceous, Eocene, shale* and *igneous; wynne grass, tamarind, bloodwood; guano, gros-michel* and *woman's tongue . . . arid* and *acid* and *peripatus; water runoffs, gas pockets* and *layers of vesicular lava – honeycombs of limestone.*

The overriding generalization was shared by everyone: The Cock Pit was an extraordinarily fruitful land mass with abundant reserves of rich soil, available water and unbelievable deposits of gases and ores.

All this was accepted as fact before the morning of the third day. McAuliff listened as Peter Jensen summed it up with frightening clarity.

'It's inconceivable that no one's gone in and developed. I dare say Brasilia couldn't hold a candle! Three-quarters of the life force is right here, waiting to be used!'

The reference to the city carved out of the Brazilian jungles made Alex swallow and stare at the enthusiastic, middle-aged, pipe-smoking mineral expert.

We're going to build a city . . . Julian Warfield's words.

Unbelievable. And viable.

It did not take great imagination to understand Dunstone now. The project was sound, taking only gigantic sums of capital to set it in motion; sums available to Dunstone. And once set in motion, the entire island could be tied to the incredible development . . . Armies of workers, communities, *one source*.

Ultimately, the government.

Kingston could not, *would* not turn it off. Once in motion – *one source* – the benefits would be overwhelming and undeniable. The enormity of the cash flow alone could subvert the parliament. Slices of the gigantic pie.

Economically and psychologically, Kingston would become dependent on Dunstone plc.

So complicated, yet so basically, ingeniously simple.

Once they have Kingston, they have the laws of the land in their vaults. To shape as they will. Dunstone will own a nation . . . R. C. Hammond's words.

It was nearly midnight; the carriers were banking the fires under the scrutiny of the two runners, Marcus and Justice Hedrik. The black revolutionary, Lawrence, was playing his role as one of the crew, subservient and pleasant, but for ever scanning the forests beyond, never allowing himself to be too far away from Alison Booth.

The Jensens and Ferguson had gone to their tents. McAuliff, Sam Tucker and Alison sat around a small bivouac table, the light of the dying fires flickering across their faces as they talked quietly.

'Jensen's right, Alexander,' said Tucker, lighting a thin cigar. 'Those behind this know exactly what they're doing. I'm no ore expert, but one strike, one hint of a mother lode, and you couldn't stop the speculation money.'

'It's a company named Dunstone.'

'What is?'

'Those behind ... the company's called Dunstone; the man's name is Warfield. Julian Warfield. Alison knows.'

Sam held the cigar between his fingers and looked at McAuliff. 'They hired you.' Tucker's statement was spoken slowly, a touch gruffly.

'He did,' replied Alex. 'Warfield did.'

'Then this Royal Society grant ... the Ministry, and the Institute, *are* covers.'

'Yes.'

'And you knew it from the beginning.'

'So does British Intelligence. I wasn't just acting as an informer, Sam. They trained me ... as best they could over a couple of weeks.'

'Was there any particular reason why you kept it a secret, Alexander?' Tucker's voice – especially as capped with McAuliff's name – was not comforting. 'I think you should have told me. Especially after that meeting in the hills. We've been together a long time, boy ... No. I don't think you acted properly.'

'He was generously proper, Sam,' said Alison, with a combination of precision and warmth. 'For your benefit, I speak from experience. The less you're aware of, the better your prospects. Take my word for it.'

'Why should I?' asked Tucker.

'Because I've been there. And because I was there. I'm here now.'

'She's tied in against Chatellerault. That's what I couldn't tell you. She worked for Interpol. A data bank picked out her name; it was made to look so completely logical. She wanted to get out of England –'

'*Had* to get out, my darling . . . Do you see, Sam? The computer was Interpol's; all the intelligence services are first cousins, and don't let anyone tell you otherwise. MI5 ran a cross-reference, and here I am. Valuable bait, another complication . . . Don't be anxious to learn too much. Alex was right.'

The ensuing silence was artificial. Tucker inhaled on his thin cigar, the unasked questions more pronounced by their absence. Alison whisked strands of hair, let down for the evening, off her forehead. McAuliff poured himself a small quantity of Scotch. Finally Sam Tucker spoke.

'It's fortunate I trust you, Alexander.'

'I know that. I counted on it.'

'But *why*?' continued Sam quietly. 'Why in hell did you *do* it? You're not that hungry. Why did you work for *them*?'

'For whom? Or which? Dunstone or British Intelligence?'

Tucker paused, staring at Alex before he replied. '*Jesus*, I don't know. Both, I guess, boy.'

'I accepted the first before the second showed up. It was a good contract, the best I'd ever been offered. Before I realized it, I was locked in. I was convinced I couldn't get out . . . by both sides. At one point, it was as simple as staying alive . . . Then there were guarantees and promises . . . and more guarantees and more promises.' McAuliff stared across the clearing; it was strange. Lawrence was crouched over the embers of a fire, looking at them. 'Before you know it, you're in some kind of crazy cell block, hurtling around the confining space, bouncing off the walls . . . that's not a very sane picture.'

'Move and countermove, Sam,' interrupted Alison. 'They're experts.'

'Who? Which?' Tucker leaned forward in his chair, holding Alison with his old eyes.

'Both,' answered the girl firmly. 'I saw what Chatellerault did to my husband. I know what Interpol did to me.'

The silence returned once more, less strained than before. And once again, Sam Tucker broke it softly.

'You've got to define your enemies, Alexander. I get the feeling you haven't done that ... present company excepted as allies, I sincerely hope.'

'I've defined them as best I can. I'm not sure those definitions will hold. It's complicated, at least for me.'

'Then simplify, boy. When you're finished, who wants you hanged the quickest?'

McAuliff looked at Alison. 'Again, both. Dunstone literally; MI5 and 6 figuratively. One dead, the other dependent – subject to recall. A name in a data bank. That's very real.'

'I agree,' said Tucker, relighting his thin cigar. 'Now, let's reverse the process. Who can *you* hang the quickest? The surest?'

Alex laughed quietly, joined by Alison. The girl spoke. 'My Lord, you *do* think alike.'

'That doesn't answer the question. Who the quickest?'

'Dunstone, I imagine. At the moment, it's more vulnerable. Warfield made a mistake; he thinks I'm *really* hungry. He thinks he bought me because he made me a part of them. They fall, I fall ... I'd have to say Dunstone.'

'All right,' replied Sam, assuming the mantle of a soft-spoken attorney. 'Enemy number one defined as Dunstone. You can extricate yourself by simple blackmail: third-person knowledge, documents tucked away in lawyers' offices. Agreed?'

'Yes.'

'That leaves enemy number two: Her Majesty's Intelligence boys. Let's define them. What's their hook into you?'

'Protection. It's supposed to be protection.'

'Not noticeably successful, would you say, son?'

'Not noticeably successful,' said Alex in agreement. 'But we're not finished yet.'

'We'll get to that; don't rush ... What's *your* hook into them?'

McAuliff paused in thought. 'Their methods ... and their contacts, I think. Exposing their covert operations.'

'Really the same as with Dunstone, isn't it?' Tucker was zeroing in on his target.

'Again, yes.'

'Let's go back a second. What does Dunstone offer?'

'Money. A great deal of money. They need this survey.'

'Are you prepared to lose it?'

'Hell, yes! But I may not have to –'

'That's immaterial. I assume that's part of the "guarantees and promises".'

'That's right.'

'But it's not a factor. You haven't stolen from the thieves. In any way can they get you indicted as one of them?'

'Christ, no! They may think so, but they're wrong.'

'Then there are your answers. Your definitions. Eliminate the hooks and the offers. Theirs. The money and the protection. Lose one – the money; make the other unnecessary – the protection. You're dealing from strength, with your own hooks. *You* make whatever offers you wish.'

'You jumped, Sam,' said McAuliff slowly. 'Or you forgot. We're not finished; we may need the protection. If we take it, we can't deny it. We'd be a joke. The Iran-Contra syndrome. Worms crawling over each other.'

Sam Tucker put down his thin cigar in the ashtray on the table and reached for the bottle of Scotch. He was about to speak, but was interrupted by the sight of Charles Whitehall walking out of a jungle path into the clearing. Whitehall looked around, then crossed rapidly to Lawrence, who was still over the coals of the banked fire, the orange glow colouring his skin a bronzed black. The two men spoke. Lawrence stood up, nodded once, and started towards the jungle path. Whitehall watched him briefly, then turned and looked over at McAuliff, Sam and Alison.

With urgency, he began walking across the clearing to them.

'There's your protection, Alexander,' said Sam quietly as Whitehall approached. 'The two of them. They may despise each other, but they've got a common hate that works out fine for you. For all of us, goddamnit . . . Bless their beautiful black hides.'

'The courier has returned.' Charles Whitehall adjusted the light of the Coleman lantern in his tent. McAuliff stood inside the canvas flap of the doorway – Whitehall had insisted that Alex come with him; he did not wish to speak in front of Alison and Sam Tucker.

'You could have told the others.'

'That will be a . . . multilateral decision. Personally, I would not subscribe to it.'

'Why not?'

'We must be extremely careful. The less that is known by the more, the better.'

McAuliff pulled out a pack of cigarettes and walked to the single nylon-strapped chair in the centre of the tent. He sat down, knowing that Charley-mon would not; the black was too agitated, trying almost comically to remain calm. 'That's funny. Alison used the same words a little while ago. For different reasons . . . What's the message from Maroon Town?'

'Affirmative! The Colonel will meet with us. What's more important – *so* much more important – is that his reply was in units of four!'

Whitehall approached the chair, his eyes filled with that messianic anxiety Alex had seen in Drax Hall. 'He made a counterproposal for our meeting. Unless he hears otherwise, he will assume it is acceptable . . . He asks for eight days. And rather than four hours after sundown, he requests the same four hours after two in the morning. *Two* in the *morning*! Diagramatically to the *right* of the setting sun. Don't you see? He *understands*, McAuliff. He understands! Piersall's first step is confirmed!'

'I thought it would be,' replied Alex lamely, not quite sure how to handle Whitehall's agitation.

301

'It doesn't matter to you, does it?' The Jamaican stared at McAuliff incredulously. 'A scholar made an extraordinary discovery. He'd followed elusive threads in the archives going back over two hundred years. His work proved out; it could have enormous academic impact. The story of Jamaica might well have to be rewritten ... Can't you *see*?'

'I can see you're excited, and I can understand that. You should be. But right now, I'm concerned with a less erudite problem. I don't like the delay.'

Whitehall silently exploded in exasperation. He looked up at the canvas ceiling, inhaled deeply, and quickly regained his composure. The judgment he conveyed was obvious: The blunt mind in front of him was incapable of being reached. He spoke with condescending resignation. 'It's good. It indicates progress.'

'Why?'

'I did not tell you, but I included a message with our request for a meeting. It was admittedly a risk but I felt – unilaterally – that it was worth taking. It could expedite our objective with greater speed. I told the courier to say the request came from ... new believers of Acquaba.'

McAuliff tensed; he was suddenly angry with Whitehall, but had the presence to minimize his anger. The horrible memory of the fate of the first Dunstone survey came to mind. 'For such a brilliant guy, I think that was pretty stupid, Charley-*mon*.'

'Not stupid. A calculated risk. If the Halidon decides to make contact on the strength of Piersall's code, it will arrive at that decision only after it learns more about us. It will send out for information; it will see that *I* am part of the unit. The elders of the Halidon will know my credentials, my scholarship, my contributions to the Jamaican story. These will be in our favour.'

Alex leaped out of the chair and spoke quietly, viciously. 'You egomaniacal son of a bitch! Has it occurred to you that your ... *other* credentials may *not* be favourable? You could be the one piece of rotten meat!'

'*Impossible!*'

'You arrogant prick! I won't have the lives of this team

302

jeopardized by your inflated opinion of yourself! I want protection, and I'm going to get it!'

There was a rustling outside the tent. Both men whipped around towards the canvas flap of the entrance. The canvas parted, and the black revolutionary, Lawrence, walked in slowly, his hands in front of him, bound by rope. Behind Lawrence was another man. In the shadowed darkness it appeared to be the runner Marcus Hedrik. In his hand was a gun. It was jabbed into the flesh of his prisoner.

The captor spoke quietly. 'Do not go for your weapon. Don't make noise. Just stay exactly where you are.'

'Who are you?' asked McAuliff, amazed that Hedrik's voice had lost the hesitant, dull tones he had heard for the better part of a week. 'You're not Marcus!'

'For the moment, that is not important.'

'Garvey!' whispered Alex. 'Garvey said it! He said there were others . . . he didn't know who. You're with British Intelligence!'

'No,' replied the large man softly, even politely. 'Two of your carriers were English agents. They're dead. And the obese Garvey had an accident on the road to Port Maria. He is dead also.'

'Then –'

'It is not you who will ask the questions, Mr McAuliff. It is I. You will tell me . . . you new believers . . . what you know of Acquaba.'

25

They talked for several hours, and McAuliff knew that for the
time being he had saved their lives. At one point Sam Tucker
interrupted, only to receive and acknowledge the plea in Alexander's eyes: Sam *had* to leave them alone. Tucker left, making
it clear that he would be with Alison. He expected Alex to speak
with them before retiring. Sam did not notice the ropes on
Lawrence's hands in the shadowed corner, and McAuliff was
grateful that he did not.

'Marcus Hedrik' was *not* the runner's name. Marcus and
Justice Hedrik had been replaced; where they were was of no
consequence insisted this unnamed member of the Halidon.
What was of paramount consequence was the whereabouts of
the Piersall document.

Always leave something to trade off . . . in the last extremity.
The words of R. C. Hammond.

The documents.

McAuliff's ploy.

The Halidonite probed with infinite care every aspect of
Piersall's conclusions as related by Charles Whitehall. The black
scholar traced the history of the Acquaba sect, but he would not
reveal the *nagarro*: the meaning of the Halidon. The 'runner'
neither agreed nor disagreed; he was simply an interrogator. He
was also a perceptive and cautious man.

Once satisfied that Charles Whitehall would tell him no more,
he ordered him to remain inside his tent with Lawrence. They
were not to leave; they would be shot if they tried. His fellow
'runner' would stay on guard.

The Halidonite recognized the intransigence of McAuliff's

304

position. Alex would tell him nothing. Faced with that, he ordered Alex under gunpoint to walk out of the campsite. As they proceeded up a path towards the grasslands, McAuliff began to understand the thoroughness of the Halidon – that small part of it to which he was exposed. Twice along the alley of dense foliage, the man with the weapon commanded him to stop. There followed a brief series of guttural parrot calls, responded to in kind. Alex heard the softly spoken words of the man with the gun.

'The bivouac is surrounded, Mr McAuliff. I'm quite sure Whitehall and Tucker, as well as your couriers, know that now. The birds we imitate do not sing at night.'

'Where are we going?'

'To meet with someone. My superior, in fact. Continue, please.'

They climbed for another twenty minutes; a long jungle hill suddenly became an open grassland, a field that seemed extracted from some other terrain, imposed on a foreign land surrounded by wet forests and steep mountains.

The moonlight was unimpeded by clouds; the field was washed with dull yellow. And in the centre of the wild grass stood two men. As they approached, McAuliff saw that one of the men was perhaps ten feet behind the first, his back to them. The first man faced them.

The Halidonite facing them was dressed in what appeared to be ragged clothes, but with a loose field jacket and boots. The combined effect was a strange, unkempt paramilitary appearance. Around his waist was a pistol belt and holster. The man ten feet away and staring off in the opposite direction was in a caftan held together in the middle by a single thick rope.

Priest-like. Immobile.

'Sit on the ground, Dr McAuliff,' instructed the strangely ragged paramilitary man, in clipped tones used to command.

Alex did so. The use of the title 'Doctor' told him the unfamiliarity was more his than theirs.

The subordinate who had marched him up from the camp

approached the priest figure. The two men fell into quiet conversation, walking slowly into the grass while talking. The two figures receded over a hundred yards into the dull yellow field.

They stopped.

'Turn around, Dr McAuliff.' The order was abrupt; the black man above him had his hand on his holster. Alex pivoted in his sitting position and faced the descending forest from which he and the runner had emerged.

The waiting was long and tense. Yet McAuliff understood that his strongest weapon – perhaps his only viable strength – was calm determination. He was determined; he was not calm.

He was frightened in the same way he had experienced fear before. In the Vietnam jungles; alone, no matter the number of troops. Waiting to witness his own single annihilation.

Pockets of fear.

'It is an extraordinary story, is it not, Dr McAuliff?'

That voice. My God! He knew that voice.

He pressed his arms against the ground and started to whip his head and body around.

His temple crashed into the hard steel of a pistol; the agonizing pain shot through his face and chest. There was a series of bright flashes in front of his eyes as the pain reached a sensory crescendo. It subsided to a numbing ache, and he could feel a trickle of blood on his neck.

'You will remain the way you are while we talk,' said the familiar voice.

Where had he heard it before?

'I know you.'

'You don't *know* me, Dr McAuliff.'

'I've heard your voice . . . somewhere.'

'Then you have remarkable recall. So much has happened . . . I shall not waste words. Where are Piersall's documents? I am sure it is unnecessary to tell you that your life and the lives of those you brought to Jamaica depend on our having them.'

'How do you know they'd do you any good? What if I told you I had copies made?'

'I would say you were lying. We know the placement of every Xerox machine, every photostat copier, every store, hotel and individual that does such work along the coast. Including Bueno, the Bays and Ocho Rios. You have had no copies made.'

'You're not very bright, Mr Halidon ... It is Mr Halidon, isn't it?' There was no response, so Alex continued. 'We photographed them.'

'Then the films are not developed. And the only member of your team possessing a camera is the boy, Ferguson. He is hardly a confidant ... But this is immaterial, Dr McAuliff. When we say documents, we assume any and all reproductions thereof. Should any surface ... *ever* ... there will be, to put it bluntly, a massacre of innocents. Your survey team, their families, children ... all those held dear by everyone. A cruel and unnecessary prospect.'

... to the last extremity. R. C. Hammond.

'It would be the Halidon's last action, wouldn't it?' McAuliff spoke slowly but sharply, stunned by his own calm. 'A kind of final ... *beau geste* before extinction. If you want it that way, I don't give a damn.'

'*Stop it, McAuliff!*' The voice suddenly screamed, a piercing shriek over the blades of wild grass, its echo muted by the surrounding jungles.

Those words ... They were the *words* he had heard before!

Stop it. Stop it ... stop it ...

Where? For God's sake, where had he heard them?

His mind raced; images were blurred with blinding coloured lights, but he could not focus.

A man. A black man – tall and lithe and muscular ... A man following orders. A man commanding but not with his own commands. The voice that had just roared was the same voice from the past ... *following orders.* In panic ... as before.

Something ...

'You said we would talk. Threats are one-sided conversations; you take turns, you don't talk. I'm not on anybody's side. I

307

want your . . . superiors to know that.' Alex held his breath during the silence that followed.

The quiet reply came with measured authority . . . and a small but recognizable trace of fear. 'There *are* no superiors as far as you are concerned. My temper is short. These have been difficult days . . . You should realize that you are very close to losing your life.'

The man with the pistol had moved slightly; Alex could see him now out of the corner of his eye. And what he saw convinced him he was on the track of an immediate truth. The man's head had snapped up at the priest figure; the man with the weapon dangling in his hand was questioning the priest figure's words.

'If you kill me . . . or any member of the team, the Halidon will be exposed in a matter of hours.'

Again silence. Again the measured authority; again the now unmistakable undertone of fear. 'And how is this remarkable exposure going to take place, Dr McAuliff?'

Alex drew a deep breath silently. His right hand was clasping his left wrist; he pressed his fingers into his own flesh as he replied.

'In my equipment there is a radio signalling device. It is standard and operates on a frequency that rides above interference. It's functional within a radius of twenty-five miles . . . Every twelve hours I send out one of two codes; a light on the miniature panel confirms reception *and* pinpoints location-identification. The first code says everything's normal, no problems. The second says something else. It instructs the man on the receiving end to implement two specific orders: fly the documents out and send help in. The absence of transmission is the equivalent of the second code, only more so. It alerts all the factions in Kingston, including British Intelligence. They'll be forced in; they'll start with our last location and fan out. The Cock Pit will be swarming with planes and troops . . . I'd better transmit the code, Mr Halidon. And even when I do, you won't know which one I'm sending, will you?' McAuliff stopped for precisely three seconds. And then he said quietly, 'Checkmate, Mr Bones.'

A macaw's screech could be heard in the distance. From somewhere in the wet forests a pride of wild pigs was disturbed. The warm breeze bent the reeds of the tall grass ever so slightly; cicadas were everywhere. All these were absorbed by Alex's senses. And he understood, too, the audible, trembling intake of breath from the darkness behind him. He could feel the mounting, uncontrollable pitch of anger.

'No, mon!' The man with the pistol cried out, lunging forward.

Simultaneously, McAuliff felt the rush of air and heard the rustle of cloth that precedes the instant of impact from behind. Too late to turn; defence only in crouching, hugging the earth.

One man tried to stop the priest figure as he lunged forward; the weight of two furious bodies descended on Alex's shoulders and back. Arms were thrashing, fingers spastically clutched; hard steel and soft cloth and warm flesh enveloped him. He reached above and grasped the first objects his hands touched, yanked with all his strength, and rolled forward.

The priest figure somersaulted over his back; Alex crashed his shoulders downward, rising on one knee for greater weight, and threw himself on the coarse cloth of the caftan. As he pinned the priest, he felt himself instantly pulled backward, with such force that the small of his back arched in pain.

The two Halidonites locked his arms, stretching his chest to the breaking point; the man with the pistol held the barrel to his temple, digging it into his skin.

'That will be *enough*, mon.'

Below him on the ground, the yellow moonlight illuminating a face creased with fury, was the priest figure.

McAuliff instantly understood the bewildering, unfocused images of blinding, coloured lights his mind had associated with the panicked words *stop it, stop it*.

He had last seen this 'priest' of the Halidon in London's Soho. During the psychedelic madness that was The Owl of Saint

309

George. The man lying on the ground in a caftan had been dressed in a dark suit then, gyrating on the crowded dance floor. He had screamed at McAuliff to *Stop . . . stop it!* He had delivered a crushing fist into Alex's midsection; he had disappeared into the crowds, only to show up an hour later in a government car on the street by a public telephone.

This 'priest' of the Halidon was an agent of British Intelligence.

'You said your name was Tallon.' McAuliff strained his speech through the pain, the words interrupted by his lack of breath. 'In the car that night you said your name was Tallon. And . . . when I called you on it, you said you were . . . testing me.'

The priest figure rolled over and slowly began to rise. He nodded to the two Halidonites to relax their grips and addressed them. 'I would not have killed him. You know that.'

'You were angry, mon,' said the man who had taken Alex out of the camp.

'Forgive us,' added the man who had cried out and lunged at the priest figure. 'It was necessary.'

The 'priest' smoothed his cassock and tugged at the thick rope around his waist. He looked down at McAuliff. 'Your recollection is sharp, Doctor. I sincerely hope your ability to think clearly is equally acute.'

'Does that mean we talk?'

'We talk.'

'My arms hurt like hell. Will you tell your sergeants to let go of me?'

The 'priest' nodded once again, and flicked his wrist in accord. Alex's arms were released; he shook them.

'My sergeants, as you call them, are more temperate men than I. You should be grateful to them.'

The man with the pistol belt demurred, his voice respectful. 'Not so, mon. When did you last sleep?'

'That does not matter. I should have more control . . . My friend refers to a hectic several weeks, McAuliff. Not only did I have to get myself out of England, avoiding Her Majesty's

310

Service, but also a colleague who had disappeared in a Bentley around a Soho corner . . . A West Indian in London has a thousand hiding places.'

Alex remembered vividly. 'That Bentley tried to run me down. The driver wanted to kill me. Only someone else was killed . . . because of a neon light.'

The priest figure stared at McAuliff. He, too, seemed to recall the evening vividly. 'It was a tragedy born of the instant. We thought a trap had been set, the spring caught at the last moment.'

'Three lives were lost that night. Two with cyanide –'

'We are committed,' interrupted the Halidonite, who looked at his two companions and spoke gently. 'Leave us alone, please.'

In warning, both men removed the weapons from their belts as they pulled Alex to his feet. As ordered, they retreated into the field. McAuliff watched them. A ragged-clothed twosome with the unlikely jackets and pistol belts. 'They not only do as you say, they protect you from yourself.'

The priest figure also looked at his retreating subordinates. 'When we are in our formative years, we are all given batteries of tests. Each is assigned areas of instruction and future responsibility from the results. I often think grave errors are made.' The man tugged at his caftan and turned to McAuliff. 'We must deal now with each other, must we not? . . . As I am sure you have surmised, I was an impermanent member of MI5.'

'An "infiltrator" is the word that comes to mind.'

'A very successful one, Doctor. Hammond himself twice recommended me for citations. I was one of the best West Indian specialists . . . I was reluctant to leave. You – and those manoeuvring you – created the necessity.'

'How?'

'Your survey suddenly contained too many dangerous components. We could live with several, but when we found out that your closest associate on the geological team – Mr Tucker – was apparently a friend of Walter Piersall, we knew we had to keep you under a microscope . . . Obviously, we were too late.'

'What were the other components?'

The priest figure hesitated. He touched his forehead, where a grass burn had developed from his fall to the ground. 'Do you have a cigarette? This very comfortable sheet has one disadvantage: There are no pockets.'

'Why do you wear it?'

'It is a symbol of authority, nothing more.'

McAuliff reached into his pocket, withdrew a pack of cigarettes, and shook one up for the Halidonite. As he lighted it for him, he saw that the black hollows in the very black skin beneath the eyes were stretched in exhaustion. 'What were the dangerous components?'

'Oh, come, Doctor, you know them as well as I do.'

'Maybe I don't; enlighten me. Or is that dangerous, too?'

'Not now. Not at this point. The *reality* is the danger. Piersall's documents are the reality. The . . . components are inconsequential.'

'Then tell me.'

The priest figure inhaled on his cigarette and blew the smoke into the soft breeze of the dull yellow light. 'The woman you know about. There are many who fear her on the Continent. Among those, one of the Dunstone hierarchy . . . the Marquis de Chatellerault. Where she is, so is an arm of the Intelligence service. The boy, Ferguson, is deep with the Craft interests; actually, they fear him. Or did. And rightly so. He never understood the calamitous economic potential of his fibre work.'

'I think he did,' interrupted Alex. 'And does. He expects to make money out of Craft.'

The Halidonite laughed quietly. 'They will never let him. But he is a component. Where does Craft stand? Is he part of Dunstone? Nothing happens in Jamaica that the soiled hand of Craft has not touched . . . Samuel Tucker I have told you about: his association with the suddenly vital Walter Piersall. Whose summons did he answer? Is he on the island because of his old friend McAuliff? Or his new friend Piersall? Or is it coincidence?'

'It is coincidence,' said Alex. 'You'd have to know Sam to understand that.'

'But we do not, you see. We only understand that among the first telephone calls he made was to a man who was disturbing us profoundly. Who was walking around Kingston with the secrets of two hundred years in his brain ... and somewhere on paper.' The priest figure looked at McAuliff – stared at him, really. His eyes in the moonlight conveyed a supplication for Alex to understand. He looked away and continued. 'Then there is Charles Whitehall. A very ... *very* dangerous and unpredictable component. You must know his background; Hammond certainly did. Whitehall feels his time on the island has come. His is the hot mysticism of the fanatic. The black Caesar come to ride up Victoria Park on nigger-Pompei's horse. He has followers throughout Jamaica. If there is anyone who might expose Dunstone – wittingly or otherwise – it could well be Whitehall and his fascists.'

'Hammond didn't know that,' protested McAuliff. 'He made it clear that you ... the Halidon ... were the only ones who could stop Dunstone.'

'Hammond is a professional. He creates internal chaos, knowing that his breakthrough can come at any instant during the panic. Would it surprise you to know that Hammond is in Kingston now?'

Alex thought for a moment. 'No ... But I'm surprised he hasn't let me know it.'

'There is a sound reason. He doesn't want you to fall back on him. He wants the forces to remain on collision courses. He flew in when word was received that Chatellerault was in Savanna-la-Mar ... You knew *that*, didn't you?'

'*He* knows it because I told Westmore Tallon.'

'And then there are the Jensens. That charming, devoted couple. So normal, so lovable, really ... who send back word to Julian Warfield of every move you make, of every person you make contact with; who bribe Jamaicans to spy on you . . . The Jensens made a huge mistake once, years ago. Dunstone stepped in and recruited them. In exchange for obliterating that mistake.'

McAuliff looked up at the clear night sky. A single elongated cloud was drifting from a distant mountain towards the yellow moon. He wondered if the condensation would disappear before it reached the shining satellite, or blur it from beneath . . . envelop it from the ground.

As he was so enveloped.

'So those are the components,' said Alex aimlessly. 'The Halidon knows a lot more than anyone else, it seems. And I'm not sure what that means.'

'It means, Doctor, that we are the silent caretakers of our land.'

'I don't recall any election. Who gave you the job?'

'To quote an American writer: "It comes with the territory." It is our heritage. We do not swim in the political rivers, however. We leave those to the legitimate competitors. We *do* try our best to keep the pollution to a minimum.' The priest figure finished his cigarette and crushed the burning end under his sandalled foot.

'You're killers,' said McAuliff simply. 'I know that. I think that's the worst kind of human pollution.'

'Are you referring to Dunstone's previous survey?'

'I am.'

'You don't know the circumstances. And I'm not the one to define them. I am here only to persuade you to give me Piersall's documents.'

'I won't do that.'

'*Why?*' The Halidonite's voice rose in anger, as before. His black eyes above the black hollows pierced into McAuliff's.

'*Mon?*' came the shouted query from the field. The priest figure waved his arm in dismissal.

'This is not your business, McAuliff. Understand that and get out. Give me the documents and take your survey off the island before it is too late.'

'If it was that simple, I would. I don't *want* your fight, god-damnit. It has no appeal for me . . . On the other hand, I don't relish being chased all over the globe by Julian Warfield's guns. Can't *you* understand *that?*'

The priest figure stood immobile. His eyes softened; his lips parted in concentration as he stared at Alexander. He spoke slowly; he was barely audible. 'I warned them that it might come to this. Give me the *nagarro*, doctor. What is the meaning of the Halidon?'

McAuliff told him.

26

They returned to the river campsite, McAuliff and the runner who had assumed the name and function of 'Marcus Hedrik'. There was no pretence now. As they neared the bivouac area, black men in rags could be seen in the bush, the early dawn light shafting through the dense foliage, intermittently reflecting off the barrels of their weapons.

The survey camp was surrounded, the inhabitants prisoners of the Halidon.

A hundred yards from the clearing, the runner – now preceding Alex on the narrow jungle path, pistol secure in his field jacket belt – stopped and summoned a Halidon patrol. He did so by snapping his fingers repeatedly until a large black man emerged from between the trees.

The two men spoke briefly, quietly, and when they were finished the patrol returned to his post in the tropic forest. The runner turned to McAuliff.

'Everything is peaceful. There was a skirmish with Charles Whitehall, but it was anticipated. He severely wounded the guard, but others were nearby. He is bound and back in his tent.'

'What about Mrs Booth?'

'The woman? She is with Samuel Tucker. She was asleep half an hour ago ... That Tucker, he will not sleep. He sits in the chair in front of his tent, a rifle in his hands. The others are quiet. They will be rising soon.'

'Tell me,' said Alex while the runner still faced him, 'what happened to all that Arawak language? The Maroon Colonel, the units of four, the eight days?'

316

'You forgot, Doctor. I led the Whitehall-mon to his courier. The Colonel of the Maroons never got the message. The reply you received came from us.' The runner smiled. Then he turned, gesturing for Alex to follow him into the clearing.

Under the eyes of the runner, McAuliff waited for the white light of the miniature panel to reach full illumination. When it did, he pressed the signal-transmitter button, holding his left hand over his fingers as he did so. He knew the concealment was unnecessary; he would not radio for aid. He would not jam the frequency with cries of emergency. It had been made clear that at the first sight of hostile forces, each member of the survey would be shot through the head, Alison Booth and Sam Tucker the first to be executed.

The remainder of the understanding was equally clear. Sam Tucker would continue to send the signals every twelve hours. Alexander would return with the runner into the grassland. From there, with the 'priest', he would be taken to the hidden community of the Halidon. Until he returned, the team was a collective hostage.

Alison, Sam, Charles Whitehall and Lawrence would be told the truth. The others would not. The Jensens, James Ferguson and the crew would be given another explanation, a bureaucratic one readily acceptable to professional surveyors: During the night a radio message from Kingston had been relayed by Falmouth; the Ministry of the Interior required McAuliff's presence in Ocho Rios; there were difficulties with the Institute. It was the sort of complication to which survey directors were subjected. Field work was constantly interrupted by administrative foul-ups.

When the priest figure suggested the time of absence would be no less than three full days, Alex demanded to know the reason for so long a period.

'I can't answer that, McAuliff.'

'Then why should I agree to it?'

'It is only time. Then, too, are we not at checkmate . . . Mr

317

Bones? We fear exposure perhaps more than you fear for your lives.'

'I won't concede that.'

'You do not know us. Give yourself the margin to learn. You will not be disappointed.'

'You were told to say three days, then?'

'I was.'

'Which presumes that whoever told you to say it expected you to bring me to them.'

'It was a distinct probability.'

Alexander agreed to three full days.

The black revolutionary, Lawrence, was rubbing a penicillin salve over Charles Whitehall's bare back. The rope burns were deep; whoever had lashed Charley-mon had done so in fever-pitch anger. The ropes on both men had been removed after McAuliff's talk with them. Alexander had made it clear he would brook no further interference. Their causes were expendable.

'Your arrogance is beyond understanding, McAuliff!' said Charles Whitehall, suppressing a grimace as Lawrence touched a sensitive burn.

'I accept the rebuke. You're very qualified in that department.'

'You are not *equipped* to deal with these people. I have spent my life, my *entire life*, stripping away the layers of Jamaican – Caribbean – history!'

'Not your entire life, Charley,' replied Alex, calmly but incisively. 'I told you last night. There's the little matter of your extra-scholastic activity. "The black Caesar riding up Victoria Park on nigger-Pompei's horse..."'

'*What?*'

'They're not my words, Charley.'

Lawrence suddenly pressed his fist into a raw lash mark on Whitehall's shoulder. The scholar arched his neck back in pain. The revolutionary's other hand was close to his throat. Neither man moved; Lawrence spoke. 'You don't ride no nigger horse, mon. You den walk like everybody else.'

318

Charles Whitehall stared over his shoulder at the blur of the brutal, massive hand poised for assault. 'You play the fool, you know. Do you think any political entity with a power structure based in wealth will tolerate *you*? Not for a minute, you egalitarian jackal. You will be crushed.'

'You do not seek to crush us, mon?'

'I seek only what is best for Jamaica. Everyone's energies will be used to that end.'

'You're a regular Pollyanna,' broke in Alex, walking towards the two men.

Lawrence looked up at McAuliff, his expression equal parts of suspicion and dependence. He removed his hand and reached for the tube of penicillin salve. 'Put on your shirt, mon. Your skin is covered,' he said, twisting the small cap onto the medicine tube.

'I'm leaving in a few minutes,' said McAuliff, standing in front of Whitehall. 'Sam will be in charge; you're to do as he says. Insofar as possible, the work is to continue normally. The Halidon will stay out of sight . . . at least as far as the Jensens and Ferguson are concerned.'

'How can that be?' asked Lawrence.

'It won't be difficult,' answered Alex. 'Peter is drilling for gas-pocket sediment a mile and a half south-west. Ruth is due east in a quarry; the runner we know as "Justice" will be with her. Ferguson is across the river working some fern groves. All are separated, each will be watched.'

'And me?' Whitehall buttoned his expensive cotton safari shirt as though dressing for a concert at Covent Garden. 'What do you propose for me?'

'You're confined to the clearing, Charley-mon. For your own sake, don't try to leave it. I can't be responsible if you do.'

'You think you have any say about anything now, McAuliff?'

'Yes, I do. They're as much afraid of me as I am of them. Just don't try to upset the balance, either one of you. I buried a man on an Alaskan job a number of years ago. Sam will tell you, I know the standard prayers.'

*　　　*　　　*

Alison stood on the river bank, looking down at the water. The heat of the early sun was awakening the late sleepers of the forest. The sounds were those of combative foraging; flyer against flyer, crawler fighting crawler. The green vines dangling from the tall macca-fat palms glistened with the moisture rising from below; fern and moss and matted cabbage growth bordered the slowly flowing currents of the Martha Brae offshoot. The water was morning-clear, bluish-green.

'I went to your tent,' said McAuliff, walking up to her. 'Sam said you were out here.'

She turned and smiled. 'I wasn't really disobeying, my darling. I'm not running anywhere.'

'Nowhere to go . . . You'll be all right . . . The runner's waiting for me.'

Alison took two steps and stood in front of him. She spoke quietly, barely above a whisper. 'I want to tell you something, Alexander T. McAuliff. And I refuse to be dramatic or tearful or anything remotely theatrical because those are crutches and both of us can walk without them. Six weeks ago I was running. Quite desperately, trying my goddamnedest to convince myself that by running I was escaping – which I knew underneath was absurd. In Kingston I told you how absurd it was. They can find you. Anywhere. The computers, the data banks, the horrid, complicated tracers they have in their cellars and in their hidden rooms are too real now. Too thorough. And there is no life underground, in remote places, always wondering. I don't expect you to understand this, and, in a way, it's why what you're doing is right . . . "Do unto others *before* they do unto you." That's what you said. I believe that's a terrible way to think. And I also believe it's the only way we're going to have a life of our own.'

McAuliff touched her face with his fingers. Her eyes were bluer than he had ever seen them. 'That sounds dangerously like a proposal.'

'My wants are simple, my expressions uncomplicated. And, as you said once, I'm a damned fine professional.'

'McAuliff and Booth. Surveyors. Offices: London and New York. That'd look good on the letterhead.'

'You wouldn't consider "Booth and McAuliff"? I mean, alphabetically –'

'No, I wouldn't,' he interrupted gently as he put his arms around her.

'Do people always say silly things when they're afraid?' she asked, her face buried in his chest.

'I think so,' he replied.

Peter Jensen reached down into the full pack and felt his way among the soft articles of clothing. The canvas was stuffed. Jensen winced as he slid the object of his search up the sides of the cloth.

It was the Luger. It was wrapped in plastic, the silencer detached, tied to the barrel and in plastic also.

His wife stood by the entrance flap of their tent, the slit folded back just sufficiently for her to look outside. Peter unwrapped both sections of the weapon and put the silencer in the pocket of his field jacket. He pressed the release, slid out the magazine, and reached into his other pocket for a box of cartridges. Methodically he inserted the magazine until the spring was taut, the top bullet ready for chamber insertion. He slid the magazine back into the handle slot and cracked it into position.

Ruth heard the metallic click and turned around. 'Do you have to do this?'

'Yes. Julian was very clear. McAuliff was my selection, his concurrence a result of that choice. McAuliff's made contact. With whom? With what? I must find out.' Peter pulled open his jacket and shoved the Luger down between a triangle of leather straps sewn into the lining. He buttoned the field jacket and stood up straight. 'Any bulges, old girl? Does it show?'

'No.'

'Good. Hardly the fit of Whitehall's uniform, but I dare say a bit more comfortable.'

'You will be careful? It's so dreadful out there.'

'All that camping you dragged me on had a purpose. I see that now, my dear.' Peter smiled and returned to his pack, pushing down the contents, pulling the straps into buckling position. He inserted the prongs, tugged once more, and slapped the bulging outsides. He lifted the canvas sack by the shoulder harness and let it fall to the dirt. 'There! I'm set for a fortnight if need be.'

'How will I know?'

'When I don't come back with my carrier. If I pull it off right, he might even be too petrified to return himself.' Peter saw the tremble on his wife's lips, the terrible fear in her eyes. He motioned for her to come to him, which she did. Rushing into his arms.

'Oh, God, *Peter* –'

'Please, Ruth. *Shhh*. You mustn't,' he said, stroking her hair. 'Julian has been everything to us. We both know that. And Julian thinks we'd be very happy at Peale Court. Dunstone will need many people in Jamaica, he said. Why not us?'

When the unknown carrier came into camp, James Ferguson could see that the runner he knew as Marcus Hedrik was as angry as he was curious. They were all curious. McAuliff had left early that morning for the coast; it seemed strange that the carrier had not met him on the river. The carrier insisted he had seen no one but wandering hill people, some fishing, some hunting – no white man.

The carrier had been sent by the Government Employment Office, a branch in Falmouth that knew the survey was looking for additional hands. The carrier was familiar with the river offshoot, having grown up in Weston Favel, and was anxious for work. Naturally, he had the proper papers, signed by some obscure functionary at GEO, Falmouth.

At 2:30 in the afternoon, James Ferguson, having rested after lunch, sat on the edge of his cot, prepared to gather up his equipment and head back into the field. There was a rustling outside his tent. He looked up, and the new carrier suddenly slapped open the flap and walked in. He was carrying a plastic tray.

'I say –'

'I pick up dishes, mon,' said the carrier rapidly. 'Alla time be very neat.'

'I have no dishes here. There's a glass or two need washing . . .'

The carrier lowered his voice. 'I got message for Fergo-mon. I give it to you. You read it quick.' The black reached into his pocket and withdrew a sealed envelope. He handed it to Ferguson.

James ripped the back and pulled out a single page of stationery. It was the stationery of The Craft Foundation, and Ferguson's eyes were immediately pulled to the signature. It was known throughout Jamaica – the scrawl of Arthur Craft, Senior, the semi-retired but all-powerful head of the Craft enterprises.

My dear James Ferguson:

Apologies from a distance are always most awkward and often the most sincere. Such is the present case.

My son has behaved badly, for which he, too, offers his regrets. He sends them from the South of France where he will be residing for an indeterminate – but long – period of time.

To the point: your contributions in our laboratories on the baracoa experiments were immense. They led the way to what we believe can be a major breakthrough that can have a widespread industrial impact. We believe this breakthrough can be accelerated by your immediate return to us. Your future is assured, young man, in the way all genius should be rewarded. You will be a very wealthy man.

However, time is of the essence. Therefore I recommend that you leave the survey forthwith – the messenger will explain the somewhat odd fashion of departure but you may be assured that I have apprised Kingston of my wishes and they are in full agreement. (The baracoa is for *all* Jamaica.) We are also in mutual agreement that it is unnecessary to involve the survey

323

director, Dr McAuliff, as his immediate interests are rightfully in conflict with ours. A substitute botanist will join the survey within a matter of days.

I look forward to renewing our acquaintance.

Very truly yours,

Arthur Craft, Senior

James Ferguson held his breath in astonishment as he reread the letter.

He had done it.

He had really done it.

Everything.

He looked up at the carrier, who smiled and spoke softly.

'We leave late afternoon, mon. Before dark. Come back early from your work. I will meet you on the river bank and we will go.'

27

The priest figure identified himself by the single name of 'Malcolm'. They travelled south on hidden routes that alternated between steep rocky climbs, winding grottos and dense jungle. The Halidonite in the ragged clothes and the field jacket led the way, effortlessly finding concealed paths in the forests and covered openings that led through long dark tunnels of ancient stone – the dank smell of deep grotto waters ever present, the bright reflection of stalactites, suspended in alabaster isolation, caught in the beams of flashlights.

It seemed to McAuliff that at times they were descending into the cellars of the earth, only to emerge from the darkness of a grotto onto higher ground. A geological phenomenon, tunnelled caves that inexorably progressed upwards, evidence of oceanic-terrestrial upheavals that bespoke an epoch of incredible geophysical combustion. The cores of mountains rising out of the faults and trenches, doing infinite battle to reach the heat of the sun.

Twice they passed hill communities by circling above them on ridges at the edge of the forest. Malcolm both times identified the sects, telling of their particular beliefs and the religious justification for their withdrawal from the outside world. He explained that there were approximately twenty-three Cock Pit communities dedicated to isolation. The figure had to be approximate, for there was ever-present the rebellion of youth who found in their intermittent journeys to the marketplace temptations outweighing the threats of Obeah. Strangely enough, as one community, or two or three, disintegrated, there were always others that sprang up to take their places . . . and often their small villages.

'The "opiate of the people" is often an escape from simple hardship and the agonizing pointlessness of the coastal towns.'

'Then eliminate the pointlessness.' Alex remembered the sights of Old Kingston, the corrugated tin shacks across from the abandoned, filthy barges peopled by outcasts; the emaciated dogs, the bone-thin cats, the eyes of numbed futility on the young-old women. The men with no teeth praying for the price of a pint of wine, defecating in the shadows of dark alleys.

And three blocks above, the shining, immaculate banks with their shining, tinted windows. Shining, immaculate, and obscene in their choice of location.

'Yes, you are right,' replied Malcolm the Halidonite. 'It is the pointlessness that erodes the people most rapidly. It is so easy to say "give meaning". And so difficult to know how. So many complications.'

They continued their journey for eight hours, resting after difficult sections of jungle and steep cliff-like inclines and endless caves. McAuliff judged that they had gone no farther than seventeen, perhaps eighteen miles into the Cock Pit country, each mile more treacherous and enervating than the last.

Shortly after five in the afternoon, while high in the Flagstaff Range, they came to the end of a mountain pass. Suddenly in front of them was a plateau of grassland about half a mile long and no more than five hundred yards wide. The plateau fronted the banks of a mountain cliff, at three-quarters altitude. Malcolm led them to the right, to the western edge. The slope of the plateau descended into thick jungle, as dense and forbidding as any McAuliff had ever seen.

'That is called the Maze of Acquaba,' said Malcolm, seeing the look of astonishment on Alex's face. 'We have borrowed a custom from ancient Sparta. Each male child, on his eleventh birthday, is taken into the core and must remain for a period of four days and nights.'

'Units of four . . .' McAuliff spoke as much to himself as to Malcolm as he stared down at the unbelievably cruel density of jungle beneath. 'The odyssey of death.'

'We're neither that Spartan nor Arawak,' said Malcolm, laughing softly. 'The children do not realize it, but there are others with them . . . Come.'

The two Halidonites turned and started towards the opposite ledge of the plateau. Alex took a last look at the Maze of Acquaba and joined them.

At the eastern edge, the contradictory effect was immediate.

Below was a valley no more than half a mile in length, perhaps a mile wide, in the centre of which was a quiet lake. The valley itself was enclosed by hills that were the first inclines of the mountains beyond. On the north side were mountain streams converging into a high waterfall that cascaded down into a relatively wide, defined avenue of water.

On the far side of the lake were fields – pastures, for there were cattle grazing lazily. Cows, goats, a few donkeys and several horses. This area had been cleared and seeded – generations ago, thought McAuliff.

On the near side of the lake, below them, were thatched huts, protected by tall ceiba trees. At first glance, there seemed to be seventy or eighty such dwellings. They were barely visible because of the trees and arcing vines and dense tropical foliage that filled whatever spaces might have been empty with the bright colours of the Caribbean. A community roofed by nature, thought Alex.

Then he pictured the sight from the air. Not as he was seeing it, on a vertical-diagonal, but from above, from a plane. The village – and it was a village – would look like any number of isolated hill communities with thatched roofs and nearby grazing fields. But the difference was in the surrounding mountains. The plateau was an indentation formed at high altitude. This section of the Flagstaff Range was filled with harsh updraughts and uncontrollable wind variants: jets would remain at a twelve-thousand-foot minimum, light aircraft would avoid direct

327

overhead. The first would have no place to land, the second would undoubtedly crash if tempted to do so.

The community was protected by natural phenomena above it and by a torturous passage on the ground that could never be defined on a map.

'Not very prepossessing, is it?' Malcolm stood next to McAuliff. A stream of children were running down a bordered path towards the lake, their shouts carried on the wind. Natives could be seen walking around the huts; larger groups strolled by the avenue of water that flowed from the waterfall.

'It's all . . . very neat.' It was the only word McAuliff could think of at the moment.

'Yes,' replied the Halidonite. 'It's orderly. Come, let's go down. There is a man waiting for you.'

The runner-guide led them down the rocky slope. Five minutes later the three of them were on the western level of the thatched community. From above Alex had not fully realized the height of the trees that were on all sides of the primitive dwellings. Thick vines sloped and twisted, immense ferns sprayed out of the ground and from within dark recesses of the underbrush.

Had the view from the plateau above been fifty feet higher, thought McAuliff, none of what he had seen would have been visible.

Roofed by nature.

The guide started across a path that seemed to intersect a cluster of huts within the jungle-like area.

The inhabitants were dressed, like most Jamaican hill people, in a variety of soft, loose clothing, but there was something different that McAuliff could not at first discern. There was a profusion of rolled-up khaki trousers and dark-coloured skirts and white cotton shirts and printed blouses – all normal, all seen throughout the island. Seen really in all outback areas – Africa, Australia, New Zealand – where the natives had taken what they could – stolen what they could – of the white invaders' protective comforts. Nothing unusual . . . But something was very different, and Alex was damned if he could pinpoint that difference.

And then he did so. At the same instant that he realized there was something else he had been observing. Books.

A few – three or four or five, perhaps – of the dozens of natives within this jungle community were carrying books. Carrying *books* under their arms and in their hands.

And the clothing was *clean*. It was as simple as that. There were stains of wetness, of sweat, obviously, and the dirt of field work and the mud of the lake . . . but there was a cleanliness, a neatness, that was *not* usual in the hill or outback communities. Africa, Australia, New Guinea or Jacksonville, Florida.

It was a normal sight to see clothing worn by natives in varying stages of disrepair – torn, ripped, even shredded. But the garments worn by these hill people were whole, untorn, unripped.

Not cast-offs, not ill-fitting stolen property.

The Tribe of Acquaba was deep within a jungle primeval but it was not – like so many of the isolated hill people – a worn-out race of poverty-stricken primitives scratching a bare subsistence from the land.

Along the paths and around the dwellings Alex could see strong black bodies and clear black eyes, the elements of balanced diets and sharp intelligences.

'We shall go directly to Daniel,' said Malcolm to the guide. 'You are relieved now. And thank you.'

The guide turned right down a dirt path that seemed to be tunnelled under a dense web of thick jungle vines. He was removing his pistol belt, unbuttoning his field jacket. The commando was home, reflected McAuliff. He could take off his costume – so purposely ragged.

Malcolm gestured, interrupting Alex's thoughts. The path on which they had been walking under an umbrella of macca-fats and ceibas veered left into a clearing of matted spider grass. This open area extended beyond the conduit of rushing water that shot out from the base of the high waterfall streaming down the mountain. On the other side of the wide, banked gulley the ground sloped towards a barricade of rock; beyond were the grazing fields that swung right, bordering the eastern shore of the lake.

In the huge pasture, men could be seen walking with staffs towards the clusters of livestock. It was late afternoon, the heat of the sun was lessening. It was time to shelter the cattle for the night, thought McAuliff.

He had been absently following Malcolm, more concerned with observing everything he could of the strange, isolated village, when he realized where the Halidonite was leading them.

Towards the base of the mountain and the waterfall.

They reached the edge of the lake-feeding channel and turned left. Alex saw that the conduit of water was deeper than it appeared from a distance. The banks were about eight feet in height; the definition he had seen from the plateau was a result of carefully placed rocks, embedded in the earth of the embankments. This natural phenomenon had been controlled by man, like the seeded fields, generations ago.

There were three crossings of wooden planks with waist-high railings, each buttressed into the sides of the embankments, where there were stone steps . . . placed decades ago. The miniature bridges were spaced about fifty yards apart.

Then McAuliff saw it; barely saw it, as it was concealed behind a profusion of tall trees, immense giant-fern and hundreds of flowering vines at the base of the mountain.

It was a wooden structure. A large cabin-like dwelling whose base straddled the channel, the water rushing out from under the huge pilings that supported the hidden edifice. On each side of the pilings were steps – again in stone, again placed generations ago – that led up to a wide catwalk fronting the building. In the centre of the planked catwalk was a door. It was closed.

From any distance – certainly from the air – the building was completely concealed.

Its length was perhaps thirty feet; its width impossible to

determine, as it seemed to disappear into the jungle and the crashing waterfall.

As they approached the stone steps, McAuliff saw something else, which so startled him that he had to stop and stare.

On the west side of the building, emerging from within and scaling upwards into the tangling mass of foliage, were thick black cables.

Malcolm turned and smiled at Alex's astonishment. 'Our contact with the outside, McAuliff. Radio signals that are piped into telephone trunk lines throughout the island. Not unlike the cellular phones, but generally much clearer than the usual telephone service. All untraceable, of course. Now let us see Daniel.'

'Who is Daniel?'

'He is our Minister of Council. His is an elective office. Except that his term is not guided by the calendar.'

'Who elects him?'

The Halidonite's smile faded somewhat. 'The council.'

'Who elects *it*?'

'The tribe.'

'Sounds like regular politics.'

'Not exactly,' said Malcolm enigmatically. 'Come. Daniel's waiting.'

The Halidonite opened the door, and McAuliff walked into a large high-ceilinged room with windows all around the upper wall. The sounds of the waterfall could be heard; these were mingled with the myriad noises of the jungle outside.

There were wooden chairs – chairs fashioned by hand, not machinery. In the centre of the back wall, in front of a second, very large, thick door was a table, at which sat a black girl in her late twenties. On her 'desk' were papers, and at her left was a word processor on a white computer table. The incongruity of such equipment in such a place caused Alex to stare.

And then he swallowed as he saw a telephone – a sophisticated, push-button console – on a stand to the girl's right.

'This is Jeanine, Dr McAuliff. She works for Daniel.'

The girl stood, her smile brief and tenuous. She acknowledged

Alex with a hesitant nod; her eyes were concerned as she spoke to Malcolm. 'Was the trip all right?'

'Since I brought back our guest, I cannot say it was wildly successful.'

'Yes,' replied Jeanine, her expression of concern now turned to fear. 'Daniel wants to see you right away. This way ... Dr McAuliff.'

The girl crossed to the door and rapped twice. Without waiting for a reply, she twisted the knob and opened it. Malcolm came alongside Alex and gestured him inside. McAuliff walked hesitantly through the door frame and into the office of the Halidon's Minister of Council.

The room was large, with a single, enormous leaded glass window taking up most of the rear wall. The view was both strange and awesome. Twenty feet beyond the glass was the midsection of a waterfall; it took up the entire area; there was nothing but endless tons of crashing water, its sound muted but discernible. In front of the window was a long, thick hatch table, its dark wood glistening. Behind it stood the man named Daniel, Minister of Council.

He was a Jamaican with sharp Afro-European features, slightly more than medium height and quite slender. His shoulders were broad, however; his body tapered like that of a long-distance runner. He was in his early forties, perhaps. It was difficult to tell: his face had lean youth, but his eyes were not young.

He smiled – briefly, cordially, but not enthusiastically – at McAuliff and came around the table, his hand extended.

As he did so, Alex saw that Daniel wore white casual slacks and a dark blue shirt open at the neck. Around his throat was a white silk kerchief held together by a gold ring. It was a kind of uniform, thought Alex. As Malcolm's robes were a uniform.

'Welcome, Doctor. I will not ask you about your trip. I have made it too many times myself. It's a bitch.'

Daniel shook McAuliff's hand. 'It's a bitch,' said Alex warily.

The minister abruptly turned to Malcolm. 'What's the report?

I can't think of any reason to give it privately. Or is there?'

'No ... Piersall's documents are valid. They're sealed, and McAuliff has them ready to fly out from a location within a twenty-five mile radius of the Martha Brae base camp. Even he doesn't know where. We have three days, Daniel.'

The minister stared at the priest figure. Then he walked slowly back to his chair behind the hatch table without speaking. He stood immobile, his hands on the surface of the wood, and looked up at Alex.

'So by the brilliant persistence of an expatriate island fanatic we face ... castration. Exposure renders us impotent, you know, Dr McAuliff. We will be plundered. Stripped of our possessions. And the responsibility is yours ... *You*. A geologist in the employ of Dunstone plc. And a most unlikely recruit in the service of British Intelligence.' Daniel looked over at Malcolm. 'Leave us alone, please. And be ready to start out for Montego.'

'When?' asked Malcolm.

'That will depend on our visitor. He will be accompanying you.'

'I *will*?'

'Yes, Dr McAuliff. If you are alive.'

28

'There is but a single threat one human being can make against another that must be listened to. That threat is obviously the taking of life.' Daniel had walked to the enormous window framing the cascading, unending columns of water. 'In the absence of overriding ideological issues, usually associated with religion or national causes, I think you will agree.'

'And because I'm not motivated religiously or nationally, you expect the threat to succeed.' McAuliff remained standing in front of the long, glistening hatch table. He had not been offered a chair.

'Yes,' replied the Halidon's Minister of Council, turning from the window. 'I am sure it has been said to you before that Jamaica's concerns are not your concerns.'

'It's ... "not my war" is the way it was phrased.'

'Who said that to you? Charles Whitehall or Barak Moore?'

'Barak Moore is dead,' said Alex.

The minister was obviously surprised. His reaction, however, was a brief moment of thoughtful silence. Then he spoke quietly. 'I am sorry. His was a necessary check to Whitehall's thrust. His faction has no one else, really. Someone will have to be brought up to take his place ...' Daniel walked to the table, reached down for a pencil, and wrote a note on a small pad. He tore off the page and put it to the side.

McAuliff saw without difficulty the words the minister had written. They were: 'Replace Barak Moore.' In this day of astonishments, the implication of the message was not inconsiderable.

'Just like that?' asked Alex, nodding his head in the direction of the page of notepaper.

'It will not be simple, if that is what you mean,' replied Daniel. 'Sit down, Dr McAuliff. I think it is time you understood. Before we go further . . .'

Alexander Tarquin McAuliff, geologist, with a company on 38th Street in New York City, United States of America, sat down in a native-made chair in an office room high in the inaccessible mountains of the Flagstaff Range, deep within the core of the impenetrable Cock Pit country on the island of Jamaica, and listened to a man called Daniel, Minister of Council for a covert sect with the name of Halidon.

He could not think any longer. He could only listen.

Daniel covered the initial groundwork rapidly. He asked Alex if he had read Walter Piersall's papers. McAuliff nodded.

The minister then proceeded to confirm the accuracy of Piersall's studies by tracing the Tribe of Acquaba from its beginnings in the Maroon Wars in the early eighteenth century.

'Acquaba was something of a mystic, but essentially a simple man. A Christ figure without the charity or extremes of mercy associated with the Jesus beliefs. After all, his forebears were born to the violence of the Coromanteen jungles. But his ethics were sound.'

'What is the source of your wealth?' asked Alex, his faculties returning. 'If there *is* wealth. And a source.'

'Gold,' replied Daniel simply.

'Where?'

'In the ground. On our lands.'

'There is no gold in Jamaica.'

'You are a geologist. You know better than that. There are traces of crystalline deposit in scores of minerals throughout the island –'

'Infinitesimal,' broke in McAuliff. 'Minute, and so impacted with worthless ores as to make any attempt at separation prohibitive. More expensive than the product.'

'But . . . gold, nevertheless.'

'Worthless.'

Daniel smiled. 'How do you think the crystalline traces

became impacted? I might even ask you – theoretically, if you like – how the island of Jamaica came to be.'

'As any isolated land mass in the oceans. Geologic upheavals –' Alex stopped. The theory was beyond imagination, made awesome because of its simplicity. A section of a vein of gold, millions upon millions of years ago, exploding out of the layers of earth beneath the sea, impacting deposits throughout the mass that was disgorged out of the waters. 'My God . . . there's a vein . . .'

'There is no point in pursuing this,' said Daniel. 'For centuries the colonial law of Jamaica spelled out an absolute: All precious metals discovered on the island were the possession of the Crown. It was the primary reason no one searched.'

'*Fowler*,' said McAuliff softly. 'Jeremy Fowler . . .'

'I beg your pardon?'

'The Crown Recorder in Kingston. Almost a hundred years ago . . .'

Daniel paused. 'Yes. In 1883, to be exact . . . so that was Piersall's fragment.' The minister of the Halidon wrote on another page of notepaper. 'It will be removed.'

'This Fowler,' asked Alex softly. 'Did he know?'

Daniel looked up from the paper, tearing it off the pad as he did so. 'No. He believed he was carrying out the wishes of a dissident faction of Maroons conspiring with a group of north-coast landowners. The object was to destroy the records of a tribal treaty so thousands of acres could be cleared for plantations. It was what he was told and what he was paid for.'

'The family in England still believes it.'

'Why not? It was' – the minister smiled – '*Colonial Service*. Shall we return to more currently applicable questions? You see, Dr McAuliff, we want you to understand. *Thoroughly*.'

'Go ahead.'

According to Daniel, the Halidon had no ambitions for political power. It never had such ambitions; it remained outside the body politic, accepting the historical view that order emerges

336

out of the chaos of different, even conflicting ideologies. Ideas were greater monuments than cathedrals, and a people must have free access to them. That was the lesson of Acquaba. Freedom of mobility, freedom of thought . . . freedom to do battle, if need be. The religion of the Halidon was essentially humanist, its jungle gods symbols of continuously struggling forces battling for the mortals' freedom. Freedom to survive in the world in the manner agreed upon within the tribe, without imposing that manner on the other tribes.

'Not a bad premise, is it?' asked Daniel confidently, again rapidly.

'No,' answered McAuliff. 'And not particularly original, either.'

'I disagree,' said the minister. 'The thought may have a hundred precedents, but the practice is almost unheard of . . . Tribes, as they develop self-sufficiency, tend to graduate to the point where they are anxious to impose themselves on as many other tribes as possible. From the Pharaohs to Caesar; from the Empire – several empires, Holy Roman, British, et cetera – to Adolf Hitler; from Stalin to your own conglomeratized government of self-righteous proselytizers. Beware the pious believers, McAuliff. They were all pious in their fashions. Too many are still.'

'But you're not.' Alex looked over at the enormous leaded glass window and the rushing, plummeting water beyond. 'You just decide who is . . . and act accordingly. Free to "do battle", as you call it.'

'You think that is a contradiction of purpose?'

'You're damned right I do. When "doing battle" includes killing people . . . because they don't conform to *your* idea of what's acceptable.'

'Who have we killed?'

Alex shifted his gaze from the waterfall to Daniel. 'I can start with last night. Two carriers on the survey who were probably picking up a few dollars from British Intelligence; for what? Keeping their eyes open? Reporting what we had for dinner?

337

Who came to see us? Your runner, the one I called "Marcus", said they were agents; he killed them. And a fat pig named Garvey, who was a pretty low-level, uninformed liaison and, I grant you, smelled bad. But I think a fatal accident on the road to Port Maria was a bit drastic.' McAuliff paused for a moment and leaned forward in the chair. 'You massacred an entire survey team – every member – and for all you know, they were hired by Dunstone the same way I was: just looking for work. Now, maybe you can justify all those killings, but neither you nor anyone else can justify the death of Walter Piersall ... Yes, Mr High and Mighty Minister, I think you're pretty violently pious yourself.'

Daniel had sat down in the chair behind the hatch table during Alex's angry narrative. He now pushed his foot against the floor, sending the chair gently to his right, towards the huge window. 'Over a hundred years ago, this office was the entire building. One of my early predecessors had it placed here. He insisted that the minister's room – "chamber", it was called then – overlook this section of our waterfall. He claimed the constant movement and the muffled sound forced a man to concentrate, blocked out small considerations ... That long-forgotten rebel proved right. I never cease to wonder at the different bursts of shapes and patterns. And while wondering, the mind really concentrates.'

'Is that by way of telling me those who were killed were ... small considerations?'

Daniel pushed the chair back in place and faced McAuliff. 'No, Doctor. I was trying to think of a way to convince you. I shall tell you the truth, but I am not sure you will believe it. Our runners, our guides – our infiltrators, if you will – are trained to use *effect* wherever possible. Fear, McAuliff, is an extraordinary weapon. A non-violent weapon; not that we are necessarily non-violent ... Your carriers are not dead. They were taken prisoner, blindfolded, led to the outskirts of Weston Favel, and released. They were not hurt, but they were frightened severely. They will not work for MI5 or MI6 again. Garvey

338

is dead, but we did not kill him. Your Mr Garvey sold anything he could get his hands on, including women, especially young girls. He was shot on the road to Port Maria by a distraught father, the motive obvious. We simply took the credit . . . You say we massacred the Dunstone survey. Reverse that, Doctor. Three of the four white men tried to massacre our scouting party. They killed six of our young men after asking them into the camp for a conference.'

'One of those . . . white men was a British agent.'

'So Malcolm tells us.'

'I don't believe a trained Intelligence man would kill indiscriminately.'

'Malcolm agrees with you. But the facts are there. An Intelligence agent is a man first. In the sudden pitch of battle a man takes sides. This man, whichever one he was, chose his side . . . He did not have to choose the way he did.'

'The fourth man? He was different, then?'

'Yes.' Daniel's eyes were suddenly reflective. 'He was a good man. A Hollander. When he realized what the others were doing, he objected violently. He ran out to warn the rest of our party. His own men shot him.'

For several moments, neither spoke. Finally McAuliff asked, 'What about Walter Piersall? Can you find a story for that?'

'No,' said Daniel. 'We do not know what happened. Or who killed him. We have ideas, but nothing more. Walter Piersall was the last man on earth we wanted dead. Especially under the circumstances. And if you do not understand that, then you're stupid.'

McAuliff got out of the chair and walked aimlessly to the huge window. He could feel Daniel's eyes on him. He forced himself to watch the crashing streams of water in front of him. 'Why did you bring me here? Why have you told me so much? About you . . . and everything else.'

'We had no choice. Unless you lied or unless Malcolm was deceived, neither of which I believe . . . And we understand your position as well as your background. When Malcolm flew out of England, he brought with him MI5's complete dossier on you. We are willing to make you an offer.'

Alex turned and looked down at the minister. 'I'm sure it's one I can't refuse.'

'Not readily. Your life. And, not incidentally, the lives of your fellow surveyors.'

'Piersall's documents?'

'Somewhat more extensive, but those, too, of course,' answered Daniel.

'Go on.' McAuliff remained by the window. The muted sound of the waterfall was his connection to the outside somehow. It was comforting.

'We know what the British want: the list of names that comprise the Dunstone hierarchy. The international financiers that fully expect to turn this island into an economic sanctuary, another Switzerland. Not long ago, a matter of weeks, they gathered here on the island from all over the world. In Port Antonio. A few used their real names, most did not. The timing is propitious. The Swiss banking institutions are breaking down their traditional codes of account-secrecy one after another. They are under extraordinary pressures, of course . . . We have the Dunstone list. We will make an exchange.'

'It for our lives? And the documents . . .'

Daniel laughed, neither cruelly nor kindly. It was a genuine expression of humour. 'Doctor, I am afraid it is you who are obsessed with small considerations. It is true we place great value on Piersall's documents, but the British do not. We must think as our adversaries think. The British want the Dunstone list above all things. And above all things, we want British Intelligence, and everything it represents, out of Jamaica. That is the exchange we offer.'

McAuliff stood motionless by the window. 'I don't understand you.'

The minister leaned forward. 'We demand an end to English influence . . . as we demand an end to the influence of all other nations – *tribes*, if you wish, Doctor – over this island. In short words, Jamaica is to be left to the Jamaicans.'

'Dunstone wouldn't leave it to you,' said Alex, groping. 'I'd say its influence was a hell of a lot more dangerous than anyone else's.'

'Dunstone is *our* fight; we have our *own* plans. Dunstone was organized by financial geniuses. But once confined in our territory, our alternatives are multiple. Among other devices, expropriation ... But these alternatives take time and we both know the British do not have the time. England cannot afford the loss of Dunstone plc.'

McAuliff's mind raced back to the room in the Savoy Hotel ... and R. C. Hammond's quiet admission that *economics were a factor. A rather significant one.*

Hammond the manipulator.

Alex walked back to the armchair and sat down. He realized Daniel was allowing him the time to think, to absorb the possibilities of the new information. There were so many questions; most, he knew, could be answered, but several touched him. He had to try.

'A few days ago,' he began awkwardly, 'when Barak Moore died, I found myself concerned that Charles Whitehall had no one to oppose him. So did you. I saw what you wrote down –'

'What is your question?' asked Daniel civilly.

'I was right, wasn't I? They're the two extremes. They have followers. They're not just hollow fanatics.'

'Whitehall and Moore?'

'Yes.'

'Hardly. They're the charismatic leaders. Moore *was*, Whitehall *is*. In all new merging nations there are generally three factions: right, left, and the comfortable middle – the entrenched hold-overs who have learned the daily functions. The middle is eminently corruptible; it continues the same dull, bureaucratic chores with sudden new authority. It is the first to be replaced. The healthiest way is by an infusion of the maturest elements from both extremes. Peaceful balance.'

'And that's what you're waiting for? Like a referee? An umpire?'

'Yes. That's very good, Doctor. There's merit in the struggle, you know; neither side is devoid of positive factors . . . Unfortunately, Dunstone makes our task more difficult. We must observe the combatants carefully.'

The minister's eyes had strayed again; and, again, there was that brief, nearly imperceptible reflection. 'Why?' asked Alex.

Daniel seemed at first reluctant to answer. And then he sighed audibly. 'Very well . . . Barak Moore's reaction to Dunstone would be violent. A bloodbath . . . chaos. Whitehall's would be equally dangerous. He would seek temporary collusion, the power base being completely financial. He could be used as many of the German industrialists honestly believed they were using Hitler. Only the association feeds on absolute power . . . absolutely.'

McAuliff leaned back in the chair. He was beginning to understand. 'So if Dunstone's out, you're back to the . . . what was it . . . the healthy struggle?'

'Yes.' said Daniel quietly.

'Then you and the British want the same thing. How can you make conditions?'

'Because our solutions are different. We have the time and the confidence of final control. The English . . . and the French and the Americans and the Germans . . . do not have either. The economic disasters they would suffer could well be to our advantage. And that is all I will say on the subject . . . We have the Dunstone list. You will make the offer to the British.'

'I go with Malcolm to Montego –'

'You will be escorted, and guarded,' interrupted Daniel harshly. 'The members of your geological survey are hostages. Each will be summarily executed should there be the slightest deviation from our instructions.'

'Suppose British Intelligence doesn't believe you? What the hell am I supposed to do then?'

Daniel stood up. 'They will believe you, McAuliff. For your

342

trip to Montego Bay is merely part of the news that will soon be worldwide. There will be profound shock in several national capitals. And you will tell British Intelligence that this is our proof. It is only the tip of the Dunstone iceberg ... Oh, they will believe you, McAuliff. Precisely at noon, London time. Tomorrow.'

'That's all you'll tell me?'

'No. One thing more. When the acts take place, the panicked giant – Dunstone – will send out its killers. Among others, you will be a target.'

McAuliff found himself standing up in anger. 'Thank you for the warning,' he said.

'You are welcome,' replied Daniel. 'Now, if you will come with me.'

Outside the office, Malcolm, the priest figure, was talking quietly with Jeanine. At the sight of Daniel, both fell silent. Jeanine blocked Daniel's path and spoke.

'There is news from the Martha Brae.'

Alex looked at the minister and then back at the girl. 'Martha Brae' had to mean the survey's campsite. He started to speak, but was cut off by Daniel.

'Whatever it is, tell us both.'

'It concerns two men. The young man, Ferguson, and the ore specialist, Peter Jensen ...'

Alex breathed again.

'What happened?' asked Daniel. 'The young man first.'

'A runner came into camp bringing him a letter from Arthur Craft, Senior. In it Craft made promises, instructing Ferguson to leave the survey, come up to Port Antonio, to the Foundation. Our scouts followed and intercepted them several miles down the river. They are being held there, south of Weston Favel.'

'Craft found out about his son,' said Alex. 'He's trying to buy off Ferguson.'

'The purchase might well be to Jamaica's advantage. And Ferguson is not a hostage high on your scale of values.'

343

'I brought him to the island. He is valuable to me,' answered Alex coldly.

'We shall see.' Daniel turned to the girl. 'Tell the scouts to stay where they are. Hold Ferguson and the runner; instructions will follow. What about the Jensen man?'

'He is all right. The scouts are tracking him.'

'He left camp?'

'He's pretending to be lost, our men think. Early this morning, soon after Dr McAuliff left, he had his carrier stretch what is called an . . . azimuth line. He had the man walk quite a distance while he reeled out the nylon string. The signals were by tugs, apparently –'

'And Jensen cut the line and tied his end to a sapling,' interrupted Alex in a rapid monotone. 'With a loop around a nearby limb.'

'How do you know this?' Daniel seemed fascinated.

'It's a very old, unfunny trick in the field. A distasteful joke. It's played on green recruits.'

Daniel turned again to the girl. 'So his carrier could not find him. Where is Jensen now?'

'He tried to pick up Malcolm's trail,' replied the secretary. 'The scouts say he came very close. He gave up and circled back to the west hill. From there he can watch the entire campsite. All means of entrance.'

'He will wait the full three days, starving and trapped by cats, if he thinks it will help him. He does not dare go back to Warfield without something.' Daniel looked at Alex. 'Did you know you were *his* choice to direct the survey?'

'I was *his* . . .' McAuliff did not finish the statement. There was no point, he thought.

'Tell our people to stay with him,' ordered the minister. 'Get close, but don't take him . . . unless he uses a radio that could reach the coast. If he does, kill him.'

'What the hell are you saying?' demanded McAuliff angrily. 'Goddamnit, you have no right!'

'We have every right, Doctor. You adventurers come to this

344

island. Soil it with your *filth*. Don't speak to me of *rights*, McAuliff!' And then, as suddenly as he had raised his voice, he lowered it. He spoke to the girl. 'Convene the Council.'

29

Daniel led McAuliff down the steps into the matted grass on the left bank of the miniature channel of rushing water. Neither man spoke. Alex looked at his watch; it was nearly eight o'clock. The rays of the twilight sun shot up from behind the western mountains in spectral shafts of orange; the intercepting hills were silhouetted in brownish black, emphasizing their incredible height, their fortress-immensity. The lake was a huge sheet of very dark glass, polished beyond the ability of man, reflecting the massive shadows of the mountains and the streaks of the orange sun.

They walked down the slope of the clearing to the stone fence bordering the grazing fields. At the far left was a gate; Daniel approached it, unlatched the large single bolt, and swung it open. He gestured McAuliff to go through.

'I apologize for my outburst,' said the minister as they walked into the field. 'It was misdirected. You are a victim, not an aggressor. We realize that.'

'And what are you? Are you a victim? Or an aggressor?'

'I am the Minister of Council. And *we* are neither. I explained that.'

'You explained a lot of things, but I still don't know anything about you,' said McAuliff, his eyes on a lone animal approaching them in the darkening field. It was a young horse, and it whinnied and pranced hesitantly as it drew near.

'This colt is forever breaking out,' laughed Daniel as he patted the neck of the nervous animal. 'He will be difficult to train, this one ... *Hyee! Hyee!*' cried the Halidonite as he slapped

346

the colt's flank, sending it kicking and prancing and snorting towards the centre of the field.

'Maybe that's what I mean,' said Alex. 'How do you train . . . people? Keep them from breaking out?'

Daniel stopped and looked at McAuliff. They were alone in the large pasture, awash with the vivid colours of the dying Jamaican sun. The light silhouetted the minister and caused McAuliff to shield his face. He could not see Daniel's eyes, but he could feel them.

'We are an uncomplicated people in many ways,' said the Halidonite. 'What technology we require is brought in, along with our medical supplies, basic farm machinery, and the like. Always by our own members, using untraceable mountain routes. Other than these, we are self-sufficient on our lands. Our training – as you call it – is a result of understanding the immense riches we possess. Our isolation is hardly absolute. As you will see.'

From childhood, Daniel explained, the Halidonite was told he was privileged and must justify his birthright by his life's actions. The ethic of contribution was imbued in him early in his education; the need to use his potential to the fullest. The outside world was shown in all its detail – its simplicities, its complications, its peace and its violence; its good and its evil. Nothing was concealed; exaggeration was not left to young imaginations. Realistic temptation was balanced – perhaps a bit strongly, admitted Daniel – with realistic punishment.

As near to his or her twelfth birthday as possible, the Halidonite was tested extensively by teachers, the Elders of the Council, and finally by the minister himself. On the basis of these examinations, individuals were selected for training for the outside world. There followed three years of preparation, concentrating on specific skills or professions.

When he or she reached sixteen, the Halidonite was taken from the community and brought to a family residence on the outside, where the father and mother were members of the tribe. Except for infrequent returns to the community and reunions

347

with his own parents, the outside family would be the Halidonite's guardians for a number of years to come.

'Don't you have defections?' asked Alex.

'Rarely,' replied Daniel. 'The screening process is most
thorough.'

'What happens if it isn't thorough enough? If there are –'

'That is an answer I will not give you,' interrupted the minister. 'Except to say the Maze of Acquaba is a threat no prison
can compete with. It keeps offenders – within and without – to
a minimum. Defections are extremely rare.'

From the tone of Daniel's voice, Alex had no desire to pursue
the subject. 'They're brought back?'

Daniel nodded.

The population of the Halidon was voluntarily controlled.
Daniel claimed that for every couple that wanted more children,
there invariably was a couple that wanted fewer or none. And,
to McAuliff's astonishment, the minister added: 'Marriages take
place between ourselves and those of the outside. It is, of course,
unavoidable and, by necessity, desirable. But it is a complicated
procedure taking place over many months and with stringent
regulations.'

'A reverse screening process?'

'The harshest imaginable. Controlled by the guardians.'

'What happens if the marriage doesn't . . .'

'That answer, too, is not in bounds, doctor.'

'I have an idea the penalties are stiff,' said Alex softly.

'You may have all the ideas you like,' said Daniel, starting
up again across the field. 'But what is of the greatest importance
is that you understand that we have scores . . . hundreds of
guardians – halfway houses – throughout the countries of the
world. In every profession, in all governments, in dozens of
universities and institutions everywhere . . . You will never
know who is a member of the Halidon. And that is our threat,
our ultimate protection.'

'You're saying that if I reveal what I know, you'll have me
killed?'

'You and every member of your family. Wife, children, parents . . . in the absence of the formal structure, lovers, closest associates, every person who was or is an influence on your life. Your identity, even your memory, will be erased.'

'You can't know every person I talk to, every telephone call I make. Where I am every minute. *No* one can! I could mount an army; I could find you!'

'But you will not,' said Daniel quietly, in counterpoint to McAuliff's outburst. 'For the same reason others have not . . . Come. We are here.'

They were standing now on the edge of the field. Beyond was the tentacled foliage of the Cock Pit forest, in shadowed blackness.

Suddenly, startlingly, the air was filled with a penetrating sound of terrible resonance. It was a wailing, inhuman lament. The tone was low, breathless, enveloping everything and echoing everywhere. It was the sound of a giant woodwind, rising slowly, receding into a simple, obscure theme and swelling again to the plaintive cry of the higher melody.

It grew louder and louder, the echoes now picking up the bass tones and hurling them through the jungles, crashing them off the sides of the surrounding mountains until the earth seemed to vibrate.

And then it stopped, and McAuliff stood transfixed as he saw in the distance the outlines of figures walking slowly, purposefully, in measured cadence, across the fields in the chiaroscuro shadows of the early darkness. A few carried torches, the flames low.

At first there were only four or five, coming from the direction of the gate. Then there were some from the south bank of the black, shining lake; others from the north, emerging out of the darkness. Flat-bottomed boats could be seen crossing the surface of the water, each with a single torch.

Within minutes there were ten, then twenty, thirty . . . until McAuliff stopped counting. From everywhere. Dozens of slowly moving bodies swaying gently as they walked across the darkened fields.

349

They were converging towards the spot where Alex stood with Daniel.

The inhuman wailing began again. Louder – if possible – than before, and McAuliff found himself bringing his hand up to his ears; the vibrations in his head and throughout his body were causing pain – actual *pain*.

Daniel touched him on the shoulder; Alex whipped around as if he had been struck violently. For an instant he thought he had been, so severe were the agonizing sensations brought on by the deafening sound of the horrible lament.

'Come,' said Daniel gently. 'The *hollydawn* can injure you.'

McAuliff heard him accurately; he knew that. Daniel had pronounced the word: not 'Halidon' but 'hollydawn'. As though the echoing, deafening sound had caused him to revert to a more primitive tongue.

Daniel walked rapidly ahead of Alex into what McAuliff thought was a wall of underbrush. Then the Halidonite suddenly began to descend into what appeared to be a trench dug out of the jungle. Alex ran to catch up, and nearly plummeted down a long, steep corridor of steps carved out of rock.

The strange staircase widened, flaring out more on both sides the deeper it went, until McAuliff could see that they had descended into a primitive amphitheatre, the walls rising thirty or forty feet to the surface of the earth.

What was the staircase became an aisle, the curving rock on both sides forming rows of descending seats.

And suddenly the deafening, agonizing sound from above was no more. It had stopped. Everything was silent.

The amphitheatre, carved out of some kind of quarry, blocked out all other sound.

McAuliff stood where he was and looked down at the single source of light: a low flame that illuminated the wall of rock at the centre rear of the amphitheatre. In that wall was embedded a slab of dull yellow metal. And on that slab of metal was a withered corpse. In front of the corpse was a latticework of thin reeds made of the same yellow substance.

McAuliff needed to go no closer to realize what the substance was: gold.

And the withered, ancient body – once huge – was that of the mystic descendant of the Coromanteen chieftains.

Acquaba.

The preserved remains of the progenitor ... spanning the centuries. The true cross of the Tribe of Acquaba. For the believers to see. And sense.

'Down here.' Daniel's words were whispered, but Alex heard them clearly. 'You will sit with me. Please, hurry.'

McAuliff walked down the remaining staircase to the floor of the quarry shell and over to the Halidonite on the right side of the primitive stage. Jutting out from the wall were two stone blocks; Daniel pointed to one: the seat nearest the corpse of Acquaba, less than eight feet away.

McAuliff lowered himself on to the hard stone, his eyes drawn to the open catafalque of solid and webbed gold. The leathered corpse was dressed in robes of reddish black: the feet and hands were bare ... and huge, as the head was huge. Allowing for the contraction of two centuries, the man must have been enormous – nearer seven feet than six.

The single torch below the coffin of gold shot flickering shadows against the wall; the thin reeds crisscrossing the front of the carved-out casket picked up the light in dozens of tiny reflections. The longer one stared, thought Alex, the easier it would be to convince oneself this was the shell of a god lying in state. A god who had walked the earth and worked the earth – two hundred years could not erase the signs on the enormous hands and feet. But this god, this man did not toil as other men ...

He heard the sounds of muted steps and looked up into the small amphitheatre. Through the entrance, hidden in darkness, and down the staircase they came, a procession of men and women separating and spreading throughout the lateral stone aisles, taking their seats.

In silence.

Those with torches stood equidistant from each other on graduating levels against opposite walls.

All eyes were on the withered body beyond the latticework of gold. Their concentration was absolute; it was as if they drew sustenance from it.

In silence.

Suddenly, without warning, the sound of the *hollydawn* shattered the stillness with the impact of an explosion. The thunderous, wailing lament seemed to burst from the bowels of rock-covered earth, crashing upwards against the stone, thrusting out of the huge pit that was the grave of Acquaba.

McAuliff felt the breath leaving his lungs, the blood rushing to his head. He buried his face between his knees, his hands clamped over his ears, his whole body shaking.

The cry reached a crescendo, a terrible screaming rush of air that swelled to a pitch of frenzy. *No human ears could stand it!* thought Alex as he trembled ... as he had never before trembled in his life.

And then it was over and the silence returned.

McAuliff slowly sat up, lowering his hands, gripping the stone beneath him in an effort to control the violent spasms he felt shooting through his flesh. His eyes were blurred from the blood which had raced to his temples; they cleared slowly, in stages, and he looked out at the rows of Halidonites, at these chosen members of the Tribe of Acquaba.

They were – each one, all – still staring, eyes fixed on the ancient, withered body behind the golden reeds.

Alex knew they had remained exactly as they were throughout the shattering madness that had nearly driven him out of his mind.

He turned to Daniel; involuntarily he gasped. The Minister of Council, too, was transfixed, his black eyes wide, his jaw set, his face immobile. But he was different from all the others; there were tears streaming down Daniel's cheeks.

'You're mad ... all of you,' said Alex quietly. 'You're insane ...'

Daniel did not respond. Daniel could not hear him. He was in a hypnotic state.

They all were. Everyone in that carved-out shell beneath the earth. Nearly a hundred men and women inextricably held by some force beyond his comprehension.

Auto-suggestion. Self-somnipathy. Group hypnosis. Whatever the catalyst, each individual in that primitive amphitheatre was mesmerized beyond reach. On another plane . . . time and space unfamiliar.

Alexander felt himself an intruder; he was observing a ritual too private for his eyes.

Yet he had not asked to be here. He had been forced in – ripped out of place – and made to bear witness.

Still, the witnessing filled him with sorrow. And he could not understand. So he looked over at the body that was once the giant, Acquaba.

He stared at the shrivelled flesh of the once-black face. At the closed eyes, so peaceful in death. At the huge hands folded so strongly across the reddish black robe.

Then back at the face . . . the eyes . . . the eyes . . .

Oh, my God! Oh, Christ!

The shadows were playing tricks . . . terrible, horrible tricks.

The body of Acquaba moved.

The eyes opened; the fingers of the immense hands spread, the wrists turned, the arms raised . . . inches above the ancient cloth.

In supplication.

And then there was nothing.

Only a shrivelled corpse behind a latticework of gold.

McAuliff pressed himself back against the wall of stone, trying desperately to find his sanity. He closed his eyes and breathed deeply, gripping the rock beneath him. It could *not* have *happened*! It was some sort of mass hallucination by way of theatrical trickery accompanied by group expectation and that damned unearthly ear-shattering sound! Yet he had *seen* it! And it was horrifyingly effective. He did not know how long it was – a minute, an hour, a decade of terror – until he heard Daniel's words.

'You *saw* it.' A statement made gently. 'Do not be afraid. We shall never speak of it again. There is no harm. Only good.'

'I . . . I . . .' Alexander could not talk. The perspiration rolled down his face. And the carved-out council ground was cool.

Daniel stood up and walked to the centre of the platform of rock. Instead of addressing the Tribe of Acquaba, he turned to McAuliff. His words were whispered, but, as before, they were clear and precise, echoing off the walls.

'The lessons of Acquaba touch all men, as the lessons of all prophets touch all men. But few listen. Still, the work must go on. For those who can do it. It is really as simple as that. Acquaba was granted the gift of great riches . . . beyond the imaginations of those who will never listen; who will only steal and corrupt . . . So we go out into the world without the world's knowledge. And we do what we can . . . It must ever be so, for if the world knew, the world would impose itself and the Halidon, the Tribe of Acquaba, and the lessons of Acquaba would be destroyed . . . We are not fools, Dr McAuliff. We know with whom we speak, with whom we share our secrets. And our love . . . But do not mistake us. We can kill: we *will* kill to protect the vaults of Acquaba. In that we are dangerous. In that we are absolute. We will destroy ourselves *and* the vaults if the world outside interferes with us.

'I, as Minister of Council, ask you to rise, Dr McAuliff. And turn yourself away from the Tribe of Acquaba, from this Council of the Halidon, and face the wall. What you will hear, staring only at stone, are voices, revealing locations and figures. As I mentioned, we are not fools. We understand the specifics of the marketplace. But you will not see faces, you will never know the identities of those who speak. Only know that they go forth bearing the wealth of Acquaba.

'We dispense vast sums throughout the world, concentrating as best we can on the areas of widespread human suffering.

Pockets of famine, displacement . . . futility. Untold thousands are helped daily by the Halidon. Daily. In practical ways.

'Please rise and face the wall, Dr McAuliff.'

Alexander got up from the block of stone and turned. For a brief instant his eyes fell on the corpse of Acquaba. He looked away and stared at the towering sheet of rock.

Daniel continued. 'Our contributions are made without thought of political gain or influence. They are made because we have the concealed wealth and the commitment to make them. The lessons of Acquaba.

'But the world is not ready to accept our ways, Acquaba's ways. Its global mendacity would destroy us, cause us to destroy ourselves perhaps. And that we cannot permit.

'So understand this, Dr McAuliff. Beyond the certainty of your own death, should you reveal what you know of the Tribe of Acquaba, there is another certainty of far greater significance than your life: the work of the Halidon will cease. That is our ultimate threat . . .'

One by one, the voices recited their terse statements:

'Afro axis. Ghana. Fourteen thousand bushels of grain. Conduit: Smythe Brothers, Cape Town. Barclay's Bank . . .'

'Sierra Leone. Three tons medical supplies. Conduit: Baldazi Pharmaceuticals, Algiers. Bank of Constantine . . .'

'Indo-China axis. Vietnam, Mekong, Quan Tho provinces. Radiology and laboratory personnel and supplies. Conduit: Swiss Red Cross. Bank of America . . .'

'South-west Hemisphere axis. Brazil. Rio de Janeiro. Typhoid serum. Conduit: Surgical Salizar. Banco Terceiro, Rio . . .'

'Northwest Hemisphere axis. West Virginia. Appalachia. Twenty-four tons food supplies. Conduit: Atlantic Warehousing. Chase Manhattan, New York . . .'

'India axis. Dacca. Refugee camps. Inoculation serums, medicals. Conduit: International Displacement Organization. World Bank, Burma . . .'

The voices of men and women droned on, the phrases clipped, yet somehow gentle. It took nearly an hour, and McAuliff began

355

to recognize that many spoke twice, but always with different information. Nothing was repeated.

Finally there was silence.

A long period of silence. And then Alexander felt a hand on his shoulder. He turned, and Daniel's eyes bore in on him.

'Do you understand?'

'Yes, I understand,' McAuliff said.

They walked across the field towards the lake. The sounds of the forest mingled with the hum of the mountains and the crashing of the waterfall nearly a mile to the north.

They stood on the embankment, and Alex bent down, picked up a small stone, and threw it into the black, shining lake that reflected the light of the moon. He looked at Daniel.

'In a way, you're as dangerous as the rest of them. One man . . . with so much . . . operating beyond reach. No checks, no balances. It would be so simple for good to become evil, evil good. Malcolm said your . . . term isn't guided by a calendar.'

'It is not. I am elected for life. Only I can terminate my office.'

'And pick your successor?'

'I have influence. The council, of course, has the final disposition.'

'Then I think you're more dangerous.'

'I do not deny it.'

30

The trip to Montego was far easier than the circuitous march from the Martha Brae. To begin with, most of the journey was by vehicle.

Malcolm, his robes replaced by Savile Row clothing, led Alexander around the lake to the south-east, where they were met by a runner who took them to the base of a mountain cliff, hidden by jungle. A steel lift, whose thick chains were concealed by mountain rocks, carried them up the enormous precipice to a second runner, who placed them in a small tram, which was transported by cable on a path below the skyline of the forest.

At the end of the cable ride, a third runner took them through a series of deep caves, identified by Malcolm as the Quick Step Grotto. He told Alex that the Quick Step was named for seventeenth-century buccaneers who raced from Bluefield's Bay overland to bury treasure at the bottom of the deep pools within the caves. The other derivation – the one many believed more appropriate – was that if a traveller did not watch his feet, he could easily slip and plummet into a crevice. Injury was certain, death not impossible.

McAuliff stayed close to the runner, his flashlight beamed at the rocky darkness in front of him.

Out of the caves, they proceeded through a short stretch of jungle to the first definable road they had seen. The runner activated a portable radio; ten minutes later a Land-Rover came out of the pitch-black hollows from the west and the runner bid them goodbye.

The rugged vehicle travelled over a criss-cross pattern of back-country roads, the driver keeping his engine as quiet as possible, coasting on descending hills, shutting off his headlights whenever they approached a populated area. The drive lasted a halfhour. They passed through the Maroon village of Accompong and swung south several miles to a flat stretch of grassland.

In the darkness, on the field's edge, a small aeroplane was rolled out from under a camouflage of fern and acacia. It was a two-seater Comanche; they climbed in, and Malcolm took the controls.

'This is the only difficult leg of the trip,' he said as they taxied for take-off. 'We must fly close to the ground to avoid interior radar. Unfortunately, so do the ganja aircraft, the drug smugglers. But we will worry less about the authorities than we will about collision.'

Without incident, but not without sighting several ganja planes, they landed on the grounds of an outlying farm, southwest of Unity Hall. From there it was a fifteen-minute ride into Montego Bay.

'It would arouse suspicions for us to stay in the exclusively black section of the town. You, for your skin, me, for my speech and my clothes. And tomorrow we must have mobility in the whites areas.'

They drove to the Cornwall Beach Hotel and registered ten minutes apart. Reservations had been made for adjoining but not connecting rooms.

It was two o'clock in the morning, and McAuliff fell into bed exhausted. He had not slept in nearly forty-eight hours. And yet, for a very long time, sleep did not come.

He thought about so many things. The brilliant, lonely, awkward James Ferguson and his sudden departure to the Craft Foundation. Defection, really. Without explanation. Alex hoped Craft was Jimbo-mon's solution. For he would never be trusted again.

And of the sweetly charming Jensens ... up to their sorespectable chins in the manipulations of Dunstone plc.

Of the 'charismatic leader' Charles Whitehall, waiting to ride 'nigger-Pompei's horse' through Victoria Park. Whitehall was no match for the Halidon. The Tribe of Acquaba would not tolerate him.

Nor did the lessons of Acquaba include the violence of Lawrence, the boy-man giant ... successor to Barak Moore. Lawrence's 'revolution' would not come to pass. Not the way he conceived it.

Alex wondered about Sam Tucker. Tuck, the gnarled rock-like force of stability. Would Sam find what he was looking for in Jamaica? For surely he was looking.

But most of all McAuliff thought about Alison. Of her lovely half laugh and her clear blue eyes and the calm acceptance that was her understanding. How very much he loved her.

He wondered, as his consciousness drifted into the grey, blank void that was sleep, if they would have a life together.

After the madness.

If he was alive.

If they were alive.

He had left a wake-up call for 6:45. Quarter to twelve, London time. Noon. For the Halidon.

The coffee arrived in seven minutes. Eight minutes to twelve. The telephone rang three minutes later. Five minutes to noon, London time. It was Malcolm, and he was not in his hotel room. He was at the Associated Press Bureau, Montego Bay office on St James Street. He wanted to make sure that Alex was up and had his radio on. Perhaps his television set as well.

McAuliff had both instruments on.

Malcolm the Halidonite would call him later.

At three minutes to seven – twelve, London time – there was a rapid knocking on the hotel door. Alexander was startled. Malcolm had said nothing about visitors; no one knew he was in Montego Bay. He approached the door.

'Yes?'

The words from the other side of the wood were spoken hesitantly, in a deep, familiar voice.

'Is that you ... McAuliff?'

And instantly Alexander understood. The symmetry, the timing was extraordinary; only extraordinary minds could conceive and execute such a symbolic coup.

He opened the door.

R. C. Hammond, British Intelligence, stood in the corridor, his slender frame rigid, his face an expression of suppressed shock.

'Good God. It is you . . . I didn't believe them. Your signals from the river . . . There was nothing irregular, nothing at all!'

'That,' said Alex, 'is about as disastrous a judgment as I've ever heard.'

'They dragged me out of my rooms in Kingston . . . before daylight. Drove me up into the hills –'

'And flew you to Montego,' completed McAuliff, looking at his watch. 'Come in, Hammond. We've got a minute and fifteen seconds to go.'

'For what?'

'We'll both find out.'

The lilting, high-pitched Caribbean voice on the radio proclaimed over the music the hour of seven in the 'sunlight paradise of Montego Bay'. The picture on the television set was a sudden fade-in shot of a long expanse of white beach . . . a photograph. The announcer, in over-Anglicized tones, was extolling the virtues of 'our island life' and welcoming 'alla visitors from the cold climates', pointing out immediately that there was a blizzard in New York.

Twelve o'clock, London time.

Nothing unusual.

Nothing.

Hammond stood by the window, looking out at the blue-green water of the bay. He was silent; his anger was the fury of a man who had lost control because he did not know the moves his opponents were making. And, more important, why they were making them.

The manipulator manipulated.

McAuliff sat on the bed, his eyes on the television set, now a travelogue fraught with lies about the 'beautiful city of Kingston'. Simultaneously, the radio on the bedside table blared its combination of cacophonic music and frantic commercials for everything from Coppertone to Hertz. Intermittently, there was the syrupy female Voice-of-the-Ministry-of-Health, telling the women of the island that 'you do have to get pregnant', followed by the repetition of the weather . . . the forecasts never 'partly cloudy', always 'partly sunny'.

Nothing unusual.

Nothing.

It was eleven minutes past twelve London time.

Still nothing.

And then it happened.

'We interrupt this broadcast . . .'

And, like an insignificant wave born of the ocean depths – unnoticed at first, but gradually swelling, suddenly bursting out of the waters and cresting in controlled fury – the pattern of terror was clear.

The first announcement was merely the prelude – a single flute outlining the significant notes of a theme shortly to be developed.

Explosion and death in Port Antonio.

The east wing of the estate of Arthur Craft had been blown up by explosives, the resulting conflagration gutting most of the house. Among the dead was feared to be the patriarch of the Foundation.

There were rumours of rifle fire preceding the series of explosions. Port Antonio was in panic.

Rifle fire. Explosives.

Rare, yes. But not unheard of on this island of scattered violence. Of contained anger.

The next 'interruption' followed in less than ten minutes. It was – appropriately, thought McAuliff – a news report from London. This intrusion warranted a line of moving print across

361

the television screen: 'Killings in London, Full Report on News Hour'. The radio allowed a long musical commercial to run its abrasive course before the voice returned, now authoritatively bewildered.

The details were still sketchy, but not the conclusions. Four high-ranking figures in government and industry had been slain. A director of Lloyds, an accounts official of Inland Revenue, and two members of the House of Commons, both chairing trade committees of consequence.

The methods: two now familiar, two new – dramatically oriented.

A high-powered rifle fired from a window into a canopied entrance in Belgravia. A dynamited car, blown up in the Westminster parking area. Then the new: poison – temporarily identified as strychnine – administered in a Beefeater martini, causing death in two minutes; a horrible, contorted, violent death ... the blade of the knife thrust into moving flesh on a crowded corner of the Strand.

Killings accomplished; no killers apprehended.

R. C. Hammond stood by the hotel window listening to the excited tones of the Jamaican announcer. When Hammond spoke, his shock was clear.

'My *God* ... Every one of those men at one time or another was under the glass –'

'The what?'

'Suspected of high crimes. Malfeasance, extortion, fraud ... Nothing was ever proved.'

'Something's been proved now.'

Paris was next. Reuters sent out the first dispatches, picked up by all the wire services within minutes. Again the number was ... four. Four Frenchmen – actually, three French men and one woman. But still four.

Again, they were prominent figures in industry and government. And the MOs were identical: rifle, explosives, strychnine, knife.

The French woman was a proprietor of a Paris fashion house.

A ruthless sadist long considered an associate of the Corsicans. She was shot from a distance as she emerged from a doorway on the St Germain des Prés. Of the three men, one was a member of the president's all-important Elysée Financial; his Citroën exploded when he turned his ignition on in the rue du Bac. The two other Frenchmen were powerful executives in shipping companies – Marseilles-based, under Paraguayan flag . . . owned by the Marquis de Chatellerault. The first spastically lurched and died over a café table in the Montmartre – strychnine in his late-morning espresso. The second had his chest torn open by a butcher's knife on the crowded sidewalk outside the Georges Cinque hotel.

Minutes after Paris came Berlin. On the Kurfürstendamm, the *Unter Schriftführer* of the Bundestag's Overseas Agency was shot from the roof of a nearby building as he was on his way to a luncheon appointment. A *Direktor* of Mercedes Benz stopped for a traffic light on the Autobahn, where two grenades were thrown into the front seat of his car, demolishing automobile and driver in seconds. A known narcotics dealer was given poison in his glass of heavy lager at the bar of the Grand Hotel, and an appointee of the *Einkünfte Finanzamt* was stabbed expertly – death instantaneous – through the heart in the crowded lobby of the government building.

Rome followed. A financial strategist for the Vatican, a despised cardinal devoted to the church militants' continuous extortion from the uninformed poor, was dropped by an assassin firing a rifle from behind a Bernini in St Peter's Square. A *funzionario* of Milan's Mondadori drove into a cul-de-sac off the Via Condotte, where his vehicle exploded. A lethal dose of strychnine was administered with cappuccino to a *direttore* of customs at Rome's Fiumicino Airport. A knife was plunged into the ribs of a powerful broker of the *Borsa Valori* as he walked down the Spanish Steps into the Via Due Macelli.

London, Paris, Berlin, Rome.

And always the figure was four . . . and the methods identical: rifle, explosives, strychnine, knife. Four diverse, ingenious *modi operandi*. Each strikingly news-conscious, oriented for shock. All killings the work of expert professionals: no killers caught at the scenes of violence.

The radio and the television stations no longer made attempts to continue regular programming. As the names came, so too did progressively illuminating biographies. And another pattern emerged, lending credence to Hammond's summary of the four slain Englishmen: The victims were not ordinary men of stature in industry and government. There was a common stain running through the many that aroused suspicions about the rest. They were individuals not immune to official scrutinies. As the first hints began to surface, curious newsmen dug swiftly and furiously, dredging up scores of rumours, and more than rumour – facts: indictments (generally reduced to the inconsequential), accusations from injured competitors, superiors and subordinates (removed, recanted ... unsubstantiated), litigations (settled out of court or dropped for lack of evidence).

It was an elegant cross-section of the suspected. Tarnished, soiled, an aura of corruption.

All this before the hands on McAuliff's watch read nine o'clock. Two hours past twelve. London time. Two o'clock in the afternoon in Mayfair.

Commuter-time in Washington and New York.

There was no disguising the apprehension felt as the sun made its way from the east over the Atlantic. Speculation was rampant, growing in hysteria: a conspiracy of international proportions was suggested, a cabal of self-righteous fanatics violently implementing its vengeances throughout the civilized world.

Would it touch the shores of the United States?

But, of course, it had.

Two hours ago.

The awkward giant was just beginning to stir, to recognize the signs of the spreading plague.

The first news reached Jamaica from Miami. Radio Montego picked up the overlapping broadcasts, sifting, sorting ... finally relaying by tape the words of the various newscasters as they rushed to verbalize the events spewing out of the wire service teletypes.

Washington. Early morning. The undersecretary of the budget – a patently political appointment resulting from openly questioned campaign contributions – was shot while jogging on a back-country road near his residence in Arlington; the weapon was a high-powered rifle, probably with a telescopic sight, fired from a hill above the road. The body was discovered by a motorist at 8:20; the time of death estimated to be within the past two hours.

Noon, London time.

New York. At approximately seven o'clock in the morning, when one Gianni Dellacroce – a reputed Mafia figure – stepped into his Lincoln Continental in the attached garage of his Scarsdale home, there was an explosion that ripped the entire enclosure out of its foundation, instantly killing Dellacroce and causing considerable damage to the rest of the house. Dellacroce was rumoured to be . . .

Noon. London time.

Phoenix, Arizona. At approximately 5:15 in the morning, one Harrison Renfield, international financier and real-estate magnate with extensive Caribbean holdings, collapsed in his private quarters at the Thunderbird Club after a late party with associates. He had ordered a pre-dawn breakfast: poison was suspected, as a Thunderbird waiter was found unconscious down the hall from Renfield's suite. An autopsy was ordered . . . Five o'clock, Mountain time.

Twelve noon, London.

Los Angeles, California. At precisely 4:00 a.m. the junior senator from Nevada – recently implicated (but not indicted) in a Las Vegas tax fraud – stepped off a launch onto a pier in Marina del Ray. The launch was filled with guests returning from the yacht of a motion-picture producer. Somewhere between the launch and the base of the pier, the junior senator from Nevada had his stomach ripped open with a blade so long and a cut so deep that the cartilage of his backbone protruded through spinal lacerations. He fell among the revellers, carried along by the boisterous crowd until the eruptions of the warm fluid that covered so many was recognized for the blood that it was. Panic resulted, the terror alcoholic but profound. Four in the morning. Pacific time.

Twelve noon, London.

McAuliff looked over at the silent, stunned Hammond.

'The last death reported was four in the morning ... twelve o'clock in London. In each country four died, with four corresponding – identical – methods of killing ... The Arawak units of four – the death odyssey ... that's what they call it.'

'What are you talking about?'

'Deal with the Halidon, Hammond. You have no choice; this is their proof ... They said it was only the tip.'

'The tip?'

'The tip of the Dunstone iceberg.'

'Impossible demands!' roared R. C. Hammond, the capillaries in his face swollen, forming splotches of red anger over his skin. 'We will *not* be dictated to by goddamn *niggers*!'

'Then you won't get the list.'

'We'll *force* it out of them. This is no time for treaties with *savages*!'

Alexander thought of Daniel, of Malcolm, of the incredible lakeside community, of the grave of Acquaba ... the vaults of Acquaba. Things he could not, would not, talk about. He did not have to, he considered. 'You think what's happened is the work of savages? Not the killings, I won't defend that. But the methods, the victims ... Don't kid yourself.'

'I don't give a *damn* for your opinions ...' Hammond walked rapidly to the telephone on the bedside table. Alex remained in a chair by the television set. It was the sixth time Hammond had tried to place his call. The Englishman had only one telephone number he could use in Kingston: embassy telephones were off-limits for clandestine operations. Each time he had managed to get a line through to Kingston – not the easiest feat in Montego – the number was busy.

'*Damn! Goddamnit!*' exploded the agent.

'Call the embassy before you have a coronary,' said McAuliff. 'Deal with them.'

'Don't be an ass,' replied Hammond. 'They don't know who I am. We don't use embassy personnel.'

'Talk to the ambassador.'

'What in God's name for? What am I supposed to say? "Pardon me, Mr Ambassador, but my name's so-and-so. I happen to be . . ." The bloody explanation – if he'd listen to it without cutting me off – would take the better part of an hour. And then the damn fool would start sending cables to Downing Street!' Hammond marched back to the window.

'What are you going to do?'

'They've isolated me, you understand that, don't you?' Hammond remained at the window, his back to McAuliff.

'I think so.'

'The purpose is to cut me off, force me to absorb the full impact of the . . . past three hours . . .' The Britisher's voice trailed off in thought.

McAuliff wondered. 'That presupposes they know the Kingston telephone, that they shorted it out somehow.'

'I don't think so,' said Hammond, his eyes still focused on the waters of the bay. 'By now Kingston knows I've been taken. Our men are no doubt activating every contact on the island, trying to get a bearing on my whereabouts. The telephone would be in constant use.'

'You're not a prisoner; the door's not locked.' Alex suddenly wondered if he was correct. He got out of the chair, crossed to the door and opened it.

Down the corridor were two Jamaicans by the bank of elevators. They looked at McAuliff, and although he did not know them, he recognized the piercing, controlled calm of their expressions. He had seen such eyes, such expressions high in the

367

Flagstaff mountains. They were members of the Halidon.

Alex closed the door and turned to Hammond, but before he could say anything, the Englishman spoke, his back still to Alex.

'Does that answer you?' he asked quietly.

'There are two men in the corridor,' said McAuliff pointlessly. 'You knew that.'

'I didn't know it, I merely assumed it. There are fundamental rules.'

'And you still think they're savages?'

'Everything's relative.' Hammond turned from the window and faced Alex. 'You're the conduit now. I'm sure they've told you that.'

'If "conduit" means I take back your answer, then yes.'

'Merely the answer? They've asked for no substantive guarantees?' The Englishman seemed bewildered.

'I think that comes in Phase Two. This is a step contract, I gather. I don't think they'll take the word of Her Majesty's obedient servant. He uses the term "nigger" too easily.'

'You're an ass,' said Hammond.

'You're an autocratic cipher,' replied McAuliff, with equal disdain. 'They've got you, agent-mon. They've also got the Dunstone list. You play in *their* sandbox . . . with their "fundamental rules".'

Hammond hesitated, repressing his irritation. 'Perhaps not. There's an avenue we haven't explored. They'll take you back . . . I should like to be taken with you.'

'They won't accept that.'

'They may not have a choice –'

'Get one thing straight,' interrupted Alex. 'There's a survey team in the Cock Pit – white *and* black – and *no one's* going to jeopardize a single life.'

'You forget,' said Hammond softly – aloofly. 'We know the location within a thousand yards.'

'You're no match for those guarding it. Don't think you are . . . One misstep, one deviation, and there are mass executions.'

'Yes,' said Hammond. 'I believe just such a massacre took

368

place previously. The executioners being those whose methods and selections you so admire.'

'The circumstances were different. You don't know the truth . . .'

'Oh, come off it, McAuliff. I shall do my best to protect the lives of your team, but I'm forced to be honest with you. They are no more the first priority for me than they are for the Halidon! There are more important considerations.' The Englishman stopped briefly, for emphasis. 'And I can assure you, our resources are considerably more than those of a sect of fanatic . . . coloureds. I'd advise you not to change your allegiances at this late hour.'

The announcer on the television screen had been droning, reading from pages of script handed to him by others in the studio. Alex couldn't be sure – he had not been listening – but he thought he had heard the name, spoken differently . . . as if associated with new or different information. He looked down at the set, holding up his hand for Hammond to be quiet.

He *had* heard the name.

And as the first announcement three hours ago had been the prelude – a single instrument marking a thematic commencement – McAuliff recognized this as the coda. The terror had been orchestrated to a conclusion.

The announcer looked earnestly into the camera, then back to the papers in his hand.

'To repeat the bulletin. Savanna-la-Mar. Shooting broke out at the private Negril airfield. A band of unidentified men ambushed a party of Europeans as they were boarding a small plane for Weston Favel. The French industrialist Henri Salanne, the Marquis de Chatellerault, was killed along with three men said to be in his employ . . . No motive is known. The marquis was the houseguest of the Wakefield family. The pilot, a Wakefield employee, reported that his final instructions from the marquis were to fly south of Weston Favel at low altitude towards the interior grasslands. The parish police are questioning . . .'

Alex walked over to the set and switched it off. He turned to Hammond; there was very little to say, and he wondered if the Intelligence man would understand.

'That was a priority you forgot about, wasn't it, Hammond? Alison Booth. Your filthy link to Chatellerault . . . The expendable Mrs Booth, the bait from Interpol . . . Well, you're *here*, agent-mon, and Chatellerault is dead. You're in a hotel room in Montego Bay. Not in the Cock Pit. Don't talk to me about resources, you son of a bitch. You've only got one. And it's me.'

The telephone rang. McAuliff reached it first.

'Yes?'

'Don't interrupt me; there is no time' came the agitated words from Malcolm. 'Do as I say. I have been spotted. MI6 . . . a Jamaican. One I knew in London. We realized they would fan out; we did not think they would reach Montego so quickly –'

'Stop running,' broke in Alex, looking at Hammond, 'MI6 will cooperate. They have no choice –'

'You damn fool, I said *listen*! . . . There are two men in the corridor. Go out and tell them I called. Say the word "Ashanti". Have you got that, mon? "*Ashantee*".'

Alex had not heard the Anglicized Malcolm use 'mon' before. Malcolm was in a state of panic. 'I've got it.'

'Tell them I said to get out! *Now*! The hotels will be watched. You will all have to move fast –'

'Goddamnit!' interrupted Alex again. 'Now you listen to me. Hammond's right here and –'

'*McAuliff*.' The sound of Malcolm's voice was low, cutting, demanding attention. 'British Intelligence, Caribbean Operations, has a total of fifteen West Indian specialists. That is the budget. Of those fifteen, seven have been bought by Dunstone plc.'

The silence was immediate, the implication clear. 'Where are you?'

'In a pay phone outside McNabs. It is a crowded street; I will do my best to melt.'

'Be careful in crowded streets. I've been listening to the news.'

'Listen well, my friend. That is what this is all about.'

'You said they spotted you. Are they there now?'

'It is difficult to tell. We are dealing with Dunstone now. Even we do not know everyone on its payroll ... But they will not want to kill me. Any more than I want to be taken alive ... Good luck, McAuliff ... We are doing the right thing.'

With these words, Malcolm hung up the telephone. Alexander instantly recalled a dark field at night on the outskirts of London, near the banks of the river Thames. And the sight of two dead West Indians in a government car.

Any more than I want to be taken alive ...

Cyanide.

We are doing the right thing ...

Death.

Unbelievable. Yet very, very real.

McAuliff gently replaced the telephone in its cradle. As he did, he had the fleeting thought that his gesture was funereal.

This was no time to think of funerals.

'Who was that?' asked Hammond.

'A fanatic who, in my opinion, is worth a dozen men like you. You see, he doesn't lie.'

'I've had enough of your sanctimonious claptrap, McAuliff!' The Englishman spat out his words in indignation. 'Your fanatic doesn't pay two million dollars, either. Nor, I suspect, does he jeopardize his own interests for your well-being, as *we* have done constantly. Furthermore –'

'He just did,' interrupted Alex as he crossed the room. 'And if I'm a target, so are you.'

McAuliff reached the door, opened it swiftly, and ran out into the corridor towards the bank of elevators. He stopped.

There was no one there.

31

It was a race in blinding sunlight, somehow macabre because of
the eye-jolting reflections from the glass and chrome and
brightly coloured metals on the Montego streets. And the profusion of people. Crowded, jostling, black and white: thin men
and fat women – the former with their goddamned cameras,
the latter in foolish-looking rhinestone sunglasses. Why did he
notice these things? Why did they irritate him? There were fat
men, too. Always with angry faces; silently, stoically reacting
to the vacuous-looking, thin women at their sides.

And the hostile black eyes staring out from wave after wave
of black skin. Thin, black faces – somehow always thin – on top
of bony black bodies – angular, beaten, slow.

These then were the blurred, repeating images imprinted on
the racing pages of his mind.

Everything ... everyone was instantly categorized in the
frantic, immediate search for an enemy.

The enemy was surely there.

It had been there ... minutes ago.

McAuliff had rushed back into the room. There was no time
to explain to the furious Hammond; it was only necessary to
make the angry Englishman obey. Alex did so by asking him if
he had a gun, then pulling out his own, furnished by Malcolm
on the night before.

The sight of McAuliff's weapon caused the agent to accept
the moment. He removed a small, inconspicuous Rycee automatic from a belt holster under his jacket.

Alexander had grabbed the seersucker coat – this too furnished

372

by Malcolm the previous night – and thrown it over his arm, concealing his revolver.

Together the two men had slipped out of the room and run down the corridor to the staircase beyond the bank of elevators. On the concrete landing they had found the first of the Halidonites.

He was dead. A thin line of blood formed a perfect circle around his neck below the swollen skin of his face and the extended tongue and blank, dead, bulging eyes. He had been garrotted swiftly, professionally.

Hammond had bent down; Alexander was too repelled by the sight to get closer. The Englishman had summarized.

Professionally.

'They know we're on this floor. They don't know which rooms. The other poor bastard's probably with them.'

'That's impossible. There wasn't time. *Nobody* knew where we were.'

Hammond had stared at the lifeless black, and when he spoke, McAuliff recognized the profound shock of the Intelligence man's anger.

'Oh, *God*, I've been *blind!*'

In that instant, Alexander, too, understood.

British Intelligence, Caribbean Operations, has a total of fifteen West Indian specialists. That's the budget. Of those fifteen, seven have been bought by Dunstone plc ...

The words of Malcolm the Halidonite.

And Hammond the manipulator had just figured it out.

The two men had raced down the staircase. When they reached the lobby floor, the Englishman stopped and did a strange thing. He removed his belt, slipping the holster off and placing it in his pocket. He then wound the belt in a tight circle, bent down, and placed it in a corner. He stood up, looked around, and crossed to a cigarette-butt receptacle and moved it in front of the belt.

'It's a signalling device, isn't it?' McAuliff had said.

'Yes. Long-range. External scanner reception; works on

vertical arcs. No damn good inside a structure. Too much interference . . . thank heaven.'

'You wanted to be *taken*.'

'No, not actually. It was always a possibility, I knew that . . .
Any ideas, chap? At the moment, it's your show.'

'One, and I don't know how good it is. An airfield; it's a farm,
I guess west, on the highway. Near a place called Unity Hall
. . . Let's go.' Alex reached for the knob on the door to the
lobby.

'Not that way,' said Hammond. 'They'll be watching the
lobby. The street, too, I expect. Downstairs. Delivery entrance
. . . maintenance, that sort of thing. There's bound to be one in
the cellars.'

'*Wait* a minute.' McAuliff had grabbed the Englishman's arm,
physically forcing him to respond. 'Let's you and I get something
clear. Right now . . . You've been *had. Taken.* Your own people
sold you out. So there won't be any stopping for phone calls,
for signalling anyone on the street. We run but we don't stop.
For anything. You do and you're on your own. I disappear and
I don't think you can handle that.'

'Who in hell do you think I'm going to get in touch with?
The Prime Minister?'

'I don't know. I just know that I don't trust you. I don't trust
liars. Or manipulators. And you're both, Hammond.'

'We all do what we can,' replied the agent coldly, his eyes
unwavering. 'You've learned quickly, Alexander. You're an apt
pupil.'

'Reluctantly, I don't think much of the school.'

And the race in the blinding sunlight had begun.

They ran up the curving driveway of the basement garage,
directly into a tan Mercedes sedan that was not parked at that
particular entrance by coincidence. Hammond and Alexander
saw the startled look on the face of the white driver; then the
man reached over across the seat for a transistorized radio.

In the next few seconds Alex witnessed an act of violence he would never forget as long as he lived. An act performed with cold precision.

R. C. Hammond reached into both his pockets and took out the Rycee automatic in his right hand, a steel cylinder in his left. He slapped the cylinder onto the barrel of the weapon, snapped in a clip, and walked directly to the door of the tan Mercedes Benz. He opened it, held his hand low, and fired two shots into the driver, killing him instantly.

The shots were spits. The driver fell onto the dashboard; Hammond reached down and picked up the radio with his left hand.

The sun was bright; the strolling crowds kept moving. If any knew an execution had taken place, none showed it.

The British agent closed the door almost casually.

'My God . . .' It was as far as Alex got.

'It was the last thing he expected,' said Hammond rapidly. 'Let's find a taxi.'

The statement was easier made than carried out. Cabs did not cruise in Montego Bay. The drivers homed like giant pigeons back to appointed street corners, where they lined up in European fashion, as much to discuss the progress of the day with their peers as to find additional fares. It was a maddening practice; during these moments it was a frightening one for the two fugitives. Neither knew where the cab locations were, except the obvious – the hotel entrance – and that was out.

They rounded the corner of the building, emerging on a free-port strip. The sidewalks were steaming hot; the crowds of gaudy, perspiring shoppers were pushing, hauling, tugging, pressing faces against the window fronts, foreheads and fingers smudging the glass, envying the unenviable . . . the shiny. Cars were immobilized in the narrow street, the honking of horns interspersed with oaths and threats as Jamaican tried to out-chauffeur Jamaican for the extra tip . . . and his manhood.

Alexander saw him first, under a green and white sign that read MIRANDA HILL with an arrow pointing south. He was a heavyset, dark-haired white man in a brown gabardine suit, the jacket buttoned, the cloth stretched across muscular shoulders. The man's eyes were scanning the streams of human traffic, his head darting about like that of a huge pink ferret. And clasped in his left hand, buried in the flesh of his immense left hand, was a transistorized walkie-talkie identical to the one Hammond had taken out of the Mercedes.

Alex knew it would be only seconds before the man spotted them. He grabbed Hammond's arm and wished to God both of them were shorter than they were.

'At the corner! Under the sign ... Miranda Hill. The brown suit.'

'Yes. I see.' They were by a low-hanging awning of a free-port liquor store. Hammond swung into the entrance, begging his pardon through the swarm of tourists, their Barbados shirts and Virgin Island palm hats proof of yet another cruise ship. McAuliff followed involuntarily; the Englishman had locked Alex's arm in a vice-like grip, propelling the American in a semicircle, forcing him into the crowded doorway.

The agent positioned the two of them inside the store, at the far corner of the display window. The line of sight was direct; the man under the green and white sign could be seen clearly, his eyes still searching the crowds. 'It's the same radio,' said Alex.

'If we're lucky, he'll use it. I'm sure they've set up relays ... I know him. He's Unio Corso.'

'That's like a Mafia, isn't it?'

'Not unlike. And far more efficient. He's a Corsican gun. Very high-priced. Warfield would pay it.' Hammond clipped his phrases in a quiet monotone; he was considering strategies. 'He may be our way out.'

'You'll have to be clearer than that,' said Alex.

'Yes, of course.' The Englishman was imperiously polite. And maddening. 'By now they've circled the area, I should think. Covering all streets. Within minutes they'll know we've left the hotel. The signal won't fool them for long.' Hammond lifted the radio as unobtrusively as possible to the side of his head and snapped the circular switch. There was a brief burst of static; the agent reduced the volume. Several nearby tourists looked curiously; Alexander smiled foolishly at them. Outside on the corner, underneath the sign, the Corsican suddenly brought his radio to his ear. Hammond looked at McAuliff. 'They've just reached your room.'

'How do you know?'

'They report a cigarette still burning in the ashtray. Nasty habit. Radio on . . . I should have thought of that.' The Englishman pursed his lips abruptly; his eyes indicated recognition. 'An outside vehicle is circling. The . . . WIS claims the signal is still inside.'

'WIS?'

Hammond replied painfully, 'West Indian Specialist. One of my men.'

'Past tense,' corrected Alex.

'They can't raise the Mercedes,' said Hammond quickly. 'That's it.' He swiftly shut off the radio, jammed it into his pocket, and looked outside. The Corsican could be seen listening intently to his instrument. Hammond spoke again. 'We'll have to be very quick. Listen and commit . . . When our Italian finishes his report, he'll put the radio to his side. At that instant we'll break through at him. Get your hands on that radio. Hold it no matter *what*.'

'Just like that?' asked McAuliff apprehensively. 'Suppose he pulls a gun?'

'I'll be beside you. He won't have time.'

And the Corsican did not.

As Hammond predicted, the man under the sign spoke into the radio. The agent and Alex were beneath the low awning on the street, concealed by the crowds. The second the Corsican's arm began to descend from the side of his head, Hammond jabbed McAuliff's ribs. The two men broke through the flow of people towards the professional killer.

Alexander reached him first; the man started. His right hand went for his belt, his left automatically raised the radio. McAuliff

377

grabbed the Corsican's wrist and threw his shoulder into the man's chest, slamming him against the pole supporting the sign.

Then the Corsican's whole face contorted spastically; a barking, horrible sound emerged from his twisted mouth. And McAuliff felt a burst of warm blood exploding below.

He looked down. Hammond's hand held a long switchblade. The agent had ripped the Corsican's stomach open from pelvis to rib cage, severing the belt, cutting the cloth of the brown gabardine suit.

'Get the radio!' commanded the agent. 'Run south on the east side of the street. I'll meet you at the next corner. *Quickly* now!'

Alex's shock was so profound that he obeyed without thought. He grabbed the radio from the dead hand and plunged into the crowds crossing the intersection. Only when he was halfway across did he realize what Hammond was doing: He was holding up the dead Corsican against the pole. He was giving *him* time to get away!

Suddenly he heard the first screams behind him. Then a mounting crescendo of screams and shrieks and bellowing roars of horror. And within the pandemonium, there was the piercing shrill of a whistle . . . then more whistles, then the thunder of bodies running in the steaming-hot street.

McAuliff raced . . . *was* he running south? *Was* he on the east side? . . . he could not think. He could only feel the panic. And the blood.

The blood! The goddamn blood was all over him! People had to see that!

He passed an outdoor restaurant, a sidewalk café. The diners were all rising from their seats, looking north towards the panicked crowds and the screams and the whistles . . . and now the sirens. There was an empty table by a row of planter boxes. On the table was the traditional red-checked tablecloth beneath a sugar bowl and shakers of salt and pepper.

He reached over the flowers and yanked the cloth, sending the condiments crashing to the cement deck, one or all smashing to pieces; he did not, could not, tell. His only thought was to cover the goddamn blood, now saturated through his shirt and trousers.

The corner was thirty feet away. What the hell was he supposed to do? Suppose Hammond had not got away? Was he supposed to stand there with the goddamn tablecloth over his front looking like an imbecile while the streets were in chaos?

'*Quickly now!*' came the words.

McAuliff turned, grateful beyond his imagination. Hammond was directly behind him, and Alex could not help but notice his hands. They were deep red and shining; the explosion of Corsican blood had left its mark.

The intersecting street was wider; the sign read QUEEN'S DRIVE. It curved upwards towards the west, and Alex thought he recognized the section. On the diagonal corner an automobile pulled to a stop; the driver peered out the window, looking north at the racing people and the sounds of riot.

Alex had to raise his voice to be heard. 'Over there!' he said to Hammond. 'That car!'

The Englishman nodded in agreement.

They dashed across the street. McAuliff by now had his wallet out of his pocket, removing bills. He approached the driver – a middle-aged black Jamaican – and spoke rapidly.

'We need a ride. I'll pay you whatever you want!'

But the Jamaican just stared at Alexander, his eyes betraying his sudden fear. And then McAuliff saw: The tablecloth was under his arm – how did it get under his arm? – and the huge stain of dark red blood was everywhere.

The driver reached for the gearshift; Alex thrust his right hand through the window and grabbed the man's shoulder, pulling his arm away from the dashboard. He threw his wallet to Hammond, unlatched the door, and yanked the man out of the seat. The Jamaican yelled and screamed for help. McAuliff took the bills in his hand and dropped them on the kerb as he pummelled the black across the pavement.

A dozen pedestrians looked on, and most ran, preferring non-involvement; others watched, fascinated by what they saw. Two white teenagers ran towards the money and bent down to pick it up.

McAuliff did not know why, but that bothered him. He took the necessary three steps and lashed his foot out, smashing one of the young men in the side of the head.

'Get the hell out of here!' he roared as the teenager fell back, blood matted instantly along his blond hairline.

'*McAuliff!*' yelled Hammond, racing around the car towards the opposite front door. 'Get in and drive, for God's sake!'

As Alex climbed into the seat, he saw what he knew instantly was the worst sight he could see at that moment. A block away, from out of the milling crowds on the street, a tan Mercedes Benz had suddenly accelerated, its powerful, deep-throated engine signifying its anticipated burst of speed.

McAuliff pulled the gearshift into drive and pressed the pedal to the floor. The car responded, and Alex was grateful for the surge of the racing wheels. He steered into the middle of Queen's Drive, on what had to be Miranda Hill, and immediately passed two cars . . . dangerously close, nearly colliding.

'The Mercedes was coming down the street,' he said to Hammond. 'I don't know if they spotted us.'

The Britisher whipped around in the seat, simultaneously withdrawing the Rycee automatic and the transistorized radio from both pockets. He snapped on the radio; the static was interspersed with agitated voices issuing commands and answering excitedly phrased questions.

The language, however, was not English.

Hammond supplied the reason. 'Dunstone has half the Unio Corso in Jamaica.'

'Can you understand?'

'Sufficiently . . . They're at the corner of Queen's Drive and Essex. In the Miranda Hill district. They've ascertained that the secondary commotion was us.'

'Translated: They've spotted us.'

'Can this car get a full throttle?'

'It's not bad; no match for a Mercedes, though.'

380

Hammond kept the radio at full volume, his eyes still on the rear window. There was a burst of chatter from the tiny speaker, and at the same instant McAuliff saw a speeding black Pontiac come over the incline in front of him, on the right, its brakes screeching, the driver spinning the wheel. 'Jesus!' he yelled.

'It's theirs!' cried Hammond. 'Their west patrol just reported seeing us. Turn! The first chance you get.'

Alex sped to the top of the hill. 'What's he doing?' He yelled again, his concentration on the road in front, on whatever cars might lie over the crest.

'He's turning . . . side-slipped halfway down. He's righting it now.'

At the top of the incline, McAuliff spun the wheel to the right, pressed the accelerator to the floor, and raced past three vehicles on the steep descent, forcing a single approaching car to crowd the kerb. 'There's some kind of park about half a mile down.' He couldn't be sure of the distance; the blinding sun was careening off a thousand metal objects . . . or so it seemed. But he couldn't think of that: he could only squint. His mind was furiously abstracting flashes of recent memory. Flashes of another park . . . in Kingston: St George's. And another driver . . . a versatile Jamaican named Rodney.

'So?' Hammond was bracing himself now, his right hand, pistol firmly gripped, against the dashboard, the radio, at full volume, against the seat.

'There's not much traffic. Not too many people either . . .' Alex swerved the car once again to pass another automobile. He looked in the rear-view mirror. The black Pontiac was at the top of the hill behind them; there were now four cars between them.

'The Mercedes is heading west on Gloucester,' said Hammond, breaking in on Alex's thoughts. 'They said Gloucester . . . Another car is to proceed along . . . Sewell . . .' Hammond translated as rapidly as the voices spoke, overlapping each other.

'Sewell's on the other side of the district,' said McAuliff, as much to himself as to the agent. 'Gloucester's the shore road.'

'They've alerted two vehicles. One at North and Fort streets, the other at Union.'

'That's Montego proper. The business area. They're trying to cut us off at all points ... For Christ's sake, there *is* nothing else left!'

'What are you talking about?' Hammond had to shout; the screaming tyres, the wind, the roaring engine did not permit less.

Explanations took time, if only seconds – there were no seconds left. There would be no explanations, only commands ... as there had been commands years ago. Issued in the frozen hills with no more confidence than McAuliff felt now.

'Get in the back seat,' he ordered, firmly but not tensely. 'Smash the rear window; get yourself a clear area ... When I swing into the park, he'll follow. As soon as I'm inside, I'm going to swerve right and stop. *Hard!* Start firing the second you see the Pontiac behind us. Do you have extra clips?'

'Yes.'

'Put in a full one. You've used two shells. Forget that goddamn silencer, it'll throw you off. Try to get clean shots. Through the front and side windows. Stay away from the gas tank and the tyres.'

The stone gates to the park were less than a hundred yards away, seconds away. Hammond stared at Alex – for but an instant – and began climbing over the seat to the rear of the vehicle.

'You think we can switch cars –'

Perhaps it was a question; McAuliff did not care. He interrupted. 'I don't know. I just know we can't use this one any longer and we have to get to the other side of Montego.'

'They'll surely spot their own vehicle ...'

'They won't be looking for it. Not for the next ten minutes ... if you can aim straight.'

382

The gates were on the left now. Alex whipped the steering wheel around; the car skidded violently as Hammond began smashing the glass in the rear window. The automobile behind swerved to the right to avoid a collision, its horn blaring, the driver screaming. McAuliff sped through the gate, now holding down the bar of his own horn as a warning.

Inside the gates he slammed on the brakes, spun the wheel to the right, pressed the accelerator, and jumped the kerb of the drive over onto the grass. He crashed his foot once again onto the brake pedal: the car jolted to a stop on the soft turf. In the distance strollers in the park turned; a couple picnicking stood up.

Alex was not concerned. In seconds the firing would start; the pedestrians would run for cover, out of the danger zone. Away from the fire base.

Danger zone. Fire base. Cover. Terms from centuries ago.

So then it followed that the strollers in the park were not pedestrians. Not pedestrians at all.

They were *civilians*.

It *was* war.

Whether the civilians knew it or not.

There was the sudden, ear-shattering screech of tyres.

Hammond fired through the smashed rear window. The Pontiac swerved off the drive, hurtled over the opposite kerb, careened off a cluster of tropic shrubbery, and slammed into a mound of lose earth dug for one of a thousand unending park projects. The engine continued at high speed, but the gears had locked, the wheels still, the horn blasting in counterpoint to the whining roar of the motor.

Screams could be heard in the distance.

From the civilians.

McAuliff and Hammond jumped out of the car and raced over grass and concrete onto grass again. Both had their weapons drawn; it was not necessary. R. C. Hammond had performed immaculately. He had fired with devastating control through the open side window of the Pontiac. The car was untouched but the driver was dead, sprawled over the wheel. Dead weight against the horn.

The two fugitives divided at the car, each to a door of the front seat, Alexander on the driver's side. Together they shoved the lifeless body away from the wheel; the blaring horn ceased, the engine continued to roar. McAuliff reached in and turned the ignition key.

The silence was incredible.

Yet, still, there were the screams from the distance, from the grass.

The civilians.

They yanked at the dead man and threw the body over the plastic seat onto the floor behind. Hammond picked up the transistor radio. It was in 'on' position. He turned it off. Alexander got behind the wheel and feverishly tugged at the gearshift.

It did not move, and the muscles in McAuliff's stomach tensed; he felt his hands trembling.

From out of a boyhood past, long, long forgotten, came the recall. There was an old car in an old garage; the gears were always sticking.

Start the motor for only an instant.

Off – on. Off – on.

Until the gear teeth unlocked.

He did so. How many times, he would never remember. He would only remember the cold, calm eyes of R. C. Hammond watching him.

The Pontiac lurched. First into the mound of earth; then, as Alex jammed the stick into R, backwards – wheels spinning furiously – over the grass.

They were mobile.

McAuliff whipped the steering wheel into a full circle, pointing the car towards the cement drive. He pressed the accelerator, and the Pontiac gathered speed on the soft grass in preparation for its jarring leap over the kerb.

Four seconds later they sped through the stone gates.

And Alexander turned right. East. Back towards Miranda Hill.

He knew Hammond was stunned; that did not matter. There was still no time for explanations, and the Englishman seemed to understand. He said nothing.

Several minutes later, at the first intersecting road, Mc-Auliff jumped the light and swung left. North. The sign read CORNICHE ANNEX.

Hammond spoke.

'You're heading towards the shore road?'

'Yes. It's called Gloucester. It goes through Montego and becomes Route One.'

'So you're behind the Dunstone car . . . the Mercedes.'

'Yes.'

'And may I presume that since the last word' – here Hammond held up the transistorized walkie-talkie – 'any of them received was from that park, there's a more direct way back to it? A faster way?'

'Yes. Two. Queen's Drive and Corniche Road. They branch off from Gloucester.'

'Which, of course, would be the routes they would take.'

'They'd better.'

'And naturally, they would search the park.'

'I hope so.'

R. C. Hammond pressed his back into the seat. It was a gesture of temporary relaxation. Not without a certain trace of admiration.

'You are a *very* apt student, Mr McAuliff.'

'To repeat myself, it's a rotten school,' said Alexander.

They waited in the darkness, in the overgrowth at the edge of the field. The crickets hammered out the passing seconds. They had left the Pontiac miles away on a deserted back road in Catherine Mount and walked to the farm on the outskirts of Unity Hall. They had waited until nightfall before making the last few miles of the trip. Cautiously, shelter to shelter; when on the road, as far out of sight as possible. Finally using the tracks of the Jamaica Railway as their guideline.

385

There had been a road map in the glove compartment of the Pontiac and they studied it. It was maddening. Most of the streets west of Montego proper were unmarked, lines without names, and always there were the alleys without lines. They passed through a number of ghetto settlements, aware that the inhabitants had to be sizing them up – two white men without conceivable business in the area. There was profit in an assault on such men.

Hammond had insisted that they both carry their jackets, their weapons very much in evidence in their belts.

Subalterns crossing through hostile colonial territory, letting the wog natives know they carried the magic firesticks that spat death.

Ludicrous.

But there was no assault.

They crossed the Montego River at Westgate; half a mile away were the railroad tracks. They ran into an itinerant tramp enclave – a hobo camp, Jamaica-style – and Hammond did the talking.

The Englishman said they were insurance inspectors for the company; they had no objections to the filthy campsite so long as there was no interference with the line. But should there be interference, the penalties would be stiff indeed.

Ludicrous.

Yet no one bothered them, although the surrounding black eyes were filled with hatred.

There was a freight pick-up at Unity Hall. A single platform with two wire-encased light bulbs illuminating the barren site. Inside the weather-beaten rain shelter was an old man drunk on cheap rum. Painstakingly they elicited enough information from him for McAuliff to get his bearings. Vague, to be sure, but enough to determine the related distances from the highway, which veered inland at Parish Wharf, to the farm district in the south-west section.

By 9:30 they had reached the field.

Now, Alex looked at his watch. It was 10:30.

386

He was not sure he had made the right decision. He was only sure that he could not think of any other. He had recalled the lone farmhouse on the property, remembered seeing a light on inside. There was no light now. It was deserted.

There was nothing else to do but wait.

An hour passed, and the only sounds were those of the Jamaican night: the predators foraging, victims taken, unending struggles – immaterial to all but the combatants.

It was nearly the end of the second hour when they heard it.

Another sound.

A car. Driving slowly, its low-geared, muted engine signalling its apprehension. An intruder very much aware of its transgression.

Minutes later, in the dim light of a moon sheeted with clouds, they watched a lone figure run across the field, first to the north end, where a single torch was ignited, then to the south – perhaps four hundred yards – where the action was repeated. Then the figure dashed once more to the opposite end.

Another sound. Another intruder. Also muted – this from the darkness of the sky.

An aeroplane, its engine idling, was descending rapidly.

It touched ground, and simultaneously the torch at the north end was extinguished. Seconds later the aircraft came to a stop by the flame at the south end. A man jumped out of the small cabin; the fire was put out instantly.

'Let's go!' said McAuliff to the British agent. Together the two men started across the field.

They were no more than fifty yards into the grass when it happened.

The impact was so startling, the shock so complete, that Alex screamed involuntarily and threw himself to the ground, his pistol raised, prepared to fire.

Hammond remained standing.

For two immensely powerful searchlights had caught them in the blinding convergence of the cross-beams.

'Put down your weapon, McAuliff' came the words from beyond the blinding glare.

And Daniel, Minister of Council for the Tribe of Acquaba, walked through the light.

32

'When you came into the area you tripped the photoelectric alarms. Nothing mysterious.'

They were in the car, Daniel in front with the driver, Hammond and Alexander in the back seat. They had driven away from the field, out of Unity Hall, along the coast into Lucea Harbour. They parked on a deserted section of a dirt road overlooking the water. The road was one of those native offshoots on the coastal highway unspoiled by trespassing tourists. The moon was brighter by the ocean's edge, reflected off the rippling surface, washing soft yellow light over their faces.

As they were driving, McAuliff had a chance to study the car they were in. From the outside it looked like an ordinary, not-very-distinguished automobile of indeterminate make and vintage – like hundreds of island vehicles, made from the parts canibalized from other cars. Yet inside the fundamental difference was obvious: It was a precision-tooled mobile fortress ... and communications centre. The windows were of thick, bullet-proof glass; rubber slots were evident in the rear and side sections – slots that were for the high-blasting, short-barrelled shotguns clamped below the back of the front seat. Under the dashboard was a long panel with dials and switches; a telephone was locked into a recess between two microphones. The engine, from the sound of it, was one of the most powerful Alex had ever heard.

The Halidon went first class in the outside world.

Daniel was in the process of dismissing McAuliff's astonishment at the events of the past two hours. It seemed important to the minister that he convey the reality of the situation. The

389

crisis was sufficiently desperate for Daniel to leave the community; to risk his life to be in command.

It was as though he wanted very much for R. C. Hammond to realize he was about to deal with an extremely sensible and hard-nosed adversary.

'We had to make sure you were alone . . . the two of you, of course. That you were not somehow followed. There were tense moments this afternoon. You handled yourselves expertly, apparently. We could not help you. Congratulations.'

'What happened to Malcolm?' asked Alex.

Daniel paused, then spoke quietly, sadly. 'We do not know yet. We are looking . . . He is safe – or dead. There is no middle ground.' Daniel looked at Hammond. 'Malcolm is the man you know as Joseph Myers, Commander Hammond.'

McAuliff shifted his gaze to the agent. So Hammond the manipulator was a Commander. Commander Hammond, liar, manipulator . . . and risker-of-life to save another's.

Hammond reacted to Daniel's words by closing his eyes for precisely two seconds. The information was a professional burden he did not care for; the manipulator was outflanked again.

'Do I have a single black man working for me? For the Service?'

The minister smiled gently. 'By our count, seven. Three, however, are quite ineffectual.'

'Thank you for enlightening me. I'm sure you can furnish me with identities . . . They all look so much alike, you see.'

Daniel accepted the clichéd insult calmly, his smile disappearing, his eyes cold in the yellow moonlight. 'Yes. I understand the problem. There appears to be so little to distinguish us . . . from such a viewpoint. Fortunately, there are other standards. You will not be needing the identities.'

Hammond returned Daniel's look without intimidation. 'McAuliff conveyed your demands. I say to you what I said to him. They're impossible, of course –'

'Please, Commander Hammond,' said Daniel rapidly, interrupting, 'there are so many complications, let us not compound them with lies. From the beginning your instructions were clear. Would you prefer we deal with the Americans? Or the French? The Germans, perhaps?'

The silence was abrupt. There was a cruelty to it, a blunt execution of pain. Alexander watched as the two enemies exchanged stares. He saw the gradual, painful cognizance in Hammond's eyes.

'Then you know,' said the Englishman softly.

'We know,' replied Daniel simply.

Hammond remained silent and looked out of the window.

The Minister of the Halidon turned to McAuliff. 'The global mendacity, doctor. Commander Hammond is the finest Intelligence officer in the British service. The unit he directs is a coordinated effort between the aforementioned governments. It is, however, coordinated in name only. For MI6 – as the prime investigatory agency – does not apprise its fellow signatories of its progress.'

'There are good and sufficient reasons for our actions,' said Hammond, still looking out the window.

'Reduced to one, is that not right, Commander? . . . Security. You cannot trust your allies.'

'Our counterparts are leak-prone. Experience has confirmed this.' The agent did not take his eyes off the water.

'So you mislead them,' said Daniel. 'You give false information, tell them you are concentrating in the Mediterranean, then South America – Argentina, Nicaragua. Even nearby Haiti . . . But never Jamaica.' The minister paused for emphasis. 'No, never Jamaica.'

'Standard procedure,' answered Hammond, allowing Daniel a brief, wary look.

'Then it will not surprise you to learn that this mistrust is shared by your foreign confederates. They have sent out teams, *their* best men. They are presently tracing down every scrap of information MI6 has made available. They are working furiously.'

Hammond snapped his head back to Daniel. 'That is contrary to our agreement,' he said in an angry monotone.

The minister did not smile. 'I do not think you are in a position to be sanctimonious, Commander.' Daniel shifted his eyes again to Alexander. 'You see, McAuliff, since Dunstone plc was a London-based conglomerate, it was agreed to give the first-level assignment to British Intelligence. It was understandable; MI5 and 6 are the best in the free world; the Commander their best. On the theory that the fewer clandestine services operating, the less likely were breaches of security, the British agreed to function alone and keep everyone informed. Instead, they continuously furnished erroneous data.' Daniel now permitted himself a minor smile. 'In a sense, they were justified. The Americans, the French and the Germans were *all* breaking the agreement, none had any intention of keeping it. Each was going after Dunstone, while claiming to leave the field to the English ... Dunstone *has* to be dismantled. Taken apart economic brick by economic brick. The world markets can accept no less. But there are so many bricks ... Each government believes that if only it can get there first – get the Dunstone list before the others ... well, arrangements can be made, assets transferred.'

Hammond could not remain silent. 'I submit – whoever you are – that we are the logical ... executors.'

'The term "logic" being interchangeable with "deserving". I will say this for your cause. God, Queen and Empire have paid heavily in recent decades. Somewhat out of proportion to their relative sins, but that is not our concern, Commander. As I said, your instructions were clear at the outset: Get the Dunstone list at all costs. The cost is now clear. We will give you the list. You will get out of Jamaica. That is the price.'

Again, the silence; once more, the exchange of analysing stares. A cloud passed over the Montego moon, causing a dark shadow to fall over the faces. Hammond spoke.

'How can we be sure of its authenticity?'

'Can you doubt us after the events of the day? Remember,

it is in our mutual interest that Dunstone be eliminated.'

'What guarantees do you expect from us?'

Daniel laughed. A laugh formed in humour. 'We do not need *guarantees*, Commander. We will *know*. Can you not understand that? Our island is not a continent; we know every liaison, conduit and contact with whom you function.' The smile from the laugh formed in humour disappeared. 'These operations will stop. Make whatever settlements you must, but then no more . . . Give – really give – Jamaica to its rightful owners. Struggles, chaos and all.'

'And' – the Englishman spoke softly – 'if these decisions are outside my control –'

'Make no mistake, Commander Hammond!' Daniel's voice rose, cutting off the agent. 'The executions that took place today began at noon, London time. And each day, the chimes in Parliament's clock tower ring out another noon. When you hear them, remember. What we were capable of today, we are capable of tomorrow. And we will add the truth of our motives. England will be a pariah in the community of nations. You cannot afford that.'

'Your threat is ludicrous!' countered Hammond, with equal fever. 'As you said, this island is not a continent. We'd go in and destroy you.'

Daniel nodded and replied quietly, 'Quite possibly. And you should know that we are prepared for that eventuality. We *have* been for over two hundred years. Remarkable, isn't it? . . . By all you believe holy, pay the price, Hammond; take the list and salvage what you can from Dunstone. You *do* deserve that. Not that you'll salvage much; the vultures will fly in from their various geographies and dive for the carrion. We offer you time, perhaps only a few days. Make the best of it!'

A red light on the panel beneath the dashboard lit up, throwing a glow over the front seat. There were the sharp, staccato repeats of a high-pitched buzzer. The driver reached for the telephone and pulled it to his ear, held it there for several seconds, and then handed the instrument to Daniel.

The Minister of the Halidon listened. Alexander saw his face in the rear-view mirror. Daniel could not conceal his alarm.

And then his anger.

'Do what you can but risk *no lives*. Our men are to pull out. *No one* is to leave the community. That is final. *Irreversible!*' He replaced the telephone in its upright recess firmly and turned in the seat. He looked first at Alexander and then at Hammond, keeping his eyes on the Englishman as he spoke sarcastically. 'British *expertise*, Commander. John Bull *know-how* ... The West Indian Specialists, MI6, Caribbean, have just received their orders from Dunstone. They are to go into the Cock Pit and intercept the survey. They are to make sure it does not come out.'

'Oh, my God!' McAuliff pitched forward on the seat. 'Can they reach them?'

'Ask the eminent authority,' said Daniel bitingly, his eyes wide on Hammond. 'They are his men.'

The agent was rigid, as though he had stopped breathing. Yet it was obvious his mind was operating swiftly, silently. 'They are in contact with the radio receivers ... the signals transmitted from the campsite. The location can be pinpointed –'

'Within a thousand yards,' cut in Alex, completing Hammond's statement.

'Yes.'

'You've got to stop them!'

'I'm not sure there's a way –'

'*Find* one. For Christ's sake, Hammond, they're going to be killed!' McAuliff grabbed Hammond by the lapels of his jacket, yanking him forward viciously. 'You *move*, mister. Or I'll kill you!'

'Take your hands –'

Before the agent could finish the obvious, Alexander whipped his right hand across Hammond's face, breaking the skin on the Englishman's lips. 'There isn't anything more, *Commander*! I want those guarantees! *Now!*'

The agent spoke through rivulets of blood. 'I'll do my best. All I've ever given you was ... our best efforts.'

'You son of a bitch!' McAuliff brought his hand back once again. The driver and Daniel grabbed his arm.

'McAuliff! You'll accomplish *nothing*!' roared the minister.

'You tell *him* to start accomplishing!' Then Alexander stopped and turned to Daniel, releasing the Englishman. 'You've got people there.' And then McAuliff remembered the terrible words Daniel had spoken into the telephone: *Risk no lives. Our men . . . pull back. No one is to leave the community.* 'You've got to get on that phone. Take back what you said. *Protect them!*'

The minister spoke quietly. 'You must try to understand. There are traditions, revelations . . . a way of life extending over two hundred years. We cannot jeopardize these things.'

Alexander stared at the black man. 'You'd watch them *die*? . . . My *God*, you *can't*!'

'I am afraid we could. And would. And we should then be faced with the taking of your life . . . It would be taken as swiftly . . .' Daniel turned up the collar of his shirt, revealing a tiny bulge in the cloth. *Tablets, sewn into the fabric.* '. . . as I would bite into these, should I ever find myself in a position where it was necessary. I would not think twice about it.'

'For God's sake, that's *you*! They're not you; they're no part of you. They don't *know* you. Why should they pay with their lives?'

Hammond's voice was startling in its quiet incisiveness. 'Priorities, McAuliff. I told you. For them . . . for us.'

'The accidents of war, doctor. Combat's slaughter of innocents, perhaps.' Daniel spoke simply, denying the implication of his words. 'Things written and unwritten –'

'*Bullshit!*' screamed McAuliff. The driver removed a pistol from his belt; his action was obvious. Alexander looked rapidly back and forth between the Minister of the Halidon and the British Intelligence officer. 'Listen to me. You said on that phone for them to do what they can. You, Hammond. You offered your . . . goddamned "best efforts". All right. Give *me* a chance!'

'How?' asked Daniel. 'There can be no Jamaican police, no Kingston troops.'

The words came back to Alexander. Words spoken by Sam Tucker in the glow of the campsite fire. A quiet statement made as Sam watched the figure of Charles Whitehall and the black giant, Lawrence, talking in the compound. *They're our protection. They may hate each other . . .*

They're our protection.

McAuliff whirled on Hammond. 'How many defectors have you got here?'

'I brought six specialists from London –'

'All but one has sold out to Dunstone,' interrupted Daniel.

'That's five. How many others could they pick up?' McAuliff addressed the Halidonite.

'On such short notice, perhaps three or four; probably mercenaries. That is only a guess . . . They would be more concerned with speed than numbers. One automatic rifle in the hands of a single soldier –'

'When did they get the Dunstone orders?' asked Alex swiftly, breaking off Daniel's unnecessary observations.

'Within the hour is our estimate. Certainly no more than an hour.'

'Could they get a plane?'

'Yes. Ganja aircraft are always for hire. It would take a little time; ganja pilots are a suspicious breed, but it could be done.'

Alex turned to Hammond. The agent was wiping his lips with his fingers . . . his goddamn fingers, as if dusting the pastry crumbs off his mouth during tea at the Savoy! 'Can you raise the people monitoring the signals from the campsite? With that radio?' McAuliff pointed to the panel under the dashboard.

'I have the frequency –'

'Does that mean *yes*?'

'Yes.'

'What is the point?' asked Daniel.

'To see if his goddamn specialists have reached them. To get the position –'

'You want our plane?' interrupted the Minister of the Halidon, knowing the answer to his question.

396

'Yes!'

Daniel signalled the driver to start the car. 'You don't need the position. There is only one place to land: the grassland two miles south-west of the campsite. We have the coordinates.'

The vehicle lurched out of the parking area, careened off the primitive border, and sped into the darkness towards the highway.

Hammond gave the frequency-band decimals to Daniel; the minister transmitted them, handing a microphone to the British agent.

There was no pick-up.

No answer over the airwaves.

'It will take time to get the plane . . .' Daniel spoke quietly as the car roared over the wide roadway.

Alex suddenly put his hand on the minister's shoulder. 'Your runner, the one who used the name of "Marcus". Tell him to get word to Sam Tucker.'

'I have instructed our men to pull out,' answered Daniel icily. 'Please remember what I told you.'

'For Christ's sake, send him back. Give them a chance!'

'Don't you mean . . . give *her* a chance?'

McAuliff wanted – as he had never wanted anything before – to kill the man. 'You had to say it, didn't you?'

'Yes,' replied Daniel, turning in his seat to look Alexander in the eye. 'Because it is related to the condition on which you have use of the plane . . . If you fail, if the woman is killed, your life is taken also. You will be executed. Quite simply, with her death you could never be trusted.'

Alexander acknowledged the penetrating stare of Daniel the Halidonite. 'Quite simply,' he said, 'my answer is easy. I'll give the firing order myself.'

R. C. Hammond leaned forward. His speech was measured, precise as ever. 'I am going in with you, McAuliff.'

Both Daniel and Alex looked at the Englishman. Hammond, in a few words, had quietly moved into a strangely defenceless position. It astonished both men.

397

'Thank you.' It was all McAuliff could say, but he meant it profoundly.

'I'm afraid that is not possible, Commander,' said Daniel. 'You and I . . . we have matters between us. If McAuliff goes, he goes alone.'

'You're a barbarian.' Hammond spoke sharply.

'I am the Halidon. And we *do* have priorities. Both of us.'

33

McAuliff nosed the small plane above cloud cover. He loosened the field jacket provided him by the driver of the car. It was warm in the tiny cabin. The Halidon aircraft was different from the plane he and Malcolm had flown from the field west of Accompong. It was similar to the two-seater Comanche in size and appearance, but its weight and manoeuvrability were heavier and greater.

McAuliff was not a good pilot. Flying was a skill he had half mastered through necessity, not from any devotion. Ten years ago, when he had made the decision to go field-commercial, he had felt the ability to fly would come in handy, and so he had taken the prescribed lessons that eventually led to a very limited licence.

It had proved worthwhile. On dozens of trips over most continents. In small, limited aircraft.

He hoped to Christ it would prove worthwhile now. If it did not, nothing mattered any more.

On the seat beside him was a small blackboard, a slate once common to grammar school, bordered by wood. On it was chalked his primitive flight plan in white lettering that stood out in the dim light of the instrument panel.

Desired air speed, compass points, altitude requirements and sightings that, with luck and decent moonlight, he could distinguish.

From the strip outside Unity Hall he was to reach a height of one thousand feet, circling the field until he had done so. Leaving the strip perimeter, he was to head south-east at 115 degrees, air speed 90. In a few minutes he would be over Mount

Carey – two brush fires would be burning in a field; he would spot them.

He did.

From Mount Carey, maintaining air speed and dropping to 700 feet, he was to swing east-northeast at 84 degrees and proceed to Kempshot Hill. A car with a spotlight would be on a road below; the spotlight would flicker its beam into the sky.

He saw it and followed the next line on the chalkboard. His course change was minor – 8 degrees to 92 on the compass, maintaining air speed and altitude. Three minutes and thirty seconds later, he was over Amity Hall. Again brush fires, again a fresh instruction; this, too, was minimal.

East-northeast at 87 degrees into Weston Favel.

Drop altitude to 500 feet, maintain airspeed, look for two cars facing each other with blinking headlights at the south section of the town. Correct course to exactly 90 degrees and reduce air speed to 75.

The instant he reached the Martha Brae River, he was to alter course 35 degrees south-east, to precisely 122 on the compass.

At this point he was on his own. There would be no more signals from the ground, and, of course, no radio contact whatsoever.

The coordination of air speed, direction and timing was all he had . . . everything he had. Altitude was by pilotage – as low as possible, cognizant of the gradual ascent of the jungle hills. He might spot campfires, but he was not to assume any to be necessarily those of the survey. There were roving hill people, often on all-night hunts. He was to proceed on course for exactly four minutes and fifteen seconds.

If he had followed everything precisely and if there were no variants of magnitude such as sudden wind currents or rainfall, he would be in the vicinity of the grasslands. Again, if the night was clear and if the light of the moon was sufficient, he would see them.

And – most important – if he spotted other aircraft, he was

to dip his right wing twice. This would indicate to any other plane that he was a ganja runner. It was the current courtesy-of-recognition between such gentlemen of the air.

The hills rose suddenly, far more rapidly than McAuliff had expected. He pulled back the half wheel and felt the updraughts carry him into a one-o'clock soar. He reduced the throttle and countered the high bank with pressure on the left pedal; the turbulence continued, the winds grew.

Then he realized the cause of the sudden shifts and cross-currents. He had entered a corridor of harsh jungle showers. Rain splattered against the glass and pelted the fuselage; wipers were inadequate. In front of him was a mass of streaked, opaque grey. He slammed down the left window panel, pulled out the throttle, went into a swift ten-o'clock bank, and peered down. His altimeter inched towards 650; the ground below was dense black . . . nothing but jungle forest, no breaks in the darkness. He retraced the leg from the Martha Brae in his mind. Furiously, insecurely. His speed had been maintained, so too his compass. But there had been slippage; not much but recognizable. He was not that good a pilot – only twice before had he flown at night; his lapsed licence forbade it – and slippage, or drift, was an instrument or pilotage problem corrected by dials, sightings or radio.

But the slight drift had been there. And it had come from aft starboard. Jesus, he was better in a sailboat! He levelled the aircraft and gently banked to the right, back into the path of the rain squall. The windscreen was useless now; he reached across the seat and pulled down the right window panel. The burst of noise from the cross-draughted openings crashed abruptly through the small cabin. The wind roared at high velocity; the rain swept in streaking sheets, covering the seat and the floor and the instrument panel. The blackboard was soaked, its surface glistening, the chalk marks seemingly magnified by the rushing water sloshing within the borders.

And then he saw it . . . them. The plateau of grassland. Through the starboard – goddamnit, *right* window. A stretch of less-black in the middle of the total blackness. A dull grey relief in the centre of the dark wood.

He had overshot the fields to the left, no more than a mile, perhaps two.

But he had reached them. Nothing else mattered at the moment. He descended rapidly, entering a left bank above the trees – the top of a figure eight for landing. He made a 280-degree approach and pushed the half wheel forward for touch down.

He was at the fifty-foot reading when behind him, in the west, was a flash of heat lightning. He was grateful for it; it was an additional, brief illumination in the night darkness. He trusted the instruments and could distinguish the approaching grass in the beam of the forelamps, but the dull, quick fullness of dim light gave him extra confidence.

And it gave him the visibility to detect the outlines of another plane. It was on the ground, stationary, parked on the north border of the field.

In the area of the slope that led to the campsite two miles away.

Oh, God! He had not made it at all. He was too late!

He touched earth, revved the engine, and taxied towards the immobile aircraft, removing his pistol from his belt as he manipulated the controls.

A man waved in the beam of the front lights. No weapon was drawn; there was no attempt to run or seek concealment. Alex was bewildered. It did not make sense; the Dunstone men were killers, he knew that. The man in the beam of light, however, gave no indication of hostility. Instead, he did a peculiar thing. He stretched out his arms at his sides, lowering the right and raising the left simultaneously. He repeated the gesture several times as McAuliff's craft approached.

Alex remembered the instructions at the field in Unity Hall. If you sight other planes, dip your right wing. *Lower* your right wing . . . arm.

The man in the beam of light was a ganja pilot!

McAuliff pulled to a stop and switched off the ignition, his

402

hand gripped firmly around the handle of his weapon, his finger poised in the trigger frame.

The man came up behind the wing and shouted through the rain to Alex in the open window. He was a white man, his face framed in the canvas of a poncho hood. His speech was American . . . Deep South. Delta origins.

'Gawd*damn*! This is one busy fuckin' place! Good to see your white skin, man! I'll fly 'em an' I'll fuck 'em, but I don' *lak* 'em!' The pilot's voice was high-pitched and strident, easily carried over the sound of the rain. He was medium height, and, if his face was any indication, he was slender but flabby; a thin man unable to cope with the middle years. He was past forty.

'When did you get in?' asked Alex loudly, trying not to show his anxiety.

'Flew in these six blacks 'bout ten minutes ago. Mebbe a little more, not much. You with 'em, I sup'ose? You runnin' things?'

'Yes.'

'They don' get so *uppity* when there's trouble, huh? Nothin' but trouble in these mountain fields. They sure need whitey, then, you betcha balls!'

McAuliff put his pistol back in his belt beneath the panel. He had to move fast now. He had to get past the ganja pilot. 'They said there was trouble?' Alex asked the question casually as he opened the cabin door, stepped on the wing into the rain, and jumped to the wet ground.

'Gawd*damn*! The way they tell it, they got stole blind by a bunch of fuckin' bucks out there. Resold a bundle after takin' their cash. Let me tell you, those niggers are loaded with hardware!'

'That's a mistake,' said McAuliff with conviction. 'Jesus . . . goddamned *idiots*!'

'They're lookin' for black blood, man! Those brothers gonna' lay out a lotta other brothers! *Eeeaww*!'

'They do and New Orleans will go up in smoke! . . . Christ!' Alexander knew the Louisiana city was the major port of entry for narcotics throughout the Southern and South-western states.

403

This particular ganja pilot would know that. 'Did they head down the slope?' McAuliff purposely gestured a hundred yards to the right, away from the vicinity of the path he remembered.

'Damned if they was too fuckin' sure, man! They got one a them Geigers like an air-radar hone, but not so good. They took off more like down there.' The pilot pointed to the left of the hidden jungle path.

Alex calculated rapidly. The scanner used by the Dunstone men was definitive only in terms of a thousand-yard radius. The signals would register, but there were no hot or cold levels that would be more specific. It was the weakness of miniaturized long-distance radio arcs, operating on vertical principles.

One thousand yards was three thousand feet – over half a mile within the dense, almost impenetrable jungle of the Cock Pit. If the Dunstone team had a ten-minute advantage, it was not necessarily fatal. They did not know the path – he didn't *know* it either, but he had travelled it. Twice. Their advantage had to be reduced. And if their angle of entry was indirect – according to the ganja pilot, it was – and presuming they kept to a relatively straight line, anticipating a sweep . . . the advantage conceivably might be removed.

If . . . if he could find the path and keep to it.

He pulled up the lapels of his field jacket to ward off the rain and turned towards the cabin door above the wing of the plane. He opened it, raised himself with one knee to the right of the strut, and reached into the small luggage compartment behind the seat. He pulled out a short-barrelled, high-powered automatic rifle – one of the two that had been strapped below the front seat of the Halidon car. The clip was inserted, the safety on. In his pockets were four additional clips; each clip held twenty cartridges.

One hundred shells.

His arsenal.

'I've got to reach them,' he yelled through the downpour at the ganja pilot. 'I sure as hell don't want to answer to New Orleans!'

'Them New Orleens boys is a tense bunch. I don't fly for 'em if I got other work. They don' lak nobody!'

Without replying, McAuliff raced towards the edge of the grassland slope. The path was to the right of a huge cluster of nettled fern – he remembered that; his face had been scratched because his hand had not been quick enough when he had entered the area with the Halidon runner.

Goddamnit! Where *was* it?

He began feeling the soaked foliage, gripping every leaf, every branch, hoping to find his hand scratched, scraped by nettles. He *had* to find it; he had to start his entry at precisely the right point. The wrong spot would be fatal. Dunstone's advantage would be too great; he could not overcome it.

'What are you lookin' for?'

'*What?*' Alex whipped around into a harsh glare of light. His concentration was such that he found himself unlatching the safety on the rifle. He had been about to fire in shock.

The ganja pilot had walked over. 'Gawddamn. Ain't you got a flashlight, man? You expect to find your way in that mess without no flashlight?'

Jesus! He had left the flashlight in the Halidon plane. Daniel had said something about being careful ... with the flashlight. So he had left it behind! 'I forgot. There's one in the plane.'

'I hope to fuck there is,' said the pilot.

'You take mine. Let me use yours, okay?'

'You promise to shoot me a couple a bucks, you got it, man.' The pilot handed him the light. 'This rain's too fuckin' wet, I'm going back inside. Good huntin', hear!'

McAuliff watched the pilot run towards his aircraft and then quickly turned back to the jungle's edge. he was no more than five feet from the cluster of fern; he could see the matted grass at the entry point of the concealed path.

He plunged in.

He ran as fast as he could, his feet ensnared by the under-brush, his face and body whipped by the unseen tentacles of

405

overgrowth. The path twisted – right, left, right, right, *right, Jesus! circles* – and then became straight again for a short stretch at the bottom of the slope.

But it was still true. He was still on it. That was all that mattered.

Then he veered off. The path wasn't there. It was gone!

There was an ear-shattering screech in the darkness, magnified by the jungle downpour. In the beam of his flashlight, deep within a palm-covered hole below him, was a wild pig suckling its blind young. The hairy, monstrous face snarled and screeched once more and started to rise, shaking its squealing offspring from its teats. McAuliff ran to his left, into the wall of jungle. He stumbled on a rock. Two, three rocks. He fell to the wet earth, the flashlight rolling on the ground. The ground was flat, unobstructed.

He had found the path again!

He got to his feet, grabbed the light, shifted the rifle under his arm, and raced down the relatively clear jungle corridor.

Clear for no more than a hundred yards, where it was intersected by a stream, bordered by soft, foot-sucking mud. He remembered the stream. The runner who had used the name of 'Marcus' had turned left. Was it left? Or was that from the opposite direction? ... No, it *was* left. There had been palm trunks and rocks showing through the surface of the water, crossing the narrow stream. He ran to the left, his flashlight aimed at the midpoint of the water.

There were the logs! The rocks. A hastily constructed bridge to avoid the ankle-swallowing mud.

And on the right palm trunk were two snakes in lateral slow motion, curving their way towards him. Even the Jamaican mongoose did not have the stomach for Jamaica's Cock Pit.

Alexander knew these snakes. He had seen them in Brazil. Anaconda strain. Blind, swift-striking, vicious. Not fatal, but capable of causing paralysis – for days. If flesh came within several feet of the flat heads, the strikes were inevitable.

He turned back to the overgrowth, the beam of light criss-

crossing the immediate area. There was a dangling branch of a
ceiba tree about six feet long. He ran to it, bending it back and
forth until it broke off. He returned to the logs. The snakes had
stopped, alarmed. Their oily, ugly bodies were entwined, the
flat heads poised near each other, the blind, pin-like eyes staring
fanatically in the direction of the scent. At him.

Alex shoved the ceiba limb out on the log with his left hand,
the rifle and flashlight gripped awkwardly in his right.

Both snakes lunged simultaneously, leaping off the surface
of the log, whipping their bodies violently around the branch,
their heads zeroing towards McAuliff's hand, soaring through
the soft leaves.

Alex threw – dropped? he would never know – the limb into
the water. The snakes thrashed; the branch reeled in furious
circles and sank beneath the surface.

McAuliff ran across the logs and picked up the path.

He had gone perhaps three-quarters of a mile, certainly no
more than that. The time elapsed was twelve minutes by his
watch. As he remembered it, the path veered sharply to the right
through a particularly dense section of fern and maidenhead to
where there was a small clearing recently used by a band of
hill-country hunters. Marcus – the man who used the name of
'Marcus' – had remarked on it.

From the clearing it was less than a mile to the banks of the
Martha Brae and the campsite. The Dunstone advantage had to
be diminishing.

It *had* to be.

He reached the nearly impossible stretch of overgrowth, his
flashlight close to the earth, inspecting the ground for signs of
passage. If he stepped away from the path now – if he moved
into underbrush that had not seen human movement – it would
take him hours to find it again. Probably not until daylight –
or when the rains stopped.

It was painfully slow, agonizingly concentrated. Bent weeds,
small broken branches, swollen borders of wet ground where
once there had been the weight of recent human feet; these were

his signs, his codes. He could not allow the tolerance of a single error.

'Hey, mon!' came the muted words.

McAuliff threw himself to the ground and held his breath. Behind him, to his left, he could see the beam of another flashlight. Instantly he snapped off his own.

'Hey, mon, where are you? Contact, please. You went off your pattern. Or I did.'

Contact, please . . . Off your pattern. The terms of an agent, not the language of a carrier. The man was MI6.

Past tense. *Was.*

Now Dunstone plc.

The Dunstone team had separated, each man assigned an area . . . a pattern. That could only mean they were in radio contact.

Six men in radio contact.

Oh, *Jesus!*

The beam of light came nearer, dancing, flickering through the impossible foliage.

'Here, *mon!*' whispered Alex gutturally, hoping against reasonable hope that the rain and the whisper would not raise an alarm in the Dunstone ear.

'Put on your light, please, mon.'

'Trying to, mon.' No more, thought McAuliff. Nothing.

The dancing beam reflected off a thousand shining, tiny mirrors in the darkness, splintering the light into hypnotically flickering shafts.

Closer.

Alex rolled silently off the path into the mass of wet earth and soft growth, the rifle under him cutting into his thighs.

The beam of light was nearly above him, its shaft almost clear of interference. In the spill he could see the upper body of the man. Across his chest were two wide straps: One was connected to an encased radio, the other to the stock of a rifle, its thick barrel silhouetted over his shoulder. The flashlight was in the left hand; in the right was a large, ominous-looking pistol.

The MI6 defector was a cautious agent. His instincts had been aroused.

McAuliff knew he had to get the pistol: he could not allow the man to fire. He did not know how near the others were, how close the other patterns.

Now!

He lashed his right hand up, directly onto the barrel of the pistol, jamming his thumb into the curvature of the trigger housing, smashing his shoulder into the man's head, crashing his left knee up under the man's legs into his testicles. With the impact, the man buckled and expunged a tortured gasp; his hand went momentarily limp, and Alex ripped the pistol from it, propelling the weapon into the darkness.

From his crouched agony the Jamaican looked up, his left hand still holding the flashlight, its beam directed nowhere at the earth, his face contorted . . . about to take the necessary breath to scream.

McAuliff found himself thrusting his fingers into the man's mouth, tearing downwards with all his strength. The man lurched forward, bringing the hard metal of the flashlight crashing into Alex's head, breaking the skin. Still McAuliff ripped at the black's mouth, feeling the teeth puncturing his flesh, sensing the screams.

They fell, twisting in mid-air, into the overgrowth. The Jamaican kept smashing the flashlight into McAuliff's temple; Alex kept tearing grotesquely, viciously, at the mouth that could sound the alarm he could not allow.

They rolled over into a patch of sheer jungle mud. McAuliff felt a rock, he tore his left hand loose, ripped the rock up from the ground, and brought it crashing into the black mouth, over his own fingers. The man's teeth shattered; he choked on his own saliva. Alex whipped out his bleeding hand and instantly grabbed the matted hair, twisting the entire head into the soft slime of the mud. There were the muffled sounds of expulsion beneath the surface. A series of miniature filmy domes burst silently out of the soggy earth in the spill of the fallen flashlight.

And then there was nothing.

The man was dead.

And no alarms had been sent.

Alexander reached over, picked up the light, and looked at the finger of his right hand. The skin was slashed, there were teeth marks, but the cuts were not deep; he could move his hand freely, and that was all he cared about.

His left temple was bleeding, and the pain terrible, but not immobilizing. Both would stop . . . sufficiently.

He looked over at the dead Jamaican and he felt like being sick. There was no time. He crawled back to the path and started once again the painstaking task of following it. And he tried to focus his eyes into the jungle. Twice, in the not-too-distant denseness, he saw sharp beams of flashlights.

The Dunstone team was continuing its sweep. It was zeroing in.

There was not an instant to waste in thought.

Eight minutes later he reached the clearing. He felt the accelerated pounding in his chest; there was less than a mile to go. The easiest leg of the terrible journey.

He looked at his watch. It was exactly four minutes after twelve midnight.

Twelve was also the hour of noon.

Four was the ritual Arawak unit.

The odyssey of death.

No time for thought.

He found the path at the opposite side of the small clearing and began to run, gathering speed as he raced towards the banks of the Martha Brae. There was no air left in his lungs now, not breath as he knew it; only the steady explosions of exhaustion from his throat, blood and perspiration falling from his head, rivering down his neck onto his shoulders and chest.

There was the river. He had reached the river!

It was only then that he realized the pounding rain had stopped; the jungle storm was over. He swung the flashlight to his left; there were the rocks of the path bordering the final few hundred yards into the campsite.

He had heard no rifle fire. There had been no shots. There were five experienced killers in the darkness behind him, and the terrible night was not over . . . but he had a chance.

That's all he had asked for, all that was between him and his command to a firing squad ending his life.

Willingly, if he failed. Willingly to end it without Alison.

He ran the last fifty yards as fast as his exhausted muscles could tolerate. He held the flashlight directly in front of him: the first object caught by its beam was the lean-to at the mouth of the campsite area. He raced into the clearing.

There were no fires, no signs of life. Only the dripping of a thousand reminders of the jungle storm, the tents silent monuments of recent living.

He stopped breathing. Cold terror gripped him. The silence was an overpowering portent of horror.

'Alison. *Alison!*' he screamed, and raced blindly towards the tent. '*Sam! Sam!*'

When the words came out of the darkness, he knew what it was to be taken from death and be given life again.

'*Alexander* . . . You damn near got killed, boy,' said Sam Tucker from the black recesses of the jungle's edge.

34

Sam Tucker and the runner called 'Marcus' walked out of the bush. McAuliff stared at the Halidonite, bewildered. The runner saw his expression and spoke.

'There is no time for lengthy explanations. I have exercised an option, that is all.' The runner pointed to the lapel of his jacket. Alex needed no clarification. Sewn into the cloth were the tablets he had seen in the wash of yellow moonlight on the back road above Lucea Harbour.

I would not think twice about it, Daniel had said.

'Where is Alison?'

'With Lawrence and Whitehall. They're farther down the river,' answered Sam.

'What about the Jensens?'

Tucker paused. 'I don't know, Alexander.'

'*What?*'

'They disappeared. That's all I can tell you . . . Yesterday Peter was lost; his carrier returned to camp, he couldn't find him. Ruth bore up well, poor girl . . . a lot of guts in her. We sent out a search. Nothing . . . And then this morning, I can't tell you why – I don't know – I went to the Jensen tent. Ruth was gone. She hasn't been seen since.'

McAuliff wondered. Had Peter Jensen seen something? Sensed something? And fled with his wife? Escaped past the Tribe of Acquaba?

Questions for another time.

'The carriers?' asked Alex warily, afraid to hear the answer.

'Check with our friend here,' replied Tucker, nodding to the Halidonite.

412

'They have been sent north, escorted north on the river,' said the man with the usurped name of 'Marcus'. 'Jamaicans will not die tonight unless they know why they are dying. Not in this fight.'

'And you? Why you? Is this your fight?'

'I know the men who come for you. I have the option to fight.'

'The limited freedoms of Acquaba?' asked Alex softly.

Marcus shrugged; his eyes betrayed nothing. 'An individual's freedom of choice, doctor.'

There was a barely perceptible cry of a bird, or the muted screech of a bat, from the dense, tropic jungle. Then there followed another. And another. McAuliff would not have noticed . . . there were so many sounds, so continuously. A never-ending nocturnal symphony; pleasant to hear, not pleasant to think about.

But he was compelled to notice now.

Marcus snapped his head up, reacting to the sound. He swiftly reached over and grabbed Alexander's flashlight and ripped it out of his hand while shouldering Tucker away.

'*Get down!*' he cried, as he pushed McAuliff violently, reeling him backwards, away from the spot where he was standing.

Seven rifle shots came out of the darkness, some thumping into trees, others cracking into the jungle distance, two exploding into the dirt of the clearing.

Alex rolled on the ground, pulling his rifle into position and aimed in the direction of the firing. He kept his finger on the trigger; a shattering fusillade of twenty bullets sprayed the area. It was over in seconds. The stillness returned.

He felt a hand grabbing his leg. It was Marcus.

'Pull back. Down to the river, mon,' he whispered harshly.

McAuliff scrambled backwards in the darkness. More shots were fired from the bush: the bullets screamed above him to the right.

Suddenly there was a burst of rifle fire from only feet away. Marcus had leaped up to the left and delivered a cross-section

413

barrage that drew the opposing fire away. Alex knew Marcus's action was his cover. He lurched to the right, to the edge of the clearings. He heard Sam Tucker's voice.

McAuliff!' Over here!'

As he raced into the brush, he saw Sam's outline on the ground. Tucker was crouched on one knee, his rifle raised. '*Where*? For Christ's sake, where's Alison? The others?'

'Go down to the river, boy! South, about three hundred yards. Tell others. We'll hold here.'

'No, Sam! Come with me ... *Show* me.'

'I'll be there, son ...' Another volley of shots spat out of the jungle. Marcus answered from the opposite side of the clearing. Tucker continued speaking as he grabbed the cloth in Alex's field jacket and propelled him beyond. 'That black son of a bitch is willing to get his tar ass shot off for us! Maybe he's given me a little time I don't deserve. He's my countryman, boy. My new *Landsmann. Jesus!* I knew I liked this fucking island. Now get the hell down there and watch out for the girl. We'll join you, don't you worry about that. The *girl*, Alexander!'

'There are five men out there, Sam. I killed one of them a mile back. They must have seen my flashlight when I was running. I'm sorry ...' With these words McAuliff plunged into the soaking-wet forest and slashed his way to the river bank. He tumbled down the short slope, the rifle clattering against the metal buttons of his jacket, and fell into the water.

South. *Left.*

Three hundred yards. Nine hundred feet ... a continent.

He stayed close to the river bank, where he could make the best time. As he slopped through the mud and the growth and over fallen trunks, he realized his magazine clip was empty. Without stopping he reached into his pocket and pulled out a fresh clip, snapping the old one out of its slot and slamming the new one in. He cracked back the insertion bar; the cartridge entered the chamber.

Gunfire broke his non-thoughts. Behind him men were trying to kill other men.

There was a bend in the narrow river. He had travelled over a hundred yards; nearer two, he thought.

... *my new Landsmann* ... Christ! Sam Tucker, itinerant wanderer of the globe, schooler of primitives, lover of all lands – in search of one to call his own, at this late stage of his life. And he had found it in a violent moment of time in the cruellest wilds of Jamaica's Cock Pit. In a moment of sacrifice.

Suddenly, in an instant of terror, from out of the darkness above, a huge black form descended. A giant arm fell vice-like around his neck; clawing fingers tore at his face; his kidneys were being hammered by a vicious, powerful fist. He slammed the rifle butt into the body behind him, sank his teeth into the flesh below his mouth, and lunged forward into the water.

'Mon! Jesus, mon!'

The voice of Lawrence cried as he pummelled McAuliff's shoulder. Stunned, each man released the other; each held up his hands, Alex's awkwardly thrusting out the rifle, Lawrence's holding a long knife.

'My God!' said McAuliff. 'I could have *shot* you!'

There was another fusillade of gunfire to the north.

'I might have put the blade in ... not the handle,' said the black giant, waist-deep in water. 'We wanted a hostage.'

Both men recognized there was no time for explanations. 'Where *are* you? Where's Alison and Whitehall?'

'Downstream, mon. Not far.'

'Is she all right?'

'She is frightened ... But she is a brave woman. For a white English lady. You see, mon?'

'I saw, mon,' replied Alexander. 'Let's go.'

Lawrence preceded him, jumping out of the water about thirty yards beyond the point of the near-fatal encounter. McAuliff saw that the revolutionary had tied a cloth around his forearm: Alex spat the blood out of his mouth as he noticed it, and rubbed the area of his kidneys in abstract justification.

The black pointed up the slope with his left hand and put his right hand to his mouth at the same time. A whistled treble emerged from his lips. A bird, a bat, an owl . . . it made no difference. There was a corresponding sound from the top of the river bank, beyond in the jungle.

'Go up, mon, I will wait here,' said Lawrence.

McAuliff would never know whether it was the panic of the moment or whether his words spoke the truth as he saw it, but he grabbed the black revolutionary by the shoulder and pushed him forward. 'There won't be any more orders given. You don't know what's back there. I do! Get your ass up there!'

An extended barrage of rifle fire came from the river.

Lawrence blinked. He blinked in the new moonlight that flooded the river bank of this offshoot of the Martha Brae.

'Okay, mon! Don't *push*.'

They crawled to the top of the slope and started into the overgrowth.

The figure came rushing out of the tangled darkness, a darker, racing object out of a void of black. It was Alison. Lawrence reached back to McAuliff and took the flashlight out of Alex's hand. A gesture of infinite understanding.

She ran into his arms. The world . . . the universe stopped its insanity for an instant, and there was stillness. And peace. And comfort. But for only an instant.

There was no time for thought. Or reflection.

Or words.

Neither spoke.

They held each other, and then looked at each other in the dim spill of the new moonlight in the isolated space that was their own on the banks of the Martha Brae.

In a terrible, violent moment of time. And sacrifice.

Charles Whitehall intruded, as Charley-mon was wont to do. He approached, his safari outfit still creased, his face an immobile mask, his eyes penetrating.

'Lawrence and I agreed he would stay down at the river. Why have you changed that?'

'You blow my mind, Charley . . .'

'You *bore* me, McAuliff,' replied Whitehall. 'There was gun-fire up there!'

'I was in the middle of it, you black son of a bitch!' *Jesus, why did he have to say that?* 'And you're going to learn what the problem is. Do you understand that?'

Whitehall smiled. 'So tell . . . *whitey*.'

Alison slapped her hands off McAuliff and looked at both men. '*Stop it!*'

'I'm sorry,' said Alex quickly.

'I'm *not*,' replied Whitehall. 'This is his moment of *truth*. Can't you see that, *Miss Alison?*'

Lawrence's great hands interfered. They touched both men, and his voice was that of a thundering child-man. 'Neither no more, mon! McAuliff, mon, you say what you know! *Now!*'

Alexander did. He spoke of the grasslands, the plane – *a* plane, not the Halidon's – the redneck ganja pilot who had brought six men into the Cock Pit to massacre the survey, the race to the campsite, the violent encounter in the jungle that ended in death in a small patch of jungle mud. Finally, those minutes ago when the runner called 'Marcus' saved their lives by hearing a cry in the tropic bush.

'Five men, mon,' said Lawrence, interrupted by a new burst of gunfire, closer now but still in the near-distance to the north. He turned to Charles Whitehall. 'How many do you want, *fascisti?*'

'Give me a figure, *agricula*.'

'Goddamnit!' yelled McAuliff. 'Cut it out. Your games don't count any more.'

'You do not understand,' said Whitehall. 'It is the only thing that does count. We are prepared. We are the *viable* contestants. Is this not what the fictions create? One on one, the victor sets the course?'

. . . The charismatic leaders are not the foot soldiers . . . They change or are replaced . . . The words of Daniel, Minister of the Tribe of Acquaba.

'You're both insane,' said Alex, more rationally than he

417

thought was conceivable. 'You make me sick, and goddamn you –'

'Alexander! *Alexander!*' The cry came from the river bank less than twenty yards away. Sam Tucker was yelling.

McAuliff began running to the edge of the jungle. Lawrence raced ahead, his huge body crashing through the foliage, his hands pulverizing into sudden diagonals everything in their path.

The black giant jumped to the water's edge; Alex started down the short slope and stopped.

Sam Tucker was cradling the body of Marcus the runner in his arms. The head protruding out of the water was a mass of blood, sections of the skull were shot off.

Still, Sam Tucker would not let go.

'One of them circled and caught us at the bank. Caught *me* at the bank ... Marcus jumped out between us and took the fire. He killed the son of a bitch: he kept walking right up to him. Into the gun.'

Tucker lowered the body into the mud of the river bank.

McAuliff thought. Four men remained, four killers left of the Dunstone team.

They were five. But Alison Booth could not be counted now.

They were four, too.

Killers.

Four. The Arawak four.

The death odyssey.

Alex felt the girl's hands on his shoulders, her face pressed against his back in the moonlight.

The grasslands.

Escape was in the grasslands and the two aircraft that could fly them out of the Cock Pit.

Yet Marcus had implied there was no other discernible route but the narrow, twisting jungle path – a danger in itself.

The path was picked up east of the river at the far right end of the campsite clearing. It would be watched; the MI6 defectors were experienced agents. *Egress* was a priority; the single avenue of escape would have automatic rifles trained on it.

Further, the Dunstone killers knew their prey was downstream. They would probe, perhaps, but they would not leave the hidden path unguarded.

But they had to separate. They could not gamble on the unknown, on the possibility that the survey team might slip through, try to penetrate the net.

It was this assumption that led McAuliff and Sam Tucker to accept the strategy. A variation on the deadly game proposed by Lawrence and Charles Whitehall. Alexander would stay with Alison. The others would go out. Separately. And find the enemy.

Quite simply, kill or be killed.

Lawrence lowered his immense body into the dark waters. He hugged the bank and pulled his way slowly upstream, his pistol just above the surface, his long knife out of its leather scabbard, in his belt – easily, quickly retrievable.

The moon was brighter now. The rain clouds were gone; the towering jungle overgrowth obstructed but did not blot out the moonlight. The river currents were steady; incessant, tiny whirlpools spun around scores of fallen branches and protruding rocks, the latter's tips glistening with buffeted moss and matted green algae.

Lawrence stopped; he dropped farther into the water, holding his breath, his eyes just above the surface. Diagonally across the narrow river offshoot a man was doing exactly what he was doing, but without the awareness Lawrence now possessed.

Waist-deep in water, the man held a lethal-looking rifle in front of and above him. He took long strides, keeping his balance by grabbing the overhanging foliage on the river bank, his eyes straight ahead.

In seconds, the man would be directly opposite him.

Lawrence placed his pistol on a bed of fern spray. He reached below and pulled the long knife from his belt.

He sank beneath the surface and began swimming underwater.

Sam Tucker crawled over the ridge above the river bank and rolled towards the base of the ceiba trunk. The weight of his body pulled down a loose vine; it fell like a coiled snake across his chest, startling him.

He was north of the campsite now, having made a wide half circle west, on the left side of the river. His reasoning was simple, he hoped not too simple. The Dunstone patrol would be concentrating downstream; the path was east of the clearing. They would guard it, expecting any who searched for it to approach from below, not above the known point of entry.

Tucker shouldered his way up the ceiba trunk into a sitting position. He loosened the strap of his rifle, lifted the weapon, and lowered it over his head diagonally across his back. He pulled the strap taut. Rifle fire was out of the question, to be used only in the last extremity, for its use meant – more than likely – one's own execution.

That was not out of the question, thought Sam, but it surely would take considerable persuasion.

He rolled back to a prone position and continued his reptile-like journey through the tangled labyrinth of jungle underbrush.

He heard the man before he saw him. The sound was peculiarly human, a casual sound that told Sam Tucker his enemy was casual, not primed for alarm. A man who somehow felt his post was removed from immediate assault, the patrol farthest away from the area of contention.

The man had sniffed twice. A clogged nostril, or nostrils, caused a temporary blockage and a passage for air was casually demanded. Casually obtained.

It was enough.

Sam focused in the direction of the sound. His eyes of fifty-odd years were strained, tired from lack of sleep and from peering for nights on end into the tropic darkness. But they would serve him, he knew that.

420

The man was crouched by a giant fern, his rifle between his legs, stock butted against the ground. Beyond, Tucker could see in the moonlight the outlines of the lean-to at the far left of the clearing. Anyone crossing the campsite was in the man's direct line of fire.

The fern ruled out a knife. A blade that did not enter precisely at the required location could cause a victim to lunge, to shout. The fern concealed the man's back too well. It was possible, but awkward.

There was a better way. Sam recalled the vine that had dropped from the trunk of the ceiba tree.

He reached into his pocket and withdrew a coil of ordinary azimuth line. Thin steel wire encased in nylon, so handy for so many things . . .

He crept silently towards the giant spray of tiny leaves.

His enemy sniffed again.

Sam rose, half inch by half inch, behind the fern. In front of him now, unobstructed, was the silhouette of the man's neck and head.

Sam Tucker slowly separated his gnarled, powerful hands. They were connected by the thin steel wire encased in nylon.

Charles Whitehall was furious. He had wanted to use the river; it was the swiftest route, far more direct than the torturously slow untangling that was demanded in the bush. But it was agreed that since Lawrence had been on guard at the river, he knew it better. So the river was his.

Whitehall looked at the radium dial of his watch; there were still twelve minutes to go before the first signal. If there was one.

Simple signals.

Silence meant precisely that. Nothing.

The short, simulated, guttural cry of a wild pig meant success. One kill.

If two, two kills.

Simple.

If he had been given the river, Charles was convinced, he would have delivered the first cry. At least one.

Instead, his was the south-west sweep, the least likely of the three routings to make contact. It was a terrible waste. An old man, authoritative, inventive, but terribly tired, and a plodding, unskilled hill boy, not without potential, perhaps, but still a misguided, awkward giant.

A terrible waste! Infuriating.

Yet not as infuriating as the sharp, hard steel that suddenly made contact with the base of his skull. And the words that followed, whispered in a harsh command:

'Open your mouth and I blow your head off, mon!'

He had been taken! His anger had caused his concentration to wander.

Stupid.

But his captor had not fired. His taker did not want the alarm of a rifle shot any more than he did. The man kept thrusting the barrel painfully into Charles's head, veering him to the right, away from the supposed line of Whitehall's march. The man obviously wanted to interrogate, discover the whereabouts of the others.

Stupid.

The *release-seizure* was a simply manoeuvre requiring only a hard surface to the rear of the victim for execution.

And it was, indeed, execution.

It was necessary for the victim to rebound following impact, not be absorbed in space or elastically swallowed by walled soft-ness. The impact was most important: otherwise, the trigger of the rifle might be pulled. There was an instant of calculated risk – nothing was perfect – but the reverse jamming of the weapon into the victim allowed for that split second of diagonal slash that invariably ripped the weapon out of the hands of the hunter.

Optimally, the slash coincided with the impact.

It was all set forth clearly in the Oriental training manuals.

In front of them, to the left, Whitehall could distinguish the sudden rise of a hill in the jungle darkness. One of those abrupt protrusions out of the earth that was so common to the Cock Pit. At the base of the hill was a large boulder reflecting the wash of moonlight strained through the trees.

It would be sufficient . . . actually, more than sufficient; very practical, indeed.

He stumbled, just slightly, as if his foot had been ensnared by an open root. He felt the prod of the rifle barrel. It was the moment.

He slammed his head back into the steel and whipped to his right, clasping the barrel with his hands and jamming it forward. As the victim crashed into the boulder, he swung the weapon violently away, ripping it out of the man's grasp.

As the man blinked in the moonlight, Charles Whitehall rigidly extended three fingers on each hand and completed the assault with enormous speed and control. The hands were trajectories – one towards the right eye, the other into the soft flesh below the throat.

McAuliff had given Alison his pistol. He had been startled to see her check the clip with such expertise, releasing it from its chamber, pressing the spring, and reinserting it with a heel-of-the-palm impact that would have done justice to Bonnie of Clyde notoriety. She had smiled at him and mentioned the fact that the weapon had been in the water.

There were eight minutes to go. Two units of four; the thought was not comforting.

He wondered if there would be any short cries in the night. Or whether a measured silence would signify an extension of the nightmare.

Was any of them good enough? Quick enough? Sufficiently alert?

'Alex!' Alison grabbed his arm, whispering softly but with sharp intensity. She pulled him down and pointed into the forest, to the west.

A beam of light flicked on and off.

Twice.

Someone had been startled in the overgrowth; some *thing* perhaps. There was a slapping flutter and short, repeated screeches that stopped as rapidly as they had started.

The light went on once again, for no more than a second, and then there was darkness.

The invader was perhaps thirty yards away. It was difficult to estimate in the dense surroundings. But it was an opportunity. And if Alexander Tarquin McAuliff had learned anything during the past weeks of agonizing insanity, it was to accept opportunities with the minimum of analysis.

He pulled Alison to him and whispered instructions into her ear. He released her and felt about the ground for what he knew was there. Fifteen seconds later he silently clawed his way up the trunk of a ceiba tree, rifle across his back, his hands noiselessly testing the low branches, discomforted by the additional weight of the object held in place inside his field jacket by the belt.

In position, he scratched twice on the bark of the tree.

Beneath him Alison whistled – a very human whistle, the abrupt notes of a signalling warble. She then snapped on her flashlight for precisely one second, shut it off, and dashed away from her position.

In less than a minute the figure was below him – crouched, rifle extended, prepared to kill.

McAuliff dropped from the limb of the ceiba tree, the sharp point of the heavy rock on a true, swift course towards the top of the invader's skull.

The minute hand on his watch reached twelve; the second hand was on one. It was time.

The first cry came from the river. An expert cry, the sound of a wild pig.

The second came from the south-west, quite far in the distance but equally expert, echoing through the jungle.

The third came from the north, a bit too guttural, not expert at all, but sufficient unto the instant. The message was clear.

McAuliff looked at Alison, her bright, stunningly blue eyes bluer still in the Caribbean moonlight.

He lifted his rifle in the air and shattered the stillness of the night with a burst of gunfire. Perhaps the ganja pilot in the grasslands would laugh softly in satisfaction. Perhaps, with luck, one of the stray bullets might find its way to his head.

It did not matter.

It mattered only that they had made it. They were good enough, after all.

He held Alison in his arms and screamed joyfully into the darkness above. It did not sound much like a wild pig, but that did not matter, either.

35

They sat at the table on the huge free-form pool deck over-looking the beds of coral and the blue waters beyond. The conflict between wave and rock resulted in cascading arcs of white spray surging upwards and forwards, blanketing the jagged crevices.

They had flown from the grasslands directly to Port Antonio. They had done so because Sam Tucker had raised Robert Hanley on the plane's radio, and Hanley had delivered his instructions in commands that denied argument. They had landed at the small Sam Jones Airfield at 2:35 in the morning. A limousine sent from the Trident Villas awaited them.

So, too, did Robert Hanley. And the moment Sam Tucker alighted from the plane, Hanley shook his hand and proceeded to crash his fist into Tucker's face. He followed this action by reaching down and picking Sam up off the ground, greeting him a bit more cordially but explaining in measured anger that the past several weeks had caused him unnecessary anxiety, obviously Sam Tucker's responsibility.

The two very young old reprobates then drank the night through at the bar of Trident Villas. The young manager, Timothy Durrell, surrendered at 5:10 in the morning, dismissed the bartender, and turned the keys over to Hanley and Sam. Durrell was not aware that in a very real sense, the last strategies of Dunstone plc had been created at Trident that week when strangers had converged from all over the world. Strangers, and not strangers at all ... only disturbing memories now.

Charles Whitehall left with Lawrence, the revolutionary. Both black men said their goodbyes at the airfield; each had places to

426

go to, things to do, men to see. There would be no questions, for there would be no answers. That was understood.

They would separate quickly.

But they had communicated: perhaps that was all that could be expected.

Alison and McAuliff had been taken to the farthest villa on the shoreline. She had bandaged his hand and washed the cuts on his face and made him soak for nearly an hour in a good British tub of hot water.

They were in Villa Twenty.

They had slept in each other's arms until noon.

It was now a little past one o'clock. They were alone at the table, a note having been left for Alexander from Sam Tucker. Sam and Robert Hanley were flying to Montego Bay to see an attorney. They were going into partnership.

God help the island, thought McAuliff.

At 2:30 Alison touched his arm and nodded towards the alabaster portico across the lawn. Down the marble steps came two men, one black, one white, dressed in proper business suits.

R. C. Hammond and Daniel, Minister of Council for the Tribe of Acquaba, high in the Flagstaff Range.

'We'll be quick,' said Hammond, taking the chair indicated by Alexander. 'Mrs Booth. I am Commander Hammond.'

'I was sure you were,' said Alison, her voice warm, her smile cold.

'May I present . . . an associate? Mr Daniel, Jamaican Affairs. I believe you two have met, McAuliff.'

'Yes.'

Daniel nodded pleasantly and sat down. He looked at Alex and spoke sincerely. 'There is much to be thankful for. I am very relieved.'

'What about Malcolm?'

The sadness flickered briefly across Daniel's eyes. 'I am sorry.'

'So am I,' said McAuliff. 'He saved our lives.'

'That was his job,' replied the Minister of the Halidon.

'May I assume,' interrupted Hammond gently, 'that Mrs Booth has been apprised ... up to a point?'

'You certainly may assume that, Commander.' Alison gave the answer herself.

'Very well.' The British agent reached into his pocket, withdrew the yellow paper of a cablegram, and handed it to Alexander. It was a deposit confirmation from Barclay's Bank, London. The sum of $1,000,000 had been deposited to the account of A. T. McAuliff, Chase Manhattan, New York. Further, a letter of credit had been forwarded to said A. T. McAuliff that could be drawn against for all taxes upon receipt of the proper filing papers approved by the United States Treasury Department, Bureau of Internal Revenue.

Alex read the cable twice and wondered at his own indifference. He gave it to Alison. She started to read it but did not finish; instead, she lifted McAuliff's cup and saucer and placed it underneath.

She said nothing.

'Our account is settled, McAuliff.'

'Not quite, Hammond ... In simple words, I never want to hear from you again. *We* never want to hear from you. Because if we do, the longest deposition on record will be made public –'

'My *dear* man,' broke in the Englishman wearily, 'let me save you the time. Gratitude and marked respect would obligate me socially any time you're in London. And, I should add, I think you're basically a quite decent chap. But I can assure you that *professionally* we shall remain at the farthest distance. Her Majesty's Service has no desire to involve itself with international irregularities. I might as well be damned blunt about it.'

'And Mrs Booth?'

'The same, obviously.' Here Hammond looked directly, even painfully, at Alison. 'Added to which it is our belief she has gone through a great deal. Most splendidly and with our deepest appreciation. The terrible past is behind you, my dear. Public commendation is uncalled for, we realize. But the highest citation will be entered into your file. Which shall be closed. Permanently.'

'I want to believe that,' said Alison.

'You may, Mrs Booth.'

'What about Dunstone?' asked McAuliff. 'What's going to happen? When?'

'It has already begun,' replied Hammond. 'The list was cabled in the early hours of the morning.'

'Several hours ago,' said Daniel quietly. 'Around noon, London time.'

'In all the financial centres, the work is proceeding,' continued Hammond. 'All the governments are cooperating . . . it is to everyone's benefit.'

McAuliff looked up at Daniel. 'What does that do for global mendacity?'

Daniel smiled. 'Perhaps a minor lesson has been learned. We shall know in a few years, will we not?'

'And Piersall? Who killed him?'

Hammond replied. 'Real estate interests along the North Coast which stood to gain by the Dunstone purchase. His work was important, not those who caused his death. They were tragically insignificant.'

'And so it is over,' said Daniel, pushing back his chair. 'The Westmore Tallons will go back to selling fish, the disciples of Barak Moore will take up the struggle against Charles Whitehall, and the disorderly process of advancement continues. Shall we go, Commander Hammond?'

'By all means, Mr Daniel.' Hammond rose from the chair, as did the Minister of Council for the Tribe of Acquaba.

'What happened to the Jensens?' Alexander looked at Daniel, for it was the Halidonite who could answer him.

'We allowed him to escape. To leave the Cock Pit. We knew Julian Warfield was on the island, but we did not know where. We only knew that Peter Jensen would lead us to him. He did so. In Oracabessa . . . Julian Warfield's life was ended on the balcony of a villa named Peale Court.'

'What will happen to them? The Jensens.' McAuliff shifted his eyes to Hammond.

The commander glanced briefly at Daniel. 'There is an understanding. A man and a woman answering the description of the Jensens boarded a Mediterranean flight this morning at Palisados. We think he is retired. We shall leave him alone. You see, he shot Julian Warfield ... because Warfield had ordered him to kill someone else. And he could not do that.'

'It is time, Commander,' said Daniel.

'Yes, of course. There's a fine woman in London I've rather neglected. She liked you very much that night in Şoho, McAuliff. She said you were attentive.'

'Give her my best.'

'I shall.' The Englishman looked up at the clear sky and the hot sun. 'Retirement in the Mediterranean. Interesting.' R. C. Hammond allowed himself a brief smile, and replaced the chair quite properly under the table.

They walked on the green lawn in front of the cottage that was called a villa and looked out at the sea. A white sheet of ocean spray burst up from the coral rock and appeared suspended, the pitch-blue waters of the Caribbean serving as a backdrop, not a source. The spray cascaded forward and downward and then receded back over the crevices that formed the coral overlay. It became ocean again, at one with its source; another form of beauty.

Alison took McAuliff's hand.

They were free.

ROBERT LUDLUM

THE ROAD TO GANDOLFO

ROBERT LUDLUM

THE ROAD
TO GANDOLFO

HarperCollins*Publishers*

For John Patrick

A distinguished writer, an honoured man, a
good friend. Whose idea this was.
With affection

A large part of this story took
place a while back. And quite a bit of
it tomorrow.
Such is the poetic licence of
Liturgical Drama.

A WORD FROM THE AUTHOR

The Road to Gandolfo is one of those rare if insane accidents that can happen to a writer perhaps once or twice in his lifetime. Through divine or demonic providence a concept is presented that fuels the fires of his imagination. He is convinced it is truly a *staggering* premise which will serve as the spine of a truly *staggering* tale. Visions of one powerful scene after another parade across his inner screen, each exploding with drama and meaning and . . . well, damn it, they're just plain *staggering!*

Out come reams of paper. The typewriter is dusted and pencils are sharpened; doors are closed and heady music is played to drown out the sounds of man and nature beyond the cell of staggering creation. Fury takes over. The premise which will be the spinal thunderbolt of an incredible tale begins to take on substance as characters emerge with faces and bodies, personalities and conflicts. The plot surges forward, complex gears mesh and strip and make a hell of a lot of noise – drowning out the work of true masters like that Mozart fellow and what's-his-name Handel.

But suddenly something is wrong. I mean *wrong!*

The author is giggling. He can't *stop* giggling.

That's horrible! Staggering premises should be accorded awed respect . . . heaven knows not chuckles!

But try as he may the poor fool telling the tale is trapped, bombarded by a fugue of voices all repeating an old *ars antigua* phrase: *You've-got-to-be-kidding.*

Poor fool looks to his muses. Why are they winking? Is that *The Messiah* he's hearing or is it *Mairzy-Dotes*? What happened to the staggering thunderbolt? Why is it spiraling out of whack in a clear blue sky, hiccuping its way to a diminished . . .*giggle?*

Poor fool is bewildered; he gives up. Or rather, he gives in because by now he's having a lot of fun. After all, it *was* the time of Watergate, and nobody could invent *that* scenario! I mean it simply wouldn't play in Peoria. At that point-in-time, that is.

So poor fool plunges along, enjoying himself immensely, vaguely wondering who will sign the commitment papers, figuring his wife will stop them because the oaf does the dishes now and then and makes a damn good martini.

The *oeuvre* is finally presented and, most gratefully for poor fool, the closeted sound of laughter is heard. Followed by screams of revolt and threats of beyond-salvage termination with extreme-prejudice.

'Not under *your* name!'

Time mandates change, and change is cleansing.

Now it's under my name, and I hope you enjoy it. I *did* have a lot of fun.

Robert Ludlum

Connecticut Shore, 1982

PART ONE

*Behind each corporation must be the singular
force, or motive, that sets it apart from any
other corporate structure and gives it its
particular identity.*
                    Shepherd's Laws of Economics:
                         Book XXXII, Chapter 12

PROLOGUE

The crowds gathered in St Peter's Square. Thousands upon thousands of the faithful waited in hushed anticipation for the pontiff to emerge on the balcony and raise his hands in benediction. The fasting and the prayers were over; the Feast of San Gennaro would be ushered in with the pealing of the twilight Angelus echoing throughout the Vatican. And the bells would be heard throughout all Rome, heralding merriment and good feeling. The blessing of Pope Francesco the First would be the signal to begin.

There would be dancing in the streets, and torches and candlelight and music and wine. In the Piazza Navonna, the Trevi, even sections of the Palatine, long tables were heaped with pasta and fruit and all manner of home-produced pastries. For had not this pontiff, the beloved Francesco, given the lesson? Open your hearts and your cupboards to your neighbour. And his to you. Let all men high and low understand that we are one family. In these times of hardship and chaos and high prices, what better way to overcome but to enter into the spirit of the Lord and truly show love for thy neighbour?

For a few days let rancours subside and divisions be healed. Let the word go forth that all men are brothers, all women sisters; and all together brothers and sisters and very much each other's keepers. For but a few days let charity and grace and concern rule the hearts of everyone, sharing the sweet and the sad, for there is no evil that can withstand the force of good.

Embrace, raise the wine; show laughter and tears and accept one another in expressions of love. Let the world see there is no shame in the exultation of the spirit. And once

11

having touched, having heard the voices of brother and sister, carry forth the sweet memories beyond the Feast of San Gennaro, and let life be guided by the principles of Christian benevolence. The earth can be a better place; it is up to the living to make it so. That was the lesson of Francesco I.

A hush fell over the tens of thousands in St Peter's Square. Any second now the figure of the beloved *Papa* would walk with strength and dignity and great love on to the balcony and raise his hands in benediction. And for the Angelus to begin.

Within the high-ceilinged Vatican chambers above the square, cardinals, monsignors, and priests talked among themselves in groups, their eyes continuously straying to the figure of the pontiff seated in the corner. The room was resplendent with vivid colours: scarlets, purples, immaculate whites. Robes and cassocks and head pieces – symbols of the highest offices in the Church – swayed and were turned, giving the illusion of a constantly moving fresco.

And in the corner, seated in a wing chair of ivory and blue velvet, was the Vicar of Christ, Pope Francesco I. He was a plain man of wide girth, and the strong yet gentle features of a *campagnuolo*, a man of the earth. Standing beside him was his personal secretary, a young Black priest from America, from the archdiocese of New York. It was like Francesco to have such a papal aide.

The two were talking quietly, the pontiff turning his enormous head, his huge, soft brown eyes looking up at the young priest in serene composure.

'*Mannaggi'!*' whispered Francesco, his large peasant hand covering his lips. 'This is crazy! The entire city will be drunk for a week! Everyone will be making love in the streets. Are you sure we have it right?'

'I double-checked. Do you want to argue with him?' replied the Black, bending down in tranquil solicitousness.

'My God, no! He was always the smartest one in the villages!'

A cardinal approached the pontiff's chair and leaned

12

forward. 'Holy Father, it is time. The multitudes await you,' he said softly.

'Who —? Yes, of course. In a minute, my good friend.'

The cardinal smiled under his enormous hat; his eyes were filled with adoration. Francesco always called him his good friend. 'Thank you, your Holiness.' The cardinal backed away.

The Vicar of Christ began humming. Then words emerged. *'Che gelida ... manina ... a rigido esanime ... ah, la, la-laa – tra-la la, la-laaa ...'*

'What are you *doing?*' The young papal aide from the archdiocese of New York, Harlem district, was visibly upset.

'Rodolfo's aria. Ah, that Puccini! It helps me to sing when I am nervous.'

'Well, cut it out, man! Or pick a Gregorian chant. At least a litany.'

'I don't know any. Your Italian's getting better, but it's still not so good.'

'I'm trying, brother. You're not the easiest to learn with. Come on, now. Let's go. Out to the balcony.'

'Don't push! I go. Let's see, I raise the hand, then up and down and right to left —'

'Left to right!' whispered the priest harshly. 'Don't you listen? If we're going on with this honkey charade, for God's sake learn the fundamentals!'

'I thought if I was standing, giving – not taking – I should reverse it.'

'Don't mess. Just do what's natural.'

'Then I sing.'

'Not that natural! Come on.'

'All right, all *right*.' The pontiff rose from his chair and smiled benignly at all in the room. He turned once again to his aide and spoke softly so that none could hear. 'In case anyone should ask, which one is San Gennaro?'

'Nobody will ask. If someone does, use your standard reply.'

'Ah, yes. "Study the scriptures, my son." You know, this is all crazy!'

'Walk slowly and stand up straight. And smile, for God's sake! You're *happy*.'

'I'm *miserable*, you African!'

Pope Francesco I, Vicar of Christ, walked through the enormous doors out on to the balcony to be greeted by a thunderous roar that shook the very foundations of St Peter's. Thousands upon thousands of the faithful raised their voices in the exultation of the spirit.

'*Il Papa! Il Papa! Il Papa!*'

And as the Holy Father walked out into the myriad reflections of the orange sun setting in the west, there were many in the chambers who heard the muted strains of the chant emerging from the holy lips. Each believed it had to be some obscure early musical work, unknown to all but the most scholarly. For such was the knowledge of the *erudito*, Pope Francesco.

'*Che ... gelida ... manina ... a rigido esanimeee ... ah, la, la-laaa ... tra-la, la, la ... la-la-laaa ...*'

CHAPTER ONE

'That son of a bitch!' Brigadier General Arnold Symington brought the paperweight down on the thick layer of glass on his Pentagon desk. The glass shattered; fragments shot through the air in all directions. *'He couldn't!'*

'He did, sir,' replied the frightened lieutenant, shielding his eyes from the office shrapnel. 'The Chinese are very upset. The premier himself dictated the complaint to the diplomatic mission. They're running editorials in the *Red Star* and broadcasting them over Radio Peking.'

'How the hell *can* they?' Symington removed a piece of glass from his little finger. 'What the hell are they saying? "We interrupt this programme to announce that the American military representative, General MacKenzie Hawkins, *shot the balls* off a ten-foot jade statue in Son Tai Square"? – Bullshit! Peking wouldn't allow that; it's too goddamned undignified.'

'They're phrasing it a bit differently, sir. They say he destroyed an historic monument of precious stone in the Forbidden City. They say it's as though someone blew up the Lincoln Memorial.'

'It's a different kind of statue! Lincoln's got clothes on; his balls don't show! It's not the same!'

'Nevertheless, the White House thinks the parallel is justified, sir. The President wants Hawkins removed. More than removed, actually; he wants him cashiered. Court-martial and all. Publicly.'

'Oh, for Christ's sake, that's out of the question.' Symington leaned back in his chair and breathed deeply, trying to control himself. He reached out for the report on his desk. 'We'll transfer him. With a reprimand. We'll send

15

transcripts of the – censure, we'll call it a censure – to Peking.'

'That's not strong enough, sir. The State Department made it clear. The President concurs. We have trade agreements pending —'

'For Christ's sake, Lieutenant!' interrupted the brigadier. 'Will someone tell that spinning top in the Oval Office that he can't have it on all points of the compass! Mac Hawkins was *selected*. From twenty-seven candidates. I remember exactly what the President said. Exactly. "That mother's *perfect*!" That's what he said.'

'That's inoperative now, sir. He feels the trade agreements take precedence over prior considerations.' The lieutenant was beginning to perspire.

'You bastards kill me,' said Symington, lowering his voice ominously. 'You really frost my apricots. How do you figure to do that? Make it "inoperative", I mean. Hawkins may be a sharp pain in your diplomatic ass right now, but that doesn't wash away what *was operative*. He was a fucking teenage hero at the Battle of the Bulge *and* West Point football; *and* if they gave medals for what he did in Southeast Asia, even Mac Hawkins isn't strong enough to wear all that hardware! He makes John Wayne look like a pansy! He's *real*; that's why that Oval Yo-yo picked him!'

'I really think the office of the presidency – regardless of what he may think of the man – as commander in chief he —'

'*Horse-shit!*' The brigadier general roared again, separating the words in equal emphasis, giving the crudity of his oath the sound of a military cadence. 'I'm simply explaining to you – in the strongest terms I know – that you don't publicly court-martial a MacKenzie Hawkins to satisfy a Peking complaint, no matter how many goddamned trade agreements are floating around. Do you know *why*, Lieutenant?'

The young officer replied softly, sure of his accuracy. 'Because he would make an issue of it. Publicly.'

'*Bing-go.*' Symington's comment sprang out in a high-pitched monotone. 'The Hawkinses of this country have a constituency, Lieutenant. That's precisely *why* our commander in chief picked him! He's a political palliative. And if you don't think Mac Hawkins knows it, well – you didn't have to recruit him. I did.'

'We are prepared for that reaction, General.' The lieutenant's words were barely audible.

The brigadier leaned forward, careful not to put his elbows in the shattered glass. 'I didn't get that.'

'The State Department anticipated a hard-line counterthrust. Therefore we must institute an aggressive counterreaction *to* that thrust. The White House regrets the necessity but at this point in time recognizes the crisis quotient.'

'That's what I thought I was going to get.' Symington's words were less audible than the lieutenant's. 'Spell it out. How are you going to ream him?'

The lieutenant hesitated. 'Forgive me, sir, but the object is not to – ream General Hawkins. We are in a provocatively delicate position. The People's Republic demands satisfaction. Rightly so; it was a crude, vulgar act on General Hawkins's part. Yet he refuses to make a public apology.'

Symington looked at the report still in his right hand. 'Does it say why in here?'

'General Hawkins claims it was a trap. His statement's on page three.'

The brigadier flipped to the page and read. The lieutenant drew out a handkerchief and blotted his chin. Symington put down the report carefully on the shattered glass and looked up.

'If what Mac says is true, it *was* a trap. Broadcast *his* side of the story.'

'He has no side, General. He was drunk.'

'Mac says *drugged*. Not drunk, Lieutenant.'

'They were drinking, sir.'

'And he was drugged. I'd guess Hawkins would know the difference. I've seen him sweat sour mash.'

'He does not deny the charge, however.'

17

'He denies the responsibility of his actions. Hawkins was the finest intelligence strategist in Indochina. He's drugged couriers and pouch men in Cambodia, Laos, both Vietnams, and probably across the Manchurian borders. He knows the goddamned difference.'

'I'm afraid his knowing it doesn't *make* any difference, sir. The crisis quotient demands our acceding to Peking's wishes. The trade agreements are paramount. Frankly, sir, we need gas.'

'Jesus! I figured that was one thing you *had*.'

The lieutenant replaced the handkerchief in his pocket and smiled wanly. 'The levity is called for, I realize that. However, we have just ten days to bring everything into focus; to make our inputs and come up with a positive print.'

Symington stared at the young officer; his expression that of a grown man about to cry. 'What does that mean?'

'It's a harsh thing to say, but General Hawkins has placed his own interests above those of his duty. We'll have to make an example. For everybody's sake.'

'An example? For wanting the truth out?'

'There's a higher duty, General.'

'I know,' said the brigadier wearily. 'To the – trade agreements. To the gas.'

'Quite frankly, yes. There are times when symbols have to be traded off for pragmatic objectives. Team players understand.'

'All right. But Mac won't lie down and play busted symbol for you. So what's the – *input*?'

'The inspector general,' said the lieutenant, as an obnoxious student might, holding up a severed tapeworm in Biology I. 'We're running an in-depth data trace on him. We know he was involved in questionable activities in Indochina. We have reason to believe he violated international codes of conduct.'

'You bet your ass he did! He was one of the best!'

'There's no statute on those codes. The IG specialists have caseloads going back much further than General Hawkins's

18

ex-officio activities.' The lieutenant smiled. It was a genuine smile; he was a happy person.

'So you're going to hang him with clandestine operations that half the joint chiefs and most of the CIA know would bring him a truckload of citations – if they could talk about them. You bastards kill me.' Symington nodded his head, agreeing with himself.

'Perhaps you could save us time, General. Can you provide us with some specifics?'

'Oh, no! You want to crucify the son of a bitch, you build your own cross!'

'You do understand the situation, don't you, sir?'

The brigadier moved his chair back and kicked fragments of glass from under his feet. 'I'll tell you something,' he said. 'I haven't understood anything since nineteen forty-five.' He glared at the young officer. 'I know you're with Sixteen-hundred, but are you regular army?'

'No, sir. Reserve status, temporary assignment. I'm on á leave of absence from Y, J, and B. To put out fires before they burn up the flagpoles, as it were.'

'Y, J, and B. I don't know that division.'

'Not a division, sir. Youngblood, Jakel, and Blowe, Los Angeles. We're the top ad agency on the Coast.'

General Arnold Symington's face slowly took on the expression of a distressed basset hound. 'The uniform looks real nice, Lieutenant.' The brigadier paused, then shook his head. 'Nineteen forty-five,' he said.

Major Sam Devereaux, field investigator for the Office of the Inspector General, looked across the room at the calendar on his wall. He got up from the chair behind his desk, walked over to it, and Xed the day's date. One month and three days and he would be a civilian again.

Not that he was ever a soldier. Not really; certainly not spiritually. He was a military accident. A fracture compounded by a huge mistake that resulted in an extension of his tour of service. It had been a simple choice of alternatives: Re-enlistment or Leavenworth.

19

Sam was a lawyer, a damn fine attorney specializing in criminal law. Years ago he had held a series of Selective Service deferments. Through Harvard College and Harvard Law School; then two years of postgraduate specialization and clerking; finally into the fourteenth month of practice with the prestigious Boston law firm of Aaron Pinkus Associates.

The army had faded into a vaguely disagreeable shadow across his life; he had forgotten about the long series of deferments.

The United States Army, however, did not forget.

During one of those logistic crunches that episodically grip the military, the Pentagon discovered it had a sudden dearth of lawyers. The Department of Military Justice was in a bind – hundreds of courts-martial on bases all over the globe were suspended for lack of judge advocates and defence attorneys. The stockades were crowded. So the Pentagon scoured the long-forgotten series of deferments and scores of young unattached, childless lawyers – obtainable meat – were sent unrefusable invitations in which was explained the meaning of the word 'deferment' as opposed to the word 'annulment'.

That was the accident. Devereaux's mistake came later. Much later. Seven thousand miles away on the converging borders of Laos, Burma, and Thailand.

The Golden Triangle.

Devereaux – for reasons known only to God and military logistics – never saw a court-martial, much less tried one. He was assigned to the Legal Investigations Division of the Office of the Investigator General and sent to Saigon to see what laws were being violated.

There were so many, there was no way to count. And since drugs took precedence over the black market – there were simply too many American entrepreneurs in the latter – his inquiries took him to the Golden Triangle where one-fifth of the world's narcotics were being funnelled out, courtesy of powerful men in Saigon, Washington, Vientiane, and Hong Kong.

20

Sam was conscientious. He didn't like drug peddlers and he threw the investigatory books at them, careful to make sure his briefs to Saigon were transmitted operationally within the confused chain of command.

No report signatures. Just names and violations. After all, he could get shot or knifed – at least, ostracized for such behaviour. It was an education in covert activities.

His trophies included seven ARVN generals, thirty-one representatives in Thieu's congress, twelve US Army colonels – light and full – three brigadiers, and fifty-eight assorted majors, captains, lieutenants, and master sergeants. Added to these were five congressmen, four senators, a member of the President's cabinet, eleven corporation executives with American companies overseas – six of which already had enough trouble in the area of campaign contributions – and a square-jawed Baptist minister with a large national following.

To the best of Sam's knowledge, one second lieutenant and two master sergeants were indicted. The rest were – 'pending'.

So Sam Devereaux committed his mistake. He was so incensed that the wheels of South-east Asian justice spun off the tracks at the first hint of influence that he decided to trap a very big fish in the corruption net and make an example. He chose a major general in Bangkok. A man named Heseltine Brokemichael. Major General Heseltine Broke-michael, West Point '43.

Sam had the evidence, mounds of it. Through a series of elaborate entrapments in which he himself acted as the 'connection', a participant who could swear under oath to the general's malfeasance, he built his case thoroughly. There could not possibly be two General Brokemichaels, and Sam was an avenging angel of a prosecutor, circling in for his kill.

But there were. Two. Two major generals named Brokemichael – one Heseltine, one Ethelred! Apparently cousins. And the one in Bangkok – Heseltine – was not the one in Vientiane – Ethelred. The Vientiane Brokemichael

21

was the felon. Not his cousin. Further, the Brokemichael in Bangkok was more an avenger than Sam. He believed *he* was gathering evidence on a corrupt IG investigator. And he was. Devereaux had violated most of the international contraband laws and *all* of the United States government's.

Sam was arrested by the MPs, thrown into a maximum security cell, and told he could look forward to the better part of his lifetime in Leavenworth.

Fortunately, a superior officer in the inspector general's command, who did not really understand a sense of justice that made Sam commit so many crimes, but did understand Sam's legal and investigatory contributions to the cause of the inspector general, came to Sam's aid. Devereaux had actually filed more evidentiary material than any other legal officer in South-east Asia; his work in the field made up for a great deal of inactivity in Washington.

So the superior officer allowed a little unofficial plea bargaining in Sam's case. If Sam would accept disciplinary action at the hands of a furious Major General Heseltine Brokemichael in Bangkok, constituting a six-month loss of pay – no criminal charges would be brought. There was just one more condition: to continue his work for the inspector general's office for an additional two years beyond the expiration of his army commitment. By that time, reasoned the superior officer, the mess in Indochina would be turned over to those messing, and the IG caseloads reduced or conveniently buried.

Re-enlistment or Leavenworth.

So Major Sam Devereaux, patriotic citizen-soldier, extended his tour of duty. And the mess in Indochina was in no way lessened, but indeed turned over to the participants, and Devereaux was transferred back to Washington, D.C.

One month and three days to go, he mused, as he looked out his office window and watched the MPs at the guardhouse check the automobiles driving out. It was after five; he had to catch a plane at Dulles in two hours. He had packed that morning and brought his suitcase to the office.

The four years were coming to an end. Two plus two. The

22

time spent, he reflected, might be resented, but it had not been wasted. The abyss of corruption that was South-east Asia reached into the hierarchical corridors of Washington. The inhabitants of these corridors knew who he was; he had more offers from prestigious law firms than he could reply to, much less consider. And he did not want to consider them; he disapproved of them. Just as he disapproved of the current investigation on his desk.

The manipulators were at it again. This time it was the thorough discrediting of a career officer named Hawkins. Lieutenant General MacKenzie Hawkins.

At first Sam had been stunned. MacKenzie Hawkins was an original. A legend. The stuff of which cults were born. Cults slightly to the political right of Attila the Hun.

Hawkins's place in the military firmament was secure. Bantam Books published his biography – serialization and *Reader's Digest* rights had been sold before a word was on paper. Hollywood gave obscene amounts of money to film his life story. And the anti-militarists made him an object of fascist-hatred.

The biography was not overly successful because the subject was not overly cooperative. Apparently there were certain personal idiosyncrasies that did not enhance the image, four wives paramount among them. The motion picture was less than triumphant insofar as it comprised endless battle scenes with little or no hint of the man other than an actor squinting through the battle dust, yelling to his men in a peculiar lisp to 'get those Godless ... [Roar of cannon] ... who would tear down Old Glory! At 'em, boys!'

Hollywood, too, had discovered the four wives and certain other peculiarities of the studio's on-the-set technical adviser. MacKenzie Hawkins went through starlets three at a time and had intercourse with the producer's wife in the producer's swimming pool while the producer watched in fury from the living room window.

He did not stop the picture, however. For Christ's sake, it was costing damn near *six mill*!

These misfired endeavours might have caused another

23

man to fade, if only from embarrassment, but not so Mac Hawkins. In private, among his peers, he ridiculed those responsible and regaled his associates with stories of Manhattan and Hollywood.

He was sent to the war college with a new specialization: intelligence, clandestine operations. His peers felt a little more secure with the charismatic Hawkins consigned to covert activities. And the colonel became a brigadier and absorbed all there was to learn of his new speciality. He spent two years grinding away, studying every phase of intelligence work until the instructors had no more to instruct him.

So he was sent to Saigon where the escalating hostilities had blossomed into a full-scale war. And in Vietnam – both Vietnams, and Laos, and Cambodia, and Thailand, and Burma – Hawkins corrupted the corruptors and the ideologues alike. Reports of his behind-the-lines and across-the-neutral-borders activities made 'protective reaction' seem like a logical strategy. So unorthodox, so blatantly criminal were his methods of operation that G-2, Saigon, found itself denying his existence. After all, there were limits. Even for clandestine activities.

If *America First* was a maxim – and it was – Hawkins saw no reason why it should not apply to the filthy world of covert operations.

And for Hawkins, America *was* first. Ir-re-fucking-gardless!

So Sam Devereaux thought it was all a little sad that such a man was about to be knocked out of the box by the manipulators who got to where they were by draping the flag so gloriously and generously around themselves. Hawkins was now an offending lion in the diplomatic arena and had to be eliminated in the cause of double-think. The men who should have been upholding the general's point of honour were doing their best to sink him fast – in ten days, to be precise.

Normally Sam would have taken pleasure out of building a case against a messianic ass like Hawkins; and regardless of his feelings to the contrary, he would build a case against him. It was his last file for the inspector general's office, and he was not going to risk another two-year alternative. But he was still sad. The Hawk, as he was known – misguided fanatic as he might be – deserved better than what he was getting.

Perhaps, thought Sam, his depression was brought about by the last 'operative' instruction from the White House: find something in the morals area Hawkins can't deny. Check to see if he was ever in the care of a psychiatrist.

A psychiatrist! Jesus! They *never* learned.

In the meantime, Sam had dispatched a team of IG investigators to Saigon to see if they could dig up a few negative specifics. And he was off to Dulles airport to catch a plane to Los Angeles.

All of Hawkins's ex-wives lived within a radius of thirty miles of each other, from Malibu to Beverly Hills. They'd be better than any psychiatrist. Christ! A psychiatrist!

At 1600 Pennsylvania Avenue, Washington, D.C. they were all novacained above the shoulders.

CHAPTER TWO

'My name is Lin Shoo,' said the uniformed Communist softly, slant-eyeing the large, dishevelled American soldier who sat in a leather chair, holding a glass of whisky in one hand and a well-chewed cigar in the other. 'I am commander of the People's Police, Peking. And you are under house arrest at this moment. There is no point in being abusive, these are merely formalities.'

'Formalities for what?' MacKenzie Hawkins shouted from his armchair – the only occidental piece of furniture in the oriental house. He put his heavy boot on a black lacquered table and flung his hand over the leather back, the lighted cigar dangerously close to a silk screen room divider. 'There aren't any goddamned formalities except through the diplomatic mission. Go down there and make your complaints. You'll probably have to get in line.'

Hawkins chuckled and drank from his glass.

'You have chosen to reside outside the mission,' continued the Chinese named Lin Shoo, his eyes darting between the cigar and the screen. 'Therefore you are not technically within United States territory. So you are subject to the disciplines of the People's Police. However, we know you will not go anywhere, General. That is why I say it is a formality.'

'What have you got out there?' Hawkins waved his cigar towards the thin, rectangular windows.

'There are two patrols on each side of your residence. Eight in all.'

'That's a big fucking guard detail for someone who's not going anywhere.'

'Small liberties. Photographically, two is more desirable

26

than one and three is menacing.'

'You taking liberties?' Hawkins drew on his cigar and again rested his hand over the back of the leather chair. The lighted butt was no more than an inch from the silk.

'The Ministry of Education has done so, yes. You will admit, General, your place of isolation is most pleasant, is it not? This is a lovely house on a lovely hill. So very peaceful, and with a fine view.' Lin Shoo walked around the chair and unobtrusively moved the panel of the silk screen away from Hawkins's cigar. It was too late; the heat of the butt had caused a small circular burn in the fabric.

'It's a high-rent district,' replied Hawkins. 'Somebody in this people's paradise, where nobody owns anything but everyone owns everything, is making a fast buck. Four hundred of 'em every month.'

'You were fortunate to find it. Property can be purchased by collectives. A collective is not private ownership.' The police officer walked to the narrow opening that led to the single sleeping room of the house. It was dark; where sunlight should have been streaming through the wide window there was a blanket nailed across the frame into the thin surrounding wall. On the floor a number of mats had been piled one on top of another; wrappings from American candy bars were scattered about and there was a distinct odour of whisky.

'Why the photographs?'

The Chinese turned from the unpleasant sight. 'To show the world that we are treating you better than you treated us. This house is not a tiger cage in Saigon, nor is it a dungeon in the shark-infested waters of Holcotaz.'

'Alcatraz. The Indians got it.'

'I beg your pardon?'

'Nothing. You're making a big splash with this thing, aren't you?'

Lin Shoo was silent for a moment; it was the pause before profundity. 'Should someone – who has for years publicly denounced the deeply felt objectives of your beloved motherland – dynamite your Lin-Kolon Memorial inside

27

your Washington Square within your state of Columbia, the robed barbarians on your Court of Supreme Justice would, no doubt, have executed him by now.' The Chinese smiled and smoothed the tunic of his Mao uniform. 'We do not behave in such primitive ways. All life is precious. Even a diseased dog, such as you.'

'And you gooks never denounced anybody, is that it?'

'Our leaders reveal only truth. That is common knowledge throughout the world; the lessons of the infallible chairman. Truth is not denunciation, General. It is merely truth. All knowing.'

'Like my state of Columbia,' muttered Hawkins, removing his foot from the lacquered table. 'Why the hell did you pick me out? A lot of people have done a lot of goddamned denouncing. Why am I so special?'

'Because they are not so famous. Or infamous, if you will—. Although I did enjoy the film of your life. Very artistic; a poem of violence.'

'You saw that, huh?'

'Privately. Certain portions were extracted. Those showing the actor portraying you murdering our heroic youth. Very savage, General.' The Communist circled the black lacquered table and smiled again. 'Yes, you are an infamous man. And now you have insulted us by destroying a revered monument —'

'Come off it. I don't even know what happened. I was drugged and you goddamned well know it. I was with your General Lu Sin. With *his* broads, in *his* house.'

'You must give us our honour back again, General Hawkins. Can't you see that?' Lin Shoo spoke quietly, as though Hawkins had not interrupted. 'It would be a simple matter for you to render an apology. A ceremony has been planned. With a small contingent of the press in attendance. We have written out the words for you.'

'*Oh, boy!*' Hawkins sprang out of the chair, towering over the policeman. 'We're back to that again! How many times do I have to tell you bastards? *Americans don't crawl!* In any goddamned ceremony, with or without the goddamned

28

press! Read that straight, you puke-skinned dwarf!'

'Do not upset yourself. You place far too much emphasis on a mere ceremonial function; you place everyone – *all of us* – in most difficult positions. A small ceremony; so little, so simple —'

'Not to me it isn't! I represent the armed forces of the United States and nothing's little or simple to us! We don't trip easy, buddy boy; we march straight to the drums!'

'I beg your pardon?'

Hawkins shrugged, a touch bewildered by his own words. 'Never mind. The answer's no. You may scare the lace-pants boys down at the mission, but you don't shake me.'

'*They* appealed to you because they were instructed to do so. Certainly that must have occurred to you.'

'Double bullshit!' Hawkins walked around to the fireplace, drank from his glass and placed it on the mantel next to a brightly coloured box. 'Those fags were cooking up something with that group of queens at State. Wait'll the White House – wait'll the *Pentagon* reads *my* report. Oh, boy! You bowlegged runts will hightail it to the mountains and then we'll blow *them* up!' Hawkins grinned, his eyes bright.

'You are so abusive,' said Lin Shoo quietly, shaking his head sadly. He picked up the brightly coloured box next to the general's glass. 'Tsing Taow firecrackers. The finest made in the world. So loud, so bright with white light when they go *bang, bang, bang*. Very lovely to watch and to hear.'

'Yeah,' agreed Hawkins, slightly confused by the change of subject. 'Lu Sin gave 'em to me. We shot off a motherload the other night. Before the fucker drugged me.'

'Very beautiful, General Hawkins. They are a fine gift.'

'Christ knows he owed me *something*.'

'But do you not see?' continued the police officer. 'They sound like – explosives. Look like – detonating ammunition, but they are neither. They are only show. Semblances of something else. Real in themselves but only an *illusion* of *another* reality. Not dangerous at all.'

'So?'

29

'That is precisely what you are being asked to give. The semblance, not the reality. You have only to *pretend*. In a short, simple ceremony with but a few words that *you* know are only an illusion. Not dangerous at all. And very polite.'

'Wrong-o!' roared Hawkins. 'Everybody knows what a firecracker is; *nobody'll* know I'm pretending.'

'Between the two of us, I must differ. It is nothing more than diplomatic ritual. Everyone will understand, take my word for it.'

'Yeah? How the hell do you know that? You're a Peking cop, not a Kissing-ass.'

The Communist fingered the box of firecrackers and sighed audibly. 'I apologize for the minor deception, General. I am not with the People's Police. I am second vice-prefect for the Ministry of Education. I am here to make an appeal to you. An appeal to your reason. However, the rest is quite true. You *are* under house arrest, and the patrois outside *are* policemen.'

'I'll be goddamned! They sent me a lace-pants.' Hawkins grinned again. 'You boys are worried, real worried, aren't you?'

The Communist sighed once more. 'Yes. The idiots who started this thing have been shipped to mining collectives in Outer Mongolia. It was lunacy; although I'll grant them you were a temptation, General Hawkins. Have you any *idea* the volumes of scurrilous attacks you've made on every Marxist, Socialist, and, forgive me, even vaguely democratically oriented nation on the face of this earth? The worst examples - I should say *best* examples of demagoguery!'

'A lot of that crap was written by the people who paid me to speak,' said Hawkins, a bit reflectively. And then he quickly added, 'Not that I didn't believe it! Goddamn, I *believe*!'

'You're impossible!' Lin Shoo stamped his foot as a child might. 'You're as insane as Lu Sin and his band of growling paper lions! May they all crack many rocks and fornicate with Mongolian sheep! You are simply impossible!'

Hawkins stared at the Communist - both at the furious

30

expression on his face and the brightly coloured box of firecrackers in his hand. He had made a decision and both of them knew it.

'I'm also something else, slant eyes,' said the lieutenant general, approaching Lin Shoo.

'No! *No!* No *violence*, you idiot —' It was too late for the Communist to scream. Hawkins grabbed the cloth of his tunic, pulled him swiftly off his feet and chopped Lin Shoo beneath the mandible.

The vice-prefect of the Ministry of Education slumped instantly into unconsciousness.

Hawkins grabbed the box of firecrackers out of Lin Shoo's hand and raced around the lacquered table into the sleeping quarters. He grabbed the blanket nailed across the window, folded back a tiny section on the edge and looked outside at the rear of the house. There were the two policemen chatting calmly, their rifles at their sides. Beyond them was the sloping hill that led down to the village.

Hawkins released the blanket and ran back into the main room, dropping immediately to his hands and knees and scrambling obstacle-style towards the front door. He stood up and silently opened it a crack. The two flanking policemen were about forty feet away and were as relaxed as the troops in the rear. What's more, they were looking down the descending road, their attention *not* on the house.

MacKenzie took the brightly coloured box of firecrackers from under his arm, ripped off the lightweight paper and shook out the connecting strings of cylinders. He wound two separate strands together, twisted both fuses into one, and removed his World War II Zippo from his pocket.

He stopped; he sucked his breath, angry with himself. Then, holding the strands of firecrackers at his side, he walked casually past the windows into the bedroom and removed his holster and cartridge belt from another nail in the thin wall. He strapped the apparatus around his waist, removed the Colt .45 and checked the magazine. Satisfied, he shoved the weapon into its leather casing as he walked out of the bedroom. He circled the armchair in front of the Han

31

Shu mantel, stepped over the immobile Lin Shoo, and returned to the front door.

He ignited the Zippo, and held the flame beneath the twisted fuse, then opened the door and threw the entwined strands on to the grass beyond the porch.

Closing and bolting the door softly and swiftly, Hawkins dragged a small red lacquered chest from the foyer and forced it against the thick, carved panel. Then he raced into the sleeping quarters and pulled back a small section of the window blanket and waited.

The explosions were even louder than he remembered; made so, he guessed, from the combined strands bursting against one another.

The guards at the rear of the house were jolted out of their lethargy; their weapons collided in midair as each whipped his off the ground. Rifles in waist-firing position, the two men raced towards the front of the house.

The moment they were out of sight, Hawkins yanked down the blanket, crashed his foot into the thin strips of wood and thinner panes of glass, shattering the entire window. He leaped through on to the grass and started running towards the fields and the sloping hill.

CHAPTER THREE

At the base of the hill was the main dirt road that circled the village. Like spokes from a wheel, numerous offshoots headed directly into the small marketplace, in the centre of the town. A semi-paved thoroughfare branched outward tangentially from the circling road and connected with a paved highway about four miles to the east. The American diplomatic mission was twelve miles down that highway within Peking proper.

What he needed was a vehicle, preferably an automobile, but automobiles were practically non-existent outside the highest official circles. The People's Police had automobiles, of course; it had crossed his mind to double back around the hill to find Lin Shoo's, but that was too risky. Even if he found it and stole it, it would be a marked vehicle.

Hawkins circled the village, keeping to the high ground above the road. They would be coming after him. He could stay in the hills indefinitely; that didn't bother him. He had bivouacked underground in the mountains of Cong-Sol and Lai Tai in Cambodia for months at a time; he could live in the forests better than most animals. Goddamn, he was a *pro*!

But it was also pointless. He had to get to the mission and let the Free World know what kind of enemy it was sucking up to. Enough was enough, goddamn it! They could send out radio messages, barricade the whole complex, and fight it out until the offshore carriers sent in air strikes to pinpoint pulverize, even if it meant blowing up half of Peking. Then the copters could come in and get them out.

Of course, the civilians would shit in their pants, but he would control them. Teach the fancy pants how to fight. *Fight! Not talk!*

MacKenzie stopped his fantasizing. Below to the right, coming around the bend in the road a quarter of a mile away was a lone motorcycle. On it was a *shee-san* police official, a kind of Chinese state trooper. The answer to a prayer!

Hawkins rose from the tall grass and started scrambling down the hill. In less than a minute he was at the edge of the dirt border. The bike was still around the curve out of sight, but he heard it coming closer. He threw himself down in the dirt in the middle of the road, drawing his legs up to appear smaller than he was, and lay perfectly still.

The motorcycle's engine roared as the driver came around the curve, then sputtered as it skidded to a stop. The *shee-san* got off the bike and whipped out the kick-stand. Hawkins could hear and feel the quick footsteps as the trooper approached.

The *shee-san* bent over him and touched his shoulder, recoiling at the recognition of the American uniform. Mac moved. The *shee-san* shrieked.

Five minutes later Hawkins had stretched the *shee-san*'s tunic and pants over his rolled-up trousers and shirt. He slipped the trooper's goggles over his eyes and put on the ludicrously tiny visor hat, using the chin strap to hold it in place, a cloth pimple sitting on the crew-cut, greyish black hair. Fortunately for his sense of well-being, he had a cigar. He chewed the end to its desired juiciness and lighted up.

He was ready to ride.

The diplomatic attaché ran into the director's office without saying a word to the secretary or even knocking at the door. The director was threading his teeth with dental floss.

'Excuse me, sir. I've just received the instructions from Washington! I knew you'd have to read them!'

The director of the diplomatic mission, Peking, reached for the cable and read it. His eyes widened and his mouth opened in astonishment. A long strand of dental floss, caught in his teeth, extended down to the desk.

*

34

He saw the road-block cutting off his entry on to the Peking highway. It was about three quarters of a mile down the semi-paved thoroughfare; a single *shee-san* patrol car and a line of troopers stretching across the road was all he could distinguish through the fogged-up goggles.

As he drew nearer, he could see that the guards were shouting to each other. One trooper stepped in front of the line and began waving his rifle in the air – hysterically – back and forth, a signal for the approaching rider to stop.

There was only one thing for it, thought Hawkins. If you're going to buy a goddamned grave, buy it *big*! Go out with all weapons on repeat-fire, blazing barrels of thunder and lightning; go out with the screams of the Commie bastards ringing in your ears!

Goddamn! He couldn't see for the fucking dust, and his goddamn *foot* kept slipping off the tiny fucking gas pedal.

He slapped his hand to his holster and pulled out the .45.

He couldn't focus worth shit, but by *Christ*, he could squeeze the trigger! He did so repeatedly.

To his astonishment the *shee-san* did not fire back; instead they dived into the mounds of dirt and sand, screaming like hysterical piglets, scampering into and over the mounds of dirt burying their asses from the fire-power of his single .45 weapon.

Goddamn! *Disgraceful!*

Unless his goggles were playing tricks with the dirt and cigar smoke and the onrushing blurs, even the trooper in front – an officer, by Christ; he had to be – even *he* didn't have the balls to fight back.

An *officer*!

MacKenzie kept the bike at top-throttle and exhausted the clip of the .45. He careened up and over a mound of dirt and sand and cascaded on to a sloping hill of grass. As the bike was in midair he glimpsed the blurs of screaming heads beneath him and wished to hell he had more ammo. He twisted the handlebars violently so he could angle down and zoom diagonally back towards the road.

Goddamn! He hit the surface again! He'd broken through the barricade! He was barrel-assing on to the Peking highway!

The flat concrete was a joy. The spinning wheels of the motorcycle hummed; the wind rushed against his face – clear, intoxicating blasts of clean, dustless air which forced the smoke of his cigar into whirling pockets around his ears. Even the goggles were clear now.

He took the next nine miles like a star-spangled meteor through an unknowing Chincom sky. Another mile and he would turn into the northern side streets of Peking. Goddamn! He was going to make it! And then, by Christ, the Commie bastards would find out what an American counter-strike was!

He raced the bike through the crowded streets and careened off the kerb at the entrance to Glorious Flower Square, the final stretch of the mission which stood at the end of the small plaza, fronting the street in alabaster, Oriental splendour. There were, as usual, crowds of Pekingers and out-of-towners milling about, waiting to catch glimpses of the strange, huge pink people that came and went through the white steel doors inside the medium-sized compound.

It wasn't much of a compound at that; there was no brick wall or high metal fence surrounding the mission. Only a thin latticework of decorative wood, lacquered against the elements, enclosing the clipped grass lawn that fronted the steps.

The protection was in the windows and doors: iron grillework and steel.

MacKenzie revved the bike's engine to maximum, figuring the noise would part the throngs of onlookers.

It did.

The Chinese scattered as he raced down the street.

And Hawkins damn near fell off the bike's saddle at what he saw in front of him; what in a sense - was rushing towards him at goddamn near fifty miles an hour on that short stretch of pavement in Glorious Flower Square.

There were *three sets of wooden barricades* – elongated horses – in front of the closed latticework gate! Each horizontal plank was a foot or so above the other, forming a receding escalator wall of thick boards backed up by the delicate, filigreed fence.

Standing in a line at port-arms were a dozen or so soldiers, flanked by two officers, all staring straight ahead. At him.

This is it, thought MacKenzie, nothing left but the gesture, the motion – the act itself.

Total defiance!

Goddamn! If he only had some ammo left!

He crouched and headed the bike right into the centre of the barricade; he twisted the bar accelerator to the maximum and pressed the foot choke all the way down.

The speedometer's needle wavered in a violence of its own as it quivered and shot up swiftly towards the end of the dial; man and machine burst through the air corridor like a strange, huge bullet of flesh and steel.

Amid the screams of the hysterical crowds and the scattering of the panicked soldiers, Hawkins yanked the handlebars furiously back and slapped the weight of his body against the rear of the saddle. The front wheel rose off the ground like an abstract, spinning phoenix – followed by a mad extension of tail and rider – and crashed into the upper section of the barricade.

There was a thunderous shattering of wood and lattice-work as MacKenzie Hawkins shot up, into – and through – the tiers of obstructions, a maniacally effective human cannonball that dragged the rest of the weapon with him.

The bike plummeted down into the path of washed pebbles that led to the steps of the mission. As it did so, MacKenzie was hurled forward, somersaulting over the bars, rolling on the tiny stones until he thudded into the base of the short flight of steps to the white steel door, the cigar still gripped between his teeth.

Any second now the Chincoms would regroup, the fusillade would begin, and the sharp chops of icelike pain

37

would commence, giving him, perhaps, only seconds before oblivion came.

But the firing did not begin. Only louder and louder screaming from the crowds and the soldiers. Oriental heads peered over the mass of wreckage, above the shattered planks, in front of the smashed latticework. Most of the soldiers who had thrown themselves on the ground were now on their hands and knees.

Yet no one fired a weapon. Then MacKenzie understood: he was, technically, within US territory. If he was shot inside the compound it might be construed as an execution on American soil. It could become an international incident. *Goddamn!* He was protected by lacepants fol-de-rol! Diplomatic niceties were keeping him alive!

He scrambled to his feet, ran up the steps to the white steel door and began punching the bell and pounding his hand on the metal panel.

There was no response.

He banged louder and kept his free hand on the bell. He yelled to those inside and after what seemed like minutes, the single rectangular slot in the door was opened.

A pair of wide, frightened eyes peered out.

'For Christ's sake, it's *Hawkins!*' roared MacKenzie, putting his screaming mouth inches in front of the panicked set of eyes. 'Open the goddamned door, you son of a bitch! What the hell are you doing?'

The eyes blinked, but the door did not open.

Hawkins yelled again, and again the eyes blinked. After several seconds the eyes were replaced by trembling lips.

'No one's home, sir,' came the quivering, unbelievable words.

'*What?!*'

'Sorry, General.'

The shaking lips were now replaced by the rapid slamming of metal. The slot was closed.

MacKenzie stood there in temporary shock. Then he started pounding once again and yelling again and punching the bell buttons so hard the Bakelite cracked.

38

Nothing.

He looked back at the crowds and the soldiers, and became aware of the screams and grins and wave after wave of giggles.

Hawkins jumped down the set of steps and began running across the lawn in front of the building. All the windows were not only shut, but the iron inner shutters had been closed behind the grillework. The whole goddamn mission was sealed tight, an enormous white, rectangular clam.

He raced around the side. It was the same everywhere: closed windows, iron shutters, grillework.

He rounded the back lawn and ran to the large rear entrance. He began pounding the door and yelling louder than he thought he had ever yelled in his life.

Finally the slot opened and another set of eyes appeared – less frightened than those in front but nevertheless wide and disturbed.

'Open this fucking door, goddamn it!'

Once more lips appeared, and now MacKenzie could see the grey moustache. It was the ambassador.

'Get away from here, Hawkins,' said the deep, anglicized voice, cultivated in the Eastern Establishment. 'You're just not operative!'

And the slot was closed.

MacKenzie stood there immobilized. Time and space fused into nothingness. He was vaguely aware that the crowds and the soldiers had moved around the latticework fence at the sides and the rear of the mission.

Without really thinking, he backed away from the entrance and looked up at the outside wall of the building and at the roof.

He could do it, using the grillework of the windows. He jumped to the first window and climbed up the grillework until he reached the next protrusion of crisscrossing bars.

In several minutes he had scaled the side of the building and pulled himself over the edge of the sloping tiled roof.

He trudged up to the apex and looked around.

The flagpole was centred in the grass on the lawn to the left

39

of the gravel path. The gently waving cloth of Old Glory undulated in the breeze in isolated splendour.

Lieutenant General MacKenzie Hawkins tested the wind and then unzipped his fly.

CHAPTER FOUR

Devereaux smiled at the doorman of the Beverly Hills Hotel, then walked around the huge automobile to the driver's side, tipped the parking attendant, and climbed in behind the wheel, the glare of the sunlight bouncing off the hood. It was all so Southern California: doormen, parking attendants, silent tips, oversized cars, and blinding sunlight.

As was the telephone conversation he had held two hours ago with the first Mrs MacKenzie Hawkins.

He had decided to begin logically, piecing together a progressive disintegration of the man. Surely a pattern would emerge; it would be easier to document this contemporary version of the Rake's Progress if he started with the subject's introduction to the really corrupt world: soft silks and money as opposed to mere killing, torture, and West Point arrogance.

Regina Sommerville Hawkins was that introduction. According to the data banks, Regina was Virginia Hunt Country, spoiled-rich out of Foxcroft and Finch. She had set her cotillion bonnet for the trophy called Hawkins in 1947, when the celebrated youthful warrior of the Bulge had further impressed the nation with dazzling feats on the gridiron. Since Daddy Sommerville owned most of Virginia Beach, and Ginny was an authentic Southern belle – money *and* magnolia, not just the fragrance – the match was easily arranged. The heroic up-from-the-ranks West Pointer was met, overwhelmed, and temporarily subdued by the lilting drawl, large breasts, and indigenous conveniences of this soft but persistent daughter of the Confederacy.

Daddy knew a lot of people in Washington, so, combined with Hawkins's own talents and track record, Regina

41

expected to be a general's wife within six months. A year at best.

In Washington. Or Newport News. Or New York. Or perhaps lovely Hawaii. With servants and uniforms and dances and more servants and ...

However, Hawkins was peculiar, and Daddy did not know *that* many people who could curb his odd behaviour. The Hawk did not want the la-de-da life of Washington, Newport News, or New York. He wanted to be with his troops. And there was a congressional on his sheet; requests were not denied lightly. Regina found herself in out-of-the-way army camps where her husband furiously trained disinterested draftees for a war that wasn't. So she decided to shed her trophy. Daddy did know enough people to make that easy. Hawkins was transferred to West Germany and Regina's doctors made it clear she could not take the climate. The distance between them just made it feasible to call the whole thing quietly off.

Now, nearly thirty years later, Regina Sommerville Hawkins Clark Madison Greenberg was living in a suburb of Los Angeles called Tarzana with her fourth husband, Emmanuel Greenberg, motion picture producer. On the phone two hours ago she had said to Sam Devereaux:

'Listen, lover, you want to talk about Mac? I'll get the girls together. We usually meet on Thursdays, but what the hell is a day?'

So Sam wrote down the directions to Tarzana and was now on his way in a rented car to Regina's manse. The car radio played *Muddied Waters*, which seemed appropriate.

He found the driveway of the Greenberg residence and entered it, ascending, he was sure, the final crest of the hills. Halfway into the property was an iron gate, operated electrically; it swung open as he approached.

He parked in front of a four-car garage. On the flat asphalt surface there were two Cadillacs, a Silver Cloud Rolls and, in rather obvious counterpoint, a Maserati. Two uniformed chauffeurs were talking idly, leaning against the Rolls. Sam got out of the car with his attaché case and closed the door.

'I'm Mrs Greenberg's broker,' he said the chauffeurs.

'This is the *place*, man,' laughed the younger chauffeur. 'Merrill, Lynch, and The Girls. That's what they ought to call it.'

'Maybe they will some day. Is that the path to the door?' Sam gestured towards a flagstone walk that seemed to disappear into a short forest of California fern and miniature orange trees.

'Yes, sir,' said the older, dignified chauffeur, as if it were important to cut short the younger man's informality. 'To the right. You'll see it.'

Sam walked down the path to the front door. He had never seen a pink door before, but if he had to see one, he knew it would be in Southern California. He pushed the doorbell and heard the chimes ring out the opening notes of the *Love Story* theme. He wondered if Regina knew the ending.

The door opened and she stood in the foyer, dressed in tight-fitting shorts and an equally tight, translucent shirt that made her huge breasts burst forward in an absolutely challenging fashion.

Though in her forties, Regina was dark haired, tanned, unlined, and lovely, and she carried her frontage with the assurance of youth.

'You're the m*a*yjor?' she asked, the rank emerging in the low, slow, flat *A* of the Hunt Country.

'Major Sam Devereaux,' he confirmed. It was silly to state the name so formally but his attention was on her two titanic challenges.

'Come on in. I reckon you figured we'd all take offence at a uniform.'

'Something like that, I guess.' Devereaux smiled foolishly, forced his eyes away from the shirt and walked into the foyer.

The foyer was short; the entrance to a huge sunken living room, the far wall of which was nothing but glass. Beyond the glass was a kidney-shaped pool surrounded by a terrace of Italian tile, bordered by an ornate iron fence overlooking the valley.

43

All this he noticed after, say, fifteen seconds. The first quarter minute was taken up observing three additional pairs of breasts.

Each pair was magnificent in its individual style. Full and Round. Narrow and Pointed. Sloping yet Argumentative.

They belonged in turn to Madge, Lillian, and Anne; Regina Greenberg made the introductions swiftly and pleasantly. And Sam automatically related the breasts – the girls – to the data in his attaché case.

Lillian was number three. Palo Alto, California.

Madge was number two. Tuckahoe, New York.

Ann was number four. Detroit, Michigan.

A nice cross-section of America.

Regina – Ginny – was obviously the oldest, not so much in appearance as in authority. For in truth, all the girls were in that vague age range between middle thirties and the next decade – a span Southern California was expert in obscuring. And each was attractive and commanding in a way slightly different from the others. And each was dressed in sexy Southern California: casual but minutely engineered for that effect.

MacKenzie Hawkins was a man whose tastes and abilities were to be envied.

The courtesies were got over with rapidly, courteously. Sam was offered a drink, which he dared not refuse in this company, and seated in a sunken bean bag from which it was impossible to rise. He managed to place the attaché case at his side, but immediately realized that the contortions required to reach over, pick it up, and open it on his lap would tax Plastic Man, so he hoped it would not be necessary.

'Well, here we all are,' drawled Regina Greenberg. 'Hawkins's Harem, as it were. What does the Pentagon want? Testimonials?'

'There's one we'll all give without reservation,' said Lillian brightly.

'Enthusiastically,' said Madge.

'*Oooh,*' said Anne.

44

'Yes, well. The general's abilities are enormous,' stammered Sam. 'I mean – well, I didn't expect to meet you all at once. Together. In a group.'

'Oh, we're a real sorority, Major.' Madge, Round and Full, sat in a bean bag next to Sam and reached over, touching his arm. 'Ginny told you. Hawkins's —'

'Yes, I understood,' said Devereaux, swiftly interrupting.

'Talk to one of us about Mac, you talk to all of us,' added Lillian – Narrow and Pointed – from across the room in a particularly mellifluous voice.

'That's right,' cooed Anne – Sloping yet Argumentative – standing outrageously in front of the centre pane of glass on the swimming pool wall.

'In the event we don't have a quorum, I act as spokeswoman,' drawled Regina Greenberg from a jaguar-skin couch against the right wall. 'That's because I was there first and have seniority.'

'Not necessarily in years, dear,' said Madge. 'We won't let you malign yourself.'

'It's difficult to know how to begin,' said Sam, who, nevertheless, plunged into the difficulty. He touched first, gently, on the abstract hardships of dealing with a highly individualistic personality. He slowly, gently explained that MacKenzie Hawkins had involved his government in a most delicate situation for which a solution had to be found. And although said government was filled with undeniable and undying gratitude for General Hawkins's extraordinary contributions, it was often necessary to study a man's background to help him – and his government – resolve delicate situations. Frequently the partially negative led to the positive, if only to balance and accentuate the affirmative.

'So you want to screw him,' recapped Regina Greenberg. 'It had to happen, didn't it, girls?'

There was a chorus of yesses and uh-huhs.

Sam knew better than to offer a flat denial; there was more intelligence – or perception in that room than might have been evident at first. 'Why do you say that?' he asked Ginny.

45

'Gawd, Major!' replied Titanic. 'Mac's been on a collision course with the high-brass pricky-shits for years! He sees through their manure piles. That's why they like it when those Northern liberals make him out a joke. But Mac's no joke!'

'Nobody thinks he's funny right now, Mrs Greenberg. Let me assure you.'

'What's Mac done?' The question was put defensively by Anne, still silhouetted splendidly at the window.

'He defaced —' Sam stopped; bad choice of word. 'He destroyed a national monument belonging to a government we're trying to maintain a détente with. Like our Lincoln Memorial.'

'Was he drunk?' asked Lillian, eyes and narrow frontage levelled at Sam; two sets of sharp artillery.

'He says he wasn't.'

'Then he wasn't,' stated Madge positively from the bean bag beside him.

'Mac can drink a whole battalion under a mess hall slop shoot.' Ginny Greenberg's drawl was punctuated by her affirmatively nodding head. 'But he never, *never* plays the whisky game to the disadvantage of that uniform.'

'He wouldn't put it into words, Major,' said Lillian, 'but it was a stronger rule than any oath he ever took.'

'For two reasons,' added Ginny. 'He surely didn't want to disgrace his rank, but just as important, he didn't like for the pricky-shits to laugh at him because of booze.'

'So you see,' stated Madge in the bean bag, 'Mac didn't do what they said he did to the Lincoln Memorial. He just wouldn't.'

Sam looked back and forth at the girls. Not one of these ex-Mrs Hawkinses was going to help him; none would utter a negative word about the man.

Why?

He struggled like hell to get out of the bean bag and tried to assume the stance of a cross-examining attorney. A very soft, gentle attorney. He paced slowly in front of the massive window. Anne went to the bean bag.

46

'Naturally,' he began, smiling, 'these circumstances, this group here, evoke several questions. Not that you're under any obligation to answer, but frankly, speaking personally, I don't understand. Let me explain —'

'Let *me answer*,' interrupted Regina. 'You can't figure out why Hawkins's Harem protects its namesake. Right?'

'Right.'

'As spokeswoman,' continued Ginny, receiving nods of assent from the others, 'I'll be brief and to the point. Mac Hawkins is one great guy – in bed and out, and don't snicker at the bed because most marriages haven't got it. You can't live with the son of a bitch, but that's not his fault.

'Mac gave us something we'll never forget because it's with us every day. He taught us to break our moulds. Sounds simple, doesn't it? "Break your mould." But, lover, it sets you *free*. "You're your own goddamned inventory," he used to say. "There's nothing you *have* to do and nothing you *can't* do; use your inventory and work like hell."

'Now, I don't think that all of us believe that's holy writ. But by gawd, he made each one of us try a lot harder. He set us free before it was chic and we haven't done badly. So, you see, there's not one of us – if Mac came knocking at the door – who wouldn't accommodate him. You dig?'

'I dig,' replied Sam quietly.

The telephone rang. Regina reached behind the couch to the French phone on the marble table. She turned to Sam. 'It's for you.'

Sam looked a bit startled. 'I left your number with the hotel but I didn't expect ...' He walked to the table and took the phone.

'He *what*?!' Blood drained from Sam's face. He listened again. 'Jesus! He *didn't*!' And then in the weariness of aftershock: 'Yes, sir. I can see he most certainly did ... I'll go back to the hotel and await instructions. Unless you'd rather turn this over to someone else; my tour is up in a month, sir. I see. Five days at the outside, sir.'

He hung up and turned to Hawkins's Harem. Those four

47

magnificent pairs of mammaries that both invited and defied description.

'We're not going to need you, ladies. Although Mac Hawkins may.'

'I'm your only contact with Sixteen-hundred, Major,' said the young lieutenant as he paced – somewhat childishly, thought Sam – the plush Beverly Hills Hotel room. 'You can refer to me as Lodestone. No names, please.'

'Lieutenant Lodestone, Sixteen-hundred. Has a nice ring to it,' said Devereaux, pouring himself another bourbon.

'I'd go easy on the alcohol.'

'Why don't you go to China instead? Of *me*, that is.'

'You do have a long, long flight.'

'Not if *you* make it, I don't.'

'In a way, I wish I could. Do you realize there are seven hundred million potential consumers over there? I'd really like to get a see-you shot of that market.'

'A who?'

'Close-up look. A real peek-see.'

'Ohh. *C-U.* Not see-you —'

'What an opportunity!' The lieutenant stood by the hotel window, his hands clasped behind his back. *Caveat consumer.*

'Then *go*, for Christ's sake! In thirty-two days I've got a permit to get out of this Disneyland and I don't want to trade my uniform in for a Chinese smock!'

'I'm afraid I can't, sir. Sixteen-hundred needs pro-PR now. All the other slambangs are gone. Some are turning out a crackerjack house organ at Dannemora ... Damn!' The lieutenant turned from the window and walked to the writing-desk where there were half a dozen photographs, five by seven. 'It's all here, Major. All you need. They're a little hazy, but they show Brand X, all right! He certainly can't deny it now.'

Sam looked at the blurred but definable telephotos from Peking. 'He almost reached, didn't he?'

'Disgraceful!' The lieutenant winced as he studied the

48

photographs. 'There's nothing left to be said.'

'Except that he almost made it.' Sam crossed to an armchair and sat down with his bourbon. The lieutenant followed him.

'Your head IG investigator in Saigon will fly his reports directly to you in Tokyo. Take them with you to Peking. They've got a lot of real dirt.' The young officer smiled his genuine smile. 'Just in case you need some final stickum for the coffin.'

'Gee, you're a nice kid. Ever meet your father?' Sam drank a great deal of his bourbon.

'You mustn't personalize it, Major. It's an objective operation and we have the input. It's all part of the —'

'Don't say again —'

'... game plan.' Lodestone swallowed the words. 'Sorry. And anyway, if you do personalize it, what more do you want? The man's a maniac. A dangerous egotistical madman who's interfering violently with peaceful pursuits.'

'I'm a lawyer, Lieutenant, not an avenging angel. Your maniac made several contributions to other – game plans. He's got a lot of people in his corner. I met with eight –*four* – this afternoon.' Sam looked at his glass; where did the bourbon go?

'Not any more, he doesn't,' said the officer flatly.

'He doesn't what?'

'Whatever constituency he had will disappear.'

'Constituency? He's a politician?' Sam decided he needed another drink. He couldn't follow this Buster Brown any longer. So why not get really drunk?

'He *peed* on the Stars and Stripes! That's a Peoria no-no!'

'Did he really reach?'

'We're sending you to China,' continued Lodestone, overlooking the question, 'in the fastest way possible. Phantom jet aircraft over the northern route, stops in Juneau and the Aleutians, into Tokyo. From there a supply carrier to Peking. I've brought all the papers you need from Washington.'

Devereaux mumbled into his bourbon. 'I don't like moo

49

goo gai pan and I hate egg rolls ...'

'May I suggest you get some rest, sir? It's almost twenty-three hundred and we have to leave for the airbase at oh four hundred. You take off at dawn.'

'Wish I'd said that, Lodestone. Nice ring to it. Five hours. And you're down the hall but not *in here*.'

'Sir?' The young man cocked his head.

'I'm going to give you an order. Go away. I don't want to see you until you come to sew in my name tags.'

'What?'

'Get the hell out of here.' And then Sam remembered and his eyes – though slightly glazed – were laughing. 'You know what you are, Lieutenant? You're a pricky-shit. A real, honest-to-God pricky-shit. Now I know what it means!'

Four hours ... He wondered.

It was worth a try. But first he needed another drink.

He poured it and walked to the writing-desk and laughed at the Peking telephotos. The son of a bitch had flair, no question about it. But he was not at the desk to look at the photographs; he opened the drawer and took out his notebook. He turned the pages and did his best to focus on his own handwriting. He walked to the telephone by the bed, dialled nine, and then the number on the page.

'Hello?' The voice was magnolia-soft and Sam could actually smell the oleander blossoms.

'Mrs Greenberg? This is Sam Devereaux —'

'Well, how're *you*?' Regina's greeting was positively enthusiastic; there was no attempt to conceal her pleasure that the caller was a man. 'We were all wondering which one you'd call. I'm really flattered, M*ay*jor! I mean, actually, I'm the elder stateswoman. I'm really touched.'

Her husband was probably out, thought Sam through the bourbon, warmed by the memory of her challenging, translucent shirt.

'That's very kind of you. You see, in a little while I'm going to go on a long, long trip. Over oceans and mountains and more oceans and islands and ...' *Jesus!* He hadn't figured out

50

how to put it; he hadn't really been sure he could dial her number. Goddamn bourbon fantasies! 'Well, it's sheecrit – *secret*. Very covert. But. I'm going to talk to your – namesake?'

'Of *cawsse*, lover! And naturally, you didn't get half a *chay*nce to ask all those important government questions. I understand, I *really do*.'

'Well, several items came up, one in particular —'

'It usually does. I do believe I should do all I can to help the government in its delicate situation. You're at the Beverly Hills?'

'Yes, ma'm. Room eight twenty.'

'Wait a sec.' She put her hand over the receiver, but Sam could hear her calling out. '*Manny!* There's a national emergency. I have to go to town.'

CHAPTER FIVE

'Major! Major Devereaux! Your phone is off the hook. That's a no-no.'

An incessant, ridiculously loud knocking accompanied Lodestone's nasal screams.

'What the gawd-almighty hell is *that*?' asked Regina Greenberg, nudging Sam under the covers. 'It sounds like an unoiled piston.'

Devereaux opened his eyes into the visual abyss of a hangover. 'That, dear patron saint of Tarzana, is the voice of the evil people. They surface when the earth churns.'

'Do you know what time it is? Call the hotel police, for heaven's sake.'

'No,' said Sam, reluctantly getting out of bed. 'Because if I do, that gentleman will call the joint chiefs of staff. I think they're scared to death of him. They're merely professional killers; he's in advertising.'

And before Devereaux could really focus, hands had dressed him, cars had driven him, men had yelled at him, and he was strapped into an Air Force Phantom jet.

They all smiled. Everyone in China smiled. With their lips more than their eyes, thought Sam.

He was met at the Peking airfield by an American diplomatic vehicle, escorted by two flanking Chinese army cars and eight Chinese army officers. All smiling; even the vehicles.

The two nervous Americans that came with the diplomatic car were attachés. They were anxious to get back to the mission; neither was comfortable around the Chinese troops.

Nor did either attaché care to discuss very much of anything except the weather, which was dull and overcast. Whenever Sam brought up the subject of MacKenzie Hawkins – and why not? he had relieved himself on *their* roof – their mouths became taut and they shook their heads in short, lateral jerks and pointed their fingers below the windows at various areas of the automobile. And laughed at nothing.

Finally Devereaux realized they were convinced that the diplomatic car was bugged. So Sam laughed, too. At nothing.

If the automobile *was* fitted with electronic surveillance, and if someone *was* listening, thought Devereaux, that person was probably conjuring up a picture of three adult males passing dirty comics back and forth.

And if the ride from the airfield seemed strange to Sam, his half-hour meeting with the ambassador at the diplomatic mission in Glorious Flower Square was ludicrous.

He was ushered into the building by his cackling escorts, greeted solemnly by a group of serious-faced Americans who had gathered in the hallway like onlookers in a zoological laboratory – unsure of their safety but fascinated by the new animal brought in for observation – and propelled quickly down a corridor to a large door that was obviously the entrance to the ambassador's office. Once inside, the ambassador greeted him with a rapid handshake, simultaneously raising a finger over his slightly quivering moustache. One of the escorts removed a small metal device about the size of a pack of cigarettes and began waving it around the windows as though blessing the panes of glass. The ambassador watched the man.

'I can't be sure,' whispered the attaché.

'Why not?' asked the diplomat.

'The needle moved a touch, but it could be the loudspeakers in the square.'

'Damn! We have to get more sophisticated scanners. Scramble a memo to Washington.' The ambassador took Sam's elbow, leading him back to the door. 'Come with me, General.'

'I'm a major.'

'That's nice.'

The ambassador propelled Sam out of the office, across the corridor to another door, which he opened, and then preceded Devereaux down a steep flight of stone steps into a large basement. There was a single light bulb on the wall; the ambassador snapped it on and led Sam past a number of wooden crates to another door in the barely visible wall. It was heavy and the diplomat had to put his foot against the surrounding cement in order to pull it open.

Inside was a long-out-of-use, walk-in refrigerator, now serving as a wine cellar.

The ambassador entered and struck a match. On one of the racks was a candle, half burned down. The ambassador held the flame to the wick, and the light swelled flickeringly against the walls and the racks. The wine was not the best, observed Devereaux silently.

The ambassador reached out and yanked Sam into the centre of the small enclosure and then pulled the heavy door almost shut, but not completely.

His lean, aristocratic features accentuated by the wavering flame of the candle, the ambassador smiled apologetically.

'We may strike you as a touch paranoid, but it's not the case at all, I can assure you.'

'Oh, no, sir. This is very cosy. And quiet.'

Sam tried to return the ambassador's smile. And for the next thirty minutes he received his last instructions from his government. It was an appropriate place to get them: deep underground, the surrounding earth inhabited by worms that never saw the light of day.

Armed with his briefcase and no courage whatsover, Devereaux walked out the mission's white steel door, to be greeted by a Chinese officer who waved at him from the foot of the path. Sam saw for the first time the evidence of wreckage – large splinters of wood, several angle irons lying about on the lawn.

The officer stood outside the border of the property and

grinned a flat grin. 'My name is Lin Shoo, Major Deveroxx. I will escort you to Lieutenant General Hawkins. My car, should you please.'

Sam climbed into the back seat of the army staff vehicle and settled back, his case on his lap. As opposed to the nervous Americans, Lin Shoo was not at all inhibited about talking. The subject quickly became MacKenzie Hawkins.

'A highly volatile individual, Major Deveroxx,' said the Chinese, shaking his head. 'He is possessed by dragons.'

'Has anyone tried reasoning with him?'

'I, myself. With great and charming persuasion.'

'But not with great or charming success, I gather.'

'What can I tell you? He assaulted me. It wasn't proper at all.'

'And you want a full-scale trial because of *that*? The ambassador said you were adamant. A trial or a lot of hazzerai.'

'Hazzerai?'

'It means trouble. It's Jewish.'

'You don't look Jewish ...'

'What about this trial?' interrupted Sam. 'Are the charges centred on assault?'

'Oh, no. That would not be philosophically consistent. We expect to suffer *physically*. Through struggle and suffering there is strength.' Lin Shoo smiled; Devereaux didn't know why. 'The general will be tried for crimes against the motherland.'

'An extension of the original charge,' said Sam, making a quiet statement.

'Far more complex, however,' replied Lin Shoo, his smile fading into resigned depression. 'Wilful destruction of national shrines – not unlike your Lincoln Memorials. He escaped once, you know. With a stolen truck he ran into the statuary on Son Tai Square. He is now charged with defacement of venerated artistic craftsmanship – the statuary he ran into was sculptured after the designs of the chairman's wife. And there can be no counter-argument concerning drugs for this. He was seen by too many

55

diplomatic people. He made great sums of noise in Son Tai.'

'He'll claim extentuating circumstances.' No harm in testing, thought Devereaux.

'As with assault, there is no such thing.'

'I see.' Sam didn't but there was no point in pursuing it. 'What could he draw?'

'How so? Draw? The sculpture?'

'Prison. What sort of prison sentence? How long?'

'Roughly four thousand, seven hundred and fifty years.'

'*What?* You might as well execute him!'

'Life is precious to the sons and daughters of the motherland. Every living thing is capable of contribution. Even a vicious criminal like your maniac imperialist general. He could have many productive years in Mongolia.'

'Now just hold on!' Devereaux changed his position abruptly to look Lin Shoo full in the face. He could not be sure, but he thought he heard a metallic click from the front seat. Not unlike the springing of a pistol's safety catch.

He decided not to think about it. It was better that way. He returned his attention to Lin Shoo.

'That's *crazy*! You know that's just plain dumb! What the hell are you talking about? Four thousand – *Mongolia?*' Devereaux's attaché case fell out of his lap; he heard – again – the metallic click. 'I mean, let's be reasonable ...' Devereaux's words drifted off nervously. He picked up the leather case.

'These are the legitimate penalties for the crimes,' said Lin Shoo. 'No foreign government has the right to interfere with the internal discipline of its host nation. It is inconceivable. However, in this particular case, perhaps, it is not entirely unreasonable.'

Sam paused before speaking; he watched the scowl on Lin Shoo's face return slightly, ever so slightly, to its previous polite, unhumorous smile. 'Do I detect the beginnings of an out-of-court settlement?'

'How so? Out of court?'

'A compromise. Do we talk about a compromise?'

Lin Shoo now allowed the scowl to float away. His smile

56

came as close to being genial as Devereaux could imagine. 'Please, yes. A compromise would be enlightening. There is strength, also, in enlightenment.'

'And maybe a little less than four thousand years in Mongolia – in the compromise?'

'Fraught with possibilities. Should you succeed where others have not. After all, it is to our natural advantage to reach a compromise.'

'I hope you know how right you are. Hawkins is a national hero.'

'So was your Speero Agaroo, Major. Your President said so himself.'

'What can you offer? Dispense with the trial?'

Lin Shoo dropped his smile, too suddenly for comfort, thought Sam.

'We cannot do that. The trial has been announced. Too many people in the international community know of it.'

'You want to save face, or do you want to sell gas?' Devereaux sat back; the Chinese officer did want a compromise.

'A little of both is a compromise, is it not?'

'What's your little? In the event I can get Hawkins to be reasonable.'

'A reduction of the sentence would be one consideration.' Lin Shoo's smile returned.

'From four thousand to twenty-five hundred years?' asked Devereaux. 'You're all heart. Let's start with probation; I'll concede acquittal.'

'How so? Probation?'

'I'll explain later; you'll like it. Give me some real incentive to work on Hawkins.' Sam fingered the top of his attaché case, tapping his nails on the leather. It was a silly thing that usually split adversaries' concentration and sometimes produced a hasty concession.

'A Chinese trial takes many forms. Long, ornate, and quite ritualistic. Or very short, swift, and devoid of excess. Three months or three hours. I can, perhaps, bring about the latter —'

57

'That *and* probation, I'll buy,' said Sam quickly. 'That's incentive enough to make me want to work real hard. You've got a deal.'

'This probation. You will have to define more legalistically.'

'Basically, you not only save face and sell gas, but you can show how tough you are and *still* be heroes in the world press. All at the same time. What could be better than that?'

Lin Shoo smiled. Devereaux wondered briefly if there wasn't more understanding beyond that smile than the Chinese cared to show. Then he dismissed the thought; Lin Shoo distracted him by asking a question and answering it before Sam could speak.

'What could be better than that? Having General Hawkins out of China. Yes, *that* would be better.'

'What a coincidence. Because that's one insignificant part of probation.'

'Really?' Lin Shoo looked straight ahead.

'You, I can handle,' said Sam, almost reflectively. 'I've still got to worry about Brand X.'

CHAPTER SIX

The cell could be seen clearly through a single pane of unidirectional glass embedded in the heavy steel door. There was a western-style bed, a writing desk, recessed overhead lights, both a desk lamp and bedside light, and a large rug on the floor. There was an open door on the right wall that led to a small bathroom, and a horizontal clothes rack on the left. The room was no more than ten by twelve feet, but all things considered, far grander than Sam had visualized.

The only thing missing was MacKenzie Hawkins.

'You see,' said Lin Shoo, 'how considerate we are; how well appointed are the general's accommodations?'

'I'm impressed,' replied Devereaux. 'Except I don't see the general.'

'Oh, he is there.' The Chinese smiled and spoke softly. 'He has his little games. He hears the footsteps and conceals himself on either side of the door. Twice the guards were alarmed and made ill-considered entrances. Fortunately, there were several to overcome the general's strength. Now all the shifts are alerted. His meals are delivered through a slot.'

'He's still trying. ...' Sam chuckled. 'He's something.'

'He is many things,' added Lin Shoo enigmatically as he approached a webbed circle beneath the unidirectional glass and pushed a red button. 'General Hawkins? Please, General, show yourself. It is your good and gracious friend, Lin Shoo. I know you are beside the door, General.'

'Up your ass, slant eyes!'

Lin Shoo released the button momentarily and turned to Devereaux. 'He is not always the essence of courtesy.' The Chinese returned to the speaker and pushed the button

59

again. 'Please, General, I have a countryman of yours with me. A representative of your government. From the armed forces of your nation —'

'You better check her goddamned purse! Maybe up her skirt! Her lipstick might be a bomb!' came the shout from the unseen general officer.

Lin Shoo turned back to Devereaux in bewilderment. Sam gently moved the Chinese out of the way, pushed the button himself, and yelled into the speaker.

'Get off it, you chicken fucker! You're a goddamn bruise on my prick! Show that hairy ass you call a face or I'll open the slop-shoot and drop in that fucking lipstick! I'll *frag* you, you miserable son of a bitch! – Incidentally, Regina Greenberg says hello.'

The immense head of MacKenzie Hawkins slowly appeared in the pane of unidirectional glass. It emerged from the side, huge, crew-cut, leather-lined. Mac's expression was one of utter consternation. A half-chewed cigar was gripped between his teeth, beneath wide, blood-shot eyes that betrayed disbelieving curiosity.

'How so? What do you say?' Lin Shoo's controlled lips were parted in astonishment.

'It's a highly classified military code,' said Devereaux. 'We only employ it under extreme conditions.'

'I will not pursue the matter; it would not be courteous. If you flip the lever on the side of the glass, General Hawkins will see you. When you feel comfortable, I shall admit you. However, I will remain outside, please.'

Sam pushed the small handle on the side of the glass; there was a click. The large, squinting face reacted with instant hostility. Devereaux had the feeling that Hawkins was observing something very obscene but unimportant: Sam, the military accident.

Devereaux nodded to Lin Shoo. The Chinese reached out with both hands, as if to pull with one and push with the other, and unlatched the door. The heavy steel panel opened; Sam walked in.

To an enormous fist that came rushing towards him, on a

direct collision course with his left eye. The impact came; the room, the world, the galaxy spun out of orbit into the shimmering of a hundred thousand splotches of white light.

Sam felt the wet cloth over his face before he felt the pain in his head, especially his eye, and he thought that was strange. He reached up, pulled the cloth away and blinked. All he saw at first was a white ceiling. The centre light hurt his head, especially his left eye. He realized he was on a bed, so he rolled over and everything came back to him.

Hawkins was at the writing desk, papers and photographs scattered about the top. The general was reading from a sheaf of stapled papers.

Devereaux did not have to move his painful head farther to know that his opened attaché case was somewhere near the general. Nevertheless, he did so and saw it at Hawkins's feet. Open and upside down. Empty. The contents in front of the general.

Sam cleared his throat. He could not think of anything else to do. Hawkins turned; his expression was not pleasant. Somehow absent was that welcoming, manly bond of recognition between comrades at arms.

'You little pricky-shits have been busy, haven't you?'

Painfully, Devereaux swung his legs over the side of the bed and touched his left eye. He touched it gently, mainly because he could barely see out of it. 'I may be a shit, General, but I'm not so little, as one day I hope to prove to you. Christ, I hurt.'

'*You* want to prove something' - Hawkins gestured at the papers and allowed himself the inkling of a cynical grin 'to *me*? With what you *know* about me? You've got moxie, boy. I'll say that for you.'

'That phrase is about as antediluvian as you are,' muttered Sam as he stood up. Unsteadily. 'You enjoying the reading material?'

'It's some goddamned record! They'll probably want to make another movie about me.'

'Leavenworth Productions. Film processed in the prison

61

laundry. You *are* a bona fide fruitcake.' Devereaux pointed to a blanket draped over the door covering the pane of unidirectional glass. 'Is that smart?' He gestured at the blanket.

'It's not dumb. It confuses them. The oriental mind has two very pronounced pressure points: confusion and embarrassment.' Hawkins's eyes were level.

The statement startled Sam. Perhaps it was Hawkins's choice of words, or maybe the quiet intelligence behind the voice. Whatever it was, it was unexpected. 'I mean it's a little useless; the room is bugged. Bugged, hell! All they have to do is push a red button and they can hear everything we say.'

'Wrong, soldier,' replied the general as he got out of the chair. 'If you *are* a soldier and not a goddamn lace-pants. Come here.' Hawkins walked over to the blanket and folded back, first, a corner on the right, then the opposite section of the cloth on the left. In both small areas were barely visible holes in the wall, now very visible with wet toilet paper shoved into the centres. Hawkins dropped the two sections of the blanket and then pointed to six additional plugs of wet toilet tissue – two on each wall, upper and lower - and grinned his leather-lined grin. 'I've gone over this fucking cell palm-spread by palm-spread. I've blocked out each mike; there aren't any others. Naturally, I didn't touch 'em before. See how careful the goddamn monkeys were? Even got one right over the pillow in case I talked in my sleep. That was the toughest to spot.'

Grudgingly, Sam nodded his approval. And then he thought of the obvious. 'If you *have* plugged every one, they'll race in here and move us. You should realize that.'

'You should think better. Electronic surveillance in close areas is wired terminally into a single unit. First, they'll figure they've got a short in the unit circuit, which will take 'em an hour to trace   if they don't have to break down the walls and can do it with sensors   and that'll confuse 'em. Then, if they rule out a short, they'll guess *I* plugged 'em and that'll embarrass 'em. Confusion and embarrassment; the pressure points. It'll take 'em another hour to figure how to

62

get us somewhere else without admitting error. We've got at least two hours. So you better do some pretty fine explaining in that time.'

Devereaux had the distinct feeling that he had better be capable of some pretty fine explaining. Hawkins was a wily pro and Sam did not relish any confrontation. Certainly not physical or, he was beginning to suspect, mental.

'Don't you want to hear about Regina Greenberg?'

'I've read your notes. You've got lousy handwriting.'

'I'm a lawyer; all lawyers have lousy handwriting. It's part of the bar exam. Also I didn't intend to have them typed up.'

'I should hope not,' said Hawkins. 'You've also got a dirty mind.'

'You've got terrific taste.'

'I don't discuss former wives.'

'They've discussed *you*,' countered Sam.

'I know the girls. You didn't get anything you could use. Not from the girls, you didn't. Anything else you got is none of my business.'

'Do I detect a moral position?'

'In my own crude way. I got a little class, boy.' Hawkins pointed to the desk; his arm, hand, and extended finger all were very steady. 'Now, start explaining that stuff.'

'What's there to explain? You've read it, you say. Do I have to tell you that it represents an airtight case of *persona non grata* on one side, and a large embarrassment for the other? If I do, I just have.' Devereaux touched his eye; it hurt like hell, so he sat down again on the bed.

'That stuff in Indochina,' growled Hawkins, walking to the desk and picking up the stapled pages, 'it's written up like I was working for the fucking gooks!'

'I wouldn't go that far. It raises certain questions as to your methods of operation —'

'That's going *that* far, boy!' interrupted the general. 'I was either working for 'em or working with *both* sides, or just pocketing half the pouch money in Southeast Asia! *Or* I was so *dumb* I didn't know what I was doing at all!'

'*Ahh!*' sang Sam in a lilting, false tremolo. 'Now we are

beginning to understand, said Alice to Cock Robin. A military, really military, man with two Congressional Medals of Honour is a dubious bet for traitor. But all that combat, all those banging noises and that scurrying behind the lines and capture and torture and primitive means of brutal survival – the cumulative effect of all *that* would certainly flip out said hero right into laughing land. Very sad, but the human psyche can take only so much.'

'Horseshit!' roared Hawkins. 'My head's screwed on a hell of a lot tighter than those fuckers who asked for all this crap!'

'Two points for the general,' said Devereaux, holding up his fingers in the *V* sign. 'I hereby state for the record that the general's head is screwed better than anyone at Sixteen-hundred. And, I might add, so is the general.'

'What does that mean, boy?'

'Oh, come on, Hawkins. You're finished! How and why it happened, I don't know. I just know that you got in the way at a rotten time; you made too much noise and you are *expendable*! Not only expendable, but a goddamned pawn that Sixteen-hundred's giving up loud and clear. You're even an *example*!'

'Horseshit, again! Wait'll the Pentagon gets wind of this!'

'They've – *it's* – already got its nostrils full. The brass noses are colliding with each other, running to the deodorant factories. You don't exist, General! Except maybe as a wayward memory.' Sam got up from the bed. The pain in the eye was spreading throughout his head again.

'You can't sell that and I won't buy it,' said Hawkins defensively, his voice indicating a slightly diminished confidence. 'I've got friends. I've got a career sheet that reads like a recruiting poster. Goddamn it, soldier, I'm a general officer who came up from the ranks – from the fucking mud in Belgium! They won't treat me this way!'

'I'm not a soldier. I'm a lawyer and I'm telling you you've been treated – with several layers of forget-me gas. Those telephotos from your buddies in Peking sealed the whole ball of wax. You've bubbled over.'

'They've got to prove it!'

'They've got that, too. I was given it in a pitch-black wine cellar about an hour ago. By a psychotic holding a candle. A very solid citizen. They've got you.'

Hawkins squinted his eyes and removed the chewed, unlit cigar from his mouth. 'How?'

'"Medical records." That's the hard evidence. Psychiatric and physical. "Stress collapse" is only the beginning. The Defence Department will issue a statement that says, in essence, you were purposely placed in ambivalent situations so they could ascertain the development. "Schizoid progression," I think it's called. Conflicting objectives like the Indochina stuff. Also those pictures of you pissing on the mission's roof have a very complicated psychiatric explanation.'

'I've got a *better* one. I was goddamned angry! Wait'll I give my version.'

'You won't get a chance to tell it. If the game plan becomes an issue, the President plans to go on the air, praise your past, show your current medical records – with heartbreaking reluctance, of course – and ask the country to pray for you.'

'Couldn't happen.' The general shook his head confidentially. '*No* one believes a president anymore.'

'Maybe not, but he's got the buttons. Not his own, maybe, but enough others. You'll be strapped down in a Nike silo, if he says so.' Sam saw that there was a metal mirror in the small cubicle that housed the toilet. He walked towards the door.

'But why should he *do* it? Why would anyone *let* him do it?' Hawkins's cigar was held limply in his hand.

Devereaux looked at the size and hue of the shiner over his left eye. 'Because we need gas,' he replied.

'Huh?' Hawkins dropped his cigar on the rug. Obviously without thinking, he stepped on it, grinding it into the surface. 'Gas?'

'It's too complicated. Never mind.' Sam pressed the sensitive flesh around his eye with his fingers. He hadn't had a mouse in over fifteen years; he wondered how long it would

65

take for the swelling to recede. 'Just accept the situation for what it is and make the best deal you can. You haven't got much choice.'

'You mean I'm supposed to lie down and *take* it?'

Devereaux walked out of the toilet, stopped and sighed. 'I'd say the immediate objective was to keep you from lying down in Mongolia. For some four thousand-plus years. If you cooperate, maybe I can pull it off.'

'Out of China?'

'Yes.'

'How much cooperation? With the gooks *and* Washington?' Hawkins's squint was very pronounced.

'A lot. All the way down the pike.'

'Out of the army?'

'No point in staying. Is there, really?'

'Goddamn!'

'I agree. But where does it get you? There's a big world out of that uniform. Enjoy it.'

Hawkins crossed back to the desk in angry silence. He picked up one of the photographs, shrugged and dropped it. He reached into his pocket for a fresh cigar. 'Goddamn, boy, you're not thinking again. You're a lawyer, maybe, but like you say, you're no soldier. A field commander sucks in a hostile patrol, he doesn't feed it, he cuts it down. Nobody's going to let me enjoy. They'll put me in that Nike silo you mentioned. To keep me from talking.'

Devereaux exhaled a long breath through his lips. 'It's just possible I can build a shield acceptable to all parties. After you went down the pike over *here*. Full confession, public apology, the works.'

'Goddamn!'

'Mongolia, General ...'

Hawkins bit into the cigar; the bullet between his teeth, thought Sam.

'What's a "shield"?'

'Off the top of my head, I figure a letter to the secretary of the army, accompanied by a tape of your reading it – verified by voice print. In the letter, *and* the tape, you state that in

moments of complete lucidity you're aware of your illness –
et cetera, et cetera.'

Hawkins stared at Devereaux. 'You're out of your mind!'

'There are a lot of Nike silos in the Dakotas.'

'Jesus!'

'It's not as bad as it sounds. The letter and the tape will be
buried in the Pentagon. Used only if you publicly make
waves. Both to be returned, say, in five years. How about
it?'

Hawkins reached into his pocket for a book of matches.
He struck one and a cloud of pungent smoke nearly fogged
out his face; but his voice was clear behind it. 'Down this
Chinese pike of yours, there's no talk about that psychiatric
bullshit. No one tries to make me out a nut.'

'Hell, no. Nothing like that. Simple fatigue.' Devereaux
paced back and forth in the small enclosure as he so often did
in conference rooms, weaving the fabric of defence. 'A little
booze, maybe; that's sympathetic, even kind of cute when the
client's a ballsy type.' Sam stopped, clarifying his thoughts.
'The Chinese would prefer an ideological approach; it'd
soften them up. You saw the light. They've been generous to
you, nice to you. The People's regime is dandy. *And* tolerant.
You didn't realize that. You're really sorry for all those nasty
things you've said for a quarter of a century.'

'Goddamn! You make me *bleed*, boy!' With a technique
that escaped Sam, Hawkins actually chewed on his cigar as
he roared. And then he removed it and lowered his voice. 'I
know, I know —. The silos or Mongolia. *Jesus!*'

Devereaux watched the man – painfully. He took several
steps towards him and spoke softly. 'You've been squeezed,
General. By righteous pieces of plastic; nobody knows that
better than I do. I've read your file and I agree with maybe one-
fiftieth of what you stand for; in many ways I think you're a
menace. But one thing you're not is a manipulator. And
you're no joke. Remember what you told the girls? You said
everyone's his own inventory. That says a lot to me. So let me
help you. I'm no soldier, but I'm a damned good lawyer.'

Hawkins turned away. In embarrassment, thought Sam.

When the words came, there was a defencelessness about them that made him wince.

'Don't know why I'm so concerned about what anybody says – or why I don't settle for a silo *or* Mongolia. Goddamn, boy, I've spent thirty-some years in this man's army. You take off the uniform – no matter what you put me into – I'm as naked as a plucked duck. I only *know* the army; I don't know anything else, not trained for anything when you come right down to it. Never spent any time with the technological – except little stuff in G-two, things like that. Don't know anything about fancy doings like "negotiations". All I know how to do is fuck up and trap pouch thieves – those Indochina reports are right about that: I outsmarted the KGU, the CIA, the ARVN, and even the sellouts on the Saigon general staff. But that's different. I can handle personnel, I suppose. But they always gave me the misfits, the stockade products; if they'd been civilians they wouldn't be allowed on the streets. I was always good with them. I could control those devious bastards; I could put myself in their slimy shoes and *use* 'em, *use* their goddamned angling. But there's nothing I can do on the outside.'

'That doesn't sound like the man who said everyone's his own inventory. You're better than that.'

Hawkins turned and faced Sam. He spoke slowly, reflectively. 'Shit, boy. You know what? The only god-damned thing I'm trained for is to be a crook, maybe. And I'd probably fuck that up because I don't give that much of a damn about money.'

'You look for challenges. Talented people always do. Money's a by-product; usually the challenge there is in the amounts, what they represent, not what they can purchase.'

'I guess so.' Hawkins took a deep breath and stretched; his resignation was coming into focus for him, thought Devereaux. He walked past Sam aimlessly, humming the opening notes of *Mairzy-Doats*. Devereaux knew from long experience with clients to let the moment subside, allow the client time to fully accept the decision.

'Wait a minute, boy. *Wait* a minute —.' Hawkins took the

cigar out of his mouth and levelled his eyes with Sam.
'Everybody wants my cooperation. The Chinks, those
assholes in Washington - probably a dozen gas conglomer-
ates. I mean they not only *want* it, they *need* it. So much so
they'll fake records, build a case —. That ball of wax got out
of *control* —'

'Now hold on. What we're faced with —'

'No, *you* hold on, boy! I'm not going to give you a hard
time. I'll make you a better deal than you thought possible.'
Hawkins shoved the cigar between his teeth, his eyes alive,
his voice thoughtful yet intense. 'I'll do exactly - *say* exactly,
whatever you bastards want me to say and do. Word for
word, gesture for gesture. I'll kiss every butt on Son Tai
Square, if you want. But *I* want two things. Out of China *and*
the army - they go together. And one thing more: three days
in the G-two files back in D.C. Just my *own*, nobody else's.
What the hell, I wrote *up* the goddamned things! A last look
at my contributions, all the guards you want. I'll be making
my final evaluations and additions. Standard procedure for
discharging intelligence officers. How about it?'

Sam hesitated. 'I don't know. That stuff's classified —'

'Not to the officer who filed it! Clandestine Operations,
Regulation seven seven five, Statute of Amendments.
Actually, he's *required* to make his final evaluations.'

'Are you *sure*?'

'Never more sure of anything in my life, boy.'

'Well, if it's standard —'

'I just gave you the regulation! It's military bible, boy!'

'Then I can't see any obstacles —'

'I want it in writing. In exchange for that letter and tape
that certifies me so fatigued I eat lizard shit. In fact, *I'll* make
the ultimatum: D.C. ussues me a written order to comply
with CO Reg seven seven five upon my return to the States,
or I'll opt for all the silos in Mongolia! I've still got a lot of
supporters back home. They may be a little squirrelly, but
they're also goddamned noisy.'

MacKenzie Hawkins chuckled; his cigar was a mangled
pulp of itself. It was Sam's turn to squint.

'What are you thinking of?'

'Not a hell of a lot, boy. You just reminded me of something. Everyone *is* his own inventory. The sum of his parts. There may *be* a big goddamned world out there. And a challenge or two.'

PART TWO

This closely held corporation — that is, the company whose investors are few, regardless of capitalization — must have at its financial core men of generous heart and stout courage, who will infuse the structure with their dedication and sense of purpose.

Shepherd's Laws of Economics:
Book CVI, Chapter 38

CHAPTER SEVEN

The People's trial went brilliantly for all concerned. MacKenzie Hawkins was the image of converted, reformed hostility; he was a manly pussycat, playing his role to perfection. On his arrival at Travis Air Force Base in California, he emerged from the plane a stoic figure and spoke clearly into the cameras, and at the crowds of press and lunatic fringers; charming the media and defusing the screeching superpatriots.

He stated simply that there came a time when old soldiers – even youngish old soldiers – should step aside gracefully; times changed and values with them. What was perfidy a decade ago was, perhaps, a proper course of action today. The military man, the military *mind* was not equipped – nor should it be trained – for great international issues. It was enough that the military man, a simple warrior in his nation's legions – *sic ... ibid ... in gloria transit ...* MacKenzie Hawkins – adhere to the eternal truths as he saw them.

It was all very refreshing.

It was all very heartfelt.

It was all bullshit.

And Mac Hawkins was superb.

It was remarked that the man in the Oval Office watched from deep down in a sunken armchair with his pet 150-pound dog, Python, protectively on his lap. He laughed and clapped his hands over Python's fur and stamped his feet and giggled and had a wonderful time. His family skipped in and laughed and clapped their hands and giggled and stamped their feet just like daddy. They weren't sure why daddy was so happy, but it was the best fun they'd had since daddy shot

73

that awful little spaniel in the stomach.

Sam Devereaux watched the transformation of Mac-Kenzie Hawkins from roaring bear to passive possum with dubious awe. The Hawk had turned into a soft-bellied mushy-beak, and what was basically lacking was the motive. Not that Sam discounted the spectre of imprisonment — Mongolia *or* Leavenworth – but once Hawkins had agreed to the plea of guilty, the public apology, the *letter* and gratuitous photographs of his bowed head during the hundred-year sentence of probation, he could have merely resumed his military bearing and let whatever storms rage that might. Instead, he went to extremes to still any controversy. It seemed as though he really wanted to fade away (terrible phrase, thought Devereaux).

Naturally, it crossed Sam's mind that Hawkins's behaviour was somehow related to Washington's quid pro quo regarding the G-2 files – the CO Regulation 775, and MacKenzie's access to them. If so, it was an unnecessary effort on the general's part; three intelligence services had looked over the files and found nothing to compromise national security. By and large the entries concerned old-hat Saigon conspiracies, some ancient European network speculations, and a slew of conjectures, rumours, and unsubstantiated allegations – dipsy-doodle nonsense.

If Hawkins honestly believed he could make a compromising dollar – and for what other purpose would he insist on CO 775? – from these out-of-date, unconfirmed recordings, there was no harm in it. What with inflation, the reduced pension he would receive, and the overall untouchability of his status, things were going to be rough enough. So nobody much cared what he did with his old files. Besides, if there was any resulting embarrassment there was also *the letter.*

'Goddamn, it's good to talk to you again, young fella.' MacKenzie's voice was loud and enthusiastic over the telephone, causing Sam to jerk the instrument away from his ear. The gesture was part audio-input, part raw fear of association.

Devereaux had left the Hawk over two weeks ago in California, just after the press conference at Travis. Sam had flown back to Washington, his discharge barely three days off, and he had spent the time wrapping up any and all desk matters that might conceivably — even *barely* conceivably — stand in the way of that glorious hour.

Hawkins wasn't a desk matter, but his mere presence was an abstract threat. On general principles.

'Hello, Mac,' said Sam cautiously. They had dispensed with the military titles at the beginning of the Peking trial. 'You in Washington?'

'Where else, boy? Tomorrow I trek over to G-two for my seven seven five. Didn't you know?'

'I've been pretty busy. There's been a lot to close out here. No reason for anyone to tell me about your seven seven five.'

'I think there is,' replied the Hawk. 'You're escorting me. I thought you knew that.'

There was a sudden, huge lump in the middle of Devereaux's stomach. He absently opened his desk drawer and reached for the Maalox as he spoke. '*Escorting* you? Why do you need an escort? Don't you know the address? I'll give you the address, Mac, I've got it right here. Don't go away. *Sergeant!* Get me the address of G-two Archives! Move your *ass*, Sergeant!'

'Hold on, Sam,' came the soothing words of MacKenzie Hawkins. 'It's just military procedure, that's all. Nothing to get uptight over. Anyway, I *know* the address; you should, too, boy and that's a fact.'

'I don't *want* to escort you. I'm a *lousy* escort! I said good-bye to you in California.'

'You can say hello again over dinner. How about it?'

Devereaux breathed deeply. He swallowed the Maalox and waved away the WAC who was his sergeant-secretary. 'Mac, I'm sorry, but I *do* have a number of things to finish up. Maybe at the end of the week; anytime actually - the day after tomorrow. At sixteen hundred hours to be precise.'

'Well, Sam, I thought we ought to go over the G-two routine for tomorrow morning. I mean you *have* to be there, son. It's in the orders. We wouldn't want anything fucked up over there, would we? *Jesus!* They wouldn't let either one of us out then.'

'Where do you want to have dinner?' asked Devereaux. He grimaced. The Maalox bottle was empty.

You're escorting me. I thought you knew that . . . It's in the orders. We wouldn't want anything fucked up over there, would we?

No, we certainly would not. Devereaux shook his head. A couple in the next booth were staring at him. He stopped and grinned foolishly; the couple whispered to each other and looked away. Their reaction was clear: You never knew who was being sentenced next.

A tall man came through the curtained arch across the room. It was Sam's turn to stare. In awe.

It was the Hawk. He was sure of it. But the tall man threading his way politely through the crowded room bore little resemblance to the dishevelled, cigar-chewing Mac-Kenzie Hawkins who had squinted at him through the glass of a Peking cell. And even less to the close-cropped Hawkins who stood ramrod straight at all times and took each step as though marching to the tune of a thousand pipers - against a strong wind.

To begin with there was the Van Dyke beard. Granted it was new, but the definition was clear and exceedingly well groomed. As was the hair; it was not only growing out, but it had been shaped by tonsorial hands so that the grey swept over the ears in waves. Very, very distinguished. And the eyes - well, one could not really see the eyes because they were covered by tinted, tortoiseshell glasses, a very light tint that was more academic, or diplomatic, than mysterious.

And the man's walk. Good God! Hawkins's ramrod military posture had been replaced by a tasteful, goddamn it, *elegant grace*. There was a softness about the whole bearing,

76

a kind of casual glide that was more Palm Beach than Fort Benning.

'I saw you watching me,' said the Hawk as he slid into the booth. 'Not bad, eh, boy? Not one of those pricky-shits stopped me. How about that?'

'I'm astonished,' answered Sam.

'You shouldn't be, son. First thing you learn in infiltration is adaptability. Not just terrain, but a good-sized accent on local customs and behaviour. It's a form of psycho-war.'

'What the hell are you talking about?'

'Behind the lines, Sam. This is enemy territory, don't you know that?'

By the time Mac Hawkins had elegantly spooned his iced vichyssoise he had reached the heart - the core the bombshell of his reason for dinner with Sam. It was explosively capsuled in a single name.

Heseltine Brokemichael. Late Major General of Command, Bangkok. Currently in limbo, Washington, D.C.

'Yes, Sam, old Brokey was with me in Korea and points east and south. Damn fine officer; a little hot-headed, but then he always had to contend with that stupid bastard cousin of his. What's that idiotic name of his? Ethelred? Can you imagine? *Two* Brokemichaels in the same goddamned army, both with freak names!'

'I'm not hungry any more,' said Devereaux quietly. The Hawk continued.

'Yes, sir, you really laid the heavy mortar on Brokey's career. He couldn't get another star on his collar if he bought all the astrologers in the Pentagon. You see, they can never be *sure*; one of the goddamned Brokemichaels is a crook, but, of course, you never proved that, either.'

'They wouldn't let me!' Devereaux's whisper carried farther than he cared to think about. The couple in the next booth stared again. Sam grinned again. 'I had the evidence; I built the case. They made me drop it!'

'And a good man was cut down just when the joint chiefs were looking kindly on him. I tell you, it's a pity.'

'Get off it, Mac. I had that bastard cold '

77

'The wrong bastard, boy. And even then you committed serious crimes to get your so-called evidence.'

'I took a calculated risk because I was damned angry. I paid for it with two years of my life in that cockadoodle uniform. And that's *it*. I want out.'

'That's too bad. I mean, I'm sorry to hear you say that because you may have to spend a little more time over at IG if I —'

'*Hold it!*' interrupted Devereaux in a whisper that bordered a roar. 'I'm out the day after tomorrow! Nothing, *nothing's* going to change that!'

'I certainly hope not. Let me finish. You *may* have to spend time if I can't talk old Brokey out of this crazy idea of his. You see, those charges against you in Bangkok weren't actually dropped; they were sort of suspended because of the complicated circumstances, and what with all those peace freaks screaming against the military. Now, Brokey doesn't hold anything against you, Sam, but he'd really like to clarify his own status, you can understand that. He figures that if he resurrects those charges, you can dig up the files and get the *right* Brokemichael — you'd *have* to or be on a rock pile — and he'd have the JCS smiling nicely on him, just like they used to. Wouldn't take more than, say, six or seven months. A year at the outside — *maybe* eighteen months if the trial was a long one, but you'd both get what you want —'

'I want *out*! That's *all* I want!' Sam wrung his napkin so tightly it squeaked. 'I *paid* for my moral indignation. It's *past.*'

'Past for you, boy. Not old Brokey.'

'The facts are *there*. I made a goddamned apology; it's in writing. The day after tomorrow, after sixteen hundred hours, I'll dictate a statement — to a civilian secretary — recapping the whole thing in one-syllable words. I will *not* reopen that case!'

'You will if old Brokey pulls out a certain Bangkok file and issues a directive for your arrest. He *is* a general officer, Sam. Even though he may have pulled duty cleaning out the fucking high-brass latrines, for all I know.'

Hawkins had pursed his lips, tsking, and shaking his head slowly; the wide, innocent eyes behind the tinted glasses, conveyed anything but innocence.

'All right, Mac. Game time is over. You said, *if* you couldn't talk Brokemichael out of this nonsense. *Can* you talk him out of it?'

'Either talk him out of it, or remove him from the scene for a couple of days. Yes, I can do one or the other. Once you've got that discharge, boy, Brokey'd have a hell of a time convincing anyone to go after you. That paper's sort of a statute of limitations, you know. But I don't have to tell *you* that.'

'No, you don't. Just tell me what rotten thing you want from me.'

The Hawk removed his tinted glasses and, elegantly, wiped the non-prescription lenses as though he were polishing jade. 'Well, as a matter of fact, I've been giving a lot of thought to my immediate future. And I think there's a place for you, but I'm not sure.'

'Don't ever be. Next week I'll be back at my desk in Boston with Aaron Pinkus Associates, the best law firm in the Bay State.'

'Well, you could take an extra few weeks. Say a month, couldn't you? *Jesus*, boy, it's been four years; what's another month?'

'Aaron Pinkus will one day be on the Supreme Court. Every day with him is an education and I'm not giving up thirty years of paid education. What do you mean, you think there's a place for me? Doing what?'

'I may need an attorney. I think you're the best I ever met.'

'I'm probably the only one you've ever met —'

'But you've got a few weak spots, young fella,' interrupted Hawkins, replacing his tinted glasses. 'I'm sorry to say that, but it's a fact. So I don't know whether to hire you or not. I have to ponder some more about you.'

'In the meantime, you'll keep Brokemichael out of the picture?'

'And you'll give some consideration to acting as my

79

attorney? Just for a couple of weeks? You see, I've got a little money saved up —'

'I know exactly how much money you've got,' broke in Devereaux sympathetically. 'I *had* to. You want advice for investments?'

'Sort of —'

'Then without qualification I'll help you. I mean that.' Sam did. After a lifetime of devotion, risk, and service, Mac had managed to amass a sum total of fifty-odd thousand dollars. No other assets whatsoever. No houses, real estate, stocks. Nothing. That and a reduced pension was all he had for the rest of his life. 'And if I can't give you the advice I think you should have, I'll find someone else who can.'

'That's mighty touching, son.'

Was there a hint of a glistening tear in this tough old-line officer's eyes? It was difficult to tell with the tinted glasses.

'It's the least I can do. It may sound corny, but it's the least any taxpayer can do for you. You've given a lot, and you've been shafted by the plastic men. I know that.'

'Well, boy,' said Hawkins, inhaling deeply, heroically, 'everyone does what he has to do in this world. At a given moment of time — *Ouch!* This goddamn faggot suit is tighter than a Memorial Day uniform.' The Hawk pulled out a folded, faded magazine from his breast pocket. The pages showing were dog-eared and marked with red pencil.

'What's that?' asked Devereaux.

'Oh, some Chincom propaganda the slants left in my cell. It's the standard Commie crap, misspelled English and all. This is an article that's supposed to show the kind of injustice that's widespread in organized religion. This here Catholic pope has a first cousin – kind of like the Brokemichaels in a way, except they don't have the same names – but they look alike. Actually they're identical, except that this pope's cousin grows a beard to hide the likeness.'

'I don't understand. Where's the injustice?'

'This cousin is a small-time singer in a minor opera company and half the time he's out of work. The Chincoms make the obvious comparison. The singer sings his heart out for the people's culture and starves half to death, while his pope cousin eats like a guinea gourmet and steals from the poor.'

'It interested you so much you marked it up?'

'Hell, no, boy. I just picked out the inaccuracies to show this priest friend of mine. It may surprise you, but I've been doing a little studying about things I haven't thought much about before. God, and the church, and things like that —. Don't you laugh, now.'

Devereaux smiled gently. 'I'd never laugh at a thing like that. I don't think it's anything to laugh at. A man's religious thoughts are not only his constitutional right, but often his very real sustenance.'

'That's a mighty nice way to phrase it. Real deep, Sam. By the way, just one thing about this Brokemichael business. Tomorrow morning at G-two. Keep your fucking mouth shut and do as I say.'

Hawkins was waiting under the canopy when Sam pulled up to the kerb in front of the hotel. He held what looked like a very expensive briefcase in one hand, opened the car door with his other and slid in. There was a broad grin on his face.

'*Goddamn!* It's a beautiful morning!'

It was not. It was cold and wet and the skies promised a heavy rain.

'Your barometer's a little off.'

'Nonsense! The day - like age - depends on how you feel, boy. And I feel just grand!' Hawkins smoothed the lapels of his tweed suit, adjusted the deep red paisley tie over the modish striped shirt, and ran his fingers delicately over the hair above his ears.

'Glad you're in such good spirits,' said Sam, starting up the car and entering the flow of traffic. 'I don't want to dampen them but you can't take a briefcase with you. You can't remove any papers. Nothing leaves the G-two offices.'

Hawkins laughed. He pulled out a cigar from his shirt pocket. 'Oh, don't worry your legal head about details,' he said, snipping off the end of the cigar with a sterling silver clipper. 'I've taken care of all that.'

'There's nothing to take care of! I'm responsible for you and I've got twenty-four hours to keep my nose clean.' Devereaux took his hostility out on the horn; the sound was returned in good measure by the surrounding vehicles.

'Jesus, you're in a foul temper. You just keep your eyes on the high ground, don't concern yourself with the flanks.'

'Goddamn it, doesn't anybody speak English anymore? What goddamned flanks? What does that mean?'

'It means what I said last night.' MacKenzie spoke as he lighted his cigar. 'Do as I say and don't make waves. By the way, would you like to know the name of the fella in charge of the G-two archives? Well, no reason for you to know, but he's a bright son of a bitch, a real genius. Didn't know what I was doing for the service when I got him out of that prison camp west of Hanoi a few years back. He's a Pointer, too. Can you beat that? Class of forty-seven. Same as me. Goddamn! The coincidences in this world —'

'No! ... No, Mac! No! No, no no! You can't! I won't let you!' Sam attacked the horn again. Viciously hammering on it. At a crippled old lady who was having a difficult time crossing the intersection. The poor, trembling thing sank her head farther into her quivering shoulders.

'Regulation seven seven five makes it clear that a legal escort is just that. An escort. Not an observer. He takes the clandestine operations officer to and from the place of examination, but he's not permitted inside the room. I guess there're a lot of dishonest lawyers, Sam.' MacKenzie took a long, savouring intake of cigar smoke.

'There's another thing that's not allowed in that room, you son of a bitch!' Devereaux slammed his hand in fury on the rim of the horn once more. The crippled old lady was now splayed out in the middle of the street. 'And that's a briefcase!'

'It is, if the officer is making his final contributions. Nobody can see those but the ranking archivist of G-two. It's classified material.'

'There's nothing *in* there!' yelled Sam, pointing at his briefcase.

'How do you know? It's locked.'

Upon entering the offices of army intelligence, Hawkins was escorted quietly, professionally, to the specific room selected for his 775, by two flanking military police. Sam took up the rear. It seemed to Devereaux as formal an exercise as an execution, except that Mac was loose and slightly slouched in his modish tweed suit, not ramrod at all. But once the four of them were inside the room, Hawkins straightened up and replaced his warm civilian tones with the harsh bark of a leather-lined general officer. He ordered the MPs to take Sam into the next room and summon their superior. The MP captains saluted, took Devereaux by the elbows silently into the adjacent room, slammed the door, locked it, checked the corridor, and walked in Wehrmacht unison out into the hallway. They locked that door, too.

He had a vague feeling of *déjà vu*; then he remembered. He'd watched a late night movie on television several weeks ago. *Seven Days in May.* He walked to the single window and looked out. And down. Through the bars. It was four storeys to the street. G-2 wasn't taking any chances with legal escorts from the inspector general's office, he thought.

There was the sound of voices from the next room. And then overly masculine laughter accompanied by eruptions of profanity. Old comrades-in-arms recalling the good old days when everyone got his ass shot off, except the generals. Sam sat down in a chair and picked up a dog-eared, worn-out copy of *Let's Stamp Out V.D. in G-2*, and read.

His reading – which was actually rather fascinating – was suddenly interrupted by the steady repetition of another sound from the examination room.

Therump-chump. Therump-chump. Therump-chump.

Devereaux swallowed several times, annoyed with himself for leaving his antacid tablets in the car. The sound he was hearing could not be confused with any other sound in his

83

frame of reference, no matter how hard he tried. It was a Xerox machine.

Why would an examination room for the processing of eyes-only classified files have a Xerox machine?

On the other hand, why wouldn't it?

The first question was infinitely more logical. A Xerox machine was a contradiction – in spirit and in fact – to the purpose of Regulation 775.

Sam went back to his reading, unable to keep his mind even on the pictures.

An hour and twenty minutes later the *therump-chumping* stopped. Several minutes after that a metallic crack of a lock was heard and the door of the examination room was opened. MacKenzie emerged carrying his expensive briefcase, now bulging and strapped together with shining steel G-2 bands, and a foot-long steel chain dangling from the crossbar.

'What the hell is that?' asked Devereaux from the chair, apprehensively and not at all kindly.

'Nothing,' replied the Hawk casually. 'Just some Fleet-Pac-Com-Sat transfer files.'

'And what the hell is that?'

'*Major,*' continued MacKenzie, raising his voice, standing suddenly very erect. 'I present Brigadier General Beryzfickoosh! *Atten ... hut!*'

Devereaux shot up from the chair and snapped his hand in salute as a barrel-chested officer with twelve rows of ribbons, an eye patch and, Sam swore, a fright wig on his head, walked swiftly into the room. The salute was returned with a vibrating flourish; the officer then extended a large, muscular hand.

'Hear you're up for discharge, Major,' said the general gruffly.

'Yes, sir,' answered Devereaux, gripping the outstretched hand.

At which instant Hawkins slapped the briefcase chain over Sam's wrist, securing the triple combination lock between the links, and barked, 'First transfer completed, General!'

'*Confirmed*, sir!' shot back the general, still holding Devereaux's hand in an iron grip, his one eye staring at Sam. 'Fleet-Pac-Com-Sat is now in your custody, Major! Prepare for second transfer!'

'For what, General?'

'Say!' The general released Sam's hand. 'Aren't you the legal prick who shafted old Brokey Brokemichael?'

Devereaux's stomach was suddenly in agony; perspiration formed instantly on his forehead, as the heavy briefcase pulled him halfway to the floor. 'There are two sides to that story, sir.'

'Goddamned right!' shouted the general. 'Brokey's and some shit-ass noncombatant's who *should* be on a stockade rock pile!'

'Now, just a minute, General —'

'*What*, soldier? You being *insubordinate*?'

'No, sir. Not at *all*, sir. I would just like to point out —'

'Point *out*!? You point your ass in the direction of that door and secure the transfer of Fleet-Pac-Com-Sat, or I'll point you right into a court-martial! For insubordination *and* incompetence!'

'Yes, sir! Right away, sir!' Sam tried to salute but the chain and the briefcase were too heavy, so he made a rapid about-face and headed for the door, which was miraculously opened by the two MP captains.

The formalities at the entrance desk were over with quickly. The steel G-2 bands securing the briefcase were some kind of symbol of authority. Devereaux signed the checkout book and the miniature camera silently took his photograph.

Out on the street, Sam turned to the Hawk. 'That guy's crazy! Another ten seconds he would have thrown me into solitary! For *what*?'

'Old Brokey's got a lot of friends,' said MacKenzie. 'Here, I'll drive.'

'Thanks.' Devereaux reached awkwardly into his pocket and gave Hawkins the keys, his hand still trembling. They walked to the parking lot and got in the car.

Fifteen minutes later, in the middle of a Washington traffic jam, Sam's nerves began to calm down. His panic at being faced with a weird, apoplectic general screwing up his discharge at the last minute was fading. But that concern was being inexorably replaced with another very genuine fear. Brought about partially by the Hawk's silence.

'Mac, now that this pile of fleet-kumquats is in my custody, what the hell am I supposed to do with them? Where's this second transfer taking place?'

'Don't you know?'

'Of course not.'

'The general thinks you do.'

'Well, I *don't*!'

'You want to go back and ask him, Sam? Personally, I don't recommend it. Not with the way he feels about you. *Jesus!* He might dig up all kinds of very serious violations. And you just got your picture taken. One thing always leads to another, you know what I mean? Like the domino theory. Your trial could last for a year or two.'

'*What the hell's in here, Hawkins?* Don't bullshit me! What *is* it?'

'Sorry, Sam. I'm afraid I can't discuss it. You understand, boy. It's classified.'

Sam sat forward on the couch, his arm stretched out over the coffee table. MacKenzie manipulated the hacksaw back and forth over the chain.

'Once I get this goddamned chain off, we can work on the lock,' said Mac comfortingly. 'It would be easier with a small blowtorch.'

'Not on *my* arteries, you son of a bitch! And thanks for not telling me you didn't have the combination.'

'Now, don't worry, I'll have it off in ten or fifteen minutes. The steel's a touch harder than I figured.'

An hour and fourteen minutes later the last links were severed, leaving one dangling chain and a triple combination lock around Devereaux's wrist.

86

'I've got to get in touch with my office,' Sam said. 'They'll expect me to check in.'

'No, they won't. You're with me. Covering my seven seven five. That's what the agreement states. One day minimum, three days maximum.'

'But we're not there.'

'We went to lunch ...' MacKenzie cleared this throat.

'I should still telephone —'

'*Goddamn*, you've no faith in me at *all*! Why the hell do you think I waited until this morning before going to G-two? You've got one day left and *I* account for your time. You can't get in trouble if you're not *there*.'

'Of course not. No trouble – just a firing squad.'

'Nonsense.' Hawkins got up from the floor, carrying the freed briefcase to the hotel writing desk. 'You're safer with me. I know those IG close-outs. You think you're winding everything up and some pricky-shit waltzes in and tells you you're not going anywhere until some brief is completed.'

Devereaux looked over at the general, now snapping the G-2 bands and opening the expensive briefcase. There was logic in Mac's madness. There *was* sure to be some ball-breaking file or other that a confused superior did not care to have left in his lap. A memorandum could be misplaced – or not read. A confrontation, even a discussion, between legal officers could not be overlooked. Hawkins definitely had a point: Sam was safer away from the office.

MacKenzie removed several hundred Xeroxed pages and put them on the desk beside the briefcase. Devereaux pointed to them and spoke cautiously, 'That's all *your* seven seven five?'

'Well, not exactly. A lot of it's open stuff that's never been closed out.'

Sam was suddenly more uncomfortable than he had been for the past three hours. 'Wait a minute. You said back at G-two that it was just raw material on people you'd run across.'

'Of people *other* people ran across. I added that, son, I really did. You were just so upset you didn't listen.'

87

'Oh, Christ! You removed raw files on subjects that weren't *yours*?'

'No, Sam,' replied the Hawk as he squared off some pages. '*You* did. It says so right at the security desk. Your signature.'

Devereaux sank back in the couch. 'You devious son of a bitch.'

'That kind of says it,' agreed Hawkins sadly. 'There were times in the field – operating way the hell behind the lines, of course – when I wondered how I could bring myself to do the things I did. But then the answer was always the same. I was trained to survive, boy. And survive I do.' The Hawk now had four piles of Xeroxes neatly to the left of the briefcase on the desk. He tapped his fingers over them as if playing a piano and then looked over at Sam pensively. 'I think you're going to do real fine. You *will* accept the temporary appointment as my attorney, won't you? It won't be for long.'

'And it's a little more complicated than investments, isn't it?' Devereaux remained well back in the couch.

'A mite, I suspect.'

'And if I refuse I don't even have to worry about Brokemichael. He's minor. Now there's a small matter of removing classified files from G-two. No statute of limitations on that little caper.'

'Don't imagine there is.'

'What do you want me to do?'

'Work up some contracts. Pretty simple stuff, I should think. I'm forming a company. A corporation, I guess you'd call it.'

Sam inhaled deeply. 'That's really kind of amusing, if it weren't so sad. Purpose and intent notwithstanding, there's a not-so-minor item called capitalization required when you form a corporation. I know your finances. I hate to disabuse you but you're not exactly in the corporate assets league.'

'No faith, that's your trouble. I expect you'll change.'

'And what does that cryptic remark mean?'

'It means I've got the assets figured out to the dollar, that's

88

what it means.' Hawkins planted his fingers over the Xeroxes in an elongated press. As if he had found the Lost Chord.

'What assets?'

'Forty million dollars.'

'*What!*' In his stunned disbelief, Sam leaped up from the couch. The dangling steel chain followed swiftly and, in a howling instant of pain, the bottom links whipped across his eye.

His left eye.

The room went around and around.

CHAPTER EIGHT

Devereaux ripped open the envelope the instant he closed the hotel door. He pulled out the rectangular slip of heavy paper and stared at it.

It was a cashier's cheque made out to his name. The amount was for ten thousand dollars.

It was absurd.

Everything was absurd; nothing made any sense at all.

He had been a civilian for exactly one week. There had been no hitches regarding his discharge; no Brokemichael surfaced, and no last-minute problems developed in the office because he had not gone to the office until an hour before his formal separation from the army. And when he arrived he not only had a patch over his left eye, but a thick bandage around his right wrist. From burns.

He had moved out of his apartment, sent his belongings to Boston, but did not follow them because a devious son of a bitch named MacKenzie Hawkins stated that he needed 'his attorney' in New York. Therefore Sam had a two-room suite at the Drake Hotel on Park Avenue, reserved and paid for. The suite was leased for a month; Hawkins thought it would be enough time.

For what? Mackenzie was not yet ready to 'spell it out'. However, Sam was not to worry; everything was 'on the expense account'.

Whose expense account?

The corporation's.

What corporation?

The one Sam would soon be forming.

Absurd!

Forty million dollars' worth of delusions that screamed for a frontal lobotomy.

And now a cashier's cheque for ten thousand dollars. Free and clear and no receipt required.

Ridiculous! Hawkins could not afford it. Besides, he had gone too far. People did not send other people (especially lawyers) ten thousand dollars without some kind of explanation. It simply was not healthy.

Sam walked over to the hotel telephone, checked the confusing litany on the pull-out tab beneath the instrument, and placed a call to MacKenzie.

'Goddamn, boy! That's no way to behave! I mean, you might at least say thank you.'

'What the hell for? Accessory to theft? Where did you get ten thousand dollars?'

'Right out of the bank?'

'Your savings?'

'That's right. Didn't steal from anyone but myself.'

'But why?'

There was a slight pause in Washington. 'You used the word, son. I believe you called it a retainer.'

There was a second pause. In New York. 'I think I said I was the only lawyer I knew who had a retainer based in the sort of blackmail that could march me in front of a firing squad.'

'That's what you said. And I wanted to correct that impression. I want you to know I value your services. I surely wouldn't want you to think I didn't appreciate you.'

'Cut it out! You can't afford it and I haven't done anything.'

'Well, boy, I believe I'm in a better position to judge what I can afford. And you *did* do something. You got me out of China some four thousand years before my parole was due.'

'That's different. I mean —'

'And tomorrow's going to be your first day of work,' interrupted the Hawk. 'Not much, but a beginning.'

There was now a long pause in New York. 'Before you say

91

anything, you should understand that as a member of the bar, I subscribe to a canon of ethics that is very specific. I'll do nothing to jeopardize my standing as an attorney.'

Hawkins replied loudly, with no pause whatsoever, 'I should hope not! Goddamn, boy, I don't want any slippery shyster in *my* corporation. Wouldn't look good on the stationery —'

'*Mac!*' roared Devereaux in exasperation. 'You didn't have stationery printed?'

'No. I just said that. But it's a hell of an idea.'

Sam did his best to control himself. 'Please. *Please.* There's a law firm in Boston and a very nice man who'll be on the Supreme Court someday who expects me back in a couple of weeks. He wouldn't look kindly on my being employed by – somebody else during my leave. And you said my work for you would be finished in three or four weeks. So no stationery.'

'All right,' agreed Hawkins sadly.

'Now, what's on for tomorrow? I'll charge you by the day and deduct it from the ten thousand and return the rest at the end of the month. From Boston.'

'Oh, don't worry about that.'

'I *do* worry. I should also tell you that I'm not licensed to practise in the state of New York. I may have to pay outside attorney's fees; depending upon what you want done. I gather it involves filing for this corporation of yours.' Devereaux lit a cigarette. He was happy to see that his hands were not shaking.

'Not yet. We'll get to that in a couple of days. Tomorrow I want you to check out a man named Dellacroce. Angelo Dellacroce. He lives in Scarsdale. He's got several companies in New York.'

'What do you mean "check out"?'

'Well, I undestand he's had business problems. I'd like to know how serious they are. Or were. Sort of find out what his current state of well-being is.'

'"Well-being"?'

'Yeah. In the sense of his being around and not in jail, or anything like that.'

92

Devereaux paused, then spoke calmly, as if explaining to a child. 'I'm a lawyer, not a private investigator. Lawyers only do what you're talking about on television.'

Again MacKenzie Hawkins replied quickly. 'I can't believe that. If somebody wants to become part of a corporation, the attorney for the company should find out if the fellow's on the up-and-up, shouldn't he?'

'Well, it would depend on the degree of participation, I suppose.'

'It's considerable.'

'You mean this Angelo Dellacroce has expressed interest?'

'In a way, yes. But I wouldn't want him to think I was being rude by making inquiries, if you know what I mean.'

Devereaux noticed that his hand now trembled slightly. It was a bad sign; better than a pained stomach but still bad. 'I've got that strange feeling again. You're not telling me things you should tell me.'

'All in good time. Can you do what I ask?'

'Well, there's a firm here in the city that my office uses - used to use, anyway. Probably still does. They might be able to help.'

'That's fine. You see them. But don't forget, Sam, we've got a lawyer–client relationship. That's like a doctor or a priest or a good whore; my name doesn't get mentioned.'

'I could do without the last reference,' said Devereaux.

Damn it. His stomach growled. He hung up.

'Angelo Dellacroce!' Jesse Barton, senior partner, son-of-founder, Barton, Barton, and Whistlewhite, laughed. 'Sam you've been away too long!'

'*That* bad?'

'Let's put it this way. If our mutual Boston friend and your erstwhile employer - I *assume* he's still your employer Aaron Pinkus, thought you were seriously considering Dellacroce for some kind of money deal, he'd call your mother.'

'That bad?'

'I'm not kidding. Aaron would question your sanity and

93

personally remove your name from the office door.' Barton leaned forward. 'Dellacroce is Cosa Nostra with a capital Mafia. He's so high in the charity rackets the cardinal invites him to the Alfred E. Smith dinner every year. And naturally, he's untouchable. He drives district attorneys and prosecutors right out of their gourds. They can't get him, but not for lack of trying.'

'Then Aaron mustn't learn of my very innocent inquiry,' replied Sam in confidence.

'Your indiscretion is safe with me. Incidentally, is it an indiscretion? This party of yours, is he really that naïve?'

Sam's stomach began to answer for him. He spoke rapidly to cover the sound. 'In my judgement, yes. I'm paying back a debt, Jesse. My client saved my ass in Indochina.'

'I see.'

'So he's important to me,' continued Sam. 'And according to you he's naïve. About this Dellacroce.'

'Don't take my word for it,' said Barton, reaching for his telephone. 'Miss Dempsey, get me Phil Jensen downtown, please.' Jesse replaced the receiver. 'Jensen's second in command at the prosecutor's office. Federal district, not municipal. Dellacroce's been a target over there ever since Phil joined; that was damn near three years ago. Jensen gave up an easy sixty thou' to go after the evil people.'

'Commendable.'

'Bullshit. He wants to be a senator or better. That's where the real money is —' The telephone rang. Barton picked it up. 'Thank you ... Hello, Phil? Jesse, I've got an old friend here; he's been away for a few years. He was asking me about Angelo Dellacroce —'

The explosion on the other end of the line reverberated throughout the office. Jesse winced. 'No, for Christ's sake, he's not involved with him. Do you think I'm crazy? ... I told you he's been away; out of the country, as a matter of fact.' Jesse listened for a moment and looked over at Sam. 'Were you in northern Italy? ... Where, Phil? ... Around Milan?'

Devereaux shook his head. Barton continued, one ear at the telephone, his words directed at Sam.

94

'Or Marseilles? ... Or Ankara? ... What about Rashid?'
Devereaux kept shaking his head.

'*Algiers*? ... Were you in Algiers? ... No, Phil, you're way off. This is very straight. I wouldn't be calling you if it was anything else, now would I? ... Simple investment stuff, very legitimate. ... Yes, I know, Phil. ... Phil says those bastards will own Disneyland next. ... Come on, Phil, that's not kosher; he'll simply walk away from him. I just wanted to confirm Dellacroce's status. ... Okay. All right. I've got it. Thanks.'

Barton replaced the phone and leaned back. 'There you are.'

'I touched a raw nerve.'

'The rawest. Dellacroce not only skipped free of an airtight indictment last week, but because of a grand jury leak, the prosecutor's office has to issue a public apology. How does that grab you?'

'I'm glad I'm not Jensen.'

'Jensen's not. His office will lay off Dellacroce for a couple of months then ring him in again. Won't do them any good; Dellacroce's got his ass in butter. He slides in and out of courtrooms.'

'But my client should stay away.' Devereaux did not ask a question.

'Several continents,' replied Barton. 'Clothes don't make the man; his investors do. Ask anyone from Biscayne to San Clemente.'

'Well, goddamn, isn't that interesting? You just can't tell anymore, can you?'

'Stay clear of him,' said Devereaux, shifting the hotel phone and reaching for the glass of bourbon on the other side of the desk. 'He's bad news and you don't want him near you.'

'I see what you mean —'

'I'd rather you said "Yes, Sam, I'll stay away from Angelo Dellacroce." That's what I'd like to hear you say.'

'See what you mean.'

'You're not listening. When you pay a lawyer a retainer

you listen to him. Now, repeat after me: "I will not go near —"'

'I know you've had a hard day, but you might put your mind to the next order of business. Just sort of think about it.'

'I'm still thinking about Angelo Dellacroce.'

'That part's finished with —'

'Glad to hear it.'

'– for the time being. Now, I want you to begin roughing out a kind of standard corporation agreement. A real legal document that has blanks for people putting in money.'

'People like Dellacroce?' Devereaux's voice made clear his position.

'*Goddamn*, forget about that guinea bastard!'

'From what I know about him I think you should refer to him as the Roman-blood-royal. But I'd rather you never referred to him again. What kind of corporation? If you want it filed in New York, I'll have to bring in another attorney. I told you that.'

'*No, sir, boy!*' Hawkins shouted the words. 'I don't want anyone else involved! Just you!'

'I made it very clear: I'm not licensed to practise here. I can't file in the state of New York.'

'Who said anything about filing? I just want the papers.'

Sam was numb. He was not sure what he was supposed to say; what he could say: 'Do you mean to tell me you retained me for ten thousand dollars to prepare legal papers you are not going to execute - strike that - *file?*'

'Didn't say I wouldn't sometime. I'm just not going to worry about it now.'

'Then why get a lawyer until you need one? And why the hell am I in New York?'

'Because I don't want you in Washington. For your own good. And when a man raises money for a corporation, he's got to have real legal-looking documents to give for it. I reversed the order of your questions.'

'I'm glad you told me. I won't pursue either one. What kind of corporation?'

96

'A regular one.'

'There's no such thing. Every company is different.'

'The kind where profits are shared. Among investors.'

'In that they're all the same. Or should be.'

'That's the kind I want. No monkey business.'

'Wait a minute.' Devereaux put down the phone and crossed to the chair where he'd left his attaché case. From it he took out a yellow legal pad and two pencils and returned to the desk. 'I'll need the specifics. I'm going to ask you some questions so I can rough out this not-to-be-filed, unexecuted legal document.'

'Go ahead, boy.'

'What's the title? The corporate name.'

'I thought about that. What do you think of the Shepherd Company?'

'Not a hell of a lot. I don't know what it means. Not that it makes any difference. Call it anything you like.'

'I like the Shepherd Company.'

'Fine.' Sam wrote out the words. 'What's the address?'

'United Nations.'

Devereaux looked at the telephone. 'What?'

'The address. Whatever the United Nations building is.'

'Why?'

'It's ... symbolic.'

'You can't use a symbolic address.'

'Why not?'

'I forgot. You're not filing. All right. The depository?'

'Who?'

'The bank. Where the corporate funds will be deposited.'

'Leave that blank. A couple of lines. There'll be several banks.'

Sam's pencil involuntarily stopped. He forced it onward. 'What's the purpose of the company?'

There was a pause in Washington. 'Give me some legal-sounding choices.'

Now a longer pause in New York. Devereaux's pencil really objected. 'Let's start with "intent".'

'Obviously, to make money.'

97

'How?'

'By having something people will pay for.'

'Manufacturing? Production of merchandise?'

'No, not really.'

'Marketing?'

'That's nearer. Keep going.'

'Where?'

'Some more words,' replied Hawkins.

'I'm not a corporate attorney but if I remember the books, a company's purpose – its motive for profit – is in one form or another of production, manufacturing, marketing, acquisition, services —'

'Hold it! That one.'

'Services?'

'That's good, but I mean the one before that.'

Sam exhaled. 'Acquisition?'

'That's it. Acquisition.'

'Acquiring at one price, disposing at a second, higher price. You're in brokerage?'

'That's very good, Sam. That's really using the old noodle.'

Devereaux pushed the pencil against its inanimate will and wrote on the pad. 'If you're a broker, there's got to be a product. Services or real estate or merchandise —'

'Of a deeply religious nature,' interrupted MacKenzie, his voice low and solemn.

'What is?'

'The product.'

Sam inhaled; it was a long breath. When he exhaled it was with a hum. 'Are you saying that you are forming a company to broker the acquisition of religious merchandise?'

'That'll do,' answered Hawkins simply.

'Artifacts?'

'That's even better.'

'For Christ's sake, *what* is?'

'"Broker the acquisition of religious artifacts." Goddamn, boy. Perfect!'

*

98

Devereaux borrowed the standard New York State forms for a limited partnership agreement from Barton. It was a relatively simple matter to transcribe his notes into the partnership forms and have the hotel stenographer re-type the pages as though they had been dictated. Things were looking up, thought Sam as he scrutinized the finished product, replete with its blank lines for investors, depositories, amounts; and the inane description of 'brokering the acquisition of religious artifacts'.

But it looked as legal as a chapter in Blackstone. Yes, Sam mused as he balanced the envelope containing the gobbledygook he was about to mail to MacKenzie Hawkins. Things *were* looking up. He'd be back in Boston with Aaron Pinkus Associates in a few days; his 'legal' work for the Hawk was finished. Altogether it had taken him nine days, some three weeks short of the month Mac had figured.

He had agreed to stay at the Drake a day or two longer, giving Mac sufficient opportunity to approve of his labours. There was no question that approval would come, and it did.

'My word, Sam, that's a mighty impressive looking document,' said the Hawk over the telephone from Washington. 'I'm downright amazed you were able to write it all up so quickly.'

'There are certain guidelines to follow; it wasn't that difficult.'

'You're too modest, young fella.'

'I'm anxious, that's what I am. Anxious to get back to Boston —'

'I can certainly understand that,' broke in Hawkins without the commensurate affirmative that would have curtailed the sudden, growing pain in Devereaux's stomach.

'*Listen*, Mac —'

'I see you made me president of the company. You didn't tell me that.'

'There were no other names. I asked you about the corporate officers and you said leave the lines blank.'

'What are those titles *secretary* and *treasurer*? Are they important?'

99

'Not if you're not filing.'

'Suppose someday I decided to?'

'The standard procedure is to combine the two. Most states require a minimum of two general partners for a limited partnership agreement.'

'But I could have more if I wanted to, couldn't I?'

'Certainly.'

'I just wanted to know what's right, Sam. Not important. It's never going to be filed. Just passes the time.'

Devereaux thought he detected a note of melancholy in Hawkins's voice. Was Mac beginning to come to grips with his own fantasies? Did he begin to understand that his irrational foray into corporate legalities was simple compensation for the absence of command decision? Sam began to relax. He actually felt sorry for this old warhorse. *Passes the time* was a euphemism for *filling up the days.* 'I'm sure it does, General.'

'Why, Sam, you haven't called me general in weeks.'

'Sorry. A slip.'

'I'll be in touch with you tomorrow, boy. You've worked hard. Have a little fun tonight. Remember, it's on the expense account.'

'As to that ten thou'. It's very generous of you but I don't want it. I don't need it. I'll deduct whatever legal expenses – stenographer, supplies, that kind of thing – and return the rest. Then there's an investment counsellor I know in Washington —'

Devereaux stopped. He realized that the click on the other end of the line had terminated the conversation.

There was no point in not having a good time. He had spent enough weekends in New York to know where the action was: the singles' bars on Third Avenue.

Sam was spectacularly successful. His catch was a nubile young thing who had come out of Omaha, Nebraska - the county seat of Henry Fonda and Marlon Brando - to scale the Broadway heights. She was terribly impressed with a lawyer who did a lot of work for Metro-Goldwyn-Warner-

Brothers when he wasn't handling contracts for *Dirty Sally* and *Masterpiece Theatre.*

Sam was impressed, too. All during the night, throughout most of the next morning, well into the following afternoon and (with time out for food and limited discussion) into the next evening.

It was 9.27 when the telephone rang; 9.29 when the nubile young thing spoke sleepily. 'Sam, the phone's on my side.'

'You're very observant.'

'Shall I get it?' she asked.

'Since it's on your side, I'd say yes.'

'You're sure?'

Sam opened his eyes. The girl had raised herself and was stretching; the sheet had fallen away. 'Make it quick,' Devereaux said.

'If you're sure.'

'I have no wife and my mother doesn't know where I am and Aaron Pinkus wouldn't be mad. Get the phone, talk fast, and hang up.'

The girl reached for the instrument; Sam reached for the girl.

'There's a man with a raspy voice who wants to talk to you. He says his name is Angelo Dellacroce.' She handed Sam the receiver.

'Hey, *you!*' The words spat from the telephone. 'You Samuel Deverooze, sec'atary-treasurer of this Shepherd Company?'

CHAPTER NINE

Former Lieutenant General MacKenzie Hawkins, twice awarded the nation's highest honour for extraordinary heroism beyond the call of duty in deadly combat against the enemy, cowered like a frightened boy at the sight of former Major Sam Devereaux, military accident.

Hawkins could see Sam getting out of the taxi at the entrance of the North Hampton Golf Club. The brass lamps on top of the stone posts flanking the drive were the only source of light; it was a cold, cloudy night and no moon could be seen. The lamps, however, gave sufficient illumination to reveal the anguished expression on Devereaux's face.

Sam was furious, MacKenzie realized that. But, he thought to himself, he had not actually lied. Not really. He never told Devereaux he *wouldn't* approach Angelo Dellacroce. Only that he had no reason to do so when Sam pressed him on the point. At that moment. Not *later*.

The secretary-treasurer title was something else. It looked terrific on the partnership agreement: *Samuel Devereaux, Esq., Counsellor-at-law, Suite 4-F, Drake Hotel, New York*, right above the line reserved for the second most important office in the Shepherd Company. It was for Devereaux's own good; he'd understand that soon enough. But at the moment Samuel Devereaux, Esq., was mad as a caged bull fenced off from heifers in heat.

The Hawk had agreed to Dellacroce's rendezvous because it suited him. The Italian was so concerned about surveillance he had insisted on meeting Mac in the middle of the fairway on hole six at the North Hampton Golf Club between the hours of midnight and one in the morning. But if

102

Hawkins had objected and changed the location to the Bell Telephone Company, Dellacroce would have capitulated.

For Dellacroce had no choice. Mac had a folder on the Mafioso that would have guaranteed a jail sentence worthy of a court in the People's Republic.

Still, a meeting at night in terrain surrounded by thick woods and streams and small lakes appealed to Hawkins. He was at home in such territory. It wasn't Cambodia or Laos, but he could sort of keep his hand in, as it were.

He flew up from Washington in the afternoon and with false identification rented a car and drove out to North Hampton. As soon as it was dark, he circled the golf club and parked at the west perimeter. Dellacroce had told him that the club was closed for the evening and the night watchman would be replaced by one of his men.

Which meant, of course, that Dellacroce would double the patrols everywhere, especially around the area of fairway six.

His pockets stuffed with coils of thin rope and rolls of three-inch adhesive, Hawkins employed an old Ho Chiminh tactic that had served him well in the past. He began his commando assault at the farthest point inside the hostile area and worked his way towards the front.

At 2300 the enemy patrols started to man their emplacements within the North Hampton Golf Club. There were nine (a few more than Mac had anticipated) spaced out in the rough by the edge of the woods on both sides of fairway six, the line of relay extending back to the clubhouse and the driveway.

One by one, Hawkins immobilized eight patrols; he removed all weapons, bound them, taped their faces – all facial muscles, not just the mouths – and rendered them unconscious with *kai-sai* chops at the base of the skull. Then he worked his way back to the ninth patrol who manned the entrance.

He saved for this man a strategy that was particularly effective against the Pathet Lao. For the guard had to be able to talk.

The man was exceedingly cooperative. Especially after Mac had sliced his trousers from crotch to cuff.

At ten minutes to midnight, Dellacroce's huge black limousine drove swiftly through the gates and up to the wide, pillared porch. In the darkness the ninth patrol, riveted to a pillar, spoke.

'Everything's fine, Mr Dellacroce. All the boys are spread good, like you said.'

The man's voice was a bit high and a little strained, but Hawkins figured rightly that Dellacroce had other things on his mind.

'Okay. Real good,' was the raspy reply as Dellacroce got out of the automobile, flanked by two heavyset bodyguards who walked like gorillas with their hands in their fur. 'Rocco, you stay here with Augie. You, Fingers, you come with me. And, Meat, you get the fuckin' car back in the lot outta sight.'

Before Dellacroce and Fingers had rounded the corner of the building, the ninth patrol was *kai-saied* out of commission. By the time Dellacroce and Fingers had disappeared across the lawn, Rocco had joined Augie in peaceful oblivion.

The gentleman named Meat was Hawkins's next dispatchee. It took nearly five minutes, but only because Meat was an experienced combat man. He did not park the limousine at the edge of the lot; instead, he had pulled to a stop in the centre. It was good positioning, thought Mac. Meat could observe all his flanks unencumbered by visual shadings or sightline obstructions. Meat was good.

But not good enough.

MacKenzie scrambled diagonally out of the parking area, over the first tee, and left through the rough towards fairway six. Since Dellacroce had made it clear he would be alone, Hawkins knew that Fingers would be hiding in the darkness, no doubt at the edge of the woods, and if he had a brain in his head, across the fairway on the east side for a superior line of fire.

But Fingers did not have much savvy. He remained in the

west rough, prone in the underbush, eliminating any rear flank observation.

Goddamn, thought MacKenzie, it was not much fun taking an asshole like Fingers.

Nevertheless, he took him. Silently. In eleven seconds.

Leaving Angelo Dellacroce alone in the middle of fairway six, the lighted end of a cigar protruding from his fat mouth, his squat body sagging at ease, his plump hands clasped behind his back as though waiting to be served a plate of linguini in a slow trattoria.

Three minutes later Devereaux's taxi was heard on the deserted back road fronting the golf club, and MacKenzie waited behind the pillar.

As Sam walked haltingly up the drive, Hawkins decided not to tell him about the immobilized patrols. It would only worry the ex-major; better to let him think Dellacroce was true to his word: he was alone on fairway six.

'God*damn!* Hello, Sam!'

Devereaux threw himself to the ground, hugging the gravel for dear life. And then he looked up; MacKenzie took out a small but powerful pencil light from his pocket and flicked it on.

The ex-major was certainly angry. His face was kind of pinched and puffed, as if it might explode right out of his skin.

'You unprincipled son of a bitch!' Sam whispered, fury and fear intermeshed. 'You lowlife! You're the most devious, despicable form of subhuman that ever lived! What the hell have you done, you *bastard?*'

'Now, now, that's no way to talk. Come on, get up; you look silly down there all splayed out ...' MacKenzie reached for Devereaux's hand.

'*Don't touch me*, you slug worm! Fucking Mongolian sheep is too *good* for you! I should have let Lin Shoo pry out your fingernails, one by one, for four thousand fucking years! Don't *touch* me!' Sam staggered to his feet.

'Look, Major —'

'Don't call me that! I don't own a serial number and I don't want to be addressed *ever* by anything *remotely* military! I'm

105

a lawyer, but I'm not *your* goddamned lawyer! Where the hell are we? How many "torpedoes" have us covered with guns?'

MacKenzie grinned. 'There's nobody, boy. Just Della-croce standing out on the fairway like a nice uncle at a backyard pasta party.'

'I don't believe you! Do you know what that gorilla told me on the phone when I said I wouldn't come out here? That goddamned hood told me my health would take a sudden turn for the worse! That's what he told me!'

'Oh, don't pay any attention to that sort of thing. Those fat slobs always talk tough.'

'Horseshit!' Devereaux peered into the darkness. 'That maniac said if I was late he'd send a basket of fruit to the hospital – *tomorrow*! And if I tried to leave town, some goon called Meat would find me before the week was up!'

The Hawk shook his head. 'Meat's pretty good, but I think you could take him. I'd put my money on you, boy.'

'I don't *want* to take him – or *any*body! And don't put any money on *me*! You're never going to see me again! I just wanted to get this over with. I want to meet this Dellacroce; tell him the whole thing's a crazy mistake! I had some typing done for you, and that's all!'

'Now listen to me, son. You're over-reacting. There's nothing to worry about at all.' Hawkins started walking across the lawn. Devereaux kept pace, his head snapping in the direction of every noise. 'Mr Dellacroce will be exceedingly cooperative. And there'll be no more tough talk, you'll see.'

'What was that?' There was a squishing sound.

'Relax, will you? I think you stepped on some dog turd. Do me a favour. Don't start explaining anything until I talk with Dellacroce, okay? It won't take me more than three or four minutes.'

'*No!* Absolutely *no*! I don't care to have a promising legal career cut short in the middle of a fairway at some Cosa Nostra golf course! These people don't play games! They

106

use bullets, and chains, and heavy cement! And rivers! What was *that?*' There was a fluttering of wings in the dark trees.

'We alarmed a bird. Let's put it this way. If you just keep your mouth shut until I'm finished, I'll pay you another ten thousand. Free and clear. How about that?'

'You're a lunatic! No, again. Because I can't spend it displacing roots in a Boston cemetery! You could offer ten million; the answer's still no!'

'That's not out of the question —'

'For Christ's sake, have yourself committed before somebody else does!'

'Then I'm afraid I'll have to put it this way. You either shut up until my business with Mr Dellacroce is finished, or tomorrow morning I call the FBI and tell them there's an ex-major walking around peddling raw-file intelligence documents he illegally removed from the G-two archives.'

'Oh, no you don't! Because I'll tell the truth. I'll tell them how you blackmailed me, then conned me, then blackmailed me again. You'd get a lighter prison sentence in Peking!'

'It surely does get complicated, doesn't it? I mean you'd be reopening the Brokemichael business. How would it look? A man violates the espionage laws because he doesn't like spending a little extra time in the service of his country. In a cushy job, not even combat. Pretty weak blackmail, I'd say.'

'You *unprincipled* —'

'I know, I know,' said the Hawk wearily. 'You keep repeating yourself. What you've got to understand is that it doesn't make a whole lot of difference to me. As you said, I've been shafted. How much more shafting can they do?'

Hawkins kept walking. Devereaux followed reluctantly, his eyes darting everywhere, his nerves obviously frayed; a series of whispered squeaks emerged from his throat until he found the words. 'Have you no decency, sir? No sense of compassion? No love of your fellowman within your heart?'

'I surely do,' said the Hawk. They cut across the third tee on to fairway six. 'Now keep that eloquent tongue of yours inactive for a while. If you don't like the way things go, then speak your piece. Can I be fairer than that?'

The overcast sky was thinning out; intermittently the moon shone through. And a hundred yards ahead they could see the squat figure of Angelo Dellacroce his hands still clasped behind his back, the lighted stub of a cigar in his mouth.

'He must have ashes all over his front,' said Hawkins quietly. Then louder, 'Mr Dellacroce?'

There was a grunt from the obese body in front of them. MacKenzie flicked on his pencil light and held it over his own head, spilling the light on his longish steel-grey hair, throwing shadows down across his precisely barbered Van Dyke.

'You're making us a target!' whispered Sam.

'Who's going to shoot?'

They approached the Italian; Mac extended his hand. Dellacroce made no move to accept it. Hawkins spoke quietly. 'Even when I accepted gook surrenders I got a handshake. Sort of separates us from the animals.'

Reluctantly Dellacroce pulled his hand from behind his back and the two shook. 'I ain't no gook and this ain't no surrender,' said the raspy voice.

'Course it isn't,' answered MacKenzie brightly. 'It's the beginning of a profitable association. By the way, this is my attorney and good friend, Sam Devereaux —'

'Mac!'

'Shut up and shake hands,' said Hawkins *sotto voce*. 'Goddamn, boys. I said shake *hands*!'

With even greater reluctance, the two hands inched towards each other, touched briefly and separated as though the owners feared infection.

'That's better,' said the Hawk enthusiastically. 'Now we can talk.'

And MacKenzie did. He started by listing the illegal activities - both foreign and domestic - of Angelo Dellacroce. It took him two minutes.

'Now, Mr Dellacroce, the reason the authorities can't catch up with you is that they don't have access to a single

108

financial clearinghouse that ties in specifically with all these here sundry enterprises. I realize it will sound strange to you, sir, but I believe I have that access. There's a bank in Geneva, Switzerland; the first three numbers of the account happen to be seven, one, five. In this account is something over sixty-two million dollars —'

'*Basta! Basta!*'

'– and the deposits were made directly from such locales as I've suggested. Now I guess you've studied the new Swiss laws relative to such accounts. They're tricky because fraud in one country may not constitute fraud in Geneva. But goddamn, would you believe there's now a way for Interpol to subpoena the records of those accounts? All the international police have to do is submit a copy of a payment – to a specific account – that's been made by a convicted narcotics dealer. And it surely is wondrous good fortune on my part to have in my possession Xeroxed copies of quite a few such payments —'

'*Basta!* You shut up!' Dellacroce roared. '*Fingers! Manny! Carlo! Dino!* Get out here! *Now!*'

There were only the sounds of the night in reply.

'There's no one there. At least no one that can hear you,' said the Hawk softly.

'*What?* — *Fingers! Figlio della prostituta!* Get out here!'

Nothing.

'Now, you and I, Mr Dellacroce, will step away from my friend and attorney, here, so we can talk real private-like.' MacKenzie touched the Italian's arm, which was instantly yanked away.

'*Meat! Augie! Rocco!* You hear me, boys? Get out here!'

'They're sleeping, too, sir,' said Hawkins kindly. 'They won't wake up for a couple of hours.'

Dellacroce whipped his head towards Mac. 'You got cops here? How many cops you got?' The questions overlapped.

'Nobody. Just me and my good friend and attorney —'

'How many? Alone you couldn't!'

'Alone, I did,' answered the Hawk.

'My best boys!'

'I'd hate like hell to see your support troops.' MacKenzie chuckled. 'Now it's time for our private talk.'

The Hawk led Dellacroce thirty feet away. He talked quietly for exactly four minutes and thirty seconds.

At which point a rasping, ear-splitting scream shattered the stillness of fairway six.

'*Mannnnaaagggiii'!*'

And Angelo Dellacroce fainted right there on the manicured grass.

MacKenzie bent over the man and gently slapped him back into consciousness.

They talked once more with the Hawk holding the obese Italian's neck as though he were a medical corpsman.

The scream came again.

'*Mannnnaaaaggggiii'!*'

And Dellacroce fainted again.

So the Hawk revived him again.

And they talked for two minutes more.

'*Mannnnaaaagggggiiii!*'

This time MacKenzie lowered the man's head on the grass of fairway six and got up. The moon had broken through the night clouds, revealing a stunned Sam staring at the sight of the fallen Dellacroce. This was it, thought the Hawk, as he walked slowly towards Devereaux. There was no point in procrastinating any longer. Sam would have to be told. There was no other way.

'Well, Sam,' began Mac with quiet confidence in the intermittent moonlight on fairway six, 'it's a pretty good start. Mr Dellacroce was eager to subscribe to the full amount reserved for him. The Shepherd Company has its first ten million dollars.'

Devereaux's knees buckled. The Hawk rushed forward and caught him before he hit the ground. The ground was not hard but MacKenzie wanted Sam to know he cared; it was always a good idea to let one's superior-adjutant know the commander was concerned for his well-being. 'Goddamn, son, you've got to stop this kind of thing! You're behaving no better than Mr Dellacroce! Now that's just not

110

proper; you're cut from a finer tunic!'

Sam's eyes were swimming around and around in the moonlight on fairway six. The words that emerged from his trembling lips were by and large incoherent, but several phrases were repeated often enough to be understood. 'Secretary-treasurer! – Oh, my God, I'm a *sec'atary-treasurer*! Ten million dollars' worth of cement! I'm in ten million dollars' worth of shit! I'll be sunk in concrete pyjamas! I'm *dead*!'

'Now, now, stop your wailin'. You're a big lawyer, fella; you shouldn't act like this.'

'I should never have met you, you squirrelly bastard! That's the only *shouldn't* of my life! Oh, my God! That killer passed out!'

'So did you. Almost. I caught you —'

'*Shhh!* Let's get out of here! I'll send him a letter – I'll get some Bellevue stationery – I'll certify you a fucking lunatic! It was all a lousy joke!'

'Oh, Mr Dellacroce knows better than that, boy!' Hawkins patted Devereaux's cheek with his right hand while, with his left, he kept an iron grip on the base of Sam's skull, inhibiting any movement above the waist. 'Dellacroce's a very religious man, most of these Italian fellas are; doesn't make any difference what they do for a living. That's separate. He knows I told him the truth.'

'What the hell are you talking about? What's religion got to do with anything? Get the fuck off my neck!'

'Religion helps a man recognize the truth. He may not like it; his *religion* may not like it, or even admit it is the truth, but because he's contemplated, the religious man can separate what's real from what's horseshit. You follow me?'

'Not for a goddamned second! My neck hurts!'

'Sorry, I'll ease up, but it's time we talk.' MacKenzie removed his hand. Instantly Devereaux bolted, but the Hawk merely rolled with him, pinning him back to the earth. 'I said we've got to *talk*, boy. You're a reasonable person; you can see the logic in that.'

'The problem,' whispered Sam, straining on the ground,

111

'is that you're *not* reasonable *or* logical! Do you know what you've done? Guys like that —' He gestured with his head; somehow, he could not use his hands. 'They freeze people for welching on their bookies! They think nothing about paying for the biggest funeral in town – for a *paisan* who held out on a skim! I *know*. I'm from *Boston*.'

'You're over-reacting again. Mr Dellacroce won't do anything like that. He knows where he stands – which is roughly in twenty feet of lye if he doesn't behave. That account in Geneva. He stole from his own people.'

Grudgingly, suspiciously, Devereaux stared at Mac in the moonlight. 'You're sure of that?'

'It was all in the G-two files. Trouble was nobody put it together. I don't think they wanted to; Dellacroce's crowd are big Pentagon supporters, what with government contracts and union affiliations —. Now, will you listen to me?'

With a reluctance born of fear, but with an assent formed in necessity, Sam nodded. The Hawk helped him up and the two men walked into the rough off fairway six. There was a large oak tree whose leaves filtered the moonlight. Sam sat down against the trunk; Mac fell to one knee in front of him, the line officer clarifying orders at a fire base.

'Remember a couple of weeks ago my telling you how I was looking into things I hadn't thought much about before? God and the church and things like that.'

'I remember saying I wouldn't laugh —' Devereaux's reply was flat, wary. A monotone.

'That was very thoughtful, boy. Well, I *was* doing some thinking, but not quite in the way you maybe considered. You and I know that ninety-nine per cent of all Commie propaganda is horseshit; everybody knows that. Ours is only – say, fifty to sixty per cent, so we're way ahead on that score. But that one per cent of the Bolshie feedback got me to wondering. About this Catholic situation. Not what people *believe*, that's their business. But how the organization operates. And it seemed to me that these Vatican fellows got such a good thing going they should spread a little more

112

around. I mean, they got investments, son. When the stock market goes up a couple of points anywhere in the world, they make zillions.'

'And if it goes down, they lose zillions.'

'Not so! The brokers get 'em out in time or they get canned from the Knights of Malta. It's part of the arrangement. And they can't get their pictures taken with the pope.'

'That *is* horseshit.'

'If it is, why do all the Catholic brokers on Wall Street have all those initials after their names. You know of any college degrees that start with the letter *K*? Malta, Columbus, Lourdes. And the saints! *Jesus!* Knights of Assisi, Knights of Peter, Matthew – it goes on for pages. It's kind of a social order. The more a fellow on the stock exchange does for the Vatican, the better the *K* after his name. And Wall Street's only one example. It's the same all over the place.'

'I think you've been reading some pretty strange books. The *Ku Klux Klanner*, maybe. Nineteen twenty edition.'

'Hell, no, I don't cotton to that shit. A man's got a right to believe anything he likes. I'm only talking about the financial part. Then there's real estate. Do you know the sort of real estate the Vatican boys have? I swear they pick up rent from the Ginza to the Gaza strips and most places in between. They own *the* prime properties in New York, Chicago, Hartford, Detroit – 'most every place where the micks, the wops, the Polacks and all those kind of people migrated. They always do it the same way. They go in early – before all the ethnics get settled – and buy up land and build a big church. Naturally, all these Ellis Islanders are nervous being in a strange place and all, so *they* build their houses near the church. In a generation or so the kids are lawyers and dentists and own automobile dealerships. So what do they do? They move out to the suburbs and go to work where they once lived, which is now the centre of *town*, the *business* district. And the church property skyrockets! It's a regular pattern, boy!'

'I'm trying to find something negative here and I can't,'

113

said Sam, staring in the shadows at the excited Hawkins. 'What's wrong with the pattern?'

'I didn't say it was wrong. I said it made for one hell of a centralized portfolio.'

'"Centralized portfolio"? You've got a new vocabulary.'

'Like you said, I've been reading. And not such strange books as you might think. You see, Sam, the product these Vatican boys manufacture – that's not meant disrespectfully, only in a business sense – doesn't change. It may have to adjust a mite now and then, take a tuck here or a nip there, but the basic merchandise stays the same. That reduces a major cost factor and allows for a continuous profit figure with no chance of negative entry —'

'"Negative entry"?'

'That's an accounting term.'

'I know it's an accounting term. How do *you* know – don't tell me. Your reading material.'

'Maggie's drawers, son.'

'What?'

'Never mind. You're on target, that's all. Now, you take an economic situation where the stock exchanges and the real estate markets hold firm, and that means you got the banks, because you control both money *and* land. Prime economic resources. And you add to that a product that requires minimum assembly alterations with maximum purchase growth – hell, boy, it's a worldwide *gold mine.*'

'You have been reading. But if you're right, why's there so much hassle over the parochial schools and *their* costs?'

'That's services, Sam. That's an entirely different entry column. I'm talking about basic portfolios, not annual operating expenditures; they fluctuate with economic conditions. Anyway, it's mostly blackmail.'

'That's succinct. They wouldn't like you in Boston.'

The Hawk shifted his weight and spoke a little more softly, but with no loss of emphasis. 'You mentioned before about something wrong. Well, I don't like to mention it because it only applies to the pricky-shit high brass and not the troops, but there is something that's got a bit of sting to it.'

'*You* found a *moral* position?'

'Morality and economics should be more related than they have been; everybody knows that. You take this political thing. Nobody's traded fire power with the Reds any better'n I have. God*damn*, nobody's going to bury me! But it strikes me that these Catholic boys in the Vatican – and that means all the powerful dioceses -- use the Bolshie excuse a mite too freely to oppose just about everything that could make things better for the peasant slobs scratching a life out of very tough ground.'

Devereaux eyed Hawkins sceptically. 'That position's a little dated. A great many changes are taking place in the Church. This new pope is opening a lot of windows. Like John the Twenty-third did.'

'Not quick enough, Sam. What the Vatican brass needs is a good shake-up in command. Something to jolt their *be*robed asses out of their lethargy.'

'You can't change a two-thousand-year pattern overnight —'

'Oh, I understand that,' interrupted the Hawk. 'And I'm glad you brought up this new pope. This Francesco. Because he's a very popular fellow. Even those who hate his guts – for doing what he's doing – know he's the biggest asset they've got in the whole damn church – that's not meant in a religious sense, of course. I don't take positions that way.'

'What positions? What sense?'

'This Francesco,' continued Mac, overlooking Devereaux's questions, 'is more than just the pope, which is enough to begin with. He's a beloved individual, you know what I'm driving at?'

'I wish you wouldn't say that.'

'He's the sort of person every man jack of a Catholic would really sacrifice for, you see what I mean?'

'I don't like that phrase, either.'

The Hawk changed knees rapidly; it was good to redistribute weight as often as possible when in an immobile position. 'Do you know the estimated total communicant membership of the Catholic Church?'

115

'The *what*?'

'How many Catholics there are in the world? Never mind, I'll tell you. Four hundred million. Now, taking the median figure of one American dollar – setting a specific date for the rate of exchange; some giving more, most less – that comes to *four hundred million dollars*.'

'What does?'

'The projected gross.'

'What projected gross?'

'Of the Shepherd Company's business services. This here "brokering the acquisition of religious artifacts". It's a clear ratio of ten to one in terms of capitalization, but naturally the profit ratio, as opposed to the gross figure, will be affected by the necessary outlay for equipment and support personnel.'

'What the hell are you babbling about?!'

'We're going to kidnap the pope, Sam.'

'Whaaat!'

'I've got a trunkful of books, boy. I've really been studying the tactical problems and I think I've got 'em licked. You see, there's this place called Chiesa di San Tommaso di Villanova in Gandolfo – pardon my lousy Italian – and the route from the Vatican is over a kind of country thoroughfare called the Via Appia Antica. It's the road to this here Gandolfo – Castel Gandolfo, they call it. These Italians, they never use one word when they can use two.'

'Whaaat?!'

'Now, don't go over-reacting. You'll wake up Dellacroce.'

'Whaaat?'

'But first we have to corral the remaining capitalization. There's thirty million more coming. I believe I've almost narrowed down the three investors, but I've still got some refining to do.' The Hawk clapped his hand over Devereaux's open mouth. 'Now, don't start that again. You keep repeating yourself.'

Devereaux's eyes bulged above MacKenzie's spread hand, but the rest of his body was frozen. Sort of a form of comatose shock, thought Hawkins. He'd seen a lot of that kind of thing when raw recruits got their first taste of a fire fight. At least Sam wasn't screaming. Or struggling. He was just plain still and kind of cold. The Hawk continued; he had only a few words left to say. The in-depth command analyses would come later. In a way he was glad Devereaux's over-reaction was so extreme. In his enthusiasm he had nearly given Sam some tactical information he was not sure he wanted Devereaux to have.

'I didn't choose you lightly. No superior-adjutant is an easy choice for a commander to make, for in many ways the SA is an extension of himself. You got it on *merit*, boy. I don't say you're ideal, you've got deficiencies. I've told you that. But, goddamn, your assets out-point your liabilities. I say that as an honest friend as well as a superior officer.

'Now, there'll be certain executive orders that you'll be asked to carry out, not always knowing precisely why they're vital. You'll just have to accept them. Command is a lonely responsibility; there's not always the time to share the reasons for one's decisions. Ask any frontline officer who sends a battalion into fire. But you'll do splendidly. I just know you will. And if by any chance you're tempted to question the orders of your superior officer, or feel that you cannot in conscience implement them, I think you should know that our investor, Angelo Dellacroce, believes that you alone, as the attorney and secretary-treasurer of the Shepherd Company, compiled that list of his illegal activities and furnished me with them. I believe that's why he didn't care to shake hands with you. Coupled with your G-two espionage violations, I'd say your position was somewhat untenable. But if I were you and had my druthers, I'd choose to fight the government treason charges rather than our investor, Mr Dellacroce. I think that Mafia bastard would cut your balls off, grind 'em up in a blender, and serve 'em as a fancy pâté at your funeral. Like you said earlier, it'd probably be an expensive funeral.'

There was no point in the Hawk holding his hand over his superior-adjutant's mouth any longer. Sam had *merfed* and *gleefed* in a spasm of panic and passed out cold.

The moonlight, filtering through the leaves of the large, sturdy oak in the rough off fairway six, cut shafts of yellow and white across Sam's young, peaceful, unmistakably strong features.

Goddamn, thought MacKenzie, the boy's going to be fine! He just needed a little time to absorb the facts. Of course, if a person didn't know any better, he'd think the son of a bitch was dead.

CHAPTER TEN

Sam Devereaux sank despondently into the hotel chair and wished he were dead.

Well, not really, but it certainly would solve a lot of problems. Of course, it was entirely possible that the state of his demise might come about whether he desired it or not. Which brought his eyes back to the insane, unfiled but filled-out limited partnership agreement between the Shepherd Company, MacKenzie Hawkins, President, and the North Hampton Corporation, Mrs Angelo Dellacroce, President; Depository: the Great Bank of Geneva, Switzerland. He held the legal document in his hand and wondered absently where his fingernails had gone.

Prominently on the first page, directly under the title of president and above the line reserved for the secretary-treasurer, was his name.

Mr Samuel Devereaux, Counsellor-at-law, Suite 4-F, The Drake Hotel, New York City.

He speculated for a moment whether he could alter the Drake's registry and then abandoned the idea. What was the point? On one flank (*flank?*) was the United States government with very specific espionage laws, and on the other was Angelo Dellacroce and his guards-of-honour with their white ties on white shirts and dark glasses and black suits and very *un*specific methods of dealing with the likes of 'squeals' such as S. Devereaux, counsellor-at-law.

Sam wondered what Aaron Pinkus would do. Then he realized what Aaron would do and abandoned that thought, too.

Pinkus would sit *Shiva* for him.

He got out of the chair and wandered aimlessly through

119

the hotel suite. What the hell *was* he going to do? What in God's name *could* he do? His gaze fell on the unsigned, typewritten note on the desk.

Copies of this limited partnership agreement have been sent by messenger to MacKenzie Hawkins, Esquire, President, the Shepherd Company, c/o The Watergate Hotel, Wash. D.C. Instructions cabled: Great Bank of Geneva. Funds transfer awaits presence Sec.-Treas., Shep. Co., Samuel Devereaux in Geneva.

He had been *cabled – internationally.*

In some marble banking hall in Switzerland, a powerful broker of international finance had no doubt already listed him as the bona fide overseer of the transfer of ten million dollars into an account of a nonfiled but very much existing company named Shepherd.

That's what he was going to do whether he liked it.or not. It was Geneva, or a lifetime of cracking rocks at Leavenworth, *or* Dellacroce justice – feet-in-cement style.

Kidnap the pope!

My God! That's what the crazy bastard said. He was going to *kidnap the pope!*

All of Mac's other insanities paled by any stretch of comparison! World War Three might be more acceptable! A simple war would be so much – well, simpler. Borders were defined, objectives properly obscured, ideologies flexible. A war was duck soup compared to 400 million hysterical Catholics; and heads of state moaning and groaning their obsequious platitudes, blaming every conceivable inimical faction, extremist or not (secretly glad to be rid of the meddling nuisance in the Vatican) and ....

My God! World War Three could be a very logical consequence of Hawkins's act!

And with that realization Sam knew what he had to do. He had to stop MacKenzie. But he could not stop him if he were in a maximum security cell in Leavenworth: who would believe him? And he certainly could not stop him if he were at the bottom of one of the deeper sections of the Hudson River, probably upstate, courtesy of Angelo Dellacroce; who would hear him?

No, the only way he could push the Hawk's insanity out of the realm of reality was to find out how the hell MacKenzie intended to pull off his papal score. The most foolish thing here would be to assume he couldn't do it. The Hawk was no joke; anyone who thought he was need only look at a few of Mac's accomplishments – including four extraordinary ex-wives who adored him, and a little matter of an initial capitalization of ten million dollars, to say nothing of military exploits spanning three decades and the same number of wars.

What the Hawk was bringing to the profession of crime were all the strategic resources, the finely honed discipline, and the leadership of an experienced general officer. MacKenzie was starting at the top; no graduate of the lineup he, but instead, a full-fledged criminal commander who had already outsacked a Mafia don in his own backyard.

The son of a bitch had flair. Christ! He had the balls of King Kong smashing the concrete off the Empire State Building as he climbed up the sides.

Kidnap the pope!

Who the hell would believe it?

Samuel Devereaux believed it, that's who believed it. What was left was for S. Devereaux, counsellor-at-law, to figure out how to stop it. And stay both alive and outside prison walls so doing. A vague idea was coming into focus, but it was still too blurred to make sense. Yet there was a core of possibility within the outlines.

'Don't be too confident,' said Sam out loud. 'You're dealing with a living, legal, spinal meningitis!'

But it *was* possible. He could pretend to go along with MacKenzie (always with great reluctance; to act otherwise would be out of character), gather in the diseased money and, at the last moment, convene the investors and blow the whole operation out of the sky. And to save his hide, there'd be a lot of 'in the case of my sudden demise, my own

121

attorneys are instructed to publicly reveal...' any number of things.

Including the translation of the Shepherd Company's 'brokering of religious artifacts'.

Who would believe it?

'*Stop that!*' Sam grabbed his wrist, startled by the sound of his own voice. He was further startled by the sound of the telephone. He raced to it like a man facing execution rushing to hear what the governor had to say.

'Goddamn! This must be the attorney *and* secretary *and* treasurer of the Shepherd Company! With assets over ten million dollars! How does that strike you?'

'It's a leading question. I'll not indulge.'

'You know something, boy? You must be a pistol of a lawyer!'

'Are you sure you want to talk over the telephone?' asked Devereaux. 'It's been given a pretty good FCC rating lately.'

'Oh, that's all right. We won't say anything we shouldn't. At least, *I* won't, and I hope to hell you know better. I just wanted to tell you that the additional copies of the partnership agreement are downstairs waiting for you. I sent them up last night with an old master sergeant I used to know —'

'Good *God*, you had *duplicates* made? You damn fool! Those copy places usually keep a set! If they're photostats there'll be negatives!'

'Not where I was. Right down here in the Watergate lobby there's a big machine. You put in a quarter for each page — *Jesus!* You should have seen the crowds gather! They're a little jumpy around here, aren't they? But nobody saw anything. It was kind of weird. Everybody staring; nobody saying anything. Except two guys from the *Washington Post* who came running in from the street —'

'All right!' interrupted Devereaux. 'The copies are downstairs. What the hell am I supposed to do with them?'

'Put 'em in your fancy briefcase, the one I gave you. Take 'em to Geneva. You won't need 'em in Switzerland, of course, but there may be one or two other stops on the way back. Namely, London; that's pretty definite. You'll be at the

Savoy for a day or two. Airline tickets and everything will be at the hotel in Geneva. When you're in London a gentleman named Danforth will call you. You'll know what to do.'

'That's a dirty pool. I won't know what to do; I don't know what I'm *doing*! You can't just put me in this crazy situation and not tell me anything. I'm carrying documents! My *name* is on them! I'm involved with the transfer of ten million dollars!'

'Now, calm down,' said the Hawk with gentle firmness. 'Remember what I told you: There'll be times when, as my adjutant, you'll be asked to carry out orders —'

'*Bullshit!*' roared Sam. 'What am I supposed to *say* to people?'

'Well, what's bullshit to one man may be sugar-coated wheat to another. If anyone presses you, you're just helping an old soldier who's quietly raising a few dollars to spread religious brotherhood.'

'That's absurd,' said Devereaux.

'That's the Shepherd Company,' said the Hawk.

MacKenzie lifted up five specific pages from the Xeroxed G-2 files scattered over the hotel bed and took them to the desk across the room. He sat down, picked up a red crayon, and proceeded to mark each copy on the top left border. One to five.

Goddamn! It was the sequence he had been looking for, the pattern he knew was there because a man can't resist going back to his first method of fortune building if the circumstances appear right. And because time minimizes the problems and pressures a person felt decades ago, especially if the profits remain.

The covert intelligence out of Hanoi three years ago had been confusing but authentic. Authentic, that is, on the bottom line; everything else was distorted.

An Englishman was making a killing by brokering hardware and ammunition to North Vietnam.

No big deal; London did not frown on trade to the Commie bloc, although there were specific regulations as to

123

war machinery. But it was a period during that screwed up, half-assed conflict when the boys in Hanoi *and* Moscow *and* Peking were running slow on the production lines. Money could be made in large bundles by anyone who could divert combat supplies into North Vietnamese ports.

One Lord Sidney Danforth had done just that.

Buying in the United States, West Germany, and France, he sailed under Chilean flag ostensibly for ports in the new African countries. Except the ships did not go anywhere near Africa. They altered their courses in international Pacific waters, sped north, refuelled in the Russian out-islands, and headed south to Haiphong as regulation-bound trading vessels.

G-2 could never prove Danforth's involvement because the Communist payments were made directly to the Chilean companies and Danforth stayed well out of sight. And Washington was not about to provoke an incident. Danforth was a powerful Englishman with a lot of clout in the Foreign Office. Nam wasn't worth it.

What had intrigued MacKenzie, however, were the two keys: Chilean flag and African ports. They were covers that had been used before. Thirty years ago. During World War II.

It was common knowledge in intelligence circles that certain South American companies with outside financing had fed war machinery to the Axis at enormous profit during the early forties. In those hectic wartime days the shipping destinations were always Capetown and Port Elizabeth because the manifest records in those harbours were chaotic at best, but usually non-existent. Scores of ships that were supposed to dock in South Africa altered courses in the southern Atlantic waters and headed into the Mediterranean. To Italy, generally.

Was it possible that one Lord Sidney Danforth had imitated his own operations of three decades past?

It was one thing to chisel a few million out of South-east Asia in the seventies, something else again to make a fortune out of the holocaust that tested the courage of the British

Lion. A man could get his name taken off the Buckingham Palace guest list pretty quickly for something like that.

It was time for the Hawk to have a transatlantic talk with Lord Sidney Danforth, seventy-two-year-old knighted paragon of British industry. And just about the wealthiest man in England.

Goddamn! The Shepherd Company was attracting some of the most interesting investors.

CHAPTER ELEVEN

The Strand was crowded. It was shortly past five o'clock; the legion of office workers were heading home.

Sam had arrived at Heathrow Airport on the 3.40 flight from Geneva and had wasted no time getting to the relaxed comfort of a Savoy suite. He needed it. Geneva had been a nightmare.

He had realized that for any future record, he had to convey a very specific ignorance as to the objectives of the Shepherd Company, cloaking this lack of knowledge in profound respect for the unnamed principals involved; especially the president, who was motivated by deeply religious convictions.

The Geneva bankers, were, at first, impressed by his humility. My God, ten million United States dollars and the overseeing lawyer only smiled and spoke convivial banalities, demurring when pressed for identities, nodding soulfully about religious brotherhood when the staggering amount was brought up. So they asked him out to lunch, where there were a lot of winks and drinks and offers of bedroom gymnastics of an incredible variety. This was, after all, Switzerland; a buck was a buck and this hard-nosed approach was not to be confused with yodelling and edelweiss and Heidi in her pinafores. Gradually, thought Devereaux, as the lunches evolved into dinners, the Geneva bankers thought he was either the dumbest attorney ever to practise before the American bar or the most implausibly secretive middleman ever to cross their borders.

He kept up the charade for three days and nights, leaving behind a half-dozen confused Swiss burgomasters, tearfully frustrated over unrequited confidences and terribly sick to their stomachs after too much industrial lubricant. And the strain on Sam was unbearable. He had reached the point where he could not concentrate on anything but his own rigid, blank smile and the necessary quiet control of his fears. He was so preoccupied with himself that when the vice-president of the Great Bank of Geneva saw him off at the airport, Devereaux just smiled and said 'Thank you' when the banker threw up over his raincoat.

In his anxiety to get the hell out of Geneva, he had left his shaving kit behind, which explained why he was now on The Strand looking for a drugstore. He walked south for a block and a half, opposite the Hippodrome, and went into the Strand Chemists. His purchases made, he headed back to the hotel, anticipating a long, warm bath, a shave, and a good dinner at the Savoy Grill.

'Major Devereaux!' The voice was enthusiastic, American, and feminine. It came from a taxi which stopped in Savoy Court.

It was Sloping yet Argumentative, the fourth Mrs MacKenzie Hawkins, the lovely lady named Anne. She hurled herself at Sam, encircling his neck with her arms, pressing her cheek and various other parts against him.

Instantly she withdrew and rather awkwardly composed herself. 'I'm awfully sorry. Gosh, that was real *forward* of me. Please forgive me. It was just so *terrific* to see a familiar face.'

'Nothing to apologize for,' said Sam, remembering that Sloping yet Argumentative had appeared to him as the most naïve, as well as the youngest, of the four wives. She had *oohed* a lot, if he recalled correctly. 'Are you staying at the Savoy?'

'Yes. I got in last night. I've never been to England before, so I spent the whole day just walking *everywhere*. Gosh, my feet are yelling at me.' She parted her very expensive suede coat and frowned at the lovely legs very much in evidence below her short skirt.

'Well, let's get you off them quickly. Into the bar, I mean.'

'I can't *tell* you! It's so *marvy* to see someone you know!'

127

'Are you here by yourself?' asked Devereaux.

'Oh yes, Don, he's my husband – now – is so darned busy with his marinas and restaurants and all those other things that he just said to me last week in LA, he said, "Annie, honey, why don't you get your pretty little ass out of the way for a while? This is going to be a heavy month." Well, I thought of Mexico and Palm Springs and all the usual places, and then I figured, damn! Annie, you've never been to London. So off I flew.' She nodded brightly to the Savoy doorman and continued as Sam gestured her through the entrance into the lobby. 'Don thought I was crazy. I mean, who do I know in England? But I think that was part of it, you know? I wanted to go someplace where there weren't all the usual faces. Somewhere really different.'

'I hope I didn't spoil it.'

'How?'

'Well, you said I was a familiar face —'

'Oh, my, no! I said familiar, but I didn't mean *familiar*. I mean, one little short afternoon at Ginny's isn't *that* kind of familiar.'

'I see what you mean. The lounge is right up those stairs.' Sam nodded towards the steps on the left that led to the Savoy's American Bar. But Anne stopped, still holding on to his arm.

'Major,' she began haltingly, 'my feet are still screaming and my neck is sore from looking up and my shoulder's aching from this darned purse strap. I'd really love to spend a little time straightening myself out.'

'Oh, sure,' replied Devereaux. 'I'm being thoughtless. And stupid. As a matter of fact I was going to do some, er, straightening out myself. I left my shaving gear in Switzerland.' He held up the bag from the Strand Chemists.

'Well, then, that's *marvy*!'

'I'll call you in about an hour —'

'Why do that? Have you seen the size of those johnnies upstairs? Wow! They're bigger than some of Don's ladies' rooms. In his restaurants, I mean. There's plenty of room. And those big, groovy towels. I swear they're terry cloth

128

sheets!' She squeezed his arm and smiled ingenuously.

'Well, it *is* a solution —'

'The only one. Come on, we'll get some drinks from room service and *really* relax.' They started for the elevator.

'It's very kind of you —'

'Kind, hell! Ginny told us you called. She positively *lorded* it over us. Now it's my turn. You were in Geneva?'

Sam stopped. 'I said Switzerland —'

'Isn't that Geneva?'

Anne's suite was also on the Thames side, also on the sixth floor, and conveniently no more than fifty feet down the corridor from his.

Switzerland. Isn't that Geneva? Several thoughts crossed Devereaux's mind, but he was entirely too exhausted to dwell on them. And, for the first time in days, entirely too relaxed to let them interfere.

The rooms were very like his own. High ceilings with real mouldings; marvellous old furniture – polished, functional – desks and tables and pictures and chairs and a sofa that would do credit to Parke-Bernet; mantel clocks and lamps that were neither nailed down nor with embedded plastic cards proclaiming ownership; tall casement windows, flanked by regal drapes, that looked out on the river with the lights of small boats, the buildings beyond, and especially Waterloo Bridge.

He was in the sitting room, on the pillowhead sofa, with his shoes off and a tall drink in his hand. The London Philharmonic was on BBC1, playing a Vivaldi concerto, and the warmth from a heater filled the room with a splendid comfort. Good things came to the deserving, thought Sam.

Anne came out of the bathroom and stopped in the frame of the doorway. Devereaux's glass was suddenly checked on its way to his lips. She was dressed – if that was the word – in a translucent sheath that at once left little to, yet completely provoked, the imagination. Her Sloping yet Argumentative breasts swelled to blushing points beneath the soft, single layer of fabric; her long, light-brown hair fell casually and

129

sensually over her shoulders, framing her extraordinary endowments. Her tapered legs were outlined under the sheath.

Without saying a word, she raised her hand and beckoned him with her finger. He rose from the sofa and followed.

Inside the huge, tiled bathroom, the enormous Savoy tub was filled with steaming water; several thousand bubbles gave off the scent of roses and wet springtime. Anne reached up and removed his tie, and then his shirt, and then unstrapped his buckle, unzipped his trousers and lowered them to the floor. He kicked them free himself.

She placed her hands on both sides of his waist and pulled down his shorts, kneeling as she did so.

He sat on the edge of the warm tub while she pulled off his socks; and she held his left arm as he slid over the side, his body disappearing under the steaming white bubbles.

She stood up, undid a yellow bow at her neck, and the sheath fell to the floor on top of the thick white rug.

She was utterly magnificent.

And she got into the tub with Sam.

'Do you want to go down to dinner?' asked the girl from beneath the covers.

'Sure,' replied Devereaux from under same.

'Do you know we slept for over three hours? It's nearly nine-thirty.' She stretched; Sam watched. 'After we eat, let's go to one of those pubs.'

'If you like,' said Devereaux, still watching her, his head on the pillow. She was sitting up now, the sheet had fallen to her waist. Sloping yet Argumentative were challenging all they surveyed.

'Gosh,' Anne spoke softly, a touch awkwardly, as she turned and looked down at Sam, who could barely see her face. 'I'm being real forward again.'

'Friendly's a better word. I'm friendly, too.'

'You know what I mean.' She bent over him and kissed him on both eyes. 'You may have other plans; things you have to do or something.'

130

'Things I want to do,' interrupted Devereaux warmly. 'All plans are completely flexible, subject only to whim and pleasure.'

'That sounds sexy as hell.'

'I feel sexy as hell.'

'Thank you.'

'Thank *you*.' Sam reached above and beyond her soft, lovely back and pulled the sheet over them.

Ten minutes later (it was either ten minutes or several hours, thought Devereaux) they made the decision: They really did need food, preceded, of course, by short, smoky drams of iced whisky, which they had in the sitting room, on the pillowed couch, under two soft, enormous bath towels.

'I think the word is "sybaritic".' Sam adjusted the terry cloth over his lap. BBC1 was now playing a Noel Coward medley and the smoke from their cigarettes drifted into the sprays of warm orange light from the fireplace. Only two lamps were turned on; the room was dreamed of in a thousand ballads.

'Sybaritic has a selfish meaning,' said the girl. 'We share; that's not selfish.'

Sam looked at her. Hawkins's fourth wife was no idiot. How in hell did he do it? Had he done it? 'The way we share, it's sybaritic, believe me.'

'If you want me to,' she answered, smiling and putting her glass down on the coffee table.

'Its not important. Why don't we dress and go eat?'

'All right. I'll just be a few seconds.' She saw his questioning expression. 'No, I will. I don't dawdle for hours. Mac once said —' She stopped, embarrassed.

'It's okay,' he said gently. 'I'd really like to hear.'

'Well, he once said that if you try to change the outside too much, you can't help but mix up the inside. And you shouldn't do that unless there's a goddamned good reason. Or if you really don't like yourself.' She swung her legs out from under her and rose from the couch, holding the towel around her body. 'One, I don't see any reason; and two, I kind of like me. Mac taught me that, too. I like *us*.'

131

'So do I,' said Devereaux. 'When you're finished, we'll go down to my room and I'll change.

'Good. I'll button your shirt and tie your tie.' She grinned and dashed through the foyer door into the bedroom. Devereaux got up naked, throwing the long towel over his shoulder, and went to the side table where the bar was set up in a silver tray. He poured a small quantity of Scotch and thought about Mac Hawkins's bathroom philosophy.

Change the outside too much – you mix up the inside.

It wasn't bad, all things considered.

The tiny white light shone between the red and green bulbs on the small panel beside Devereaux's door. Sam and the girl saw it simultaneously as they walked down the corridor and approached his suite. It was the sign that a message was at the front desk for the guest. Devereaux swore under his breath.

Goddamn it! Geneva had not been erased *that* quickly. Or so completely, either. The least Hawkins could do was to let him get a decent night's sleep!

'One of those lights was on for me this afternoon,' said Anne. 'I came back to change my shoes and found it; it means you have a phone call.'

'Or a message.'

'Mine was a call. From Don in Santa Monica. I finally got him back; you know, it was only eight o'clock in the morning in California.'

'Nice of him to get up and phone.'

'Not so. My husband owns two things in Santa Monica: a restaurant and a girl. The restaurant's not open at eight in the morning; forgive my bitchiness. I think Don just wanted to make sure I was really seven thousand miles away.' Anne smiled up at him naïvely. He was not sure how to respond, all things considered.

'Seems like a lot of trouble for, well, for checking up.' Sam snapped on the light switch in his foyer. Beyond, the sitting room lamps were on, as he had left them five hours ago.

'My husband suffers from a mental illness peculiar to cheap strayers. As a lawyer, I'm sure you're familiar with it.

132

He's paranoid about getting caught. Not morally, you understand; when he's juiced up, he flaunts *that* part. Just financially; he's scared to death some court will make him pay big if I opt for out.'

They walked into his sitting room; he wanted to say something but, again, all things considered he was not sure what it should be. He chose the safest. 'I think the man's out of his mind.'

'You're sweet, but you didn't have to say it. On the other hand, I suppose it's the safest thing you *could* say —'

'Let's find another subject,' he interrupted quickly, indicating the couch and the coffee table with the Savoy-supplied newspapers on it. 'Sit down and I'll be with you in a minute. I haven't forgotten: You button the shirt and tie the tie.' Sam started for the bedroom door.

'Aren't you going to call the desk?'

'It can *wait*,' he answered from the bedroom. 'I have no intention of letting anything interfere with a quiet dinner. Or for that matter, showing you a pub or two, if they're still open when we're finished.'

'You really should find out who's trying to reach you. It could be important.'

'*You're* important,' shouted Sam, removing a tan double-knit suit from the awkward hangar in his suitcase.

'It could be something vital,' said the girl from the sitting room.

'*You're vital*,' he replied, selecting a red-striped shirt from the next layer of clothes.

'I can't *ever* not answer a phone, or check for messages, or call back even a name I never heard of; that's being *too* casual.'

'You're not a lawyer. Ever tried to get a lawyer the day after you've hired him? His secretary is trained to lie with the conviction of Aimee Semple McPherson.'

'Why?' Anne was now standing in the bedroom doorway.

'Well, he's got your money; he's scrounging around for another fee. What the hell, your case probably entails an exchange of letters with the opposing attorney, other

133

explanations notwithstanding. He doesn't want complications.'

Anne approached him as he slipped on the red-striped shirt. She nonchalantly began buttoning it. 'You're a very cool Clyde. Here you are in strange country —'

'Not so strange,' he broke in smiling. 'I've been here before. I'm your tour guide, remember?'

'I mean, you've just come from Geneva where you obviously had a bad time —'

'Not so bad. I survived.'

'— and now someone is desperately trying to find you —'

'What's desperate? I don't know anybody so desperate.'

'For Christ's sake!' The girl yanked his collar as she fastened it. 'Things like this make me nervous!'

'Why?'

'I feel responsible!'

'You shouldn't.' Devereaux was fascinated. Anne was very serious. He wondered ...

And the telephone rang.

'Hello?'

'Mr Samuel Devereaux?' asked the precise voice of a male Britisher.

'Yes, this is Sam Devereaux.'

'I've been waiting for your call —'

'I just got in,' interrupted Sam. 'I haven't checked my messages yet. Who is this?'

'At the moment, merely a telephone number.'

Devereaux paused, annoyed. 'Then I should tell you, you would have waited all night. I don't return calls to telephone numbers.'

'Come, sir,' was the agitated reply. 'You're not expecting any other caller of consequence.'

'That's a little presumptuous, I think —'

'Think whatever you like, sir! I'm in a great hurry and quite put out with you. Now, where do you wish to meet?'

'I don't know that I want to. Fuck off, Basil, or whatever the hell your name is.'

The pause was now on the other end of the line. Sam could

hear heavy breathing. In seconds the telephone number spoke. 'For God's sake, have pity on an old man. I've done you no harm.'

Sam was suddenly touched. The voice had cracked slightly; the man was desperate. He remembered Hawkins's last conversation. 'Are you —'

'No *names, please!*'

'All right. No names. Are you recognizable?'

'Extremely. I thought you knew that.'

'I didn't. So we meet someplace out of the way.'

'Very much so. I thought you knew that, too.'

'Stop saying that!' Devereaux was as much annoyed with Hawkins as he was with the Englishman on the telephone. 'Then you'd better choose it, unless you want to come to the Savoy.'

'Impossible! That's kind of you. I have several apartment buildings in Belgravia. One's the Hampton Arms; do you know it?'

'I can find it.'

'Good. I'll be there. Flat four seven. It will take me an hour to get into London.'

'Don't hurry. I don't want to meet in an hour.'

'Oh? At what time then?'

'When do the pubs close these days?'

'Midnight. A little over an hour.'

'Shit!'

'I beg your pardon?'

'I'll see you at one o'clock.'

'Very well. The Hampton security will be alerted. Remember, no names. Just flat four seven.'

'Four seven.'

'And, Devereaux. Bring the papers.'

'What papers?'

'The pause was longer now, the English breathing heavier. 'That goddamned agreement, you *ass.*'

The girl not only accepted the fact that their dinner would be short and that he had to leave the hotel, but she seemed positively elated.

135

Sam was wondering less and less. The *why* escaped him, but the *what* was becoming clearer. He agreed to have a nightcap with her when he returned. The hour was unimportant, Anne said; she gave him a key.

The taxi stopped at the kerb in front of the Hampton Arms. At Sam's mention of flat four seven, he was led by a doorman in a series of swift, secretive movements that took him through service doors, a short back staircase, a freight elevator, and the delivery entrance of the flat.

An ominous looking man with a north country accent asked for identification and then led Sam through a pantry, a large living room, a hallway, and finally to a small dimly lit library where a rather ugly little old man sat in the shadows by the window. The door closed. Devereaux stood, adjusting his eyes to the light and the unattractive ancient in the armchair.

'Mr Devereaux – naturally,' said the wrinkled old man.

'Yes. You must be the Danforth Hawkins spoke of.'

'Lord Sidney Danforth.' The ugly little person spat out the ugly words, then suddenly his voice was syrup. 'I don't know how your employer pieced together what he did, nor do I for a moment admit *anything*; it's all so preposterous. And so long ago. Nevertheless, I am a good man, a charitable man. Quite a *wonderful* man. Give me the damned papers!'

'What?'

'The agreement, you insufferable bastard!'

Stunned, Sam reached into his breast pocket where he had a folded copy of the Shepherd Company's limited partnership. He crossed to the ugly little person and gave it to him. Danforth swung out a portable desk panel from somewhere at the side of the armchair and snapped on a bright worklight at the top of the board. He grabbed the papers and started scanning them.

'Fine!' said Danforth, wheezing, flipping over the pages. 'They say absolutely *nothing*!' The little Britisher reached for a pen and began filling in the black lines. When he had finished, he refolded the papers and handed them distastefully to Devereaux. 'Now, get out! I am a marvellous man, a

136

magnanimous provider; a humble multi-millionaire whom everyone adores. I have richly deserved the extraordinary honours heaped upon my person. Everybody knows that. And nobody. I repeat, *nobody* could conceivably associate me with such madness! I am only – spreading brotherhood – do you understand me? *Brotherhood*, I say!'

'I don't understand anything,' said Sam.

'Neither do I,' replied Danforth. 'The transfer will be made in the Cayman Islands. The bank is listed and the ten million will be shifted within forty-eight hours. Then I'm through with you!'

'The Cayman Islands?'

'They're in the Caribbean, you ass.'

CHAPTER TWELVE

He could see the tiny white light shining fifty feet down the Savoy corridor. He did not have to get any closer to know it was the door to his rooms; avoiding it was a second, very good reason to let himself into Annie's suite.

'If that's not you, Sam I've got problems,' she called from the bedroom.

'It's me. All your problems are happy ones.'

'I like those kind.'

Devereaux walked into the large bedroom with the windows overlooking the river. Anne was sitting up, reading a brightly coloured paperback by the light of the table lamp. 'What's that?' he asked. 'It looks impressive.'

'A marvellous history of Henry the Eighth's wives. I got it at the Tower this morning. That man was a monster!'

'Not really. A lot of his troubles were geopolitical.'

'In his crotch they were!'

'That's more historically sound than you may think. How about a drink?'

'You've got to make a phone call first. I promised; first thing you did when you got back.'

The girl turned a page calmly. Sam was not only astonished, he was curious. 'What did you say?'

'MacKenzie called. All the way from Washington.' She turned another page.

'MacKenzie?' Devereaux could not help himself; he roared. 'Just – *MacKenzie called*! You're sitting there like you heard from room service and tell me MacKenzie called. How do *you* know he called? Did he call *you*?'

'Really, Sam, stop being so uptight.' Cold as ice, she

turned another goddamned page. 'It's not as though I didn't know him. I mean, after all —'

'Oh, no! Spare me the odious comparisons! I just want to know about this extraordinary coincidence that has you seven thousand miles from home taking a telephone call from an ex-husband who's calling *me* – three thousand miles from New York.'

'If you'll calm down, I'll tell you. If you won't, I'm just going to keep on reading.'

Devereaux thought about how much he wanted a drink, but he suppressed his anger and spoke quietly. 'I'm calm and I would very much like to have you speak. Please speak.'

Anne put the book down on her lap and looked up at him. 'To begin with, Mac was every bit as uptight as you are when I got on the line.'

'How *did* you get on the line?'

'Because I was worried.'

'That's why, not how.'

'If you recall, and I think you will if you try real hard, you left me at the table downstairs. You were running late and I insisted. I told you I'd sign the check and go upstairs. Am I right so far?'

'I owe you for dinner. Go on.'

'A nice young man in white tie and tails came to the table and said there was an urgent transatlantic call for you. Are they always so dressed up?'

'It's a Savoy custom. What did you say?'

'That you wouldn't be back until very late; I wasn't sure of the time. He seemed upset so I asked him if I could help. He said the caller was a General Hawkins from Washington, and I think the rank and the city made him nervous. Mac always does that; it gets better telephone service. So I told him not to worry about a thing. I'd talk to the old fart. He liked that.' Anne returned to her book. 'Now, go call him. The number's on the desk in the other room. It's also on the desk in your place and also downstairs. I'm very flattered that you got it here first.'

139

It *was* possible, Sam reflected. Unlikely but within the scope of possibility, as certain radio waves indicated the possibility of additional civilizatïons in galactic space. 'What did Hawkins say? How was he uptight?'

'Oh, just that I was *here*, I suppose,' said the girl, reluctantly taking her eyes off the page. 'He started swearing and yelling and giving orders. I said, "Mac," I said, "go wash your mouth out with brown soap!" I always used to tell him that. I mean he uses language we stayed away from in Belle Isle. Anyway, he calmed down and started to laugh.' Anne's eyes drifted upward, at nothing. She was remembering, thought Sam, and those memories were not cold ones. 'He asked me if I'd got rid of the fancy gigolo waiter yet – that's what he calls Don – and if not, *why* not. And how you were such a nice fellow. You know, Mac thinks a great deal of you. Anyhow, it is very important that you call him back. I said it'd be awfully late; maybe not until three in the morning. But he said that was all right; it would only be ten o'clock in Washington.'

'Can't it wait until morning?'

'No. Mac was very emphatic. He said if you thought about putting it off I should tell you it had something to do with an Italian gentleman who was asking for you.'

'Did he add that he was in the undertaking business?'

'No. But I think you should call him. If you want privacy, you can use the phone in the other room.'

'Goddamn, boy! Isn't it a real small world! There you are halfway across the globe and who do you run into but little old Annie. Not that she's old, you understand —'

'I understand,' interrupted Sam, 'that you've got greetings for me from Dellacroce. What did you tell your deeply religious friend now? That I crucified Jesus?'

'Hell, no. That was just a little psych-prod, in case you were reluctant to return my call. I haven't even talked to Dellacroce. I don't think he's in favour of any further communications. Does that make you feel better?'

Devereaux lit a cigarette. It helped cover the slight pain

140

that was developing in his stomach. 'I'll tell you the truth, Mac. It simply makes me nervous that you called me at all. It makes me feel that you are about to say something that will not bring me any closer to Boston, or my mother, or my real employer, Aaron Pinkus; that's the way your psych-prod makes me feel.'

There was a long series of audible tsks from MacKenzie Hawkins in Washington. 'You are a very suspicious person. It must be the lawyer in you. How did everything go with Danforth?'

'He's a madman. He blows out hot and cold like a psycho. He also signed the papers; he's in for ten million for reasons I can't possibly imagine. The bank's in the Cayman Islands, which is, I assume, the reason for your telephone call.'

'You mean you think I'd ask you to go to the Caymans?'

'It crossed my mind.'

'I wouldn't do that. The Caymans aren't any fun. Just dinky little hot spots with lots of banks and pricky-shit bankers. They're trying to make the place into another Switzerland. ... No, I'll fly down there myself and take care of it. And you've got another ten thousand added to your account. Thought you'd like to know that.'

'*Mac!*' Devereaux's stomach experienced a sharp, stinging sensation. 'You can't *do* that!'

'It's easy, boy. You just make the cashier's cheque out for deposit only.'

'That's not what I mean! You have no *right* putting money into my account!'

'The bank didn't argue —'

'The bank wouldn't argue! *I* argue! I *am* arguing! Christ, don't you understand? It means you're paying me!'

'One-tenth of one per cent? Goddamn, boy, I'm cheating you!'

'I don't *want* to be paid! I don't want anything to *do* with any money from you! That makes me an *accessory*!'

'I don't know anything about that, but it's surely not right for one person to call upon the time and the talents of another person and not pay him for it.' Hawkins's voice had the ring of a quiet evangelist.

'Oh, shut up, you son of a bitch,' said Devereaux, recognizing the inevitability of defeat. 'Outside of Danforth, why did you call?'

'Well, now that you mention it, there's a fellow in West Berlin I'd like you to talk with.'

'Wait. Don't tell me,' interrupted Sam wearily. 'The airline tickets and the hotel reservations will be at the Savoy desk before I can say kippered herring.'

'By morning, anyway.'

'Okay, Mac, I know when I'm hung.' He was getting in deeper. Somehow, some way, some time, Sam thought, he would have to climb out.

MacKenzie wrote out the figure numerically.
$20,000,000.00
Then he wrote it in words:
Twenty million dollars.
Strange, but it had no real effect on him. It was merely a means, not an end in itself. Although it had occurred to him that he could easily call it an economic day, wrap it up, and retire to the south of France. Certainly, neither Dellacroce nor Danforth would sue. Not bloody likely. But that wasn't what it was all about; the money was both a conveyance and a by-product. And in its way, a legitimate form of punishment. The two marks deserved their losses.

But time was running short and he could not allow himself to get sidetracked. Summer was only a few months away; there was an enormous amount of work to do. The selection and training of the support personnel would be time-consuming. The leasing and stocking of the manoeuvre site would be difficult, especially the covert purchasing of equipment. The manoeuvres themselves would take a number of weeks. All told, there was a great deal to accomplish in a short time. Because of this it was a natural temptation to veer from the initial strategy and go with less than the full capitalization, but it would be wrong. That's for sure. He had set the figure of forty million not merely for the numerical symmetry to the four hundred million (although it certainly looked proper on the limited partnership agreement, in the blank lines he had filled out), but because forty million took care of *everything*, including last-extremity contingencies.

Otherwise known as quick-witted evacuation of the fire base.

It would have to be forty million. He was just about ready for his third investor.

Heinrich Koenig, Berlin.

Herr Koenig had not been easy. Whereas Sidney Danforth had overworked his modus operandi in Chile, and whereas Angelo Dellacroce had been just plain sloppy with regard to his Mediterranean payments and entirely too ostentatious in his manner of living, Heinrich Koenig had made no obvious errors, and lived the quiet life of a country squire in a peaceful rural town twenty-odd miles from Berlin.

But twenty-two years ago Koenig had played an enormously dangerous game brilliantly. A game that not only netted him a fortune but also ensured the capitalization and ultimate success of his various business enterprises.

During the height of the Cold War, Koenig was a double agent-cum-blackmailer. He began by secretly informing on single agents to both sides, then extorting cash – financed through opposing intelligence channels – from those seeking protection from exposure. Soon he was issued exclusive international, nontariff 'franchises' for his new companies from scores of countries dependent upon the economic goodwill of both giant factions. Finally, with the grace of Mephistopheles, he forced Washington, London, Berlin, Bonn, and Moscow into declaring his companies *outside* the regulatory legalities that governed other industries. Koenig accomplished this by explaining to each that he would inform the others of its past activities.

And then, to the profound relief of many governments, Koenig retired. He had built his empire on the trampled bodies – deceased and paralysed – of half the bureaucratic

143

and industrial population of Europe and America. He had remained untouchable because of the very real terror of chain reaction-reprisal. What bureaucrat, what under-secretary, what minister or statesman (indeed, what head of a government) would allow access to the horrors of Pandora's box? So, in retirement, Koenig remained as safe as during his halcyon days of furious activity.

Fear was Koenig's clout. But there was no fear or clout if a man didn't give a good goddamn about reaction or reprisals – governmental, industrial, or international.

And naturally this was Hawkins's weapon.

For there was an international army of victims who would quick-march for the kill if they thought they could do so with impunity, if everyone realized his past sins were known to everybody else. Complete disclosure was Mac's threat.

Koenig would certainly see the logic of this approach; it was the absence of it that had guaranteed his fortunes. He surely could foretell the effects of several hundred lengthy cablegrams sent simultaneously to several hundred in-habitants of the corridors of power throughout the world. Oh, yes! Koenig would be convinced, the instant a barrage of names, dates, and activities was rattled off to him.

MacKenzie picked up the raw-file Xeroxes from the bed, keeping the piles in sequence, and carried them to the coffee table in front of the couch. He sat down and with the red crayon he began circling two or three items on each page.

Things were going beautifully. It was all a question of making a realistic appraisal of one's capabilities and the logistics available to complement those abilities. Simple inventory. He picked up the Xeroxes, moved to the desk, and arranged the papers properly in front of the telephone. He was ready to calmly, dispassionately recite a record of international duplicity that would cause Genghis Khan to blush.

Heinrich Koenig would part with ten million dollars.

His eyes rimmed with black circles of exhaustion, Devereaux went through customs at Berlin's Tempelhof

Airport, fully prepared to have his forehead stamped by the officiously barking neo-Nazi who inspected his papers and luggage. Christ, he thought, give a German a rubber stamp and he went wild.

At one point he stared in amazement at the contents of his own suitcase. Everything was folded neatly and arranged tidily as though packed by Bergdorf Goodman, and he simply did not pack suitcases that way. Then through the fog of dislocation, he remembered that Anne had taken care of everything. She not only had packed for him, she had also accompanied him to the cashier's desk and helped him settle his bill.

She had done all this, reflected Sam, because he was not in condition to do much for himself. The insanity of his predicament had led him into a battle with a bottle of Scotch. He lost. The only thing he did remember to do was to airmail the goddamned limited partnership agreement to Hawkins.

Berlin's Kempinsky Hotel was a Teutonic version of New York's old Sherry-Netherland with a slightly harsher interior; the overstuffed lobby chairs seemed cast more in concrete than leather. Still, it screamed money, polished dark wood, and terribly proper clerks Sam knew hated his weak, democratically oriented, and inferior guts.

The front desk dispensed with him efficiently and swiftly. He was escorted by a disagreeable, ageing SS Oberführer who treated his suitcase as though it contained bagels and lox. Once inside the suite (it was enormous; Mac Hawkins did send him first class) the Oberführer snapped up the shades in the various rooms with the authority of a man used to issuing commands to a firing squad. Devereaux, fearing for his life, grossly overtipped him, saw him to the door as if he were a visiting diplomat and bid him a gracious *auf Wiedersehen*!

He opened his suitcase. Anne had possessed the foresight to wrap a full bottle of Scotch in a Savoy towel. If there was ever time to ingest the indigestible, it was now. Not much; just enough to get the motor running.

145

There was a knock on the door. Sam was so startled he coughed a mouthful of whisky over the bed. He corked the bottle and furiously looked for a place to hide it.

Under the pillow! Covered by the bedspread! He stopped. What was he doing? What the hell was the matter with him? What was *happening* to him? *Goddamn you, MacKenzie Hawkins!*

He took a deep breath, and calmly placed the bottle on the dresser top. He took another deep breath, opened the door, and promptly, involuntarily, expelled every bit of air in his lungs.

Standing in the door frame was the blonde Aphrodite from Palo Alto, California, catalogued in his memory as Narrow and Pointed. The third Mrs MacKenzie Hawkins. Lillian.

'I knew it was you! I said to the man at the desk that it *had* to be you!'

Sam was not sure why he had catalogued Lillian as Narrow and Pointed. 'Narrow' did the lady an injustice. Perhaps it was a relative adjective, subject to the immediate visual comparison to the other six.

Devereaux was thinking these absurd thoughts and – he was aware – staring like a twelve-year-old at his first *Artists and Models* magazine, while Lillian sat across from him, explaining that she had flown into Berlin three days ago to attend a two-week course in gourmet cooking.

Of course, it was unbelievable. After all, he was a skilled attorney. He had analysed scores of crime-ridden mentalities, stripping away the layers of fraud from sophisticated deceivers on all levels of the social jungle. In spite of his drained mind and body, he was not a man to be conned easily and he would let the third Mrs MacKenzie Hawkins know that – in *spades*! He stared at her harder, then mentally shrugged. What the hell!

'So there we are, Sam. I may call you Sam, mayn't I? It's amazing what an interest in really fine cooking can lead to.'

'But entirely plausible, Lillian! That's what makes

146

coincidences truly – well, coincidental!' Sam laughed quasi-hysterically, doing his best to control his eyes. He was simply too exhausted to be successful; he just gave up and let his eyes roam freely.

'And I can't think of a better way to see Berlin. If we're lucky, we can find an indoor tennis court! I hear the hotel has a swimming pool; perhaps a gymnasium —' Lillian stopped and Devereaux felt deprived; in his spent condition he was enjoying the soft, breathless, aural massage. 'I may be taking far too much for granted. Are you travelling alone?'

He knew he shouldn't. He *shouldn't*.

'More alone than I've ever been in my life.'

'Well, we certainly can't have that. If you don't mind my saying so, you look dreadfully tired. I think you've been working half to death. You really need someone to look after you.'

'I am only a warm shadow of my substance. ...'

'You poor lamb. Come over here and let me rub your shoulder blades. It does wonders, it really, really does.'

'I am a wasted vestige. I am filled with vacuum and molten lead. ...'

'You're exhausted, my lamb. That's the good boy; stretch out and put your head on Lilly's lap. Oh my, your temples are so warm. And your neck muscles are much too tense. There, that's better; doesn't it feel better?'

It did. He could feel her nimble fingers unbutton his shirt and the gentle hands moving about his chest, caressing his flesh with the touch of angels. What the hell. He opened his eyes, his sight was filled with the unbearable loveliness of two magnificent breasts inches above his face.

'Do you like hot tubs filled with lots of soap bubbles that smell like roses and springtime?' he whispered.

'Not actually,' she whispered back. 'I'm partial to warm showers. Straight up, as it were.'

Sam smiled.

CHAPTER THIRTEEN

The fragrance permeated the air around him; he did not need to open his eyes to know its source.

If he was able to reconstruct the previous evening with any accuracy – and the quiescence below his waist convinced him that he could – they had spent most of the night in the Kempinsky shower.

Sam opened his eyes. Lillian was beside him, sitting up against the pillows with a pair of horn-rimmed glasses perched on her lovely upturned nose. She was reading from an enormous piece of frayed cardboard, the white sheet covering her chest but not for an instant obscuring the shafts beneath.

'Hello,' he said quietly.

'Good morning!' She looked down at him and positively beamed. 'Do you know what time it is?'

The blonde creature *was* a healthy type, he considered. It must be all that California surfboarding, or perhaps MacKenzie Hawkins had taught her to do pushups. 'My watch is under the covers with my wrist. I do not know what time it is.'

'It's twenty after ten. You slept for eleven hours. How do you feel?'

'Are you telling me we went to bed – I was asleep – by eleven thirty last night?'

'You could be heard at the Brandenburg Gate. I kept shoving you to stop your snoring. You were positively operatic. How's your head?'

'Fairly secure, as a matter of fact. I wonder why?'

'All that steam. And exercise. Actually, you weren't capable of drinking a great deal. I think your bloodstream went into revolt.' Lillian picked up a pencil from the bedside table and lightly checked the menu.

'You smell terrific,' he said after several moments of looking up at her, remembering the sightlines from her lap and the touches of angels over his chest.

'So do you, lamb,' she replied, smiling, removing her glasses, and gazing down at Sam. 'Do you know, you have a very acceptable body?'

'It has its points.'

'I mean you have a fundamentally sound physique, moderately well proportioned and coordinated. It's really a pity you've let it disintegrate.' She tapped her glasses against her chin like a doctor studying postoperative conditions.

'Well, I wouldn't go so far as to say disintegrate. I played lacrosse once. I was pretty good.'

'I'm sure you were, well over a decade ago. Now look here —' Lilly put down her glasses and peeled the blankets away from Devereaux's chest. 'See here. And *here* and here and *here*! Absolutely no tone whatsoever. Muscle pockets that've had no discernible use for years! And *here*.'

'Ouch!'

'Your latissimi dorsi are positively non-*existent*. When was the last time you exercised?'

'Last night. In the shower.'

'That aspect of your condition cannot be debated. But it's a minor part of the whole being —'

'Not to me it isn't!'

'— relative to the muscular network. Your body is a temple; don't let it crumble and decay with misuse and neglect. Spruce it up! Give it a chance to stretch and breathe and be useful; that's what it's meant for. Look at MacKenzie —'

'I object! I don't want to look at MacKenzie!'

'I'm speaking clinically.'

'I knew it,' mumbled Devereaux in defeat. 'I can't escape him. I'm possessed.'

'Do you realize that Mac is well over *fifty*? And take his body. It's taut. It's a coiled spring toned to perfection ...'

Lilly's eyes drifted up at nothing. As Anne's had done at

149

the Savoy. She was remembering, as Anne had remembered – and those memories were not cold.

'Well, for God's sake,' said Sam. 'Hawkins spent his whole life in the army. Running and jumping and killing and torturing. He had to stay in shape so he could stay alive. He had no choice.'

'You're wrong. Mac understands the meaning of full capacity, experiencing the total potential. He once said to me – well, never mind, it's unimportant.' The girl removed her hand from Devereaux's chest and reached for her glasses.

'No, please.' The bedroom in the Kempinsky might have been a bedroom in the Savoy. But the wives were not interchangeable; they were very individual. 'I'd like to hear what Mac said.'

Lilly held her glasses in both hands, fingering the stems pensively. '" Your body should be a realistic extension of your mind, pushed to its limit but not abused."'

'I liked the "change the outside, mix up the inside" better —'

'What?'

'Something else he said. Maybe I don't understand; the intellectual and the physical are poles apart. I might imagine I could fly off the Eiffel Tower, but I'd better not try it.'

'Because that wouldn't be realistic; it would be abusive. But you might train yourself to scale down it in record time. *That* would be the realistic, *physical* extension of your imagination. And it's important to attempt it.'

'Scale down the Eiffel Tower?'

'If flying off is a serious consideration.'

'It's not. If I follow this pseudoscholastic doggerel, you're saying that if you think about doing something you should actually translate it as much as possible into physical terms.'

'Yes. The main thing is not to remain inert.' Lilly waved her arms in emphasis; the sheet plummeted down.

Unbearably lovely, thought Devereaux. But at the moment untouchable; the girl was in debate.

150

'This is either far more complicated or much simpler than it sounds,' he said.

'It's more complicated, believe me,' she answered. 'The subtlety is in the obviousness.'

'You believe in this challenge concept, don't you?' Sam said. 'I mean it's fundamentally the necessary satisfaction of meeting the challenge, isn't it?'

'Yes, I suppose it is. For its own sake; to try to reach out for what you can imagine. To test your potential.'

'And you believe that.' There was no question implied.

'Yes, I do. Why?'

'Because at this moment my imagination is working so hard I can't stand it. I feel the necessity of physical expression; to test my potential. Within reasonable limits, of course.' He rose from his base camp until he sat facing her, their eyes level. He reached out and took her glasses, folded them, and dropped them over the side of the bed. He held out his hand and she gave him the menu.

Lillian's eyes were bright, her lips parted in a half smile. 'I was wondering when you were going to ask.'

And then the Nazi telephone rang.

The voice on the other end of the line belonged to a man brought up in his formative years watching all those war movies from Warner Brothers. Every syllable dripped evil.

'Ve do not - vill not - cannot shpeak on der telephone.'

'Go across the street and open a window. We'll shout,' replied Devereaux irritably.

'Der time ist der essence! You vill go down to der lobby, to der fart chair in front of der vindow, on der richt of der hentrance! Under der arm carry a folded copy of *Der Spiegel*. Und you vill be crossing der legs every twenty seconds.'

'I'm sitting down?'

'You vould look foolish crossing der legs standing up, mein Herr.'

'Suppose someone's sitting in the chair?'

The pause conveyed both anger and confusion. There followed a short, strange sound that gave rise to the image of

151

a small pig squealing in frustration. 'Remove him!'was the reply that followed the squeal.

'That's silly.'

'You vill do as I say! Dere is no time to argue! You vill be contacted. Fifteen minutes.'

'Hey, wait a minute! I just got up. I haven't had breakfast; I've got to shave —'

'Fourteen minutes, mein Herr!'

'I'm hungry!'

The connection was broken by a loud click on the line. 'To hell with him,' said Devereaux, turning back in anticipation to the extraordinary Lillian.

But Lillian was not where she should have been. Instead, she was standing on the other side of the bed in Sam's bathrobe.

'To coin a phrase, my darling, we were saved by the bell. You have things to do, and I really must get ready for class.'

'Class?'

'Die erstklassige Strudelschule,' said Lilly. 'Less expert but probably more fun than the Cordon Bleu in Paris. It starts at noon, We're over in the Leipziger Strasse; that's past Unter den Linden. I really should hurry.'

'What about – *us*? And breakfast and – don't you shower in the morning?'

Lilian laughed; it was a nice, genuine laugh. '*Die Schule* day is finished by three-thirty. I'll meet you back here.'

'What's your room number?'

'Five eleven.'

'I'm five nine.'

'I know. Isn't that marvellous.'

'Or something ...'

The confusion in the Kempinsky lobby was absurd. 'Der fart chair in front of der vindow' *was* occupied by an elderly gentleman whose close-cropped, bejowled head kept nodding down into the folds of neck flesh as he dozed. On his lap, unfortunately, was a folded copy of *Der Spiegel*.

The elderly man was, at first, annoyed, then furious at the

two men who flanked his chair and told him in no uncertain terms to get up and come with them. Twice Sam tried to intercede, explaining as best he could that he, too, had a folded copy of *Der Spiegel*. It did no good; the troopers were interested only in the gentleman sitting in the huge armchair. Finally, Devereaux stood directly in front of the two contacts and every twenty seconds, crossed and uncrossed his legs.

At which point the bell captain came up to Sam and in perfectly good, loud English gave him the directions to the men's room.

Whereupon a large woman with a striking resemblance to Dick Butkus approached the trio around the armchair and began hitting the two Gestapo men with both a hatbox and an extremely large, black leather handbag.

There was only one thing for it, thought Devereaux. He grabbed one of the contacts around the neck and pulled him away from the fire zone.

'You crazy son of a bitch! *I'm* the one! You're from Koenig, aren't you?'

Thirty seconds later Devereaux was propelled out of the Kempinsky entrance and into a nearby alley.

Halfway down the alley, taking up most of the space between the buildings, was an enormous open truck with a canvas tarpaulin stretched across the rear rigging poles. Under the tarpaulin, from deck to canvas, were hundreds of crates piled on top of one another, filled with thousands (it seemed like thousands) of screeching chickens.

There was a narrow corridor in the centre of the van between the crates. It led to the rear window of the cab. In front of the window were two tiny stools.

'Hey, come on! This is ridiculous! It's - goddamn it, it's unsanitary!'

His escorts nodded Germanically and smiled Germanically, and Germanically heaved Sam up into the tiny corridor and shoved him down the eighteen-inch passageway towards the stools.

All around him sharp beaks pecked at his person. The

noonday sun was completely blanketed out by the heavy canvas tarpaulin above. The odour of chickenshit was unbearable.

They drove for nearly an hour into the countryside, stopping every now and then to be looked over by cooperative East German soldiers who waved them on, pocketing *Deutschmarks* as they did so.

They entered a large farming complex. Cattle were grazing in the fields, silos and barns could be seen, barely, through the opening of the tiny passageway between the crates and the flying feathers at the rear of the truck.

Finally they stopped. Escort number one grinned his Germanic grin and led Sam into the sunlight.

He was marched into a large barn that reeked of cattle urine and fresh manure. He was led – Germanically – down a crisscross series of turns through the stinking building until they came to an empty stall. A row of blue ribbons denoted the residence of a prize steer.

Inside, sitting on a milking stool, surrounded by piles of bull-shit, was the heavyset man Sam knew was Heinrich Koenig.

He did not get up; he sat there and stared at Devereaux. In his tiny eyes, surrounded by folds of blemished flesh, were thunderbolts.

'So. ...' Koenig remained immobile, drawing out the word disdainfully, waving the escorts away.

'So?' replied Sam, his voice cracking slightly, aware of the wet chicken droppings on his back.

'You are the representative from this monster, General Hawkins?' Koenig pronounced the word 'general' with a hard Germanic *G*.

'I'd like to clear that up, if I may,' said Devereaux with false laughter. 'Actually, I'm just a slight acquaintance, barely know the man. I'm a low profile attorney from Boston; actually not much more than a law clerk. I work for a little Jewish man named Pinkus. You wouldn't like him. My mother lives in Quincy and through the strangest coincidence —'

154

'Enough!' A very loud fart could be heard in the vicinity of the milking stool. 'You are the contact, the intermediary, with this devil from hell!'

'Well, as to that, I would have to debate the legal association; said association subject to the clarification of intent with regard to foreknowledge. I don't believe —'

'You are a jackal, a hyena! But such dogs bark loudly if the meat is sufficient. Tell me. This Hawkins. He is a Gehlen operation, *nein*?'

'A who?'

'Gehlen!'

Devereaux remembered. Gehlen was the master spy of the Third Reich who bought and sold for all factions after the war. It would not do for Koenig to think there was any connection between Hawkins and Gehlen; for it would mean there was a link to one Sam Devereaux, who was way out of his league.

'Oh, I'm sure not. I don't think General Hawkins ever heard of what's-his-name. I know *I* haven't.' The chicken-shit was melting under Sam's shirt, all over his fevered back.

Koenig rose slowly from the milking stool, a second flatus loudly proclaiming his ascent. He spoke with quiet, intense hostility.

'The general has my reluctant respect. He has sent me a babbling idiot. Give me the papers, fool.'

'The papers —' Sam reached into his jacket pocket for another Xerox copy of the Shepherd Company's limited partnership agreement.

The German fingered the papers silently, squeezing each one as he flipped it. His audible reactions were blunt: a combination of farts and grunts.

'This is outrageous! A great injustice! Political enemies everywhere! All wishing only to destroy me!' Beads of saliva formed at the corners of Koenig's mouth.

'I agree wholeheartedly,' said Devereaux, eagerly nodding his head. 'I'd throw it away if I were you.'

'You would like that? All of you. You are all out to get me! My great contributions that kept peace in the world, enemies

155

in constant touch, that opened hot lines and red lines and blue lines between the great powers – these are forgotten. Now you whisper behind my back. You tell lies about non-existent bank accounts, even my humble places of residence. You never concede that I earned every *Deutschmark* I possess! When I retired, none of you could tolerate it; you did not have me to kick around any longer! And now this! The injustice!'

'Oh, I understand.'

'You understand nothing! Give me something to write with, you idiot.'

He farted and signed.

CHAPTER FOURTEEN

The bells of the Angelus pealed in solemn, vibrant splendour. They echoed throughout St Peter's Square, floated above Bernini's marble guardians, and were heard in quiet celebration beyond the dome, deep in the Vatican gardens. Seated on a bench of white stone, looking up at the orange rays of the descending sun, was a corpulent man with a face best described as having weathered seven decades good-naturedly, if not always peacefully. The face was full; but the peasant quality of the bone structure under the folds of flesh would tend to deny that the face was pampered. The man's eyes were wide and large and brown and soft; they held nearly equal parts of strength, perception, resignation, and amusement.

He was dressed in the splendid white robes of his office. The highest office of the Holy Apostolic Catholic Church, the descendant of Peter himself, the Bishop of Rome, the spiritual commander of 400 million souls throughout the earth.

Pope Francesco I, the Vicar of Christ.

Born Giovanni Bombalini in a small village north of Padua in the first years of the century. It was a birth that was recorded sketchily, at best, for the Bombalinis were not affluent. Giovanni was delivered by a midwife who, as often as not, forgot to report the fruits of her labours (and her patient's labours) to the village clerk, secure in the knowledge that the church would do *something*; christenings made money. Actually Giovanni Bombalini's emergence into this world might never have been legally recorded at all except that his father had a wager with his cousin Frescobaldi, three villages to the north, that his second child would be a male. Bombalini Senior wanted to take no chances that his cousin Frescobaldi would renege on the bet, so he went to the village hall himself to report the birth of a male child.

As it happened, part of the wager was that Frescobaldi's wife - who was expecting in the same month - would *not* give birth to a boy. But of course she did, and the bet was cancelled. This child, Guido Frescobaldi, was born - according to the sketchy records - two days after *his* cousin, Giovanni.

Early in his life Giovanni showed signs of being different from the other children of the village. To begin with he did not care to learn his catechism by verbal repetition; he wanted to *read* it, *then* memorize it. This upset the village priest for it smacked of precociousness and somehow was an affront to authority, but the child would not be denied.

The ways of Giovanni Bombalini were indeed extraordinary. Although he never shirked his labours in the fields, he was rarely too tired to stay up half the night reading whatever he could get his hands on. When he was twelve he discovered the *biblioteca* in Padua, which was hardly the library in Milan, nor Venice, nor certainly Rome, but it was said by those who knew Giovanni that he read every book in Padua, then Milan, then Venice. By which time his priest recommended him to the holy fathers in Rome.

The church was Giovanni's answer to a prayer. And as long as he prayed a great deal - which was easier, though no less time-consuming than labouring in the fields - he was allowed to read more than he ever thought would be allowed him.

By the age of twenty-two, Giovanni Bombalini was an ordained priest. Some said the best-read priest in Rome, an *erudito fantastico*. But Giovanni did not possess the properly stern visage of a proper Vatican *erudito*; nor did he assume the proper attitudes of certainty with regard to everyday truths. He was forever finding exceptions and flexibilities in liturgical history, pointing out (some said mischievously) that the writings of the church found their strength in honest contradictions.

At twenty-six Giovanni Bombalini was a sharp pain in the large Vatican ass. Aggravated further by his matured appearance, which was the antithesis of the gaunt, academic image so desired by Rome's *eruditi*. He was, if anything, the caricature of a field peasant from the northern districts. Short of stature, stocky, and wide of girth, he looked like a farmhand more at home in the goat stables than in the marble halls of the various Vatican *collegia*. No amount of theological erudition, or good nature, or, indeed, deep belief in his church could counteract the combined aggravation of his mind and appearance. So posts were found for him in such unlikely locations as the Gold Coast, Sierra Leone, Malta, and, through an error, Monte Carlo. An exhausted Vatican dispatcher misread the name Montes Claros and inserted Monte Carlo - no doubt because he had never *heard* of Brazil's Montes Claros - and the fortunes of Giovanni Bombalini turned.

For into the cauldron of high stakes and high emotions wandered the simple looking priest with the bemused eyes, gentle humour, and a head packed with more knowledge than any twelve international financiers put together. He'd had little to do in the Gold Coast, Sierra Leone, and Malta, so he had occupied his time, when not praying or teaching the natives, by subscribing to scores of reading services and adding to his already extraordinary memory bank.

It is common knowledge that people who live with constant motion, and high risk, and a great deal of alcohol, occasionally need spiritual consolation. So Father Bombalini began to comfort a few stray lambs. And to the amazement of these first few strays, they found not so much a simple priest who outlined penance, but a most amusing fellow who could discourse at length on almost any subject: economic conditions of world markets, historical precedents for anticipated geopolitical events, and, particularly, food. (Here he favoured the more basic sauces, eschewing the artifices of the often inappropriate *haute cuisine*.)

Before too many months had passed, Father Bombalini was a regular guest at many of the larger hotel suites and great houses of the Côte d'Azur. This rather odd-looking, rotund prelate was a marvellous raconteur, and it always made everyone feel better to have him around before going out to covet – successfully – his neighbour's wife.

And a number of excessively large contributions to the church were made in Father Giovanni's name. With increasing frequency.

Rome could no longer overlook Bombalini. The exchequers of the Vatican treasury said so.

The war found Monsignor Bombalini in various Allied capitals and occasionally attached to various Allied armies. This was brought about for two reasons. The first was his adamant deposition to his superiors that he could not remain neutral in light of the known Hitlerian objectives. He catalogued his thesis with sixteen pages of historical, theological, and liturgical precedents; none but the Jesuits could understand it, and they were on his side. So Rome shut its eyes and hoped for the best. The second reason for his wartime travels was that the international rich of Monte Carlo in the thirties were now colonels and generals and diplomats and ambassadorial liaisons. They *all* wanted him. There were so many intra-Allied requests for his services that in Washington, J. Edgar Hoover marked Bombalini's file: *Highly Suspect. May be a fairy.*

The postwar years were a time of rapid acceleration up the Vatican ladder for Cardinal Bombalini. Much of his success was due to his close friendship with Angelo Roncalli, with whom he shared a number of unorthodox views, as well as a penchant for decent, but not necessarily exclusive, wine and a good game of cards after the evening prayers.

As he sat on the white stone bench in the Vatican gardens, Giovanni Bombalini – Pope Francesco – reflected that he missed Roncalli. They had accomplished much together; it had been good. And the similarities of their respective ascendencies to the chair of St Peter never ceased to amuse him. Roncalli, John, would have been amused, too; no doubt, was, of course.

They were both compromises offered by the stern,

160

orthodox constituencies of the Curia to quiet the fires of discontent within the global flock. Neither compromise expected to reign very long. But Roncalli had it easy; he had only theological arguments and undeveloped social reformers to contend with. He didn't have damn fool young priests who wanted to marry and have children and, when of other persuasions, run homosexual parishes! Not that any of these personally bothered Giovanni; there was absolutely *nothing* in theological law or dogma that actually prohibited marriage and offspring; and, as far as the other, if love of fellowman did not surmount biblical ambiguities, what had they learned? But, Mother of God, the fuss that was made!

There was so much to do – and the doctors had made it clear that his time was limited. It was the only thing they *were* clear about; they could isolate no specific illness, no particular malady. They just conferred and confirmed that his 'vital signs' were slowing down at an alarming rate. He had demanded openness from them; Mother of God, he had no fear of death! He welcomed the rest. He and Roncalli could plough the heavenly vineyards together and take up their baccarat again. At last count Roncalli owed him something over six hundred million lire.

He had told the doctors that they looked too long in their microscopes and too little at the obvious. The machine was wearing out; it was as simple as that. Whereupon they nodded pontifically and uttered sombrely: 'Three months, four at the most, Holy Father.'

Doctors. *Basta!* Veterinarians with *cugini* in the Curia! Their bills were outrageous! The goatherders of Padua knew more about medicine; they had to.

Francesco heard the footsteps behind him and turned. Walking up the garden path was a young papal aide whose name escaped him. The youthful priest carried a clipboard in his hand. There was a painted crucifix on the underside; it looked silly.

'Your Holiness asked that we resolve some minor matters before the vesper hour.'

'By all means, Father. What are they?'

161

The aide rattled off a series of inconsequential functions, ceremonial in nature, and Giovanni flattered the young prelate by requesting his opinion on most of them.

'Then there is a request from an American periodical, *Viva Gourmet*. I would not mention it to the Holy Father except that the inquiry was accompanied by a strong recommendation from the United States Armed Forces Information Service.'

'That is a most unusual combination, is it not, Father?'

'Yes, Your Holiness. Quite incomprehensible.'

'What was the request?'

'They had the effrontery to ask the Holy Father to submit to an interview with a lady journalist regarding the pontiff's favourite dishes.'

'Why is that an effrontery?'

The young prelate paused; he seemed momentarily perplexed. Then he continued with confidence. 'Because Cardinal Quartze said it was, Holy Father.'

'Did the learned cardinal give his reasons? Or, as usual, did he commune with God all by himself and simply deliver the divine edict?' Francesco tried not to overdo his perfectly natural reaction to Ignatio Quartze. The cardinal was a loathsome fellow in just about every department. He was an *erudito aristocratico* from a powerful Italian-Swiss family, who had the compassion of a disturbed cobra. Looked like one, too, thought Giovanni.

'He did, Holy Father,' replied the priest. And the instant he spoke, the aide was struck by a sudden embarrassment. 'He – he —'

'May I suggest, Father,' said the pontiff with graceful understanding, 'that our splendidly berobed cardinal offered the opinion that the pope's favourite dishes were less than impressive?'

'I – I —'

'I see he did. Well, Father, it is true that I subscribe to simpler cooking than does our cardinal with the unfortunate nasal drip, but it is not due to lack of knowledge. Merely lack of, perhaps, ostentation; not that our cardinal, who is

162

afflicted with that unfortunate eye that strays to the right as he talks, is ostentatious. I don't believe it ever crossed his mind.'

'No, of course not, Holy Father.'

'But I think that during these days of high prices and widespread unemployment, it might be a fine idea for your pontiff to outline a number of inexpensive, though I assure you, quite excellent dishes. Who is the journalist? A lady, you say? Don't ever tell anyone I said it, Father, but they are not the best cooks.'

'No, surely not, Your Holiness. The nuns of Rome are strenuous —'

'Galvanizing, Father. Positively galvanizing! Who is the journalist from this gourmet periodical?'

'Her name is Lillian von Schnabe. She is American, from the state of California, married to an older man, a German immigrant who fled Hitler. As coincidence would have it, she is currently in Berlin.'

'I merely asked who she was, Father. Not her biography. How do you know all this?'

'It was in the recommendation from the United States Army Information Service. The military think highly of her, apparently.'

'More than apparently. So, her husband fled Hitler? One does not turn away from such compassionate women. Coupled with the state of food prices – a number of inexpensive papal dishes is called for. Set up an appointment, Father. You may tell our resplendent cardinal, who suffers from the unfortunate affliction of a high-decibelled wheeze, that we truly hope our decision is not an affront to him. *Viva Gourmet*. The Lord God has been good to me; it is a mark of recognition. I wonder why its correspondent is in Berlin? There's a monsignor in Bonn who makes an excellent *Sauerbraten*.'

'I swear, you've got feathers in your teeth!' said Lillian as Sam walked into the room.

'It's better than chickenshit.'

163

'What?'

'My business contact had a strange method of transportation.'

'What are you talking about?'

'I want to take a shower.'

'Not with *me*, honey!'

'I've never been so hungry in my life. They wouldn't even
stop for a – what the hell is it? A strudel. Everything was *ein,
zwei, drei*! *Mach schnell!* Christ, I'm starved! They really
think they won the war!'

Lillian backed away from him. 'You are the filthiest, most
foul-smelling man I've ever seen. I'm surprised they let you in
the lobby.'

'I think we goose-stepped.' Sam noticed a large white
business envelope on the bureau. 'What's that?'

'The front desk sent it up. They said it was urgent and they
weren't sure you'd stop for messages.'

'I can only conclude your ex, the fruitcake, has been busy.'
Devereaux picked up the envelope. Inside were airline
tickets and a note. He didn't really have to read the note; the
airline tickets said it all.

Algiers.

Then he read the note.

'*No!* Goddamn it, *no!* That's less than an hour from now!'

'What is?' asked Lillian. 'The plane?'

'What plane? How the hell do *you* know there's a plane?'

'Because MacKenzie called. From Washington. You can
imagine his shock when I answered —'

'Spare me your inventive details!' roared Devereaux as he
raced to the telephone. 'I've got several things to say to that
devious son of a bitch! Even convicts get a day off! At least
time for a meal and a shower!'

'You can't reach him now,' said Lillian quickly. 'That was
one of the reasons he called. He'll be out for the rest of the
day.'

Sam turned menacingly. Then he stopped. This girl could
probably cut him in two. 'And I suppose he offered a
suggestion as to why I should be on that plane. Once he got

over the shock of hearing your lovely voice, of course.'

Lillian looked puzzled. It crossed Devereaux's mind that the puzzlement was not entirely genuine. 'Mac mentioned something about a German named Koenig. How anxious this Koenig was for you to leave Berlin – one way or the other.'

'The less controversial method being Air France to Paris and from Paris to Algiers?'

'Yes, he did say that. Although not in those exact words. He's terribly fond of you, Sam. He speaks of you as a son. The son he never had.'

'If there's a Jacob, I'm Esau. Otherwise, I'm fucked as Absalom.'

'Vulgarity isn't called for —'

'It's the only thing that *is* called for! What the hell is in Algiers?'

'A sheik named Azaz-Varak,' answered Lillian Hawkins von Schnabe.

Hawkins left the Watergate in a hurry. He had no desire to talk to Sam; he had absolute faith in Lillian, in all the girls, actually. They were doing their jobs splendidly! Besides, he was to meet with an Israeli major who, with any luck, could put the final pieces of the puzzle together for him. The puzzle being Sheik Azaz-Varak. By the time Devereaux reached Algiers a telephone call would have to be made. The Hawk could not make it without that final item which would ensure the last of the Shepherd Company's capitalization.

That Azaz-Varak was a thief on a global scale was nothing new. During the Second World War he sold oil at outrageous prices to the Allies and the Axis simultaneously, favouring only those who paid instantly in cash. This did not make him enemies, however; instead, his policies engendered respect, from Detroit to Essen.

But the war was ancient history. That war. It was Azaz-Varak's behaviour in a far more recent conflagration that interested Hawkins: the Mideast crisis.

Azaz-Varak was nowhere to be found.

While oaths were hurled across the lands of the Middle

165

East, and the world watched armies clash against armies, and crisis-laden conferences took place, and outrageous profits were made, the greediest sheik of them all claimed to have a case of shingles and went to the Virgin Islands.

Goddamn! It didn't make sense! So MacKenzie went back into Azaz-Varak's raw files and studied them with the eye of a professional. He began to find the pattern in the years between 1946 and 1948. Sheik Azaz-Varak had apparently spent a considerable amount of time in Tel Aviv!

According to the reports, his first few trips were made quite openly. It was supposed that Azaz-Varak sought Israeli women for his harem. Thereafter, however, Azaz-Varak continued to fly into Tel Aviv, but not openly, landing at night in outlying airfields that could accommodate his most modern and expensive private planes.

More women? Hawkins had researched exhaustively and was unable to unearth the name of a single Israeli female who ever went back to the sheikdom of Azaz-Kuwait.

Then, what had Azaz-Varak been doing in the state of Israel? And why had he travelled there so frequently?

MacKenzie's breakthrough came, strangely enough, from information supplied by naval intelligence on the island of St Thomas, where Azaz-Varak had fled during the Mideast war. There, he tried to buy up more property than anyone wished to sell. Rebuffed, he became furious.

The islanders had enough trouble. They did not need Arabs with harems and slaves. Jesus! *Slaves!* The very idea sent the bureau of tourism into apoplexy; visions of all that kitchen help in revolt were positively nauseating. Azaz-Varak was systematically prevented from buying two buckets of sand. When it was suspected he was trying to negotiate through second and third parties, covenants were included that would have made Palm Beach green with envy and the ACLU purple with rage. Simply put: no fucking Arabs could own, lease, sublease, visit, or trespass.

So in his frustration, the acquisitive sheik angrily, and hastily, brought in an American holding company called the Buffalo Corporation and tried to negotiate through it. There *were* laws and St Thomas was a United States possession. And it did not take much research on Hawkins's part to uncover the fact that the Buffalo Corporation – address: Albany Street, Buffalo, New York; telephone: unlisted – was a subsidiary of an unknown company called Pan-Friendship, main office: Beirut; telephone: also unlisted.

Subsequent overseas calls to several Israeli clearing-houses made stunningly clear what Azaz-Varak had been doing during all those visits to the Jewish homeland. He owned half the real estate in Tel Aviv, much of it in the poorer sections of town. The sheik was a Tel Aviv slumlord.

The Buffalo Corporation collected rents from all over the city. *And* if the Israeli major – who was in ordnance and supply – confirmed a report the Hawk had received from some old Cambodian buddies in the CIA, the Buffalo Corporation was also in another business. One that held most unfortunate implications for the owner of said Buffalo Corporation, insofar as he was the very Arab who scared hell out of the realtors in St Thomas.

The report was simple; all MacKenzie needed was one military official to corroborate it. For the CIA boys learned that a major expeditor of petro-chemicals and fuel for the army of Israel during the Mideast war was a little-known American company called the Buffalo Corporation.

Sheik Azaz-Varak not only owned half the real estate in Tel-Aviv, but at the height of the conflict, he fed the Israeli war machine so the maniacs in Cairo wouldn't damage his investments.

It was the sort of information that simply demanded a long-distance call, thought MacKenzie Hawkins. To the sheikdom of Azaz-Kuwait.

Devereaux appreciated the sympathy from the Air France stewardess, but he would have appreciated food more. There were no supplies in the galley of the 727, a condition that would be corrected in Paris. Apparently – and there was no way to be sure he understood correctly – the Boche catering trucks that serviced Air France had been tied up in a Russian

167

induced traffic jam on the autobahn, and what had been left in the galley had been stolen by the Czechoslovakian ground crew in Prague. And besides, the food was better in Paris.

So Sam smoked cigarettes, caught himself chewing bits of tobacco, and tried to concentrate on the doings of MacKenzie Hawkins. His seatmate was some kind of Eastern religious, perhaps a Sikh, with brown skin tinged with grey, a very small black beard, a purple turban, and darting eyes that were as close as a human's could be to those of a rat. It made thinking about MacKenzie easier; there would be little conversation on the trip to Paris.

Hawkins had raised his third ten million. And now there was an Arabian sheik who was the fourth and final mark. Whatever it was that MacKenzie had culled from the raw files had the effect of thermonuclear blackmail. Christ! *Forty million!*

What was he going to *do* with it? What kind of 'equipment and support personnel' (whatever the hell *they* were) could possibly cost so much?

Granted one did not kidnap a pope with a dollar and a quarter in his pocket, but was it necessary to cover the Italian national debt to do it?

One thing was certain. The Hawk's plan for the kidnapping included the exchange of extraordinary sums of money. And whoever accepted such sums were *ipso facto* accessories to the most outrageous abduction in history! It was another avenue he, Sam, could explore. And a pretty good one at that. If he could obtain the names of even a few of Mac's suppliers, he could scare them right out of the picture. Certainly the Hawk was not going to say to someone: *Yes, I'll buy that railroad train because I'm going to kidnap this pope fellow and it'll be a big help.* No, that was hardly the way of an experienced general officer who had drugged half the pouch couriers in Southeast Asia. But if he, Sam, reached that same someone and said: *You know that train you're selling to that bearded idiot? It's going to be used to kidnap the pope. Have a good night's sleep* – well, that was something else again. The train would not be sold. And if he

168

could prevent a train from being sold, perhaps he could prevent other supplies from reaching the Hawk. MacKenzie was army; lines of supply were paramount to any operation. Without them whole strategies were altered, even abandoned. It was military holy writ.

Yes, reflected Devereaux, gazing out into the German twilight from the foodless Air France plane, it was a very decent avenue to explore. Coupled with his first consideration – finding out how the Hawk intended to pull off the kidnapping, and the second consideration – finding out what specific blackmailing material MacKenzie held over his investors, the suppliers were a third, powerful ingredient. In preventive medicine.

Sam closed his eyes, conjuring up visions of long ago. He was in the basement of his home in Quincy, Massachusetts. On the huge table in the centre of his room was his set of Lionel trains, going around and around, weaving in and out of the miniature shrubbery and over the tiny bridges and through the toy tunnels. But there was something strange about the sight. Except for the engine and the caboose, all the other vehicles were marked identically: 'Refrigerator Car. Food.'

At Orly Airport, the passengers to Algiers were told to remain on the plane. For Devereaux nothing mattered once he saw the white truck pull up alongside the aircraft and men in white coats transferring immaculate steel containers into the galley. He even smiled at Rat Eyes beside him, noticing as he did so that his seatmate's purple turban had slipped somewhat over his brown forehead. Sam might have said something – he'd learned long ago that even strangers appreciated it when you told them their zippers were open – but since several other turbaned acquaintances who'd boarded at Orly had come up to pay their respects and had said nothing, Devereaux felt it wasn't his place. Besides most of the other purple turbans seemed a touch lopsided. Perhaps it was a custom indigenous to the particular religious sect.

Regardless, all Sam could think about were the immaculate steel trays, now securely in the Air France galley broilers, sending out deliriously inviting wafts of *escalope de veau, tournedos, sauce Béarnaise*, and, if he was not mistaken, steak *au poivre*. God was in his heaven and on Air France as well. Good Lord! Devereaux vaguely calculated the hours since he'd eaten: It was nearing thirty-six.

Unintelligible words droned over the cabin loudspeakers; the 727 taxied out on to the field. Two minutes later they were airborne and the stewardesses went about the business of distributing the most meaningful literature Sam could think of: menus.

His order took up more time than anyone else in the cabin. This was partially due to the fact that he salivated and had to swallow as he spoke. There followed an agonizing hour. Normally it was not agonizing to Sam, for it was taken up with cocktails. But today he could not drink. His stomach was too empty.

At length, dinner approached. The stewardess went down the aisle spreading the miniature tablecloths, placing the napkin-enclosed silverware, and reconfirming the choice of dinner wines. Sam could not help himself; he kept craning his neck over the edge of the seat. The scents from the galley were driving him crazy. Every odour was a banquet to his nostrils; the juices ran down his throat at each recognizable smell.

And naturally it had to happen.

The weird looking Sikh beside him lunged from his seat and unravelled his purple turban. Out of the cloth fell a large, lethal revolver. It crashed to the deck of the aircraft; Rat Eyes lunged down, retrieved it, and screamed.

'Aiyee! Aiyee! Aiyee! Al Fatah! Al Fatah! Aiyee!'

It was the signal; a screeching symphony of 'Aiyees' and 'Fatahs' could be heard behind first class, throughout the tube of the long fuselage. From somewhere in his trousers, Rat Eyes pulled out an extremely long, murderous looking scimitar.

Sam stared numbly. In complete defeat.

So the man wasn't a Sikh. He was an Arab. A goddamn fucking Palestinian Arab.

170

What else?

The stewardess now faced the murderous blade; the barrel of the huge pistol was jammed between her breasts. She did her best, but the terror could not be concealed.

'On the wires! On the wires to your captain!' screeched the Palestinian. 'This aircraft will proceed to Algeria. This is the wishes of Al Fatah! To Algiers! Only Algiers! Or you will all die. *Die! Die!*'

'*Mais, oui, monsieur,*' screamed the stewardess. 'The aircraft *is* proceeding to Algiers! *That* is our destination, monsieur!'

The Arab was crestfallen. His wild, piercing eyes became temporary pools of dull mud, the frustration conveyed by the tiny dots of questioning chaos in the centre of the mud.

Then the eyes sprang back once more to the vivid, cruel, violent exuberance.

He slashed the air with the huge scimitar and waved the pistol maniacally.

His demonic, defiant screams were worthy of shattering the high-altitude glass, but fortunately did not.

'*Aiyee! Aiyee! Arafat!* Hear the word of *Arafat*! Jewish dogs and Christian pigs! There will be no food or water until we *land*! *That is the word of Arafat!*'

Deep within the recesses of Sam's subconscious a small voice whispered: *You're fucked, babe.*

171

CHAPTER FIFTEEN

The stage manager winced; two violins and three horns went sour during the crescendo of 'Musetta's Waltz'. The act's finale was ruined. Again.

He made a note for the conductor who he could see was smiling blissfully, unaware of the grating dissonance. It was understandable: the man's hearing wasn't so good anymore.

As the stage manager looked out, he saw that the spotlight operator had dozed off again; or had gone to the toilet. The shaft of light was angled down, immobile, into the pit – on a confused flautist – instead of on Mimi.

He made a note.

On the stage itself was another problem. Two problems. The swinging gates into the café had been hung upside down, the pointed tops inverted so that they vee'd up from the floor, providing the audience a clear view behind the scenery where numerous bare feet were being rubbed and not a few extras scratched themselves in boredom. The second problem was the step unit on stage left; it had become unhinged so that Rodolfo's leg plummeted down into the open space causing his tights to rip up to his crotch.

The stage manager sighed and made two more notes.

Puccini's *La Bohème* was being given its usual performance by the company. *Mannaggia!*

As he finished putting three exclamation points after his twenty-sixth note of the evening, the assistant box-office manager approached his lectern and handed him a message.

It was for Guido Frescobaldi, and because any distraction was preferable to watching the remainder of the act, the stage manager unfolded the paper and read it.

Instantly, involuntarily, he caught his breath. Old

172

Frescobaldi would have a fit – if it was possible for Guido to *have* a fit. There was a newspaper reporter in the audience who wanted to meet with Frescobaldi after the performance.

The stage manager shook his head sadly, recalling vividly Guido's tears and protestations when the last (and only) newspaper reporter interviewed him. There were two reporters actually: a man from Rome and a silent Chinese colleague. Both Communists.

It was not the interview that had upset Frescobaldi, it was the article that came out of it.

Impoverished Opera Artist Struggles for People's Culture as Cousin, the Pope, Lives in Indolent Luxury off the Honest Sweat of Oppressed Workers!

That had been for openers. The front page headlined the story in the Communist newspaper, *Il Popolo*. The article had gone on to say that diligent investigative reporting on the part of *Il Popolo*'s journalists – ever alert to the inequities of capitalism's unholy alliance with savage organized religion – had uncovered the crass injustice done to this look-alike relative of the world's most powerful and despotic religious leader. How one Guido Frescobaldi sacrificed for his art while his cousin, Pope Francesco, stole everyone blind. How Guido contributed his great talent for the good of the masses, never seeking material rewards, satisfied only that his contributions uplifted the spirit of the people. So different from his cousin, the pontiff, who contributed nothing but new methods to extract money from the frightened poor. Guido Frescobaldi was the earthly saint; his cousin the subterranean villain, no doubt with orgies in the catacombs, surrounded by treasures.

The stage manager did not know a great deal about Guido's cousin, or what he did in the catacombs, but he did know Frescobaldi. And *Il Popolo*'s reporter had etched a portrait that was somewhat at variance to the Guido they all knew. But it was *this* Guido the world outside of Milan read about. *Il Popolo* stated in an editorial that the shocking story was to be reprinted in all the Socialist countries, including China.

Oh, how Frescobaldi had screamed! His roars had been the protestations of a thoroughly embarrassed man. The stage manager hoped that he could catch Guido during the act change and give him the message, but it was not always easy to find Guido during an act change. And it was useless to put the note in the dressing room for he would never see it.

For the role of Alcindoro was Guido Frescobaldi's moment in the operatic sun. It was his single triumph in a lifetime devoted to his beloved *musica*. It was proof that tenacity really did overshadow talent.

Guido was usually so moved by the events on stage – as well as his own performance – that he waddled in a trance behind the scenery until the confusion of an act change was over, his eyes invariably moist, his head held high in the knowledge that he had given his all for the audience of La Scala Minuscola, the fifth-string company of the world-renowned opera house. It was both a training ground and a musical cemetery, allowing the inexperienced to flutter their vocal wings and the over-the-hill to stay occupied until the Great Conductor summoned them to that glorious festival in the sky.

The stage manager reread the note to Guido. In the audience that night was a lady journalist named Signora Greenberg who wished to chat with Frescobaldi. He had been recommended to her by no less a distinguished source than the United States Army *Informazione Servizio*. And the stage manager knew why this Signora Greenberg included the recommendation in her note. Ever since the Communists wrote that terrible article, Guido refused to talk to anyone from the newspapers. He had even grown a huge walrus moustache and beard to lessen the likeness between himself and the pontiff.

The Communists were stupid. *Il Popolo*, through habit, was always picking a fight with the Vatican, but they soon learned what everyone else knew: Pope Francesco was not a man to vilify. He was simply too nice a fellow.

Guido Frescobaldi was a nice fellow, too, thought the stage manager. Many a late night they had divided bottles of wine together; a middle-aged signaller of cues and the elder character actor who had given his life for music.

What a drama was in the *real* story of Frescobaldi! It was worthy of Puccini, himself!

To begin with, he lived only for his beloved opera; all else was inconsequential, necessary solely to keep body and musical soul together. He had been married years ago. And six years later his wife had left him, taking their six children with her back to her native village near Padua and the security of her father's not immodest farm. Though Frescobaldi's circumstances, which by tradition meant the circumstances of his family, had not been destitute. And if his own income was currently less than adequate for *him*, it was by choice, not necessity. The Frescobaldis were actually quite well off; their cousins, the Bombalinis, had been sufficiently wealthy to allow their third son, Giovanni, to enter the church, and God knew that took a little money.

But Guido turned his back on all things clerical, mercantile, and agricultural. He wanted only his music, his opera. He badgered his father and mother to send him to the academy in Rome, where it was soon discovered that Guido's passion far outdistanced his talents.

Frescobaldi had the Latin fire and the soul, perhaps, but he also possessed a rotten musical ear. And Papa Frescobaldi was getting nervous; so many Guido associated with were *non stabili* – they wore funny clothes.

So at the age of twenty-two, Papa told Guido to come home to the village north of Padua. He had been studying in Rome for eight years; no noticeable progress had been made. No jobs – at least in music – had been offered, no musical future seemed to hold promise.

Guido did not care, however. It was the total immersion in things musical that counted. Papa could not understand. But Papa would no longer pay, so Guido came home.

The elder Frescobaldi told his son to marry his nice village cousin, Rosa Bombalini, who was having a little trouble finding a husband, and Papa woud give Guido a *fonografo* for a wedding present. Then he could listen to all the music

175

he wished. Also, if he did not marry Cousin Rosa, Papa would break his ass.

So for six years, while his cousin and brother-in-law, Father Giovanni Bombalini, studied in the Vatican and was sent to strange places, Guido Frescobaldi endured a forced marriage to the three hundred-pound bundle of self-indulgent hysteria named Rosa.

On the morning of his seventh anniversary, he gave up. He awoke screaming; he smashed windows, broke furniture, threw pots of linguini against the walls, and told Rosa that she and her six children were the most repulsive human beings he had ever met.

Basta!

Enough was enough!

Rosa gathered the children together and fled to the village farm; and Guido walked downtown to his father's pasta shop, picked up a bowl of tomato sauce, heaved it in Papa's face and left Padua forever. For Milan.

If the world would not let him be a great operatic tenor, he at least would be near great singers, great music.

He would clean toilets, sweep stages, sew costumes, carry spears. Anything.

He would make his life at La Scala!

And so it had been for over forty years with Frescobaldi. He had risen slowly but happily from toilets to brooms, from stitching to spears. Finally he was awarded those first few words on stage - *Not so much to sing, Guido! More like talk, you see?* - and the sheer openness of his emotion made him an instant favourite of less discriminating operagoers. Of La Scala Minuscula. Where the ticket scale was lower.

In his way Frescobaldi became a beloved fixture as well as a devoted participant. He was always available to help in rehearsals, to cue, to stand in, to recite, and his knowledge was formidable.

Only once in all the years did Guido cause any trouble for anyone, and it wasn't really his fault. That, of course, was the *Popolo* attempt to embarrass his cousin, the pope. Luckily, the Communist writer had not discovered Frescobaldi's

176

early marriage to the pontiff's sister. It would have been difficult for him, however, because Rosa Bombalini had died of overeating three decades earlier.

Hurriedly, the stage manager made his way to Frescobaldi's dressing room. He was too late. The lady speaking to Guido surely was the Signora Greenberg. She was very American and, indeed, very well endowed. Her Italian was a little strange, however. Her words were drawn out like yawns, but the lady did not appear sleepy.

'You see, Signor Frescobaldi, the purpose will be to counteract those nasty things the Communists wrote.'

'Oh, yes, *please!*' cried Guido imploringly. 'They were infamous! There is no finer man in the world than my dear cousin, *Il Papa*. I weep for the embarrassment I caused!'

'I'm sure he doesn't feel that way. He speaks so well of you.'

'Yes – yes, he would,' replied Frescobaldi, the moisture clouding his blinking eyes. 'As children we would play in the fields together, when our families visited. Giovanni – excuse me, Pope Francesco – was the best of all the brothers and cousins. He was a good *man* even as a *boy*. Does that make sense? And brains!'

'He'll be happy to see you again,' said the Signora. 'We haven't scheduled the exact time yet, but he hopes you'll meet with him for the photographs.'

Guido Frescobaldi could not help himself. Although he lost not a dram of dignity, he wept – quietly, without a sound or a gesture. 'He is such a kind man. Did you know that when that terrible magazine came out he sent me a note, in his own hand. He wrote to me: "Guido, my cousin and dear friend: Why have you hidden yourself all these years? When you come to Rome, please call on me. We will play some bocce. I put a course in the garden. Always, my blessing, *Giovanni*."' Frescobaldi dabbed his eyes with the edge of the makeup towel. 'Not a hint of anger or even displeasure. But of course I would never disturb so great a personage. Who am I?'

'He knew it wasn't your fault. You understand that your cousin would rather not have it known that we're planning

177

this anti-Communist story. With politics the way they are —'

'Not a *word*!' interrupted Guido. 'I say *nothing*. I wait only to hear from you and I shall come to Rome. If need be – and I am scheduled to perform – I shall allow my understudy to take my place. The audiences may throw vegetables, but for Francesco, *anything*!'

'He'll be touched.'

'Did you know,' said Frescobaldi, leaning forward in the chair, lowering his voice, 'that under this moustache of mine, the face is very like my exalted cousin's?'

'You mean you *really look alike?*'

'It was ever so since we were children.'

'It never would have crossed my mind. But now that you mention it, I do see a resemblance.'

The stage manager closed the door silently. It had been partially open; they had not seen him and there was no point in interrupting. Guido might be embarrassed; the dressing room was small. So Frescobaldi was going to see his cousin, the pope. *Buonissimo!* Perhaps he might beseech the pontiff to allocate some funds to La Scala Minuscola. They could use the money.

The singing was really terrible.

'Aiyee! Al Fatah! Arafat!'
The screaming Palestinian revolutionaries dashed through the exit doors and down the steps to the concrete of Dar el Beida airport. They hugged and kissed each other and slashed at the night air with their blades. One unfortunate had his finger sliced off in the rejoicing, but it did not cause much concern. Under the leadership of Rat Eyes the group made a dash for the fence that surrounded the field.

No one tried to stop them. Indeed, the searchlights were swung in their direction to help them see their way over the fence. The authorities understood that it was desirable for the idiots to leave the field this way. If they walked into the terminal and out through the doors, a large degree of face would be lost. Besides, the quicker they left the better. They were doing nothing for the tourist trade.

The instant the final Palestinian raced out of the aircraft, Sam had lurched into the Air France galley. To no avail. In the midst of crisis, Air France had kept its head, and its financial acumen. The gleaming metal trays were in place for the next contingent of passengers.

'I paid for some goddamned food!' yelled Sam.

'I'm sorry,' said the stewardess, smiling blankly. 'Regulations prohibit the serving of food after landing.'

'For God's sake, we were hijacked!'

'Your ticket reads Algiers. We are in Algiers. On the ground. After landing. There can be no food.'

'That's inhuman!'

'That is Air France, monsieur.'

Devereaux staggered through the Algerian customs. He held four American five-dollar bills in his hand, separated as though they were playing cards. Each of the four Algerian inspectors down the line took one, smiled, and passed him on to the next man. No luggage was opened; Sam grabbed his suitcase off the conveyor and looked frantically for the airport restaurant.

It was closed. For a religious holiday.

The taxi ride from the airport to the Aletti Hotel on Rue de l'Enur El Khettabi did nothing to calm his nerves or soothe his agonizingly empty stomach. The vehicle was ancient, the driver more so, and the road down into the city steep and filled with winding curves and hairpin turns.

'We're terribly sorry, Monsieur Devereaux,' said the dark-skinned desk clerk in overly precise English. 'All of Algiers is in a state of fasting until the sun rises in the morning. It is the will of Mohammed.'

Sam leaned over the marble counter and lowered his voice to a whisper. 'Look, I respect everyone's right to worship in his own way, but I haven't eaten and I've got a little money —'

'Monsieur!' The clerk's eyes widened in Algerian shock as he interrupted and drew himself up to his full height of roughly five feet. 'The will of Mohammed! The way of Allah!'

179

'Good Lord! I don't believe my *eyes!*' The shout came from across the Aletti lobby. The light was dim, the ceiling high. The figure was obscured in shadows. The only thing Sam knew was that the voice was deep and feminine. And deeply feminine. Perhaps he had heard it before, he could not be sure. How could he be sure of anything - at that moment - in such an unlikely spot as an Algerian hotel lobby - during an Algerian religious holiday - in the last stages of starvation. All was beyond sureness.

And then the figure walked through the hazy pools of light, led by two enormous breasts that cleaved the air in majestic splendour.

Full and Round. Naturally; why did he even bother to act surprised? Ten million - thirty million, forty million dollars no longer shocked him. Why should the sight of Mrs MacKenzie Hawkins, number two?

She pressed the cool, wet towel on his forehead; he lay back on the bed. Six hours ago she had taken off his shoes and socks and shirt and told him to lie back and stop shaking. In truth, she'd *ordered* him to stop shaking. And while he was at it, to stop babbling incoherently about crazy things like Nazis and chicken droppings and wild-eyed Arabs who wanted to blow up airplanes because they flew where they were supposed to fly. Such talk!

But that had been six hours ago. And during the interim she had taken his mind off food, and MacKenzie Hawkins, and some sheik named Azaz-Varak, and - oh my God! - the *kidnapping of the pope!*

She had reduced the dimensions of the whole insanity to the simpler proportions of a terrifying nightmare.

Her name was Madge; he had remembered that. And she had sat next to him on the bean bag in Regina Greenberg's living room; and she had reached over to touch him every time she emphasized a point. He remembered that distinctly because each time she had leaned toward him, Full and Round seemed to burst out of her peasant blouse, as they seemed now about to burst out of the silk shirt she wore.

180

'Just a bit longer,' she said in her deep, somewhat breathless voice. 'The desk clerk promised you'd be the first tray out of the kitchen. Now just relax.'

'Tell me again.'

'About the food?'

'No. About how come you're here in Algiers. It'll take my mind off the food.'

'Then you'll just start babbling again. You simply won't believe me.'

'Maybe I missed something —'

'You're teasing me,' said Madge, leaning over dangerously, adjusting the towel. 'All right. Short and to the point. My late husband was the leading West Coast importer of African art. His gallery was the largest in California. When he died he had over $100,000 tied up in seventeenth-century Musso-Grossai statuary. What the hell am I going to do with five hundred statues of naked pigmies? I mean *really*! You'd do just what I'm doing. Try to stop the shipment and get your money back! Algiers is the clearing house for Musso-Grossai — Now, damn it! There you *go* again!'

Devereaux could not help himself. Tears of laughter rolled down his cheeks. 'I'm sorry. It's just that it's so much more *inventive* than a sudden London vacation from a philandering husband. Or a gourmet school in Berlin. My God, it's beautiful! Five hundred naked pigmies! Did you think it up, or did Mac?'

'You're too suspicious.' Madge smiled gently, knowingly, and lifted the towel from his forehead. 'That's no way to live. Here, I'll soak this with some cool water. Breakfast should be here in fifteen or twenty minutes.' She rose from the bed and looked over at the window in silent thought. The orange rays of the new day were streaming through the window. 'The sun's up.'

Devereaux watched her; the dawn's light washed over her striking features, heightening the sheen of her auburn hair and adding a soft, deep glow to her face. It was not a young face but it had something better than youth. An openness that accepted the years and could laugh gracefully at them.

There was a directness that touched Sam.

'You're a terrific looking person,' he said.

'So are you.' She replied quietly. 'You've got what an old friend of mine used to call a face you'd like to know. Your eyes level. My friend used to say "watch the eyes, especially in a crowd; see if they listen". Actually, Mac said it. A long time ago. I suppose that sounds silly, eyes listening.'

'It doesn't sound silly at all. Eyes do listen. I had a friend who used to go to Washington cocktail parties, and he'd repeat the word "hamburger" over and over again - just "hamburger", nothing else. He swore that ninety per cent of the time the people around him would say things like, "Very interesting. I'll check the statistics on that"; or "Have you mentioned it to the undersecretary?" He always knew who'd say those things because their eyes were moving so fast; you see, he wasn't very important.'

Madge laughed softly; their eyes locked and she smiled. 'He sounds very important to me.'

'You're a *nice* person, too.'

'Yes, I try to be.' She looked over at the window again. 'MacKenzie also said that too many people run from their perfectly natural inclination to be concerned human beings. As if concern was a sign of weakness. He said: "Goddamn, Midgey, *I'm* concerned and no son of a bitch better call *me* weak!" And no one ever did.'

'I suppose being concerned is another way of being nice,' added Devereaux, mulling over the latest homily.

'There's no better way,' said Madge, carrying the towel into the bathroom. 'I'll be out in a minute.'

She closed the door. Sam repeated the words to himself: *Too many people run from their perfectly natural inclination to be concerned human beings.* MacKenzie was a man of more complications than Devereaux cared to think about. At least, until breakfast arrived.

The bathroom door opened. Madge stood in the door frame and smiled deliberately, a sense of marvellous fun in her eyes, very much aware of the picture she presented. She no longer wore her skirt. Instead her breasts were now

182

lovingly encased in an ivory-coloured brassiere made of webbed lace. Below, her short slip accentuated the curve of her hips and bore witness to the soft white flesh that touched – and wanted to be touched - between her upper thighs.

She walked around to the side of the bed and took his immobile hand. She sat down gracefully and leaned over, her incredible spheres touching him, sending electricity through him causing him to suddenly inhale very short breaths. She kissed him on the lips. She pulled back and undid his belt and with the swift, graceful movements of a dancer, pulled down his trousers.

'Why Major, you have been thinking nice thoughts —'

And the Algerian terrorist telephone rang.

The galaxy went out of whack again. Sanity vanished in a sudden rush of hysteria. Sweet reason and laced brassieres and soft flesh were no more. Instead, screams in Arabic, commands that threatened unbelievable violence should they be disobeyed.

'If you'll stop yelling about pigs and dogs and vultures for a second, maybe I can figure out what you're trying to say,' said Sam, holding the phone away from his ear. 'All *I* said was that I couldn't come down right now.'

'I am the emissary from Sheik *Azaz-Var*ak!'

'What the hell is that?'

'Dog!'

'It's a dog? You mean a puppy dog?'

'Silence! Azaz-Varak is the god of all khans! The possessor of the desert winds, the eyes of the falcon, the courage of all the lions of Judea, the prince of thunder!'

'Then what does he need me for?' ventured Sam hesitantly, reluctantly recognizing the name of the Hawk's fourth mark. The final ten million. Jesus! He thought about it now with no more emphasis than ten boxes of Pop Tarts!

'Silence, dog! Or both your ears will be cut from your head and placed with hot irons up your unspeakable.'

'Now, goddamn it, that's not friendly! You talk nicer or I'm going to hang up; there's a lady here.'

'Please, Mr Deveroo,' said the Arabic voice, suddenly

quite gentle with a trace of a whine. 'In the name of Allah –
for the love of Allah, do not be difficult. It will be *my* ears in
unspeakable places if you are difficult. We must leave for
Tizi Ouzou immediately.'

'Tizi - who?'

'Ouzou, Mr Deveroo.'

'Ouzou? Did you say Ouzoo?'

Suddenly, without any warning whatsoever, the most
unexpected thing Sam could imagine happened. Madge
grabbed the telephone from him.

'Give me that!' she ordered. 'I know Tizi Ouzou; my
husband and I stayed there once. It's a dreadful place! –
Listen here, whoever you are, you'd better have a damn good
reason to ask my friend to go to Tizi Ouzou. It's the
godforsaken end of nowhere! Without a decent hotel *or*
restaurant, to say nothing about toilet facilities!'

The girl held the phone to her ear, nodding briefly every
three or four seconds. The whine on the line became very
audible.

'Really, Madge, I can handle —'

'Be quiet. This son of a bitch isn't even Algerian. ... Yes.
Yes. ... All right. Then we'll *both* be down! ... Take it or
leave it, you desert gnat, that's the only way it's going to be.
... They're *your ears*, sweetie. ... And one other thing. The
minute we get there, I want a huge meal waiting for my friend
here, do you understand? ... And no biscuits of camel dung,
either! All right. Five minutes.'

She hung up and smiled at Devereaux, who was mostly
naked and completely pale.

'That was very generous of you, but it's not necessary —'

'Don't be silly. You don't know these people; I do. You
have to be firm, they're quite harmless, despite those
goddamned knives. Besides, do you think I'd let you out of
my sight for a minute? After I've seen what nice thoughts
you've been thinking? And in your condition.' She leaned
over and kissed him again. 'It's really very touching.'

Devereaux realized that in his weakened condition he

184

might be subject to hallucinations; but he was not prepared for the two robed Arabs that met them in the Aletti lobby.

Peter Lorre and Boris Karloff. Quite a bit younger than the more recent photographs Sam remembered, but otherwise unmistakable.

The next twenty minutes were a blur. Yet he *had* to be able to think clearly. Azaz-Varak (*who*ever and *where*ver he was) signified the last of the investors. He had to begin putting together the pieces of his counterstrategy.

Peter Lorre sat in the front seat next to Boris, who drove. The car sped through the streets and careened dangerously around the corners of early morning Algiers. They were halfway up a winding, steep hill when Devereaux realized they were heading for Dar el Beida airport.

'We going on a plane?' asked Sam apprehensively.

Madge answered beside him. 'Oh, sure, sweetie. Tizi Ouzou's like two hundred miles east. You wouldn't want to drive. Remember, I've *been* there.'

Devereaux looked at her. He wondered, and whispered. 'I remember. What I can't understand is why you're here. Do you know what you're involved with? Do you know what you're *doing*?'

'I'm trying to be helpful.'

'So was Rose Mary Woods.'

The interior of the helicopter was only slightly smaller than the main level of Pennsylvania Station. Pillows were everywhere and beside each seat was an elaborate water pipe attached to the wall with a kind of Bunsen burner underneath it. An open galley was at the rear.

And after three minutes in the air, Sam was given the first sustenance he could recall. A small cup of acrid, black liquid that vaguely smelled of coffee, but more of bitter liquorice mixed with stale sardines.

He drank it in one swallow, grimaced, and looked at the tiny person wrapped in sheets who had poured it for him. The tiny person manipulated several wheels around the water pipe in the wall and held a match to the burner beneath. A long rubber tube with a mouthpiece was reeled

185

from somewhere and held out for Sam.

He took it and wondered. It probably would not do him any good, but on the other hand it was something to put in his mouth, and nothing of that nature at this point could be any worse than the numbed agony he was experiencing. He inserted the mouthpiece between his teeth and drew on it.

It wasn't smoke exactly; it was more a vapour. Sweet and pungent at the same time. Really very pleasant. Actually quite delightful. Rather diverting in its way.

He drew more heavily; and then more rapidly; he looked across at Madge, sitting opposite him in a bank of pillows. 'Would you mind, my dear?' he heard himself saying calmly. 'Please remove all your clothes.'

'I'd go easy on that,' replied the girl in her most provocative, breathless whisper.

Was she whispering? Her voice seemed to arrive at his ears on different levels of sound.

'Your blouse first, if you please.' Again he was not quite positive he had said what he heard himself saying. 'Then perhaps if you would remove your skirt while performing a small, undulating dance. That would be very accommodating.'

'Put that damn thing down.'

'It's up?' He could actually smell her perfume. And the pains were gone from his stomach. Instead he could feel a surging force of great strength pulsating throughout his body. He was capable of giant deeds; he was – what was it? – the possessor of the desert winds. A prince of thunder, a hurler of lightning. With the courage of all the lions of Judea.

'That's not a Lucky Strike you're pulling on. It's pure hashish.'

'Who ...?' The information reached that small section of his brain that was functioning. *What the hell was he doing?* He spat out the mouthpiece and tried to stabilize the aircraft; it had to be the helicopter because *something* was suddenly going around and around. The lion of Judea was shrinking; a mangy pussycat was taking its place.

And then he heard the whining words of Peter Lorre, who had walked back from the pilot's area. 'We are on a heading south-south-east of Tizi Ouzou.'

'How come?' Madge was upset and did not bother to conceal it. 'You said Tizi, not someplace else. I've got friends on Rue Joucif, you fly! My late husband did a lot of favours for the Algerian government!'

'A thousand nights of blissful pardons, lady of Deveroo, but my government is Azaz-Kuwait. My sheik is the sheik of all sheiks, the god of all khans, the eyes of the falcon, the courage —'

'*When you're calling mee, calling meee, calling meeee!*' Sam suddenly found himself bursting forth in song; at least, it sounded like him. It *was* a song.

'Shut up, Major!' shouted Madge.

'*Alone - alonnnnne on this night that was meant for —*'

'Will you be quiet!' yelled the girl.

'It seemed appropriate,' mumbled Sam.

'Where are we going?' asked Madge of the whining Arab, who was looking at Devereaux as though the American should be watched closely.

'Seventy miles south-east of Tizi Ouzou is a stretch of desert that is traversed only by Bedouin tribes. It is very remote and lends itself to confidential rendezvous. An eagle's tent has been spread for the sheik of all sheiks, the god of all khans. Azaz-Varak, the magnificent, is flying in from his holiest of kingdoms to meet with the unspeakable dog named Deveroo.'

'*When I'm calling yoooo – Deverooo – only yooooo —*'

'Will you shut up!'

CHAPTER SIXTEEN

There were maps everywhere, covering the Watergate bed, spilling over the coffee table, scattered about the floor, propped up against the bureau mirror, and draped over the hotel sofa. There were gasoline road maps, railroad maps, elevation charts, geological and vegetation carto-analyses; even aerial photographs from sequential altitudes of 500, 1,500, 5,000, and finally 20,000 feet.

These plus 363 ground-level photographs of every inch of the terrain under study.

Nothing could be left to chance.

Five minutes ago he had made his final decision. The real estate broker from the highly confidential, international firm of Les Châteaux Suisses des Grands Siècles would be arriving imminently. Naturally, secretly; the first law of Les Châteaux Suisses was absolute secrecy.

Mac had selected a remote château in the canton of Valais, south of Zermatt, in the countryside near Champoluc. The surrounding lands - two hundred acres - were in the cartographical shadow of the Matterhorn and were virtually inaccessible.

What was uppermost in his mind were two factors. The first was terrain. It would have to come as close as possible to duplicating Ground Zero, as Hawkins had decided to name it. Every turn and curve and rise of the road; each slope and hill that might play a part in the approach to or the escape from Ground Zero would have to be simulated as precisely as possible. Manoeuvres were useless if the training grounds did not reflect the combat zone.

The second factor was the inaccessibility. His base of operations, as Mac had come to think of the leased property,

188

had to be completely concealed from the outlying country roads as well as from the air. The area had to be one where huge pieces of equipment could be hidden in seconds; where a complement of at least a dozen men could live and train for a minimum of eight weeks.

The château in question possessed these specifics. And it was not that far from Zürich. The Shepherd Company's capital would be transferred to Zürich. Devereaux would have to see to this centralization of finances. As well as the vetting of the château's lease.

There was a discreet knock at the hotel door. MacKenzie stepped carefully over the maps and photographs on the floor and went to it. He stood close to the panel and spoke.

'Monsieur D'Artagnan?' Les Châteaux Suisses used pseudonyms all the time.

'*Oui, mon général*,' was the quiet reply from the corridor.

Hawkins opened the door and a middle-aged, nondescript, portly man entered. Even his slightly waxed moustache was nondescript, thought MacKenzie. He'd be a tough fellow to spot in a crowd; there was absolutely nothing outstanding about him.

'I see you have pursued the information we sent you,' said Monsieur D'Artagnan in an accent formed west of Alsace-Lorraine. He was obviously a man who wasted no time on the amenities, and the Hawk was grateful for that.

'Yes, I have. I've made my decision.'

'Which property?'

'Château Machenfeld.'

'Ahh, *Le Machenfeld! Magnifique   extraordinaire!* What history has been played on its rolling fields; what battles won and lost in front of its towering parapets of granite! And the indoor plumbing has been kept most functioningly modern. An exquisite choice. I congratulate you. You and your coterie of religious brothers will be very happy.' D'Artagnan removed the fattest envelope Hawkins had ever seen from his inner jacket pocket. The highly secretive firm did not carry briefcases, Mac remembered; so much confidential information crammed into one repository was too dangerous. The brokers carried only those papers of immediate concern.

'Are those the leasing arrangements?'

'*Oui, mon général*. All completed and ready for your chosen and agreed-upon mark. And the six months' deposit, of course.'

'Well, before we get to that, let me go over the conditions —'

'There are *new* ones, monsieur?'

'No. I just want to make sure you understand the old ones.'

'But, my *général*, everything *was* understood,' said D'Artagnan, smiling. 'You dictated the specifications; I transcribed them myself, as is our policy, and you approved the transcript. Here. See for yourself.' He handed Hawkins the papers. 'I think you know we would never alter our clients' demands. We have only to fill in the specific château and cross-check to make sure the demands are not in conflict with the owner's conditions of lease. I have done so with all potential locations; there are no conflicts.'

MacKenzie took the papers and picked his way between the maps and photographs to the sofa. With one hand he removed two huge elevation charts and sat down.

'I want to be positive that what I'm reading is what I heard.'

'Ask any questions you wish. As is the policy of Les Châteaux Suisses des Grands Siècles, each broker is completely familiar with all conditions. And when our business is concluded, the papers are microfilmed and placed in the company vaults in Geneva. We suggest you make similar arrangements with your copies. Untraceable.'

Hawkins read aloud. 'Whereas the party of the first part, hereafter known as the lessee, takes possession *in-nomen-incognitum....*' Mac's eyes skimmed downward. 'In the

190

absence of ... *communicatum-directorum* between the party of ... and the party of.... Goddamn! You boys got your training in clandestine operations.'

D'Artagnan smiled; the waxed moustache stretched a little. 'Ask your questions, monsieur.'

And so it began.

Les Châteaux Suisses des Grands Siècles was nothing if not thorough and specific – in the language of a lease that would never from that moment on see the light of day.

To begin with all identities were held sacrosanct, never to be divulged to any individual, organization, court, or government. No law, national or international, superseded the agreement; *it* was the only law. Payments were made to the firm either in cash or treasurer's cheques; in the case of the Shepherd Company, from a Cayman Island depository.

Whenever explanations of 'source' were desirable, they would be expedited where necessary and in the interests of controlling outside curiosity. In the case of the Shepherd Company, the sole explanation of 'source' was a loose federation of international philanthropists interested in the study and promulgation of an historic religiosity.

All supplies, equipment, transportation, and services would be expedited in complete confidentiality by Les Châteaux Suisses des Grands Siècles and consigned to branch offices in Zermatt, Interlaken, Chamonix, or Grenoble. Any and all deliveries of consequence to Le Château Machenfeld would be made between the hours of midnight and 4 a.m. Drivers, technicians, and labourers, where possible, would be from the ranks of the Shepherd Company's brotherhood, who would be sent down from Le Machenfeld to the branch offices. In the absence thereof, only employees of Les Châteaux Suisses who had no less than ten years' acceptable service with the firm would be assigned the deliveries.

All payments were to be made in advance, based on book

retail value, with a surcharge of 40 per cent for the confidential services of Les Châteaux Suisses.

'That's a lot of per cent,' said MacKenzie.

'It's a very wide boulevard,' replied D'Artagnan. 'We don't avail ourselves to those who drive in narrow streets. We think our consultation fee is ample proof of this.'

It was, thought the Hawk. The 'consultation fee' - applied against whatever lease was arrived at, *if* a lease *was* signed - was $500,000.

'You do mighty fine work, Mr D'Artagnan,' said Hawkins, taking up a fountain pen.

'You're in good hands. In a few days you will, as it were, vanish from the earth.'

'Don't worry. Everybody I know - that's *everybody* - will be extremely grateful never to hear from me again. Seems I generate complications.' The Hawk laughed quietly to himself. He signed his name: *George Washington Rappaport*.

D'Artagnan left with MacKenzie's treasurer's cheque drawn on the Cayman Island's Admiralty Bank. The amount was for $1,495,000.

The Hawk picked up a handful of photographs and walked back to the hotel sofa. As he sat down, however, he knew he could not dwell on the majesty of Machenfeld. There were other immediate considerations. Machenfeld would be worthless without the personnel to train within its borders. But former Lieutenant General MacKenzie Hawkins, twice winner of the Congressional Medal of Honour, knew where he was going and how to get there. Ground Zero was several months away. But the journey had begun.

He wondered how Sam and Midgey were doing. Goddamn, that boy was getting around!

The helicopter descended, dropping straight down and causing torrential clouds of sand to blast up in increasingly furious layers from the desert floor. So thick was the enveloping storm that the only way Sam knew they had landed was the jarring thud of the undercarriage as it met and was swallowed by the dunes.

They had been in the air somewhat longer than had been anticipated. There had been a minor navigational problem: The pilot was lost. It had to be the pilot since it was unthinkable to admit the possibility that the eagle's tent of Azaz-Varak was in the wrong place. But at last, they saw the complex of canvas below.

The sand settled and Peter Lorre opened the hatch. The desert sun was blinding. Sam held Madge's arm as they stepped out of the aircraft; if the sun was blinding, the sand was boiling. 'Where the hell are we?'

'Aiyee!' 'Aiyee!' 'Aiyee!' 'Aiyee!'

The screams were everywhere, and from everywhere there was rushing movement. Turbaned Arabs, their sheets flying in the wind like a hundred white sails, raced out of the various tents towards them. Peter Lorre and Boris Karloff flanked Sam, gripping his arms as if displaying an animal carcass. Madge stood in front, somewhat protectively, thought Devereaux uncomfortably, as though she were about to give instructions to a slaughterhouse butcher. The racing battalion of sheets and turbans formed two single lines that created a corridor leading slightly uphill in the sand to the largest of the tents, about fifty yards away.

Peter Lorre's nasal shriek filled the air. 'Aiyee! The eye of the falcon! The hurler of lightning! The god of all khans and the sheik of all sheiks!' He turned to Sam and screamed even louder. 'Kneel! Unworthy white hyena!'

'What?' Devereaux wasn't arguing; he just thought the sand would melt his trousers.

'It is better to kneel,' said the deep-throated Boris Karloff, 'than to find yourself standing on stumps.'

The sand was, indeed, uncomfortable. And Sam, in an instant of real human concern, wondered what Madge was going to do; she wore a very short skirt above her desert boots. He squinted and looked at her.

He need not have indulged in human concern, he thought. Madge was not kneeling at all. Instead she had moved slightly to the side and was standing erect. She was spectacular.

'Bitch,' he whispered.

'Keep your head,' she answered quietly. 'That's meant figuratively – I think.'·

'*Aiyee!* Behold the prince of thunder and lightning!' shrieked Peter Lorre.

There was movement at the tent at the end of the corridor of abus and turbans. Two minions swept back the front flap and prostrated themselves on the ground, their faces in the sand. From the shadowed recesses emerged a man who was a major disappointment, a walking anticlimax, to the dramatic preparations for his entrance.

The prince of thunder and lightning was a spindly little Arab; peering out from the shrouds was about the ugliest face Devereaux had ever seen. Below the outsized, narrow, hooked nose, Azaz-Varak's lips were curled – actually *curled* – so that his thin black moustache seemed fused to his nostrils. The pallor of his skin (what could be seen) was a sickly beige, which served to emphasize the dark, deep circles under his heavy-lidded eyes.

Azaz-Varak approached, lips pressing, nostrils sniffing, head bobbing. He looked only at Madge. When he spoke there was a certain authority in his whine.

'The wives of the lion's lair, the royal harem – none understand the awesome responsibilities that befall my generous person. Would you like a camel, lady?'

Madge shook her head with a certain authority of her own. Azaz-Varak continued to stare.

'Two camels? The aeroplane?'

'I'm in mourning,' said Madge respectfully but firmly. 'My wealthy sheik passed away just after the last crescent moon. You know the rules.'

The heavy-lidded eyes of Azaz-Varak were filled with disappointment; his curled-up lips smacked twice as he replied. 'Ahh, it is the awesome burdens of our faith. You

194

have two crescents of the calendar to survive. May your sheik rest with Allah. Perhaps you will visit my palaces when your time has passed.'

'We'll see. Right now, my escort is hungry. Allah wants him to protect me; he can't do that if he faints.'

Azaz-Varak looked at Sam as though studying the pre-slaughtered carcass. 'He has two functions, then. One worthy, one despicable. Come, dog. To the eagle's tent.'

'That's where the food is, isn't it?' Devereaux smiled his best, most ingratiating smile as he scrambled to his feet.

'You will partake of my table when our business is concluded. Pray to Allah that it is finished before the northern snows come to the desert. Did you bring the unmentionable agreement?'

Devereaux nodded. 'Did you bring any hot corned beef?'

'Silence!' shrieked Peter Lorre.

'Lady,' said Azaz-Varak, addressing Madge, 'my servants will see to your every wish. My palaces are lovely; you would like them.'

'It's tempting. We'll see where I am in a month or so.' She winked at Azaz-Varak. His lips went through a series of wet pressings before he snapped his fingers and proceeded towards the eagle's tent.

The minutes stretched into quarter hours, those to the inevitable hour, and then two more of them. Devereaux honestly believed he had reached the end. A promising legal career was being snuffed out, starved out, in the middle of some godforsaken stretch of desert, seventy miles south of a ridiculously named place called Tizi Ouzou in North Africa.

What made the ending so ludicrous was the sight of Azaz-Varak poring over each sentence of the Shepherd Company's limited partnership papers, with eight to ten screeching Arabs looking over his shoulder, arguing vehemently among themselves. Every page was treated as though it were the only page; every convoluted --

and unnecessary – legalism torn apart for a meaning that was not there. Sam saw clearly the terrible irony: the esoteric, legalistic nonsense that was the essence of every lawyer's livelihood was keeping him from his own survival.

An insane thought went through his pained brain: if all legal documents were written to be understood between meals – all meals postponed until said understanding was clear – the state of justice would be on a much higher plane. And most lawyers of his acquaintance out of work.

Every now and then one of Azaz-Varak's ministers would carry over a page and point to a particular paragraph, asking him in excellent English what it meant. Invariably Devereaux would explain that it was a standard clause – which invariably it was – and not important.

If it was not important, why was the language so confusing? Only significant items were in confusing words; otherwise there was no need for the confusion.

And, too, good things were stated clearly; unworthy things were often obscured. Did standard mean unworthy?

And so it went. Until at one point Sam screamed.

Nothing else; he simply screamed.

Azaz-Varak and his gaggle of ministers looked over at him. They nodded as if to say, 'Your point is well taken.' And then went back to screaming at each other.

At the instant the darkness started to cloud his vision, his last look at living things, thought Sam, he heard the words, whined by the sheik of sheiks.

'The northern snows have reached the desert, unspeakable one. These foul papers are like camels' prints in storms of sand: They are without meaning. Not any meaning that would bring the wrath of Allah, or certain international authorities. My generous, all-knowing person has signed them. Not that I subscribe to the despicable suggestion made to my ear, but only to help unite the world in love, you hated dog.'

Azaz-Varak rose from the mountain of pillows beneath

him. He was escorted to a screened-off section of the enormous tent by several hunched-over ministers and disappeared beyond the silks.

Peter Lorre came up to Sam, the limited partnership agreement in his hands. He gave it to Devereaux and whispered, 'Put this in your pocket. It is better that the eye of the falcon not fall on it again.'

'Is falcon edible?'

Perplexed, the tiny Arab looked at Sam. 'Your eyeballs are swimming in their sockets, Abdul Deveroo. Have the faith of the Koran, first paragraph, book four.'

'What the hell is that?' Sam could hardly speak.

'"The feasts were brought among the unbelieving infidels and no longer were they unbelieving."'

'Does that mean we eat?'

'It does. The god of all khans has ordered his favourite: boiled testicle of camel braised with the stomach of desert rat.'

'*Aiyeeeeee!*' Devereaux blanched and leaped up from the floor of the eagle's tent. The spring had been sprung; there was nothing left but self-annihilation. The end was at hand; the forces of destruction called for his finish in an explosion of violence.

So be it. He would meet it swiftly. Surely. Without thought, only blinding fury. He ran around the pillows and over the rugs and out on to the sand. It was sundown; his end would come with the orange sun descending over the desert horizon.

Boiled testicles! Stomach of rat!

'Madge! *Madge!*'

If he could only reach her! She could bring back news of his demise to his mother and Aaron Pinkus. Let them know he died bravely.

'*Madge!* Where are you?!'

When the words came he felt stirrings of bewilderment that were contradictory to the last thoughts of those who were about to perish.

'Hi, sweetie! Come on over. Look what I've got *here*. It's a *gas!*'

Sam turned, his ankles deep in sand, his caked lips trembling. Fifty yards away a group of Arabs were gathered around the front of the helicopter, all peering into the pilot's cabin.

In a trance of confusion, Devereaux staggered towards the bewildering sight. The Arabs squealed and grumbled but let him through. He gripped the ledge of the window and peered inside. It was easy; the aircraft had sunk into the dune upon landing.

It was not his eyes, however, that were assaulted. It was his ears.

There was a continuous, deafening crackle of static from the helicopter's panel that filled the small enclosure like jack hammers in a wind tunnel. Madge was in the co-pilot's seat, her blouse neckline lowered another several buttons.

Then he heard the words riding through the static and Sam froze, his hunger and exhaustion replaced momentarily by a kind of hypnotic terror.

'Midgey! Midgey, girl! You still there?'

'Yes, Mac, still here. It's just Sam. He's finished with what's-his-name.'

'*Goddamn!* How is he?'

'Hungry. He's a very hungry boy,' said Madge, expertly manipulating switches and dials on the radio panel.

'There'll be plenty of time for rations later. An army travels on its stomach, but first it's got to evacuate the fire zone! Before it gets its ass shot off! Does he have the papers?'

'They're sticking out of his pocket —'

'He's a fine young attorney, that boy! He'll go far! Now, get out of there, Midgey. Get him to Dar el Beida and on that plane for Zermatt. Confirm, and over and out!'

'Roger confirm, Mac. Out.' Midge whipped through several dozen switches as though she were a computer programmer. She turned her face to Devereaux and beamed.

'You're going to have a nice rest, Sam. Mac says you really deserve a vacation.'

'Who? Where ...?'

'Zermatt, sweetie. It's in Switzerland.'

PART THREE

The smooth-running corporation is largely de-pendent on its executive personnel, whose back-grounds and allegiances are compatible with the overall objectives of the structure and whose identities can be submerged to the corporate image.

Shepherd's Laws of Economics:
Book CXIV, Chapter 92

CHAPTER SEVENTEEN

Cardinal Ignatio Quartze, his thin, aristocratic features bespeaking generations of *noblesse oblige*, stormed across the rugs of his Vatican office to the large balconied window overlooking St Peter's Square. He spoke in fury, his lips compressed in anger, his nasal voice searing like the screech of a bullet.

'The Bombalini peasant goes too far! I tell you he is a disgrace to the college which - God help us all - elevated him!'

The cardinal's audience was a plump, boyish-looking priest who sat, as languorously as his habit allowed, in a purple velvet chair in the centre of the room. His pink cheeks and pursed, thick lips bespoke, perhaps, a less aristocratic background than his superior but no less a love of luxury. His speech was more a purr than a voice.

'He was and remains only a compromise, Cardinal. You were assured his health would not permit an extended reign.'

'Every *day* is an extension beyond endurance!'

'He has certain ... humilities that serve us. He has quieted much hostile press. The people look upon him warmly; our worldwide contributions are nearly as high as they were with Roncalli.'

'Please! Not that name! What good is a treasury that expands and contracts like a thousand concertinas because the Holy See subsidizes everything he can put his fat peasant hands on! And we don't need a friendly press. Division is far better to solidify our own! Nobody understands.'

'Oh, but I do, Cardinal. I really do -'

'Did you see him today?' continued Quartze as if the priest had not spoken. 'He openly humiliated me! In audience! He questioned my African allocations.'

'A patently obvious ploy to appease that terrible black man. He's forever complaining.'

'And afterwards he tells jokes *jokes*, mind you to the Vatican guard! And waddles into the museum crowds and eats an ice *eats* an *ice*, mind you offered by some Sicilian brood mare! Next he'll drop lire in the men's room and all the toilet seats will be stolen! Such indignities! What he does to the bones of St Peter! They will turn to dust!'

'It cannot be very long, my dear Cardinal.'

'Long enough! He'll deplete the treasury and fill the Curia with wild-eyed radicals!'

'You are the next pontiff. The negative reactions of the broad middle hierarchy support you. They are silent, but resentments run deep.'

The cardinal paused; his mouth curved slightly downward as he stared out into the square, his jaw jutted forward below the dark hollows of his deep-set eyes. 'I do believe we have the delegates. Ronaldo, get me the plans for my villa at San Vincente. It calms my nerves to study them.'

'Of course,' said the priest, rising from the purple chair. 'You must remain calm. And when summer comes you will be rid of the Bombalini peasant. He will stay at Castel Gandolfo for at least six weeks.'

'The *plans*, Ronaldo! I'm very upset. Yet in the midst of chaos, I remain the most controlled man in the Vatican —. The plans, you transvestite!' screamed the cardinal.

The moment the papal aide with the ever present clipboard left the room, Pope Francesco I got out of the elevated, high-backed, white velvet chair (a repository that would have frightened Saint Sebastian) and sat next to the lady from *Viva Gourmet* on the couch. He was struck immediately by the beauty of her voice; it was warm and lilting. Very lovely. It befitted such a healthy looking woman.

The aide had suggested that the interview be limited to twenty minutes; the pontiff had suggested that it should end

204

when concluded. The lady journalist had reddened slightly with embarrassment, so Giovanni put her at ease by switching to English and asking her if she thought there was a market for clipboards with crucifixes painted on the underside. She had laughed while the aide, who did not understand English, stood by the door, his clipboard clutched to his breast like a plastic stigmata.

The aide would have to be replaced, thought the pope. He was another young prelate seduced by the pretensions of Ignatio Quartze. The cardinal was too obvious; he was moving his charges into the papal apartments before the papal funeral was arranged. But Francesco had made up his mind: the Church was not going to be left in the pontifical hands of Ignatio Quartze. To begin with, they held the chalice at Mass as though wringing the neck of a chicken.

The interview with *Viva Gourmet*'s Lillian von Schnabe was productive and pleasant. Giovanni expounded on two of his favourite subjects: that good, substantial meals could be created from inexpensive stock and flavoured with simple, spiced sauces; and that in these difficult days of high prices it was a mark of distinction – to say nothing of Christian brotherhood – to share one's table with one's neighbour.

Mrs von Schnabe saw immediately what he was trying to communicate. 'Is this a form of "the loaves and the fishes", Your Holiness?'

'Let us say He was not preaching to the wealthier sections of Nazareth. A number of His miracles were based in sound psychological principles, my dear. I open my basket of fruit, you open your basket of pasta; we have fruit *and* pasta. The simple addition alone gives variety. Variety we rightly equate with more rather than less.'

'And the diet's improved,' agreed Lillian, nodding.

'*Perfetto*. You see? Two *principii*: reduce the cost and share the supply.'

'That sounds almost socialistic, though, doesn't it?'

'When stomachs are empty and prices are high, labels are foolish. In the *Borsa Valori* – the stock exchange, you call it

205

they are not prone to open baskets; they sell them. It is fitting that they do so, considering the nature of their labours. But I do not address such people. They eat at the Grand Hotel, on each other's expense accounts. I believe that, too, is a derivative of the "loaves and fishes" principle.'

They discussed numerous recipes based on the village dishes from the pope's past. Giovanni could see that the nice lady with the lovely voice was impressed. He had done his nutritional homework; carbohydrates, proteins, starch, calories, iron, and all kinds of vitamins were to be found in his recipes.

Lillian filled half a notebook, writing as rapidly as the pope spoke, stopping him occasionally to clarify a word or phrase. After nearly an hour had passed, she paused and asked a question Giovanni did not understand.

'What about your own *personal* requirements, Your Holiness? Are there any restrictions or specific necessities called for in the meals brought to you?'

'*Che cosa?* What do you mean?'

'We are what we eat, you know.'

'I sincerely hope not. I am in my seventh decade, my dear. An excess of onion or olive or pimento. ... But such information is not needed for your article. People my age quite naturally gravitate to and regulate their personal needs in this area.'

Lillian put her pencil down. 'I didn't mean to pry, but you're so fascinating a man – and I *am* considered one of the best nutritional experts in America. I suppose I just wanted to approve of the way your kitchen treats you.'

Ahh, thought Giovanni Bombalini, *how many years it has been since a lovely person of the opposite gender has been concerned about him! He could not remember, it was so long ago! Pinched-faced nuns and officious nurses, yes. But so attractive a lady, with such a lovely voice. ...*

'Well, my dear, these outrageous doctors *do* insist on certain foods. ...'

Lillian picked up her pencil.

And they talked for another fifteen minutes.

206

At the end of which time there was a knock on the door of the papal apartment. Francesco rose from the couch and returned to the elevated, high-backed, white velvet chair that belonged in one of those Cinecittà biblical spectaculars.

An agitated Cardinal Ignatio Quartze stood in the doorway, a handkerchief dabbing his aquiline nose, noises emerging from his throat. 'I am sorry to interrupt, Holy Father,' he said in both Italian and high dudgeon, giving the word 'holy' a rather profane but eminently courteous connotation, 'but I've just been informed that Your Holiness has seen fit to disagree with my instructions regarding the convocation of the Bankers for Christ.'

'"Disagree" is too strong a term. I merely suggested that the convocation committee reconsider. To occupy the Sistine Chapel for two days at the height of the spring tourist season seems unwarranted.'

'If you will forgive my contrary observation, the Sistine is the most favoured *and* frequented site we possess. All convocations of merit convene there.'

'Thus denying thousands every year of its beauty. I'm not sure there's merit in that.'

'We are *not* an amusement park, Pope Francesco.' Strange noises continued to come from the area of the cardinal's throat; he blew his nose with aristocratic vigour.

'I sometimes wonder,' replied Giovanni. 'We sell such a diversity of baubles everywhere. Did you know there's a stand featuring rhinestone rosary beads?'

'*Please*, Your Holiness. The Bankers for Christ. They *expect* the Sistine. We are finalizing extremely important matters.'

'Yes, my dear Cardinal, I received the memorandum. "Accruals for Jesus" is somewhat laboured, I think, but I suppose there are certain tax advantages.' Giovanni's attention was suddenly drawn to Lillian. She had closed her notebook politely but firmly; she was anxious to leave. *Ahh*, it had been such a pleasant interlude! And Quartze was not going to spoil it; he could wait. He addressed the attractive lady with the lovely voice. In English, of course; a language

207

only barely understood by Quartze. 'How rude we are. Do forgive us. The agitated cardinal with the propellers in his nasal passages has once again found my judgements lacking.'

'Then I would have to say *his* judgement left much to be desired,' said Lillian, rising from the couch and placing her notebook in her purse. She looked into Giovanni's eyes and spoke softly with feeling. 'I suppose this isn't a proper thing to say but since I'm not Catholic, I'll say it anyway. You're one of the most attractive men I've ever met. I hope you're not offended.'

Giovanni Bombalini, Pope Francesco, Vicar of Christ felt the stirrings of memories of fifty years ago. And they were good. In a profoundly sacred sense – for which he was grateful. 'And you, my dear, possess an honesty – however erroneous your present opinion – that walks in the warm light of God.'

'If I do, it's because I was taught by someone quite like you, I think. Although a few would recognize the similarity.'

'I am flattered. This – someone, give him the blessings of a farmhand-priest.'

Lillian smiled. She started for the door, where Quartze's handkerchief fluttered a tattoo in front of his agitated face and the sounds of mucus still could be heard beyond his aquiline nose and very thin lips. The prelate sidestepped to let her pass, doing his best to ignore her. So Lillian paused briefly, forcing him to look at her. When he did so, she winked.

As she closed the door the words from Pope Francesco were clear and firm. For in his anger, the pontiff raised his voice, in English.

'Talk to me not of the Sistine, Ignatio! Instead, discuss these plans I requested for your waterfront home at San Vincente! What are "security arrangements"? They include a *steam bath?*'

Hawkins had reserved both seats in the first-class section of the Lufthansa 747. Since he needed elbow room, there was no point in inconveniencing a fellow passenger. This way, he was able to place the folders beside him for quick referrals.

He had specifically chosen the night flight to Zürich. The travellers, by and large, would be diplomats, bankers, or corporate executives used to transatlantic flights; they would use the night for sleep, not socializing. He would have a minimum of interruptions.

For selections would have to be made, offers of recruitment dispatched immediately from Zürich.

MacKenzie's briefcase contained assorted personnel profiles from which he would choose his troops. They were the last of the files he had Xeroxed at the G-2 archives. Those fortunate enough to be chosen would be his brigade; his personal army that would be privileged to engage in the most unusual manoeuvre in modern military history.

And each soldier would return from the engagement one of the richest men in his part of the world.

For, where possible, they would be from separate parts of the world. For the inviolate condition of recruitment was that none would ever acknowledge the existence of the others once the engagement was completed. It would be better if they came from different places.

The dossiers in the Hawk's briefcase were those of the most accomplished double and triple agents in the US Army data banks. And there was a common denominator running through each file: All were in forced retirement.

The state of double and triple agenting was at a low ebb. The experts described in the dossiers had not had really gainful employment for some time, and for such men inactivity was anathema. It meant not only a loss of prestige within the community of international criminals, but also a reduced scale of living.

The prospects of $500,000 per man would not be lightly dismissed. And each potential recruit was worth it. Each was the best at his speciality.

It was all a question of logistics. Think – then *out*-think. Every function handled by an expert, every move timed to the split second.

209

And that required a commander who demanded flawless precision from his troops. Who trained them to perform at peak efficiency levels. Who did not stint when it came to equipment and simulation; who would duplicate as far as technically possible the *exact conditions* projected for the assault. In essence, a general officer of the first rank. Himself. *Goddamn!*

Once the brigade was selected and assembled, Mac would outline the basic strategy. Then he would allow his officers to offer suggestions and refinements. A good commander always listened to his subordinate officers but, of course, reserved final judgement for himself.

The weeks of training would show where the strengths and weaknesses lay; the objective was merely to eliminate all weakness.

The fewer troops the better, but not so few as to impair the efficiency of the mission. Which was why there was only one payment for each soldier: $500,000. There would be no rewards if they were caught. At least, not the kind they were after. There *would* be certain family allotments in the case of capture. It was the sort of thing all armies had learned to take for granted. Men performed better under combat conditions if their minds were free of concern about their families. It was a good thing, too. It was another proof of separation between the species.

The Shepherd Company would bank funds for dependants in advance of Ground Zero; to be deducted, of course, from all final payments upon the successful completion of the operation.

Goddamn! He was not only pro, he was a very thorough pro at that! If those idiots in the Pentagon had turned over the whole US Army to him, they would not be having all that trouble with volunteer enlistments. The Pentagon prickyshits did not really understand 'the book'. If a soldier took the book for what it was and didn't try to bend it politically, or find ambiguities to hide behind – well, it was a goddamned good book. Flawed but workable.

He had no time to think about pricky-shits. He had about

refined his brigade. The required areas of expertise were seven: camouflage, demolition, sedative medicines, native orientation, aircraft technology, escape cartography, and electronics.

Seven experts. He had narrowed the dossiers down to twelve. Before he reached Zürich he knew he would have the seven. It was just a question of reading and rereading. He would send out his offers from Zürich, not from the Château Machenfeld; nothing could be traced to Machenfeld.

He even had to be careful in Zürich. Not with regard to traces, however; he could handle that problem. But he had to make damn sure he didn't run into Sam Devereaux. Sam was due within hours of his own arrival; he wasn't ready for Sam's kind of panic. He could handle *that* problem better within the confines of Machenfeld.

But then, thought the Hawk, he didn't really have anything to worry about. Devereaux was the girls' problem and they had – each and every one – carried out their assignments with real know-how.

Goddamn! They were splendid! A man had to count himself fortunate, indeed, to have such a quartet of fine women behind him. 'Behind every great man. ...' they said. Behind *him* there wasn't *one* fine lass, there were *four*.

And a grander, more upstanding group of girls there never were! Sam was a lucky fellow and he didn't know it. Hawkins made a mental note to tell him when he saw Sam at Machenfeld.

Tomorrow, if the schedule held.

Devereaux walked down the station platform looking for the correctly numbered railway car. The task was made difficult because he could not stop belching. He had eaten his way from Tizi-whatever-the-hell-it-was, through Algiers, past Rome, into Zürich. Madge had seen him off at Dar el Beida airport admitting no more than their good-byes than she had saying hello in the Aletti Hotel room.

211

But Sam had made up his mind not to speculate any further about the girls. Whatever propelled them to do what they did for the Hawk could be left to Krafft-Ebing; he had other things to concentrate on.

The capitalization of forty million dollars was committed. Hawkins now had his marbles (no, he did not have his marbles, but that was another question), and he would start playing the game. The Hawk would begin his final arrangements, make his purchases, recruit his – what was it? – 'support personnel'.

Jesus! Support personnel!

So he could kidnap the pope!

Oh, my God! The whole world was an enormous fruitcake!

There was only one thing to bear in mind, one objective to keep in focus: How to stop MacKenzie Hawkins.

Two objectives: Stay out of jail himself. And out of the homicidal clutches of the Mafia, the Peerage, the Nazis, and particularly those Arabs who wanted to stuff his unmentionables into unspeakables.

He found his compartment, the sort made famous by Rex Harrison and Margaret Lockwood. Shadows and black velvet collars and the incessant *therumping* of the metal wheels against the metal tracks below signifying the ineviatable approach of terror. And large windows on the sliding doors, with curtains suddenly drawn back revealing the faces of evil.

Night Train, Orient Express – with slow dissolves to hands inching into folds of dark overcoats, ever so slowly withdrawing the black steel of murderous pistols. The train started.

'Well, ah declare! Ah said to myself, Ah simply *don't beleeeeve it*! It's the *mayjor*! Right here in *l'il ole Zürich*!'

There was no reason to be the least astonished. After all, *Titanics* was on schedule.

Regina Sommerville Hawkins Clark Madison Greenberg stood in the corridor outside the railroad compartment and spoke through the wood-framed window. She slid the door open and filled the small enclosure with remembrances of magnolia blossoms. Sam sat down calmly by the window, amazed at his own casualness. 'Your timing's nothing short of brilliant. The train rolls and so do you. If I tried to get off at Lucerne I have an idea you'd start screaming "rape"!

'Why, what a peculiar thing to say. I hope you haven't forgotten the Beverly Hills Hotel; I never will.'

'My memories have no beginnings, no middles, no ends. The world fornicates in a thousand broken mirrors; we abuse ourselves in the reflections of Sodom and Gomorrah....

'Now, tell me why you just *happen* to be in Zürich. At the Hauptbahnhof, on this particular train, in this particular car.'

'Oh, that's easy. Manny's shooting a picture in Geneva. For UA. I think it's so porn they had to make it outside the States.'

'That's Geneva; this is Zürich. You can do better than that. Let's have it for Hawkins's Harem. A little imagination, please.'

'Honestly! Now you're downright offensive!' Regina swept her vicuña back and placed her hands defiantly on her hips. Two cannons had Devereaux in their sights. 'I don't think you've got a damn thing to complain about. We root ourselves up out of *very* comfortable circumstances, traipse *all* over the world, subject ourselves to every kind of inconvenience – *rush, rush, rush* - check on everything – look after you, body *and* soul - make sure no one hurts you – see to your every comfort —. Oh, Lawdy, what more could we do?! And for what? Abuse! Just plain, big ole abuse!'

Regina dropped her defiant pose and began to cry. She opened her purse, withdrew a Kleenex, and sat down opposite Sam, dabbing her eyes.

A lost, hurt little girl.

'Hey, come on. That's not fair.'

As are most men, Sam was helpless before a tearful woman.

Regina sobbed; her chest throbbed. Devereaux got out of his seat and knelt in front of her. 'It's okay. It's all right. Don't cry, please.'

Between subsiding gasps, the girl looked at him gratefully. 'Then you don't hate me? Say you don't hate me.'

'How could I hate you? You're lovely – and sweet – and for Christ's sake, please stop crying.'

She put her face next to his and her lips against his ear. 'I'm sorry. It's just that I'm exhausted. The pressure's been simply God-awful. I've stayed by the telephone night and day, always worryin' – and, of course, wonderin'. I really missed you.'

Ginny's coat was like a warm, comforting blanket between them. The huge, soft lapels came close to enveloping Devereaux's arms. She took both his hands and guided them between the folds of thick fabric and placed them on the softer, warmer, more comforting swells of loveliness that were beneath the silk of her blouse.

'That's better. Stop crying now.' It was all he could think to say, so he said it softly.

She whispered into his ear, causing all kinds of things to happen to his metabolism. 'Do you remember those marvellous old English movies that took place on trains like this?'

'Sure. Rex Harrison saving Margaret Lockwood from the evil Conrad Veidt —'

'I think you can slide the door closed and lock it. And there are curtains. ....'

Devereaux rose from the floor. He locked the door, closed the curtains, then turned back to Regina. She had removed her vicuña coat and spread it invitingly over the soft seat of the railroad compartment.

Beneath them the *therumping* sounds of the metal against metal signified the inexorable journey, the beat somehow sensual. Outside, the lovely countryside of Switzerland whipped by, bathed in a Swiss twilight.

'How much time do we have before we reach Zermatt?' he asked.

'Enough,' she replied, smiling. She began unbuttoning her silk blouse. 'And we'll know. It's the last stop.'

CHAPTER EIGHTEEN

Hawkins registered at Zürich's Hotel D'Accord with a counterfeit passport. He'd purchased it in Washington from a CIA agent who realized the courts would not let him write a book when he retired; the man also offered a selection of wigs and hidden cameras but MacKenzie demurred. On settling into the room, his first act was to go right down to the lobby again and negotiate with the head switch-board operator: cash for cooperation. Since the cash was one hundred dollars, it was agreed that all his calls and cablegrams would be routed through her board.

He returned to the room and spread the seven dossiers (his final selections) over the coffee table. He was immensely pleased. These men were the most devious, experienced *provocateurs* in their fields. It was now merely a question of enlisting them. And MacKenzie knew he was an exceptionally qualified recruiter.

Four he knew he could reach by phone. Three by cable. Admittedly, the telephone contacts would be difficult, for in no case would one call find the expert in. But he would reach them by using various codes from the past. One call would be made to a Basque fishing village on the Bay of Biscay; another to a similar coastal town in Crete. A third would be placed to Stockholm, to the sister of the espionage expert who was currently living as a minister of the Scandinavian Baptist Church. The fourth call would be to Marseilles where the man sought was employed as a tugboat pilot.

And the geographical diversity! In addition to those he could reach by telephone (Biscay, Crete, Stockholm and Marseilles), there were the cablegrams: to Athens, Rome,

216

and Beirut. What a spread! It was an intelligence director's dream!

MacKenzie took off his jacket, threw it on the bed, and withdrew a fresh cigar from his shirt pocket. He chewed the end to its proper consistency and lighted up. It was just nine-fifteen; the afternoon train to Zermatt was at four-fifteen.

Seven hours. Now that was a good omen if ever one existed! Seven hours and seven subordinate officers to recruit.

He carried the three dossiers to the desk and arranged the files in front of the telephone. The cablegrams would be sent first.

At precisely twenty-two minutes to four the Hawk replaced the telephone and made a red check mark on the dossier titled *Marseilles*. It was the last of the phone contacts; he needed only two replies – to the cables to Athens and Beirut. Rome had responded two hours ago. Rome had been out of work longer than the others.

The calls had gone smoothly. In each case the initial conversations with the middlemen – and women – had been reserved, polite, general, almost abstract. And with each MacKenzie employed just the right words, quietly, confidentially. Each expert he had wanted to reach called him back.

There had been no hitches with anyone. His proposals were couched in the same universally understood language; the term *yellow mountain* the springboard. It was the highest score an agent could make for himself. The *yellow mountain* figure was a 'five hundred key' with advance funds banked against contingencies. The *security controls* included 'inaccessible clearing-houses' that maintained no connections with international regulatory agencies. The *time factor* was between six and eight weeks, depending on the 'technological refinements called for in the sophisticated engineering process'. And finally, as leader, his own background encompassed wholesale service to entire governments in most of Southeast Asia, proof of which could be confirmed by several accounts in Geneva.

He had done his research well. To a man, they all needed

217

to mine the *yellow mountain.*

Hawkins got up from the desk and stretched. It had been a long day and it wasn't over yet. In twenty minutes he would have to leave for the railroad station. Between now and then he would speak with the switchboard operator and give her instructions for those callers who might try to reach him. The instructions would be simple: he had reserved the room for a week; he would return to Zürich in three days. The callers could contact him there, or leave numbers where they could be reached. MacKenzie did not want to return to Zürich, but Athens and Beirut were exceptional recruits.

The telephone rang. It was Athens.

Six minutes later Athens was in.

One more to go.

The Hawk moved his untouched luggage to the door and repacked his briefcase, leaving Beirut's dossier in a separate, easily accessible spot. He looked at his watch: three minutes to four. There was no point in procrastinating any longer. He had to leave for the station. Returning to the desk he dialled the switchboard operator and told her he wanted to leave a few simple instructions —

The operator interrupted politely.

'Yes, of course, mein Herr. But may I take them later? I was about to ring your room. An overseas call has just come in for you. From Beirut.'

Goddamn!

Sam opened his eyes. The sun was streaming through the huge French doors: the breeze billowed the drapes of blue silk. He looked around the room. The ceiling was at least twelve feet high, the fluted columns in the corners and the intricately carved mouldings of dark wood everywhere bespoke the word 'château.' It all came into focus. He was in a place called Chateau Machenfeld, somewhere south of Zermatt. Outside the thick, sculptured door of his room was a wide hallway with Persian prayer rugs scattered over a glistening dark floor, and muted candelabra on the walls. The hallway led to an enormous winding staircase and a

218

proliferation of crystal chandeliers above a great hall the size of a respectable ballroom. There, among priceless antiques and Renaisssance portraits, was the entrance – gigantic double doors of oak opening on a set of marble steps that led to a circular drive large enough to handle a funeral for the chairman of General Motors.

What had Hawkins *done*? How did he do it? My God, why? What was he going to use such a place for?

Devereaux looked at the sleeping Regina, her dark brown hair lying in waves over the pillow, her California-tanned face half buried under the eiderdown quilt. If she had any answers, she wouldn't tell him. Of all the girls, Ginny was the most outrageously manipulative; she had orchestrated him down to the moment of sleep. Partially, granted only partially, because he was fascinated by her. There was a will of steel beneath the soft magnolia exterior; she was a natural leader who, as all natural leaders, took delight in her leadership. She used her gifts, mental and physical, with imagination and boldness, and a considerable dash of humour. She could be the strong and moral proselytizer one moment, and the lost little girl in the middle of burning Atlanta the next. She was the laughing, provocative siren in the plantation moonlight, and with the flick of a switch, a conspiratorial, whispering Mata Hari giving orders to a suspicious looking chauffeur in the shadows of the Zermatt railroad station.

'*Mack Feldmann's ass is in the bitter seltzer!*'

To the best of Sam's recollection those had been the words Ginny had whispered to the strange man in the black beret, with the gold front tooth, whose catlike eyes riveted themselves to the front of her blouse.

'*Mack's in felt!*' had been the whispered reply. '*His sight's in an auto bomb's flower pot!*'

With that less-than-articulate rejoinder, Ginny had nodded, grabbed Devereaux's arm, and propelled him into the Zermatt street.

'Carry your suitcase in your left hand and whistle something. He'll turn into an alley and we'll wait at the

219

corner for him to bring out the car.'

'Why all the nonsense? The left hand. The whistling —'

'Others are checking. To make sure we're not being followed.'

The *Orient Express* syndrome was being somewhat overdone, Sam had thought at the time, but nonetheless he'd switched the suitcase to his left hand and started whistling.

'Not *that*, you ninny!'

'What's the matter? It's some kind of hymn —'

'Over here it's called "Deutschland Über Alles"!'

He'd switched to 'Rock of Ages' as another man, this one in a real Conrad Veidt overcoat complete with velvet lapels, came up to Regina and spoke softly.

'*Your warts are in the wagon.*'

'*Mack Feldmann's ass surely has sweet shekels,*' she had answered quietly, rapidly. And within seconds a long black automobile raced out of the dark alley and they had climbed in.

That was how the tortuous, two-hour drive had begun. Miles of winding, uphill roads cut out of the Swiss mountains and forests, intermittently illuminated by the eerie wash of moonlight. Until they reached some kind of massive gate that wasn't a gate; it was an honest-to-god *portcullis*. In front of a *moat*.

A real moat! With heavy planks and the sounds of water below. Then another winding, uphill road that ended in the enormous circular drive in front of the largest country house Sam had seen since he toured Fontainebleau with the Quincy Boy Scouts. And even Fontainebleau didn't have parapets. This place did, certainly high and definitely stone, with the sort of cutout patterns one associated with *Ivanhoe*.

Quite a place, Château Machenfeld. And he had only seen it at night. He wasn't sure he wanted to see it in daylight. There was something frightening about the mere thought of such a massive edifice when related to one MacKenzie Hawkins.

But where did the château fit in? What was it for? If it was going to be the son of a bitch's command post, why didn't he

220

just rent Fenway Park and be done with it? It had to take an army of minions to keep the place running; minions talked. Ask anyone at Nuremberg or in Sirica's courtroom.

But Regina wouldn't talk. (Of course, she wasn't a minion; in no way did the word fit.) Yet he had tried. All the way down from Zürich – well, perhaps not every moment – and half the night in Machenfeld – perhaps less than half – he had done his best to get her to tell him what she knew.

They had sparred verbally, each talking obliquely, neither coming to grips with any positive statements that could lead to any real conclusions. She admitted – she had no choice – that all the girls had agreed to turn up in the right places at the right times so that he, Sam, would have company and not be led into temptations that could be debilitating on such a long businees trip. And have someone trustworthy to take messages for him. And watch out for him. And where goddamned cotton-pickin' hell was the harm in *that*? Where was he going to find such a concerned group of ladies who had his best interests at heart? And kept him on schedule?

Did she know what the *business trip* was about?

Lawdy, no! She never asked. None of the girls asked.

Why not?

Landsakes, honey! The Hawk had told them not to.

Couldn't any of them draw ... certain inferences? I mean, my God, his itinerary wasn't exactly that of a New England shoe salesman.

Honeychile! When they were married to the Hawk – individually, of course – he was always involved with top-secret army things they all knew they shouldn't ask questions about.

He wasn't *in* the army now!

Well-live-and-die-in-Dixie! That's the *army's* fault!

And so it went.

And then he began to understand. Regina was no patsy. None of the girls was. *Fall guy* was not in their collective vocabulary. If Ginny, or Lillian, or Madge, or Anne knew anything concrete they weren't about to say so. If they perceived a lack of complete integrity, each put on blinkers,

221

and her own particular activity remained unrelated to any larger action. None certainly would discuss anything with *him*.

There was another problem in the midst of the Hawk's insanity: Sam genuinely liked the girls. Whatever the whack-a-doo furies were that drove them to do MacKenzie's bidding, each was her person, each an individual, each – God help him – had an honesty he found refreshing. So, if he did spell out what he knew, the instant he did so they were accessories. To a *conspiracy*. It didn't take a lawyer to know that. What was he thinking about; he *was* a lawyer.

As of this ... point in time ... each girl was clean. Maybe not like a hound's tooth; maybe not even like a wino's bridgework, but legally it could be argued that each had operated in a vacuum. There was no conspiracy under the circumstances.

Thank you, Mr Defence Attorney. The bench suggests that you reclaim your tuition from law school.

Sam got out of the ridiculously oversized, canopied bed as quietly as possible. He saw his shorts halfway across the room towards the French doors, which was where he was heading, anyway, and briefly wondered why they were so far from the bed. Then he remembered, and he smiled.

But this was morning, a new day, and things were going to be different. Ginny had given him one specific to hang on to: Hawkins would arrive by late afternoon or early evening. He would use the time until then to learn whatever he could about Château Machenfeld. Or more precisely, what the Hawk was planning for Château Machenfeld as it related to one Pope Francesco, Vicar of Christ.

It was time for him to mount his own counterstrategy. Hawkins was good, no question about it. But he, Sam Devereaux from the Eastern Establishment's Quincy-Boston axis, wasn't so bad, either. Confidence! Mac had it; so did he.

As he put on his shorts, the obvious first move in his counterstrategy came into focus. It wasn't just obvious, it was blatant; bells rang! Such an extraordinary place

222

(mansion, estate, compound, small country) as Machenfeld would demand an unending series of supplies to keep it functioning. And suppliers were like minions, they could see, and hear, and bear witness. The Hawk's proclivity for massiveness could be the most vulnerable aspect of his plans. Sam had considered disrupting Mac's supply lines as *one* of his options, from a military point of view, but he had no idea how positively logical it was. It might be all he needed.

He'd circulate rumours as massively dangerous, as gigantically outrageous, as the sight of Machenfeld itself. He'd start with the servants, then the suppliers, then everyone else who came near the château, until a state of isolation was brought about and he could come to grips with a deserted Hawkins, and – *what the hell was that noise?*

He walked rapidly to the French doors and through them to the small balcony beyond. It overlooked the rear of Château Machenfeld. He assumed it was the rear; there was no circular drive below. Instead, there were gardens in spring bloom, with gravelled paths and latticed arbours and scores of small fishponds carved out of rock. Beyond the gardens were green fields that merged into greener, darker forests, and in the distance were the majestic Alps.

The noise continued, spoiling the view. He could not, at first, determine where it came from, and so he squinted in the sunlight. And instantly wished to hell he hadn't. Because he could now see what was making the noise.

One, two, three ... five, six ... eight, nine! Nine assorted – *insanely* assorted – vehicles were slowly going down a dirt road that bordered the fields, progressing south towards the surrounding forests.

There were two long black limousines, a huge earth-moving bulldozer, an outsized tractor with pronged forks in front, and five – goddamn it, yes, five motorcycles!

It didn't take a lot of imagination to get the picture. The Hawk was about to enter manoeuvres! He had bought himself his own personal *papal motorcade*! Plus equipment that could shove the ground around into any design he liked: The route of said papal motorcade!

223

But he hadn't even arrived at Machenfeld! How the hell was he able to – and what the hell was *that*?

In his anger and confusion, Devereaux gripped the balcony, shaking his head in frustrated bewilderment. His eyes were arrested by an extraordinary sight fifty yards away.

Within a kind of patio, outside a pair of open doors that looked like the entrance to some sort of enormous kitchen, stood a large man wearing a chef's hat, who was in the process of checking off items from a thick sheaf of papers in his hand. In front of the man was a mountain of crates and cartons and boxes that must have reached the height of fifteen feet!

Lines of supply, *shit*!

There wasn't anything left in Europe for Hawkins to buy. There was enough food down there to eliminate half the famine on the Ganges! The son of a bitch had requisitioned enough rations for an army, goddamn it, an army setting out on a two-year bivouac!

Limousines, motorcycles, bulldozers, tractors, food for the entire Lost Battalion! Sam's counterstrategy move number one was shot to hell by a parade of nine idiotically assorted vehicles and some gasping eccentric in a chef's hat.

The only state of isolation in the foreseeable future was from any and all lines of supply. They were totally unnecessary.

That left the minions. The dozen or so servants that had to be around to keep Machenfeld afloat. Kitchens, gardens, fields (that probably meant barns, maybe livestock), and at least thirty to forty rooms with cleaning and waxing and polishing and dusting. Christ! There *had* to be a staff of twenty!

He'd begin right away. Perhaps with the drivers of the nine vehicles; convince them to get the damn things off the château's grounds before it was too late. Then he'd rapidly go from one group of servants to another. Let them know in ominous terms, which meant legal terms, that if they knew what was good for them they'd get the hell out of

224

Machenfeld before all the agents of Interpol descended.

All the food in Switzerland wouldn't do the Hawk any good if there was no one on the premises. To *run* the premises. And a few well-chosen words to those manning the vehicles, words like 'international violations', 'personal accountability', and 'life imprisonment', would surely cause that stream of motorcycles and limousines and trucks to barrel-ass back over the moat into safer territory.

Sam was so preoccupied with his new strategy that he wasn't really aware that his undershorts kept sagging, causing him to hold them up with a free hand. He was forced to be aware of it now because as he gripped the railing his shorts had plummeted down to his ankles. Swiftly, he retrieved his modesty, noting with a degree of self-satisfaction that the games with Ginny Greenberg must have been pretty damned exciting indeed. But it was no time for pleasant reminiscence; there was work to do. His watch read nearly eleven; he hadn't realized he'd slept so long – the games were not only exciting, but exhausting. He had barely five or six hours to get everybody out. Such a large staff of servants probably had lots of personal belongings. That would mean transportation, perhaps more complicated than he had considered. But one thing had to be clear: when the minions left the grounds of Machenfeld, they were *not to return*. For *any* reason. Anything less would weaken his basic premise: Machenfeld was a threat to everyone who remained, therefore no one was to do so.

Evacuation!

The château was to be deserted!

Then what the hell was MacKenzie going to do?

Stew in his cigar juice, *that's* what he was going to do!

It was merely a question of logistics and execution.

Goddamn! Logistics and execution! He was beginning to *think* like the Hawk! And have the confidence of the Hawk! Be bold! Be outrageous! Take fate by the balls and. ...

Shit! Before anything could happen, he had to get dressed. He raced through the French doors into the room. Ginny stirred and moaned a little and then buried her head farther

into the eiderdown quilt. He stepped out of the torn
underwear, and crossed quietly to his suitcase which was on
an overstuffed armchair against the velour-covered wall.

It was empty.

There wasn't a goddamned thing in his suitcase.

He looked around for the closet.

Closets. There were four.

Empty. Except for Ginny's dresses.

Shit!

He ran as quietly as possible to the sculptured door and
opened it.

Sitting across the wide hallway was the black beret with
the gold front tooth and catlike eyes which were now focused
on Sam's lower extremities. In the confusion that, perhaps,
was understandable. The sneer was not.

'Where are my clothes?' whispered Devereaux, partially
closing the door, leaning against it.

'In the *launtree*, mein Herr,' replied the black beret in an
accent formed in some Swiss canton run by Hermann
Göring.

'Everything?'

'Courtesy of Château Machenfeld. All was dirty.'

'That's ridiculous!' Sam tried to keep his voice low. He did
not want to wake Ginny. 'Nobody asked me —'

'You were asleep, mein Herr,' interrupted the black beret,
grinning suggestively, his gold tooth gleaming. 'You were
very tired.'

'Well, now I'm very angry! I want my clothes back. Right
away!'

'I cannot do that.'

'Why not?'

'It is the *launtree's* day off.'

'What? Then why did you take them?'

'I told you, mein Herr. They were dirty.'

Sam stared at the catlike eyes across the hallway. They
had narrowed ominously; and the gold tooth was no longer
seen because the grin had disappeared, replaced by an

226

adamant mouth. Sam closed the door. He had to think. Quickly. As Mac would say, he had to weigh his options. And he had to get out.

He did not consider himself a brawler, yet he was not a physical coward. He was a pretty big fellow, and regardless of what Lillian said in Berlin, he was in fair shape. Still, all things considered it was a good guess that the black-bereted maniac across the hall could beat the shit out of him. Even naked, he could not leave by the stairs.

Option One considered and rejected.

That left the windows, more specifically the small balcony beyond the French doors. He grabbed his shorts off the floor, put them on, held them up, and walked silently outside. The room was three storeys off the ground, but directly below was another balcony. With sheets, or drapes, tied together he could make it with reasonable safety.

Option Two was feasible.

He went back inside and studied the drapes. As his mother in Quincy would say, they were spring drapes. Silk, billowy, not strong. Option Two was fading. Then he looked at the bed sheets, ignoring the inviting sight of Regina who was now more outside the eiderdown quilt than under. If the sheets were combined *with* the drapes, this would probably hold him. Option Two was re-emerging.

Battle dress.

That was a problem. There was nothing *but* dresses.

So, assuming Option Two succeeded and he reached the ground, he had Options Three and Four to consider. And as he considered them there was a sinking feeling in his stomach. He could race around Machenfeld in underwear that kept falling down to his ankles or he could put on one of Ginny's Balenciaga prints and hope the zipper held.

A man running around spreading alarms in dishevelled underwear, *or* a Paris original, was not likely to be taken too seriously. There might even be Options Five and Six to contend with: be locked up, or raped.

227

Shit!

He had to keep his head; he had to get hold of himself and think things out. Slowly. He could not allow a minor item like clothing to stand in the way of evacuation. What would the Hawk do? What was that goddamned term he used so frequently?

Support personnel! That was it!

Sam raced back out on the balcony. The man in the chef's hat was still checking off items on his list. It'd probably take him a week.

'Pssst! Pssst!' Devereaux leaned over the railing, remembering at the last instant not to let go of the underwear. 'Hey, *you*!' he whispered loudly.

The man looked up, startled at first, then smiled broadly. *'Ahh! Bonjour, monsieur! Ça va?'* he shouted.

Sam held his finger to his lips. 'Shhh!' He gestured for the chef to come closer.

He did so, carrying his papers, making a last notation as he walked. *'Oui, monsieur?'*

'I'm being held prisoner!' whispered Devereaux with solemn urgency and much authority. 'They've taken my clothes. I need *clothes*. And when I get down I want you to get everyone who works here into the kitchen. I've got some very important things to say. I'm a lawyer. *Avocat.*'

The man in the chef's hat cocked his head. *'Je ne comprends pas, monsieur. Désirez-vous le petit déjeuner?'*

'Who? – No. I want clothes. *See?* All I've got is this, *these*.' Sam stretched his torn undershorts so they could be seen between the rails; then he pointed to his legs. 'I need pants, *trousers*! Right away. *Please!*'

The expression on the man's face changed from bewilderment to suspicion. Perhaps even distaste mingled with hostility. *'Vos sous-vêtements sont très jolis,'* he said, shaking his head, turning back towards the patio and the crates of food.

'Wait! Wait a minute!'

'The chef is French, mein Herr, but not *that* French.' The

voice came from below, from the balcony directly underneath. The speaker was an immense, bald man with shoulders nearly as wide as the depth of the railing. 'He thinks you are making a most peculiar offer. I can assure you he's not interested.'

'Who the hell are *you*?'

'My name is unimportant. I leave the château when the new master of Machenfeld arrives. Until then his every instruction is my command. His instructions do not include your clothing.'

Devereaux had an overpowering urge to let his shorts fall and copy Hawkins's action on the roof of the diplomatic mission in Peking, but he controlled himself. The man on the balcony below was huge. And obviously couldn't take a joke. So instead he leaned over and whispered the words conspiratorially.

'Heil Hitler, you fucker!'

The man's arm shot forward; his heel clicked like the bolt of a rifle. *'Jawohl! Sieg heil!'*

'Oh, shit!' Sam turned and walked back into the room. In exasperation, he kicked off his shorts. Then he absently studied them as they lay on the floor. Perhaps it was the angle of the fabric, he was not sure. But suddenly they looked strange.

He bent down and picked them up.

Christ! What games?

The elastic waist had been cut deliberately in three places! The incisions were *incisions*, not tears. There were no loose threads or stretched cloth. Someone had taken a sharp instrument and sliced the goddamn things! On purpose. Immobilizing him by the simplest method possible!

'Lawdy! What's all that shoutin' about?' Regina Greenberg yawned and stretched, modestly pulling the eiderdown quilt over her enormous breasts.

'You bitch,' said Devereaux in quiet anger. 'You devious bitch!'

'What's the matter, honeychile?'

'Don't "honeychile" me, you Southern retardant! I can't get *out* of here!'

Ginny blinked and yawned again. She spoke with calm authority. 'You know, Mac once said something that's been a comfort to me all through the years. He said, when the mortars are falling all around you and things look terrible – and, believe me, there were times when the world looked pretty terrible to me – he said, think of the good things you've done, the accomplishments, the contributions. Don't ponder your mistakes or your sorrows; that only puts you in a depressed state of mind. And a depressed state of mind is not equipped to take advantage of that one moment that could arise and save your ass. It's all a question of mental attitudes.'

'What the hell has that bullshit got to do with the fact that I don't have any clothes?'

'Not an awful lot, I guess. It's just that you sounded so depressed. That's no way to face the Hawk.'

Devereaux started to answer blindly, angrily. Then he stopped, looked at the sincerity in Ginny's eyes and began again. 'Wait a minute. "Face the Hawk." You mean you want me to fight him? *Stop* him?'

'That's your decision, Sam. I only want what's best for everyone.'

'Will you help me?'

Ginny was pensive for a moment, then replied firmly. 'No, I won't do that. Not in the way you're thinking. I owe MacKenzie too much.'

'Lady!' burst out Devereaux. 'Do you have *any idea* what that lunatic is up to?'

Mrs Hawkins number one looked at him with an expression of suddenly imposed innocence. 'A lieutenant doesn't question a general officer, Major. He can't be expected to understand the intricacies of command —'

'Then what the hell are we talking about?'

'You're a smart fellow. The Hawk wouldn't have promoted you if you weren't. I just want him to have the finest advice he can get. So he can do whatever it is he wants to do the best way possible.' Ginny rolled over under the eiderdown quilt. 'I'm really very sleepy.'

And Devereaux saw them on the bedside table next to her head.

A pair of scissors.

CHAPTER NINETEEN

'Sorry about the clothes,' said the Hawk in the huge drawing room. Sam glared and retied the curtain sash he used as a belt around the eiderdown quilt. 'You'd think the laundry would have more than one key, wouldn't you? These big fancy places don't trust anyone; shows the kind of house guests they must be used to, I suppose.'

'Oh, shut up,' mumbled Devereaux, who found it necessary to double-loop the sash because the silk kept slipping. 'The laundress *will* be here in the morning, I presume.'

'I'm sure of it. She's one of the few who go home at night. To the village. That'll change, of course; there'll be a lot of changes.'

'Just tell me there'll be *one* change and I'll go back and have dinner with Azaz-Varak.'

'Come on now, Sam, you've got a one-track mind. Let's get on to other things. You sure you don't want a shirt and a pair of trousers? Just take me a minute to go upstairs. ...' Hawkins made a gesture past a dozen or so overstuffed, antimacassared armchairs towards the great hall.

'No! I don't want anything from you! – I take that back. I *do* want something. I want you to call off this crazy business and let me go home!'

MacKenzie bit off the chewed end of his cigar, spitting it between the feet of a suit of armour. 'You *will* go home, I promise you that. The minute you centralize the company finances and make a few deposits that can be tapped under certain conditions, I'll drive you to the airport myself. That's the word of a general officer.'

'It's the reasoning of a brain soaked in linseed oil! Do you

232

have any idea what you're asking me to do? That's not chopped liver you're talking about, it's *forty million dollars*. I'm marked for life! They'll have a record sheet on me in every Interpol headquarters and police station in the civilized world! You don't put your name on forty million dollars' worth of bank transfers and expect to go back to a normal law practice. Word gets out.'

'That's not so, and you know it. All that Swiss banking stuff is confidential.'

Devereaux looked around to make sure no one else was within hearing. 'Even if it's supposed to be, it's not *going* to be once a ... certain attempt is made to snatch a ... certain person in Rome! And that's *all* it will be! An attempt! You'll have your ass in a net, and every contact you've made since China will be put under a microscope and my name will surface and so will forty fucking million dollars in Zürich and that's the *ballgame!*'

'Now, goddamn, boy, we've been over that! Your job's finished now. Or will be soon's you take care of the money. You don't have to be involved anymore. And you're *clean*, son. You're a hundred per cent Clorox!'

'I'm not.' Devereaux choked as he whispered and clutched the eiderdown quilt. 'I just *told* you: The minute *you're* nailed, *I'm* nailed!'

'For what? Say you happened to be right – which I don't for a second consider remotely possible -- what can they nail you for? Banking funds for an old soldier who told you he was raising money to support an organization dedicated to spreading religious brotherhood? Let me ask you a question, Mr Attorney. Could you, under oath, testify to any wrongdoing?'

'You're *insane!*' broke in Sam, stumbling slightly as he stepped forward. 'You *told* me! You're going to kidnap —' Devereaux stopped and made charade-like gestures that included hauling a body over his shoulder and the sign of the cross.

'Well, *hell*, boy, there are *oaths* and there are *oaths*! Be reasonable. Anyway, that's hearsay. Not admissible.'

233

Sam closed his eyes; he began to understand what martyrdom was all about. He continued, his whisper strained but controlled. 'I walked out of those archives with that fucking briefcase chained to my wrist!'

'Outside of that,' mumbled MacKenzie. 'Anyhow, that's army stuff; neither of us has much use for the army. Anything else?'

Devereaux thought. 'Circumstantially; it's the mother-loving end. There hasn't been a single aboveboard transaction.'

'That's objective,' said Hawkins, shaking his head, confirming his own judgement. 'There's been no violence; no one's lied. No theft, no collusion. Everything voluntary. And if the particular methods *seem* unusual, that's the prerogative of every individual investor, as long as he doesn't infringe on the rights of others.' Mac paused and held Sam's eyes. 'There's something else, too. You said yourself that a lawyer's first responsibility was to his client, not abstract moral dilemmas.'

'I said that?'

'You surely did.'

'That's not bad —'

'It's goddamned eloquent, that's what it is. You've got a silver tongue in your head, young man.'

Sam stared back at the Hawk, trying to see beneath his guile. But it wasn't guile; he meant what he said. And since personal sincerity was the momentary leveller, Devereaux decided to be personally sincere.

'Listen to me,' he said quietly. 'Say you go through with this – this insanity, because that's what it is, you know. Say you really do it. You actually kidnap the pope and get away with it. Even for a few days. Do you know what might happen? What you could trigger?'

'Surely do. Four hundred million green samolians from four hundred million howling mackerel snappers. No offence intended, just a harmless phrase.'

'*No*, you gung-ho son of a bitch! There'd be international *revulsion*! And *recrimination*. And then mainly *accusations*!

234

Governments would point their fingers at other governments! Presidents and chairmen and prime ministers would use blue lines and red lines and then very *hot* lines. And before you know it, some asshole recites a code from a tiny black box in a briefcase because he didn't like what some other asshole said. Jesus, Mac! You could start World War Three!'

'*Goddamn!* Is that what you've been thinking about?'

'It's what I've tried *not* to think about.'

Hawkins threw his cigar into the cavern that was the Machenfeld fireplace and stood arms akimbo, a flame dying in his eyes. 'Sam, boy, you couldn't be farther from the truth. You know, son, war isn't what it used to be. Hasn't any spirit to it anymore. Bugles and drums, and men caring for men, and hating an enemy because he can hurt the things you love. That's all gone now. Now it's buttons and shifty-eyed policitians who blink a lot and wave their hands without meaning very much. I hate war. I never thought I'd hear myself say it, but I'm saying it and learning it now. I'd never allow a war.'

Devereaux bored into the Hawk's eyes; he would not let MacKenzie look away. 'Why should I believe that? Everything you've done reeks of con. Immense con. Why should a war stop you?'

'Because, young man,' replied Hawkins quietly, returning Sam's stare in full measure, 'I just told you the truth.'

'All right. Suppose you provoke one without meaning to?'

'*Goddamn!* Now you're pushing me too far!' MacKenzie strode from the fireplace to a second suit of armour to the right of the mantel. The face piece was open so he slammed it shut. 'I put in damned near forty years and got fucked by the plastic men! *Your* words, boy! Now, I don't feel sorry for myself because I knew what I was doing, and was accountable for my actions! But, goddamn, don't ask me to feel sorry for *them* or be accountable for their *stupidity!*'

So much for personal sincerity, thought Devereaux. Like Options One, Two, Three, and Four in the morning, it was shot to hell. This time in a burst of self-righteousness. There was nothing for it but to find another way. One would present itself, Sam was convinced of that. The Hawk had a way to go before the pontiff of the Catholic Church blessed the edelweiss at Machenfeld. Something would turn up; and Option Seven – Options Five and Six happily avoided – was coming into focus. For the moment he had to calm MacKenzie down and under no circumstances lose his confidence. And then Mac did have a point. A legal point.

He, Sam, was clean. Legally clean. In every other way the mud was an inch thick, but in evidentiary considerations, he was not a good case for any prosecutor.

'Okay, Mac, I'm not going to fight you. You were screwed and I did say it, and I believe you. You hate war. Maybe that's good enough. I don't know anymore. Personally, I just want to go back home to Quincy, and if I read about you in the papers, I'll remember the words of a scarred but honest warrior spoken in this room.'

'A tongue of silver, boy! I admire that.'

'As long as it's not a head of lead, I'll accept that. Do you have the papers for the Zürich bank?'

'Don't you want to hear the amount I've ... accrued for your participation? How do you like that "accrued"? I'm a corporate president, you know; we don't fuck around with second-rate vocabularies.'

'I'm impressed. What's the entry figure?'

'The what?'

'The accrual; that's the noun root of the verb "to accrue".'

'Smartass shavetail. What do you say to a half a million dollars?'

Sam could not say anything. He was numb. He saw his hand move in astonishment, and he watched it with a certain fascination, not sure if the appendage belonged to him. It must have; when he thought about jiggling the fingers, they jiggled.

A half a million dollars.

What was there to think about? It was as insane as everything else. Including the fact that he was not indictable.

It was Monopoly time. Let's buy *Boardwalk* and *Park Place.*

Stop. Go To Jail.

Why worry?

It didn't do any good anyway.

'That's reasonable – severance pay,' Sam said.

'That's all you've got to *say*? With what I banked for you in New York, you can hire that Jewish fella and he'll be happy to take the job.' MacKenzie was the injured party. He obviously expected Devereaux to practise a little bit of his well-advertised overreaction.

'Let's say I'll erupt with enthusiasm when I'm looking at those figures – in a bank book – in Boston – with my mother sitting across the room complaining about the new management at the Copley Plaza. Okay?'

'Do you know something?' said Hawkins, his eyes squinting. 'You're kind of weird.'

'*I'm* kind of. ...' Devereaux did not finish the sentence. There was no point.

There was the abrupt, episodic clicking of high heels. Regina Greenberg walked through the cathedral arch into the drawing room. She was dressed in a beige pants suit, the rather severe jacket buttoned over Titanics. She looked, well, rather efficient, thought Sam. She smiled briefly and addressed Hawkins.

'I've met with the staff. Five will stay. Three couldn't; they'd have to live in the village and I explained that wasn't acceptable.'

'I hope they weren't hurt.'

Ginny laughed confidently. 'Hardly. I spoke to each individually, and gave all three two months' wages.'

'The rest understand the conditions?' MacKenzie reached into his pocket for a fresh cigar.

'And their bonuses,' said Ginny. 'Minimum three months. All with families to explain that they've been hired for resident staff work in France for the duration. No questions are to be asked.'

'No different from overseas duty,' commented the Hawk,

nodding his head. 'And the money's a hell of a lot better than combat pay – without a weapon in sight.'

'The logistics are in your favour, too,' continued Ginny. 'Only two of the five are married. Not too happily, I gather. They won't miss, or be missed.'

'We'll have to get women, though,' countered MacKenzie, 'for R and R. I'll scout the grounds later; spec out tent arrangements – far enough away from the manouevres, of course. And the counsellor here is going into Zürich to take care of several financial items for me. What do you think, Sam? How long do you figure it will be before you're finished?'

Devereaux had to force himself to consider the Hawk's question. He was stunned by the obvious control MacKenzie wielded over Ginny. According to the data banks, she had divorced MacKenzie over twenty years ago; yet here she was deferring to him like a schoolgirl with a crush on her teacher.

'What did you say?' Sam knew the question but wanted a few seconds to evaluate.

'How long will Zürich take?'

'A day. Maybe a day and a half, with no hitches. A lot will depend on the account clearances. I think the transfers are coded through Geneva, but I may be wrong about that.'

'Can "hitches" be eliminated with a little honey in the pot?'

'Probably. Relinquishing-of-interest could apply. The time period's minor but the sums aren't. The depositories would pick up several thousand – on paper. That might act as a general incentive.'

'Goddamn, son, you hear yourself? You hear how *good* you are?'

'Elementary bookkeeping. A trial lawyer figures litigation with banks is prime meat. They've got more ways to lie to themselves – and everybody else – than anyone since tribes started to barter. A decent attorney simply picks the lie he knows will suit him best.'

'You hear that, Ginny? Isn't that boy something?!'

'You're mighty impressive, Sam; I've got to admit it. And, Mac, since the *may*jor here's got everything under control,

238

maybe I could go up to Zürich with him and kind of keep him company.'

'Why, that's a splendid idea! Don't know why I didn't think of it.'

'I can't imagine how it escaped you,' said Devereaux quietly. 'You're all heart.'

From all points of the compass the Hawk's subordinate officers arrived. They were met at the Zermatt railroad station by the bereted, gold-toothed, cat-eyed chauffeur whose name was Rudolph. And Rudolph had a hectic two days.

Crete showed up first, without incident. That is, he managed to cross international boundaries under the scrutiny of very professional authorities without incident (but with a forged passport) and got as far as the Zermatt station, where his troubles erupted. For Rudolph refused to acknowledge Crete to be Crete in spite of the proper identity markings on his clothing, and consequently would not let him into his Italian taxi.

Because, for reasons that escaped Hawkins, none of the G-2 data bank entries on Crete had established the fact that he was Black. Yet there it was. Crete was a brilliant aeronautical engineer, a Soviet sympathizer as long as the Ruskies paid him, a defected espionage agent complete with a doctor's degree and very black skin. Rudolph was totally bewildered, so MacKenzie had to use some very harsh language over the telephone with Rudolph, and finally the bereted maniac let the *Schwarzer* in the back seat of his car.

Marseilles and Stockholm were next. They flew in together out of Paris because they met each other on the previous night at Les Calavados on the Boulevard Georges Cinque and renewed an old acquaintanceship that went back to the days when both were making money from the Allies and the Axis. They were delighted to discover that they were both on a trip to the same yellow mountain in Zermatt. Rudolph had no trouble with Stockholm and Marseilles because they spotted him before he spotted them and they

239

criticized him for his stupidity at being obvious.

Beirut did not take the train from Zürich; he hired an ambulance, instead. He had his reasons; they went back to several contraband run-ins with the Zürich police. So he flew in to Geneva, drove a rented car in the name of a socially elite transvestite, dropped it in Lausanne, contacted l'Hôpital des Deux Enfants in Montreux and leased the ambulance, ordering it to transport him as a coronary wishing to spend his last days in Zermatt. He timed everything to the Zürich train however and all would have gone smoothly except for Rudolph. Unfortunately, Rudolph had a flat tyre on the back roads of Machenfeld, and in his subsequent haste to reach the Bahnhof on time he had a minor collision in the railroad station's parking lot. With the ambulance.

Therefore it was difficult for Rudolph to identify the highly agitated coronary patient, who climbed out of the rear door yelling about imbeciles, with the figure whose markings identified him as Beirut.

But Rudolph was beginning to shrug more and more. The master of Machenfeld, he was beginning to suspect, was not all there in the head. And neither were the people he was sent up to Zermatt to meet.

And the lovely lady of his late-night dreams, the beautifully breasted Fräulein, had left the château for several days. Things were not the same.

Rome and Rudolph got along splendidly. Rome lost his luggage on the train. The combined chaos of finding his three suitcases and his contact from the château proved a strain nearly too much for Rome. Rudolph sympathized and allowed him to sit in the front seat on the trip to the château.

Biscay was extremely secretive. Once he displayed the coded identification (a pair of white gloves with black roses stitched on the back) Biscay excused himself to go to the men's room and disappeared through a window. After an hour, Rudolph's impatience turned to curiosity and the curiosity, in turn, became panic when he discovered the men's room empty. He tried to remain inconspicuous as he looked in nooks and crannies and luggage bins. Biscay followed him discreetly. And it was only after Rudolph called Machenfeld in panic that Biscay, listening from an adjacent booth, decided that his contact was authentic.

Biscay sat in the back seat, and Rudolph did not say a single word all the way to Machenfeld.

The last to arrive was Athens. If Biscay was suspicious, Athens was paranoid. To begin with, he pulled the emergency cord on the train, stopping it in the freight yards just outside the station. Conductors and engineers ran through the cars looking for the emergency, while Athens jumped off and raced over the tracks to the platform, where he concealed himself behind a concrete pillar. It was not difficult for Athens to spot Rudolph.

The train finally proceeded into the station. Rudolph examined all the disembarking passengers; Athens could see his anxiety. When there was no one left on the platform but railroad personnel, Athens approached Rudolph from the rear and tapped him on the shoulder. As he did so, he displayed his identification (a red kerchief) and gestured for Rudolph to follow him.

At which point, Athens raced back to the end of the platform, jumped down on to the tracks and started running towards the freight yard. He soon outdistanced Rudolph and started a series of *I-See-You's* between the immobile cars.

Five minutes later a distraught Rudolph was being comforted by the energetic Athens as they walked out of the freight yards towards the taxi.

And as MacKenzie Hawkins watched the car approach from the ramparts of Machenfeld, he congratulated himself once more on his professionalism. Seventy-two hours had passed since he had begun making his coded contacts from the D'Accord; and in that seventy-two hours every one of his subordinate officers was physically on the premises.

Goddamn!

Based on the accepted principle that larceny goes a long way in the banking business, Sam's trip to Zürich – more

241

specifically his trip to the Staats Bank to centralize the Shepherd Company's capital – was so successful so rapidly that he would be able to catch the early afternoon train back to Zermatt. And since Regina Greenberg was out shopping, he left a message for her at the Hotel D'Accord: *Have gone bowling. Will be home late.*

He wanted those hours on the train by himself; to think, to refine. For Option Seven was becoming more sharply defined as the hours passed. Due mainly to the papers he carried out of the bank given him by a perspiring trust officer who was considerably richer than he was before he'd met Sam.

Among the fourteen documents, four pertained to the account transfers from Geneva, the Cayman Islands, Berlin, and Algiers – minus accrued interest, of course; one listed the total assets of the Shepherd Company, with its bond of confidentiality, its codes of release and the account number; one was in the name of the family Devereaux (Sam did not explain it and the banker had asked no questions, treating the item as though it did not exist); and eight separate documents defined eight separate trusts.

One of these accounts was larger than the others and within it were four individual sets of figures ... obviously meant for four individuals. It did not take much reflection on Devereaux's part to identify them: Mrs Hawkinses one, two, three, and four.

That left seven trusts, each with an identical maximum figure.

Seven.

The Hawk's *support personnel.*

MacKenzie had recruited seven men to kidnap the pope. (Sam couldn't imagine that any were women; the Hawk's four ex-wives were capable of *anything* calling for feminine skills.) These seven were his – what was it? – subordinate officers. MacKenzie had allowed that his subordinate officers would be arriving at Machenfeld shortly.

'What do you mean "subordinate officers"?' Devereaux had asked.

242

'The troops, son, the troops!' The Hawk had replied, the flame reignited in his eyes.

'What do you mean "shortly"?'

'We're on blue alert, boy. That means all posts are manned, contact expected from here on in.'

'Like in a few days?'

'Maybe sooner, depending on enemy counterpersonnel blockades. Our troops will have to cross hostile territory on their way to base camp.'

'What the fuck are you talking about?'

'Nothing you have to be concerned with. Just bring back that money stuff from Zürich. Before I give my first briefing on the mission, I want my subordinate officers to see for themselves just how thoroughly command centre has taken care of their interests. It'll give 'em a real sense of purpose, of comradeship; it emanates from the top, you know. It always has.'

That was the other reason why Option Seven was coming into focus. *Bring back that money stuff ... before I give my first briefing ... command centre has taken care of their interests.*

The Hawk's troops had been recruited without knowing precisely what the war was all about. Militarily speaking there was nothing unusual in that, but considering the enormity of the projected enemy's resources – namely, the whole world – a few well-chosen words like, *'Do you realize what this maniac intends to do? Kidnap the pope!'* and *'You're dealing with a certified mental case!'* and *'You're commander is a fruitcake!'* and *'This lunatic shot the jade balls off a Chinese monument.'* – things like that could very well make the support personnel look to other fields of endeavour.

It was a question of timing. And psychology. If Sam read him correctly, Hawkins was going to hit his subordinate officers with a double-barrelled salvo: a highly technical, strategically 'feasible' description of the abduction, *and* bona fide documents from the Staats Bank du Zürich that guaranteed each man a fortune, *regardless of outcome*! It

243

would be a tough act to cripple, but that's what Option Seven was all about.

Sam would reach the subordinate officers *first*. He would shoot off canons of doubt regarding the Hawk's fundamental sanity. There was nothing more frightening to criminal underlings than the possibility that their employers were unbalanced. Lack of balance meant lack of judgement, no matter how well disguised. And lack of judgement could spell ten-to-twenty-to-life; in this case, probably a long rope and a blindfold.

Even the criminal element in Europe had to have heard of the paranoïd general who was thrown out of China. It wasn't that long ago. And when he had finished this part of his oral summation, Sam would place his high card on the table.

High? There were none higher. It was irresistible.

For on the train to Zermatt he would go through the documents from the Staats Bank du Zürich, specifically the trust accounts, and write out all the numbers and the sequential codes of release, and put them on seven pieces of paper.

He would give each man a card with the information written on it. Each could leave Château Machenfeld without so much as sitting through a meal, head for Zürich – *and claim his money.*

Each subordinate officer would make a fortune! For doing absolutely nothing. Irresistible!

Giovanni Bombalini, the Vicar of Christ, walked out into his beloved garden to be alone. He did not wish to see anyone, or talk with anyone. He was angry with the world, *his* world, and when one was angry it was always best to meditate.

He sighed. If he was to be truthful with himself, he had to admit he was angry with God. It was so senseless! He raised his eyes to the afternoon sky and a single word emerged plaintively from his lips.

'Why?'

He lowered his head and continued down the path. The

sprays of lilies were in spring bloom, greeting life.

As he was about to leave it.

The doctors had just delivered their collective report. His vital signs were diminishing with increased acceleration. He had no more than six or seven weeks.

Death itself was easy. Good heavens, it was a relief! *Life* was the struggle. But struggle or no, he had not consolidated the necessary forces to carry on his and Roncalli's work. He needed more time; he needed the authority of the office to bring divergent factions closer together. Why could not God understand that?

Eh, my beloved Lord? Why? Just a little more time? I promise not to lose my temper. Nor will I insult the nasal-toned – pardon, most Holy Father – the cardinal or his band of antediluvian thieves. Six months would do nicely. Then I shall rest in the arms of Christ with grateful devotion. Five months, perhaps? Much could be accomplished in five months ....

Giovanni tried with all his heart to perceive a heavenly response. If there was one, it was too weak to get through his vital signs.

Perhaps, dear Father, if you would speak to the Holy Virgin? She might find more eloquent words to convey my supplication. It is said that women are more persuasive in these matters ....

Still nothing. Just a minor pain in his knees which meant the weight was hard on his old bones and he should sit for a while. What was it that lovely *giornalista* had said? There were certain exercises —

Basta! All he needed was to collapse doing push-pulls. Ignatio Quartze would roll his body under the bed and they would not find him for a week. In the meantime, Quartze would pack the Curia.

The pontiff reached his favourite white bench and lowered himself on the cool stone. A breeze came from the garden walls, fluttering the leaves of the tree above him. Was it a sign? It *was* refreshing. Then the breeze stopped; the still air returned and the fluttering of leaves was replaced by footsteps clattering over the path.

It was the new papal aide. A young Black priest from the diocese of New York City, a brilliant student who had done much good work in the Harlem districts. Francesco had sought out just such a deserving young prelate – over considerable opposition. It was a small part of a large design.

'Your Holiness?'

'Yes, my son. You look agitated. What's the matter?'

'I think I did something quite wrong. I was bewildered and you weren't in your rooms and there didn't seem to be anything else to do. I'm very sorry.'

'Well, now, we don't know the extent of this calamity until you describe it. You didn't, by any chance, find Cardinal Quartze in my closet and call the guards?'

The Black priest smiled. Ignatio had made clear his disapproval of the aide's appointment. Francesco took every opportunity to lessen the insult.

'No, Your Holiness. I heard your private telephone ringing. The one in the drawer of your bedside table; it just kept ringing.'

'It would, my son,' interrupted the pontiff. 'It is not connected to the Vatican switchboard. A minor indulgence. So you answered it. Who was calling? Only a few old friends and an associate or two of long standing have the number. There is no great harm in what you did. Who was it?'

'A monsignor in Washington, Holy Father. He was very upset —'

'Ahh, Monsignor Patrick Dennis O'Gilligan! Yes, he calls frequently. We play chess together long distance.'

'He was very excited – and he thought I was *you*. He didn't give me a chance to speak. He rattled on so fast I couldn't stop him.'

'Yes, that sounds like Paddy; he's had his problems. The Berrigans again? Those two keep busy —'

'No, Holy Father. Much worse. The *President* called him. Something about the confidence of the confessional, and whether it was *admissible*. He wants to *convert*, Holy Father!'

246

'Che cosa? Madre di Dio!'

'It gets worse, Your Holiness. Sixteen White House aides want to find Jesus right away. Under certain conditions of Vatican privilege and something called Christian immunity.'

Giovanni sighed. There was *so much* to do.

Four months, oh Lord?

CHAPTER TWENTY

The unfamiliar faces had one thing in common, thought Sam. Very muscular bodies. As though each enjoyed the outdoors, kept in trim by moving rocks under the eyes of the penitentiary guards. And speaking of eyes, that was another thing in common. All their eyes seemed a little sleepy at first, the lids half closed. But it was only appearance. On closer examination the eyes could be seen spinning in their sockets like pinballs caught between magnets; very little went unobserved.

There was a tall, blond man who looked like he jumped out of a television commercial for Scandinavian cigars; a Black who nodded silently a great deal and spoke an English refined in university lecture rooms; another dark-skinned fellow with distinctly sharp, northern features whose accent was like all those people in formal clothes at the Savoy; two Frenchmen who had something to do with boats; a long-haired man in very tight trousers who strutted when he walked like a tango dancer, aware of his ass – unmistakably Italian; and finally, a rather wild-eyed Greek who wore a red kerchief and kept telling jokes no one quite understood.

There was a soft-spoken politeness among them that was positively unctuous, complemented by manners that seemed born of breeding and wealth, were it not for the shifty eyes. They certainly were very much at home in the huge drawing room of Château Machenfeld, where the Hawk had everyone gather before the late dinner.

Gathered, but in the interests of international security, not introduced. No names were used.

Sam had returned to the château at seven. It would have been an hour earlier but he had to walk the last three miles

248

because no taxi out of Zermatt was allowed to travel beyond certain zones and Rudolph was nowhere to be found. When Sam called information for Machenfeld's telephone number, he discovered there was no such place.

It all might have taken the heart out of him, but Option Seven kept him going. He knew when a case was won.

MacKenzie had greeted him with mixed feelings. The Hawk was pleased that he had brought back the financial papers so promptly, but felt that his treatment of Regina was most ungentlemanly. She was a fine girl, and now Sam could not properly say good-bye to her.

Why not?

Because her luggage had been sent to the airport. Ginny was on her way back to California, with a stop in Rome to look at the museums.

So much for Ginny, thought Devereaux. He was a little sad, but there was Option Seven to think about. And he began to think the timing was perfect.

MacKenzie told him that there would be no business discussed the first evening. Just social chitchat and strolls through the gardens and cocktails and dinner and brandy. Why? Because the troops would like a chance, he believed, to size each other up, check their rooms for bugs, oil their weapons, and generally assure themselves that Machenfeld was no Interpol trap. Sam could expect to hear noises during the night; most of the men would carry out their own surveillance, and that was good because they would undoubtedly run into one another and realize further that everything was on the up-and-up.

In the morning, when all were refreshed, the Hawk would hold his first briefing. Before he did that, however, he would certainly take the time to say good-bye to Sam. He was going to miss his young friend, no question about it. But the word of a general officer was his bond; it was the glue that held his battalions together.

Devereaux's work was finished. Rudolph would drive him into Zermatt, where he'd take the morning train to Zürich and the late-afternoon flight to New York.

There was one thing Sam should be aware of, however, just in case he became nervous or was afflicted with hypertension. For the next month or so, several associates of the Shepherd Company's first investor, Mr Dellacroce, would stay in close touch with him. Their names were Fingers and Meat, Hawkins believed; it was just a temporary arrangement, no offence intended.

Yes. Sam understood. There was no point in MacKenzie being redundant.

Devereaux had terminated the conversation, saying he would shave and shower the sweat of three mountain miles off him, and return for cocktails.

In his room, Sam found the scissors Ginny had used on his underwear and cut out seven strips of paper five inches long, one inch wide. He wrote out the identical message on each.

Vitally important you meet with me in my room – third floor, rear of house, last door in the north hallway on the right. 2.00 a.m. sharp. Your life depends on it. I am a friend. Remember two o'clock this morning!

He folded the strips of paper neatly so they fitted into the palm of his hand and put them in his jacket pocket. He then removed the seven index cards from his briefcase, the ones with the account numbers and sequential codes-of-release written on them and put them in his trousers pocket. They were his high cards. Irresistible!

He returned to the drawing room downstairs and put to use all the social graces a fine Boston upbringing provided. He shook hands with the men.

And passed each his message.

By one thirty in the morning he was ready. The Italian came first, his hands encased in sheer, skintight black gloves, his feet laced in balletlike slippers with ridged rubber soles. And then, one by one, the rest showed up in apparel not much different. There was a proliferation of gloves, and soft shoes or sneakers, and black sweaters, and narrow trousers with thick belts holding thicker knives, and small holsters

250

with single straps across small pistols, and in several cases coils of wire.

Altogether a very professional group of psychopaths, thought Sam, as he told them with quiet, not completely heartfelt authority to relax and get comfortable, and smoke if they wished.

Since they all *were* relaxed, and most smoking already, he wasn't sure it was a good opening. But the best summations were those that built from quiet even awkward beginnings.

So he began. Softly, at first. Starting with man as a tribal being, looking to the heavens for meaning beyond his daily battle for survival, finding solace in that which he could not really comprehend, because there was comfort in primitive faith. There was structure, an organization to natural phenomena, and that meant there had to be a force, a mind, a profound all-knowing intelligence that conceived the whole. Yet could never be truly understood.

There was beauty in that lack of understanding, for men strove beyond themselves for the all-seeing, all-knowing force that created the earth, created *them*, knew *them* – loved *them*.

Without this search, man was an animal. With it he reached out, and compassion became a part of him.

Sam explained that symbols and titles were not important in themselves, for correlations could be drawn between all religions. The essence was the differentiation between good and evil. But symbols and titles held mystical meaning, and profound comfort, for millions everywhere. Faith. The poor and the oppressed prayed to them, held them in reverence and hope. And for millions these symbols were the warm light in their unceasing winters of darkness.

Devereaux paused. It was the moment for a crescendo.

'Gentlemen, facing you is a crime of such monstrous proportions, a crime of such profound evil – a crime which *cannot possibly succeed* and can only lead each of you to your death, or to a life endured, not lived, in a brutal prison cell. For within the walls of this château is a man who would

251

rob you of your most priceless possessions! Your *freedom*! Your *very lives*! For he conceives the *impossible*. In his unbalanced – woefully unbalanced – mind he is convinced he can overcome the swift and terrible reaction, the vengeance, of the entire world! He expects to lead you into the gaping jaws of oblivion. He intends to kidnap the pontiff of the Catholic Church! He is, in a word, *insane!*'

Sam stopped. He bored his eyes into the face of each man. Cigarettes were suspended in midair, mouths were open in disbelief, eyelids were stretched stares conveying a paralysis born of shock.

He had them! The jury was in the palm of his hand! The phrases had come out like thunder!

It was time for his high cards. Those irresistible figures and sequential code words that would make each man in the room rich. Very, very rich. For doing nothing but avoiding the risk of oblivion.

'Gentlemen, I realize the state of shock you're in and it pains me to see it. It pains me to have caused it. As that great Roman, Marcus Aurelius, observed: We must all do what we have to do, at the moment fate demands that we do it. But as the Indian prophet, Baga Nishyad, also observed: Buckets filled with tears can be spread over grain and the rice will grow like jewels. I do not have jewels, gentlemen, but I do have riches for each of you. Deserved rewards. Sums of money that will lessen your pain, and send you back to the lands of your choice, to live in freedom, freedom from fear, from oblivion. And from want. Here. I pass among you these small index cards. Each is a passport to your personal nirvanas. Let me explain.'

And Sam did.

And the seven subordinate officers studied the cards, glancing at one another as they did so.

'Do you speak French?' asked one of the Frenchmen.

Devereaux laughed – a touch too gaily he felt. 'Not really.'

'Thank you,' said the Frenchman, turning to the others. '*Vous parlez tous français?*'

To a man they nodded affirmatively.

So they all began speaking French.

Quietly. Rapidly. Until seven heads nodded once again affirmatively. Sam was touched; he knew they were trying to find a way to thank him.

Which was why he was bewildered when two of the men suddenly approached and grabbed him, spun him around, and began wrapping his wrists in wire.

'What the hell are you doing?' he yelled. 'What are you doing to my hands? And what the hell is that?'

He gestured his head at the red kerchief the Greek had whipped from his neck and was now twirling.

'And what the hell are they?!'

He referred to a number of metallic cracks that sounded strangely like weapons being inspected.

'We have that compassion you spoke of, monsieur,' said the Frenchman. 'We offer the choice of a blindfold before we execute him.'

'*What!?*'

'Be brave, signore,' said the Italian.'We all know this business. We accept the odds or we do not play.'

'Ya,' added the Viking. 'It is a game. Some vin. Some lose. You lost.'

'*Whaaat?!*'

'Take him down to the patio,' said the second Frenchman. 'We'll tell the staff it's target practice.'

'*Mac! Maac! Maaac!*' He was led down the hallway. Several pairs of hands clapped themselves over his mouth; he bit them. '*For Christ's sake! Hawkins! Where the fuck are you?!*'

Again the hands clamped over his face. The cordon marched with precision down the hallway towards the magnificent winding staircase. Devereaux again forced his mouth open and bit furiously at the flesh around his teeth; hands and arms whipped back momentarily. It was enough for Sam to kick out behind him and for an instant free himself.

He raced and plunged bodily down the curving steps, tumbling over and over as he fell.

'Hawkins! You son of a bitch, get out here! These maniacs want to shoot me!'

He bounced over the treads, careened against the wall, and plummeted shoulders over backside down into the last straightaway. His shouts were progressively blurred, but the overall meaning was unmistakable.

'Blindfolds – ouch! Pistols! Goddamn – you – oh – ohh –. Hawkins! Uhu! Jesus – my head!'

He reached the bottom of the staircase, a dishevelled heap. The Hawk strode through the cathedral arch from the drawing room, a cigar clenched between his teeth, several folded maps in his hand. He looked at Sam on the floor and then up at the band of subordinate officers.

'Goddamn, boy! This changes *everything*!'

Once again his clothes were taken. Only now there weren't even any dresses in the closet. His meals were brought up by Rudolph.

The Hawk explained that it had taken a command counterdecision to save his life; and the troops did not like it one bit.

'For a fact, I nearly had a mutiny on my hands before the brigade set its colours,' Hawkins had told him the next morning.

'Set its what? Never mind, don't tell me.'

'I mean it, son. I had to take stern measures and let them know right off that in matters of extreme prejudice, no authority – regardless of consensus – exceeded that of a field general. It was touch and go for a while, but I've handled the roughest in my day. Those pups, good as they are, weren't any match. It's in the eyes, boy. Always the eyes.'

'I don't understand,' Devereaux had moaned sincerely. 'I spelled everything out beautifully. I unravelled the whole ball of wax. The background, the motive. Jesus! Even the money! I had them!'

'You had nothing,' the Hawk replied concisely. 'You made two big mistakes. To begin with, you assumed that such a group of men, such a fine contingent of officers, would accept money surreptitiously, without earning it —'

'Get off it!' Devereaux had roared his interruption. 'You can't sell the honour-among-thieves bullshit because I won't buy it!'

'I think you're misjudging, boy, but if that's the way you see it, there's your second mistake to consider.'

'What mistake?'

'One of the oldest traps in Interpol is to set up a hot bank account and send someone after it. I'm surprised you didn't know that. You set up seven all at once.'

Sam had retreated under the eiderdown quilt and pulled it over his head. Unfortunately, he could not block out MacKenzie's words.

'You know, Sam, life is a series of compartments, some related to each other, most separate. But every once in a while these parallel compartments, as I call them, have to acknowledge one another's existence. Now, you saved my life in Peking. You brought to bear your skills and your experience and kept me from that oblivion I hear you talked about. And last night, here in Switzerland, I saved *your* life. Using what skills and experience *I* have. We're even. Our compartments in this area aren't parallel anymore. So don't fuck up, son. I can't be responsible. And that's the word of a general officer.'

By the end of two weeks, Sam was sure he'd lose what was left of his sanity. The mere thought of clothes drove him mad. Throughout his life clothes were an accepted part of living – sometimes pleasant, even ego-fulfilling – but they had not been a subject he ever dwelled on for any length of time.

That's a nice jacket; the price is okay. Get it. Shirts? His mother said he should get shirts. What's wrong with Filene's? So I'm a lawyer. Okay, J. Press. Shirts and grey flannels. Socks? His bureau drawer somehow always had socks in it. And shorts and handkerchiefs. A suit was a pretty big occasion, the few times in his adult life when he went out and bought one. Still, he'd never been tempted to have one tailor-made. And in the goddamned army, his civilian jackets and trousers were on hand only because they meant a change from the goddamned uniform. No. Clothes had never been a major factor in his life.

They were now.

But necessity - part of which was not losing one's sanity - was the mother of invention. And truer words were never said. So Sam began to invent, and the thesis of his invention was that he was undergoing a sincere change of position.

It had to be gradual, based on available alternatives. Since he was so completely, intrinsically, *legally* enmeshed in the Shepherd Company's operations and since all avenues of separation had been blocked, what was the point of fighting any longer? Life *was* compartmentalized; and he was locked into a big vault named MacKenzie Hawkins - which also held some forty million dollars, which was a lot of chopped liver.

Maybe, just maybe, his negative approach was self-defeating, all things considered. Perhaps, just perhaps, he should be putting his energies into productive channels; find areas where he could contribute. After all, there was one indelible bottom line. If the Shepherd Company got blown up, a hell of a lot of shrapnel would find its way into the hide of the second and only other corporate officer of record.

These were the conjectures he began to put into words – haltingly, without much conviction at first – during MacKenzie's daily visits at the start of the third week. But he realized that simply saying them was not very persuasive. The Hawk had to see his mind working, observe the transformation.

By Wednesday he had built up to the following:

'Mac, have you considered the legal aspects after - you know, after —'

'Ground Zero's good enough. What legal aspects? Seems to me you've obliged nicely in that department.'

'I'm not so sure. I've been involved in a fair amount of plea bargaining. From Boston to Peking.'

'What are you talking about?'

'Nothing. I was just - oh, nothing.'

By Thursday, this: 'There could be consequences after . . . this Ground Zero . . . that you haven't thought out. A cancer could be growing on the presidency of the Shepherd Company that ultimately may cripple the office.'

'Spell it out, boy.'

'Well. . . . No, never mind. It's conjecture. What was all that noise this afternoon? It sounded very exciting.'

The Hawk squint-eyed him before being pulled into the question. 'Goddamn, it was exciting,' he answered after several seconds. 'Nothing like the evolvement of precision in manoeuvres! It fires up a man's heart! What the hell were you talking about? This cancer stuff.'

'Oh forget it. The old legal brain was just wandering. Are the manoeuvres really all that . . . top drawer?'

'Yeah . . .' Hawkins rolled the cigar from one side of his mouth to the other. 'They're all right, I guess.'

On Friday: 'How was the practice today? Sounded great.'

'Practice? Goddamn, it's not practice, it's manoeuvres!'

'Sorry. How were they?'

'A little sloppy; we've got some minor difficulties.'

'Sorry, again. But I've confidence in you. You'll straighten things out.'

'Yeah . . .' The Hawk paced at the foot of the bed, his cigar a mashed pulp. 'I may have to pick up a few diversion troops. Two or three, that's all. I wasn't concentrating. And, goddamn, Sam, I would have been on-the-barrel-sight except for the trouble you've caused!'

'I told you. I really regret all that. *I* wasn't concentrating —'

MacKenzie stopped and blurted out the words. 'Do you mean that?'

'Yes,' replied Devereaux slowly, with conviction. 'The first thing a lawyer learns is to deal with facts, hard evidence. All of it, not just the bits and pieces. I isolated. I'm truly sorry.'

'I won't pretend to understand that bullshit, but if you feel the way I think you're saying, what the hell were you talking about yesterday? And, damn it, the day before. Those "consequences" after Ground Zero.'

257

Bingo! as they said in Boston, thought Devereaux to himself. But he showed no emotion; he was the calm, probing attorney with his client's best interests at heart. 'All right. I'll spell it out. I know those trust accounts, Mac. Excluding the one major trust, which I gather is yours, your seven men can draw (or have their consigners draw) up to three hundred thousand on the basis of the first code releases. The second code releases are on a printout sheet in one of the other documents. The printout requires your countersignature and I assume you'll send it to Zürich just before you leave for Ground Zero. Am I right so far?'

'I really skull-sessioned that trust business. What's wrong?'

'Nothing. Yet. With the second release each man has a total of five hundred thousand, correct? That's his fee, right? A half a million for Ground Zero. Everybody the same.'

'Not bad for six weeks' work.'

'There are other things to consider. Plea bargaining on a large scale can include more than immunity. And not just through writing a book, although I understand a lot of cash is funnelled through publishers these days.'

'What are you talking about?' The Hawk squashed his cigar out on the bedpost.

'What's to prevent any or all of your subordinate officers from going straight to the authorities - through inter-mediaries, of course - and making separate deals? After the fact. They have your money; they avoid prosecution because they cooperate. Remember, we're talking about one of the biggest scores in history. They could make a few thousand on top of what they've got.'

MacKenzie's squinting eyes suddenly widened in relief. And self-satisfaction. There was definitely a sense of triumph in his grin. 'Is that what you've troubled yourself over, boy?'

'Don't make light of it —'

'Hell, no, I won't. And I didn't. None of my men would do anything like that. Because they're going to want to disappear like jackrabbits running from a brush fire. They

258

won't surface anywhere for fear of colliding with *each other*.'

'Now *I* don't understand,' said Sam dejectedly.

The Hawk sat on the bed. 'I've covered all that, son. Sort of in the same way I lashed you to the loaded howitzer. You gave me the idea. I intend to say good-bye to each officer separately. And with each I'm going to hand him an open-faced bearer bond worth an additional half million. And tell him *he's* the *only* one getting it. Because like a good general officer I've kept my combat logs, and in rereading them I realized the mission could not have been successful without *his* particular strategic contributions. They're hung. Both ways. A man won't inform on a crime that couldn't have been committed without *his expertise* – especially when it's worth an additional half million – and he sure as shit doesn't want his fellow conspirators to know he got preferential treatment to the tune of half a million.'

'My God!' Sam could not stop the admiration from creeping into his voice.

'Clausewitz makes it clear that you don't engage the Berber in the same way you do battle with the king's dragoons. It's a question of applicable tactics.'

Devereaux, once again, was struck by the Hawk's sheer boldness. He spoke softly, barely above a whisper, 'You're talking about – Jesus! – three and a half million dollars!'

'That's correct; you add real quick. And a million apiece for the girls, that's four more million. Plus the original compensation for the officers, another three and a half. And for your information, though I should probably reconsider, I've got another bearer bond for you. That's a million on your paysheet.'

'*What?*'

'I kind of suspected you never understood the forty-mill capitalization. I didn't just come up with a figure, you know. That sum was arrived at after very careful deliberation. I got a booklet from the Securities and Exchange Commission which told what to look for in sound corporate financing. You see, before the company even *markets* its services, we have a preoperation salary outlay of close to fifteen million;

then there was the capitalization expenses, including travel and front money and finder's fees – I kinda screwed you on that, son, but I knew you had good things coming – and the corporate real estate and the equipment indigenous to the marketing sources ....'

Involuntarily, Sam's ears distorted the sound waves. Isolated phrases such as 'aircraft purchases estimated at five million', and 'shortwave communication relays coming in at a million-two', and 'refurbishing, and supplies', and 'additional company offices' – all these came through with sufficient clarity to make Sam wonder where he was. Stark naked under an eiderdown quilt somewhere in Switzerland, or fully clothed in a boardroom somewhere in the Chrysler Building. Unfortunately for the state of his stomach, everything came together with the Hawk's brief summation.

'This SEC booklet was very specific about liquid assets available for reserve capital. It recommended a point spread of twenty to thirty per cent. Then I checked out the custom-of-the-trade practices with limited partnership agreements and found that the overcalls were generally ten to fifteen per cent, which struck me as inadequate. So I skulled a bit and decided on twenty-five per cent. And that's what we've got. The budget projections prior to marketing come to just about thirty million. Taking that as the base figure, you add ten for contingency. That makes forty million and that's what I raised. Damned sound economics, I'd say.'

Devereaux was temporarily speechless. His mind was racing but no words came. MacKenzie the military fruitcake was suddenly Hawkins the conglomerate financier. And that was more frightening than anything he had previously considered. Military principles (or lack thereof) when combined with industrial principles (of which there was a lack thereof) did a military-industrial complex make. The Hawk was a walking military-industrial complex!

If there was strident urgency in Sam's stopping Mac-Kenzie before, it was tripled now.

'You're invincible,' said Sam finally. 'I rescind all my previous reservations. Let me join you, really join you. Let me earn my silly million.'

CHAPTER TWENTY-ONE

Each officer had been assigned a colour, in French. Not only was French spoken by everyone, but the sounds of the colour words were more distinctive in French than in any other language.

The American Negro from Crete was *Noir*, of course. The Viking from Stockholm, *Gris*; the Frenchman from Biscay was *Bleu*; while his countryman from Marseilles was *Vert*; the dark-skinned non-Black from Beirut was *Brun*; Rome was *Orange*; and finally, Athens was *Rouge*, in honour of his ever present kerchief. To instil a sense of discipline and identity among the men, the Hawk further insisted that the word 'Captain' precede each colour.

This aspect of authority and identity was desirable because MacKenzie's second command by necessity stripped his men of their specific individualities. For Ground Zero's assault was to be made in stocking masks. Head and face hair were to be at a minimum; skins powdered or bleached to medium Caucasian hues, and all ambulation which, no doubt, had been studiously disguised, drastically changed.

The men accepted the order without question. Razors and scissors and bleaching agents went to work; none had any desire to stand out any more distinctly from his fellow officers than basic nature dictated. There was security in anonymity, and they knew it.

The manoeuvres progressed into the fourth week. The forest road bordering the Machenfeld field had been shaped to conform as accurately as possible to the site of Ground Zero; boulders had been moved, trees uprooted, whole areas of bush transplanted. A second location had been selected and cosmeticized: a winding, narrow, back road that descended a relatively steep hill in the woods.

In redesigning both these sites the men worked from enlarged photographs – 123 photographs, to be exact – sent by an agreeable tourist in Rome by the name of Lillian von Schnabe. However, Mrs von Schnabe did not take credit for her films. As a matter of fact, the rolls were sent undeveloped by two relays of couriers unknown to each other and delivered to a bewildered Rudolph in Zermatt. In several cases of tampons. Rudolph put the strange cargo in the trunk of his Italian taxi, underneath the tools. A man had his dignity to consider.

On the third day of the fourth week the Hawk scheduled the first complete run-through of the assault. By necessity it was a start-stop hold-to-position exercise as the men switched around, assuming the pivotal roles of the adversary. Motorcycles raced, limousines sped, figures in stocking masks leaped from their stations to perform the tasks assigned. Using a stopwatch, MacKenzie clocked each phase of the manoeuvre; he had developed eight basic phases for the entirety, from incursion to escape. And goddamn, his officers were progressing beautifully! They knew that the overall success of Ground Zero depended on the complete success of each individual assignment within each specific phase. The concept of failure was not attractive.

Which was why the captains objected unanimously to the Hawk's prime tactical innovation: total absence of hand weapons. A well-placed knife or a rapidly exercised garrotte had served them all in past skirmishes, more often than not being the difference between survival and capture. But MacKenzie was adamant: It would be both guarantee and proof that no harm would come to the pope until the ransom was paid. Therefore, all pistols, knives, coils, foot studs, knee cleats, finger points – even pig-iron knuckles – were eliminated. Forbidden, too, were any forms of hand-to-hand above the level of basic jukato.

Eventually, they accepted the limitations. 'In Sweden there is a saying,' intoned Captain Gris in his Nordic lilt. 'One Volvo in the garage is worth a lifetime of passes on the

Scandinavian railroad. I shall accommodate the commander.'

'Oui,' agreed Captain Bleu, the Frenchman from Biscay. 'For the recompense involved, I shall sing them to sleep with Gascogne lullabies, if it is required.'

But lullabies were not required. Instead, sleep was to be induced by half-inch hypodermic needles dispensing solutions of sodium pentothal. Each officer would be outfitted with a thin bandolier across his chest, which carried tiny hypodermic needles in small rubber receptacles – where once had been bullets. They were easy to extract swiftly. If administered properly, within a three-inch diameter on the lower right area of the neck, the anaesthetic would take effect in seconds. The problem was merely to immobilize the victims for those brief moments until the drug caused collapse. It was not a difficult problem and since there'd be considerable noise from the vehicles, even a partial scream or two might go unnoticed.

So the officers, heeding the words of wisdom from Gris and Bleu, re-evaluated their objections to the Hawk's order. In a way it was a challenge; and none were interested in lifetime passes on the Scandinavian railroad. Not when he could own a fleet of Volvos.

Each captain's expertise was called on. Captain Gris and Bleu were masters of camouflage and escape cartography. Captain Rouge was an expert in demolition; he had personally blown up six piers in the Corinth strait when it was rumoured the American fleet was sailing in. Sedative medicines were a speciality of the Englishman, Captain Brun, who had darkened his skin for a life in Beirut; most narcotics held interest for him. Aircraft technology and electronics were covered brilliantly. The first, of course, was the bailiwick of Captain Noir, whose exploits in Houston – and Moscow – were legend. The second was the province of Captain Vert, who found it necessary in Marseilles to devise an extraordinary variety of radio communications. It was such a busy port; and Interpol was always underfoot.

Lastly, native orientation was left to Captain Orange, who

knew Rome like the back of his constantly gesturing hand. He would write out full descriptions of eight innocuous-looking sets of clothing that blended into the current dress, and further, he would provide a minimum of four separate methods of transportation, using public conveyances where feasible, to the site of Ground Zero. For during the final days of the fourth week, each captain was to travel to Rome and personally survey the assault area.

The airfield at Zaragolo would be no problem; they agreed to that. And neither would the helicopter at Ground Zero. It could be flown in the night before the assault. Gris and Bleu assured them the camouflage would be undetectable.

Goddamn, thought MacKenzie as he snapped the stopwatch at the end of the manoeuvre's Phase Eight. Twenty-one minutes! In another day or so it would get to the optimum eighteen. He felt a surge of pride in his once bemedalled chest. His machine was emerging as one of the finest ministrike forces in the military books.

Even the three privates (the diversionary-troops) were splendid. They had but two functions: scream and lie still. But as was proper for the lowest enlisted ranks, they knew nothing. They had been recruited by Captain Brun from the poppy fields high in the Turkish hills, to which they would return the instant Ground Zero was terminated. They'd been hired to perform at a fixed price, did not care to know anything and, naturally, were housed by themselves in enlisted quarters and did not eat at the officers' mess.

They were called simply: Privates One, Two, and Three.

The run-through completed, the officers gathered around the Hawk beside the huge blackboard he'd set up on an A-frame in the field. Sweat was pouring through their stocking masks. Those in priestly habits took them off carefully, studying them for repairs that might be needed; and the inevitable cigarettes and matches came out of pockets. No lighters; fingerprints could be lifted from lighters.

The three privates, naturally, went off by themselves. In sight but not within hearing. Enlisted personnel were not privy to tactical analyses; it was not proper.

The analyses began. Although immensely pleased Hawkins did not dwell on the positive; he told them their mistakes, marking up the blackboard with his criticisms with such sharp authority that the officers cowered like rebuked children.

'Precision, gentlemen! Precision is everything! You must never allow your concentration to lapse, even for a second! Captain Noir, you're cutting your time too close between Phase One and your station in Phase Six. Captain Gris, you had trouble with your cassock over the uniform. Practise it, man! Captains Rouge and Brun, your execution of Phase Five was just plain sloppy! Take out that radio equipment! Go over your moves! Captain Orange! Yours was the most serious lapse of all!'

'*Che cosa?* I make *no* mistakes!'

'Phase Seven, Captain! Without the proper execution of Phase Seven, the whole mission goes up in mortar smoke! That's the *exchange*, soldier! You're the one who speaks Italian best. I put this Frescobaldi in the pope's car and take the pope. Where the hell were *you?*'

'In position, *Generale!*'

'You were on the wrong side of the road! And Captain Bleu, for an expert at camouflage, you stuck out like a plucked duck in your Phase Four station! *Cover*, man! Use the foliage for cover!'

'Now, as to this latrine rumour that some of you are unhappy over Phase Eight, the escape routes to Zaragolo; that a few of you figure we should have two copters at Ground Zero. Well, let me tell you, there's no contingency for radar, gentlemen. One small bird with Italian air force markings, flying low, can get through. Two choppers would be picked up on a scanner. I don't think any of you cotton to having your asses a thousand feet in the air, surrounded by the whole guinea air force. No offence, Captain Orange.'

The captains looked at each other. They'd obviously discussed Phase Eight among themselves, and since the small helicopter at target centre was lifting out only the

Hawk, the pope, and the two pilots, they had grumbled. But the commander painted a convincing picture. The escape routes on the ground had been exhaustively analysed by Gris and Bleu, who were not only the best in the business, but who would be using them as well. It was conceivable that the ground was safer.

'We withdraw our objections,' said Captain Vert.

'Good,' said MacKenzie. 'Now let's concentrate on —'

It was as far as he got. For in the distance, across the south field, running through the grass was the figure of Sam Devereaux in sweat pants, shouting at the top of his lungs.

'One, two, three, four! What do we like to *jog* for? *Good* health, *good* health! Five, six, seven, eight! Get the weight! Out of the freight! Four, three, *two*, *one*! Jogging is a lot of fun!'

'*Mon Dieu!*' cried Captain Bleu. 'The soft-headed one never stops! He has carried on so for five days now!'

'Before we rise in the morning!' added Gris. 'During rest periods, whenever there is a peaceful moment he is below the window, shouting.'

The other captains joined in a chorus of agreement. They had accepted the general's decision not to shoot the idiot, even grudgingly allowed that there was no harm in letting the fool out of the room to exercise – as long as two guards from the Machenfeld staff were assigned to him. The jackass wasn't going anywhere; not in sweat pants, with no top, over a high barbed-wire fence that led only to impenetrable Swiss mountain forests. But they had drawn the line regarding the clown's participation in Ground Zero.

So here he was, trying to impress them with his training. A pathetically poor athlete who cannot make the team, but will not stop trying.

'All right. All right,' said the Hawk, suppressing a laugh. 'I'll talk to him again, make him quiet down. He's just doing it for your benefit, you know. He really wants to join the big fellas.'

He was driving them all crazy, and he knew it. Of course

there were times when he thought he might collapse from exhaustion, but the knowledge that his grotesqueries were having their desired effect kept him going. Everyone avoided him, some actually ran at the sight of him. His insane behaviour had become an irritating, aggravating joke. Already three dogs which had appeared out of nowhere to guard him were taken from the corridor outside his room to the staff quarters below because of their incessant barking. And he made it a point to run by the staff area repeatedly. The hounds, themselves weary of being screamed at for their perfectly natural reaction, now merely raised their heads and stared with hatred at him from behind the gates as he passed by.

As did the staff – and MacKenzie's officers. Sam was a loud nuisance, a joke that had worn thin. What was happening, of course, was that he was being taken for granted. And in a few days he would take advantage of that scorn.

Although he was not allowed to eat with Mac and his band of psychopaths, the Hawk was considerate enough to continue visiting him every day in the late afternoon when Sam was brought back to his room and the sweat pants removed. Devereaux understood. Hawkins needed a sounding board for his enthusiasms. And, bragging, he dropped the information that he and his men would be away for a day or two to execute a surveillance check of Ground Zero. They would then return for any last-minute alterations of strategy.

But Sam shouldn't be concerned. He would not be lonely at Machenfeld. What with the guards, and the dogs, and the staff.

Sam smiled. For when the Hawk and his freaks left the château, it was his own personal Ground Zero. He had begun to prime his guards, the wild-eyed Rudolph and some obvious killer with no name. He had convinced Rudolph and No Name on several occasions to sit in the middle of a field as he ran around it. It was not difficult; they were grateful to be stationary. They simply sat in the grass with two ominous looking pistols trained on him as he jogged and intermittently stopped to perform callisthenics. On each occasion he had gradually widened the distance between him and his guards so that this afternoon he was nearly 250 yards away from them.

The army had taught him *something* about small weapons; he knew that there was no handgun that was any damned good beyond thirty yards. Not in terms of accuracy; scatter shot was something else, but he had to take *some* chances. Stopping the Hawk was the kind of objective that in war made heroes of unheroic soldiers. What had MacKenzie said? 'It's commitment. Nothing takes its place. All the ammo in the world can't be a substitute....'

Sam was committed. The prospects of World War III loomed larger every day.

His plan was simple, and relatively safe. He had been tempted to give it an option number, but his options had not been noticeably successful so he decided against it. He would jog here in the south field, as he was doing now, where the bordering forest was thickest and the grass higher than in the other pastures. He would widen the distance between himself and the guards as he had done this afternoon and institute intermittent callisthenics. Among them pushups. Which naturally brought him close to the ground, below the level of the grass.

At the proper moment, he would crawl away as fast as he could towards the forest, then race to the fence. However, when he reached the fence, he would *not* climb it. Instead, he would remove the sweat pants - properly torn - and throw them over. And then, if all went as it should, if Rudolph and No Name were racing in several directions at once, he would scream as though severely hurt and get the hell out of the area. Into the thickest woods.

Rudolph and No Name would naturally run to the spot at the fence, see the sweat pants on the other side, and undoubtedly take the appropriate actions: One would go over the fence, while the other raced back to the château for the dogs.

At which point Sam would wait until he heard the

barking. Then he would return to Machenfeld, go in through the door, steal clothes and a weapon. From that point to an automobile in the circular drive, and a pistol to threaten the gatekeeper, had to be clear sailing.

It had to be!

What could go wrong?

The Hawk wasn't the only one capable of strategies. He'd learn not to mess with a Boston lawyer who worked for Aaron Pinkus!

The shouts interrupted his thoughts. He was within sight of the manoeuvre area; he could see the strange looking road signs and the vehicles. Rudolph and No Name were yelling at him to come back. Naturally, he would oblige; he was not permitted to observe manoeuvres.

'*Sorry fellas!*' he yelled breathlessly as he reversed direction, his legs pounding the soft earth. 'Let's head down to the gate and back and call it a day!'

Rudolph and No Name grimaced and got up from the grass. Rudolph gave him a finger; No Name a thumb to the teeth.

Sam made it a point every afternoon to end his jogging with a run down to the main gate. It was a good idea to study the premises as thoroughly as possible in anticipation of his escape. It was conceivable that he might have to operate the mechanism himself, depending upon the state of panic at the moment. If it was maximum (as MacKenzie would say) the gate might even be left open.

He contemplated this possibility as his feet clattered over the boards of the moat, when suddenly his musings were replaced by a feeling of discomfort. For down at the gate a long, black limousine was being admitted with much bowing and obsequious grinning on the part of the gatekeeper. And when he heard the words shouted from the driver's seat as the automobile was expertly whipped out of the gate towards him, he froze and instantly considered drowning himself in the Machenfeld moat.

'I don't belive it!' yelled Lillian Hawkins von Schnabe at the wheel. 'Sam Devereaux in *sweat pants*! God almighty,

270

you took my advice. You're toning up that wreck of a vessel you live in!'

And if he considered drowning himself at Lillian's words, the next voice he heard drove him to the railing.

'You surely look better than you did in London!' shouted Anne from Santa Mónica, Mrs Hawkins number four – Sloping yet Argumentative. 'Your little trip must have done you a world of good!'

CHAPTER TWENTY-TWO

Devereaux's escape plan did not become unglued as had Options One to Four. Neither was it bypassed as Options Five and Six had been. Nor had it exploded in a torrent of abuse as was the fate of Option Seven. It was, however, postponed.

He suddenly had two additional guards to contend with, one of whom was as much a shock to the Hawk as both were to Sam. MacKenzie admitted it. Casually, without letting it upset his schedule; merely using the reality to bolster his overall strength – turning a liability into an asset.

'Annie's got a problem, counsellor,' the Hawk said back in Devereaux's room. 'I think you might give it some legal thought. Do something about it when this is over.'

'All problems pale into insignificance —'

'Not hers. You see, Annie's family – the whole god-damn family – spent more time *in* prison than *out* of it. Mother, father, brothers – she was the only girl – they had record sheets that took up most of the precinct files in Detroit.'

'I never came across any of that. It's not in the data banks.' Devereaux was momentarily sidetracked from his own concerns. MacKenzie wasn't trying to con him, now. There was no fire in the eyes, only sadness. Truth. But there *hadn't* been any mention of a criminal record in Anne's dossier. If he remembered correctly, she'd been listed as the only daughter of two obscure Michigan school teachers who wrote poetry in medieval French. Parents deceased.

'Course not,' said the Hawk. 'I changed all that for the

272

army. And everybody else, mainly her. It was a big hangup for the girl; it was holding her back.' MacKenzie lowered his voice, as if the words were painful, but nevertheless a reality that could not be brushed aside. 'Annie was a hooker. She fell into poor ways – very artificial ways for her – when she was growing up. She worked the streets. She didn't know any better then. She had no home life, most of the time no home. When she wasn't hooking she'd spend her time in libraries, looking at all the pretty magazines, imagining what it would be like to live decent. She was constantly trying to improve herself, you know. She never stops reading, even now, always after bettering herself. Because underneath there's a very fine person. There always was.'

Sam's memory went back to the Savoy. Anne in bed with a huge, glossy paperback of *The Wives of Henry VIII* on her lap. Then later, the words spoken with such conviction in the foyer doorway as she was about to get dressed. Words that meant a great deal to her. Devereaux looked up at the Hawk and repeated them quietly. '"Don't change the outside too much or you'll mess up the inside." She said you told her that.'

MacKenzie seemed embarrassed. It was obvious he had not forgotten. 'She had problems. Like I just said, underneath there was a very fine person she didn't recognize. Hell, *I* did. Anybody would.'

'What's her legal problem?' Sam asked.

'This goddamned gigolo-waiter husband of hers. She's stuck with that fucker for six years; helped him go from a hot-pants beach boy to owning a couple of restaurants. She *built* those restaurants. She's damned proud of them! And she likes the life. Overlooking the water, all those boats, nice people. She lives decent now, and *she did it*.'

'So?'

'He wants her out. He's got himself another woman and he doesn't want any lip from Annie. A quiet divorce and just get the hell out.'

'She doesn't want the divorce?'

'That's immaterial. She doesn't want to lose the

restaurants! It's principle, Sam. They represent everything she's worked for.'

'He can't simply take them. There's the property settlement to consider, and California laws are rough as hell.'

'So's he. He went back to Detroit and dug up her police record.'

Sam paused. 'That's a legal problem,' he said.

'You'll work on it?'

'There's not much I can do here. It's a confrontation problem, big attack variety. Fire for fire, dig up counter-accusations.' Devereaux snapped both his fingers – the legal *Wunderkind* making a brilliant decision. 'Tell you what. Let me out of here and I'll fly straight to California! I'll hire out one of the best LA private detectives – like on television – and really go after this prick!'

'Good thinking, boy,' replied the Hawk, clucking his tongue in respect. 'I like that aggressive tone; you bear it in mind for later. Say, in a month or two.'

'Why not *now*? I could —'

'I'm afraid you can't. That's out of the question. You're here for the duration. Talk with Annie, though. Learn what you can. Maybe Lillian can help; she's a resourceful filly.'

With these words MacKenzie dispensed with his liability and gained an asset: Sam now had two additional people to keep an eye on him. He might outwit Rudolph and No Name; the girls were something else again.

Within hours after their arrival, however, it was apparent to Sam that Lillian would have very little time to pay attention to him. In her usual forthright manner she plunged into furious activity, commandeering two of the Machenfeld staff to help her. The work began first thing in the morning when the brigade went out for manoeuvres.

Upstairs. In the top floor rooms and on the ramparts of the château.

There was the banging of hammers and the whirring of

saws and the cracking of plaster. Furniture was carried up and down the long winding staircase; those pieces too large or too awkward were raised and lowered by pulleys and ropes over the outside walls. Scores of potted plants and bushes and small trees were placed around the battlements – seen from the ground by Sam for he was not permitted above the third floor. Paints and brushes and panels of wood were transported daily by Lillian and her two helpers and when Sam could no longer politely ignore her labours, he asked her what she was doing.

'A little arranging, that's all,' she replied.

Finally, crates of crushed stone and washed gravel were hoisted up the wall, accompanied by several concrete benches and (if Sam was not mistaken, and being from Boston he was not) a marble *prayer stall.*

It was suddenly very clear to Devereaux exactly what Lillian was doing. She was turning the top floor and the ramparts of Château Machenfeld into a full-fledged papal residence! Complete with apartments and gardens and prayer stalls!

Oh, my God! A papal residence!

Anne, on the other hand, spent most of her time with Sam. Since MacKenzie had deemed it improper for the girls to eat at the officers' mess – it was diversionary for women to break bread with a strike force prior to combat – Anne and Lillian were assigned their meals in Devereaux's room, Sam under the eiderdown quilt, of course. But Lillian was rarely there; she spent most of her time upstairs – arranging.

So Sam and Anne were thrown together. On a surprisingly platonic basis. True, he had made no pass, but she made no offer either. It was as though both understood the insanity whirling around them, neither wanting the other to be involved, each, in a very real sense, protecting the other. And the more they talked together, the more Sam began to understand what MacKenzie meant about Anne. She was the most genuine, guileless person he had ever met

275

in his life. All the girls were devoid of artifice, but there was something different about Annie. Whereas the others had reached certain plateaux, conscious of their worth, Anne was not satisfied. There was about her a delightfully irreverent sense of purpose that proclaimed for all the world to hear that she *could* expand, *could* experience – but *good heavens*! one did not have to be *gloomy* about it.

Devereaux recognized his imminent danger; he could get really sidetracked. He began to think that he had been looking for this girl for about fifteen years.

And he *couldn't* think about that. Another plan had come into focus. One he knew would work.

The very day Hawkins and his brigade of banana captains took off for Ground Zero!

The last sweet and sour strains of the orchestra filled the theatre. Guido Frescobaldi took his curtain calls, wiping a tear from his eyes. He had to shed his art and think of things plenipotentiary now. He had to hurry to his dressing room and lock up his makeup box.

The call had come! He was going to Rome! He was going to be embraced by his beloved cousin, the most beloved of all popes, Giovanni Bombalini, Francesco, Vicar of Christ! Ohh! Such blessings had come to him! To be reunited after all these years!

But he could say nothing. Absolutely *nothing*. That was part of the arrangements. It was the way Bombalini – *Madre di Cristo* – Pope Francesco wished it, and one did not question the ways of so munificent a pontiff. But Guido did wonder just a little bit. Why did Giovanni insist that he tell the management that small lie that he was going to visit family in Padua, not Rome? Even his friend, the stage manager, had winked when he told him.

'Perhaps you might ask your *family* to pray to Saint Peter for a little sacred lire, Guido. The box office has not been good this season.'

What did the stage manager know? And when did he know it?

It was not like the Giovanni of old to be secretive. And yet who was he, Frescobaldi, to doubt the wisdom of his beloved cousin, the pope.

Guido reached his small dressing room and began to take off his costume. As he did so his eyes fell on his Sunday church suit, pressed and hanging neatly in the centre of the wall. He was going to wear it on the train to Rome. And he suddenly felt ungrateful and ashamed of himself.

Giovanni was being so *good* to him. How could he even *think* a compromising thought?

The lady journalist who was bringing them together had asked for all his measurements. Every last one. When he asked why, she told him. And he had wept.

Giovanni was buying him a new suit.

The Hawk and his subordinate officers returned from Rome. The final check of Ground Zero had gone off without a hitch; no alterations were required.

Further, all intelligence data had been gathered and processed. Using basic surveillance techniques employed in hostile territories, Hawkins had donned an enemy uniform (in this case a black suit and a clerical collar) and obtained a Vatican pass, and identification that certified him to be a Jesuit doing an efficiency study for the treasury. He had free access to all calendars and personnel schedules. From apartments to barracks.

They all confirmed the Hawk's projections.

The pope would leave for Castel Gandolfo on the same day he had chosen for the past two years. He was an organized man; time was to be allocated properly with regard to needs and functions. Castel Gandolfo expected him, and he would be there.

The pope would use the same modest motorcade he had employed previously. He was not a wasteful or pretentious

277

man. One motorcycle point with two front and rear flanks. Basic. The limousines were restricted to two: his own, in which his most personal aides accompanied him; and a second, for secretaries and lesser prelates, who carried his current working papers.

The route of the motorcade was the scenic road he had spoken of with feeling whenever he mentioned Gandolfo: the beautiful Via Appia Antica, with its rolling hills and remnants of ancient Rome along the way.

Via Appia Antica. Ground Zero.

The two Lear jets had been delivered to Zaragolo. It was an airfield for the rich. The small Fiat sedan, which was the diversion equipment for the Turk privates, had been purchased by Captain Noir, in the name of the Ethiopian embassy. It was parked in an all-night garage next to a police station, where the crime rate was at a minimum.

Guido Frescobaldi was on his way to Rome. Regina would handle him. She'd put him up at a *pensione* she rented called The Doge, on the Via Due Macelli, right near the Spanish Steps, and take good care of the old man until the morning of the assault. And first thing that morning she'd load him up with a thiopental solution that would keep him on a harmless high for damn near twelve hours.

The Hawk planned to pick Guido up in the Fiat on his way to Ground Zero. Of course, Regina would have him properly dressed by then, with a very large overcoat that covered his fancy clothes. Skirts, really.

There was only one last item to take care of. The two limousines used in manoeuvres had to be driven to a place called Valtournanche, several miles northwest of the Alpine town of Champoluc. To a little-used private airfield frequented by the jetsetters heading for their ski chalets. The limousines were a natural. They were registered to nonexistent Greeks, and the Swiss *never* bothered Greeks who could afford such automobiles.

Lillian could take care of the transfer. Oversee it, actually. She could use the two men who had helped her shape up the

278

pope's BOQ. Once the cars were in position they could vanish along with Lillian. Mac, of course, would give them bonuses.

He'd get rid of Rudolph, too, and that psycho, what's-his-name, the minute they were back from Ground Zero and the pope was safely - secretly - in his quarters. The chef had to stay; what the hell, even if he did find out who he was cooking for, he was a French Huguenot wanted by the police in sixteen countries.

That left Anne. And Sam, of course.

He could handle Sam. Sam was so lashed to that loaded howitzer he was part of the casing. But he couldn't figure out Annie. What was the girl up to? Why wouldn't she leave? Why had she used his own oath against him?

'You gave your solemn word that if ever any of us came to you in need, you'd never abandon us. You'd never allow an injustice to be done if you could prevent it. I'm here. I'm in need, and an injustice has been done. I've nowhere else to go. Please let me stay.'

Well, of course, he had to. After all, it was the word of a general officer.

But *why*? Could it be Sam?
Goddamn!

So he would die in Gandolfo. It could be worse, thought Giovanni Bombalini, gazing out the windows of his study. A half century ago all he had to look forward to was a gravesite in the Gold Coast, preceded by a long, drawn-out Last Rites ceremony delivered half in Latin, half in Kwa with swarms of flies circling his head. Gandolfo certainly held advantages over that exit.

He would be able to work better, too, at Gandolfo; use the weeks left to straighten out his own affairs, which were minimum, and do his best to set a course for the immediate future of the Church. He would bring with him several hundred analyses of the most powerful dioceses throughout the world and issue scores of promotions; balancing, but balancing in favour of younger, more vigorous perspectives.

Which often had nothing to do with youth.

He had to keep reminding himself that the intractable old guard was not to be scorned, and should not be. The old war-horses had gone through ecclesiastical battles unknown to the vast majority of those who screamed for reform and change. It was not easy to alter the philosophies of a lifetime. But the *fine* old war-horses knew when to step aside and graze in the pastures, ready with an affectionate eye to offer advice when asked, compassion regardless. The others – the Ignatio Quartzes of the world – needed a push.

Pope Francesco decided that among his last acts would be a little pushing. It would take the form of a Last Rites Dissertation to be read to the Curia after his death, and then made public. It was a bit presumptuous, he supposed, but if God did not want him to complete it, He could always summon him at His will.

He had begun the dissertation, dictating to the young Black priest. And he had sent a papal memorandum to every office in the Vatican appointing his young aide as executor of his personal effects in the event he was called to the arms of Christ.

Giovanni was told that Ignatio Quartze threw up for nearly an hour after receiving the papal instruction. It must have wreaked havoc with the cardinal's nasal passages.

'Your Holiness?' The young Black aide came through the door of the bedroom carrying a suitcase. 'I can't find the miniature chessboard. It's not in the drawer with the telephone.'

Giovanni thought for a moment, then coughed an embarrassed laugh. 'I'm afraid it's in the bathroom, Father. Since Monsignor O'Gilligan solved his conversion problems by explaining penance, he's been an absolute terror in his moves. Concentration was required.'

'Yes, sir.' The young priest smiled as he put down the suitcase. 'I'll put it in the vestment trunk.'

'Are we about packed? I say "we", but you've done the work.'

'Almost, Holy Father. The pills and the tonics will stay in my briefcase.'

'A little fine brandy could do just as well.'

'I have that, too, Your Holiness.'

'You are truly a man of God, my son.'

281

CHAPTER TWENTY-THREE

RIGIRATI! COSTRUZIONE!

The large metal sign was secured to the centre of the wooden barrier, that stretched across the width of the back country road.

It looked very official, right down to the last tiny red reflector, and the imposing insignia of Rome's municipal government. It also officially closed off a section of the Via Appia Antica to all approaching vehicles, offering instead a detour cut out of the forest down the Appian hill. And since this particular stretch of the Appian road was the narrowest on the entire route, there was no feasible alternative to the detour if the vehicles in question were larger than the smallest Fiat. Not even the size of the Fiat sedan which the Hawk had driven out of the garage next to the police station and which now lay overturned at the bottom of the hill.

Any larger automobile would not have room to turn around. To reverse direction a driver would have to steer his car backward for the better part of a mile, over countless potholes and around numerous blind curves. Of course the same driver might opt for negotiating the wide expanses of fields that regularly interrupted the Appian forests, but they were filled with rocks and mounds and intermittent stone walls, some built in ancient times. The fields were not only treacherous, but it was against the law to drive on them.

These thoughts went through Captain Noir's head, his black face powdered under the stocking mask, as he lay motionless in the bushes off the side of the road beyond the

282

barrier. He had heard the sounds of the motorcycles in the distance.

All was ready.

Ground Zero had arrived.

The location was perfect. Only trees and fields and hills; the general had planned well. The abduction could probably be carried out on this isolated stretch of road without the detour but in some ways the detour was the most important aspect of Ground Zero. The vehicles *could* turn around by inches – but they wouldn't. They would use the detour.

Still, in case they didn't, Captain Noir held in his hand a piercing, high-frequency whistle. Its use meant that Plan Able, Phase One, Positions One to Three were aborted, instantly implementing Plan Baker, Phase Double Zero, Positions One Hundred and One to One Hundred and Ten: abduction farther up Appia.

Down the road beyond the barrier, the blue helmet with the white cross enamelled on the steel stood out like an enormous jewel in the Italian sunlight. It was on the head of the motorcycle patrolman in front of the papal column; the Vatican point, as the general termed him. The uniformed officer was travelling at medium speed; any faster on the old road would be uncomfortable for those in the limousines.

The patrolman spotted the barrier with the large official sign and drove up to it. Captain Noir held his breath. The officer jumped off his motorcycle, kicked out the stand, and walked up to the obstruction. He raised his eyebrows in bewilderment, looked beyond the barricade for signs of construction and grumbled unintelligibly.

He turned and held up his hands. The lead automobile had reached a point approximately a hundred feet from the barrier.

The patrolman returned to his idling bike, mounted, swung the bars, drove swiftly to the lead limousine, and spoke excitedly to those inside.

The rear door opened; a priest in a black cassock got out. He and the patrolman walked back towards the barrier, their attention on the sloping road down the Appian hill.

There was rapid, indistinguishable chatter between them; and then a series of gestures that conveyed only indecision. The priest turned, picked up the cloth of his cassock, and trotted back past the lead car to the papal limousine.

Captain Noir could not see too well, but the slight Appian breeze carried the sounds of more excited chatter. Noir swallowed and gripped the high-frequency whistle in his hand.

Then to his great relief he heard laughter. And the priest returned to the lead car, nodded his head, gesturing to the left at the patrolman, and climbed back into the limousine.

An adventurous decision had just been made; the general knew his enemy.

The motorcade turned left down the hill, led by the patrolman. All the vehicles entered cautiously, at very slow speeds, and when the two rear motorcycles reached the first curve on the slope, Noir got out of the grass and raced to the barrier, pulling it across the opening of the detour. He ripped off the top sign revealing the second:

DINAMITE! FERMA! PERICOLO!

He had done it! By God, he'd done it! He had escaped from Machenfeld and was on his way to Rome, and if everything held firm, no one would know he was gone until morning! Then it would be too late! The Hawk would be on his way to Ground Zero!

There was no way they could know he was gone. Unless they broke down the door to his room, which was highly unlikely under the circumstances. Anne wasn't talking to him; she'd stamped off to her room in the south wing. He had provoked an argument that could be heard on the peaks of the Matterhorn, eliciting language from her she must have learned from her felonious family.

Rudolph and No Name wanted absolutely nothing to do with him. Especially proximity. After the battle with Anne he had proceeded to complain to his guards of sudden, agonizing pains in his groin. He had doubled up and screamed.

'Oh, Jesus! It's Kuwaiti encephalitis! I saw it in the Algerian desert five weeks ago! Oh, my God! I caught it! The testicles swell like basketballs, but heavier! I've got to have a doctor! Get me a doctor!'

'No doctor. No outside communications until the master of Machenfeld returns.' Rudolph was stern.

'Then you better watch it!' Sam continued. 'It's highly contagious!'

Whereupon he had fainted, clutching himself through the sweat pants. Panicked, No Name and Rudolph moved back swiftly against the wall in the drawing room. Revived but in agony, Sam crawled out of the room and up the staircase. To meet his Maker in peace, and with enormous testicles.

Rudolph and No Name stayed well behind until Sam reached his room and closed the door. When he opened the door for one last time – he saw that his guards were far down the hallway with double handkerchiefs tied around their faces, aerosol cans of disinfectant billowing clouds of spray around them.

The coast was clear! For a beautiful, foolproof exit from Machenfeld.

Lillian and two of the staff were driving the limousines to an airfield somewhere south. He'd overheard the Hawk explaining the route to Mrs Hawkins number three; the trip was four hours long and it was vital that she position the vehicles on a road by the west highway of the airfield.

An airfield!

That meant aeroplanes! And aeroplanes flew to Rome!

285

And even if they didn't – or wouldn't – there were telephones! And radios!

His new plan had jelled instantly. He would be inside the trunk of the second limousine, the one being driven by a member of the château staff. It had been a simple matter to jam the lock of the vehicle's trunk while he had been saying goodbye to Lillian, helping her with the suit-cases.

As soon as his guards disappeared in the cloud of disinfectant, Sam tied three blankets together, scaled down to the ground from the balcony, raced to the limousine in the drive, and crawled into the trunk.

Once inside, he wrapped the blankets around his upper body, grateful he still had his sweat pants, and waited. He was counting on nature to provide him with a shortcut to his objective and he was not disappointed.

The limousines sped through the gate and the trip had begun. After three and a half hours of bouncing, plunging, climbing, and racing through the Swiss mountains, Sam heard the rapid blasts of the lim-ousine's horn. Within seconds there'd been a corres-ponding reply in the distance, from the lead automobile, and the car slowed down and stopped. The driver got out quickly. Devereaux could hear the footsteps outside the trunk. And then he'd heard the unmistakable muted splashing.

He opened the trunk, climbed silently out, and hit the urinating Swiss with a jack handle.

Before a half minute had passed, Devereaux had removed the man's trousers, jacket, shirt, and shoes. Pulling on the trousers and the jacket – enough to obscure him in the night darkness – he had raced around to the door and leaped into the driver's seat, tapping the horn twice as a signal to resume the trip.

Lillian honked back, and started off immediately.

The airfield at Valtournanche (that's what the sign had said) did present a minor problem, but it was more than compensated for by the extraordinary sum of money Sam found in the jacket he had taken from the Swiss. Five thousand dollars, American! The Hawk must have given the staff member a bonus!

It automatically gave birth to another, incredible plan! A magnificent finale!

He could stop the Hawk without the police! Without the authorities! Stop him cold, dismantle Ground Zero and disperse the brigade all at the same time! With no firing squads or hangmen or life imprisonment in the offing! It was perfect. Beyond error.

There was a curve in the road on the west border of the airfield. Sam slowed his limousine, and the instant Lillian's vehicle rounded the turn, he stopped the car, turned off the ignition, grabbed the shirt and the shoes, jumped out, and raced into the woods.

He waited in the darkness for the inevitable. Lillian's automobile could be heard in reverse gear. She and her escort got out and ran back to the abandoned second car.

'Isn't that the limit!' Lillian was angry. 'The ungrateful worm chickened at the last moment! And after Mac gave him all that money. Well, it doesn't surprise me. His neck muscles had no tone; it's always a sign of weakness. Come on! Get in! We're almost there.'

An hour later Devereaux, dressed in a leather jacket and baggy trousers oddly too large for his frame, was counting out $2,500 to a stunned pilot in a Valtournanche hangar, the fee for a rushed, unscheduled flight to Rome. Sam had chosen a man quite a bit smaller than himself, with no apparent muscle tone whatsoever. Pilots who took this kind of employment were not generally considered to be of the highest moral character. He didn't care to be rolled and dropped off into an Alpine mountain pass.

But he had made it! They were airborne! They'd reach Rome well before dawn. And then he, Sam Devereaux, the finest young attorney in Boston, would deliver the best summation of his career.

*

287

Captains Gris and Bleu, dressed in tight-fitting police uniforms, stood erect and motionless behind the trunks of two Appian maples on opposite sides of the winding road – motionless except for their right hands, which they flexed at their sides, thumbs caressing the short hollow needles that protruded from the inverted rings.

As the commander had predicted, the two motorcycles at either side of the papal limousine had dropped back and now rode parallel in front of the bikes flanking the rear. And again, as the commander had projected, the noise was deafening.

One by one the vehicles passed. As the final two patrolmen came between the two maple trees, Gris and Bleu leaped out, hammerlocked both men with their left arms, and each plunged a small needle into his man's neck.

Within seconds the patrolmen were limp.

Gris and Bleu lowered the motorcycles between their legs and dragged each body off into the underbrush. Together they entered the woods and raced diagonally downhill through the tangled foliage to position themselves for their next assignment. Secreted in these positions were the cassocks they would slip over their uniforms.

Captains Orange and Vert lay on their stomachs across from one another hidden by the tall weeds. Their posts were at the start of the second curve on the descending side road. Through the dense reeds they saw – and smiled as they did so – that the two final motorcycles failed to appear. Their other team of patrolmen struggled to keep their bikes upright, riding behind the second limousine.

Captain Orange crossed himself as the pontiff's vehicle passed.

Captain Vert spat. It was long past time for the Church to install a *French* pope; the Italians were pigs about that.

288

The papal car turned into the final downhill curve. Orange and Vert sprang up and out and executed the practised manoeuvres with lightning-swift dispatch against the motorcycle escorts.

The patrolmen collapsed; the papal limousine was entering the turn at the base of the Appian hill. There were only seconds remaining before the detonations of Phase Four, the smoke bombs from the overturned Fiat. Orange and Vert ran to their next assignment – the most prestigious of all: Phase Seven. Phases Five and Six, the destruction of the communications equipment and the sedation of the papal entourage, would be occurring any second.

Phase Seven was the zenith of Ground Zero: the exchange of the popes. Guido Frescobaldi for Giovanni Bombalini.

The explosions from the Fiat were positively frightening; the screams of the hysterical Turks terrifying. The Hawk grinned in appreciation. *Goddamn!* What a beautiful sight! All that smoke and noise and – well, the screams were overdone.

The motorcade stopped in shock, agitated voices swelling. One motorcycle and two limousines in an isolated back country road bordered by a steep hill on the south side and a tall, thick forest on the north.

Optimum, observed the Hawk, holding a weaving Guido Frescobaldi in the bushes.

Captain Noir reached his post and signalled Captains Rouge and Brun; they were strung out at ten-yard intervals, prepared for the moment to implement Phase Five: the destruction of all communications equipment.

It came.

The single Vatican policeman jumped off his motorcycle and ran towards the smoking Fiat with the trapped, screaming passengers. Every door of both limousines was swung open. The drivers and the priests screamed and waved their hands and shouted orders at everyone and no one, then ran towards the overturned car.

Now!

Dressed as priests, Noir, Rouge, and Brun dashed from their hidden recesses. Brun and Rouge plunged into the front seat of the first limousine, ripping out every wire in sight. Noir raced to the second automobile, the papal car, and dived through the open door towards the equipment.

Suddenly a hand lashed out over the seat, followed by an arm extending from a white cassock. But the hand and the arm were not white. They were *black*!

And the grip that held Noir's neck – accompanied by the swift, hard rabbit punches that hammered his head – was a street tactic Noir knew well. It was indigenous to a plot of turf called Harlem!

Noir wrenched his aching, pounding head and was suddenly, astoundingly, face to face with a brother!

A *brother* in the honkey white robes of the Church!

It went against Noir's grain to coldcock a brother, but there was nothing for it. The Catholic kid was good, but he hadn't taken advanced training above 138th Street and Amsterdam. Noir twisted his thumb and forefinger into the sensitive flesh; the Black priest screamed and released Noir's head as Noir yanked him halfway over the seat. He sighed as he chopped the Catholic kid at the base of the skull. He immediately went about his business, ripping wires and smashing dials. The fat old honkey in white robes – the *man*, himself, figured Noir – leaned forward and pulled the kid into the back seat, cradling the kid's head as if the kid was really hurt.

'He'll be okay, pops. I don't know how you boys do it. I *swear* I don't! The Baptists got his turf tide up in ribbons. They've got *rhythm*! Course, you've got the cops....'

Son of a bitch! What the hell else could go wrong? What other delays were concealed in the blinding sunlight of Rome's Leonardo da Vinci Airport? It was a nightmare

290

being played out in the bright morning without benefit of sleep!

The goddamned, dwarf son of a bitch of a pilot from Valtournanche insisted that his aircraft be cleared by the narcotic inspectors! Nobody gave a damn if a plane flew in six vaults of stolen gold, or undeclared diamonds, or eyes-only defence plans for all of NATO, as long as there wasn't a joint on board! No amount of protesting on Sam's part made any difference whatsoever – Well, yes it did. It caused him to be stripped and searched.

'Per favore, signore. Where is your underwear? Where did you leave it? – Search the plane again!'

'That's crazy!' screamed Devereaux. 'How could a pair of shorts —'

'Che cosa?' inquired the capitano suspiciously.

'Shorts!' Sam outlined a pair of briefs. 'Where could I hide ...'

'Ah haaa,' interrupted the capitano. 'The mountain Swiss wear long underwear. With pockets. And flaps. And many buttons. Buttons are hollow.'

'I'm not Swiss! I'm American!'

The capitano's eyebrows shot up as he lowered his voice. 'Ah haaa — Mafia, signore?'

And so it went until Sam had dispensed ten one-hundred-dollar American bills, which happened to coincide with the end of the capitano's shift, whereupon Sam was released.

'Where can I get a taxi?'

'Have your money exchanged first, signore. No taxi has change for American one-hundred-dollar bills.'

'I don't have any hundreds left. Only five hundreds.'

'Then they will call the police. For certainly such money cannot possibly be authentic. You will need lire.'

Oh, my God, the police! thought Sam. The police and hysterical taxi drivers were the last thing he wanted. They definitely were not part of his grand finale to thwart the Hawk.

And so he spent the better part of an hour in the exchange

291

line only to be told by the lady with a moustache that bills of such denominations had to be examined by specto-graphs.

'Thank you, signore,' said the face of fur finally. 'We have processed these under four different machines. They are very nice. Here is your lire. Do you have an empty suit-case?'

It was 9.45. Still time! A taxi into Rome took about an hour when one considered the traffic, and then perhaps a half hour to get to the southern outskirts where he could pick up the Via Appia.

The ride down the Appia couldn't be more than twenty minutes or so. He would recognize the signs he had seen during manoeuvres, he was sure of that. He'd reach Ground Zero with at least a half hour to spare!

He'd stop the Hawk, prevent World War III, eliminate the spectre of life imprisonment, and go home to Boston with a real Swiss bank account!

Goddamn! If he had two cigars, he'd smoke them both at the same time!

He ran across the terminal to the door under the signs that read Taxi in three languages. He raced breathlessly on to the concrete.

Up and down the whole area were hundreds of immobile dollies filled with luggage. Groups of men were gathered in the street, close to riot.

Sam approached a tourist. 'What's going on?'

'Goldanged guinea bastards called a cab strike!' Sam backed away. He had several hundred thousand lire stuffed in his pockets like football pads. There had to be somebody in one of the parking lots with an automobile.

He found him. At twenty minutes past eleven. And offered money. The faster he drove the more thousands of lire he would get. The man agreed.

11.32! He would make it!

He had to!

It was the summation of his life!

292

Why was he kidding himself? It was his life.

Gris and Bleu pulled at the clerical ropes around their cassocks. They were on their knees, concealed by the dense underbrush and cascading branches at the base of the hill by the edge of the old road. Both were prepared to spring through the foliage to execute Phase Six, the immobilization of the motorcade. The overturned Fiat was directly in front of them, the smoke billowing everywhere, the five papal aides, the two chauffeurs and the remaining patrolman all making genuine attempts to reach the screaming Turks.

The numbers presented no problem. Once Gris and Bleu joined the smoke-engulfed mêlée, they would work swiftly, their church habits adding to the confusion. It would be a simple matter to incapacitate one adversary, then another. Rouge would join them on the west flank, intercepting anyone who might discover the conspiracy prematurely, and make a dash for the limousines.

Now!

Gris and Bleu lunged out of the brush into the confusion of smoke, screams, and flailing arms, their wide cassocks billowing, rings at the ready.

One by one the members of the papal entourage collapsed to the ground, beatific smiles on their peaceful faces.

'Tie them! Give me some cord!' yelled Gris to the Turks as the three 'victims' crawled out of the windows and from under the car.

'Not tight, you maniacs!' added Bleu harshly. 'Remember what the commander said!'

'*Mon Dieu!*' roared Bleu suddenly, grabbing Gris's shoulder, pointing to the ground beyond the rising smoke. '*Qu'est-ce que c'est que ça?*'

In the middle of the road, halfway to the limousines, lay Rouge flat on his back, one arm raised, the wrist bent, as though frozen in mid-pirouette. The stocking mask could

293

not disguise the expression of Olympian repose underneath. In the confusion, he had tripped over his cassock, plunging his needle into his stomach.

'Quick!' yelled Gris. 'The antidote! The general thinks of everything!'

'He has to,' said Bleu.

'*Now!*' ordered the Hawk, holding Guido Frescobaldi, who had suddenly raised his voice in song.

Across the dirt road, Mac could see Orange crossing himself as he leaped out of the bushes towards the papal limousine. It was wasted motion, he thought; the pope was not going to attempt any escape. He had helped his aide down on the seat and was getting out of the car, his face wrathful.

The Hawk took Frescobaldi by the hand, and led him towards the limousine.

'I bid you good day, sir,' said the Hawk to the pope. It was a proper military salutation for a surrender.

'*Animale!*' roared the pontiff in a roll of thunder that reverberated throughout the Appian forests and hills. '*Uccisore! Assassino!*'

'What's that?'

'*Basta!*' The thunder cracked again. And the lightning was in Francesco's eyes; the eyes of a giant in the body of a mortal. 'Take my life! You kill my beloved children! The children of God! You slay the *innocenti*! Send me to Jesus! Kill me, too! And may God have mercy on your soul!'

'Oh, for Chri— for heaven's sake, shut up! Nobody's going to kill anybody.'

'I see what I see! The children of God are slain!'

'That's plain horseshit! Nobody's hurt, and nobody's going to get hurt.'

'They are all *morto*,' said Francesco, with less conviction, his eyes darting everywhere in bewilderment.

'No more than you are. We wouldn't be tying them up if they were, would we? Orange! Over here!'

'*Si, Generale.*' Orange came around the hood of the limousine, crossing himself repeatedly.

'Get that coloured boy out of the car. Must be a house guest of the pope here.'

'That man is a *priest*. My personal aide!'

'You don't say? Must be a fine lad with the choirs. Easy, Orange,' said MacKenzie as the Italian pulled the unconscious Black prelate from the automobile. 'Put him in the brush and loosen that big robe. It's too damn hot for ponchos.'

'You mean,' asked Giovanni incredulously, 'they're all alive?'

'Certainly, they're alive,' replied MacKenzie, signalling Vert to prepare Frescobaldi for the exchange; the pope's double sat serene.

'I don't believe you! You've murdered them!' roared the pope suddenly.

'Will you keep quiet!' The Hawk did not ask a question. 'Listen to me. I don't know how you handle your command, but I assume you can tell if a soldier's alive or not.'

'*Che cosa? ...*'

'Captain Gris!' yelled MacKenzie to the masked Scandinavian tying up a priest by the hubcaps of the first limousine. 'Lift that man up and bring him here, please.'

Gris complied. MacKenzie took the pontiff's right hand.

'Here! Put your fingers on the side of the throat next to the collar bone. Now, see? Do you get pulse?'

The pope's eyes narrowed, his concentration on the touch. 'The heart —. Yes. You speak the truth. The others? They are the same? The hearts beat?'

'I gave you my word,' said the Hawk sternly. 'I must reprimand you, sir. Opposing commands do not lie when capture is secure. We're not animals, sir. But we haven't much time.' The Hawk gestured for Vert to bring over the narcotized Frescobaldi. 'I'm afraid we'll have to change some of your clothes. I'll have to —'

MacKenzie stopped. Pope Francesco was staring at Frescobaldi. It was the first moment he had taken cognizance of the singer who was clean shaven and now, without his moustache, looked more like Giovanni Bombalini than did Bombalini himself.

'Guido! It is Guido Frescobaldi!' The pontiff's voice could have been heard in the Bay of Naples, so loud was his roar. 'Guido, my own flesh! My blood! It is Guido! *Madre di Dio!* You are a part of this – this heresy?!'

Signor Guido Frescobaldi smiled.

'*Che gelida ... manina ... a rigido esanine ... ah, la-la ... la-laaa. ...*'

'It's him, all right, but he's been a little out of things since this morning. And will be for a while longer. Come on, now. We've got to get some of that hardware off you and on him. Captain Orange? Captain Vert? Give Mr Francesco a hand.'

'*There!*' The Hawk spoke in the tones of a victorious general officer. He held the grinning Guido Frescobaldi by the shoulders, admiring the final result. 'He looks real fine, doesn't he?'

Francesco, transfixed, could not help himself. '*Jesus et Spiritus Sanctus.* The ugly Frescobaldi is myself. It is a miracle of God.'

'Two like-spits in the gunnery pool, Mr Pope!'

The pontiff was barely audible. 'You put ... Frescobaldi ... in the *chair* of *St Peter?*'

'For about two hours with luck – by my calculations.'

'But *why?*'

'Nothing personal. I understand you're a very nice fellow.'

'But why? In the name of God, *why*? That is no answer.'

'Didn't expect it to be,' replied the Hawk. 'I just don't want you screaming your head off. You've got a mighty loud voice.'

'Then I shall be – screaming my head out – if you do not tell me ... *Aiyeeeee! ...*'

'All right! All *right*! We're kidnapping you. Holding you

for ransom. You'll be fine; no harm will come to you and that's the word of a general officer.'

The conference was interrupted by Captains Gris and Bleu, who raced up and snapped to attention.

'The area is secured, General,' barked Gris.

'All sedations are completed,' added Bleu. 'We are prepared to move.'

'Good! Let's move then. *Troops!* Evacuate the area! Prepare to execute escape procedures! By your numbers! *Move!*'

As if on cue, the sounds of the revving helicopter could be heard from the camouflaged area fifty yards away from the centre of Ground Zero.

And then there was another sound. From the road at the top of the Appian hill: A car screeching to a halt.

'*Stop!*' came a plaintive wail from the woods. 'For Christ's sake, *stop!*'

'*What?*'

'*Mon Dieu!*'

'*Che cosa?!*'

'*I say!*'

'*Tokig!*'

'*Bakasi!*'

'*Shit!*'

Sam stumbled down the old dirt road on the hill. He came racing around the last curve and fell to one knee.

Giovanni Bombalini watched in astonishment; automatically he gave the kneeling figure his rather confused benediction, '*Deus et filius —*'

'Will you shut up!' MacKenzie glared at Francesco. '*Goddamn*, Sam! What the hell are you doing here? You're supposed to be sick as a *dog —*'

'*Listen* to me, everybody!' broke in Sam. 'Everyone gather around!' He struggled to his feet; the captains stood where they were, their faces betraying a certain insensitivity. 'Escape! Run for your lives! Leave this man alone! It's a trap! Machenfeld has fallen! It happened last night! Hundreds of Interpol police are swarming. ...' Sam's jaw

297

was suddenly a gaping orifice as he stared at the Hawk. *'What did you say?'*

'You're a real pistol, son. I respect your moxie, like I said before. But I can't say you have much respect for my know-how.' MacKenzie snapped one of the straps that crisscrossed his chest over his field jacket. It was attached to a large leather case that was lashed over his hip. 'No assault operation ever stays out of contact with its command centre. Not since 1971, anyway. Hell, I used to patch relays from Ly Sol in Cambodia right straight down to the Mekong units.'

'What?'

'Tri-arced, high-frequency radio contact, boy. Set a schedule and receive-send simultaneously. You're *dated*, Sam! As of an hour ago the only thing swarming around Machenfeld were butterflies. I don't know how you did it, but you're mighty lucky you got here alone.... Come to think of it, you'd be a damned fool to get here any other way. – All right, men! Resume Phase Eight! – Come on, Sam. You're going for a ride. And I tell you this now, boy. Any more trouble and I'm going to open a door at two thousand feet and you can fly by yourself!'

'Mac, you can't! Think of World War *Three*!'

'Think of a nice free-fall – without a parachute – straight into a plate of spaghetti!'

And then there was another sound. A frightening one. From the top of the hill. From the road again.

The captains and the Turks froze.

The Hawk whipped his head around – and up – towards the Via Appia.

The pontiff said one word.

'Carabinieri.'

The whining, jarring, two-note scream of the Italian state police sirens could be heard in the distance. Drawing nearer.

'Goddamn! How?!' What the hell *happened*? Sam, you *didn't*!'

'My God, *no*! I didn't! I *wouldn't*!'

298

'I think there is a – miscalculation, signore,' said Pope Francesco softly.

'*What?* What mother – what miscalculation?'

'The motorcade was to stop at the small village – well, not so *much* a village – of Tuscabondo. It is a mile or so past the *deviazione*, your detour.'

'Jesus!'

'He can be merciful, Signor Generale.'

'Those bastards will be swarming the hills, the fields. Goddamn!'

'And the air, Generale,' said Captain Orange excitedly, breaking out in a sweat under his mask. 'The *carabinieri* have fleets of *elicotteri*. They are the *pazzi* of the sky!'

'Jesus H. Christ!'

'*Figlio di Santa Maria* – *Figlio di Dio* – He is the way, *Generale.*'

'I told you to shut up. *Men!* Check your maps! Quickly! Gris and Bleu, evaluate escape routes E-Eight and E-Twelve. Our previous routes were faster but more exposed. Deliver your decision in one minute! Orange and Vert. Give me Frescobaldi! Join the others! Sam, you stay here!'

The screams of the sirens were nearer, almost at the intercept point of the Appia. Frescobaldi, weaving in MacKenzie's grip, sang louder.

'Signore.' Giovanni Bombalini took a step towards MacKenzie. 'You speak the word of a general. You have great sincerity when you say it.'

'What? Yes, of course. You're not much different, I suspect. Command's a big responsibility.'

'Indeed it is. And truth is responsibility's right arm.' The pope looked once more at the unconscious figures of his motorcade, each body comfortably stretched out, none harmed. 'And compassion, naturally.'

The Hawk was barely listening. He was holding Frescobaldi, keeping an alert eye on a stunned Sam Devereaux, and watching Captains Gris and Bleu make their final evaluations over the maps. 'What are you talking about?'

'You say you have no wish to inflict harm on my person.'

'Of course not. Wouldn't get much ransom for a corpse. Well, maybe with *your* people —'

'And Frescobaldi is as strong as an ox,' said the pope, as much to himself as to MacKenzie, while studying the half-conscious Guido. 'He always was. Signor Generale, if I said I would go with you without interference, perhaps even in the spirit of cooperation, would you grant me a small request? As one commander to another?'

The Hawk squinted at the pontiff.

'What is it?'

'A brief note, only several words – in English – to be left with my aide. I would want you to read it, of course.'

MacKenzie took out a combat pad from his field jacket, ripped off a page, unclipped the waterproof pencil and handed both to Francesco. 'You've got fifteen seconds.'

The pope put the paper against the limousine and wrote swiftly. He gave the page back to the Hawk.

I am safe. With God's blessing I shall reach you as the chess-playing O'Gilligan reaches me.

Honkey.

'If it's a code, it's pretty piss-poor. Go ahead, put it in the coloured fella's pocket. I like that part that says you're safe.'

Giovanni ran to the figure of his papal aide, stuffed the note under his cassock and returned to the Hawk. 'Now, Signor Generale, you waste time.'

'What?'

'Put Frescobaldi in the limousine! Hurry! Inside is a briefcase. With my pills. Get it, please.'

'*What?*'

'You would last five minutes in the Curia! Where is the *elicottero?*'

'The copter?'

'Yes.'

300

'Over there. In a clearing.'

Captains Gris and Bleu had completed their swift conference. Gris called out. 'We have briefed the men, General. We go! We meet at Zaragolo!'

'*Zaragolo!*' said the pontiff. 'The airport at Monti Prenestini?'

'Yes,' answered the Hawk, staring with sudden concentration on Pope Francesco. 'What about it?'

'Tell them to stay north of Rocca Priora! There are battalions of police in Rocca Priora.'

'That's east of Frascati —'

'Yes!'

'You heard him, Captains! Outflank Rocca Priora! *Now, scramble!*' roared the Hawk.

'*No!*' screamed Sam, backing away on the road, looking up at the hill. 'Everybody's crazy! You're out of your minds! I'm going to stop you. All of you!'

'Young man!' Giovanni stood erect and addressed Sam pontifically. 'Will you please be quiet and do as the general says?!'

Noir emerged from the clearing. 'The bird's ready, General! We've got a clean lift-off area.'

'We've also got an extra passenger. Get the counsellor, Captain. You might show him a needle, if you can manage it.'

'With real pleasure,' said Noir.

'One dosage, Captain!'

'Shit!'

And so Giovanni Bombalini, the Holy Father of the Catholic Church, and MacKenzie Hawkins, two-time winner of the Congressional Medal of Honour, put Guido Frescobaldi into the papal limousine and ran like hell through the Appian forest to the helicopter.

It was difficult for Francesco. The pontiff swore mildly at Sebastian, the patron saint of athletes, and finally in desperation pulled up the skirts of his habit, displaying rather thick peasant legs, and damn near beat MacKenzie to the aircraft.

301

The Lear jet soared above Zaragolo's cloud cover, Captain Noir at the controls, Captain Rouge in the co-pilot's seat. The Hawk and the pope sat in the forward section, across from one another, each by a window.

Bewildered, MacKenzie glanced over at Francesco. He knew from long years of experience that when command was stymied, the best thing to do was to do nothing, unless the combat at hand required immediate counter-strike.

Such was not the case now. The problem was that Francesco did not behave like any enemy the Hawk had ever fought.

Goddamn!

There he sat, his heavy robes unbuttoned down to his undershirt, his shoes off, and his hands folded casually across his wide girth, looking out of the Lear's window like some kind of happy delicatessen proprietor on his first aeroplane ride. It was amazing. And confusing.

Goddamn!

Why?

MacKenzie realized that there was no point in wearing his stocking mask any longer. The others had to, for their own protection, but for him it made no difference.

He removed it with a grateful sigh. Francesco looked over at him, not unpleasantly. The pope nodded his head, as if to say, Nice to meet you face to face.

Goddamn!

MacKenzie reached into his pocket for a cigar. He lifted one out, bit off the end, and pulled out a book of matches.

'*Per favore?*' Francesco was leaning towards him.

'What?'

'A cigar, Signor Generale. For me. Do you mind?'

'Oh, no, not at all. Here you are.' Hawkins extracted a second cigar from the pack and handed it to the pontiff. And then, as an afterthought, reached into his other pocket for the clipper.

But it was too late.

Francesco had bitten off the end, spat it out – somehow

302

without offence – taken the matches from Mac's hand, and struck one.

Pope Francesco, the Vicar of Christ, lighted up. And as the circles of aromatic smoke rose above his head, the pontiff sat back in the seat, crossed his legs under his habit, and enjoyed the scenery below.

'*Grazie*,' Francesco said.

'*Prego*', replied MacKenzie.

PART FOUR

The ultimate success of any corporation is dependent upon its major product or service. It is imperative that the projected consumer be convinced through aggressive public relations techniques that the product, or service, is essential – to his very existence, if possible.
Shepherd's Laws of Economics:
Book CCCXXI, Chapter 173

CHAPTER TWENTY-FOUR

Sam sat in the cushioned, wrought iron chair at the northwest corner of the Machenfeld gardens. Anne had picked the spot after careful deliberation; it was the area of the gardens that provided the best view of the Matterhorn whose peak could be seen in the distance.

It had been three weeks now since the awful thing: Ground Zero.

The captains and the Turks had departed – for unknown parts of the world, never to be heard from again. The staff had been reduced to one cook, who helped Anne and Sam with the housecleaning and the gardens. MacKenzie was not very good at either chore, but he did take turns driving into the village for the newspapers. Too, he checked daily with the high-priced doctor he had flown in from New York, just in case. The doctor, a specialist in internal medicine, had no idea why he was being paid such extraordinary sums of money to do absolutely nothing but live lavishly in a lakeside residence, and so in the spirit of the AMA he accepted the unreported cash and did not complain.

Francesco (Sam could not bring himself to say pope) had settled comfortably into the sealed-off top-floor apartments and could be seen daily walking on the ramparts through his rooftop gardens.

MacKenzie had really done it! He had won the biggest military objective of his career.

And he was currently, through a convoluted series of extraordinarily complex, untraceable conduits, making his ransom demands of the Vatican. Ultrahigh-frequency radio codes arcing from the Alps to Beirut to Algiers; relayed by desert and ocean towers from Marseilles, to Paris, to Milan, and so on to Rome.

According to the schedules he had imposed, the Vatican reply was to be radioed out of Rome and relayed from Beirut by 5 p.m.

MacKenzie had left Machenfeld to drive to the isolated transmission centre – a lone cabin high in the upper Alps, in which was installed the finest, most sophisticated radio equipment obtainable. It had been delivered to Machenfeld by Les Châteaux Suisses but put into operation by the Hawk himself. No one but MacKenzie knew the location of the mountain retreat.

Oh, my God! Five o'clock this afternoon! Sam forced his thoughts away from the awful thing.

There was movement up at the château. Anne had walked out the terrace door carrying the usual large, glossy picture book under her arm and a silver tray with glasses on it in her hands. She started across the lawn to the gardens. Her walk was firm, feminine; a graceful, natural dancer oblivious to the subtle rhythms inherent in her grace. Her light brown hair fell casually, framing the clear pink skin of her lovely face. Her wide, bright blue eyes reflected whatever light they faced.

He had learned something from all the girls, thought Devereaux. Something different and individually their own – gifts to him. And if a normal life was ever to return, he would be grateful for their gifts.

But perhaps he had learned the most important thing from Anne: Try for improvement – but don't deny what's past.

There was laughter on the lawn. Anne was looking up at the ramparts where Francesco, dressed in a colourful ski sweater, was leaning over the parapet.

It had become their private game, Anne's and Francesco's. Whenever the Hawk was out of sight they held conversations. And Sam was sure – because Anne would not deny it – that she had made numerous trips up to his private apartments bringing him glasses of chianti, which was specifically forbidden from his diet. Anne and Francsco had become good friends.

Several minutes later that judgement was confirmed. Anne placed the silver tray with the drinks on the table next to Sam. Her eyes were smiling.

'Did you know, Sam, that Jesus was a very practical, down-to-earth person. When he washed Mary Magdalene's feet, he was letting everybody know she was a human being. Maybe a very fine one, in spite of what she used to do. And that people shouldn't throw rocks at her because maybe their feet weren't so clean, either.'

MacKenzie climbed the final precipice by means of an Alpine hook. The last two hundred yards of the spiralling summit road were too deep with mountain snow for the motorcycle, so it was faster to make the final ascent directly. It was eleven minutes to five, Zürich time.

The signals would commence in eleven minutes. From Beirut. They would be repeated after an interval of five minutes, to double-check for decoding errors. At the end of the second series he would confirm reception by transmitting the air-clearance code to the relay in Beirut: four dashes, repeated twice.

Once inside, the Hawk started the generators and watched with satisfaction as the myriad wheels spun with a smooth whirring sound within the casing, and the dials began registering *output*.

When the two green lights went on, signifying maximum performance, he plugged in the single electric heater, feeling the warmth of the glowing coils. He reached over to the powerful shortwave equipment, flipped on the receiving switches and turned the amplifier spools to high volume. Three minutes to go.

He walked to the wall. Slowly he began to turn a handle, hearing the gears mesh. Outside, beyond the iron grillework of the tiny window, he could see a webbed disc swing out and up on its track.

309

He returned to the radio receiving panel and revolved the parallel megacycle and tetracycle dials with delicate precision. The voices of a dozen languages emerged from the amplifiers. When the needles were in the exact parallel cycle points there was a silence. One minute to go.

MacKenzie took out a cigar from his pocket and lighted up. He inhaled with real contentment and blew out the smoke in ring after ring.

Suddenly the signals were there. Four short, high-pitched dashes; repeated once. The channel was cleared.

He picked up a pencil, his hand poised above a page of notepaper, prepared to write out the code as it was beamed from Beirut.

The message terminated, the Hawk had five minutes to decode. To convert the signals into numbers, then transfer the numbers into letters and the letters into words.

When he had finished, he stared in disbelief at the Vatican reply.

It was impossible!

Obviously, he had made several errors in receiving the Beirut transmission.

The signals began again.

The Hawk started writing on a fresh page of notepaper.

Carefully.

Precisely.

The transmission ended as it began: four dashes, repeated once.

MacKenzie put the decoding schedule in front of him. He believed he had memorized it thoroughly, but this was no time to make a mistake. He cross-checked every dot, every dash.

Every word.

There were no errors.

The unbelievable had happened.

Relative to the insane request regarding the contribution of four hundred million American dollars, by assessing worldwide dioceses on the basis of one dollar per communicant, the treasury of the Holy See is in no position to consider such a request. Or any request at all for this particular charity. The Holy Father is in excellent health and sends his blessings in the name of the Father, the Son, and the Holy Spirit.

Ignatio Quartze,
Cardinal Omnipitum,
Keeper of the Vatican Treasury

The Shepherd Company suspended operations.

MacKenzie Hawkins walked the grounds of Château Machenfeld, smoking his cigars, staring blankly at the infinite beauty of the Alps.

Sam made an accounting of the corporation's monetary assets, exclusive of the properties and equipment. Of the original capitalization of $40,000,000, there remained $12,810,431.02.

Plus a contingency expense fund of $150,000, which had not been touched.

Not bad at all. Especially since the investors, to a panicked vulture, refused reimbursement. They wanted nothing whatsoever to do with the Shepherd Company or any of its management personnel. None would even bother to file for tax losses as long as Shepherd's corporate executives promised – on the Bible, *Burke's Peerage*, *Mein Kampf*, and the Koran – never to get in touch with him again.

And Francesco, now sporting a Tyrolean hat along with his favourite ski sweater, was allowed out of the top-floor apartments. For the sake of everybody's sanity, it was agreed to refer to him as Zio Francesco, somebody's uncle.

Since he showed no inclination to go anywhere or do anything other than enjoy the company, Zio Francesco roamed freely. There was someone always nearby, but not to prevent escape; for assistance. He was, after all, in his seventies.

The cook was especially taken with him, for he spent long periods in the kitchen, helping with the sauces, and every once in a while asking permission to fix a particular dish.

He made one request of the Hawk. The Hawk refused it.

No! Absolutely no! Zio could not telephone his apartment in the Vatican! It made no difference whatsoever that his telephone was private or unlisted *or* concealed in the drawer of his bedside table! Telephone calls could be traced.

Not if they were radioed, insisted Francesco. The Hawk had impressed them all, frequently, by telling them about his complicated methods of communicating with Rome. Of course, a simple telephone call would not have to be nearly so complex. One little relay, perhaps.

No! All that spaghetti had gone to Zio's head. His brain was soft.

The Hawk's was softer, perhaps, suggested Francesco. What progress was the general making? Were not matters at a stalemate? Had not Cardinal Quartze outflanked him?

How could a telephone call change that?

How could it make things any worse? persisted Francesco. The Hawk could be at the radio, his hand on a switch, prepared to break the connection should Zio say anything improper. Was it not more advantageous to the general for at least two people to know he was alive? That the deception was *truly* a deception? There certainly was nothing to lose, for the Hawk had already lost. And possibly there was something to gain. Perhaps four hundred million American dollars.

Besides, Guido needed help. This was no criticism of his cousin, who was not only strong as a bull but a most gentle and thoughtful person. But he was new at the job and would certainly listen to his cousin Giovanni Bombalini. Helped, of course, by Giovanni's personal aide, the young American priest from Harlem.

The situation might *not* be remedied overnight – for there were matters of health and logistics to be considered. But when all was said and done, what alternative did the Hawk *have*?

He obviously had none. And so MacKenzie came down from the Alpine cabin one afternoon carrying three canvas-wrapped cartons of radio equipment and proceeded to install the instruments in a Machenfeld bedroom.

When all was completed, the Hawk issued an irrevocable command. Only he and Zio Francesco were allowed inside during radio transmissions.

That was fine with Anne and Sam. They had no desire to be there. The cook thought everybody was crazy and went back to the kitchen.

And at least twice a week from then on – very late at night – the huge disc antenna was wheeled out and raised above the battlements. Neither Sam nor Anne knew what was being said or whether anything was being accomplished, but often when they sat in the gardens to talk and look at the glorious Swiss moon, they heard great peals of laughter from the upstairs room. The Hawk and the pope were like small boys thoroughly enjoying a new game.

A secret game, played in their personal clubhouse.

Sam sat in the garden absently looking at his copy of *The Times*. Life at Château Machenfeld had become routinized. For instance, every morning one of them would drive into the village to pick up the newspapers. Coffee in the gardens with the newspapers was a wonderful way to start the day. The world was such an unholy mess; life was so peaceful at Machenfeld.

The Hawk, having discovered the existence of riding trails on the property, purchased several fine horses and rode frequently, sometimes for hours at a time. He'd found something he'd been looking for, thought Sam.

Francesco discovered oil painting. He would trek over the fields in his Tyrolean hat with Anne or the cook, set up his easel and paints, and render for posterity his impressions of the Alpine splendours. That is, when he wasn't in the kitchen, or teaching Anne to play chess, or debating – always pleasantly – with Sam over points of law.

There was one thing about Francesco that nobody talked about, but all knew had something to do with his attitude. Francesco had not been a well man when he was taken out of the Appian hills. Not well at all. It was the reason Mac had insisted on the availability of the New York specialist.

But as the weeks went by, Francesco seemed to improve in the Alpine air.

Would it have been the same, otherwise?

No one, of course, would speculate, but Francesco had said something at dinner one evening that registered on them all.

'Those doctors. I shall outlive every one of them! They would have had me buried a month ago.'

The Hawk responded with a coughing fit.

And Sam? What of him?

Whatever it was, he knew that it included Anne.

He looked at her now in the late morning sun, sitting in the chair reading the newspaper, the ever present book on the table beside her. *A Pictorial History of Switzerland* was the title today.

She was so lovely, so gloriously – herself. She'd help him become a better lawyer, by making the law seem not so important.

Now he began to think of other things.

Like reading quietly. Understanding. Evaluating.

Like – Judge Devereaux.

Oh, Boston was going to like Anne! His mother would like her, too. And Aaron Pinkus. Aaron would approve wholeheartedly.

If Judge Devereaux ever got back to Boston.

He'd think about that – tomorrow.

'Sam?' said Anne, looking over at him.

'What?'

'Did you read this article in the *Tribune?*'

'What article? I haven't seen the *Tribune*.'

'Here.' She pointed but did not give him the paper. She was engrossed. 'It's about the Catholic Church. All kinds of things. The pope has called a Fifth Ecumenical Council. And there's an announcement that a hundred and sixty-three opera companies are being subsidized, to elevate the spirit of creativity. And a famous cardinal – my God, Sam – it's that Ignatio Quartze! The one Mac yells about.'

'What about him?'

'It seems he's retiring to some villa called San Vincente. Something to do with papal disputes over Vatican allocations. Isn't that strange?'

Devereaux was silent for several moments before he replied. 'I think our friends have been very busy up on the ramparts.'

In the distance were the sounds of galloping hooves. Seconds later MacKenzie Hawkins emerged on the dirt road from beyond the trees and the fields where only weeks ago manoeuvres were held. He reined in his horse and trotted up to the northwest corner of the gardens.

'Goddamn! Isn't it a glorious day? You can see the peak of the Matterhorn!'

There was the music of a triangle coming from the other direction. MacKenzie waved; Devereaux and Anne turned and saw Francesco on the terrace outside the kitchen door, the triangle and the silver bar in his hands. He was dressed in a large apron, the Tyrolean hat firmly on his head.

Zio Francesco called out.

'Lunch, everybody! The *speciale di giorno* is *fantastico*!'

'I'm hungry as a horse!' roared back the Hawk as he patted his mount. 'What've you got, Zio?'

Francesco raised his voice to the Alpine hills. And there was music in his words.

'My dear friends. It's *Linguini Bombalini!*'

315

EPILOGUE

MacKenzie Hawkins, pleasantly surfeited with Zio's linguini and the splendid *chianti classico* Francesco had his cousin, Frescabaldi, ship to the railroad station in Zermatt, the Hawk wandered across the Alpine pasture to the edge of the field, its glorious view of the majestic mountains as always moving him. It was another ritual that had become part of his day. A few minutes alone, really alone, without even his horse beneath him, or the sound of human voices, only the rustle of the tall grass caressed by the gentle Alpine breezes. He needed these moments, for a man had to face both his accomplishments and his failures by himself, accepting the results without regret as long as he knew he had done his best with what was in him.

Regarding Zio, he had both lost and he had won. He had hardly reached the four hundred million dollars he envisioned, but what was left of the forty million capitalization wasn't exactly C-rations. Yet he had won something else, something far more important, a restored, healthy, *vital* Pope Francesco the First, the Pontiff who wanted more than anything else to finish the job started by John the Twenty-Third. To blow the cobwebs out of the Catacombs and bring his church into the twenty-first century. Zio would have to go back, they both had agreed to that without telling the others – sometime soon, somehow. They could work it out. Somehow.

Well, that was just goddamned *fine* for Uncle Zio, but what about *him*, what about the Hawk? What the hell was *he* supposed to do? Sit on his ass in Edelweiss and let the world pass as he *vegetated*?

316

'Find another cause, Mac, perhaps a somewhat more earthly one,' had suggested Francesco. 'The world abounds with them, and you have extraordinary talents my son – '

'Cut the "my son" crap, Zio.'

'Sorry, it goes with the office. If I had so many "sons", I'd make an extraordinary mockery of celibacy – which I intend to bring up one day. It's really so unnatural, so foolish, and nothing explicit in the Scriptures.'

'Maybe I should just keep you here before they hang you in St Peter's Square.'

'No, no, I must go back . . . But what about you, my friend. What *will* you do?'

The Hawk had not replied, for he had no answer then. He thought about it now, gazing at the breath-taking skyline of the snow-capped Alps, when suddenly, an eagle swooped down from some unseen high altitude perch in search of ground-bound prey that would sustain it.

An *eagle*. A lone eagle, soaring in splendour and splendid freedom, the master of the air and the earth, its wingspread incredible and mesmerizing. The magnificent bird circled in the winds, descending lower and lower, then abruptly dove with marvellous speed into a field below . . . Something *happened*! The eagle's massive wings were flapping furiously – it was caught, something had snared it, binding it to the ground! Then, in agonizing moments, the bird broke free, its movements frantic until it found the unencumbered air and soared aloft.

MacKenzie stared across at the would-be killing field, wondering what had caused the near tragic occurrence. The answer came in seconds: two men were racing out of a nearby cluster of brush, obviously annoyed that their decoyed trap malfunctioned. They picked up the lethal animal-covered instrument, one throwing it into the grass in disgust.

The incident brought back memories to the Hawk, images from long ago when he was a young officer posted to a Ranger training base somewhere in the hills of Nebraska or

317

Iowa, or was it Kansas? – no it was Nebraska. The eagle itself was not the sole prodder of these memories, but the great bird was a large part of it because of what it somehow historically stood for in pictures and symbols, even in name. Full headdresses crowning the heads of once powerful chiefs, the single, double and triple feathers earned by deeds of bravery by the young tribal males.

The American Indian.

There had been an Indian reservation perhaps twenty miles from the secret training base, certainly no secret to the Indians who pathetically came to beg whatever they could from the strapping, well-fed troops. So pathetic were these pilgrimages, that many of the young Rangers, the Hawk among them, trekked over to the reservation to get a clearer understanding. It was a *disgrace*! These original inhabitants, the *owners* of the land, lived in abject poverty, scandalously shafted by the white invader! Naturally the Rangers stole the Quartermaster bare and until the soldiers left for scaling cliffs on D-Day, the Indians lived better than any of them could remember.

The *American Indian* – screwed by the same kind of pricky shits who threw General MacKenzie Hawkins out of the army! That noble savage would be his *cause*! It might take months, even years, but *goddamn*, it was a quest worth serving.

The Hawk turned and raced back across the field, the tall grass whipped by his gathering speed. He saw Francesco by the vegetable garden, watering his precious herbs. 'Zio, *Zio*, I've *got* it!'

'What have you got, my son – forgive me, I mean Mac?'

'I'm going to free our American Indians, I mean *really* set them *free*!'

'They are in *chains*?' asked the bewildered Francesco, his watering-can drenching his Lederhose.

'Worse, they're in economic bondage, shafted by the white pricky shits!'

'Sometimes you can be obtuse, MacKenzie – '

318

'Don't you *see*, Zio? It's my grail, my quest, my *cause*! Hell, it might take me a long time, maybe even a few years, but the right *shaftees* are there, I know it, I *feel* it!'

'May this humble country priest bless in advance those you would free from this bondage? . . . In the name of the Father, the Son, and the Holy Ghost, pray to your Maker, my children. The Hawk is on your horizon.'